8W $4.95

PENGUIN BOOKS

NEVER LOOK BACK

Lesley Pearse's previous novels are *Georgia, Tara, Charity, Ellie, Camellia, Rosie* and *Charlie*, the last two of which are also published in Penguin. She was born in Rochester, Kent, but has lived in Bristol for the last twenty-five years. She has three daughters.

Never Look Back

Lesley Pearse

PENGUIN BOOKS

PENGUIN BOOKS

Published by the Penguin Group
Penguin Books Ltd, 27 Wrights Lane, London W8 5TZ, England
Penguin Putnam Inc., 375 Hudson Street, New York, New York 10014, USA
Penguin Books Australia Ltd, Ringwood, Victoria, Australia
Penguin Books Canada Ltd, 10 Alcorn Avenue, Toronto, Ontario, Canada M4V 3B2
Penguin Books (NZ) Ltd, Private Bag 102902, NSMC, Auckland, New Zealand

Penguin Books Ltd, Registered Offices: Harmondsworth, Middlesex, England

First published 2000
1 3 5 7 9 10 8 6 4 2

Set in 9/11pt Monotype Palatino
Phototypeset by Intype London Ltd
Printed in England by Clays Ltd, St Ives plc

I dedicate this book to my youngest daughter Jo, for having enough faith to believe I could drive us all the way from Missouri to the West Coast of America without getting lost and cheerfully assisting me in the enormous research needed for this book. I hope it will be a permanent reminder of the laughs we had along the way.

And to Elizabeth 'Toots' Olmsted in Oregon, for remaining a dear friend for nearly thirty years and retaining enough interest and devotion to scour American bookshops for my research material. Who would have thought when we met working for Yellow Pages all those years ago that our lives would take us so far apart, yet our hearts and minds would stay so firmly linked!

Acknowledgements

To Harriet Evans and Louise Moore not just for their skill and tact in editing my work but for their joyful enthusiasm, encouragement and warm friendship. I love you both.

To Peter Bowron, John Bond, Nicky Stonehill and the rest of the team at Penguin who have worked so hard on my behalf. I appreciate it more than mere words can say.

To Marcy and Alan Culpin of Denver, Colorado, for their extensive knowledge of American history and for digging around to find the answers to my more obscure questions. I hope you will enjoy the finished work and look back to that dinner party, so long ago now, when I first told you of my ideas. You inspired me more than you realized.

Special thanks to the knowledgeable and astoundingly helpful staff in: The American Museum, Claverton, Bath, England; The Lower East Side Tenement Museum, Manhattan; South Seaport Museum, Manhattan; New York Public Library; Ellis Island Immigrant Museum, New York Harbour; The National Frontier Trails Centre, Independence, Missouri; Fort Laramie, Wyoming; The Emigrant Trail Museum, Truckee, California.

It would be impossible to list all of the vast number of books I read during my research but some were so particularly outstanding and stimulating they deserve a special mention: *The Historical Atlas of New York City* by Eric Homberger; *San Francisco from Hamlet to City* by Roger W. Lotchin; *The Prairie Traveler* by Captain Randolph B. Marcy; *Women of The Gold Rush* by Elizabeth Margo; *How the other Half Lives* by Jacob A Riis. His haunting, very early photographs of the poor in New York, along with the graphic descriptions of the way they lived, gave me tremendous insight into how it was for the disadvantaged in the nineteenth century; *Low Life* by Luc Sante; *Women's Diaries of the Westward Journey* by Lillian Schissel; *Soiled Doves* by Anne Seagraves; *The*

Way West and *The Civil War* by Geoffrey C. Ward; *Foreign and Female* by Doris Weatherford.

A final special thank-you to all those kind and helpful people I met briefly along my own 'trail' across America in motels, hotels, restaurants, laundrettes, bars, streets and places of historical interest. I remember you all with fondness, if not all your individual names. But especially Kate Deline and Ken from Illinois, the bikers who rescued me when I ran out of petrol in the middle of the Nevada desert. Bless you!

Prologue

New York 1900

'Is she crazy?' Fanny Lubrano whispered to her father as he came back from settling the old lady into a seat up in the bows of their tug.

It was a grey March day, the blustery wind coming straight in off the Atlantic, and even in the shelter of the wheel-house it was very cold.

'She has to be crazy to offer me a hundred dollars,' Giuseppe replied, the expression on his weather-beaten face one of utter bewilderment. 'But she sure don't sound like she is!'

Before making ready to cast off, they looked down through the wheel-house window at the old lady. She had the style and poise of the rich women who lived on Fifth Avenue, swathed in a sable coat and matching hat; yet that sort of woman wasn't likely to want a trip round New York Bay in an old tug.

Fanny said she thought the lady was too fashionably dressed for someone of advanced years, and her dainty side-buttoned boots were hardly suitable for a boat trip. Giuseppe was more concerned that she had no companion, and he found her tense stance and the way her eyes scanned the waterfront very suspicious.

'What if she *is* crazy, Pa, and her folks are out looking for her?' Fanny said suddenly. 'I know she got out of a fancy carriage and the driver said he'd wait for her, but if she catches a chill, we'll be blamed.'

Giuseppe pushed back his cap and scratched his head. 'I guess if we don't take her, someone else will, and maybe rob her too. Besides, she seems to know what she's doing, and about river craft. Asked me how long I'd been working the harbour, about you and where we lived. Goddam it, Fanny, I want to please her, she was right kindly, but maybe I oughtn't to have taken her money, a hundred dollars is a whole lot too much.'

Fanny half smiled at that. Her father looked tough, but he had a soft centre. The elderly, children and the very needy always plucked at his heart strings. She had long since lost count of the loans he'd made to his brothers and sisters which were never repaid; that was one of the reasons why they still lived in a cramped East Side tenement.

'That fur cost a whole lot more than we can make in a couple of years.' She shrugged. 'We never asked her for that much, did we? She offered it. So I reckons we'd better look lively and cast off afore she changes her mind.'

As the tug chugged along past the busy wharves, the old lady took a deep breath of the smoky, fishy-smelling air and smiled at the memories it evoked. Fifty-eight years had passed since she arrived here as a seventeen-year-old immigrant, staying for five years before moving on, and the place had changed dramatically in the intervening years. In her time South Street was crammed with graceful sailing ships, bowsprits half-way across the cobbled quay and drying sails flapping and crackling in the wind. The warehouses, grain stores, saloons and sailors' boarding-houses had been mostly rickety wooden places built in a higgledy-piggledy fashion. Now the ships were mostly steamers, the buildings all of fine, sturdy brick – only the smell, the sounds of rumbling carts, the sailors and stevedores yelling to one another were the same.

Prosperity shone out all over Manhattan. Where she remembered farm land, now there was street after street of elegant brownstone houses. Buildings so high she got a crick in her neck looking up at them, sidewalks paved and the streets well lit. People travelled in overhead trains, and there was even talk of running one underground too. They had huge shops they called department stores which sold everything from furs and carpets to a length of elastic or a set of buttons.

In her time Central Park had been swampy waste ground, and the most desperate of the Irish labourers who built the Croton Aqueduct, that miracle which brought piped clean water to the city, squatted there in squalid shanties with their pigs and goats. The park was wonderful, and she was so glad that the people of the city had somewhere serenely beautiful to escape to, but to her mind the new Brooklyn Bridge was more splendid. While nature had created the true magic of the park, the bridge was an entirely man-made miracle, engineering and artistry working hand in hand to make something which looked fragile and beautiful, yet was strong enough to withstand the elements and the heaviest of traffic.

She felt no sorrow that the city bore little resemblance to the one she arrived in over half a century ago, for she was no longer the excited, wide-eyed girl who had fallen in love with its honest, brash and bold exuberance.

They had both been changed by circumstance, ambition, greed, and powerful men. Yet that honesty she had loved it for was still in place. She hoped she'd retained hers too.

Hearing a peal of girlish laughter, she glanced over her shoulder to the wheel-house. It pleased her to see the tug owner and his daughter working so happily together. They could of course be laughing at her, but that didn't matter.

She had selected this boat purely out of sentimentality on hearing Giuseppe was a widower, and that he worked with his daughter. Her father had been a river man on the Thames, and they had been very close too. When she'd seen their open, friendly faces she doubled the amount she had first intended to offer. The money she'd given them would put extra food on their table, maybe the girl could buy herself a pretty dress. She remembered only too well how young girls ached for something frivolous.

There hadn't been so many Italians here when she first landed, the immigrants then were predominantly English, Irish and German. Yet from 1845 and onwards, Italians, Poles, Russians, Jews and a great many other races had come here in their hundreds of thousands, each nationality adding further spice and character to the crowded city.

Yet Giuseppe didn't speak with an Italian accent, so he must have been born here, and perhaps his mother had been Dutch or German to give him those blue eyes and fair hair. His daughter – Fanny, he'd said her name was – reminded her of herself at seventeen. Thick blonde hair, eyes as blue as forget-me-nots, and a similar sturdy, no-nonsense look about her. It seemed strange that she wore men's clothes, but then she supposed a long dress on a boat was hardly practical. Besides, she herself had resorted to wearing men's pants a few times back in '49 out in the West when it wasn't safe to look too feminine in a town overrun by hard-drinking, gold-seeking men.

As the tug approached the Staten Island Ferry her heart quickened, for just behind it was State Street, where she'd lived when she first arrived here. Sadly the quaint little wooden house and some of its neighbouring fine Federal houses had been demolished to make way for offices and warehouses. Few people lived in this neighbourhood now, they had all moved further uptown. Wall Street was now a street of banks and financial institutions; Trinity Church at the top of it, which had so many memories for her, was one of the few remaining old buildings. She thought it sad that the church's elegant spire, the highest landmark when she arrived here, would soon be hidden by the giant buildings New Yorkers seemed to love so much. But then Americans didn't appear to have nostalgia for old places.

Yet Castle Clinton was still much the same, though in her time it had been an island, reached by a walkway from the Battery. The shore area had been reclaimed for many years now, filled in with tons of rubble and grassed over to make Battery Park. Castle Clinton had become a clearing-house for immigrants, now it was an aquarium, but back in 1842 it had been a concert hall, with a green around it, and it was there she met Flynn O'Reilly.

She closed her eyes for a moment, remembering his first kiss. It seemed odd that after all these years she could still recall the magic of it, and all the turbulent emotions he awakened in her heart.

'I wonder what would have happened,' she thought aloud.

'To who, ma'am?'

She was startled to find the young girl at her elbow looking quizzically at her. Yet she wasn't embarrassed. One of the few advantages she'd found in becoming old was the freedom to do and say exactly what she pleased, even talk to herself.

'To me, if I'd run off with my first love,' she explained with a wide smile. 'My life might have turned out quite different.'

Fanny was delighted the old lady seemed to want to talk. Aside from intense curiosity about this odd passenger, her working life was male dominated, and she often longed for female company.

So, armed with a warm rug as an excuse to strike up a conversation, she'd approached her to see if she was cold.

'Was he rich?' she asked, keeping her tone light.

The old lady shook her head, her faded blue eyes twinkling with merriment. 'Oh no, just a poor Irish lad.'

'Then it's a good thing you didn't run off with him,' Fanny retorted. 'There sure as hell ain't many Irish men who make their fortune. But there's many a brewery made one from their drinking.'

'They might drink, but they sure can love,' the old lady replied reflectively. 'I think I'd sooner have passion than riches.'

Fanny was thrown for a moment. While well used to her own kind making earthy comments about the opposite sex, she hadn't expected a remark like that from a real lady. She offered the rug, explained that the wind would get up once they were out in the bay, tucked it around the lady's lap, and then, taking a deep breath, she blurted out her question. 'Why did you want to come out here, ma'am?'

The old lady looked appraisingly at Fanny for a moment. She was wearing a threadbare, far too large seaman's coat and a striped muffler wound round her head and neck. The tip of her nose was red with cold, yet her blue eyes sparkled with interest. She thought it was yet another thing they had in common, she had always been incurably inquisitive too.

'I guess old age makes you sentimental. I wanted to see all the changes,' she said, waving one gloved hand towards the shore. 'You see, honey, I was your age when I first came to New York, I only spent a few years here, but it kinda coloured and shaped my whole life. Now I've got a yen to go home, and I want new memories to take with me along with the old ones.'

'Which state would "home" be?' Fanny asked.

The old lady laughed, not a dainty little tinkle, but a deep, throaty belly-laugh.

'Which state would home be?' She repeated the question, mimicking Fanny's accent. Then laughed again. 'Honey, you have pleased me. For half a century I've done my damnedest to sound and act like an American. But everyone I ever met guessed I was English the moment I opened my mouth. Then just when I'm about to leave, you take me for a Yank. Bless you.'

'Well, I'll be jiggered,' Fanny said, sinking down on to the bench beside her. She had noticed something unusual about the woman's speech, but in New York there were as many different accents as there were saloons. 'I had the notion you were from one of them fancy mansions up on Fifth Avenue! Do tell me about yourself. That is, if you've a mind to.'

'My name's Matilda Jennings,' the old lady said in a crisp, clear voice. 'I have come from a fancy mansion today, but I was born seventy-four years ago in a part of London that's as bad as anything you've got here on the Lower East Side.'

Fanny's mouth dropped open in shock. She hadn't met many English people, but those she had spoken to had created an image in her mind that England was filled with castles, palaces and grand mansions. Not one of them had ever admitted it had slums too. But surprised as she was by that, she was more astounded to hear this woman's age. Where she lived people rarely reached sixty and looked ancient long before that. Yet this woman had walked on to the tug unaided, her step was sprightly, and though her face was lined, it had a softness, her skin a clarity that a woman of twenty years younger would envy. 'You're kiddin' me?' she retorted. 'You can't be that old!'

Matilda didn't reply immediately, but instead slowly peeled off her soft leather gloves and held her hands out to Fanny. 'So what do you see there?' she asked.

Fanny's own hands were calloused from hauling ropes, red-raw with the wind and water, yet the old lady's proved that age could be even more cruel than the elements. They were big hands for such a dainty, slender woman, the backs puckered with wrinkles and engorged purple veins. Her knuckles were swollen and misshapen, and a couple of nails were missing, leaving ugly scar tissue.

'You've had to work very hard,' Fanny said in a low voice, stunned because she hadn't expected that. She turned the hands over and looked at the palms, running one finger over the skin which felt very dry and crackly, like leaves in the fall. They *were* the hands of a very old woman, yet as she held them, suddenly she didn't feel as if there was a half-century separating them.

'They are ugly, and better out of sight,' Matilda said reflectively, slipping her gloves back on. 'But they tell you a great deal about my life, you can probably guess that they've scrubbed floors and dug fields, but there's a lot more hidden. They've soothed babies, shot guns, driven wagons, buried the dead and plenty more besides.'

Fanny wanted to ask how she eventually got rich enough to afford such a lovely coat, but she knew that was too impertinent.

'Once I began to make money,' Matilda continued, 'I spent a fortune on creams and potions, but it was too late, nothing could make my hands pretty again. I was so ashamed of them I always wore gloves. But I'm old now, and vanity fades, just like heart-aches do. So I tend to look at them and remind myself that it wasn't my brain or my looks which got me through the bad times, just these hands and my will. I was lucky they were both so strong.'

Fanny felt a surge of intense admiration for the plain-speaking English lady. She had grown up surrounded by immigrants, and mostly they were the kind that ran out of ambition and energy a few weeks after they got off the boat. They stayed in their squalid, overcrowded tenements, and as the years went by they blamed others for their poverty and lack of success. Yet this woman in her expensive furs was proof not only that with a will, courage and determination anyone could make it out of the Lower East Side to Fifth Avenue, but that you could still retain kindness, and humility too.

'I thought at first you were crazy,' Fanny said hesitantly, all at once very ashamed for prejudging her. 'I'm sorry.'

Matilda took the girl's hand in her gloved one and squeezed it. 'Fanny, perhaps I *am* crazy, wanting to smell the East River on a cold March day, and see sights I know will stir up painful memories. Even crazier for wanting to go back to a country I've almost forgotten, and almost certainly outgrown. But when you're as old as me you get that way. I have a hankering to see if the river Thames is as wide as I remember, if the Tower of London can still scare me. I guess too I want to die in my own country where no one knows about the more scandalous parts of my history.'

Fanny's eyebrows shot up into two inverted Vs.

Matilda chuckled at her shocked expression. 'Oh yes, Fanny, I've been quite a girl in my time, but that's a long story and much as I'd love to tell you about it, this might be my last chance to look at the old sights and remember how it all came about.'

Fanny knew that was a signal for her to go. She wasn't hurt

for she sensed Matilda meant exactly what she'd said. She got up and tucked the rug more securely around her. 'I'm real glad I met you, ma'am,' she said. 'You enjoy your trip and if you want anything just holler.'

'I knew I was right to choose this boat,' Matilda said with a warm, appreciative smile. 'You put me in mind of myself as a young girl.'

Fanny went back to the wheel-house and Matilda concentrated on the view across the bay. The sky was dark grey, the wind strong and bitterly cold, but that suited her, she didn't want warmth and bright sunshine slanting her mind towards only the happier memories.

As Giuseppe steered towards Ellis Island, she found her eyes remained glued to the majestic Statue of Liberty, even though it had no place in her past. It had been erected only a few years ago, just as Ellis Island with its new immigration department was a recent development. Yet goose bumps came up all over her as she gazed on it, staggered by not only its vast proportions, but the sheer beauty of it. She hoped it would give all those poor huddled masses arriving in America the comfort and inspiration that were intended.

Giuseppe slowed right down as they approached Ellis Island. The huge new immigration building was impressive with its domes and spires, yet it was already dubbed the 'Isle of Tears'. A German steamer had just docked and a thick stream of passengers was pouring down each of the gangways. Although she knew their voyage across the Atlantic had taken less than half the time her own had, as the tug drew nearer she could see from their pale, drawn faces and the stoop of their shoulders that for most of them the journey had been an unspeakable nightmare of overcrowding, rotten food and sickness.

She began to cry as she thought about what was in store for them. While the rich got swept straight into New York, with no thought that they might be undesirable in some way, the poor had first to pass through 'assessment'. How many of those black-coated men with long whiskers who looked hardly capable of carrying their own baggage would make it through the stringent medical? Then there were the literacy and competence tests for others to stumble on. In her time all were welcome. Maybe that welcome didn't run to decent homes or well-paid work, but at least they didn't face the humiliation of being turned around and sent home because they didn't fit the bill of what the American Government perceived as ideal immigrants.

Even above the sound of the sea, wind, seagulls and the tug's engine, she could hear the pitiful cries of hungry and sick children. Women with frightened eyes clutched babies to their breasts, scanning the sky-line on the other side of the bay in hope that the relatives who urged them to come would be there to greet them.

Sadly Matilda knew they had more misery and shocks in store for them. New York might be prosperous but a great deal of that wealth had been made out of people just like these. She knew the evils of those appalling East Side tenements built by unscrupulous speculators, their only thought to wring as many dollars a square foot out of them as they could. If she had her way she'd force those men to live there too. She wondered how long it would take to break the new arrivals, living in tiny dark rooms, one tap between four families and a privy shared by the whole block.

Yet today these immigrants would be lucky if they even got one of those hell-holes. Most would end up tonight sleeping in some squalid flop-house in conditions even more crowded and unsanitary than on that ship. Unless they were very smart they'd be robbed of their money and possessions too. There were infectious diseases to contend with, many of their children wouldn't survive a year, let alone to adulthood. If they thought they were starting a new life where racial, social and religious prejudice didn't exist, they were sadly mistaken. America was for the brave. It took a strong body, a stout heart and determination to make it.

Matilda shook herself out of such pessimistic thoughts. For those who had the will it really was a country where dreams could come true. Just a few miles outside the busy cities was a land of incredible beauty. She hoped that every poor immigrant trudging into that building today would get to see its sparkling rivers, its mountains, forests and endless prairies. They had arrived too late to see real wilderness as she had – the vast herds of buffalo were gone now, the Red Indians who had survived had been robbed of their hunting grounds and pushed into reservations. Trains sped people from coast to coast and the paths that had been taken by the early pioneers in their covered wagons had all but disappeared. But there was still so much to thrill, so much opportunity for those with the nerve to grasp it.

An hour or so later as the tug chugged back towards the piers in East River, Matilda wiped away the last of her emotional tears and turned her mind to her future.

She had experienced so much in this land – joy and sorrow, poverty and riches, great love and passion too. So many of those she'd loved were dead, their graves marking places she could never forget. Yet on balance the good memories outweighed the bad. She had had so many dear, good friends, lovers who had filled her heart with bliss, and she'd seen and done things few women of her generation could even imagine. Even the immense evil she'd encountered, the terrible anguish and pain, was in soft focus now, only the happiness, humour and sweetness remained important to her.

She was ready now for what lay ahead. Tomorrow she would book a passage home to England, a first-class cabin where a steward would wait on her, imagining she'd been born to such luxury, and she'd spend the voyage polishing up her role as a grand lady.

It pleased her to think that the stories of London Lil would remain in American folklore for all time, but she must leave her here, kiss Lil goodbye and forget her.

Up in the wheel-house Giuseppe was at the helm, and Fanny was silently watching Matilda. Several times during the last hour she had seen the woman crying and her heart went out to her. She wished she knew her full story. Was she a widow? Did she have children and grandchildren? Or was that Irishman she'd spoken of the only real love in her life?

But as she watched, Matilda stood up and moved right into the bows. She bent over, one hand supporting herself on the rail, while with the other she appeared to be fumbling under her coat.

Fanny didn't draw her father's attention to this, thinking perhaps Matilda was adjusting her stockings. But suddenly there was something small and bright red in the woman's hand. She brought it up to her lips, appeared to kiss it and murmur something to it. Then, lifting her arm, she threw it into the sea.

As Matilda sat down again, Fanny slipped out of the wheel-house and looked over the side of the tug. The small red article was bobbing along on the surface of the water. Not a handkerchief or scarf, as she'd expected, but a red satin garter!

Fanny knew it must have some special significance to the old lady, perhaps a memento of her first love. She would give anything to know the full story.

Chapter One

London 1842

As Matilda Jennings wearily turned into Finders Court at seven in the evening, she caught a fleeting glimpse of a tuft of flame-red hair as its owner bobbed down behind a handcart. No one but her two half-brothers had such fiery hair, and if they were hiding from her it meant they'd been up to mischief.

'Luke! George! Come 'ere at once, if you know's what's good fer you,' she yelled.

Matilda was sixteen and a flower-seller. She was dirty and exhausted from a long day which had started at four that morning in Covent Garden market, yet despite having walked London's streets all day hawking her wares, she still managed to exude a defiant air of robust vitality.

Her blue dress was ragged, muck-splattered from filthy streets, her calico pinafore heavily stained. But her thick, butter-coloured hair was neatly braided beneath a mob-cap, her cheeks were rosy, and when she gave one of her ready smiles her bright blue eyes sparkled.

Most of the people who bought Matilda's flowers probably assumed she was a country girl, perhaps selling produce from her own garden. They wouldn't know the pink cheeks were caused by wind burn, or that the merry smile was just part of her salesmanship. There was a bony, malnourished body beneath the voluminous dress and petticoat, her shawl hid her shoulders invariably stooped from the cold, and once her basket was empty she hobbled home painfully in worn-out boots to the kind of tenement that would make her flower-buying customers shudder.

Finders Court was ten two- and three-storey ramshackle houses leaning drunkenly on each other around a tiny squalid yard. The upper windows, many of them boarded up with bits of wood and rags, almost touched the ones opposite. Each house had some ten or twelve small rooms, and most of these were occupied by more than one family. It was just off Rosemary Lane, London's largest second-hand clothes market, and just a few minutes' walk from the Tower of London and the river Thames.

At dusk on a chilly March evening, as always the court was teeming with noisy activity, costermongers trying to entice the frowzy women in grubby caps leaning out from upper windows to come down and buy the remaining goods on their handcarts, groups of dirt-smeared dock workers discussing the day's work, or the lack of it. Old men and women were flopped down on doorsteps, taking a rest before staggering up the stairs with their sacks laden with the proceeds of a day's scavenging work. Ragged children manned the water pump, filling their buckets and jugs, while younger siblings fought and played around them.

With only one privy shared by upwards of five or six hundred people, slop pails emptied along with rotting rubbish from windows, the stench was overpowering. Donkeys and horses were tethered overnight and it was quite a common occurrence for a pig to be rooting around in the yard too.

As the owner of the red hair remained hidden behind the cart, Matilda yelled again, louder this time, in a strident tone which reminded her uncomfortably of the boys' mother, Peggie. Perhaps they heard the similarity too, and knew Matilda was just as capable of giving them a good hiding, for this time both boys emerged somewhat nervously.

''Ow many times 'ave I told you to get up 'ome and set the fire afore I get back?' she yelled, side-stepping other children in her path and grabbing Luke, the older boy, by the ear. She would have caught George too, but she was hampered by her basket. 'Your father will be 'ome soon for his supper and he wants a cuppa tea before he goes out again.'

Luke was ten, George eight. Skinny, foxy-faced little runts with nothing in common with their older sister but identical bright blue eyes. Matilda had looked after them from birth, but since Peggie died four years ago she had taken on the role of mother. She had loathed Peggie, and often she disliked her brats too, but for her father's sake she did her best for them.

As she hauled Luke closer to her, the smell of him made her gag. 'Whatcha bin up to?' she gasped.

He didn't need to admit it. The stench was unmistakable. 'You dirty little sod, you've bin collecting pure again!' she exclaimed in horror.

'Pure' was dog's excrement. The lowest of the low collected it up and sold it to the tanners to treat their leather. There were a great many disgusting ways for poor people to make a living in London, but this one was the worst in her book.

Putting down her basket, she dragged both boys by the ears to the pump where a simple-minded lad from across the court was filling a bucket. She commanded him to continue pumping and pushed Luke right under the stream. Grasping his hair firmly with one hand, and using a rag she kept in the pocket of her pinafore, she scrubbed him down, hair, face, body, right down to his filthy bare feet.

'It's freezin',' he wailed, his teeth chattering as she finally let him go to grab George and give him the same treatment. Luke's thin worn shirt and ragged breeches were stuck to his scrawny frame and he shook himself like a dog, showering her with water. 'We only did it for you, Matty. We got a whole sixpence.'

If that explanation had come from almost any other child Matilda might have been touched. But Luke was a habitual liar and already an incorrigible rogue. She knew that if she hadn't spotted him, he and his brother would have nipped off to spend the money on themselves, probably waiting until she'd fallen asleep before crawling into the bed beside her in their stinking condition.

As so many people were watching and listening, Matilda didn't make any reply until she'd got both boys, still dripping and shivering, up the rickety stairs to their room at the top of the house.

'Take your clothes off and put your night-shirts on,' she said curtly as she closed the door. 'I'll deal with you in a minute when I've got the fire going. And don't even think of running out or you'll be sorry.'

The room was very dark because one of the two small windows was broken and had been replaced with a piece of wood. There was little furniture: an iron bed in which she and the boys slept – Lucas, their father, had a makeshift one, a flour sack filled with straw – a bench, a rough wood cupboard and a small table were all there was apart from their father's chair. It was solid oak with arms and seat smooth with years of constant use and Lucas jokingly called it the Bosun's chair. It was the only thing of any value they owned.

Matilda lit the candle first, then, taking it over to the fireplace, she raked the old ashes to one side, hastily dipped a bit of rag into the oil pot, and lit it from the candle, laying a few twigs over it. She didn't look round at the boys behind her, but she guessed by their silence they were signalling to one another, trying vainly to work out some plan to get out again tonight. But even they wouldn't dare run out in their ragged night-shirts which barely covered their bony bottoms, and they hadn't another change of clothes.

In a few minutes she'd got the fire going well, slowly adding more dry wood, then small pieces of coal. She held her icy hands to the blaze while she prepared what she was going to say to her brothers.

Appalling as Finders Court would be to someone from the upper classes, Matilda took some comfort in knowing it was one of the better tenements in the neighbourhood. At least here no one operated a penny-a-night shelter for the absolute down-and-outs. She knew of courts where there were as many as thirty people huddled in one filthy room, without even a blanket to cover themselves. In those, runaway children and orphans as young as five or six slept alongside criminals, prostitutes, beggars and the feeble-minded, and their corruption began from their first night in such places.

Matilda was an intelligent and sensitive girl. Spending her days in the better areas of London, she had observed every aspect of the huge divide between rich and poor. It wasn't just that the rich had grand houses, servants and ate well; their children were protected.

Most of London's poor relinquished all responsibility for their children long before they even reached Luke's age, turning them out and expecting them to find work to keep themselves. While Matilda wasn't against Luke or George working – after all, she'd started as a flower girl at ten – both she and her father believed it was their duty to hold the boys close to them in a family home until such time as they were mature enough to cope alone with the temptations and dangers of London.

With this in the forefront of her mind she turned to them. With their faces clean for once and shivering violently, they looked pitiful. Matilda pulled up the bench to the fire and ordered them to sit down.

'Jennings have never collected pure,' she said firmly, taking up a position at the side of the fire, her hands on her hips. 'Jennings have always been watermen. Being a waterman is a respected craft, like being a carpenter or a builder, and it's been passed down from father to son for five or six generations. So what do you think Father will do when I tells 'im what 'is sons 'ave been doing?'

''E'll strap us,' George snivelled, his eyes wide with fear.

'That's what you deserve,' she said, nodding her head. 'But it will break 'is 'eart, that's what. Collecting pure is a job for beggars. It's worse than scavenging in the sewers, as nasty as pickin' pockets. We ain't got much, but us Jennings 'ave always 'ad pride. That's why we don't share this room with no other family. We pays our three and sixpence each week and we 'olds our 'eads up. There's folks in this court what thinks we is 'oity-toity, but that's because they're jealous of us. You go out grubbing around picking up that stinking stuff, and you shame our family name.'

'But we was only thinking of you,' Luke whined, his red hair and white face suddenly very vulnerable and angelic-looking in the glow from the fire. 'We knows you needs the money.'

'Your father and me earn enough to keep us,' she said, softening a little and reminding herself they were only little boys. 'What we want is for you to go to Miss Agnew's every day, so you learns to read and write like me. That way you can get a proper trade when you're older.'

'Reading and writing ain't got you nuffin but sellin' flowers,' Luke retorted with some belligerence. 'You could do that if you was a blind cripple.'

'Maybe it's all I can do now, but at least I ain't selling meself like some of the girls around 'ere,' Matilda retorted angrily. Luke was a cruel little swine, he always had a knack of answering back with something that would hurt her. 'I goes to smart places, it's clean work and the flowers smell nice. Ladies and gentlemen buys them off me.'

Luke merely sneered, his sharp features so very like the rats which scuttled up and down the stairways. He had the mentality of a rat too. Quick, sly and vicious. He didn't seem to have inherited anything from his honest and kindly father. He didn't even show any interest in following the family trade.

'I don't like school,' George said, his eyes filling with tears. 'I can't do it and Miss Agnew beats us around the 'ead.'

Matilda sighed deeply. George was slow in comparison to his older brother, and she felt for him. There were no real schools for the children of the very poor, though she'd heard it rumoured there were men in the Government who believed there should be. All there was were dame schools, where women like Miss Agnew passed on their knowledge of the rudiments of reading, writing and sums, in one tiny room, to any child who turned up with the required ha'penny a day. Matilda had been taught by Miss Agnew herself and knew how cruel she could be, but to her it had been worth it. She read anything she could get her hands on, usually only religious tracts or news sheets she found in the streets, because real books were too expensive, but only last week she'd bought the first instalment of *Oliver Twist* by Mr Charles Dickens, and she could hardly wait to get the second part.

She could write a good hand, add up and multiply – if she could just get a job in a shop she'd be made for life. The trouble was that looking the way she did now, with her ragged dress and boots with holes in them, no one would take her on, not even as a scullery maid. She was on a treadmill, and until she found a way of earning enough to buy some decent clothes, she knew she couldn't get off it.

'If you try 'arder Miss Agnew won't beat you,' she said wearily. 'Now, promise me you'll go to 'er tomorrow? Or I'll tell Father what you've bin up to.'

They gave their promise, but she knew it was an empty one. They could see nothing in learning for them, earning a few pennies was far more satisfying. They might not collect pure again in a hurry, but they'd be down with the other mudlarks in the Thames in a day or two, scavenging for anything they could sell to the marine shops – nails, rivets, bones and bits of timber. She might as well talk to the wall.

She filled the kettle with water her father had drawn from the pump before he'd left for the river, then put it on the fire. Out of her basket she pulled the four mutton pies she'd bought on the way home. They were usually a penny each, but she'd got all four for tuppence as the pie man had a lot left unsold. With a nice thick slice of bread and a juicy orange each it was a good supper by Finders Court standards.

'Give us the sixpence then,' she said, holding out her hand. 'And while you're finding it, bring the wet clothes over 'ere and I'll 'ang 'em up to dry. You ain't goin' anywhere else tonight.'

Luke gave her a malicious look as he handed it over, and she guessed he would attempt to steal it back before the night was over, so she reminded herself to hide it well once he was asleep. It wouldn't be the first time she'd woken in the morning to find her apron pocket had been dipped into and a few of her precious pennies gone.

Wringing the clothes out of the window first, she then hung them over a piece of twine above the fire. The boys' clothes were even more ragged than her own, the seats of their breeches so patched there was nothing more to sew patches to. She hated to see them barefoot too, but their feet were as hard as nails and they wouldn't wear a pair of boots now, even if there was money enough to buy some.

The boys were just tucking into their pies and the kettle was boiling when they heard their father's heavy tread on the stairs. Matilda put a spoonful of tea into a tin jug, added the water and put it down on the table to draw. A couple of minutes later Lucas Jennings came in.

He was a short, stocky man with powerful shoulders and arms from a lifetime of wielding oars to ferry his passengers out on the river. His face was as brown and crinkled as a walnut, making him look older than his forty years. Like most men's of his class, his teeth were blackened stumps, and his fair hair was long and sparse. But his vivid blue eyes were what most people noticed first about him, and his clothes. His rough black pilot's coat and thin canvas trousers were a common uniform in his profession, but the clean red and white spotted neckerchief and black cap trimmed with gold braid signified he maintained his pride in a craft which had taken seven years of apprenticeship to learn before taking up his freedom at Waterman's Hall.

The weariness of the man was apparent in his slow movements and bent shoulders, but he smiled with affection at his children sitting at the candlelit table. 'Now, there's a sight to gladden the heart,' he said in his croaky voice. 'Three clean faces and supper on the table.'

Matilda moved towards him, kissed his cheek and took his coat to hang it on the nail on the back of the door. 'Did you 'ave a good day, Father? It were nice and sunny, weren't it?'

Spring was late in coming this year, only two days more of March to go and until today it had rained for what seemed like weeks.

'It were a fair one, Matty,' he sighed, sitting down in his chair and holding out his hands to the fire to warm them. 'The sun brought more folk out right enough, and made the river look purty again, but so many of them just walk across the bridges now instead of hiring us. It ain't like the old days.'

Lucas and the other licensed watermen's trade had been going into a decline for years now. In his grandfather's time only the most experienced men could be trusted to get their passengers safely through the narrow arches of London Bridge. Ships had moored up in the middle of the river, so that the men were busy all day taking the passengers to shore. But now London Bridge had been rebuilt anyone could safely get a boat through it, and the steam ships moored at piers now, so the passengers could walk off. Even the visitors to London who had once delighted in taking a boat to see the sights on the river were scarce, they didn't like the swell from the steamers.

Lucas took the big earthenware mug Matilda handed him and sipped the hot, black brew appreciatively. He would be out again in an hour, for the night trade on the river was the most lucrative, with passengers paying double fare to get to the entertainments on the South Bank in a hurry. But working nights had its own dangers: drunken young fools showing off by standing up and rocking the boat, and occasionally falling in, to say nothing of the blaggards who often tried to rob him when he got them to the other side. But Lucas wasn't so concerned with his own safety, what troubled him about night work was leaving his children alone. Finders Court had become ever more dangerous in recent years. Matilda was a pretty girl, and he'd seen the way some of his male neighbours eyed her up.

'You boys bin down in the mud again?' he asked, spotting the steaming clothes above the fire. ''Ow many times 'ave I told you to keep away from it?'

Matilda handed her father his supper on a tin plate. 'No, they ain't,' she said. 'They was just a bit mucky, so I washed 'em.' She paused for a second, casting her brothers a warning glance. Lucas was a kind man and a good father, but he wouldn't think twice about beating them if he knew the truth. 'I 'ad a good day today,' she went on, deftly changing the subject. 'Made three shillings all but a penny. I got primroses and violets, 'cos I was one of the first up the market this morning.'

Lucas's face clouded over at the reminder that she began her day while he was still fast asleep. While he was very proud of his hard-working daughter, he still felt a deep sense of guilt that through his stupidity in taking up with Peggie, he'd inadvertently blighted Matilda's life.

Her mother Nell had died in childbirth, leaving him with a sickly baby to take care of along with five-year-old Matilda and his two older sons John and James who were ten and nine at the time. Immersed in grief for the wife he had loved so much, and unable to cope with his children alone, when Peggie, a seventeen-year-old girl who had only recently come to live at the court, offered to help him out with the new baby, it never occurred to him to be wary.

Before he knew what was happening, she had moved in with him. He ought to have been suspicious when the children seemed cowed by her and reluctant to stay indoors. But he was so grateful Peggie was looking after his baby that he chose to ignore their behaviour, believing it was purely due to them missing their mother.

With hindsight he should have told Peggie to go when baby Ruth died a couple of months later. But his need to have the comfort of a woman in bed beside him was stronger than the niggling doubts about her suitability as a step-mother. By the time Luke was born, he knew the personal things of Nell's and items of furniture which had disappeared hadn't been stolen as Peggie claimed, but sold by her to buy gin. He knew too that she hadn't one-tenth of the housekeeping skills that Nell had had, and that she was often too harsh with his other children, but he was trapped by his conviction that a man had to take care of a woman once she bore him a child.

Soon after George was born two years later, Peggie was drunk almost all the time, and Matilda became nursemaid to Lucas's two youngest sons. The older boys, John and James, were absenting themselves as much as possible because of Peggie's drunkenness and Lucas was relieved when they finally went off to sea. Life in the navy was cruel, but the prospects were better than he could offer them working on the river, and he had no wish for them to hang around in London and witness their father being humiliated by a slatternly woman.

Four years ago, Peggie died. Drunk as usual, she had fallen in the path of a coach and horses. Lucas didn't shed one tear for her, by then he knew she sold herself to any man for the price of a glass of gin. But it was sad to see Matilda saddled with even more responsibility for Luke and George. She deserved better.

'You're a good girl,' Lucas said, reaching out for his daughter and pulling her close to him. 'So much like yer ma, I wish I could do more for you.'

As her father's hand slid round her waist to squeeze her, a lump came up in Matilda's throat. He rarely spoke of Nell any more, but the few words he did say made it clear he still thought about her a great deal and reproached himself that their life together hadn't turned out the way they had planned.

Lucas was just nineteen back in 1818 when he first saw Nell down at Greenwich. He was sitting in his boat, waiting for the return of his passenger he'd brought down from Westminster Bridge to collect some papers from a shipping office. She was standing on the quay watching the boats, and he was immediately captivated by her country girl rosy cheeks and golden hair. Lucas had never been one for girls, he always found himself tongue-tied and awkward in their presence, but when this one smiled at him, he felt brave enough to climb out of the boat and ask if she wanted him to call her a ferry.

She said she just enjoyed watching the boats on the river as it made a pleasant break from her work as a parlourmaid. Her voice was different from London girls', as pretty as her face, soft and melodious, and when Lucas remarked on it, she laughed and said she came from Oxfordshire originally. She had come to work for a sea captain here in Greenwich when she was thirteen, and in seven years with him she had worked her way up from scullery maid to her present position.

Lucas found himself searching out fares to Greenwich after that, just in the hope of seeing her again, and it soon became apparent to him by the number of times she was there, waiting on the quay, that she felt the same way. She was so refreshing, a happy girl who spoke of her job and employer with affection and pride and considered herself very fortunate. As Lucas had two more years to go of his apprenticeship to his father before he got his own freedom of the river, he knew it was folly even to think of courting a girl, but he fell deeply in love with her, and she with him.

They both took so many risks – Nell might have been discharged without a reference if she was caught slipping out to meet him for an hour in the evenings just to walk with him in Greenwich Park, and Lucas would have been skinned alive by his father if he knew he left his boat unattended when he should have been working. But just to see one another, to kiss and hold hands made the risks worthwhile.

They made love for the first time one Sunday afternoon. The sea captain had gone away to the country with his wife for a few days, and Nell was allowed the whole day off. Lucas rowed her up the river to show her Lavender Hill, and there in a field with the sweet perfume of the lavender fields filling their nostrils, they couldn't hold back any longer.

Silas, Lucas's father, pronounced him a fool when he told him he wanted to get married. Aside from the fact few working men bothered with a legal marriage, he said his son was too young to take the responsibility for a woman. But he softened when he met Nell, charmed by her decency, pretty face and soft voice. Perhaps too he saw advantages for himself, for he had lived alone with his son for some five years since his wife had died, and his own health was fading.

Starting married life in two rooms in Aldgate, shared with her new father-in-law, wasn't what Nell had hoped for, but she was already carrying Lucas's child and her nature was optimistic and warm-hearted. They made plans that when Lucas finished his apprenticeship, they would find themselves a place of their own.

She scrubbed out the two rooms, made curtains for the

windows, cooked, washed and mended their clothes, and Silas often remarked when he saw beeswax polish on the floor that she was the best homemaker he'd ever known. A year after John was born, James arrived too, and even though times became harder because Silas was often too sick to work, they were very happy. Then just a few months after Lucas got his freedom of the river, Silas died, and Nell became pregnant again.

Lucas sold Silas's old boat, and hid the money in a box under the floorboards. He worked all the hours he could, and each day he added another shilling or two to their hoard, so his and Nell's dream came closer to realization. Soon they would be able to sell his boat too and buy a larger one with smart new paint which would attract a far better class of customer, and finally get a small house of their own further up the south side of the river by Lavender Hill.

It was a fire which laid waste their dream. In the winter of 1823, just a month before the new baby was due, the wooden house in Aldgate that Lucas had lived in for his entire life was razed to the ground, along with three adjoining ones. Fortunately Nell was out with both the boys, then aged four and three, and only one old man trapped on the top floor perished, but they lost everything, furniture, bedding and most importantly their savings.

Perhaps it was the terrible shock that made Nell go into labour too early, but they had only just found the room in Finders Court when it started. The baby girl only lived for a few hours, and Nell lay on a pile of straw, the only protection from the cold, and cried pitifully.

Lucas did his best for his family, but it seemed to him that was the point when fate turned against them. The Thames froze over so he had no work, and both boys and Nell got sick. Even later that year, when Lucas was earning again, Nell was only a shadow of her former self, weary and despondent because Finders Court was so crowded, dirty and noisy. It wasn't until Matilda was born in the autumn of 1826 that she gathered herself and tried to make their humble room a home. Lucas could remember promising her he would still find a way to get them a real house, but he never earned enough again to save.

Just before Nell died, she begged Lucas to make sure Matilda learned to read and write, so she would have a chance of a better life. Looking back, Lucas realized it was the only promise he ever made to Nell that he'd managed to keep.

Matilda's lips on his cheek brought him out of his reverie. 'You've done all you could for me,' she said softly. 'And you're a good man. Things will get better, just you see. We got our 'ealth and strength.'

Lucas left to go back to the river when he'd finished his supper Luke and George climbed into bed to keep warm and asked Matilda to tell them a story.

'I don't know that you deserves one,' she said, but smiled as she said it. Rested after supper, in the soft glow of the candle, her cap and pinafore washed and drying ready for the morning, she could find it in her heart to love them. They were little rogues, but then maybe they needed to be tough and wily to survive. Hadn't she learnt at an early age to pinch a few pennies from Peggie to make sure they got some dinner?

'Tell us about if you was Queen,' George said, his eyes half closing already with sleepiness, red hair shining like newly scrubbed carrots in the candlelight.

Matilda laughed as she combed her hair through. George loved stories and the more fanciful the better. 'Well, I'd be a happy Queen,' she said. People always remarked how the young Queen Victoria had a plain and miserable face. She thought this was very strange, after all Victoria was only twenty-three and she'd been brought up with everything anyone could wish for. 'I'd want all the people to be happy too, especially the poor ones, so I'd spend lots of money building them 'ouses, find good jobs for them all and give cartloads of food away each day. Every little boy would get a new suit of clothes, and all the girls would get a new frock. Of course if I was Queen you'd be princes, so you'd live with me in the palace and ride in a coach with black 'orses.'

'You wouldn't be Queen in that case,' Luke interrupted, his expression one of utter scorn. 'I'd be King.'

'It's only make-believe,' she reproached him. 'Us Jennings have got about as much chance of becoming royalty as father of finding a lump of gold in the Thames.'

Matilda was woken by the church clock striking four. It was so very tempting to cuddle closer to her brothers and go back to sleep, but if she did that the best flowers would have been sold by the time she got to Covent Garden. She crept out of bed and fumbled for her clothes in the pitch darkness. She couldn't see her father, but she knew he was there by his loud snoring. She dressed quickly, two flannel petticoats over her shift, wool stockings and her dress, then felt her way over to the fireplace to find her pinafore and cap. They were still damp, but they'd soon dry once she got outside. She groped her way over to the cupboard to pull a lump of bread off last night's loaf, then retrieved the money she'd tied up in a bit of rag and hidden from Luke, and finally picking up her boots, cap, pinafore and, shawl, she put them into her basket and crept out of the room.

Her boots she put on outside the door, but she waited until she'd washed her face and hands down at the pump in the yard before combing and plaiting her hair and finishing her dressing. She wrapped her shawl around her, criss-crossing it across her chest and tying the ends behind her back, then, with her basket over her arm and money in her pocket, set off for Covent Garden, munching at her bread.

At half past seven she was sitting with a group of other flower-girls on the steps of St Martin-in-the-Fields. She had bought a dozen bunches of violets and another dozen of primroses for two shillings, some paper for a ha'penny, and the twine she'd picked up for nothing around the stalls; now she was dividing them up into small posies and arranging a few leaves around them. She could make them into thirty-six posies for a penny a time, giving her a profit of a shilling at worst, often a great deal more when the sun shone and gentlemen gave her extra. The sun was shining now, melting the slight frost, and she felt sure today was going to be a good one.

The other girls were mostly much younger than Matilda, some only nine or ten. Many of them were barefoot, all more ragged and dirty than Matilda, and one was crippled, with one leg much shorter than the other.

As usual there was little conversation between the girls, just a nod and a smile as yet another joined them. Six years ago when Matilda had first begun selling flowers she had found this silence disconcerting, but she understood it now. Every single one of them had a hard luck story to tell, yet they were mostly so similar that no one wanted to hear them. They grouped here every morning to gain a little comfort in being with their own kind, that was enough. Matilda would sometimes help a younger girl with her posies, remembering how hard she'd found it to make them look pretty when she first started, but she steeled herself against any further involvement. Occasionally she recognized a face as belonging to the younger sister of a girl she'd known some years earlier, but she'd learned never to inquire about them. Flower-girls had a habit of turning into prostitutes at fourteen or so.

At eight o'clock Matilda made her way slowly up the Haymarket towards Piccadilly. She found this part of London curious as it changed so much during the course of the day. Now in early morning it was busy with shop girls and businessmen rushing to work, side-stepping the many street sweepers and scavengers. Occasionally she was lucky enough to sell a couple of posies to men at this time of day, but mostly people were in too much of a hurry to stop. By noon a different class of people emerged, ladies and gentlemen arriving in carriages and cabs for luncheon and shopping. There would be throngs of young, pretty girls too, hoping to catch the eye of a gentleman.

Until a couple of years ago Matilda had admired and envied these girls, fresh from the country, in their fashionable clothes, dainty boots and flower-trimmed bonnets, but she was shocked when she eventually discovered they were in fact 'gay' – the name given to prostitutes. She knew now that in just a few short years, unless they were very lucky, these same girls would be much worse off than she was, riddled with disease, old before their time and forced to seek their customers down by the docks or in the dark, festering alleys of Seven Dials.

In the evening as the theatres and fun palaces opened, the Haymarket was an even more lively and colourful place. Ladies in sumptuous hooped gowns and glittering jewels, accompanied by gentlemen in opera hats and frock-coats, were out for a night's entertainment. Sword swallowers, tumblers and jugglers flocked to the area, and the air was laden with aromas of roasting chestnuts, shellfish and sweetmeats. Music came from every corner, the hurdy-gurdy man, singers and street musicians all competing with one another for the pennies thrown by the rich.

Yet busy Oxford Street with its elegant shops was a better

place to sell flowers and that was Matilda's destination today. She knew the sun would lure out the shoppers, and the sight of fresh spring flowers loosened the purse-strings of even frugal housewives. With luck her basket would be empty by two in the afternoon.

At one o'clock Matilda's bright smile was no longer a forced one and her cry of 'Sweet smellin' violets, buy a posy for yer lady, sir,' was almost a song. She had only four posies left to sell, and three times during the morning men had given her a whole sixpence without expecting change. She thought she might get off soon to go and look for a pair of boots in Rosemary Lane, the hole in the bottom of her present ones was growing so big she might as well not be wearing any.

Her expectations that the sunshine would bring people out had been more than fulfilled. The pavements were packed with jostling crowds and the carriages, hansoms, broughams and horse-drawn omnibuses disgorged more every minute. She was warm for once, she'd even been compelled to remove her shawl and put it into her basket. She might be very hungry and thirsty, but that was almost a delight knowing she had enough money in her pinafore pocket to buy a treat of a meat pie and a glass of ginger beer on her way home.

Matilda was just moving across the pavement towards the street to waylay an elderly gentleman with a much younger woman on his arm, when out of the corner of her eye, to her left, she saw a little girl emerge from a shop, toddling intently towards the kerb. She was a pretty little thing between two and three, with dark curly hair bobbing beneath her white bonnet, in a pink flounced dress and lace-trimmed pantaloons. Matilda was distracted from her original intention of selling the gentleman some flowers purely by the child's apparent glee at the busy street before her. She had clearly slipped away unnoticed from her mother or nursemaid.

The child moved very quickly despite her long clothes, and although the crowd was very dense around her, no one appeared to be aware of her presence. Matilda's protective instincts were tugged, and she began to push her way through the crowd towards the child. But as she moved, the sound of cantering horses' hooves and the jingling of harness made her turn her head. To her dismay a carriage pulled by four horses was coming hurtling down the street. She looked back towards the child and saw she had reached the kerb and paused, but she was clapping her hands together with excitement as she too saw the horses coming closer. She was much too young to sense the danger and it was more than likely that she would step out.

Dropping her basket to the ground, Matilda yelled out a warning and darted forward, frantically pushing people out of her way. The coach and horses were so close now she could smell them and almost feel the heat from them on her back. Then to her horror the little girl stepped out into the street, directly in their path.

Matilda's own safety didn't even cross her mind, she leaped right out into the street and snatched the child up by the waist. She heard a frenzied whinny behind her, but her thoughts were all for the child. As she felt a glancing blow against her back, it catapulted her forward, and she tossed the child towards the pavement.

A strong smell of ammonia was the next thing Matilda was aware of, and she recoiled from it instinctively.

'Can you hear me?' she heard a male voice say close to her, and as she regained her senses she found herself lying on the ground and a man was supporting her head and holding a bottle of smelling-salts to her nostrils. Confused for a moment, she thought she'd fainted from hunger and that the memory of rushing to rescue a child was just a kind of dream.

''Course I can,' she replied. 'And stop sticking that up me nose.'

She heard someone laugh nearby and suddenly became aware of a large crowd of people all looking down at her. The man supporting her had black curly hair and a clerical collar. He was very young for a priest, with doleful, dark eyes. 'What's your name?' he asked.

'Matilda Jennings,' she replied and struggled to sit up. 'Was there a little girl?'

'Yes, there was,' he said. 'But thanks to you she's now safe with her mother.'

It was a relief to know she hadn't imagined it. 'Her ma ought to be horsewhipped letting go of 'er 'and,' she said indignantly. 'Where is she? I'll give 'er a piece of me mind.'

A loud peal of laughter from the watching crowd incensed

her. 'What are they laughing for?' she asked. 'It ain't funny! That little tot could 'ave bin trampled on.'

'I think they are laughing from relief that you are not only unhurt but forthright enough to speak out,' the man said with a weak smile. 'What you did was exceptionally brave. Now, let me help you up.'

As he took her two hands to help her to her feet, Matilda winced at a pain in her back. Someone in the crowd shouted out that she needed a doctor.

Matilda was used to living by her wits. She wasn't above pretending to shiver to gain sympathy on a cold day, or to stand outside a bakery looking longingly at the bread until she was handed some. Instinctively she knew this was a situation she could use to her own advantage. 'My back, my back,' she exclaimed, making an exaggerated grimace of agony as she clutched her sides. 'It dun 'alf 'urt! What's up wif it?'

A woman moved closer to Matilda. She was plump and kindly looking, wearing the kind of plain dress and straw bonnet which suggested she was a cook or a housekeeper.

'The horse's hoof caught your shoulder,' she said. 'It's torn your dress and it's bleeding badly. It needs bathing.' To Matilda's astonishment the woman then turned to the priest with the smelling-salts and wiggled her finger at him, her round face bristling with indignation. 'You and your wife should take care of her, sir. It were your little girl she saved, weren't it?'

Matilda looked at the man in shocked surprise. She had assumed he was just a passer-by who because of his calling had stopped to help. Yet priests didn't get married and have children!

He must have guessed what she was thinking because he not only agreed he was the child's father, but added that he was a Church of England parson. Matilda also noted now that he was trembling and ashen-faced. But any sympathy she felt for him was tempered by the possibility of a reward. She pretended to sway on her feet as if about to faint.

'Look at her!' the woman said, catching hold of Matilda's arm. 'She's had such a terrible fright. She might have been killed.'

'I'll take her into the shop so she can sit down,' the parson said quickly, and before Matilda could as much as blink, he had picked up her abandoned basket and was leading her into a draper's shop.

Outside on the street Matilda wasn't afraid of anyone, not even the police who often moved her on during the day, but as she was led through the doors and saw the long polished wooden counter, bales of wools and cottons and piles of bed linen, her nerve left her. The elegantly dressed customers all took a step back in alarm, the assistants' faces tightened with disapproval. She knew that to them she was just a beggar and quite likely to be verminous too, certainly not a person to be brought into a high-class establishment.

Matilda's first thought was to run back out. She didn't think her injury was much more than a graze, and even the pleasing prospect of a cup of tea, and perhaps a shilling as a reward, wasn't worth humiliation.

'I can't come in 'ere, sir, they won't like it,' she whispered, but if he heard her, he ignored her protest and whisked her right to the back of the shop where his wife, flanked by two women assistants, was sobbing noisily, clutching the little girl to her bosom as if terrified someone was going to snatch her from her.

The parson let go of Matilda's arm and moved closer to his wife. 'Dry your eyes, Lily my dear,' he said soothingly. 'Tabitha is quite safe now, and we must think of the brave person who saved her from injury.' He turned his head back to Matilda and beckoned for her to come forward. 'Look, here she is. Her back is hurt and I think she's in shock.'

Matilda didn't know what 'in shock' meant, not until the woman passed her daughter to her husband and stood up to embrace Matilda. It wasn't just a slight touch of the arms or an inclination of the cheek either, but an impulsive, full-blown hug.

'My dear, words can't express my gratitude,' she gasped out, dabbing at her wet face with a handkerchief. 'I only realized Tabitha had run out when I heard a shout from the street. I ran like the wind to the door, just in time to witness what you did. You must think me appallingly rude and ungrateful, but I just pulled my angel from the person who had caught her, and ran back in here with her. Whatever must you think of me?'

Matilda was so bowled over that a real lady could bring herself to explain her actions and to hug a mere flower-girl that she was stuck for words. She remembered being told that when Peggie was knocked down by the horses, the coachman didn't even stop until he got around the corner. He'd said later that 'he didn't wish to distress his lady passengers with the sight of blood'. Even her father had said he hadn't expected anything more of gentry.

But then this woman wasn't exactly gentry, she had a nice gentle voice and a good manner about her, but her dress and bonnet were plain and she wore no jewellery. In fact she was unremarkable in every way, slight and thin, with small, sharp features and dull brown hair beneath her bonnet.

'I understand, missis,' Matilda said awkwardly. 'You was just worried about yer little 'un. I 'ope she weren't 'urt with me grabbing 'er like that?'

The woman looked across at her daughter wriggling in her husband's arms and smiled with affection. 'Not a mark on her, and completely unaware what trouble she caused. But let me see to you, my dear. We must get you some tea, and look at your injuries.'

In the next five or ten minutes Matilda felt as if she had woken to find herself in a different world. A cup of very sweet tea was put in her hands, the women from the shop were casting almost envious glances at her, and the parson was introducing himself and his wife to her as if she was someone of quality.

He was the Reverend Giles Milson, his wife Lily, and she was informed that Tabitha, their only child, had just turned two. Their church was St Mark's in Primrose Hill and they lived in the parsonage. Lily Milson, as she tried to examine Matilda's back through the torn dress, said she must come home with them in a cab so the wound could be properly examined and bathed.

Matilda was perturbed by this offer. It was common knowledge that Church people only offered charity as a ruse to give the recipient a lecture on the Scriptures. Rosemary Lane was a favourite haunt of missionaries and Bible thumpers, who stood on corners ranting about hell-fire and damnation. She'd heard, too, that girls who turned to them for help were often ravished. What she wanted was to be given a couple of shillings and sent on her way.

Yet a small voice inside her whispered that she might be better off for going along with these people. If nothing else she might get a decent dinner out of them. Perhaps even a few old clothes.

Matilda's customary self-restraint failed her in the cab. Whether it was because it was her first ride in a cab, little Tabitha smiling beguilingly and reaching out for her, or the Milsons' solicitous questions about how she felt, she didn't know. But suddenly she was crying.

'I'm sorry,' she kept repeating, covering her face with her hands. 'I don't know what's up wif me.'

Lily Milson was still feeling tearful herself, and indebted to this girl for saving her child, so her heart welled up with compassion for her. As the tears streamed down the girl's cheeks, so the dirt was washed away, and it seemed to Lily this was God's way of showing her that but for the lottery of birth, she too could have been one of life's unfortunates, instead of sitting here in a carriage, in clean and decent clothes, with a loving husband and beloved daughter beside her.

Lily hadn't always thought herself fortunate. Back in Bristol, as a middle child among eight, no one had ever taken much interest in her. She was timid and plain, with no real talents. Her father, Elias Woodberry, was a prosperous wool merchant and although he made much of his five sons, the daughters were largely ignored and left in the hands of the servants. Although her mother was distant with all her children, male or female, she seemed actively to dislike Lily, constantly complaining that she had no spirit or even looks to commend her.

At twenty-five, still unmarried and in her parents' eyes set on spinsterhood, Lily had become an embarrassment, so she was often sent off to various relatives as an unpaid governess to their children for long periods. One of these relatives was her father's younger brother, an impoverished parson in nearby Bath. Yet far from being a punishment to be sent there, it was a pleasure – her Uncle Thomas was a kindly man, his wife Martha affectionate and grateful for any help with her five lively children. It was while there that she met Giles, a new curate at Uncle Thomas's church. He was three years older than her, also with no fortune as he was the youngest of six, but the moment she looked into his dark, soulful eyes, she fell for him. He was a true humanitarian, who had chosen the Church rather than the military as a career, because he fervently believed his mission in life should be to help the poor and needy.

If Lily had met Giles at her parents' home she doubted he would have found anything to like about her, much less love. There she was a scorned mouse with no conversation or opinion. But no one belittled her at Uncle Thomas's, they praised her gentle nature, applauded her knowledge of books and loved her for her happy delight in their children. After several months of visits, when Giles sheepishly told her he was falling in love with her, she told him he had only seen the best of her there and perhaps he ought to see her in her own home before making such statements. He laughed and said he was seeing her as she really was, and he didn't think he would like her parents very much anyway.

It was the happiest day of her life when Giles asked her to marry him. He pointed out that he had little to offer her, that even when he was given his own church they would never have the luxury she'd been brought up with, all he could give her was his love. That was all Lily wanted.

Shortly after their wedding, which her father arranged with almost indecent haste, Giles was sent to London, to St Mark's in Primrose Hill, to be curate to the frail Reverend Hooper, a widower of seventy. On the Reverend Hooper's death a year later, Giles took over as parson and they had the small parsonage to themselves.

Lily found being a parson's wife empowered her. Visiting the sick in the parish, organizing Sunday school for children, and persuading the more wealthy parishioners to donate money for charitable causes, weren't tasks to her, but a fulfilling joy. To be her own mistress at last, admired for the very qualities her family had scorned, and to have a passionate and adoring husband was like being reborn. She loved Primrose Hill – in many ways it was like Bristol and Bath with its fine Regency houses – yet here she had position and even some authority. Walking up on to the hill and seeing the panoramic views of London across Regent's Park was an unfailing delight. Giles often reminded her sharply that just outside their parish there were terrible areas where two and even three families lived in one room, where life expectancy was seldom beyond thirty-five, and over half the babies died in infancy, but because Lily hadn't seen it with her own eyes, it didn't trouble her.

Tabitha's birth was Lily's moment of triumph. At thirty-one, after four years of waiting and hoping, she had resigned herself to never becoming a mother. But fear was her joy's uninvited companion. Suddenly Giles's tales of infant deaths, of cholera, smallpox and all those other monstrous diseases took on terrifying proportions. Although she needed help, she refused to have any other servant than Aggie, the housekeeper they had inherited from the Reverend Hooper, for fear they might bring pestilence into her home.

But now, as Lily looked across the cab at Matilda struggling to compose herself, all at once she realized that today's near tragedy was a warning to her. There had been many times in the past year when she'd become fraught with trying to cope with a lively toddler alone. Today she'd only been distracted for a moment, yet that was all it took for Tabitha to get out of the shop and into danger. How ironic it was too that although Oxford Street was full of women much like herself, her child should be rescued by one of the class she feared.

Deeply ashamed of herself, Lily reached across the cab and patted Matilda's arm. 'Shock makes us all cry,' she said gently. 'But you'll feel better when you've had some food and I've got that wound cleaned up for you.'

Matilda had been to Primrose Hill selling her flowers many times in the past, but it looked and felt quite different alighting from a cab. The big houses with their marble steps and gleaming brass on their front doors had always seemed threatening before, now they looked welcoming.

Sometimes in her braver moments she had slunk down basement steps to try to sell her wares to the cook or housekeeper, and most times she was shouted at and told never to come back again. But now she was actually being asked in, not through a servants' entrance either, but through the front door.

It didn't matter that it was the smallest house in the square, just a plain two-storey one tacked on to the churchyard. It was a real house, the first she'd ever been in.

The front door was opened by an elderly, fat woman with bristles on her chin, wearing a snowy-white apron and ruffled cap, but her bright smile faded as she saw Matilda with her employers.

'This is Matilda Jennings, Aggie,' Giles said, ushering her in before him. 'She saved Tabitha's life this morning and got hurt, so we've brought her home. I know what a good nurse you can be, so perhaps you'll take a look at her injuries and give her a meal.'

'Yes sir,' the woman replied, although her stiff expression remained. 'But the dinner's been waiting this last half-hour, it's ready to serve.'

Lily brushed past the older woman with Tabitha in her arms. 'I can serve the dinner,' she said in an impervious tone. 'You see to the girl.'

Perhaps it was as well Matilda was struck dumb by the kitchen she was led into, for Aggie's disapproving scowl might well have made her utter some cheek.

It was large and bright, full of sunshine, the cleanest room she'd ever seen. A large scrubbed table stood in the centre, and instead of just an open fire to cook on, it was inside a contraption fitted with doors. Matilda had seen advertisements for such things and knew it was called a 'stove' but she'd never seen one before. A dresser was full of dainty china, shelves trimmed with red and white checked scallops, even the cooking pots looked nice hanging from hooks.

'So what happened to Miss Tabitha?' Aggie almost spat at her, the minute she'd closed the door behind them. 'And I don't want no lies either. The Reverend might be easy to fool. But I'm not.'

Matilda wasn't surprised by this response, cooks and housekeepers were notorious for shielding their employers. In as few words as possible she explained what had occurred.

Aggie slumped down on to a chair and looked astonished. 'You jumped in front of a galloping horse?'

It wasn't so much a gallop as a canter, but there were four of them, so Matilda nodded.

Aggie's face softened and she touched her eyes with the bottom of her apron, all hostility gone. 'Well I never,' she exclaimed. 'You were a brave girl. No wonder Madam brought you home. I'd better look at your wounds.'

The smell of meat and gravy wafting around the kitchen was so tantalizing Matilda was tempted to ask for food first, but she wasn't brave enough. She turned round so the older woman could view her back.

Aggie tutted but touched the wound gently. 'Your dress is all stuck to it, and it's none too clean either. I think you could be doin' with a bath, miss.'

Some time later when Matilda was at last allowed to sit at the table with a plate of stewed lamb and vegetables in front of her, she wondered for a moment if she was dreaming all this. Was she really eating this huge dinner? Had she really had a real bath? Was the clean grey dress she was now wearing really for her?

It was a house of miracles, that much she was sure of. Aggie had taken a fruit pie out of the stove, all perfect and golden just like the ones in the bakeries. Out in the scullery next to a sink there was a big tub thing with a fire beneath it which Aggie called the boiler, she'd turned a tap and drawn out hot water into a pail to fill a tin bath. Matilda was shocked to find she was expected to take off all her clothes and climb into it. A bath to her was just a wash-down all over, when her brothers and father were out, and she washed her hair under the pump outside.

Aggie had overseen the whole thing, including washing her hair for her. She'd tutted over the wound on her shoulder and said she hoped it wouldn't leave a scar. Matilda wondered why anyone would worry about a scar on her back, it wasn't as if she'd ever go around in a low-cut dress like ladies did.

But as if washing with proper soap wasn't enough, after she'd dried herself, and had ointment put on her back, Aggie came back into the scullery bringing a whole armful of Lily's old clothes for her, not just a dress but a cotton shift, two flannel petticoats, a pair of stockings and boots. There was even a pair of drawers, something Matilda hadn't ever worn before. The boots were just a bit big, but that didn't matter, they were comfortable, with no holes in them.

She felt like a lady. Clean, sweet-smelling and lovely.

Aggie glanced over her shoulder at the young girl eating her dinner and winced as she saw the way she used only the knife and pushed the food on to it with her fingers. But she had cleaned up well, her hair was as shiny as buttercups now it was washed, hanging loose over her shoulders. A pretty little thing with her sweet smile and her lack of cheek. Aggie hadn't even seen any lice on her, and she'd looked hard enough.

Aggie had been housekeeper at the parsonage for eighteen years. The Reverend Hooper had taken her on when she was widowed and left with four small children. In those days the children came with her to work, sitting out here in the kitchen or playing in the garden while she cleaned, washed and cooked for the old man. When the Milsons arrived nearly seven years ago, she had resented them bitterly. She had been used to doing everything her own way, in fact she'd come to treat the parsonage as if it were her own home. But Lily Milson changed all that. Suddenly it was 'Spring-clean that room,' 'This needs a good polish,' And 'That isn't the way I like this or that cooked.' She was forever in the kitchen, poking her nose into every last thing. Yet Aggie came round to her when she saw the tender way the woman cared for old Reverend Hooper when he became sick.

Aggie admitted now that Lily had turned out to be an almost perfect parson's wife. She fully supported her husband's work in the parish, showing kindness and understanding to those in need. No one was better at smoothing ruffled feathers than she was. She had endless patience with the difficult wealthy parishioners who believed the parson was their sole property, and worked tirelessly at making the parsonage more comfortable and inviting. Since she'd arrived she'd made new curtains, covers for old chairs, and introduced Aggie to new dishes to cook. Her only real fault was that she was so pernickety about trifles. Nothing must be wasted, not a crust of bread or left-over vegetables. If there was one small mark on her husband's surplice it had to be boiled, starched and ironed again. Everything had to gleam, be it floors, furniture, glass or silver. To her dirt was the Devil.

Yet something had changed in her since Tabitha was born. While ecstatically happy with her long-awaited child, she seemed so troubled and fearful too. She could change like the weather, one day kind and thoughtful to everyone, the next a shrew. One minute she was complimenting Aggie on her cooking, the next everything was wrong. But the worst was her ridiculous fears about disease – she seemed to think the little one was so fragile that even a common housefly might kill her!

When Aggie thought what her children had to contend with in their early days, hunger, cold, rats climbing over them while they slept, left alone for hours while she tried to find work to keep them from the poor-house! Yet they'd grown up healthy, all off her hands now, one in the navy, one in Australia, and the two girls married off with homes of their own. In her view Tabitha was overprotected, fussed over from morning till night, and that was far more unhealthy than a bit of dirt.

'Reverend and Mrs Milson want to see you when you've finished,' Aggie said as she passed the girl a slice of gooseberry pie. She wanted to say she was sorry for being so frosty at first, she of all people had no right to be like that with someone poor. But Aggie wasn't one for retracting anything. Besides, she was never going to see the girl again and she had her position to think of. 'So mind your manners, and don't go calling her "missus", it's madam and sir!'

Matilda wasn't sure of the exact meaning of 'manners'. Was it just saying please and thank you? Or was there more to it? As she made her way up the narrow hallway to the parlour at the front of the house where Aggie said she was to knock, then wait to be called in, she wondered if she was supposed to curtsey, or was that only to proper gentry?

She thought this house was splendid. There was a lovely lavender smell and everything was shiny, from the banisters to the floor beneath her feet. She didn't much care for the pictures, though, they were all dark and gloomy, especially a long narrow one of a lot of men sitting along a table, all looking at a man in the middle with sort of sunrays round his head. If she ever got rich enough to live in a house like this, she'd have bright paintings of happy scenes.

'Come in!' Giles Milson called out in answer to her tentative knock.

The first thing that struck Matilda about the sitting-room was how hot it was, the fire blazing as though it was mid-winter. The walls too were a deep dark red which made it seem even hotter, and there was so much furniture she could barely see more than a foot or two of floor.

The parson was sitting in a high-backed chair on one side of the fire, his wife on the other in a lower one. Matilda supposed Tabitha had been taken upstairs for a rest.

The couple both stared at her for a moment before speaking, then Lily excused herself. 'I beg your pardon, Matilda, it's just that you look so different with your hair loose. What a pretty colour it is!'

Matilda could only blush and drop her eyes to the floor. All she wanted now was to retrieve her basket and get home. She hoped they weren't going to lecture her about going to church before they let her go.

Giles was so taken aback by the girl's new appearance he found himself tongue-tied. The face of the girl he'd brought round with smelling-salts hadn't really registered in his mind, only that he was indebted to her. Even during the cab ride home all he'd really observed about her was her speedwell-blue eyes, and her dirt-engrained hands. Yet this girl in front of him had more in common with one of his parishioners' daughters than a waif from the slums. Her skin was pink and white, her pretty yellow hair shone like ripe corn, and she wore his wife's old dress with more style than Lily ever gave it.

'How is your back, Matilda?' he managed to get out.

'Just dandy, sir,' she replied, she hadn't the heart to continue the pretence of being badly hurt. 'These clothes you give me is lovely and the dinner was nice too.'

Giles was struck by her appreciative candour and the way she looked him right in the eye as she replied. An idea which had seeded in his mind over dinner suddenly seemed much less preposterous.

'Do sit down,' he said, beckoning to a chair between his wife and himself. 'Mrs Milson and myself would like to know a little more about you. Perhaps you could start by telling us where you live, and about your family?'

Matilda groaned inwardly, convinced that this was his way of leading up to the expected lecture on God. But as she was wearing clothes they'd given her and she had a full belly, that seemed a small price to pay for telling them anything they wanted to know.

She launched into a brief family history, including the death of Peggie which she admitted was through her drunkenness, hastily pointing out her father wasn't a drinking man and how he wished he could afford to find herself and her brothers a better home.

Lily asked how long she had been selling flowers, and seemed shocked to hear she'd started it at ten.

'Ten ain't so young,' Matilda said earnestly. 'I see's girls every day as young as five or six. But I went to school, see. Father wanted me to read and write so I'd 'ave a better chance like.'

There was a little gasp at this and Lily's eyes opened wide in surprise. 'You can read and write?' she said.

'And do sums,' Matilda said with some pride. 'But I like reading best, when I can get 'old of a book.'

She wondered what she had said wrong when the couple exchanged glances.

'I loves flowers too,' she added defensively. 'It's bloomin' 'ard getting up at four to get to the market in the middle of winter, but I tells meself at least it's clean work, not like working down at the tips, sifting rubbish all day.'

Madam raised her eyebrows. 'Sifting rubbish?' she repeated. 'Why would anyone do that?'

Matilda wanted to smile. She had forgotten that people like these knew nothing of the darker side of London. 'They sift through it for stuff to sell,' she explained. 'Bones, metal, sometimes they even get lucky and find valuables someone has thrown out by mistake. Then the dust left behind goes to make bricks.'

'How intriguing,' Lily replied, but she held a handkerchief to her nose almost as if to ward off the imagined smell in such a place. 'I had no idea.'

Giles cleared his throat. 'What sort of work would you really like, Matilda? I mean if you could choose?' he asked, giving her a penetrating look.

Matilda had often heard stories about young girls being lured away from their homes and families with a promise of a better job, never to be seen again. It was said these girls were sold abroad as white slaves. It crossed her mind she should be very careful in case that's what these two had in mind. It was a bit strange they'd brought her to their house and wanted to know so much.

'To be the Queen would be dandy,' she joked to hide her sudden nervousness.

Giles smiled. He found this girl puzzling, by rights she ought to be either cowed or wily enough to be demanding something of them. Yet apart from a slight wariness in her eyes as she answered their questions, she seemed innocently comfortable.

'I'd be 'appy to work in a shop or be a maid,' Matilda added quickly. 'But I don't s'pose anyone would take me on. I don't look or sound right, do I?'

There was no reply to this. Giles just looked at his wife and raised his eyebrows. She thought that was confirmation they agreed with her.

In point of fact, before Matilda had been summoned, the Milsons had been discussing how they should reward this girl. Lily had felt a shilling, a few groceries and the clothes they'd already given her were sufficient. Giles had pointed out that would be no lasting good, and suggested asking one of their wealthier parishioners to take her on as a scullery maid, or perhaps get her a position in the big laundry in Camden Town. But now, faced with her clean and neat appearance, the intelligence in her face, the lack of evasion to their questions, and discovering she could read and write, it seemed to Giles that she was heaven-sent as a nursemaid for Tabitha.

Giles knew only too well that he was being impulsive, and that he should consult his wife before speaking out. Yet if he did he knew she'd throw up a hundred different objections. Even if he could persuade her to consider it seriously, during the waiting period Matilda would be back selling flowers and probably lost to them for good.

Throwing caution to the wind, Giles decided to act on his own initiative. Lily would doubtless punish him for it with one of her long, cold sulks afterwards, but he told himself that the end justified the means, Lily needed help with Tabitha, and quickly.

'How would you like to work here, Matilda, as a nursemaid for Tabitha?' he blurted out. 'Mrs Milson has been under a great strain with her duties as parson's wife and mother. I believe you would be ideal for us.'

'Would I like to work here?' Matilda forgot herself and bounded out of her chair. 'I'd like it more than anything in the whole world.'

Giles heard Lily's sharp intake of breath, felt her anger at his not consulting her first, but faced with the girl's exuberance, he knew he'd made a rational decision.

'Have you ever been to church, or read the Scriptures?' Lily said in a starchy tone. She liked the look of the girl herself, and was so grateful to her for saving Tabitha she felt she must be rewarded, but she was deeply shocked by her husband's impetuosity. Yet a wife couldn't speak out in public against her husband. She would have to wait until they were alone to upbraid him for it.

'Never 'ad no time or the clothes for church,' Matilda beamed. 'Not since me mother died, anyways. But I learned to read from Miss Agnew's Bible. I liked the story of David and Goliath.'

Lily pursed her lips in disapproval. She didn't like the Bible thought of in the same light as a 'penny dreadful'. 'Of course if you do come here as nursemaid we shall have to instruct you on the Scriptures,' she said tartly.

The sharpness of the woman's tone cooled Matilda's excitement. All at once she saw that the offer had come only from the parson, not his wife, and although she wanted to work here so badly she would sell her soul for it, she knew that without Lily's approval of her she'd be out on her ear at the first mistake she made.

'I'll 'ave to talk about it to my father first,' she said after a moment's reflection. 'I mean, if I ain't there, who'll mind the boys?'

Giles guessed the real cause of her prevarication and such sensitivity endeared her to him even more.

'Of course you must speak to your father,' he said, casting a warning glance at his wife. 'Just as my wife and I must be in complete agreement. Suppose you come to see us again on Sunday afternoon at three? Perhaps your father could accompany you too. Then if everything is agreeable on all sides, you could start then.'

Matilda knew she had only a second or two to charm Lily into agreement. She turned towards the woman and gave her most winning smile. 'I know I don't look or sound like a nursemaid. But you'd never 'ave to be afeared wif me lookin' after your baby. I's got eyes in the back of me 'ead where little 'uns is concerned. And I could learn your ways, madam, real quick.'

'Yes, I've no doubt you could, Matilda.' Lily gave a tight little smile in return 'We'll see you on Sunday.'

Chapter Two

Lucas listened to Matilda's description of the dramatic events of her day with a fixed half-smile. The story's amusement value came only from her keen observations in both the draper's shop and the parsonage. He was only too aware his daughter might have been maimed for life by the horses, but smiling was one way of hiding his real feelings.

'But 'ow can I go and work for 'em, Father?' she sighed as she got to the end of the tale. She leaned her elbows on the table, wearily supporting her head with her hands and looked at him beseechingly. 'What about the boys?'

Lucas took a deep breath before replying. It was bitterly ironic that Matilda should suddenly get some good fortune on a day when he had been dwelling on how he'd failed all his children. It wasn't so much that he was unable to provide any more than basic necessities, there were families far worse off than they were. It was more shame at what he'd become in the past few years.

Once he'd been as kindly and generous-spirited as she was, he had cared about people, friends, passengers and neighbours. But somewhere along the line he'd grown bitter and heartless – was it any wonder his two younger sons were fast turning into a couple of little villains? He couldn't remember when he'd last taken them out on the river, or even checked how they were doing at school. He wasn't much of a father.

Because of this he'd come home early today. His intention was to take all three of them out, buy Matilda a new bonnet, shirts and breeches for the boys and later in the evening take them in his boat along to Vauxhall Gardens for a treat.

But Matilda was all rigged out like a lady's maid, with an offer of a job. The boys were out and hadn't been seen all day.

'Don't you fret about the boys,' he said carefully. He guessed they were up to some mischief and would delay coming back until he'd gone out again this evening. 'They's my worry, not yourn. If this parson and his wife are decent sorts, you must go to them.'

'But I'll miss you, Father,' she said, and her eyes filled with tears.

Lucas's heart melted. Matilda was the only good thing in his life, a living memory of her mother and the happiness he'd shared with her. Without Matilda to come home to every day he felt he had no purpose in life, no reason to keep striving. Yet he knew it was selfish to hold her here, he must think only of her future and happiness.

'I'll miss you an' all,' he said, but managed to smile as he said it. 'But I'd sooner miss you than have you tramping the streets every day with flowers.'

Matilda threw herself into his arms and sobbed.

Lucas wished he was able to put his feelings into words. He loved all his children. As babies he'd fed and bathed them, walked the floor with them at nights when they were sick. Even though John and James were gone now and in all likelihood he'd never see them again, they were still in his heart. Yet what he felt for Matilda was different. He didn't understand why he felt so afraid for her, but not the boys. Just the thought of her being handled roughly by some oaf made him feel sick to the stomach. London was so full of danger – the gin palaces, the penny gaffs, procuresses looking for sweet-faced girls to debauch, young gentlemen prowling the streets searching for innocents to seduce. But how could he warn her of these dangers without tainting her mind?

'Your mother would want this for you,' he murmured against her hair. Just the clean smell of her reminded him poignantly of Nell. 'She'd be so proud of you.'

Matilda stayed in the safety of his arms, sensing the conflict inside him and loving him still more because he was so strong. 'Will you come with me on Sunday?' she whispered.

''Course I will,' he whispered back. 'I'll polish up me boots and put a clean shirt on for it. And if I don't like the looks of 'em, I'll bring you straight back.'

On Sunday morning Matilda woke to the sound of church bells. She had gone to bed last night brimming over with joy that it was probably her last one in Finders Court. But now as she saw a dust-filled sunbeam slanting on to the foot of the bed, and knew she was seeing it for the last time, all at once she felt very scared and she wasn't so sure she wanted the Milsons to take her on.

She might only be a lowly flower-girl to people like them, but here in the court she was treated with respect. Being literate set her apart, people often called on her to read or write something for them, and that made her feel good about herself. Here too there was always someone to call on in times of trouble, there were neighbours who remembered her mother with fondness and looked up to her father. Who would she turn to in Primrose Hill?

She lay in bed listening to the sound of her brothers' and father's breathing, and reminded herself that tonight she would be sleeping alone, in a room where rats, mice, bugs and lice would never dare enter. After today she would never again have to use the stinking privy down in the yard, she had seen the Milsons' one and it was as clean and sweet-smelling as their kitchen. She would never go hungry, wear boots with holes, or stand for hours on icy streets until her hands and feet were numb. So maybe Mrs Milson would be hard on her until she learned her ways, and she didn't much fancy the idea of being forced to pray and study the Scriptures, but it couldn't be worse than getting up at four in the morning to walk to Covent Garden.

At half past twelve Matilda was ready to leave. She had so little to take with her, a spare shift and a petticoat bundled up in her pinafore, and two shillings in her pocket. She had made a pot of porridge for them all and fried some bacon, yet she was barely able to eat hers for a lump in her throat. The dishes and porridge pot were washed, the beds tidied and the floor swept. Her empty flower-basket sat in the corner silently reproaching her.

Luke and George were sitting on the bench intently watching their father shave. They were both wearing the new shirts and breeches he had bought them in Rosemary Lane the previous afternoon. The clothes might only be second-hand, but they were clean and unpatched, and for once the boys looked decent, even if they wouldn't stay clean for long.

'I wish you's could come and see where I'm going to work,'

she said to them, ruffling their hair with affection. 'The parsonage is so lovely, all clean and bright. Maybe if you saw it you'd understand why I keep on to you both to go to school, you see, the Milsons wouldn't want me there if I couldn't read and write.'

Both boys had been unusually quiet and helpful this morning. Luke had fetched water and even emptied the slop pail, the first time she remembered him doing so without being asked. George had polished his father's boots.

'Will you come back to see us?' Luke asked in a surprisingly quavery voice.

''Course I will,' she promised. 'Every chance I get.'

'I'll miss you telling us stories,' George said, and his eyes were swimming with tears.

Matilda was too choked up to reply to this, she hadn't expected the boys to show any sorrow she was going. She turned away to look in the piece of broken looking-glass on the mantelpiece and tied the strings of the new straw bonnet Father had bought her yesterday, and struggled to control herself.

Lucas put on his coat and brushed it down. The atmosphere in the room was as bad as if someone had died. 'We'd better be off now. It's a long walk,' he said. Then, turning to the boys, he wiggled a warning finger at them. 'Mind you keep out of mischief. I want you back in here by five o'clock and the fire lit, or you'll get no supper.'

'Promise me you'll go to school and keep out of trouble,' Matilda begged the boys as she bent to hug and kiss them.

'We will,' Luke replied, clinging to her like a limpet.

As Matilda walked down the stairs with the sound of George crying behind her, she felt her heart was breaking. She knew that within half an hour they'd be off out with the other urchins in the court, and they'd never keep their promise about school, or keeping out of mischief. Sadly she suspected that within a week or two Father would be coming home to an empty, dirty room, and he'd lose the will to drag his sons in. How long would it be before he began stopping off in an ale-house on the way home, rough company and drink preferable to facing an empty, lonely room?

Father and daughter hardly spoke as they cautiously picked their way through the maze of narrow, foul-smelling alleys towards King's Cross. In this area Sunday was little different to any other day. Shops and businesses might be closed, but there wasn't the respectful hush which fell on the rest of London, or any display of best clothes to set the day apart. Costermongers advertised their wares with strident voices, the hurdy-gurdy man and street musicians competed, ragged children played in the dirt and women yelled at each other from upper windows. Knowing that she was leaving all this behind her, Matilda's thoughts see-sawed between elation and sorrow. It was ugly. So vile, cruel and noisy that she couldn't understand why she felt even the slightest regret at leaving it. But these streets and alleys, however mean and ugly, were home, she had a clear identity here and knew what was expected of her. In Primrose Hill she'd be an ignorant foreigner. She almost hoped the Milsons had had second thoughts about her.

Lucas was trying very hard not to liken this walk to the last steps to the gallows. But that was what it felt like. True, he would be free to retrace his steps later this afternoon, he would still have his sons and his livelihood, but his daughter would be chopped out of his life from the moment he said goodbye to her. It had to be that way, all or nothing, if Matilda was to make a better life for herself. He hoped he was man enough to let her go, that his courage wouldn't fail him at the last kiss. He had pulled Nell down, he wasn't going to repeat it with his Matty.

But as they walked through Camden Town towards Regent's Park and the air grew gradually sweeter, both their spirits rose at the sight of pretty cottages, fine houses and blossom-laden trees. Whole families were out in the sunshine, mothers in ribbon-trimmed bonnets on their husbands' arms, their children dressed in Sunday best walking sedately in front of their parents for an afternoon in the park. Carriages and broughams rolled past at a leisurely pace, ladies in silks and satins sat under parasols, their escorts in top hats and winged collars.

'It's a great many years since I've been up this way,' Lucas said reflectively, taking Matilda's hand and tucking it into his arm just like a gentleman. 'Your ma and I used to come out 'ere sometimes when we was first married. She liked to look at the grand houses and the ladies' fashions. We used to make out we 'ad a little cottage by the park.'

Matilda stole a sideways look at her father. He had looked so grim earlier, his weather-beaten face furrowed by frowns. He still wasn't smiling, his tone was gruff, but there was a gentler expression on his face and he was looking around as eagerly as she was.

'Did you know you loved her right off?' she asked. She was puzzled by the mechanics of courtship, love and romance. Right from a very young girl in Finders Court she'd seen far more brutality between men and women than love and tenderness. She had heard from other flower-girls that men were only nice till they 'got it'. Yet the few books she'd read all spoke of love being beautiful, and she had always sensed that was the way her parents had felt about one another.

'I suppose I must 'ave,' he said and gave a little bashful laugh. 'I knows I couldn't wait to see 'er again anyways. I wore me arms out rowing over to Greenwich where she worked. She were the only girl fer me.'

'Did you love Peggie too?' she asked cautiously, fully expecting him either to evade the question or tell her to mind her own business. He didn't ever speak of Peggie.

'No, I never,' he said, much to her surprise. 'And seeing as you've brought the subject up, I'll warn you, don't you ever dally with a grievin' man. They ain't right in the 'ead for a bit. They wants to replace the one they've lost, and it don't work.'

Matilda digested this bit of wisdom silently. She had never been short of male admirers, hardly a week passed without some lad asking her to go to one of the penny gaffs with him to see the shows. She had seen through the doors of such places, and the raucous drunkenness, the noise and stink of them repelled her. Yet even if a lad was to offer some less crude entertainment, she doubted she'd agree to go. Perhaps she was peculiar, most girls of her age were already living with a man, yet she hadn't met one she even liked enough to kiss.

'Doing it', as the other flower-girls referred to sex, sounded so ugly, yet she had always held on to the notion that it must be different if you loved the man and he loved you back. But how would she know that for sure?

'How does a girl know when a man loves her truly?' she asked tentatively.

Lucas glanced at his daughter, wondering what prompted such a question. Nell would have known how to answer it, but he guessed in her absence he would have to try to think what she'd have said.

'When 'e wants what's right for ' er, I suppose,' he said. 'When 'e'd row right across the river just to look at 'er face and never think 'ow far it were. When 'e'd give 'is life willingly for 'er.'

Matilda's eyes prickled with tears. She knew somehow that her father's words were the truth about love, and until a man could offer her that, she wouldn't settle for anything less.

As Matilda and Lucas were making their way to Primrose Hill, Giles and Lily were sitting in the parlour digesting their Sunday luncheon, and speaking tentatively about the imminent arrival of Matilda.

'I do agree she has a certain charm,' Lily said cautiously. 'But you were so hasty, Giles. We really know nothing about her.'

'I think we know everything which is important,' he said evenly. 'She is brave, selfless, honest, and very anxious to improve her station in life. She has a sense of humour, and she is forthright. Tell me, Lily, what was it you didn't like about her?'

'The way she spoke,' Lily said quickly and made a little shudder. 'I know she can't help that, but it reminds me of where she comes from.'

Giles half smiled. He knew Lily was imagining a filthy hovel infested with rats. 'Aggie doesn't speak very much better than Matilda,' he said. 'She goes home at night to a place I doubt you'd wish to live in. You don't distrust her because of it. So tell me what you *did* like about the girl.'

Lily had spent the last couple of days thinking of nothing else but this girl. She was deeply indebted to her for saving Tabitha, and like Giles she had been taken by the girl's forthright manner and her enthusiam too. She knew that most of her trepidation was due to fear Tabitha might be tainted in some way by being cared for by a stranger. No man, not even one as sensitive as Giles, could understand such deep-rooted maternal fears.

'I liked the way she looked, such pretty hair and eyes. I liked the way she was so honest about her family too. I approved of her saying she'd soon learn my ways.'

Giles grinned, glad to hear a positive response. 'It seems to me, Lily, that the good in her far outweighs the bad. So let's just keep open minds when she arrives with her father. I dare say we'll learn a great deal more about the girl once we've met him.'

'And if I shake my head at you, you promise you'll say you've changed your mind?' she pleaded.

Giles sighed. 'I promise,' he agreed. 'But you must promise to be reasonable.'

Giles's first reaction on opening the door to Matilda and her father was surprise that Lucas Jennings wasn't the dirty, coarse-looking brute he'd expected. The man was not only clean and tidy but his clear blue eyes had an honest expression. 'I'm very pleased you came with Matilda,' he said, holding out his hand to the man. 'I'm Reverend Milson, do come in.'

Lucas swept off his cap, and awkwardly shook the man's hand before crossing the threshold. 'Pleased to meet you, sir,' he said, his voice strained and more croaky than usual because he was in the presence of a man of the cloth. 'It was right decent of you to offer my girl a position.'

'Mrs Milson and myself are indebted to Matilda for saving our little one's life,' the parson replied. He wondered if the man was going to turn down the offer because he couldn't manage without her. 'We fervently hope that you'll find everything favourable here today and agree to leave Matilda with us.'

Lucas didn't reply for a moment. He held his cap tightly between his hands, wringing it nervously. 'She's a good girl and she deserves a chance in life,' he said eventually.

Giles was humbled by that response. Watermen were renowned for being a proud and tough breed, not given to taking any kind of charity. For Jennings to come here and admit another man could give his only daughter more than he could, proved he was an intelligent and loving father. Yet sensing the man was unused to taking a servile role, and might even become hostile should he have to remain in it for long, Giles took them straight into the parlour where his wife was sitting with Tabitha on her knee.

After introducing Lily to Jennings, and asking both him and his daughter to sit down, Giles rang the bell. 'I thought we'd just have tea together while I explain the duties we'd expect Matilda to undertake,' he said.

Aggie brought in a tray of tea, and while placing it on a low table in front of her employer she winked at Matilda reassuringly.

The wink suggested there was nothing to be frightened of, but Matilda felt sweat break out all over her as she saw the dainty tea cups. Suppose she or her father dropped one and disgraced themselves? Three days earlier this room had looked fascinating and inviting, now it seemed claustrophobic with all its furniture, pictures and pieces of china. She didn't belong here, she'd never get used to it, and she had a strong desire to run out of the door and back to Finders Court where at least she could move freely without knocking into something.

Her panic was heightened by the strained silence. Madam sat white-faced and anxious, clutching her child to her. Her husband perched on the edge of his seat, running one finger around his dog-collar as if at a loss where to begin. Lucas was looking intently at a painting on the wall, and the tick of the clock on the mantelpiece seemed very loud.

It was little Tabitha who broke the ice. As her mother put her down on the settee to pour the tea, she wriggled off and ran straight over to Lucas, smiling engagingly and holding up her arms for him to pick her up.

'So you've come to see me, eh!' Lucas forgot his nerves and his face broke into a broad, appreciative smile. 'Well, you are a purty little thing, just like my Matty said you were.'

He scooped her up on to his lap and settled her into the crook of his arm, just as he had done with all his children at the same age. She looked up at him and patted his face with a chubby hand, as if she'd decided they were friends.

The tea pot rattled in Lily's hand. She opened her mouth to order the child off his lap, but closed it just as rapidly as Lucas spoke to her daughter.

'Now, you've got to be a good girl for my Matty,' he said, tickling her chin. 'No mischief. No running away!'

Matilda's heart missed a beat at the older woman's initial fearful reaction, but at her father's tender words to the small girl all at once she felt a rush of warmth come into the room. Both parents smiled and visibly relaxed.

It was a good moment, and Matilda had never felt prouder of her father. In one entirely instinctive gesture, he'd wiped out the line between their classes and showed her the way to win the Milsons' approval. All she had to do was love their child.

'I had quite forgotten you are used to small children, Mr Jennings,' Lily said, her small, pinched face suddenly looking almost pretty. 'Of course one tries to prevent them from being over-friendly to strangers, but it seems Tabitha is a good judge of character.'

'Takes me back to when Matty was small,' Lucas said, looking down fondly at the little girl. 'She'd wriggle on to me lap the moment I sat down. The boys was more distant like.'

Matilda sat in astounded silence as her father and Lily continued to chat about children. She had never imagined that her father was capable of conversing with those outside his own class and certainly not about domestic matters. It wasn't until the tea had been passed round that Giles brought the subject back to Matilda's duties.

'Your main role will be to look after Tabitha in the nursery,' he said. 'But at times when she is sleeping or with Mrs Milson, we'd like you to give Aggie a hand around the house too.'

By the time the clock on the mantelpiece struck three, Matilda had drunk two cups of tea, and eaten three small sandwiches and an iced bun. She was aware that Lily wasn't as keen to employ her as her husband appeared to be, but all the same she'd explained Tabitha's daily routine from when she rose at around seven-thirty to her going to bed at six, and the way she said things like 'And I'll expect you to tidy the nursery, or wash her napkins' implied she'd already made up her mind Matilda was to stay.

The duties sounded very light, after all she'd been used to looking after two small children single-handedly right since she was a child herself, without any of the luxury she would have here. It was true she had never used an iron or cleaned silver, and her cooking skills were very limited, but she was sure she could soon learn these things.

Giles said he would pay her five shillings a month and she could have every Tuesday afternoon off as long as she was home by nine at night.

When Lucas heard the clock chime he sensed he must be the one to finalize everything. He was more than convinced his daughter would be well treated here, but like Matilda he had noticed a certain coolness on Lily's part. 'I hope I'm not rushing you, but I have to get back to my boys,' he said, getting to his feet. 'Now, is Matilda suitable for you both, or does she come back with me?'

Giles took a quick glance at his wife and she nodded back at him in agreement.

'She certainly is suitable, Mr Jennings,' Giles said, getting up from his chair and taking a step nearer to shake the man's hand. 'So if it's agreeable with you we'd like her to start now. I just hope you can manage your boys without her.'

Lucas was relieved by the man's eagerness. He thought Matilda would soon bring his wife round, there weren't many she didn't charm. 'Don't you worry none about them,' he replied with a broad smile which showed his blackened teeth. 'I'll manage fine. Now you be good, Matty. And keep up your reading.'

'I'll see to that,' Lily spoke up, smiling up at him from her position on the couch. She couldn't describe herself as entirely happy with Matilda, her speech grated on her ears and the way she ate and drank was sickening. But Giles was after all an excellent judge of character, and if he truly believed Matilda was right for Tabitha, then it must be so.

Matilda hadn't said anything to find fault with, but then she hadn't said much at all, just looked around her with wide eyes. But Lily was taken with Mr Jennings. He was a decent man with a great deal of dignity. She had been dreading this interview, half expecting the man to steal the teaspoons or spit on the floor, so she'd been pleasantly surprised he knew how to behave in polite company. That at least suggested Matilda could adjust to being here. 'Now, Matilda, why don't you show your father out,' she said, her tone much warmer. 'I'm sure you'd like a couple of minutes alone together?'

At the front door Matilda hugged her father, trying hard not to cry.

'Don't you give them no cheek,' Lucas said in a hoarse whisper as he held her tightly. 'Learn all you can from them and become a lady.'

'I'll come and see you on my afternoon off,' she whispered.

To her surprise he caught hold of her shoulders, gave her a little shake, and his expression was suddenly very fierce.

'Oh no, Matty. You don't come there no more.'

She thought he meant he didn't want to see her any longer,

and the tears she'd tried so hard to suppress broke through. 'You don't want me no more?' she sobbed

''Course I wants you,' he said gruffly. 'I just meant you wasn't to come there. I'll meet you on Tuesdays at five by Holy Joe's.'

'But why, Father?' she asked in bewilderment. 'I thought you'd want me to come 'ome and make you supper.'

For a moment he just looked at her, and his blue eyes so like her own were sad and bleak.

'You's out of that place now and I don't want you coming nowhere near it again,' he said eventually. 'Never look back. Not never.'

Later that evening Matilda lay in bed in the little room just off the nursery, happily savouring the warmth, room to move, utter silence and the sweet-smelling starched sheets against her skin. Back in Finders Court there was only one worn, dirty blanket on the bed, sheets were an unknown luxury, warmth came from her brothers' small bodies, and she often woke itching all over from bed bugs.

Her nursemaid's uniform, a plain dark blue dress, was hanging behind the door and a crisp white starched apron and cap lay on the back of a chair in readiness for tomorrow. She had been in the parsonage less than eight hours, yet in that short time she'd been bombarded with so many items and experiences previously unknown to her that although she was exhausted and so very comfortable, she couldn't sleep for thinking about them.

It might be the smallest, most insignificant house in the square, yet to her it was vast. Aside from the parlour, kitchen and scullery she'd seen previously there was a dining-room and a room with a desk and lots of books which Giles called his 'study'. Upstairs there were four rooms. The nursery was at the front of the house with Matilda's small room leading off it, across the landing was the Milsons' room, and there was yet another spare one behind it. Every room had so much furniture – chests, chairs, odd little tables that served no purpose but to hold ornaments – and everything polished so they shone like glass. When she thought of the way people lived back in Finders Court, with two families to nearly every room, it seemed very unfair that just one small family could have all this to themselves.

Oil lamps were something she'd only seen from a distance until today, but Lily had shown her how to fill them, trim the wicks and light them. Each one could light up a room like a dozen candles. In the nursery there was a contraption in front of the fire called a guard, to prevent Tabitha burning herself. Meat was kept in a wire safe to keep the flies off it, even the sugar had a little muslin cap trimmed with beads to cover it. She didn't think she'd ever get used to the huge amount of plates and dishes used in this house – at home they had one tin plate each, scraped so clean they hardly warranted washing. Sugar tongs, butter knives, bowls and dishes for things she'd never heard of. Even the chamber-pots here were decorated with pretty flowers!

Matilda saw it as much more than a job, it was a place of great opportunity. Giles said she could read any book which took her eye, and Lily was going to teach her to sew, while Aggie would show her how to cook and launder. It was all so exciting. As for little Tabitha, she was the most adorable, sweet-natured child she'd ever met.

There was only one small grey cloud. Matilda had noticed Lily wince at her on several occasions today, and she thought that was because she didn't talk like her or eat very dainty. Yet she wasn't going to let that bother her too much; if she watched and listened to Lily very carefully, she thought she could quickly learn her fancy manners and nice way of talking.

Now, as she thought over all the events of the day, the reasons behind her father saying he didn't want her to visit her old home became clearer. Her own mother had come up from the country to work in a nice house like this one, and if she hadn't fallen in love with a waterman, her life might have continued to be secure and comfortable. Matilda had been too young when her mother died to know if she had regretted marrying Lucas, but clearly he thought he had let his wife and family down. Now that this chance had come for his daughter to better herself, he didn't want anything to hold her back from climbing up the ladder of opportunity.

She supposed that his advice to 'never look back' was wise and kindly meant. But did he really think she could forget her past and origins that easily? Surely all those hard times had given her something which was worth carrying on into a new life?

As Matilda was dropping off to sleep, Lily Milson was wide awake in bed beside her husband, fraught with anxiety about her new nursemaid.

'She eats like a savage, Giles,' she whispered in the dark. 'She tears at food, chews with her mouth wide open, and the noise she made drinking!'

'She can't help it, no one has ever taught her,' Giles said comfortingly. 'Just think of how good she is with Tabitha. She bathed her tonight with as much tenderness and care as you do.'

'But what if Tabby picks up the way she speaks and eats?'

He slid his arm around his wife and cuddled her into his shoulder. 'We correct them both together,' he said evenly. 'Now go to sleep, dear. Between us we'll make something of her. She's strong, capable and intelligent. I believe we've found an uncut diamond.'

Giles could feel how stiff and tense his wife was. She was clearly going to be awake half the night imagining terrible horrors, but knowing there was nothing more he could say to reassure her, he pretended to fall asleep.

He loved Lily for her sweetness, lack of vanity and her home-making skills, but there were times when he felt he might have been better advised to marry a more worldly and robust woman. She worried about the most trivial of things, and since Tabitha was born she'd been so fearful and agitated. She was well suited to being a parson's wife here at St Mark's where most of his parishioners were the class of people she'd been born into, but how would she manage when he had to move on elsewhere?

The past few years in Primrose Hill had been very pleasant, but Giles hadn't taken the cloth to secure himself wealth or comfort. In his view St Mark's could get by just as well with an elderly parson who liked to preach to the already converted and he should be sent somewhere that was more of a challenge.

He had already discussed this at length with the Bishop of London who agreed with his views, but Lily was the stumbling block. Her apprehension about Matilda was an exact reflection of her attitude towards all the poor. She was filled with compassion for them, she cared about injustice as much as he did, yet she was so repelled by dirt and the possibility of disease that she was likely to become ill herself if forced to live in close proximity to them.

Giles had been stunned three days ago when she not only embraced Matilda for saving Tabitha, but insisted she came home with them. But although Lily found pleasure in seeing the girl transformed by a bath and new clothes, if he hadn't forcefully insisted they give her a chance as nursemaid, Lily would have considered she'd done her duty and happily sent the girl back to the slums without another thought.

Perhaps it was exactly that which had provoked Giles's impulsive offer, though he hadn't thought along those lines at the time. If Matilda proved herself here, and helped his wife to overcome her fears, then Lily might be more willing to consider moving on. Maybe the Lily he'd married would re-emerge again too when she had less work to do – it had been such a very long time since she'd responded to him with any passion.

The Bishop had said that America was desperate for young, enthusiastic English clergymen, and in Giles's heart of hearts he felt that was the path God wanted him to follow. But he also wanted Lily to take that path with him willingly and joyfully.

A week later, on Sunday morning, Matilda was in St Mark's Church with Tabitha and Lily, looking up at the Reverend Milson in the pulpit. She thought he looked quite beautiful with his shiny black curls almost touching the shoulders of his starched white surplice, and she felt very proud of herself for ironing it so well.

When her mother was alive she vaguely remembered being taken to a church on Sundays, and being made to say prayers before going to sleep. The only time Matilda had been in one since her death was either to shelter from the rain, or when she'd been lured in by a missionary with the promise of a hot drink and a bun.

She thought this church was lovely, especially the windows with colourful pictures on the glass. It smelled of polish and flowers, and it felt very good to be seated right up at the front with the gentry, instead of tucked away at the back with the other poor people. She wished she dared turn round and look at everyone, the rustle of silk gowns, the smells of scent were all so enticing, but she knew Lily would take her to task later if she didn't appear to be engrossed in what the Reverend was saying.

His sermon was on the sin of avarice, a word she wanted to

understand, but she had long since lost the thread because Tabitha kept distracting her. She was sitting between Matilda and her mother, wriggling and pushing her feet at the pew in front. She looked a picture in a yellow dress with matching pantaloons and bonnet, but Matilda was now very well aware this little girl wasn't as sweet as she looked, she needed a firm hand.

Lily was another who wasn't all she seemed. She had a gentle manner, she was fair and kindly in most ways, but she was so very fussy. Nothing escaped her sharp eyes, not a wisp of hair coming from Matilda's cap, not a speck of dust on the furniture. She checked all tradesmen's bills several times, every item of clean laundry was scrutinized for remaining stains. For all Matilda knew perhaps all real ladies carried on this way, yet it seemed to her that Lily was in some way unhappy underneath, as if there was something wrong in her life so she had to work twice as hard to pretend everything was fine.

Aggie's biggest complaint against Lily was the way she wouldn't allow anything to be wasted. She said that a lady shouldn't demean herself by being so frugal. Matilda wasn't entirely sure which side she stood on. Having spent most of her life hungry she was glad to see that left-over meat and vegetables were made into soup, that stale bread made a pudding, yet she couldn't help thinking that if she were Lily, she'd give those scraps to the starving beggars on the street.

Matilda was brought back to the sermon when she heard the word 'gluttony'. She had been chastized several times during the week for what Lily called 'an unladylike appetite'. But how could she help it when she'd spent so much of her life being hungry? The meals Aggie prepared made her mouth water long before she sat down to eat them, and there were so many wonderful tastes she'd never experienced before. Oxtail soup, so spicy and rich she wanted gallons of it. Meaty gravy poured over roast potatoes, rice pudding and chocolate cake. Even at night when she was called into the parlour for prayers, she found herself thinking about what Aggie had planned for the next day's dinner.

Along with discovering that neither Tabitha nor Lily was quite what she expected, her duties had turned out to be a great deal heavier too. In fact at the end of the day she was often more exhausted than she'd been as a flower-girl. Lily's passion for cleanliness involved a tremendous amount of work. Hot water had to be carried upstairs in pails for washing, and then down again to be emptied. Every chamber-pot had to be scalded after emptying, linen had to be boiled.

It took a good hour to get Tabitha ready in the morning, washing her from head to foot after she'd done her business on the chamber-pot, brushing her hair, then dressing her in all those underclothes and petticoats, even before her dress. If she wet herself during the day, which she often did, everything had to come off again.

Mealtimes were a long, tedious torture when she found herself under close scrutiny from Madam. While trying to suppress her desire to wolf down her own food, she had to remember the countless rules. She could hardly believe there were so many: knives only to be used for cutting and pushing food on to the fork, the right hand for a glass, lips closed while chewing, fruit pips to be put on the spoon, not spat out. On top of this she also had to help Tabitha, and she had to be cajoled into eating anything.

It had crossed Matilda's mind many times in the last week that the upper classes could learn a lot from the poor, especially where children were concerned. Very small children soon learned the folly of wetting themselves once they were uncomfortable. They ate anything put in front of them because they didn't know when they'd get the offer of food again, and they would play a lot more happily without so many clothes hampering them. Poor Tabitha in all her petticoats could barely sit down on the nursery floor to play with her doll, and when out in Regent's Park or Primrose Hill in the afternoons, she couldn't run off any steam. It was no wonder she could be so fractious.

Of course Matilda wouldn't dare voice such thoughts, any more than she'd dare show any irritation when Lily constantly kept coming into the nursery to check what she was doing. Instead she counted her blessings, whether that was being instructed in ironing while Tabitha had a nap before dinner, or an hour of washing up with Aggie while Tabitha spent some time with her parents. She was learning skills every minute she spent in the house.

The best bits of the day were the afternoon walk, and the hour before Tabitha's bedtime. Then she could be herself, telling the little girl stories, playing with her, just like she'd done with her brothers. The evenings were the worst time. Even when she wasn't asked to clean silver or mend something, and she could read, she still felt dreadfully lonely. It was then she'd think about her family and worry about how they were managing without her. Sometimes she even missed the noise in the court and wished she was back there.

But now as she sat here in the church, clean, well fed, and with Tabitha's small hand in hers, she felt happy. She was sure Lily was beginning to trust her. Once she'd learnt to eat and talk like her, and stopped being greedy, Madam might even get to like her.

Catching something about 'sharing what you have with those less fortunate', she glanced up again at the Reverend and found he was looking right at her, a faint smile on his lips. She smiled back. Lily might have turned out to be difficult to please, and very puzzling, but he was a real gent. He didn't go on about God as she'd expected, and he always thanked her for anything she did for him, even if it was only taking his coat and hat when he came in. Many times this week he'd sought her out alone to see how she was getting on and he seemed pleased she was learning so fast. He'd even lent her his leather-bound book of *Oliver Twist* to read, because she'd confided she'd only read the first instalment and was desperate to read the rest. She liked his soft, dark eyes, the fullness of his lips, and his long, slender fingers. She thought Lily must be the luckiest woman in the world to have him as her husband.

'Hold Tabby's hand securely and wait for me,' Lily ordered Matilda as they left the church after the service. 'I have to speak to some of the parishioners.'

Matilda was delighted to wait in the churchyard while Lily joined her husband by the door. It was an ideal opportunity to study the people Giles called 'his flock'.

They did bear a similarity to sheep she'd seen over on the south side of the river. They were herded close together, and they bleated greetings to the parson and his wife as they passed them. She wondered fleetingly if any of the fine-looking gentlemen in their shiny top hats, tail-coats and crisp white linen were the same ones she'd sometimes observed in the Haymarket with a 'gay girl' on their arm. If they were, she could hardly blame them for the wives seen here were a drab bunch. Their gowns were disappointingly sombre, greys and blues in the main, one or two had flower-trimmed bonnets and hats, but she'd seen far prettier ones in the Haymarket.

A tugging on her hand made her look down at Tabitha. 'We go home now, Matty,' she said, her small face screwed up with indignation at being forced to stand and wait.

'We have to wait for your mama and papa,' Matilda replied, but bent down and picked the little girl up in her arms. 'Just be good a little longer. Smile nicely at the people.'

Matilda was very aware she was being observed from all quarters and it made her feel very uncomfortable. Aggie had told her in confidence that everyone around here knew Lily wouldn't take on a nursemaid before because of her terrible fear of disease being brought into the house. The curious stares and half-smiles suggested that she would be a subject of gossip over dinner. She hoped no one would speak to her, if they heard her voice they'd immediately guess her origins. Yet even as she thought that she wondered why it should matter to her. A week ago it had never even crossed her mind to pretend she was anything but a waterman's daughter. Was she getting ideas above her station?

It was very warm on Tuesday when Matilda left the parsonage for her first afternoon off. She was wearing another new dress that Lily had given her that morning, and it was the prettiest thing she'd ever seen – pale blue sprigged with white flowers, pin-tucks on the bodice and little pearl buttons. Maybe it was faded in places and worn around the hem and under the arms, but with the straw bonnet her father had given her she felt grand and ladylike. She almost wished she could go to Finders Court just so all the neighbours would stare at her. But she didn't dare disobey her father.

She took her time, looking in shop windows as she went, more to admire her appearance in the reflection of the glass than from interest in the goods on display. It was almost five as she approached St Joseph's Church, or Holy Joe's as everyone she knew called it. Her father was there already, sitting on a bench outside. The church was bordering on the notorious Seven

Dials district, an area of the very worst tenements and rookeries, far more dangerous and squalid than Rosemary Lane, but she supposed he'd chosen to meet her here in the leafy sanctuary of the churchyard because the roads which led to it were wide and comparatively safe. She broke into a run to greet him and he got up to hold out his arms as he did when she was small.

'Well, don't you look a picture!' he said once he'd disengaged himself from her fierce embrace. 'I can see they are feeding you well, you look so bonny.'

He smelled strongly of the river, that curious oily scent which she'd scarcely noticed when she was at home.

'Had a bit of an accident this mornin',' he said as he saw her looking down in surprise at his damp trousers and squelching boots. 'Damn fool Lascar sailor, been on the opium pipe I shouldn't wonder. He asked me to catch up with 'is ship what left 'alf an hour since in Wapping. I nearly killed meself to get 'im to it. Then just as I was pulling alongside, and 'is mates is throwing down one of them rope ladders from the side, he jumps up like a madman and topples the boat over.'

Matilda laughed. A day on the river was never without incident and such stories were once the best part of her day. 'But you're dry up 'ere,' she said, touching his shirt and waistcoat – he wasn't wearing his usual pilot's coat.

'I went 'ome and changed that part,' he laughed. 'A fine fool I looked too, soaked to the skin. Who'd want to get in a waterman's boat wif 'im looking like that?'

'What 'appened to the Lascar, did you leave 'im to drown?' she giggled.

'He scrambled up the side of the ship like a monkey,' Lucas said. 'Good job I got his fare before we set off!'

''Ow's business bin?' she said, then, remembering Lily's lessons, she repeated it correctly. 'How has business been, Father?'

Lucas spluttered with laughter and offered her his arm in an exaggerated gesture of gallantry. 'Just dandy, my fine young lady. Now, shall we find a suitable seat for quality folk?'

They found another bench in a secluded part of the graveyard. It seemed the police must have just done their rounds because there was no sign of the usual beggars and tramps curled up asleep in the bushes.

Matilda told him all her news in one long and excited monologue, her speech fluctuating between her old manner and the one her new mistress was training her to use. It took Lucas back to when Nell used to report on what the Captain ate for his dinner, who he entertained and how much wine they drank. For she too used to see-saw between her country girl's speech and the way she heard English spoken in the Captain's house. It was a jolt hearing Matilda speak of such things as sheets on her bed. Until now Lucas had forgotten that luxury Nell had introduced him to – she had grieved more about the loss of her bed linen than anything else after the fire.

'Madam says I am to have a bath every week on Saturdays,' she ended up, her eyes as big as mill-stones. 'Every week, Father! I won't have any skin left in a few months.'

Lucas laughed. Nell had been one for baths when they lived in Aldgate. One of his sweetest memories was coming in from the river one night and finding her half-asleep in it, all pink and rosy and sweet-smelling. He'd wanted to make love to her immediately, but she insisted he had to get into the water first. She'd washed him from head to foot like a small child. That night was one of the most memorable in their time together.

He pulled himself out of that reverie. It didn't do to think too deeply about Nell, it only saddened him to remember what came in later years. And how lonely he felt now.

'So you're 'appy there?' he asked.

'Yes, I'm happy.' She smiled because she'd remembered to sound the 'h', and her eyes shone. 'But I do miss you and the boys.'

'Don't waste your time thinking about us,' he said brusquely. 'We're doing fine without you.'

Her face fell at this and Lucas felt ashamed. Yet if he was to tell her the truth – that the boys had been out scavenging every day, that their room hadn't been swept or a fire lit since the day she left – she'd only be distressed. Giving them a beating was pointless, they were looking for an excuse to slip off to one of the rookeries where they could get an apprenticeship in thieving and villainy.

'Luke's bin better since you went,' he lied. 'Reckon 'e thinks 'e's all grown up now. But tell me about this book you've bin reading.'

Matilda sensed he was hiding the truth and she wanted to tell him that Charles Dickens wrote about the poor like them, and that he fully understood the danger small boys could fall into in London. But to do so would only make him unhappy knowing she'd guessed the truth, and anyway her father knew those perils even better than she did, so instead she made him laugh with a description of Mr Bumble, the beadle.

'Maybe I could bring the book with me one day and read some of it to you,' she said. Her father could read a few simple words and sign his own name, but that was the extent of his schooling.

'That'd be grand,' he said, his eyes sparkling. 'But it's time you went now, you've got a long walk and I've got to get back to the river.'

He walked part of the way with her, she looked so pretty he was afraid for her walking the streets alone.

'Give Luke and George my love,' she said as they parted just before Camden Town. 'Could you get 'em to come an' all next week?'

'I'll try,' he replied, without much conviction. 'Now, go straight back. No loitering.'

She kissed him and clung to him for a moment, breathing in that familiar and comforting smell she'd grown up with. She might find living in the parsonage more pleasant than Finders Court, it was good to feel she'd taken a step up the ladder, but if her father asked her to come back home because he needed her, she knew she wouldn't hesitate.

'I love you, Father,' she whispered. She had never said that to him before, but perhaps she had to leave him to see it for herself.

'I love you too, Matty,' he whispered back. 'And I'm so very proud of you an' all. Now, skip off 'ome and keep yer nose clean, along wif that silver they gets you to polish. Who knows, you might end up owning some of yer own one day.'

It was on a sultry night in August five months after Matilda started work at the parsonage that she heard a frenzied shriek from Lily. Giles had been out all evening, so Matilda and Lily had said their customary prayers at half past nine alone, and then Matilda had come up to bed, leaving the older woman reading in the parlour.

Imagining that someone had broken into the house and was

now hurting her mistress, Matilda leaped out of bed and rushed out on to the landing. But on hearing Giles's deep voice she faltered at the top of the stairs, shocked to think they could fight like her old neighbours.

There was no fresh air anywhere. All the upstairs windows were wide open, but no cooling breeze was coming in, only bad smells from the drains. It was almost like being back in Finders Court except there was no noise outside.

It hadn't rained for over four weeks, and each day it had grown steadily hotter. The milk had to be boiled so it wouldn't go bad, butter turned to oil and Lily was so suspicious of fish and meat now that they'd been eating only vegetables and eggs for the past week. Not that anyone wanted to eat much. Tabitha was sickly and listless, Lily looked close to fainting all the time, even Aggie who rarely complained said she didn't think she could bear the heat in the kitchen much longer.

When news of a cholera epidemic in Seven Dials reached the neighbours' ears, most of them packed up and went out to friends and relatives in the country. Lily implored her husband to let her and Tabitha go down to Bath to her uncle's home, but he said it was her duty to stay here.

At first Matilda thought this was what the row was about, for she heard Lily shout out, 'You are being so selfish, Giles. Have you thought what might happen to Tabby?'

It was hard to catch Giles's reply, but it sounded like 'Why should anything happen to her there that wouldn't happen here?'

Lily's reply was very strange. 'There's savages there. They scalp people, and all those foreigners and convicts too.'

Matilda didn't think they could be talking about Bath, from what she'd heard about that place it was very calm and elegant. She moved away from the top of the stairs, but hung over the banisters on the landing to listen.

'New York doesn't have any savages,' Giles said in a strained, weary voice. 'And they stopped transporting convicts there some years ago. As for foreigners, London is full of them too.'

It was only two days ago that Matilda learned New York was a city in America. She had been dusting in the study where a book lay open on the desk. A picture of a steamship caught her eye, and as all sailing craft interested her, she took a closer look. Beneath the picture it said, 'The *Great Western* steamship designed by Isambard Kingdom Brunel, setting out from Liverpool to New York'.

'But I couldn't bear it,' Lily cried out. 'Are you really so cruel, Giles, that you'd uproot your wife and child from our comfortable home and force us to follow your whim?'

'May I remind you, Lily, that I am God's servant,' he said in an icy voice. 'If it is His will that I must take his word to America then it is no whim, I am duty bound to go. If you believe that to be cruel because you are bound by the comfort of this house, then all I can say, Lily, is that you are not a fitting wife for a clergyman.'

Matilda could hardly believe what she was hearing. Until tonight she had only heard Giles speak to his wife with gentleness. But even through her astonishment at his harsh tone, and the subject they were speaking of, she couldn't help but wonder where this left her.

The parlour door was suddenly slammed shut, and thinking Lily was about to rush upstairs to her bedroom, Matilda fled back to her bed.

Lily didn't come upstairs, and as the house was suddenly silent again, Matilda realized that they must both still be in the parlour and had shut the windows for fear of someone overhearing them.

Panic overwhelmed her as she lay there in the dark. If the Milsons were going to America, what would happen to her?

In five months she had achieved so much. Lily no longer criticized her table manners, and only occasionally did she pull her up on her speech. She could bake pies – Aggie said her pastry was as light as her own – make a cake, she could sew almost as neatly as her mistress and she'd read dozens of books. With all those accomplishments she could almost certainly get another position, but she had grown to love Tabitha as if she were her own child.

She had won Lily's trust when Tabby had croup and she stayed up night after night attending to her. She'd got the child to eat well, taught her nursery rhymes and some of the letters of the alphabet. Tabby loved her back too, they were as comfortable and happy together as if they were related. Could Giles really be so unkind as just to show her the door without any thought for the growing bond between them?

Aggie had curtly told her many times how lucky she was. She said that in most households the nursemaid was on the same level as a scullery maid, while she was treated almost like a relative. Matilda knew this was true – she ate with her employers, had the run of the house, she could read their books and sit out in their garden. Lily even confided in her sometimes, particularly about Tabitha.

She wept then. Finders Court had become a hazy memory, just as hunger, cold and being dirty had. Was she pulled out of all that just to be shoved back in there again?

Lily stayed in her room the following morning. When she hadn't appeared by the time Aggie had prepared breakfast, Matilda took Tabitha into the dining-room. Giles was there alone.

'Good morning, sir,' she said. It was even hotter than the previous day. Aggie had opened the windows wide as soon as she'd come in, but there was no early morning breeze to banish the smell of the drains.

'Mrs Milson is a little unwell,' he said, his face stern and unsmiling. 'After you've finished your breakfast you can take a tray up to her. I shall be out all day today. Try and keep Tabby quiet so Mrs Milson can rest.'

Matilda knew by his expression that he wasn't going to make any conversation. She sat Tabitha on her chair, fastened a napkin around her neck and put her bowl of bread and milk in front of her.

'Don't want that,' Tabitha said churlishly, pushing it away.

'You will eat it,' Matilda replied, putting it back in front of her. 'If you don't you'll get nothing else.'

Matilda sensed that Giles was looking at her. She willed Tabitha not to make a scene today, she was tired and drained after having spent most of the night awake. Refusing to give the child any alternative had been the way she'd got her to eat; mostly if Matilda was firm enough she buckled down eventually and ate what was put in front of her.

'Don't want it,' she said, pushing it away again, but this time she pushed it so hard the dish toppled and spilt the contents on the tablecloth.

'Naughty girl,' Matilda exclaimed, scraping it back into the bowl. 'Look at the mess you've made on the cloth. You deserve a spanking.'

'Don't you ever threaten violence to my daughter,' Giles burst out. 'Lift a finger to her and you'll be out of this house immediately.'

'Looks like I'll be out on me ear anyway,' she retorted, shocked by his unexpected ferocity.

As soon as the words were out she wanted to claw them back. Being insolent was something neither of the Milsons tolerated, and what's more she'd let slip she'd been eavesdropping.

'I'm sorry, sir,' she said quickly, blushing furiously. 'I never thought what I was saying. 'Course I wouldn't smack Tabby, it were just said hasty like because I was cross. I didn't mean to listen to what you and Madam was saying last night either, but I couldn't help it, your voices were so loud.'

There was a hostile silence for a few moments, and Tabitha used the opportunity to push the bread and milk even further away.

'It's too hot for her to eat that,' Giles said eventually, and taking a piece of bread he spread it with butter and honey, cutting it into tiny pieces for her. 'There, Tabby, eat this,' he said, standing up to put the plate in front of her.

'Why would you think you'd be "out on your ear", when we go to America?' he asked with a touch of sarcasm once Tabitha had begun to eat the bread. 'Don't you have any faith in me, Matilda?'

She hung her head, ashamed of herself. 'Well, the new parson here might not need a nursemaid,' she said meekly.

'That's very true, but I would find you another job.'

Matilda knew her fears to be of little importance, but she felt a need to explain them. 'But it's Tabby, sir, I really love her and I think she loves me an' all. Nobody else is going to be as nice as you and Madam either. Are they?'

Giles hardly knew what to say. Matilda was an enigma. She'd come from the gutter but she had the pride of a duchess. In the five months she'd been here, she'd managed to speak better, develop ladylike manners and learn a host of new skills, but she hadn't really grasped that servants were supposed to be subservient.

She had opinions she aired, she had ideas of her own. 'Self-assured' was how Lily described her, and she had come to depend on Matilda's sound judgement. When Tabitha had croup it was Matilda who knew to hold her near a steaming kettle. She knew to wash a sticky eye with salt water, and refused to let Lily dose her child with a patent cough mixture because she said it had dangerous things in it. She was right, it transpired later when a doctor friend admitted it contained laudanum.

The truth of the matter was, Matilda was invaluable. If Lily was called away, she had no fears that her child would be neglected in her absence. It was entirely true that Tabitha loved her too, indeed she would often run to her in preference to her mama. Matilda was a good influence on the child too, patient, caring but very firm. Wilful Tabitha got away with far less with her than she did with her parents.

Yet it was Matilda's remark that nobody else was going to be as nice as them that struck him most. However hard he looked for a position for her, he knew only too well he couldn't promise she would get the same treatment she did here. The reality was that she would be overworked, treated like dirt beneath her employers' feet and never valued. That really saddened him because he knew young Matilda wouldn't keep her lips buttoned if things went badly.

'Nothing is settled yet,' he said, and knew he was a coward because he couldn't admit to her or his wife that he was dead set on going. 'So don't go worrying your head about "maybes".'

Matilda just looked at him, clear blue eyes unwavering and all-seeing. 'You are going, sir, I knew that last night when I heard you talking,' she said, her voice calm and measured. 'So maybe you'd better take me along too, because Madam won't be able to cope alone with Tabby in a strange country, and that means you won't be able to give your time to others.'

Giles knew any other employer would slap a servant down for such impudence, but he couldn't. Her eyes held no guile, her voice contained no malice or threat. She was speaking the truth.

'That's for me to decide,' he said sharply, getting up from the table. 'You are getting above yourself, Matilda.'

'I'm sorry, sir.' She dropped her eyes from his in an effort to look demure.

Giles left the room quickly. He'd thought when Matilda saved Tabby's life that it was the hand of God, now he was certain. His wife thought him cruel, his friends thought him mad, but this young girl was offering him blind allegiance because she'd come to care for him and his family. The truth of the matter was that this girl was exceptional in every way. She had brought peace and sunshine into the parsonage, calmed Lily's nervous disposition, indeed her presence was beneficial to the happiness and security of the whole family.

He would be a fool not to take her with them.

Chapter Three

'That's it, over there,' Lucas said, leaning on his oars for a moment to point out a cottage on the opposite bank of the Thames, some 400 yards ahead. 'And if I ain't much mistaken that's Dolly coming out to meet us!'

Matilda turned in her seat in the bows to look, and to her delight, her father's new home was even prettier than he'd described. It was white-painted clapboard with a thatched roof, the large garden sloping right down to the river. They were still too far away for her to see Dolly distinctly, yet the welcoming way she was rushing down towards the landing stage, merrily waving both arms, made Matilda's heart leap with joy for her father.

It was early January, bitterly cold with a stiff wind whipping up the water, and it had been a long ride from Chelsea where her father had picked her up. Matilda withdrew one hand from the new shawl the Milsons had given her for Christmas, waved back, then quickly tucked it back inside. The Milsons had given her two days' holiday so she could visit her father and meet his new woman. Yet the sparkle in her eyes and the roses in her cheeks were not entirely due to the cold or excitement at seeing her father. She was bursting with momentous news, but she felt she must hold it back and wait for an appropriate time to break it to him.

Last August with its stifling hot weather had been a kind of watershed in both their lives. In that month she had heard about the Reverend Milson's intention to move to America, her father had met Dolly, and her brothers had run away from home. Matilda had been deeply troubled by all three events, but now six months later it seemed as if everything had turned out for the best and luck was smiling on the Jennings family at last.

Luke and George had run off after being given a beating by their father for picking pockets. He guessed they were hiding in one of the hundreds of rookeries in Seven Dials but all his attempts to find them came to nothing. Countless old hags and their bully boys made a business of luring children into their lairs by offering them food and shelter. Once they had got them firmly in their clutches they trained them as thieves, taking most of the proceeds.

Around the same time Lucas met Dolly Jacobs. He had been rowing a party down the river towards the village of Barnes one hot afternoon, and one of their number suggested stopping off for refreshments at Willow Cottage tea garden.

Lucas stayed in his boat while the group sat at tables in the pleasant riverside garden with their tea and cakes, but a little later, the woman who owned it brought him down a jug of ginger beer. Lucas related later to Matilda what a nice, jolly woman she was, and how he had offered to drop in again before long and repair an old rowing boat she had moored on her landing stage.

The friendship between her father and Dolly grew as he repaired the boat, and before long he was calling on her regularly to do more odd jobs. Dolly and her late husband had owned a very successful cake shop in Cheapside. Around five years ago they had sold their shop and retired to Willow Cottage because of Mr Jacobs's ill health. Sadly he had died a year after moving there. Dolly had been left well provided for but she was lonely, so she opened up her garden and parlour as a tea garden.

Matilda was concerned at first that this little widow might be using her father, for she couldn't imagine why else a woman in her position would befriend a humble waterman. But she knew her father was very lonely, and as it seemed to be taking his mind off fretting about the boys, she kept her fears to herself.

It was at the end of October that they got news of George, through a carter named Mr Albert Gore out in Deptford. Gore had caught both brothers stealing from his wagon, and though Luke had managed to give him the slip, he had felt sorry enough for George to take him home with him for a meal and a bath. From what George told the carter about his older brother and his family situation, he realized that the easily led boy had been forced into thieving by Luke.

As Mrs Gore was very taken with George, they kept him with them, and eventually got a note to Lucas saying they were prepared to give him a permanent home in return for helping on their cart. Lucas went straight over to Deptford, determined to take George home, but when he found they were respectable, kind people and his youngest son was very happy with them, he agreed that George would be safer with them, well away from Luke's bad influence.

It transpired that Luke was beyond rescue. Although only just eleven years old, since running away from home he had embraced all the nastiest aspects of London's underworld, revelling in drinking and dog fights and showing great admiration for all crime. He boasted he was going to become a 'cracksman', and as he had already served his apprenticeship at pick-pocketing and was working at night with two older burglars as their 'boy' – his role being to wriggle through small windows and let the others in through the front door to plunder the house – Lucas knew that within a short time Luke probably would indeed progress to far more serious crime, if not blowing safes. Sadly he knew then it was futile to spend any further time or energy pursuing him.

Later, in November, Lucas said he was going to live with Dolly and in future would work that stretch of the river. Although it was common enough for the working classes to live together without marrying, Matilda was surprised and a little shocked that a seemingly respectable widow would do such a thing, she just hoped that Dolly wouldn't turn out to be another Peggie, and give her father more grief. Yet he did seem so very happy and excited, and even if it meant she wouldn't be able to see him so often, she was very glad he had found someone to love and was finally leaving Finders Court.

'Now, isn't she a fine-looking woman?' Lucas said as they approached the landing stage, his croaky voice softer with affection. 'I calls 'er me apple dumpling.'

Matilda looked up at the woman waiting for them and thought his pet name for her was appropriate. She was small and round with a sweet, unlined face wreathed in a beaming smile. Although her hair was grey and Matilda knew her to be as old as her father, she had a youthful gaiety about her which even the oversized men's boots and coat she was wearing couldn't conceal.

'Looks like you've fallen on your feet, Father,' she whispered.

'Oi! I pays me way,' he said with some indignation.

As soon as the boat was secured, Dolly rushed them straight towards the cottage, clucking over how cold they both looked and how she'd made a beef and oyster pie for their dinner. As they went up through the garden Matilda saw hens, geese and ducks, and a pen of rabbits. She wondered if they were just pets, she couldn't imagine Dolly killing them.

Dolly ushered Matilda straight into a large, warm kitchen which smelled deliciously of meat pie. She had a stove just like the one at the parsonage and on the table was a newly baked cake. From the beams on the ceiling hung bunches of dried herbs and flowers, there were dozens of jars of preserves on a shelf and even more china than Matilda had seen at the Milsons' sitting on the dresser. It was bright, clean and very homely. Clearly she wasn't another Peggie.

'Sit yerself down,' Dolly ordered, taking Matilda's shawl from her shoulders and pointing to a chair by the stove. 'And you should be wearing something warmer than that in this cold weather. I've got a coat upstairs that will fit you. I'll get it later when we've had a cup of tea and a chat. But bless me, I haven't even said how nice it is to meet you at last, or happy New Year.'

Matilda smiled as the woman smacked a hearty kiss on her cheek. She wondered if she always talked as much. 'It's nice to meet you too,' she said. 'And I'm sure it's going to be a happy New Year for all of us.'

Dolly shed her man's coat and boots, making a complaint about how muddy the garden was and how she longed for spring to arrive. Her dress was a sober dark blue with a small lace collar, but the material and cut of it wouldn't have looked out of place on one of the richer women at the church. She was curvaceous rather than fat, and as she lifted her dress to slip into a pair of dainty indoor shoes, Matilda noted her shapely ankles.

Lucas pulled up the Bosun's chair that had been in their old room and sat down beside his daughter. 'I told Dolly this was me dowry,' he joked. 'Looks well in 'ere though, don't it?'

'As if it was made for here,' Matilda agreed. She sensed her father was embarrassed that it was the only thing he had to offer Dolly.

'Lucas is made for here too,' Dolly said as she made a pot of tea. Her eyes were dark brown and twinkled merrily as she smiled. 'Heaven knows, I don't know how I managed without him. He's a real wonder, he can fix anything. And I want to say before we go any further that you must think of here as home now, Matty. Lucas and me might not be wed, but me heart's set on him and so his children are my children too.'

'We're gonna get wed though,' Lucas said, and reached out to squeeze his daughter's hand. 'We thought in the spring, when the blossom's out. How d'you feel about that?'

Dolly put the tea pot down on the stove and looked anxiously at Matilda as if expecting disapproval.

'I think that's the best news I've ever heard,' Matilda said. Her eyes were prickling and she hoped she wasn't going to disgrace herself by crying. She might not have known the woman for longer than ten minutes, but just the warmth flowing between the couple, Dolly's kind words about his children and the security her father would gain by marrying her were enough to dispel any doubts in her mind. 'I just hope you make it before I leave London. You see, the Milsons have asked me to go to America with them.'

She wished she hadn't blurted it out like that when her father's ruddy colour suddenly drained away. 'America!' he exclaimed. 'Oh no, Matty!'

Because of the boys' disappearance last August, she hadn't told him anything about her employer's intention of going to New York, besides, it wasn't mentioned again after that night, not in her hearing anyway, so she'd begun to think Giles had abandoned the idea.

'Take this tea, afore you go on,' Dolly said, pushing a mug into her hands. 'And don't you look so sour-faced, Lucas. It's a great chance for Matty. Now, just let me cut a slice of cake for you both and we'll have the whole story if you please.'

The cake was still warm, and rich with raisins and spices. Matilda thought it was the best she'd ever eaten, it put Aggie's and her own efforts to shame.

'It was only on Christmas Day they asked me to go with them,' Matilda began. 'They asked me into the parlour to give me my present, that lovely brown shawl. I nearly burst into tears at that, but then blowed if they didn't make me sit down because they said they had another surprise for me.'

She paused for a moment to get her breath back. 'Well, then

Sir just came out with it. Said they'd decided to go to America in April and would I like to go with them. Oh, Father!' she exclaimed, reaching out to touch his knee. 'Sir was so lovely. He said, "We think of you as one of our family now, Matty. None of us wants to go without you." Well, I did cry then, and Madam, she gave me one of those soft looks she gives Tabby. She said she hoped it wouldn't make you unhappy, but if I didn't like it I could always come home again. Sir's so excited, Father, he keeps saying what a big adventure it will be, and showing me maps and things about America.'

She paused again, suddenly aware that her father looked stunned and so very sad. 'I don't like to leave you, Father,' she went on, taking his hand and rubbing it between her two. 'But if I don't go, what are the choices for me? Another nursemaid's job perhaps with a family that won't be so good to me, or being a maid or a shop girl.'

'She's right,' Dolly said stoutly, giving Lucas no time to chip in with his opinion. 'A slave to someone who will never appreciate her! If I'd been offered such a chance when I was Matty's age I'd have been off without thinking twice. We keep hearing that things is going to improve soon, but I've been hearing that all me life and so have you, Lucas. The truth of the matter is that the rich get richer and the poor get poorer. America's got to be a whole lot better.'

Lucas looked at his daughter. Apart from her hands moving on his, she was sitting as stiff as a plank, her eyes pleading with him to agree she should go. He looked at Dolly who gave him an encouraging smile. 'You go with my blessing if it's what you really want,' he said slowly and thoughtfully. 'I told you once before, Matty, to never look back, and I meant it. If I can't be 'ollering with 'appiness right now for you, well, it's just that it will be 'ard not to see you grow into a woman, see you get married to some fine fella and a brood of little 'uns around yer skirts.'

'I'm not going for ever,' she said, shocked that he thought he was never going to see her again. 'I'll come back when the Milsons do.'

'You won't, me darlin',' he said softly. 'You'll get stuck in over there, I knows that. From what I've 'eard it's a big brave country, a fitting place for a brave girl like you. Just you write to us and tell us all about it. Dolly can read as good as you and she'll write back for both of us.'

'Now, afore you get settled in that chair, let me show you round,' Dolly said, anxious to lighten the atmosphere. She held out a hand to Matilda. 'I've got the bed all aired for you.'

After the parsonage the cottage seemed very small. Just the kitchen with a little scullery leading off it, and the parlour which Dolly used as the tea room when it was too cold or wet for people to sit in the garden. It looked very bare and cold after the warm kitchen, with only half a dozen small tables and chairs in it and a glass-domed stand in which, she explained, she put her cakes on display.

'I won't open it up again till Easter,' she said. 'Lucas has just given it a new coat of whitewash, and I've taken the curtains down for a washing. But it looks real pretty with the tables laid nice and a few flowers.'

Dolly's bedroom went right across the front of the cottage and Matilda had to stoop down to see the river out of the windows set in the sloping ceiling. It too was very bare, just a brass bed covered in a gaily coloured patchwork quilt and a chest of drawers, but spotlessly clean and smelling of lavender.

'You like the smell?' Dolly asked as Matilda bent to sniff a bowl of it on the chest. 'That's yer father's doing. He brought back great clumps of it in the summer, he said he thought it was the best perfume in the world.'

The room Matilda was to sleep in had clearly been specially prepared for her. It was smaller than the front room, and much less austere. Frilly print curtains hung at the small window, the patchwork quilt on the iron bed was all worked in pinks and blues, and a rag rug softened the waxed floorboards.

'I rushed to finish that quilt when I knew you were coming,' Dolly said. 'You might be going to America, lovey, but this is your room anyway. Lucas told me so much about you, right from when we first met. But you are even nicer and prettier than he said. No wonder he's so proud of you.'

Matilda wished she felt able to hug Dolly. Somehow her home encapsulated all those dreams and hopes she knew from her father that he'd once shared with Nell before she was even born. Tragic as it was that her mother hadn't survived to realize any of them, it was good to know Lucas would live out his days in peace and comfort with a loving woman worthy of him.

'I'm so glad Father found you,' she stammered out. 'I won't feel so bad about going away knowing he's got you.'

Later, after the delicious beef and oyster pie, Lucas went out to work in his boat again, and Dolly spoke of how she felt about him as she and Matilda sat by the stove.

'He's everything I ever wanted,' she said, her small face looking dreamy and young. She had unusually good teeth for a woman of her age, small, white and even with none missing, and now she was wearing a frilly mob-cap with her grey hair hidden she could pass for ten years younger. 'It's funny how things turn out sometimes. When I was a young girl I dreamed of falling in love with a rich, handsome man who would rescue me from being poor. I was very poor too,' she laughed, seeing Matilda's look of surprise. 'Much worse off than you were, lovey. I tell you, there was ten of us all living in what weren't much more than a stable, and the animals shared it at night too. At ten I was sent to work in the laundry of a big house nearby and if it hadn't been for seeing how rich people lived I expect I would have ended up with a life just like my mother's.

'Well, like I said, I kept dreaming of this rich man who would save me, and I suppose that's just what Mr Jacobs did, though he weren't handsome or rich and I never fell in love with him. He came to the house once when they were having this big party, he made lovely cakes and pastries, you see. I reckon it was his baking that attracted me, I always was a greedy little sod. Well, we chatted a bit, I found out he made a good living selling his cakes and stuff to the gentry for their parties, and he must have taken a shine to me right off, because he said he needed an assistant.'

'Was he English?' Matilda interrupted. Dolly didn't draw breath once she got started.

'Born here, but his folks were Austrian Jews,' she said. 'They were pastry-makers too. Anyway, that's how it started. I went to work for him, and when he tried the funny business on I said he'd have to marry me first.'

Matilda's eyes opened wide with surprise. She hadn't expected something so cool and calculated of Dolly. 'Well, he was no oil painting,' Dolly chuckled, and her double chin wobbled. 'Small, scrawny, with a beaky nose and not much hair. He was already thirty then.'

'And how old were you?'

'Sixteen,' she said and grinned. 'Don't get me wrong, Matty. I was fond of him. I admired his skill at baking and he was a kind, decent man. So I married him. Good job I did, or I wouldn't be sitting here now in this nice cottage with a bit of security behind me. But I earned it. I worked eighteen hours a day once he got the shop in Cheapside.'

'You didn't love him though?'

'Not like in a romantic way,' the older woman smiled. 'We were good friends, and we were snug together. He taught me all I know including how to read and write. I missed him too when he passed on. But there were times I regretted not marrying a man I felt some passion for, and that I never had the luck to bear any children. Oh heavens! I am running on! I didn't mean to give you me life story. What I started out to say was that when Mr Jacobs died I thought that was me finished an' all. I'd lost my looks and I thought I was much too old to even hope of happiness with another man. Then along came Lucas, with his lovely blue eyes, and my heart went all fluttery.'

Matilda wasn't sure she liked to be told Dolly felt passionate towards her father. It didn't seem quite proper.

'I'm glad for you both,' she managed to get out.

Dolly laughed. 'I've made you blush, that's bad of me, but I wanted you to know how it is for us. I think you and me are very alike, Matty, sort of direct, 'cept you don't talk so much! You speak so nice, you've got nice manners, and I know from yer father it's none of his doing. I managed to pick up me airs and graces along the way, an' all, I certainly weren't born with 'em. Don't you go marrying a man just for his money though! Try and fall for someone who's got some by all means, even true love can fly out the window when you're hungry. But don't just look at the money, make sure he's kind and he makes you laugh.'

By the time Matilda was ready to leave with her father the following afternoon, she found she could hug Dolly spontaneously. She was a real treasure, kind, generous and so very lovable. Her personality filled the little cottage, her laughter and chatter was like being wrapped in a warm blanket. To see the woman tenderly buttoning Lucas's coat for him and tying a warm muffler round his neck before he went out brought a lump to Matilda's throat. It was touching to see how she valued the little things he did for her too, like making her an early cup of tea or putting the ashes from the stove on to the path outside to make it less slippery for her.

Matilda felt she could go to America now with a happy heart. Dolly and Lucas would grow old together, treasuring what they had together because both of them knew what it was to live without it.

'Make the wedding at the beginning of April,' Matilda urged Dolly as she took her leave at the door. Although it was only half past three it was already nearly dark, and biting cold. Dolly had given her the coat she promised, it was dark blue serge with a rabbit collar, but although it was very much warmer than her shawl, by the time they got to Chelsea she'd probably be frozen stiff. 'And will you try and get George to come too?'

'I will,' Dolly replied, flinging her arms around her and enveloping Matilda in a smell of lavender. 'It will only be a quiet affair, just us and a few friends I've made along here. But just you remember this is your home too. If you change your mind about America, you can come here. Now go, before you make me cry.'

'So what do you reckon on Dolly?' Lucas said as they got to midstream. He had to shout as the wind was strong and blowing his words away.

'She's just perfect for you,' Matilda replied, pulling one of his rugs around her. 'I think as Reverend Milson would say you ought to get down on your knees and thank the good Lord.'

'I 'ave, Matty. I 'ave,' he said, his face breaking into the broadest smile. 'All I wish was that I met up with 'er when yer mum died instead of Peggie.'

'You once told me "Never dally with a grievin' man",' Matilda said, quick as a flash. 'So I'm glad you didn't meet her then, however much I would have liked her as a mother.'

'That's true,' he chuckled. 'Glad you remember your old man's pearls of wisdom.'

*

Three months later, in mid-April, Matilda was in the guest bedroom at the parsonage with Lily, trying to get the huge leather cabin trunk closed. She put her whole weight on it but the lock and catch stayed stubbornly two inches apart. 'It's not going to shut, Madam,' she said wearily. 'There's too much in it.'

Lily put down the evening dress she was folding on the bed alongside other clothes and linen she wanted to take, and added her weight to the lid, but it made no difference. It still wouldn't close.

'We'll have to take out that blue counterpane,' she sighed. 'I don't suppose we'll need that immediately, so maybe it can go in with the things to follow us.' She slumped down on to the bed and covered her face with her hands. 'Oh Matty, I'm so sick of all this!' she wailed.

Matilda was very tempted to tell the woman to buck up and stop feeling sorry for herself. At Christmas she had seemed happy enough at going, but since then she'd gradually worked herself up into a lather of anxiety about it. Every day she seemed to find some new complaint or worry, refusing even to try to look on the bright side. She seemed to imagine that the whole of America was a wasteland where people lived in shacks without any comforts or even shops to buy things. She wanted to take absolutely everything she and her husband owned, not just clothes, books, bed linen and china, but dozens of lengths of material to make clothes for the future too. So far the trunk had been packed and unpacked six times.

Yet Matilda did feel some sympathy – her mistress was settled here in Primrose Hill and she loved the parsonage. Her husband had arranged it all with little thought for her feelings, fears for her daughter, or the long sea voyage, and Lily was now close to breaking down from sheer panic.

Matilda flung back the lid of the trunk and lifted a few things out, putting them on the bed. 'I'll do it,' she said. 'Why don't you go and lie down for a while, you look so tired.'

Lily hesitated. She wasn't just tired but completely exhausted. She hadn't had a decent night's sleep in months for worrying about what lay ahead and Giles just didn't seem to care that she was distraught. Matilda was the only person who appeared to understand how she felt and she wanted to voice her appreciation.

It was so very ironic that this girl whom she had initially feared should become so invaluable to her. She worked so tirelessly and cheerfully, not just at the jobs she was employed to do, but instinctively turning her hand to anything that was needed. In truth Lily knew she was far more than a nursemaid – adviser, companion, friend and family member now. She didn't know how she would have got through these past few weeks without her help.

'I can't leave it all to you,' she said in a small voice. 'You've done so much already.'

Matilda was touched by the gratitude in the woman's voice. She had thought all the extra washing, ironing and mending she'd done recently had gone unnoticed. 'There's not so much left to do now,' she said with an encouraging smile. 'You go and lie down. It's nearly time to get Tabby up from her nap. I'll take her out for a little walk so it's nice and quiet for you.'

'You are a good, kind girl, Matty.' Lily impulsively reached out and touched the girl's arm. 'I'm so very glad you are coming with us.' She turned and hurried away then, leaving Matilda bug-eyed with amazement.

In three days they would be taking the stage-coach to Bristol so that the Milsons could say goodbye to their respective families, then a week later they would be taking a ship from the port there. Matilda hoped that once they were on their way Lily would cheer up and perhaps even start to enjoy the adventure of the trip.

Yet despite the apparent enthusiasm Matilda was displaying to everyone, she had her own private fears and doubts. Last week while over in Barnes for the wedding, she'd almost been tempted to stay there for good. Dolly could do with a waitress for the summer, and to see that riverside garden bright with daffodils, cherry blossom and the weeping willows with their new pale green leaves unfurling made America much less appealing.

But she steeled herself against backing down by reminding herself that Tabitha needed her and it was the chance of a lifetime. At least she had the memory of that lovely wedding tucked away in her heart. Of Dolly in a pale lemon dress with a matching hat, and her father in a borrowed frock-coat. And little George! It had been so good to be with him again, and such a shock to see him in long breeches and a boiled shirt, his red hair neatly cut. He was quite the little man, talking about his work on the wagon delivering goods, grooming the horses and how much he liked Mr Gore the carter and his wife. Getting away from Luke was the best thing that ever happened to him. Now he had a chance of growing up as honest and decent as his father.

'Can we go up to the top of the world?' Tabitha asked as they left the house for the afternoon walk. It had been raining that morning, but now the sun had come out and the air smelled clean and fresh.

Matilda giggled. That was Tabitha's name for the top of Primrose Hill, in her innocence she thought that the view from there was of the entire world.

'We'll go just as long as you don't ask to be carried on the way back,' she replied.

In a year Tabitha had gone from a merry, waddling baby to a somewhat serious little girl. Her baby fat had disappeared, leaving her a little too thin, and aside from the melting brown eyes she'd inherited from her father, every other feature was turning into a copy of her mother's. Her once button-like nose had grown a little sharp, even her dark hair which had once curled so readily now had to be coaxed with rags or it just hung limply. Aggie had recently, and rather unkindly, pointed out she wasn't going to be the beauty her parents anticipated, but plain or pretty, Matilda adored her. She was so quick, she questioned everything, and even at only three and a half she had a mind of her own.

'Why is Mama lying down again?' Tabitha asked, frowning as she looked up at Matilda.

She spoke just like an adult now, yet a year ago she couldn't manage more than a few words.

'Because she's tired,' Matilda said with a smile. 'Getting ready to move across the ocean is very tiring work, my little lady.'

'But you and Aggie do all the work,' Tabitha said pointedly. 'Mama doesn't do anything much, and she's always crying.'

That was a very astute comment for someone so young but Matilda knew she must be careful how she replied to it, as Tabitha was prone to repeating things.

'Well, Aggie and I are servants,' she said in an even tone. 'That means we are paid to do work for your mama, but even if she isn't cleaning or cooking she still has a great many other things to do. And if she cries sometimes it's just because she's sad to be leaving England.'

'But why? We'll all be there with her,' Tabitha said. ''Cept Aggie. Why can't she come too?'

'Because Aggie has a family of her own, and besides, she has to look after the new parson and his wife when we've gone,' Matilda said. To her mind the sooner Lily got away from Aggie and her alarmist views that America was a dangerous place full of savages and convicts, the happier her mistress would be. 'I expect we'll have a new housekeeper when we get to New York. It will be better to have an American woman anyway because she'll be able to tell us things about the place so we can find our way around.'

Tabitha said nothing more until they reached the top of Primrose Hill. They stopped as always to look at the view. For weeks now the city had been shrouded in fog, and on walks up here they'd been unable to see beyond a few hundred yards. But today's good weather meant they could see almost to infinity.

Matilda silently drank it all in, the green of Regent's Park at the bottom of the hill, the elegant church spires dotted all over the city, the silver glint of the Thames, and the huddled masses of houses, shops and businesses in between. She had walked most of the area within her view selling her flowers, envied those who lived in the grand houses, and pitied those poor souls who lived on the streets without any shelter. It was only now that she was leaving London, perhaps never to return, that she realized how deeply it was engraved on her heart and how much the people she was leaving behind meant to her.

Somewhere on the river her father in his gold-trimmed cap and pilot's coat was bent over his oars, straining every muscle to get his passengers quickly to their destination. As she looked south-west she imagined Willow Cottage with the tables set out in the gardens and Dolly in her clean white apron and cap waiting on her customers. Straight ahead was where George was, and she hoped he would stay with the Gores to manhood and maybe even take up the carter's trade one day for himself.

Luke was somewhere in the east, but she refused even to contemplate what he was doing.

Way out of sight further eastwards was the Thames estuary and the sea beyond. She wondered where John and James's ships were and tried to recall what her two older brothers looked like. She remembered they were fair-haired and blue-eyed like her, but they were men now, not the skinny boys she'd clung to when they left for a life at sea some ten years earlier. She hoped they would return to London one day and seek out their father. Perhaps fate would even take them to America and she could meet up with them again.

'I love you all,' she whispered to herself, her eyes filling with tears. 'I might be going thousands of miles away, perhaps never see any of you again, but you'll be in my heart for ever.'

'Why are you crying?'

Tabitha's high-pitched voice brought her back to the present. She looked down to see the small girl was staring up at her with a concerned expression on her little face.

'I'm not crying, my eyes are watering,' Matilda replied, wiping her face on her sleeve, and she smiled and picked the child up. 'I was just thinking how pretty London looks from here and looking towards where each of my family is.'

She ran through them all for Tabitha's benefit. 'Where's New York?' the child asked, squirming in Matilda's arms.

'You can't see it from here, it's miles away, right over a big ocean.'

'Will we come back here one day when I'm big?'

'I hope so, Tabby,' Matilda said, nuzzling her cheek against the little girl's. 'But you being big is as far off as America.'

Tabitha let out a wail as the *Druid* began slowly to move away from its moorings on Bristol's quayside. It was being pulled by watermen in rowing boats. They would guide the 360-ton, three-masted barque out of the floating harbour before horses towed it the rest of the way down the river Avon, through the gorge and out to the Bristol Channel where it could unfurl its sails. Giles had explained to her that big ships found it hard to navigate in and out of the port, owing to the high rise and fall of tides, and this was the main reason why the steamship the S. S. *Great Western*, which had been built here a few years earlier, now plied its trade across the Atlantic from either Portishead or Liverpool.

'Whatever's wrong?' Matilda asked in alarm, sweeping Tabitha up into her arms. She glanced nervously towards the child's parents who were standing a few feet from her, engrossed in waving and shouting last-minute messages to the members of their family on the quay. Lily had become quite cheerful in the last few days and Matilda didn't want her to be upset before they even left the port.

'I don't like it,' Tabitha sobbed into her shoulder, almost strangling her with her arms. 'I want to go home.'

'We *are* going home,' Matilda said, lifting the child back a little so she could see her face. 'To a new home, in another country. But this ship is going to be our home too for a while. I'm with you, so is your mama and papa. It's going to be like a holiday.'

The Milson party and a couple called Smethwick were the only saloon passengers, as the *Druid* was a merchant ship taking bricks, copper sheets and ironmongery to New York. There was a group of ten or twelve people, plus their children, in what Giles called 'steerage', which Matilda understood to mean they had cabins down in the ship's hold. They too were up on the deck waving goodbye to their relations – they looked like very poor people and she supposed that this was why Lily had warned her Tabitha wasn't to mix with their children.

'I don't like the way it moves.' Tabitha pouted and looked above her head at the tall masts, furled sails and rigging. 'I don't like all that stuff either.'

As Matilda's childhood had been dominated by the Thames, and she had been out on many different craft in all weathers, she saw nothing to be frightened of. Sailors to her were all men like her father, tough, strong and utterly reliable.

'The movement is lovely,' she said. 'Like being gently rocked. Those things up there are just the sails, later on the sailors will pull them up on to the masts and the wind will catch them to drive us along. There's nothing to be scared of. Captain Oates and his crew will look after us. Now, let's stand at the rail and wave goodbye. Your grandfather, grandmother and lots of your aunts, uncles and cousins are watching, you don't want them to think you are a baby, do you?'

Tabitha hated being thought of as a baby more than anything and her tears stopped instantaneously.

'Why aren't Grandmother and Grandfather Woodberry there too?' she asked.

Matilda wasn't sure how to answer that question. Lily's parents had been very cool to their daughter and son-in-law for the whole of their visit. She had the distinct impression the Woodberrys didn't approve of them for some reason. They had taken no interest in Tabitha, and when Lily had suggested Matilda should share her bedroom, as it was a floor above their own, her callous grandparents had expressed scorn that a three-year-old might be frightened and utter horror at such familiarity with a servant, banishing Matilda down to the basement to share a tiny windowless damp room with their scullery maid.

Only one of Lily's brothers, Abel, had come with his wife and two children to see her off, despite most of the rest of the family living only a walk from the quay. If it hadn't been for Lily's Uncle Thomas, his wife and five children, plus most of Giles's family coming over from Bath for the day, it would have been a very sorry departure.

'The Woodberrys are old,' Matilda said cautiously, though she was still smarting at the way they had treated her. 'I expect they find saying goodbye in a public place upsets them.'

This seemed to satisfy Tabitha and she leaned forward in Matilda's arms to wave frantically to her aunts, uncles and cousins from Bath who had made a great fuss of her.

Matilda was very relieved that she'd managed to avert a tantrum, for she wanted to stay on deck and savour the last sight of Bristol. The city had enchanted her, and even if the Woodberrys had treated her like a diseased stray dog, and upbraided their daughter for allowing a mere nursemaid to think she was of some importance, she'd had plenty of time during the week to explore this busy and exciting port.

Having never been further out of London than the villages of Hampstead in one direction and Barnes in the other, on the way here in the stage-coach she had been astounded by the distance between London and Bristol and the many, many miles of fields, rolling hills and woodland with hardly a house in sight.

Giles had been amused by her ignorance and he'd pointed out she hadn't seen anything yet for the trip across the ocean took an average of thirty-four days. Once they arrived in Bristol Matilda was even more surprised to find the people spoke quite differently to Londoners, and that the port she knew to be one of the greatest in England should be such a pretty place.

It was so much more vibrant, so close-packed and colourful in comparison to the Port of London. Now they were some thirty or forty yards from the quay, looking back it resembled a narrow street filled with ships. A virtual forest of masts, many with their sails opened to dry in the warm sunshine. Dodging around the big ships were dozens and dozens of smaller craft.

The houses on the quayside were very different from the dilapidated shacks she was used to in London's port. These were fine merchants' houses, many of which she was told had been built two centuries ago. Carriages, broughams and all manner of carts trundled along in front of them. Men pulled things which looked like sledges too, for it was easier to move heavy goods such as casks of wine and sherry on metal runners over the cobbles than to use wheels. Added to all this bustle and the ensuing noise, there were so many people – sailors, dockers, tradespeople, gentlemen in stove-pipe hats overseeing loading, and scores of ragged children running around among them all.

As the ship slid through the water, gradually gathering speed, the faces of the waving crowd became indistinct, but to compensate Matilda was presented with a more panoramic view of the city. High up above the smells, noise and confusion of the docks were the grand houses of Clifton. These were where the people lived who'd brought prosperity to Bristol with wine, tobacco, slavery and shipping. Now, in the bright sunshine, the magnificent curved terraces could be seen as their designers had intended, proud and so very elegant. Only in Greenwich had she seen anything to compare with it, for that was beautiful too. The rest of London was so flat that from the river you could only see the ugliness and poverty of the people who scraped a living along its banks.

If Matilda hadn't taken the opportunity to explore Bristol she might have been fooled into thinking the entire city was as pleasant as Charlotte Street where the Woodberrys lived. That too was perched up on a hill with a fine view of the docks and the green fields beyond the river Avon, yet far enough away for the stink and noise of the docks not to trouble them.

Yet just five minutes' walk from their splendid four-storey house, through a narrow lane, had led her into a maze of steep, fetid alleys, as bad as anything she'd seen around Rosemary Lane. Almost naked children with running sores stood in dark doorways, their bleak eyes reflecting the misery of their lives. She had seen old soldiers, crippled and maimed from injuries in the French war, gin-soaked ragged women lying in doorways, babies in their arms, oblivious to their surroundings. It had appalled and repelled her, and she had to remind herself that just a year ago such things were everyday sights for her.

It was a sobering thought that just by chance, by being there when Tabitha ran out in front of that carriage, her life had been changed miraculously. She had forgotten what hunger felt like, what it was to live amongst filth, and for gentlefolk to avert their eyes from her as she tried to sell them her posies.

Yet if in Primrose Hill she had been tempted to think she was almost a lady now, because she'd learnt manners and how to speak better, and the Milsons treated her almost like an equal, the affluent Woodberrys had brought her back to reality with a jolt. She *was* a servant, a very lowly one at that, her well-being and security were entirely dependent on her employers, and if one day she failed to please them, or they no longer needed her, she might very well find herself thrown back into the slums again.

Holding the wriggling, excited child more securely in her arms, she looked up defiantly at those splendid houses on the hill and made a silent vow to herself. She wasn't going back to any slums. She wasn't going to stay a servant all her life either, only as long as it suited her. They said that America was a land of opportunity, so she must always keep an eye out for hers. Like her father had said that day when he kissed her goodbye at the parsonage, 'Never look back.' From now on she was going to look forwards and upwards.

Chapter Four

Giles Milson supported Lily in his arms as the *Druid* sailed into New York Bay. 'Doesn't that spectacular view make you feel better?' he asked.

They had been at sea for forty-one days, and it was now mid-June and a hot, sunny afternoon, but Lily was so weak from seasickness that all she could do was ask how long it would be before they docked.

'I don't know exactly, we have to be tugged in, but I'm sure that in an hour or two you'll be safe in your new home, and this long voyage will be something to look back on in wonder.'

Matilda, who was standing a few feet away, holding Tabitha in her arms, heard what he said and smiled to herself. She thought that the only 'wonder' Lily would ever feel about her forty days at sea was surprise that she had lived to see its end.

Lily had started to complain of seasickness almost the minute the ship got under sail in the Bristol Channel, and this had continued throughout the journey. Time and again her husband, the Captain and Matilda had tried to urge her up on deck for fresh air, because it would have helped her recover, but she had refused even to attempt it, stubbornly staying in the stuffy stateroom, even on the many calm, balmy days when the ship hardly moved. Even now, when she should be happy to see the New York sky-line, she was crying against her husband's chest.

Matilda wanted to whoop and shout with excitement, for the scene in front of her was awe-inspiring. The bay was vast, yet it was crowded with boats – huge steamers, sailing ships of every kind and size, tugs, fishing boats and ferries. Looking beyond those under sail, there were hundreds more docked at wharves on both sides of the island of Manhattan. Sea birds screeched a welcome overhead and the bright, hot June sunshine picked out the vivid colours of ships' flags, giving the scene a carnival appearance.

'Where's our house?' Tabitha asked. Like Matilda she hadn't been troubled by sickness, and her face was tanned a deep brown from hours up on deck throughout the voyage.

'I don't know,' Matilda replied. 'Shall we ask your papa?'

She moved closer to her employers, but before allowing the child to repeat her question to her father, Matilda asked how her mistress was feeling.

'A little better now,' Lily sniffed, her eyes dull and pink-rimmed. 'But I shan't be myself until my feet are on firm ground again. I don't think I'll ever want to look at a ship again. I can't even hold my child in my arms!'

'You don't need to, Mama,' Tabitha said, squirming in Matilda's to be put down. 'I'm a big girl now. Captain Oates said I could be his first mate.'

Both the child's father and Matilda laughed. Tabitha had won the hearts of the entire crew, from the Captain right down to the ordinary seamen. For her the voyage had been pure enchantment – sleeping in a bunk, eating meals as the ship tossed and rolled, climbing the steep companionways, and seeing whales and porpoise from the deck. Even during bad storms, when the ship had pitched alarmingly, she had been unperturbed, but then her childish innocence of how cruel the sea could be and her blind faith in the sailors had protected her.

Matilda might have found the voyage as exciting as Tabitha if she hadn't been forced to spend so many hours cloistered in the state-room with her mistress, holding bowls as she retched, sponging her down and cleaning up after her. Her sympathy was stretched to breaking-point because she felt the woman was doing nothing to help herself and indeed wallowing in self-pity. At times the only way she could stop herself from saying what she thought was out of gratitude that she shared a cabin with Tabitha and wasn't down with the steerage passengers.

She had been appalled to find that these passengers were all crowded into a section of the ship which couldn't even be honoured with the title of 'cabin'. It was in fact just a dark, dank hold, roughly furnished with narrow wooden bunks, men, women and children all in together regardless of the fact that they were three or four separate families. With scarcely any ventilation, one meal a day – a pot of foul-smelling, greasy stew

– and only being allowed up on deck at certain times of the day, it wasn't surprising they were all very sick.

Matilda didn't think she could ever forget the horror she had encountered when she went in there with Giles when one of the women, fearing for her child's life, had asked for a priest. The stench hit her first, worse than anything she'd ever encountered in Finders Court, and she'd had to cover her mouth and nose to prevent herself gagging. In the dim light of one lantern she saw the floor was awash with vomit and excrement. Hollow eyes turned to her, the passengers being unable to lift their heads from their saturated straw mattresses, and their pitiful groaning was heart-rending.

She had taken the two-year-old boy out of there, washed him, and tried to get him to drink some boiled water. But her tender care didn't help. He died a couple of hours later, and his parents were too weak even to climb up on to the deck to attend their little son's hasty funeral.

Matilda suspected that, but for Giles's timely intervention, there could have been more deaths. The following day he insisted that the Captain got everyone out of the hold on to the deck, and had the crew remove the foul mattresses and scrub the area out with vinegar.

Yet the Captain refused to give the passengers better food – the only concession he made was to allow them up on deck for longer periods than before. Thankfully the weather turned calmer, and there were no more deaths.

But Matilda didn't think she could ever forget that little boy she'd nursed, or how callous Lily had been about his death. She had berated her husband and Matilda for exposing themselves to infection, and in fact said that if Tabitha became sick she would hold them responsible.

Thankfully the trials of the voyage were ended, and with land ahead Matilda was prepared to try to forget such things. 'Tabitha wants to know where our house is,' she said.

'I don't know myself exactly,' Giles said, smiling down at his daughter as he held his wife. 'But come up here beside us and I'll tell you what landmarks I do know.'

Tabitha climbed up on a coil of rope beside him.

'See that church?' he said, pointing to a tall steeple towering above all the other buildings on the sky-line. 'That must be

Trinity Church because I was told it's a navigational aid to sailors. That's the church we're going to. So I expect our house will be somewhere near.'

'Its very near the wharves,' Lily said in a quavery voice.

Matilda had to look away so her mistress wouldn't see her smile. She thought Lily was an expert in pessimism.

'Well, of course it is,' Giles replied in a cheerful tone. 'The church dates back to 1698, at that time it would have been the heart of the settlement here. It's because New York is such a safe harbour that the city has prospered and grown so large.'

'Well, I hope we don't have to put up with drunken sailors and all that kind of unpleasantness,' Lily said with a pout. 'As a young girl in Bristol, I used to find it quite frightening and I'm sure Tabitha will too.'

'I will not, Mama,' Tabitha piped up. 'I like sailors.'

'Do you know who is coming to meet us?' Lily asked her husband as they walked down the gangplank on to the quay.

Matilda's head was swivelling this way and that, bombarded by sights, sounds and smells that were so very reminiscent of the Port of London, and indeed Bristol. Yet it was so hot that everything seemed magnified and very bewildering.

The smell of fish was overpowering, the wheels of carts, cabs and carriages rattled across the cobbles like rumbling thunder, and the men loading and unloading ships seemed to be shouting at the top of their voices. The ships' bowsprits reached half-way across the street, sails left to dry flapped in the breeze, and the quayside was littered with everything from bales of cotton to baskets of live hens and even pigs.

'Reverend Kirkbright did say he might not be able to come personally. But he assured me in his letter that we would be met and taken to our accommodation,' Giles replied, shading his eyes from the sun as he looked around. 'I dare say they'll pick us out at any minute. So we must stay right here so they can identify us.'

Five or ten minutes passed, long enough for one of the crew to bring out their trunk and other luggage and put it down beside them. Lily sat down on the trunk and opened her parasol, urging Tabitha to come under the shade too.

Matilda was growing nervous, not because she felt threatened in any way, but because she could see by Lily's face that she was working herself up into a paddy. A young couple had rushed up to the Smethwicks the moment they came off the ship. They were already leaving in a carriage, their luggage strapped on the back. To her right one of the steerage families were being warmly welcomed by a crowd of friends or relatives, on her left the mother of the little boy who had died was sobbing in the arms of a much younger man, and Matilda guessed that this was the brother who had urged her and her husband to come here. The Milsons had disembarked quite some time before either of these families. There were dozens of people just hanging around, but mostly they were working men in rough clothes, or women in shawls and caps, hardly the kind of people who would be sent from a church.

'Isn't there someone you could ask?' Lily said, covering her nose with a lace handkerchief and looking as if she might just pass out at any minute. Yet the moment Giles made to move away, she called him back. 'No, you can't leave us, it isn't safe.'

Matilda guessed she was further intimidated by a group of negroes sitting on the back of a handcart smoking pipes. She doubted her mistress had ever seen a black man before. She hadn't seen many herself, but Giles had told her a great deal about slavery in the Southern states during the voyage, and explained that while the Northern states had freed theirs some years earlier, little had been done to help them find employment in rural areas and they tended to flock into the big cities looking for work.

They waited and waited in the hot sun. A drunk lurched up to them and appeared to be asking them for money, but as he spoke a foreign language he could merely have been passing the time of day. A man rolling a barrel came dangerously close to running Matilda down with it, and a rough-looking character in a derby hat, chewing something brown and disgusting-looking which he spat noisily on to the ground, approached Giles and offered him accommodation nearby. They heard at least a dozen different languages spoken, and saw two men roll out of a public house wrestling like prize fighters.

Giles kept pacing up and down, glancing at his watch and at his wife's tense expression, and although from time to time he reassured her that someone would arrive any minute, it was quite clear he had no idea what to do for the best.

At last, some hour after they'd left the ship, a man drove up in a trap.

'Reverend and Mrs Milson?' he asked, reining in the horse.

Giles assured him they were and the ruddy-faced man with a bulbous nose jumped down and introduced himself as Mr MacGready. He made no apology for arriving so late, but said that they'd been expected several days earlier. He went on to say he was to take them directly to their house on State Street, and Reverend Kirkbright would call on them as soon as he was able.

He was a bumptious little man with a Scots accent and he made no effort to welcome them, just helped Lily up into the trap, bundled Tabitha in after her and left Matilda to climb up unassisted.

'Take the other end of the trunk,' he ordered Giles curtly and together they hauled it up on to the back.

Sitting in the back with Lily and Tabitha, Matilda couldn't hear what passed between Giles and MacGready as they drove out of the docks. Yet she could see her master's face in profile and it seemed to her that he wasn't pleased at what he was being told.

Their destination turned out to be quite near to the wharf, but as the roads were congested with carts, gigs and cabs, it took over half an hour to reach it, and at every jolt, every strident cry from street traders, or the sight of yet another seedy looking public house, Lily let out a disapproving sniff.

Matilda personally thought it all looked fascinating. It had a great deal in common with the part of London she'd grown up in, in as much as there were thousands of people milling around, noise and the strong odours of horse droppings, drains and rotting rubbish. Yet the vast majority of the people here were well dressed, the shops were invitingly well stocked, and it had a bold, brash quality which appealed to her. Rickety wooden houses and warehouses stood alongside much grander buildings, and a glance into little lanes off the main street showed many very elegant houses. She felt she could be happy here, it was exciting, colourful, and the working men didn't look as subservient as they did at home. She hoped that meant there wasn't such a big division between classes and that it really was a place of great opportunity for everyone.

'Is this to be our house?' Lily asked as MacGready pulled up the horse outside a narrow clapboard house in dire need of a coat of paint and its shutters mended. It was tucked in on the end of a row of fine-looking five-storey houses which were very similar to Georgian ones at home. They had imposing steps up to their front doors, and newly painted railings. Their house looked like a poor relation.

'Yes, ma'am,' MacGready said as he jumped down. 'It's all quality folk live here, so you'll be fine.'

That remark sounded very like sarcasm to Matilda and she wondered if the man was always so rude to strangers. She was soon to find MacGready had no social graces or sensitivity. He hauled the trunk in through the front door which led directly into a gloomy parlour, and left it there in the middle of the floor. 'There's wood, and coal for the stove in a shed in the yard,' he said curtly. 'The oil for the lamps is there too. They've left a few groceries on the table. You're lucky there's a water pump out in the yard, only put in a few months since. But I'll be getting on my way now if you don't mind.'

'Where is the housekeeper?' Lily asked, her voice trembling.

MacGready glanced at Matilda holding Tabitha in her arms. 'Ain't one servant enough for you?'

He was gone, slamming the door behind him before any of them could say anything in reply.

Lily slumped down on to a couch in shock. Her husband looked stunned. Only Tabitha seemed unconcerned, but then she was almost asleep in Matilda's arms.

'It reminds me of houses in the country back home,' Matilda said, determined to avert her mistress from any further bouts of crying. 'Once I've given it a bit of polishing and unpacked everything it will be real cosy. Won't it, sir?'

Giles looked a bit startled to be addressed. He was clearly deep in his own thoughts, perhaps smarting at the lack of welcome.

'Yes, of course it will, Matty,' he replied. 'Now, shall we look around, dear?' he said to his wife.

When she didn't reply or even move from the couch, Matilda put Tabitha next to her. 'I'll go with Sir,' she said. 'You stay here and get your breath back.'

Their tour of the house was brief and silent. It consisted of a large kitchen behind the parlour and a tiny scullery beyond that. The shady yard had a brick path down to the privy. By a narrow staircase tucked behind a door in the kitchen they reached the two main bedrooms, then up a further flight of stairs were two more smaller attic ones.

It was clean, the furniture plain and functional, but the beds weren't made up and there was a musty smell as if it hadn't been lived in for some months. Had Matilda ever been offered such a house for her family she would have been overjoyed at her good fortune, but she couldn't see the Milsons appreciating its simple charms when they were used to so much larger and grander accommodation.

'It's smaller than I expected,' Giles reported back to his wife as they came back downstairs. 'But it's quite adequate for our needs.'

Matilda looked sharply at her master. He had made no comment about anything as they looked around, his remark seemed quite calm and resigned, yet she had a feeling he was angry.

Giles was in fact seething. He was a humble man by nature, he didn't believe his family's status or his calling should give him preferential treatment. But back home a new parson, particularly with a wife and small child, would be greeted warmly, refreshments offered and their new home sparkling a welcome. MacGready, who appeared from the little he'd said to be nothing more than a church caretaker, had been insufferably rude, implying that Milson's new role would not be as parson, but some kind of lowly assistant to the Reverend Darius Kirkbright. If it wasn't for being afraid to leave Lily and his child, he would be straight off now to see the man and give him a piece of his mind.

But Lily seemed to be almost in a trance. Aside from the hand stroking her child's hair as she slept with her head on her mother's lap, she was motionless and mute, her eyes full of fear.

Giles had no idea how to deal with her, and that made him feel even more wretched because he'd insisted on coming to America despite all her protests. Was he a brute who thought only of his own desires? Or was she at fault in not supporting him? Back home he'd been so sure of himself, believed he had been called here by a higher power. Now he was not so certain of that, maybe it was sheer vanity to think he was so important.

'What shall I do first, sir?' Matilda asked. 'Shall I make the beds, or light the stove so we can have a cup of tea?'

He shrugged helplessly. Matilda had been his rock on the voyage, using her own initiative whenever a problem arose, seldom troubling him with anything. He knew that he and his wife should be taking charge again now, but he had no domestic skills, and it didn't look as if Lily was capable of even taking her own shawl off.

'I'll light the stove, then,' Matilda said, as if she realized his plight. 'You stay here and rest, I'll see to everything.'

Giles sank down beside his wife and child as Matilda disappeared into the kitchen. He felt very ashamed of giving way to melancholy and self-doubts. But he was exhausted, his well of enthusiasm had run dry, and right at this moment he could very well understand why so many men resorted to drink to cheer them.

Once Matilda had pulled up the kitchen blind and the early evening sunshine flooded in, she was cheered by seeing the kitchen was every bit as well equipped as the one back in Primrose Hill, and larger too. It was awful that the water had to be drawn from a pump outside, she'd grown so used to turning on a tap in the scullery back in Primrose Hill, and she'd imagined that here in America everyone would have an indoor water supply. But at least it was a private pump, not one for the whole street.

The stove, on the other hand, was twice the size of the one she was used to, with three separate ovens and a tap on one side which meant it probably heated water too, but she supposed it must work in the same way. Fortunately it turned out to be much easier to lay and light than the old one, and within minutes she had a good blaze going. She went out into the yard, filled the kettle from the pump and put it on the stove, then, aware it was very quiet in the parlour, she took a peep round the door.

Tabitha was still fast asleep across her mother's lap, her father cradling his wife in his arms. Both adults looked utterly dejected.

Alarmed, she turned back to the kitchen to find cups and saucers and as she laid a tray, it suddenly occurred to her what Giles had actually meant by 'It's smaller than I expected.' He would have no study, the kitchen would have to serve as dining- and living-room too.

In fact MacGready's rude words about 'one servant being enough' were true. A third woman in such a small house would be more of a hindrance than help. Matilda didn't really mind if this meant she had to be both nursemaid and housekeeper, but she knew Lily would see it as a step down the social scale.

Going back into the parlour, she asked Giles for the keys of the trunk so she could get the bed linen out. 'I'll make up the beds while I'm waiting for the kettle,' she said. 'Now, shall I put Tabitha up in the attic room next to me, or in the room by you?'

'I don't know,' Giles answered wearily, his eyes dark and forlorn. 'You do what you think is for the best.'

'How is Mrs Milson?' Giles asked as Matilda came back down the stairs much later in the evening, after seeing both her mistress and Tabitha into bed. He looked haggard with weariness and she guessed that while she was upstairs he had been thinking over the events of the day and blaming himself for everything.

'Sleeping now,' Matilda replied, forcing her usual wide smile. 'Though she said the mattress is lumpy, and I probably didn't shake it enough before making up the bed. But it's better than the ones on the ship, and I dare say after a good night's sleep she'll feel a whole lot better in the morning.'

Lily had rallied round after a cup of tea, enough to look upstairs and come into the kitchen with a view to making some supper. Already weakened by sickness on the boat, the disappointment about the house and lack of welcome, when she found the bread left for them was hard, and the butter melted to mere oil, she became distraught.

Matilda had never expected that she would ever need to use old standbys from Finders Court, but faced with hard bread and eggs as the only food available, she quickly beat up the eggs, cut thick slices of bread and dropped them into it, then fried them golden-brown.

Tired as Tabitha was, she ate two large pieces with relish. Giles ate three and pronounced them delicious. Lily cautiously ate one, and cheered up enough to say what a clever idea it was and maybe it would make a good breakfast dish. But then, just as Matilda was convinced Lily was on the mend, she went into the scullery and saw two large beetles.

Screaming at the top of her voice, she tore right through the kitchen into the parlour where she jumped up on the couch. It took both Matilda and Giles to coax her down, and even some half an hour later she was still hysterical.

'I do hope she'll be better tomorrow, Matty,' Giles said, his dark eyes huge and sorrowful. 'I feel so responsible. Do you think it's going to be terrible here too?'

This was the first time Matilda had ever seen a weak side to her master. He had always taken charge of everything important, and he appeared to sail through his ministry work and his role as husband and father with the confidence of a man who knew everything. On the ship, he'd been the one who made them all laugh in tense moments. His often boyish exuberance was infectious, his interest in people endearing, the ship's crew had dropped his full title to an affectionate 'Rev'.

'No, of course it's not going to be terrible,' she said quickly. She was close to collapse herself – making the beds, unpacking clothes, cooking and having to keep up a bright front for everyone else had drained all her earlier energy. 'Once I've got the house straight, and Madam unpacks all her little treasures, it will be fine.'

'I didn't know it would be like this,' he blurted out, holding his head in his hands. 'I came here to work with the poor, Matty. But I didn't think we'd have to live like them.'

Matilda felt her heart swell up with sympathy for him. On the trip out here they'd often talked up on deck, and she had come to see that his motive for coming to America wasn't for adventure or self-advancement. He had spoken forcefully against slavery and the huge divide between rich and poor. He wanted education for everyone, child labour to be stamped out, and decent housing for the working classes. His wife had given him hell for the whole voyage and now he was beginning to doubt himself too.

'If you think the poor live like this,' she said teasingly, 'then you don't know much about the subject. Look around you, sir! This house might look a bit gloomy and drab right now, but that's because it's got nothing personal in it. The furniture is decent enough, so are the rugs and curtains. Once I've polished the floor it will be lovely.'

As she said those reassuring words, she glanced around her and realized it was in fact the truth. With Lily's lace chair-backs on the buttoned-backed armchairs, her pictures and ornaments softening the bareness, it would be very like the parlour back home. 'Why don't you go to bed now, sir? You look all in.'

He looked up at her, dark eyes boring into her. 'Thank God I brought you with us, Matty! Your strength is so reassuring and I think I'm going to be leaning on you for some time as I've got a feeling Mrs Milson isn't going to be much help to me for a while. You do know she's punishing me for bringing her here?'

It was the first time he had ever admitted even obliquely that his wife hadn't wanted to come. Even when it was obvious that she was wallowing in self-pity on the ship, he'd kept up the pretence that her only problem was the seasickness.

Although Matilda was touched that he felt able to confide in her, she didn't think she should side with him against his wife. 'I'm sure that's not true,' she said starchily. 'She's just frail, and scared about everything. But she'll be fine in a day or two. Now, off to bed with you, I'll make sure everything's locked up.'

After he'd gone upstairs, Matilda opened the door on to the back yard and sat on the step looking up at the night sky. It seemed very strange to think that the stars up there were the same ones as over England, yet she was thousands of miles away. It didn't feel a foreign place, not here in the darkness. The distant sounds of rumbling carriage wheels could be in Camden Town or anywhere. She wondered then what those beetles were – a sixth sense told her they were some kind of vermin, even though she'd seen nothing quite like them in England. Maybe she could ask someone tomorrow.

Suddenly she remembered that they hadn't said any prayers tonight. Giles would be upset about that when he realized. Putting her hands together, she said a quick one for all of them, that Lily would wake up feeling better, that Giles would get the welcome he deserved, and that Tabitha would behave for the next few days while they had so much to do.

'And make me strong enough for all of us,' she added.

Matilda woke when the early morning sun hit her in the face.

Creeping out of bed, leaving Tabitha still sleeping peacefully, she went over to the small window and looked out. She doubted Lily would approve that she'd slept with the child, but last night it had seemed the sensible thing to do, in case Tabitha woke and was frightened to find herself in a strange room.

Her spirits soared when she saw a glimpse of the sea between the two houses opposite. Yesterday evening she hadn't even looked out of the window, and during the carriage ride here she had supposed they were going away from the sea, not towards it. MacGready had said that New York became unbearably hot in July and August, he'd also ghoulishly mentioned epidemics of cholera, and tuberculosis being rife in the slums, which no doubt added to Lily's unhappiness. But if they were by the sea, with fresh air, they wouldn't come to any harm.

Matilda had coaxed the stove back into life, scrubbed the scullery and kitchen floors, polished and dusted the parlour, and she was still down on her knees polishing the floor when she was startled by Tabitha asking her what she was doing.

She looked up to see the little girl standing in the kitchen doorway. Her dark hair was cascading over her white nightgown, her cheeks rosy from sleep, and she looked far more like her father for once.

'Making it look like home,' Matilda replied, getting up on to her feet. 'But I've just about finished now. I hope you weren't scared when you woke up to find yourself all alone? I left you there and came down because you were fast asleep.'

Tabitha gave one of her wide smiles and came running to hug her. 'Why would I be scared? I'm a big girl now.'

'Well, sometimes it takes a while to get used to a new house,' Matilda said, picking the child up to kiss her. 'Do you see I've unpacked some of Mama and Papa's things?' She waved her hand towards the mantelpiece where the clock and a couple of china shepherdesses were sitting. 'But we'll have to wait till your papa comes down to put the clock right. I don't know what the time is.'

She guessed by the increased sound of traffic from outside that it was around eight, and if so it was time she got breakfast started. She was looking forward to Giles and Lily seeing what she'd done. Now that sunshine was coming in through the parlour windows and everywhere gleaming with polish, it looked like a different room. 'Shall we get you bathed before Mama comes down?'

Matilda hadn't found a bath, there wasn't even one outside in the yard, but there was a huge fish kettle in the scullery big enough to sit Tabitha in.

Tabitha thought it was a huge joke to be sitting in a fish kettle, and after washing her Matilda left her to play with a tin mug and a couple of spoons while she put the kettle on and laid the kitchen table.

Giles came down as she was drying Tabitha on her lap in the kitchen. She had never seen him looking so unkempt, his shirt was crumpled and he had thick dark stubble on his chin, he hadn't even combed his hair. He looked more like her father used to in the mornings than a parson.

'If you give me a moment I'll get you some hot water,' she said. 'I think you're too big to bathe in a fish kettle!'

Tabitha thought that was very funny and burst into peals of laughter. Giles laughed too.

At once Matilda felt easier. Giles had always liked jokes, and if he'd got his sense of humour back they'd all be fine.

'Washing and shaving are the least of my worries right now,' he said. 'I thought I'd take a quick walk and see if I can find some fresh bread for breakfast. Perhaps I ought to try and find a bath too.'

'Let me do that,' Matilda said eagerly. She was dying to explore. 'I can dress Tabby quickly and she could come with me.'

Giles frowned. 'I think I ought to check out how safe it is around here first,' he said.

'Do you think there might be savages with bows and arrows waiting round the corner?' she said teasingly.

He smiled. 'Didn't I tell you about the cannibals and wild animals? How very remiss of me, Matty,' he joked, looking and sounding much more like his old self. 'Maybe we could all go together. There's safety in numbers.'

'Then perhaps you'd better spruce yourself up first,' she said archly, forgetting for a moment who she was talking to. 'I mean, it wouldn't do for the new parson to be seen like that!'

He smiled, and patted her shoulder. 'What would I do without you, Matty? Always the voice of reason!'

'It's a lovely place, Mama,' Tabitha said excitedly as they ate breakfast over an hour later. 'We saw the sea, and we went in a shop and lots of people lifted their caps to Papa.'

Matilda looked cautiously at her mistress, trying to gauge her mood. She had come downstairs fully dressed a few seconds after they arrived home but she'd merely sat down in the parlour and apart from replying to her husband's question about whether she'd slept well, she said nothing more.

Aggie had always made porridge for breakfast, but Matilda wasn't convinced that the stuff the man in the shop called oatmeal was the same, and besides, it took too long to cook, but she'd got more eggs and some sausages, along with quite a selection of fruit.

'You've done very well for us, Matty,' Lily said after a few minutes. 'Was the food in the shop like home?'

'No, it wasn't,' Matty admitted. 'There seemed so much more than we are used to and there were vegetables and fruits I've never seen before. I think we'll have to get someone to explain everything to us.'

'There's bound to be women at the church who will put us straight,' Giles said and patted his wife's hand affectionately. 'I asked the man in the shop what Americans ate for breakfast, and he mentioned buckwheat pancakes with maple syrup. That sounds rather good.'

Lily sniffed, her mouth pursed with disapproval, but Matilda noted she had eaten all of her scrambled egg and sausage, and she was reaching out eagerly for a peach. Matilda had never even known there was such a fruit until last summer when one of Giles's brothers came up from Bath and brought some with him that he had managed to grow in a sheltered part of his garden. She had shared one with Tabitha and thought it was the most heavenly thing she'd ever tasted. But these American ones looked even better, they were as big as oranges and very soft.

Lily cut hers up delicately with a knife and removed the stone, then tasted a small portion cautiously. 'Umm,' she murmured, then smiled properly for the first time in weeks. 'It's wonderful.'

That peach was the first thing that pleased Lily in America, and just an hour after breakfast the ice man called. Both Giles and Lily had looked at each other in astonishment, and the man had to explain that they had a tin-lined box out in their scullery which if they bought ice from him each day would keep their food fresh during the hot weather.

It was Giles who agreed to buy a lump and as he packed the butter, cheese and milk into it, his wife and Matilda stared in disbelief. But as the temperature rose that first day into the high eighties, and they found the butter was still firm and the milk fresh and cold, they all saw it as something miraculous.

By midday Lily was showing signs of returning to her old self, running her finger along shelves in the kitchen for dirt, putting out her lace chair-backs, and talking about getting hold of some jars to bottle peaches for the winter. Matilda took Tabitha upstairs for a nap at two in the afternoon, and she was still upstairs with her, lining the linen cupboard shelves with fresh paper out on the landing, when the front-door bell rang.

As Lily and Giles were in the parlour, arranging their pictures on the wall, and they'd already said they expected there might be some visitors, she didn't rush down, but waited to be called if they required tea. She heard a booming male voice, and a much softer lady's one, and assuming it must be the Reverend Darius Kirkbright and his wife come to welcome the Milsons, she carried on with her work.

As the door from the kitchen to the staircase was closed, when Lily moved in there with the other woman Matilda couldn't hear what was being said, only the gentle murmur of their voices. It pleased her to think her mistress had some female company at last. Aside from herself, there had only been Mrs Smethwick on the ship, and she had been so snooty that even if Lily had been feeling up to talking to someone, she doubted they would have had anything in common.

The cupboard shelves finished and the clean linen stacked, Matilda made for the small attic room next to her own. The Milsons had decided earlier that this should be Tabitha's, so Giles could have the second room on the first floor as his study. It was a bare little room with a polished wood floor, and the only furniture a narrow iron bed, a chest of drawers and wash-stand, but with some pretty curtains, a rag rug and counterpane from home and Tabitha's dolls and other toys it could soon be made more homely.

Matilda had opened the windows wide earlier that morning and given the feather mattress a good shaking. The room smelled nice and fresh now and a breeze coming in from the sea had kept it cool. She made up the bed, put Tabitha's clothes in the drawers, then began unpacking a box of toys.

In all she must have been up there for some half-hour when the child woke in Matilda's room and came out to find her, dressed only in her petticoat, her hair sticking to her head with perspiration.

'What do you think of your room, Tabby?' Matilda asked her.

Tabitha climbed up on to the bed and tried it out. 'Nice,' she said. 'At night I can pretend I'm still on the ship and the wind's coming in the porthole.'

Matilda laughed. She was a great believer in wide open windows when it was hot, but Lily always insisted on closing them at night because she had the idea night breezes were loaded with pestilence. 'Mama won't let them stay open, not at night, and if I see you leaning out I'll get bars put on them. Now, shall we put your clothes back on and you can go and see Mama and Papa, they've got some visitors but I'm sure they'd like to meet you too.'

Tabitha pulled a face. 'Can't we go out for a walk?'

'Later perhaps when it's cooler,' Matilda replied. The heat was draining – she understood now why all the other houses in the street had their shutters closed while the sun was at its hottest. She wished too she had something cooler to wear, she'd been glad of the thick navy-blue serge dress on the ship but it was much too hot now and she hadn't dared say anything to Lily in case it set her off again.

'Will it always be hot like this?' Tabitha said, as Matilda washed her face and neck with cool water.

'No, your papa said it's very cold here in the winter,' she replied as she slipped the child's dress over her head and buttoned her up.

'Is Mama ever going to be happy again?'

Matilda's heart sank. Once early on during the voyage Tabitha had asked her the same thing and she thought she'd managed to convince the child her mother was only sick, not unhappy. Clearly Tabitha knew the difference.

'Of course she is,' she said stoutly. 'She was only poorly yesterday because she was very tired and because everything was strange. She's fine now, talking to her visitors, but you can see for yourself. I'll just brush your hair then take you down there.'

Matilda hesitated outside the kitchen door. Back in Primrose Hill her position in the household had been clearly defined – apart from any cleaning duties or mealtimes, she stayed in the nursery or the kitchen unless summoned by either of the Milsons ringing the bell. But there was no bell here, Tabitha's room was far too small to be called a nursery, and with her mistress being forced to use the kitchen, she didn't know where she was expected to go when they had visitors.

Knocking tentatively, she put her head round the door and asked if she should bring Tabitha in. The two women were sitting at the table sharing a pot of tea. It was unbearably hot from the stove, even though the window and back door were wide open.

'Of course, Matty,' Lily said with unexpected warmth. 'Do come in, both of you, and meet Mrs Kirkbright. This is my daughter Tabitha, and her nursemaid Matilda,' she added for her visitor's benefit.

Tabitha ran in, she was always glad to greet anyone new.

'Good afternoon, Mrs Kirkbright.' Matilda bobbed a little curtsey and hoped that was appropriate. She guessed the wife of the Reverend Kirkbright, stout and matronly in a lilac dress and matching bonnet, was a great deal older than her mistress. Yet she looked very pleasant, she had large, soft brown eyes and her smile was welcoming. She hadn't come empty-handed either – on the table was a whole pile of foodstuffs, including a currant cake, jars of preserves and a cooked chicken. 'I thought you might like to see Tabby, but unless there is something you want me to do down here, I'll go back upstairs and finish unpacking your clothes.'

'Do stay, Matty,' Lily said. 'Mrs Kirkbright has been telling me about American food and the best places to buy it. I can't take it all in, but maybe you can.'

It was a surprise not to be sent packing, and perhaps that was what made Matilda so impulsive. 'Aren't you both terribly hot?' she asked. 'Wouldn't you like to sit outside in the yard? It's cool and shady there, and I scrubbed off the bench there this morning.'

Mrs Kirkbright laughed. 'No wonder you brought her with you,' she said, looking at Lily. 'I've never managed to find any servant who acted on their own initiative. I *am* roasting in here, but I wouldn't have dreamt of saying so.'

'I didn't think it quite seemly to invite you out there,' Lily said to Mrs Kirkbright, giving Matilda a piercing look as if to remind her how close it was to the privy. 'Of course at home my husband would have taken Reverend Kirkbright into his study for their private talk, leaving us with the parlour, or even the dining-room. But if you'd be more comfortable out there, perhaps we should move.'

To her consternation Matilda realized she had acutely embarrassed her mistress. She hoped she wouldn't get into trouble for it later. Yet the yard was very cool and oddly attractive for a place which had clearly been ignored by previous occupants of the house. Overshadowed by neighbouring taller houses and with a central sad-looking tree, it was entirely in deep shade. Matilda had not only scrubbed the wooden bench that morning, but swept the path too. The remaining area of hard-packed soil was covered in a densely packed low-growing weed which, though not a lawn, at least gave an impression of one. As the privy and shed were covered with creepers, the lush greenness was welcome after the heat of the kitchen.

'Oh, this is better,' Mrs Kirkbright said, smiling as she sank down on to the bench and fanned at her face. 'What us poor women have to endure in the summer with our long dresses, petticoats and stays!'

Lily smiled, but Matilda knew she thought it improper of Mrs Kirkbright to mention underclothes.

Matilda brought out a kitchen chair for herself and placed it some feet away from the two older women, but she was pleasantly surprised to see how Mrs Kirkbright scooped Tabitha up on to her lap without a thought to crumpling her fine gown.

In fact as the woman chatted she seemed refreshingly lacking in snobbery, addressing both the child and Matilda as if they were part of her own family. She said that although she and her husband were English, and they missed some things about home, they had been here for twelve years and had no intention of ever going back. 'It's such a vibrant, exciting country,' she said earnestly. 'People are rewarded here for their effort and hard work, even a dirt-poor immigrant from Ireland or Germany can make something of himself if he's a mind to. Many of our wealthier parishioners bemoan the difficulty in getting good domestic staff, but in my view such a situation shows a clear desire for people to be their own masters, and that is an excellent thing.'

She moved on then to explain the differences between American and English food. 'Very few people here have a big dinner at noon as they do in England,' she said. 'You'll find it too hot in the summer to want to eat much anyway. Far better to eat a hearty breakfast of eggs, bacon and buckwheat pancakes, and then a good dinner in the cool of the evening. They eat more meat here, everything from corned beef to bullock's hearts and calf's head, and the seafood is very good and plentiful. One of the puddings I must give you the recipe for is pan dowdy – it's apples, sugar and spices baked in a deep crust and absolutely delicious.'

As she spoke of vegetables like squash and baked beans, Matilda asked how she should cook these. 'I'll write it all down for you when I get home and drop it round,' Mrs Kirkbright said. 'Many things in the general store are similar to those we use back in England but they just call them different names. You'll soon catch on.'

Turning to Lily, she said, 'You'll find other women much more sociable here, my dear. We do use calling cards, just like at home, but the social life is mostly much less formal. Very often us women drop in on one another once we've become good friends. I hope, Lily, that you will feel able to do this with me, for we have much in common.'

It was at this point that Matilda began to wonder why Mrs Kirkbright hadn't mentioned moving to her new parish. She sounded very much as if she was here to stay. But if that was the case, where would it leave Giles? Knowing it wasn't her place to ask such things, she kept quiet and just listened to the woman's vivid descriptions of the shops. 'You can buy almost any household goods in Pearl Street,' she said. 'That's just a walk from here, but don't be tempted to walk much further north than that, as there are some very unpleasant areas beyond. I expect my husband will be telling yours about that side of New York right now, I just hope it doesn't frighten him.'

Florence Kirkbright was correct, her husband had launched into an impassioned speech about the darker side of New York. But rather than being frightened, Giles found it soothed his earlier disappointments and brought back his conviction that God had led him here for something very special.

The Reverend Darius Kirkbright was straight-talking yet very courteous. His height – he was well over six feet tall – fresh complexion, full-moon face and snow-white hair swept back from a massive forehead all seemed to point to a man of strong character.

'I am very sorry that the Bishop of London led you to believe you would be taking over from me as parson, or minister as we call the role here,' he said after Giles had admitted he'd been angry the previous day. 'Perhaps the misunderstanding arose because I asked for a specific kind of minister, and went to great pains to say that I didn't want an unworldly novice. The kind of man I wanted wouldn't be concerned with his status.'

Giles thought at first that this was a reprimand because he'd commented on how small the house was, and a reminder that no clergyman should be looking for material comforts like a fine parsonage. But as Darius went on to apologize for not meeting him personally from the ship, ruefully admitting he knew they must have felt abandoned and hurt, and explained that he had been called away because one of his oldest parishioners was dying, it became clear to Giles that this man had all the right priorities. He too would have put a dying man's needs before those of a young, healthy family.

But perhaps the most heart-warming aspect of this big man was his directness. He didn't linger on apologies or idle smalltalk, but went straight on to tell Giles exactly what he thought about New York.

'There is a shameful situation here in this city,' he said, fixing Giles with eyes that demanded attention. 'While there are many powerful rich men with high ideals and a strong moral sense, there are many more who care nothing about the common good, and profit for themselves is gained at the expense of the workers they exploit. These latter ones worm their way into positions of authority, they grease palms, they manipulate.

'You might say that it is the same the world over, and so that may be, but you will notice after a short time in this city that the republican simplistic virtues are being lost, and an imperial culture of excess, greed and power is creeping in. Tomorrow you will see this for yourself in Fifth Avenue, grandiose mansions with white marble, Corinthian pillars, and silver ornamentation on their front doors.'

Giles raised his eyebrows. He was a little surprised to hear such puritanical views from an English clergyman.

Darius smiled, perhaps reading his mind. 'I don't despise wealth, not at all. And some of these mansions have been built by good men who are philanthropists responsible for donating money to worthy causes. But most are owned by scallywags, and their wealth is the result of evil.

'While I cannot stop such men, much less take away their wealth and give it back to those they robbed, I believe we must show our disapproval, ostracize them from society in the hopes that such action will deter others from emulating them. I also believe we must all take responsibility for the plight of the poor, and do everything in our power to alleviate their misery.'

Giles listened very carefully. He learned that Trinity Church was a rich one, with a large majority of the parishioners first- and second-generation Americans from English and Dutch stock. These were the men who had made New York what it was today, and who had big plans for its future.

'I fear, though,' Darius went on, 'that these white, Anglo-Saxon Protestant people have a mind to create a kind of supremacy, from which any other kind are barred. I may be a white, Anglo-Saxon Protestant myself, just as you are, Giles, but we share the same God as the Catholics. I believe too that all men, be they Irish, Pole, Jew, Negro or Italian, are his children and as such they should have equal rights. I cannot sit back and watch any of these discriminated against purely because of the colour of their skin, language or religion.'

Giles was growing excited at finding a man who shared his views.

'I agree wholeheartedly,' he said. 'But how can we help those who do not attend our church?'

'Through a broader ministry,' Darius said with a faint smile. 'We do not need to be Bible-thumping missionaries seeking converts, we just show the love of God at the simplest level, schools for children of the very poorest, food for the starving, foundling homes, English classes for those who do not speak our language. And we raise money for these projects and assistance by pricking the consciences of those rich but devout Christians who have not yet discovered the joy of giving.'

Giles beamed. It was only then that Darius began to shock him. 'Take a look at those Fifth Avenue mansions, Giles, walk up and down and feel the opulence, then take yourself off to an area called Five Points immediately after,' he said. 'It's not far from here, but it could be another country, the difference is so great. It is hell come to earth, Giles, far worse than anything you may have seen in London, I think the worst slum area in the world. At the centre of it is an old brewery where it is estimated over a thousand people exist.'

'Exist?' Giles repeated.

'Yes, exist. You can't call it live for they huddle together like crazed animals in their rags, in dark, putrid rooms, without fire, means to cook food, sanitation or even the scantiest of furniture. Many are reluctant to leave there even briefly, for fear someone will steal their place. Every kind of horror you can imagine goes on in there, and ones we wouldn't dare to imagine. It is Hades, Giles. And most people in New York aren't even aware of it.'

'But what can we do about it?' Giles said weakly.

'We can make known its horrors, get it pulled down and decent housing built in its place, but that brewery is only the centre of Hell, all around it are rookeries so dense that even the police fear to go in there. There are tens of thousands of people living around there – each week when another immigrant ship comes in, the numbers swell even higher. Epidemics of cholera and yellow fever flash through there from time to time, fires break out and kill a few more of the unfortunates, but still it remains, the boundaries expanding daily. When I asked the Bishop of London for a good man to join me, I didn't want a mealy-mouthed young whippersnapper who revels in taking Bible classes, but a man like St George, prepared to fight the dragon and slay him.'

Giles gulped. He had been in New York for only twenty-four hours, and much of that time had been spent in wishing he hadn't come. Now, before he'd even had time to get his bearings, see the church, walk around the streets and meet the parishioners, he was being asked to show his colours. All he could think of was how lucky it was Lily had gone out of the room with Mrs Kirkbright.

'Well, Giles! Are you a St George?'

'My sword is a little rusty,' Giles said with a faint smile. 'I share your convictions, I hope I can be the man you want beside you. But I have to say I am somewhat taken aback right now.'

To his surprise Darius began to laugh uproariously.

'Good man,' he said. 'If you'd leapt up and pulled a sword out of the closet you'd have had me worried. I like a man who has the courage to admit he needs time to take stock. I had no intention of dragging you off to that hell-hole tonight.'

Giles found himself laughing too, if only from relief. 'I ought to warn you, sir,' he said, 'my wife is a little squeamish, so I'd be grateful if when the ladies come back in you didn't tell her about this place, not today anyway.'

Darius's eyes twinkled. They were brown, but flecked with amber, reminding Giles of a cat's. 'Of course. Our little ladies have to be protected from sights that would offend and frighten them. My suggestion is that we take the comfortable route, you meet our parishioners, you and your wife socialize and make friends, and learn to love New York as myself and my wife do. Then later, once you've found your feet, we will make our plans for rooting out this evil together.'

The sun was like a huge orange fireball, slowly sinking into the sea, as Lily and Giles went for a walk along to the Battery later that same evening. The red sails of fishing boats out on the bay made a pretty sight, and Lily was cheered a little by the many elegantly dressed couples strolling arm-in-arm towards Castle Clinton, an old fort on the foreshore that the Kirkbrights had told them was now used for concerts.

'Maybe it won't be quite as bad here as I feared,' she said in a slightly disbelieving voice, looking wistfully at the many fine houses and fancy carriages. 'Reverend Kirkbright and his wife are very kind, I'm sure they'd understand if we told them the house we've been given isn't suitable for us.'

Her anxiety had grown after Florence Kirkbright had mentioned that this part of lower Manhattan was gradually sinking in tone because the wealthy former residents had begun moving further uptown to newly built areas like Gramercy Park. Lily couldn't actually see any visible signs of decay. Even the little ragamuffins playing down on the shore looked picturesque rather than squalid. But a minister's wife wouldn't say such a thing without good reason.

'I don't think I can do that,' Giles said. 'A clergyman has to accept what he is given, Lily, you know that.'

'But I don't think the Kirkbrights live in a modest house. Florence mentioned a cook and a maid, we know they have a carriage too because we will be going out in it tomorrow with them. If you are really not just a mere curate but sharing the work at the church as joint ministers, surely you should have a similar household?'

Giles sighed deeply. 'I suspect Kirkbright is independently wealthy and that his house is not owned by the church, but is his own,' he said.

This temporarily silenced Lily. Back in England parsons received a stipend according to the wealth and size of their parish. Many clergymen had private means to supplement this often meagre amount, but Giles had no such private income. They had been fortunate in Primrose Hill in that it was a wealthy parish, and her careful housekeeping had meant they lived well. She hadn't for one moment imagined that by coming to America they would live in reduced circumstances.

'Please don't look for problems,' Giles begged her. 'Tomorrow after the tour of the city we'll be having dinner with them, and meeting some of the parishioners. When you married a clergyman you knew we would never have riches, but I think we should both be very grateful for all the privileges that go with my work.'

Lily knew that was as close as he'd ever get to telling her to be quiet and accept her lot in life joyfully. She wondered what it was he and the Reverend Kirkbright had talked about today that had suddenly made Giles so happy. Just the fact that he hadn't shared it with her meant it was something slightly covert and therefore more cause for anxiety.

'I've never been sorry I married you, Giles,' she said in a small voice. This was entirely true, she loved him as much now as she had on their wedding day. 'I just wish I could be all the things you really wanted in a wife.'

Giles looked down at her small, strained face and tried to

remember when she'd last laughed, really laughed the way she used to. She no longer responded to his caresses, her glances at him were often accusing, yet she wouldn't or couldn't speak of what was troubling her. Was it his fault? Perhaps it was unseemly for a man of the cloth to desire his wife, to remember with longing those passion-filled nights in the early days of their marriage? Lily was the only woman he'd ever made love to, the only one he wanted, so he could make no comparisons. Was there truth in what other men said, that they took a mistress so they didn't *bother* their wife? Could the root cause of her unhappiness be just that, she wished he wouldn't trouble her?

But how could he speak of such delicate things? To do so might create an even wider chasm between them. All he could do was love and protect her, and try to control his own urges.

'You are everything I want in a wife, Lily,' he said, squeezing her arm. 'Just try a bit harder not to close your mind to everything which is new. Our life here might very well turn out to be far better and more worthwhile than the one we had in London. Let's strive for that together.'

Chapter Five

'I think it's high time, Matty, that you made some friends for yourself,' Lily said unexpectedly as they were hanging a new set of curtains in the parlour. 'We've been here for nearly three months now and it isn't right that you never have any fun.'

Matilda was standing on a chair, balanced on top of a wooden box, and she nearly fell off with surprise. Back in England her mistress wouldn't have considered 'fun' important to a servant's well-being, but then a great many of her previously rigid ideas had been softened since they came to America. She had retained her fussiness, her fear of disease and insistence on utilizing every scrap of food. She still lapsed into long sulks, but she had adapted to living in a small house, sometimes it seemed that she was even happier doing most of the cooking herself.

Back in England her mistress would never have taken a bath in the kitchen, yet once she saw how much time and effort were required for Matilda to haul pails of hot water up to the bedrooms, she announced that in future they would all take their baths downstairs. She didn't take fright any longer when she heard a foreign accent or saw a black face, and she even admitted to enjoying the odd glass of sherry, when once any kind of alcohol had been the gateway to Hell. She had been alarmed at first by American women's informality – they called her by her Christian name and dropped by uninvited. But slowly she'd grown to accept this was the way here, and at times she admitted to liking it.

Yet the biggest change in her attitude was the way she treated Matilda. She asked rather than ordered her to do something and even showed concern if she looked tired or off-colour. Maybe this was partly because she'd been told that English-speaking, good, reliable servants were almost impossible to find in New York, but perhaps mainly because Matilda alone appreciated what her mistress had lost by leaving England.

Back in England a parson was on a social level with doctors, barristers and other professional men, and the difference in their respective incomes was of no consequence. Lily as a parson's wife was a 'lady' and therefore was treated with the utmost respect.

Here in America a minister had little social status, unless of course he was wealthy like the Reverend Kirkbright. For shy little Lily Milson, it was painful to have to accept invitations to smart parties by the well-intentioned Kirkbrights, only to find herself ignored by most of the other guests. Giles could hold his own, he was after all young, handsome and a very interesting man, but Lily would just wilt into a corner, only too aware she was unfashionably dressed, and plain.

Giles had stated before they left England that American men treated their wives with far more respect than English men, and on the face of it they did appear to do so, at least in public. But from what Matilda had gleaned from overheard conversations between women here in this house, in reality American men in their homes were even more egotistical than the English. They told their wives nothing about their business interests, the assumption being that women were too delicate, too anxious for such things, and expected them instead to concentrate on traditional womanly skills – housekeeping, child-rearing and making life more comfortable for their men.

It seemed Giles was embracing this way of thinking too, for although he was still as kind and gentle with Lily as he'd always been, he seldom talked about his ministry work at home, and never included Lily in any part of it other than when she accompanied him to social events.

So perhaps it wasn't surprising that two women in a strange new country, living under very cramped conditions, had become something more than mistress and servant. They talked a great deal, about Tabitha, books, cooking and their neighbours, they reminisced about home, and often took walks together with Tabitha to explore their new city.

At night Giles often had to go out, and Lily would join Matilda in the kitchen, or on hot evenings, out in the back yard. Matilda might still call Lily 'madam', she still obeyed her implicitly and did the main brunt of the household chores, but the truth was that Matilda was more than Lily's equal. She was the one who haggled for lower prices in the shops, the one who wasn't afraid of anything, not even those beetles she now knew were cockroaches. It was she who decided the day's menu, for housekeeping money was tighter here than it had been in England and she knew how to stretch it. Each time Lily confided her worries to Matilda, the bond grew stronger between them.

'But where would I go to make friends?' Matilda asked. The last time she'd had a friend was when she was a child in Finders Court – once she began selling flowers there was no time for such things.

'There's a dance for young people at the church each Saturday evening.'

'I can't dance,' Matilda objected.

'From what I understand they don't do anything more difficult than a polka and I could teach you to do that.'

'What if no one asked me to dance?' Matilda said fearfully.

'I don't think that's likely to happen,' Lily smiled. 'But if you don't like that idea, what about the Bible class the Deacon runs on Wednesday evenings?'

Matilda pulled a face.

'Other girls in service go there,' Lily said reprovingly. 'It wouldn't hurt you to know a little more about the Scriptures either.'

On the following Wednesday Matilda went to the Bible class in the vestry of Trinity Church. She hadn't the remotest interest in the Bible, but she did like the idea of making some friends of her own.

As she had half expected it was very, very dull, Mr Knapp the Deacon was a thin little man with a high-pitched voice and a squint, and of the eleven people there seven were women, and only two of those her age, the other five being well over thirty and Germans. The four men were Germans too; from what Matilda gathered they saw this class as an opportunity to improve their English.

The class broke up at eight-thirty, and as Matilda got up to leave, one of the two younger girls, dark-haired and pretty, wearing a plain navy-blue dress much like her own, grinned at her. 'Say! Do you work for the new minister?' she asked.

Matilda smiled and agreed she did.

'Well, I'm real pleased to meet you,' the girl said, her dark eyes alight with genuine interest. 'I'm Rosa Castilla, Mrs Arkwright's maid. You know she met your mistress when she first arrived from England and when I heard tell she'd brought a maid with her I hoped I might run into you sometime. Can we walk home together?'

After such a tedious evening Matilda was overjoyed to meet someone in a similar position to herself. As they left the church and made their way down Wall Street, she told Rosa her name, and explained that she used to be just a nursemaid, but now did housekeeping too.

'I surely wouldn't stand for that,' Rosa exclaimed, looking horrified. 'I'd say I was quitting.'

'I like it better really,' Matilda replied. 'I get to do the shopping and I like cooking. Besides, I'm fond of my mistress and she relies on me.'

It was the first time she had ever voiced how she felt about her mistress. She hadn't even mentioned it to her father and Dolly in letters. But saying it kind of clarified her feelings and made her feel good.

'You're fond of her?' Rosa's dark eyes opened wide in astonishment. 'I never heard of anyone even *liking* the people they work for. I can't stand Mrs Arkwright, I'd surely poison her if I knew how.'

Matilda laughed at such unabashed honesty. Lily, who rarely made disparaging remarks about anyone, had described Mrs Arkwright as 'formidable', so she guessed the woman did give Rosa a tough time.

'I'd leave tomorrow if I had another job to go to,' the girl went on. 'But my folks depend on my wages, so I have to stick it.'

She went on to tell Matilda that she was born in Italy and her parents had emigrated here twelve years ago, when she was five. 'They aren't doing too well,' she said with a sigh. 'They used to run a bakery together and we lived upstairs, but when Mama got the consumption the owners threw us out. Now Papa works in the Fishmarket and they live in a room nearby. I don't mind handing over my wages 'cos they need it, but I get real scared sometimes that Mama might die. I don't know if I could stand to go back home and look after the five little ones.'

Matilda had explored the seedy area around Fulton Fishmarket and she could guess the conditions Rosa's family lived in were much like the ones she'd once known. 'Then you must make it clear they can't depend on you,' she said, imagining how she would have felt if she'd been compelled to go back to Finders Court after growing used to Primrose Hill. 'I might sound a bit heartless, but once you're back there, you'll probably be stuck for life.'

Rosa looked surprised. 'You sound like you know how it is,' she said.

'I do,' Mathilda replied and quickly told her about where she came from, and how her luck changed.

'You know, you're real nice. I thought English girls were all stuck up,' Rosa said and tucked her hand through Matilda's arm. 'Can we be pals?'

'I hope so.' Matilda felt a tingle of excitement run down her spine. Although she hadn't given it much thought, she was a little lonely and this friendly, outspoken girl seemed a perfect companion. 'Do you get much time off?'

Rosa wrinkled her nose. 'Only Sunday afternoons to go and see my folks and Wednesday evening. But then I can't do much with that because she makes me go to the Bible class, same as she makes me go to *her* church on Sunday.'

There was something about '*her* church' which made Matilda look sharply at the other girl. 'Where's yours then?'

Rosa giggled and her dark eyes flashed with mischief. 'Can you keep a secret?'

Matilda smiled. 'I think so.'

'You have to swear you won't tell this one because I'd be thrown out if Mrs Arkwright found out.'

'Cross my heart and hope to die if I tell,' Matilda agreed.

'I'm a Catholic really. I told a lie to get the job because the Arkwrights hate Catholics. Do you think that's wicked of me?'

To Matilda, who had been brought up without any religion in her life, she found it peculiar that so many people made a big issue out of it. 'No, I don't,' she said. 'I think the wicked ones are the Arkwrights for being so un-Christian.'

'The nobs are all like that, they look down their haughty noses at Catholics. Mind you, I wouldn't go to church at all if I wasn't forced to. I don't really believe there is a God, if there was, why would he make people suffer so?'

'I used to think that too,' Matilda said thoughtfully. 'But Reverend Milson is the kindest, most caring man I ever met, and he kind of makes me believe, just because he does.'

Rosa giggled, nudging her in the ribs with her elbow. 'You sound like you're a bit in love with him?'

'I love him for what he is,' Matilda said without any embarrassment. 'I'd like to marry a man just like him.'

'I'd like to marry anyone who would look after me,' Rosa said, her dark eyes suddenly doleful. 'But the only boys I ever meet are the ones that live by my folks, and I ain't marryin' one of them, 'cos they ain't got nothing to offer.'

That remark struck a real chord. Matilda remembered only too well how she'd felt about the boys around Finders Court.

'There must be somewhere a couple of beauties like us could meet some decent ones,' she replied half-jokingly. 'Mrs Milson said they have a dance at the church on Saturdays. Do you think there might be some there?'

Rosa pulled a face. 'I reckon most of 'em would be German immigrants. I can't be doing with someone who don't speak English, not even if he's respectable.'

Matilda thought that was a bit bigoted. She had heard her master claim on many an occasion that Germans were among the most industrious immigrant nationalities in the city, and as she'd seen tonight, they worked hard at learning the language too.

'Do you think Mrs Arkwright would let you have a Saturday night off anyway?' she asked.

'Maybe if she knew I was going to something at the church.' Rosa's eyes sparkled with mischief again. 'I suppose dancing with a German lad is better than sitting in the basement cleaning silver!'

They parted at the end of State Street, promising to meet again next week at the Bible class. Matilda skipped along the street, feeling absurdly happy.

It was just two days later that Matilda accidentally discovered New York's darkest side. It was her afternoon off and as it was warm and sunny, but not too hot, she decided to walk to Greenwich Village. She had heard that this was the place where the rich had built summer houses to escape to when there were epidemics in the city. Lily had wistfully reported after visiting there once that it was very pretty with little farms and lots of trees.

Had the Milsons been at home Matilda would have asked them the route to take over to the west side of the island. But Lily had been invited with Tabitha to luncheon by a new acquaintance, and Giles had been gone since ten that morning.

She set off along Pearl Street looking in the shop windows as she went, and she was so wrapped up in her thoughts about going out with Rosa that she failed to notice how far she had gone. It was only when she noticed she was now entering a very shabby area that she remembered the cautionary advice from Mrs Kirkbright, on her first day here, that this neighbourhood was unpleasant. She took a left-hand turn to make her way westwards, but as this seemed to be no improvement, she turned right.

She suddenly found herself in a narrow, unpaved street which was ankle-deep in filth. Ancient sagging frame houses leaned crazily against each other and although there was a wooden sidewalk, that was rotten, with great, dangerous holes. Yet more striking than the filth and dilapidation was the total change in atmosphere. Even in bright sunshine it felt dark and menacing.

It was perverse curiosity which made her continue rather than turn back to Pearl Street. She wanted to know everything about this city, and she couldn't do that unless she saw all its aspects, good and bad.

Yet as she continued to walk further into the maze of winding alleys, and it grew steadily worse, instinct told her she had made a grave mistake coming here alone. The smell of excrement was so strong she found herself holding her breath and gingerly picking her way holding her skirts up. There seemed to be an equal number of black and white people, but as everyone was so dirty and ragged, their colour was hardly noticeable. Hollow-eyed, tow-haired women with babies at their breasts, slumped in doorways, eyed her with deep suspicion. Almost naked children with hard, adult eyes and festering sores on their limbs began to follow her, and again and again she saw inebriated men relieving themselves openly, turning to look at her and shouting ribald comments.

There were men and women lying insensible on the ground,

a man with no legs trying to haul himself along with just his arms, and a child of Tabitha's age completely naked devouring a piece of bread which she'd obviously found abandoned in the dirt.

Pigs rooted in the muck, but they bore no resemblance to the fat, pink ones she knew from England; these were skinny, ugly, fearsome creatures caked in filth. Alongside them were dogs so thin and mange-ridden she could see every rib, and as they snarled and snapped at each other, she became alarmed that they might very well attack her.

She had always believed there could be no worse place in the entire world than London's Seven Dials, yet terrible as that was, and however many vile atrocities were committed in its dark, dank alleys and rookeries, it had a vibrant, bustling quality which was entirely lacking here. A pall of apathy hung in the air, the disease lurking in every dark corner was palpable, and it was strangely quiet, as if the residents were in a kind of trance.

She shuddered to think what it must be like at night, in rain or in the depth of winter, for there was not one pane of glass in any window, and parts of roofs were missing. She sensed that each of those sagging doorways led to rabbit warrens of evil rooms, each one home for dozens of people. The 'grog shop' on each corner was a testimony to how the residents coped with their deprivations; even the cries from babies were so weak she guessed that few of them would survive infancy.

It grew even worse the further she went, the buildings closer together, the filth underfoot deeper, the stench so bad she could scarcely breathe, and now she was frightened because she was aware she'd lost her bearings entirely. To ask the way out was unthinkable, she knew from Seven Dials that when someone revealed themselves as a nervous stranger they would be led to a dark alley and robbed. She had no more than a few cents on her, but just a glance at the rags people were wearing was enough for her to know her boots and clothes alone were sufficient reason to attack her.

'You mustn't show your fear,' she whispered to herself. 'Keep your head up, walk quickly and purposefully. You will get out.'

Yet as a man in a broken-down stove-pipe hat lurched towards her with a cudgel in his hand, she lost her nerve entirely. His toothless grin was bestial, reminding her of a man who lived for a time in Finders Court who made a living from dog fights. She dodged past him, her heart beating so fast she felt it might burst.

'Come 'ere, me little darlin'', she heard him say, and she picked up her skirt and began to run blindly. In her terror she imagined not just him, but packs of men were chasing her. She darted into an alley only to find herself in a tiny court and caught in what felt like a giant spider's web.

She screamed involuntarily, flaying her arms around as something flapped in her face. It was the sound of her own terrified yell which brought her out of her blind panic. Looking around, she saw she had merely run into a mass of washing lines, festooned with millions of dirty rags. She had seen such things before countless times in London, rag-pickers collected them from rubbish dumps, hung them up to dry them off, then sold them again in bulk. She hadn't been chased either, the only people watching her were a group of dirty children, and they were probably as frightened by her scream as she was to be there.

Pulling herself together, she resolved she had to get away from here as quickly as possible. Seeing a boy of about six or seven with red hair, standing apart from the other children, and wearing nothing more than a man's ragged shirt, she beckoned to him.

'Yeah! Whatcha want?' he said suspiciously as he sidled nearer her.

At a distance he had reminded her of her two younger brothers, purely because of his hair colour, but the resemblance ended there. He had a defeated look her brothers had never had, lack-lustre eyes, and he was so caked in ingrained dirt he couldn't have been washed in months.

Taking one cent from her pocket she held it out to him. 'Show me the way back to Pearl Street and I'll give you this,' she said.

He looked her up and down as if trying to surmise if she had more, and how he could best rob her. 'My father is a policeman,' she said, looking him squarely in the face. 'So don't try anything. Now, do you want the money?'

He stared at her silently for what seemed like forever, then nodded and held out his hand.

Matilda shook her head. 'Not till you get me there.'

'Whatcha come in here for?' he asked with a sullen expression. 'We sure ain't nowhere near Pearl Street.'

'I was trying to find my father and I lost my way,' she said. 'Now, are you going to take me?'

'I'll get yer to Broadway, that ain't far,' he said. Then, without waiting to hear if that would do, he set off at a trot a couple of yards in front of her. He led her through a fetid alley so narrow her arms touched the walls either side, across another wider street and out into a wide main thoroughfare busy with cabs and carriages. Across the street was a huge, strange-looking fortress-like building.

Matilda breathed a heartfelt sigh of relief to see civilization again. 'This is Broadway?' she asked for she knew that name, Giles had said it was one of the first proper roads to be built by the Dutch and it ran right from Lower Manhattan all the way up through the island.

The boy nodded, holding out his hand for the money.

'What's your name?' she asked.

'Sidney,' he said, his eyes on her hand rather than her face.

'Well, thank you for bringing me here, Sidney. What's that building over there?' she asked, pointing to the fortress.

'The Tombs,' he said, glancing at it fearfully. 'Now, give us the money.'

'What goes on in there?' she asked. Despite its rather splendid almost ancient Egyptian architecture, she could sense it had some awful purpose.

'The prison, ain't it,' he said. 'Now, give us the money.'

Matilda handed over the coin. 'Have you got parents, Sidney?'

He shook his head.

'So who looks after you?'

'Me,' he said, frowning as if he didn't understand why anyone should ask such a question. Matilda put her hand back into her pocket and brought out the rest of the money she had there, six cents in all. 'Buy yourself something to eat,' she said, putting it into his filthy hand. But before she could ask him anything more, he raced away, back into the alley where he clearly felt more secure.

As Matilda made her way home down Broadway she felt sick and shaky. She had believed her childhood in Finders Court was a kind of protection against shock. Yet what she'd just seen made the slums of London and Bristol look like paradise.

She looked around her in bewilderment at the well-fed, fashionably dressed people going about their business in Broadway. The street was congested with fancy carriages, shops were stuffed to capacity with every kind of luxury imaginable and enough food to feed countless armies. Yet just five minutes away people were living in conditions worse than animals, without even the most basic of necessities like clothes and food.

Were all these prosperous-looking people unaware of what was so close to them?

Matilda found she couldn't eat anything that evening. The thick pork chop on her plate reminded her of the pigs she'd seen earlier in the day, the vegetable dish piled high with roasted potatoes and carrots was like a silent reproach that she should be offered so much when that boy Sidney was starving. When Tabitha left the crust of her bread uneaten, she had a mental picture of the child she'd seen snatching stale bread from the filth in the street.

'Have you been eating pastries while you were out this afternoon?' Lily asked, giving her a scathing look.

'No, I just don't feel quite right,' she said, hoping her mistress wouldn't press her.

'Maybe you'd better take a dose of castor oil before going to bed,' Lily replied 'You look a little peaky.'

After prayers later in the evening Lily retired for the night, leaving her husband reading in the parlour and Matilda in the kitchen making the oatmeal for the morning.

She was just placing it in the stove when Giles came in. 'What's troubling you this evening, Matty?' he asked. 'I've never known you refuse food or stay silent for so long. Yet I know you aren't ill, whatever Mrs Milson might think.'

She hesitated, afraid he might be angry with her if she told him the truth.

'Are you homesick?'

'No,' she said, amazed that he'd think of such a thing. She thought about her father and Dolly a great deal, and missed them, but London to her was a place of hardship, the only really good memories of it were connected with the Milsons. 'This is home to me now.'

'I'm very glad to hear that,' he said with a smile. 'But if this is your home, that makes you part of my family, therefore you should be able to tell me what's ailing you.'

He sat down at the table and folded his arms, waiting for her reply. In the year and a half Matilda had worked for him she had come to see he wasn't a man to be fobbed off easily. He was intuitive, curious, and persistent. Those dark eyes of his looked deep into people's souls, she could swear sometimes he even heard thoughts. But she also knew he used these abilities only to help people, not to intimidate them.

'I'm not ill or homesick,' she said. 'Just troubled by something I saw today. I think if you'd seen it too, you wouldn't have been able to eat either.'

She sat down opposite him, took a deep breath and blurted it all out, her eyes cast down at the table. It was only when she had got to the part where she thought the man with the cudgel was going to hurt her that she dared look up. He was resting his head on one hand, his fingers smoothing his brow as if what he was hearing was distressing him.

'He didn't hit me,' she said quickly. 'I ran for it, and I got a boy to show me the way out. But it was such a terrible place, sir, I know if you were to see it you'd want to do something about it.'

When he didn't reply immediately she felt very uncomfortable. 'I'm sorry, sir,' she whispered, assuming he thought she was being presumptuous. 'I'm being what Madam calls "uppity".'

'You aren't being uppity at all,' he said in a strained voice. 'I wish everyone in New York could see what you have seen and react to it as you have done. Of those who have seen it, most believe the conditions are appropriate for the animals who dwell there.'

'You have seen it then?' she said in surprise.

'Oh yes, Matty, I have. You are right, it's the most Godforsaken, terrible place I have ever encountered. I can only feel relief right now that you got out without being hurt, for believe me, as well as the conditions there being an affront to a supposedly civilized city, it is an extremely dangerous place to go into alone and unprotected.'

'But if you've been in it too, how could you keep quiet about it?' She was staggered that he could sound so calm.

'Why didn't you come straight home and tell Mrs Milson about it?'

Matilda looked at him – one of his eyebrows was raised questioningly, a half-smile playing at his lips.

'She would have had hysterics,' she said. 'I wouldn't have put it past her to lock me in the shed outside too, until she was sure I hadn't brought some disease home.'

He gave a tight little laugh. 'That's exactly why I haven't spoken of it at home, and she would have made me promise that I would never go there again. So we both understand why neither of us could talk about it. But tell me, Matty, now that you've seen the horrors of Five Points, for that's what it is called, what do you think should be done about it?'

'Get the people out into proper houses, feed them and burn the place to the ground.'

He smiled. 'You echo my first thoughts about it. But I soon discovered I had to think with my head, not my heart,' he said. 'To find a real solution to the problems there, we have to act logically and dispassionately.'

'How can anyone be dispassionate about it?' Her voice rose indignantly.

'Well, first one has to look at the underlying reasons as to how that place came about, and why,' he said, spreading his hands out on the table. 'America has enough room for tens of millions of people and its government has an open-door policy to anyone who wants to come here. Yet there are no agencies to make sure there is work and housing for all. And no checks are made to see that immigrants have enough money to keep themselves and their families while they look for work.

'Now, those ramshackle houses you saw today were once decent, one-family homes, but as the owners' wealth increased, they moved out, further uptown and rented out their old houses. The newly arrived immigrants couldn't afford to pay rent for a whole house, so they took just one room. Those who didn't find a job immediately were soon forced to share that one room with another family, to pay the rent.

'When each one of those houses becomes home for fifty people or so, and the landlord makes no repairs, it soon escalates into a slum situation. Those that are in work will find somewhere less crowded to move on to, but the poor devils at the bottom of the heap have no choice but to stay and put up with the conditions.'

Matilda nodded in understanding. Finders Court was just the

same. The only happy person was the landlord who lived miles away and sent someone else to collect the rents.

'But why doesn't someone stop the landlords exploiting the poor?' she asked.

'Maybe because those landlords have become rich and powerful,' he said wryly. 'I dare say that if one was to check out who owns those properties we'd find many of them sitting on the city council and in every seat of authority.'

'But that's wicked,' she said in horror.

Giles shrugged. 'It is, but who will speak out against them, Matty? No one, not even those with a degree of humanity and charity, really wants the people who live in Five Points now living next door to them. That place is out of sight and out of mind, and therefore an ideal spot in most people's minds for the flotsam and jetsam who can't or won't work.'

Matilda thought of Seven Dials back in London. She knew only too well that most of its residents chose to live there because they were amongst their own kind. But then they were thieves, prostitutes and beggars.

'But they can't all be bad people in Five Points,' she said. 'Almost everyone I saw looked so sick and hungry.'

'They are, Matty. What you saw today are those at the very bottom of life's ladder, without the strength or will to climb to the next rung. You may have noticed that around half of them were Negroes, the other half are mainly Irish. Now, why do you think that it is just those two races there, not some English, Italians or Germans?'

Matilda shrugged. 'I don't know.'

'People in this city would be very quick to suggest it is because Negroes and Irish are indolent by nature,' he said with a sneer. 'It makes them feel better to make such sweeping statements because they don't want to take any responsibility for the atrocities which have been heaped on these two races. The English have been abusing the Irish for centuries, and the Americans have enslaved the black men. So what the Irish and Negroes have in common is that they both come from backgrounds of extreme deprivation. Hunger and appalling living conditions are nothing new to them. They arrive here in the city with nothing more than the clothes on their backs, and the only place where they can find shelter is amongst their own.'

'Why can't they find jobs?'

'The strong, bright and ambitious do. For every Irish man or woman who ends up in Five Points there are another hundred who have risen above their backgrounds, you will find them driving cabs, running businesses, in just about every field you can think of. It's the same for the Negroes too, though they have even more prejudice to overcome, and mostly end up in manual or domestic work. But for the unlucky ones who end up in Five Points it becomes a trap. You once said to me you couldn't get a better job than selling flowers because of your clothes and the way you spoke. It's much like that for them.'

'But I got out of it because you helped me,' she said. 'Surely that's all we have to do for them.'

'Matty,' he said wearily, 'we are talking about people who are in the main deficient in some way. Most are illiterate, with no skills, others are sick, and that place brutalizes them all.'

'I'm sure they could be taught to do something,' she said angrily. 'People can't just ignore them.'

'I agree,' he said gently. 'But how do we reach out to those who have sunk so low that they seek only the oblivion of drink? We aren't talking about fresh-faced young girls and boys who are eager to grasp any opportunity, but sick, worn-down people who have mainly lost all sense of morality. Five Points is a cesspit, Matty. People are murdered there nightly, thieving and prostitution are often their only means of survival.'

'But surely the children could be saved,' she said weakly, thinking of her brother George.

Giles looked at Matilda and seeing the same anguish in her eyes that he felt in his own heart, he wanted to let her into the plans he and Darius Kirkbright had been working on for the past few weeks. Yet the thought of Lily asleep upstairs completely unaware that his ministry work had taken him into such unsavoury places troubled him greatly. How would she react if she discovered he had confided in a servant but not in her?

'The orphans could be rescued,' he said hesitantly, trying to sound as if the thought had only just occurred to him. 'I believe there are hundreds of them, tiny ones sometimes less than three years old, just rooting around in the muck. I suppose they could be rounded up and taken to somewhere they could be cared for.'

Matilda was just about to say what a sound idea that was when it suddenly dawned on her that the authoritative way he'd spoken about the problems in Five Points meant he'd been in and out of there many times. Knowing him as she did, there was no way that he would walk away from what he'd seen.

'You've already planned to do it, haven't you?' she blurted out.

He blushed and looked away.

'Oh, sir!' she exclaimed. 'You've been working on this for weeks, haven't you? What on earth will Mrs Milson say when she finds out? She thinks you've been off visiting the sick and mixing with the toffs at the church.'

Although she was shocked, his hangdog expression made her want to laugh. She had seen that look on her brothers' faces when she caught them out at something.

'I cannot bring myself to think how she'll react,' he said in a low voice. 'I daresay she'll threaten to take Tabitha and go back to England. But I have to do it, Matty. A man cannot turn his back on such mammoth suffering and still call himself a man. If Mrs Milson had married a soldier she would expect him to go into battle. I am one of God's soldiers, and this is my battle. Would she have me desert my duty just for peace and harmony at home?'

Matilda's heart swelled up with admiration for him. He wasn't brash like Darius Kirkbright, who truly believed a wife should comply with her husband's wishes. Giles was a sensitive man who believed marriage should be a true partnership. Now she saw why he hadn't been talking about his work at home, and she could understand perfectly how troubled he must be by being forced to conceal what he was doing, just to keep his wife content.

'You are right to fight for those poor people,' she said softly. 'But you are wrong to keep it from Madam, however much she might not like it. She has a kind heart, sir, she loves you for what you are too, and though she probably will throw a fit, I think she'll accept it in time, and help you too.'

He put his elbows on the table and covered his face with his hands for a moment. Matilda watched him, knowing he was wrestling with his conscience.

It was some time before he spoke again. 'My dear Matty,' he

said eventually, 'you are wise beyond your years sometimes, and I agree in principle with everything you've said. But I know my wife better than anyone, and I know what would happen if she got only the briefest glimpse of what you saw today. Her fear of dirt and disease is deeply rooted, the real reason she refused to come out of the cabin on the ship was because of those steerage passengers. It was just their presence which made her sick.'

Matilda was tempted to laugh and say he was being silly, but then she recalled Lily had been looking at them fearfully while they were all still on the deck as they sailed down the river Avon. She had always refused Tabitha permission to go up on deck at times when they were allowed up there too. And that was why she was so hard when that little boy died.

'Maybe that's so, but she's got better since then,' she said stoutly.

'No Matty, she hasn't.' He shook his head. 'She feels safe in this house, and mixing with the gentlefolk at church. Aside from her glimpse of the dock area when we arrived she imagines that all of New York is much the same as it is around here. I don't doubt she would assist me in fund-raising for the poor, or the opening of a Foundling Home, just as long as I glossed over the details of the recipients of that charity. I know if the real horrors of it all were revealed to her, she'd – ' He broke off suddenly, as if afraid to say what he feared.

Matilda was just about to retort that Lily would never leave him for that, when suddenly she realized that wasn't what he imagined at all. Just the deeply troubled expression in his eyes spelled it out, what he was afraid of was pushing his wife over the edge into insanity!

If any other man had hinted at such a thing she would have laughed at him. But Giles Milson was a man who really knew about people, and his own wife better than anyone. She had witnessed Lily's hysterics and her dark moods so many times herself, and a gut feeling told her he could be right.

'Is there anything I could do to help?' she asked.

He gave her a long and thoughtful look before replying. 'Matty, you've put me in a precarious position. On the one hand I'm very glad to find I have an ally in you, but on the other it also means that if I am to continue with my work I have to ask you to assist me in shielding Mrs Milson from this. But that will put you in an impossible situation too.'

'Not really,' she said with a shrug. 'I know what you are doing is a good thing. Keeping quiet about it is the least I can do. I just wish I could do something more practical.'

When he didn't reply Matilda wondered if that was the wrong answer. Should she swear never to tell Madam?

'You could do something more,' he said eventually. 'You could work alongside me.'

Matilda's mouth fell open. 'How? I'm just a nursemaid.'

'It's the talents that come with nursemaiding I need,' he said with a wry smile. 'I saw how you reacted to that sick child on the ship, remember. I watched you pick him up, wash him and try to feed him, I saw your tears when he died.'

'You don't mean you want me to help in Five Points, do you?' Her voice rose in her surprise.

'Who better, Matty? I know you won't recoil from a dirty child because you were one yourself once. You know too what it is to be lifted out of hunger and poverty. You aren't squeamish, you have courage and common sense. Do you think you could help in rounding up some of those orphans?'

Matilda wondered fleetingly if he was the one on the edge of insanity. He had told his wife nothing, and now he was proposing to take her servant to help him. She quickly pointed this out to him.

To her further surprise he laughed. 'But don't you see that would allay her fears somewhat? She already knows that the church has given funds to open a Foundling Home out in New Jersey. It's almost ready to receive children. If I tell her that Reverend Kirkbright and I have located some children in need of care and attention, and that we want your help in taking them to the home to ease their distress, she would never imagine they were anything other than ordinary orphans, grieving for their mothers, and she would be only too happy for you to help.'

Matilda didn't know what to think now. In one way it sounded such terrible deceit. Yet how could it be wicked to rescue sick, hungry children? Especially as the Reverend Kirkbright was involved in the plan?

'Tell me about this Home?' she asked.

He leaned closer to her, his eyes shining with excitement. 'It's to be called "Trinity Waifs' and Strays' Home", and it will be funded by the parish. It's a sturdy house, surrounded by open countryside, it was once used as a quarantine hospital. As I said, it's almost ready, equipped and staffed.' He paused for a moment, looking into her eyes. 'Our biggest problem is reaching the right children to fill it, and getting them out of Five Points. As you probably know far better than I do, children living on the streets are suspicious of everyone, even more so of clergymen. With a young woman like yourself with us, someone who can speak their language, listen to their fears, and explain what we are trying to do for them, that problem could be solved.'

Matilda sat for a moment in stunned silence. She applauded what he was intending to do, she wanted to be part of it. Yet she knew this would involve going into that terrible place again and again, and coming home to face her mistress without letting on what she'd seen. Could she really do that?

'But what about the risk of infection sir?' she said quietly. 'No one can reach those children and bring them out of there keeping them at arm's length. They *will* all be lousy, they may very well be carrying diseases which you or I could bring home to Tabitha. I'm not afraid for myself, only her and Mrs Milson.'

Giles suddenly knew he was right to involve Matilda. Much as he'd always been convinced he was right to rescue these children, keeping it from Lily had put him under such strain that sometimes he felt he couldn't carry on. By sharing it now, his conviction had come back, and he suddenly saw the road ahead clearing for him. Taking Matilda along with him would ease any of Lily's suspicions. He felt the way he had at twenty, full of vigour and enthusiasm.

'We have what you might call a half-way house set up,' he said. 'A doctor will be there to help us. And we'll take every precaution.' He reached out and took her hand in his. 'Now, could we be partners?'

She felt a sudden warmth run through her veins like hot syrup. Maybe it would be safer to refuse, to say she'd say nothing to her mistress, but she wasn't going to assist him in any way. But she couldn't forget what she'd seen earlier today, or refuse to help a man intent on saving small children.

'You'll just tell Madam I'm helping you to take children to the

Home?' She needed that confirmation if Lily questioned her in private.

'Nothing more. We'll make it sound like a Sunday school outing,' he said with a smile.

She took her hand away from his, spat on it, and held it out again. 'That's how they seal bargains down in Seven Dials,' she laughed.

He smiled, spat on his own hand, then gripped hers.

'Partners!' they said together.

Chapter Six

'This is it,' Giles said, flicking back the hood of his oilskin cape as he and Matilda approached a crumbling, disease-looking dilapidated corner shop just inside Five Points. 'You'll soon see why everyone calls these places "grog shops". It might say "Groceries" on the window, but inside there's precious little food in evidence.'

It was a week ago that she saw this area for the first time, but the warm, sunny weather had ended just two days ago with a heavy storm and it had been raining ever since. Now the narrow streets and alleys were a stinking bog of glutinous mud. Even the pigs and dogs were trying to shelter against walls and in doorways, and aside from the sound of rain cascading from broken roofs and guttering there was utter silence, as if all the human residents had gone into hibernation.

As they stepped inside the shop, a scrawny little man with a pock-marked face and filthy apron shuffled out from behind his barrels and crates of bottles. It stank of cheap liquor but it was at least preferable to the far worse smell out on the street.

'Good day to you, Reverend.' The man gave them a fawning smile. 'Brought a little helper today, have we?'

'This is my assistant, Miss Jennings,' Giles replied in a crisp, businesslike voice. Although this Irishman had promised to direct him to where the orphaned children congregated, Giles didn't trust him. During previous conversations he'd had strong suspicions the man's knowledge of the children's habits wasn't prompted by kindly interest, but far more likely because he was in fact a procurer for the many brothels along the Bowery. 'We've brought some bread and apples with us for the children. So if you could point us in the right direction to find them we won't take up any more of your time.'

''Tis almost certain they are in the cellar of Rat's Castle,' the man said, looking intently at Matilda. 'I saw one of the bigger lads crawling in as I went past this very morning. Don't suppose they've moved on, not in this rain.'

Giles blanched, Rat's Castle was every bit as bad as the Old Brewery that Kirkbright had told him about when he first arrived in New York. Like that place, only the most desperate for some kind of shelter would go in. A policeman had informed him it got its name because of the innumerable escape routes from it which had been devised by the criminals who squatted there. He also said that on one police raid they had found three bodies of people who had been murdered, along with another four who'd died of natural causes. All these bodies had been left to rot in the cellars along with the stinking effluent of some three or four hundred people

Thanking the man, Giles left with Matilda, but once out on the street he turned to her, his face drawn with anxiety. 'Maybe we ought to wait for better weather when we can find the children out on the streets. Rat's Castle is an evil place, Matty. I can't take you in there.'

Matilda thought for a moment. Lily had fully accepted her husband's story that he was going out today to visit four children who had been cared for by a neighbour since their mother died, to see if they were suitable for the new Waifs' and Strays' Home. There was no reason why she shouldn't believe this to be true, even back in London Giles often took on such roles from time to time. She had willingly agreed that Matilda should go with him, and had even pulled out a few outgrown clothes of Tabitha's to help out. However, she would be suspicious if they returned saying they hadn't located the children. Giles wasn't any good at outright lies, and Lily would be quizzing them both all evening.

Not liking to voice her real thoughts, Matilda looked up at the leaden sky. 'We might have a long wait for better weather,' she said. 'It's the start of autumn, sir, and before long it will turn cold. Besides, I'm not easily shocked.'

Giles was heartened by her desire to get on with it at any cost. She looked like a street waif herself today with an oilskin cape like his, a very worn dress and shawl, and her hair tightly braided under a mob-cap. They had dressed for this excursion at Dr Kupicha's house just beyond Five Points, and they would return there to wash and change back into their own clothes before returning home. The doctor had warned them that this wasn't complete protection from carrying any infection home, but it was the best precaution he knew.

'Well, we'll just go and reconnoitre the place,' Giles said. 'We might not be able to get in there anyway. Not if there's a few bully boys keeping watch.'

Rat's Castle stood at the end of a narrow passageway, and as they approached it they paused, both intimidated by its desolate appearance. To Matilda it was very reminiscent of rookeries she'd seen in Seven Dials, and judging by the many windows, pointed eaves and fancy, twisted chimney pots, the half-timbered building had once been the home of someone wealthy. But now there were gaping holes in the walls, the timbers were rotting and all the windows were boarded up. The buildings all around it had been built at a later period but they were equally dilapidated, and what must have been a stable was leaning crazily to one side, rain water gushing down what was left of the slate roof.

There was no front door, just a gaping hole as if someone had wrenched it and its frame out for firewood. Taking a step closer, Matilda saw that the staircase at the back of a dark, rubbish-filled hall had gone the same way. The banisters had gone completely and what was left of the stairs was almost swaying in the breeze.

The smell made her gag, and she had to move back again so she could breathe.

'At least there's no one guarding it,' Giles said. 'But I don't really know how to get in, Matty. I tried to get up that staircase once before a few weeks ago and one of the treads gave way on me.'

'That man in the shop said he saw the boy crawling in,' she said. 'That might mean from outside somewhere.'

'Let's look around the side then,' Giles replied and led the way through a thicket of tall weeds and straggly bushes.

'It's funny how quiet it is everywhere,' Matilda said thoughtfully, picking her way carefully as there was human excrement everywhere.

'I find silence more nerve-racking than hearing shouting and fighting,' Giles said in a low voice. 'Somehow it shows the depth of despair they've sunk into.'

As they skirted around a particularly large bush they suddenly found themselves in a kind of small clearing where the weeds were stamped down. Ahead of them was a narrow but well-trodden path, presumably starting from somewhere behind the house.

'Look!' Matilda said, noticing what looked like a burrow dug into the ground at the base of the house. 'I bet that's the way.'

Gingerly she pulled at some branches lying over it. They came away easily to reveal a hole some two feet high by three feet wide in the lathe and plaster wall of the house.

Matilda looked at her master in consternation, but he grinned in reassurance and fished into his sack for the lantern he'd brought with him.

'I'll lower this in and take a look,' he said in a low voice. Matilda watched as he lit the candle inside and knelt down in front of the hole. 'Here goes,' he whispered, and lowering the candle into the hole he leaned right inside.

He withdrew almost immediately. 'They are there,' he exclaimed with an expression of horror on his face. 'Down in the cellar. Dozens of them.'

'Let me see,' she said, and as he got up she took his place, stretching out her arm so the light of the lantern lit up the dark cavern. But what she saw made her almost drop the lantern and her heart contracted with pity. Dozens of pairs of eyes fixed on the light from above, tiny white faces caught in the beam.

The smell from within there was appalling but she couldn't back away. 'I've come to bring you some food,' she called out. 'Can I come in?'

She didn't wait for a reply or even to consult her master, but crawled on in holding the lantern firmly. There was some sort of box beneath the hole, then a crude and wobbly stairway made of crates down to their level, some fourteen or fifteen feet below, but her overwhelming desire to help these little mites wiped out her fear, and her disgust at the evil stench. As her feet touched the ground she found it was three or four inches deep in water.

Holding the lantern higher, she moved nearer to the children. They were huddled together so tightly in just one small spot that she could only assume it was the only part of the floor not under water. 'I have a man with me from the church,' she said, speaking slowly and clearly so as not to frighten them. 'He is a good, kind man who wants to help you, and he has a sack of food with him, will you let him come in too?'

'I knows you.' A voice came from behind the main body of children. 'You're that lady what was scared in Rag-Pickers.'

'Sidney?' she said in astonishment. The voice was familiar, but it was too dark to see if it was the same red-headed boy.

'Yeah, it's me,' he said, and she saw a movement as if he'd been lying down and was now getting up. 'She's the one that give me six cents,' he said to his companions.

Suddenly there was a disturbing flurry of movement and for a moment she thought she was going to be attacked. 'I haven't any money on me,' she said quickly. 'But the man with me has bread and apples. I'm just going to call him in.'

She turned her head to see Giles was already gingerly climbing in.

'This is Reverend Milson,' she said, very relieved to find the children weren't about to set upon her, but just sitting up. 'He is a minister at Trinity Church. My name is Matty and we've both come to help you.'

She heard a splash as Giles reached the water. 'I'm just going to light another candle so I can see you,' he said, and Matilda noted his voice was shaking. 'Then I want you all to tell me your names and how old you are. After that I'll give you some food.'

'I already know Sidney over there,' Matilda said, thinking it might give Giles a little more confidence. 'So perhaps he'll tell us who everyone is. Will you do that, Sidney?'

'I don't know all the babbies' names,' he said.

As Giles lit the second candle and Matilda saw the full horror of their condition and ages, her stomach heaved. They were only little tots, yet their drawn faces and bleak eyes made them look like little old wizened men. Not one she could see wore anything which resembled clothes, just rags draped about them. Their hair was matted and their limbs like sticks. One small boy who had stood up to look at her had only a piece of sacking round him and his rib-cage protruded like the dogs' out in the street. At a quick count she thought there were eighteen children, and Sidney at six or seven was by far the eldest.

He rolled out the names of the older ones, 'Annie, John, Oz, Harry, Meg,' then went on to use nicknames which suggested that perhaps these children had been orphaned or abandoned so young they didn't know their real name. 'Blackboy, Pig, Rat, Fish and Injun.'

Matilda took the sack of food from Giles and began to hand out the bread. A sea of hands waved at her and a chorus of 'Me' broke out, but the moment they had a lump of bread in their hands silence fell as they devoured it.

Matilda's stomach lurched again, but this time it was purely from horror that anyone could eat in such conditions. She guessed that the water they were standing in was sewage – Giles had told her a couple of nights before that all the cellars around here were flooded with it when it rained. Hearing a squeak, she looked up to see a beam across the cellar roof was teeming with rats. When she cast her eyes nervously around there were dozens more, on ledges, in corners, their bright beady eyes watching her intently. Shudders ran down her spine and she just had to hope that the unexpected candlelight would keep them at bay.

At the back of the cellar was a door. She wondered what lay behind it. Only after all the bread was gone and the apples handed out did she dare to ask Sidney.

'The old 'uns don't let us go in there,' he said. 'They don't use this one 'cos it's always wet.'

'Do you always sleep in here?' Giles asked him.

'Not likely,' he said, managing a surprisingly cheerful grin. 'Mostly I goes down Battery Park. Only come here 'cos it's raining. See, we built a platform for us.' He bent down to pick up some rags under his feet and revealed planks laid on top of bricks. 'We would have done it all, but the old 'uns would turf us out and take it.'

Matilda's feet were turning to ice now that the water had seeped right into her boots. She was wearing warm clothes, yet she felt very cold, she supposed it was only by huddling together that the children managed to sleep. It didn't bear thinking what it would be like for them in winter.

'Have any of you got mothers and fathers?' Matilda asked. Most shook their heads, but the youngest just stared at her with large, sad eyes.

To try to find out for certain, she began asking them individually, getting them to say their name, age and what had happened to their parents. Sidney said he was eight. Annie said she was six, and her mother had died a while ago, she didn't think she had a father. Oz, whose full name was Oswald Pinchbeck, said he had lived with his aunt but she went away, and he wasn't sure how old he was.

Each child was so much like its neighbour – the dirt, rags and emaciated body – that Matilda thought she'd never be able to put a name to each face. They could tell her so little about themselves, 'dunno' was the most common word. She thought that this building was aptly named 'Rat's Castle' for they were like rats, foraging for food and sleeping in packs, so ignorant of the way the rest of the world lived that they had no conception of the idea of families, care, and certainly not love.

She let Giles tell them about his plan to take them to a 'Home'. He spoke well, painting a picture of comfort and warmth and happy futures for all of them. Yet although it should have brought joy into their little faces, Matilda was distressed to see their eyes narrow with suspicion.

'It isn't a prison like The Tombs,' Matilda said, bending nearer to the group. 'It's a real house with warm fires, beds and good food. You'll have a school there, wear real clothes and boots on your feet. You can learn to read books, have toys to play with. No one will ever hurt you again.'

There were no questions, just blank stares, but some of the older ones looked to Sidney as if expecting him to be their spokesman.

'Sidney,' she said in a commanding voice. 'You've met me before and I trusted you enough to lead me out of Five Points. Do you think you can trust me?'

He nodded.

'That's good. I knew you were a smart boy, so I want you to take charge of all the others. In two days' time we're going to come back here at the same time and wait outside. I want you to bring all these children with you and we'll take you to a doctor's house close by, where you can all have a big dinner, a wash and some new clothes. Then later we'll take you to that new Home we've told you about. Now, do you think you can make them all come with you?'

'Dunno,' he said doubtfully.

'They'll think you are a real hero when they see where you take them to,' she said persuasively.

'I dunno if I wants to live in a Home,' he said. 'Ain't got much time for folks telling me what to do.'

Matilda remembered how she had been reminded of her brother Luke when she first saw him. Clearly he had a similar mentality.

'Well, you're such a big boy that maybe you can manage without warm clothes and good food. So I'll do a deal with you. You bring the little ones and have some dinner with them, but if you don't want to stay, you can come on back here.'

He didn't reply, just looked at her with hard eyes.

'The little ones will get sick this winter if they stay here,' she said, pointing to the tots at the front of the group. 'Even if you think there's nothing in it for you, let them have a chance to be fed and mothered.'

Knowing she'd said enough to make him think, and any further attempts to tempt him might create suspicion, she turned to go.

'Just think, warm beds, big hot dinners and proper clothes,' she said as she clambered up the wobbly stairs behind her master. 'No more old 'uns to push you about. No rats climbing over you!'

An hour later Giles and Matilda had both washed and changed back into their own clothes, and were sitting with the doctor in his consulting room having a cup of tea and discussing what they'd seen.

Dr Tad Kupicha was from Poland, a slender, frail-looking man of over sixty with sad blue eyes and thinning white hair. He had come to America some thirty years ago with his young wife Anna. They had three daughters; one had died from measles as an infant, then ten years later he lost the other two and his wife in a cholera epidemic. Losing his entire family had turned him into something of a crusader for the poor.

Giles had been introduced to him through Darius Kirkbright, and in just a few weeks they had become close friends through their shared interests. Kupicha was one of the few doctors in New York who ran a free clinic, and he campaigned tirelessly against slum landlords and the lack of sanitation in the city.

'Do you think this boy Sidney will get the children to come?' Giles asked him.

The doctor shrugged. 'I can't say, Giles. They learn at an early age never to trust adults. But I'm hopeful from what you've told me. It was a stroke of luck Matty had met the boy before, I daresay he was impressed by her bravery at going in there, and felt he could trust her. But we'll just have to wait and see.'

'Could we manage them all, if they do come?' Matilda asked with some eagerness. The room in the basement where she had changed had been prepared already with two large tin baths, innumerable pails standing in readiness, and enough children's clothes donated by church people to dress them all. But eighteen children, each one lousy and possibly some of them sick too, was a tall order to deal with all at once.

'Of course we'll manage.' Kupicha smiled at her. 'And when we see them clean, and their bellies full, with hope in their little faces, the struggle will all have been worthwhile.'

It was only later that evening that Matilda became aware that by entering into this clandestine act of mercy with her master, her relationship with him had changed irrevocably. While she saw nothing heroic about climbing into that cellar, he did. On the journey home he falteringly tried to tell her that if she hadn't gone in there first, he would have made some excuse and turned tail. He also said that he could never have put his plan to the children as succinctly as she had.

While she didn't believe that, she was aware the children might have bolted if he'd gone in alone, and it made her glow to think she'd been so useful to him. Then when they reached home, she found another surprise waiting for her. Lily had the evening meal all ready, the table laid, and she almost *waited* on Matilda. Later, while they were washing the dishes together, Lily confided in her that she felt terribly ashamed that she hadn't offered to go with her husband, but talking to children who had just lost their mother was so desperately sad, and she knew she'd be more of a hindrance than help. She tentatively asked what the children were like and what age they were. Matilda said they were little raggamuffins, aged between three and seven. She even told her the eldest was called Sidney, with red hair, and that they would be calling to collect them in two days' time to take them out to New Jersey. She hoped that omissions weren't as bad as lies.

Late that night as Matilda lay in her warm bed, listening to the rain hammering down, she found she couldn't sleep. It seemed so shameful to be lying in warmth and comfort while those poor little waifs were huddling together like piglets in a sty, and her conscience was pricking her at entering into a plan with her master which involved deceiving her mistress.

She tried to reconcile herself to her present comfort by telling herself that it was because she had experienced the hopelessness of poverty, cold and hunger herself that she wanted to help these children. Yet for some reason her mind kept throwing up memories that reminded her she wasn't so very noble.

Hadn't she always insisted on sleeping in the middle of the bed during the winter, so her brothers' bodies kept her warm? Then there were the times when she hadn't enough money to buy all three of them a hot pie, so she'd bought just one for herself, eaten it before she got home, and let them eat the stale bread left from the morning.

Yet if she hadn't eaten those pies, or been unable to sleep for the cold, she wouldn't have had the strength or will to get up and sell flowers the next day. Likewise, nothing good would come of telling Lily the whole, unvarnished truth, however much it appeased her conscience. Giles's plan was a truly honourable one, and if it succeeded, by the end of the week those children would be properly cared for, well on their way to a new happy life. Wasn't that more important than a neurotic woman's sensitivity?

'Of course it is,' she whispered to herself. 'Now, stop agonizing about it.'

Two days later, at three o'clock in the afternoon, Matilda and Giles were back outside Rat's Castle. The rain had stopped on the previous day, blown away by strong winds, but there was a distinct autumnal nip in the air, and no sign of any children.

'They've decided not to come,' Giles said gloomily as he paced up and down anxiously.

'Not necessarily,' Matilda replied. 'I doubt if any of them can even tell the time. We just have to be patient.'

His frown was swept away by a grin. 'I suppose you learned your patience selling flowers?'

'You don't need patience for that, just persistence,' she laughed. 'But I'm not a patient person anyway. I want everything to happen immediately.'

Just then Sidney came around the corner, alone. 'There you

are,' she said in triumph to her master. 'I expect he's come alone with the idea of negotiating some new deal for himself, probably money.' She waved at Sidney and walked towards him.

As she got closer, she could see by the boy's stance that he was very unsure of himself. He was shifting from one foot to the other, and clutching at a piece of old sacking he was wearing like a cape.

'Hullo, Sidney,' she said, wondering what she should do if it was money he wanted. 'Where are the others?'

'Back there.' He waved one arm vaguely towards an alley. 'The old 'uns threw us out of the castle last night.'

'Well, you won't need that place any more,' she said with a smile. 'A real bed for you tonight.'

His eyes narrowed. 'What's in it for you?' he almost spat at her.

His cynicism reminded her of Luke. He had never understood that some people did things without thought of personal gain.

'To see you all happy and well cared for,' she said, trying not to get angry.

'Why?'

Matilda shrugged. 'Because I had a hard life when I was a little girl,' she said. 'It didn't get better until I met him,' she said, pointing back to Giles who was watching them from a few yards away. 'He took me off the streets and back to his house to look after his little girl. Now we want to make things better for all of you too.'

Sidney's taut expression marginally softened, but it was clear he needed more persuasion.

'I told you one lie when I first met you, when I said my father was a policeman. That was just because I was scared and lost,' she admitted. 'But Sidney, I promise you faithfully that little fib was the only one I will ever tell you,' she went on. 'Reverend Milson is the kindest, most honest man I've ever met. Believe me, you can trust him. He's been working for some time getting this Home ready for you all. It's the best chance in life anyone's going to offer you.'

Again Sidney didn't reply for a moment, he shifted from foot to foot, and clutched at the sacking around his shoulders. 'Yeah, but he won't be at the place he's going to take us to,' he retorted eventually. 'Nor you.'

All at once Matilda guessed he'd consulted someone else, perhaps even an adult, and they'd filled his head with nasty ideas. She remembered how when Mr and Mrs Milson had been talking to her that first day in the parlour at Primrose Hill she'd suddenly had that fear about the white slave trade. Sidney knew even less about her and the Reverend than she had about the Milsons. It showed he was more intelligent than she'd imagined, to be so cautious.

'Reverend Milson will be checking on the Home all the time,' she said. 'And there'll be nobody wicked working there, if that's what you think, because he's helped pick them all. But Sidney, whatever nasty suspicions you might have, use your brain. Could anything be worse than how you live now?'

The hard expression on his face melted and all at once she saw just a confused little boy. He'd taken on the role as leader of the children, but he was too young for such responsibility. Instinctively she stepped closer to him and drew him to her, just as she so often had with her brothers.

'Sidney, this is an evil place,' she said softly, holding him tight. 'But the whole world isn't like it. Just trust me to show you and your friends a better place.'

His hair was crawling with lice, but she averted her eyes from them. Lifting his chin with one hand, she looked right into his eyes. His face was so dirty it was difficult to see beyond the grime, but his eyes were amber-coloured and very lovely. 'Trust me, Sidney!' she implored him.

He leaned his face into her breast and she knew he was crying. 'I need you with the little ones to help them get used to it,' she said, aware she mustn't let him lose his position of authority. 'You must go and get them now, tell them there's nothing to be scared of. In just a short while you'll all be sitting down to eat the best soup you've ever eaten.'

He turned and ran from her without another word.

Matilda looked back at Giles and shrugged her shoulders. 'I guess I said something wrong,' she said, tears welling up in her eyes.

'We'll wait anyway,' he said, coming closer and patting her shoulder. 'From where I was standing, I don't believe you frightened him off.'

They waited and waited. The wind was cold, and people came

shuffling by eyeing them balefully. One man came right up to Matilda and spat a great brown glob of chewed tobacco at her feet. He said nothing, but the offensive act suggested he was telling them to push off or else.

Then just as they were looking despairingly at one another, Sidney reappeared, and following him was the little band of children. Neither of them was prepared for such a distressing sight. They had only seen these waifs in semi-darkness, when the full extent of their physical condition could only be guessed at. They were almost naked, filthy with matted hair, limbs so thin it was difficult to imagine how they could walk, faces taut with fear and gaunt with hunger.

'Suffer little children to come unto me,' Giles said softly, and when Matilda turned to him she saw he had tears running down his cheeks.

The basement kitchen was so hot with the stove fired up to heat the hot water that at times Matilda thought she would pass out, yet each time she looked around her she managed to find a little more energy. Two children in each bath, the already scrubbed ones wrapped in a blanket on one side of the room, the last two dirty ones on the other waiting patiently for their turn. All of them had been given a bowl of good soup and bread before the bathing began. Clean or dirty now, they were content to be in the warm and dry with a full belly.

It had been necessary to shave all their heads, their hair was too matted to deal with the lice any other way, and they couldn't be dressed until the doctor had examined each of them. But shaven as they were, at last they had distinct, individual faces. Four of them were black children, three with perhaps one black parent, the rest ghostly white. Every one of them was badly bruised, scarred and had evidence of rat bites, and it was apparent when one five-year-old squatted down in the corner of the room to relieve herself that none of them had even the most basic idea of personal hygiene.

Dr Kupicha's housekeeper, a stout German woman called Eva, couldn't bring herself to help wash the children, so Matilda had to do it alone, while Giles shaved heads with the doctor. But Eva did keep the hot water and soap coming, and as real children emerged from under the caked filth, she did agree to dry them, even going as far as sitting the youngest ones on her knee.

Sidney was the first to be bathed, picking his second in command Oz to join him. Matilda had laughed aloud to see the surprise on the others' faces as Sidney's face came clean to reveal a crop of freckles, and when they saw him nimbly jumping out of the bath when he was finished, their relief that he was still all in one piece was palpable.

'Your turn now.' Matilda beckoned the last two small boys into the bath, and smiled to herself as she saw Eva whisk up the blanket they'd been sitting on to take it outside.

Eva spoke only a few words of English, and Matilda could only guess at the meaning of some of the exclamations she'd made during the afternoon's work. She suspected they ran along the lines of 'How will I ever get my kitchen clean again?' and 'Has the doctor lost his mind bringing this rabble in here?'

But rabble or not they were docile, several had cried in the bath, but before long the tears had turned to timid smiles. Matilda was pretty certain they wouldn't stay this well behaved. She hoped the helpers they'd got at the home had plenty of patience, because she had a feeling they'd be tried and tested in the next few weeks.

'You are very late,' Lily exclaimed when they arrived home after ten at night. 'I've been so worried. Where on earth have you been all this time?'

She was in her night-gown with a shawl around her shoulders and her hair unbraided. Clearly she had attempted to go to bed but was unable to sleep for worry.

'It took longer to get to New Jersey than I anticipated,' Giles said. Matilda was astounded he could lie so glibly. 'And we didn't feel we could just turn around and leave without seeing the children settled in first. I'm afraid we'll have to return tomorrow again too, as we've heard there are another group of children to take. I'm so sorry you've been worried, my dear, but these things happen.'

The anxiety left Lily's face. 'I'm just glad you are both safe. But you look exhausted,' she said, putting one hand affectionately on each of their cold cheeks. 'What a trial you must have had! I've left you some bread and cheese in the kitchen, and there's some hot coffee in the pot, but I'll go on up to bed now, if you don't mind.'

Matilda didn't dare catch Giles's eye until she had heard the bedroom door shut upstairs and the bed creak. She uncovered the bread and cheese and poured them both coffee.

'I seem to learn something new about you every day,' she said at length. 'I never imagined back in Primrose Hill that you could shave children's heads. Or tell lies to your wife.'

'I didn't either,' he said, and grinned weakly. 'You know what I was really frightened of?'

'What?' Matilda asked, putting the coffee down in front of him.

'That she'd say she could smell something funny on us. I can still smell that stuff we painted on their heads.'

'Me too,' Matilda smiled. 'I guess it's just in our noses for all time. A penance for telling fibs.'

They ate their bread and cheese in companionable silence.

'The doctor thought they were robust little devils in the main,' Giles said at length. 'But he didn't like the look of the one they called "Injun" or one of the youngest girls, they'd both got badly infected chests. I hope they all behave tonight. It would have been much better if they'd gone straight to New Jersey.'

When it was decided it was too late to take the children there, they'd made a makeshift bed of straw and blankets for them in one of the other cellar rooms next to the kitchen. Eva had not been pleased by this development, and Matilda had offered to stay all night with them, but the doctor had said that was unnecessary.

'I just hope they use the pails we put in,' Matilda said with a sigh. She had lectured them all on the subject before she left, but though the older ones understood and seemed to want to please her, she didn't think the little ones had taken it in.

'Sidney's a bright lad, he'll keep them in order,' Giles said with a smile. 'It was a stroke of luck you'd met him before, and I think he'll prove very useful in helping us track down more children.'

Matilda laughed.

'What's amused you?' Giles asked in surprise.

'Sidney. He reminds me of my brother Luke in many ways. I think he'll need watching like a hawk.'

She hadn't told either Giles or Lily much about her brothers, but now, after such a day, she wanted to, if only to make Giles see that for every three or four children who could be helped, there would be one whom no amount of tender care would save. 'I think we can inherit badness, just as we can looks and brains,' she said with a wry smile. 'I don't believe it's all down to our upbringing.'

'Maybe Sidney will be gone by the morning then.' Giles shrugged. 'I just hope he doesn't take the doctor's silver with him.'

'I only said he reminded me of Luke,' Matilda said, trying to make him understand. 'It's just his colouring and his quickness. But I don't think he's a bad lad. If he was, he would have demanded money before bringing the children to us. And he wouldn't have cared where we were taking them. I think we're going to find him quite an interesting character.'

Her words were proved quite true the next day. All the children were still fast asleep when Giles and Matilda got back to the doctor's house at eight the next morning, except for Sidney who leaped up the moment they came through the door of the basement room.

'I was scared you wasn't coming back,' he said, his amber eyes lighting up with relief to see Matilda again.

'I told you I was,' she said reprovingly, patting his shaven head. 'I'm coming all the way to New Jersey to see you settled in. Now, were they all good last night?'

'Ruth's wet herself,' he said, pointing to one of the very small girls still fast asleep. 'She always did that in the castle. That's why no one liked to sleep by her.'

'Well, she's only little,' Matilda said. No one had been able to tell her anything about this child, not even her name. They guessed she was around two and a half, though she was so thin and small she looked much younger. Dr Kupicha had named her Ruth the previous day, and it was pleasing to hear Sidney use the name, a sign, she thought, that he did have a real sense of responsibility for all these children.

'But I got the others to use the pail,' he said proudly. 'I'm in charge, see.'

'Then you'd better get them all up now,' she said, her voice softening with a surge of affection for him. 'But now you'll all have to learn to use the privy outside, because that's much better than a bucket. After that you must all wash your faces and hands before having breakfast.'

'Wash again!' he said in amazement, his eyes nearly popping out of his head.

'Yes,' she laughed. 'Or there won't be any breakfast.'

'I thought we'd done all the hard part yesterday,' Giles admitted wearily to Matilda, as they rode back in the cart to the ferry across the Hudson river. 'I never expected so many problems. Do you think they will all settle down?'

Matilda turned her head to look back at the house. It was a plain stone-built building of three floors, surrounded by tall trees, built originally as a pest house for people with infectious diseases. Seen now at dusk, with a cold blustery wind coming in from the Atlantic Ocean, it had a forbidding, bleak appearance. They could almost feel the ghostly presence of all those poor souls who had been taken out there and mostly left to die.

Yet however harsh it looked from her seat in the cart, however far removed it was from the cosiness of their little house in State Street, Matilda knew the children inside it were in a place of safety at last.

'Of course they will settle down,' she said. 'You can't expect children who've never had any kind of discipline before to fall in line immediately. If you'd taken me somewhere like that, instead of to the parsonage in Primrose Hill, I would have legged it straight away.'

'You thought it was that bad?' he said in horror.

She laughed. 'Well, all those spotless floors, the rows of beds and that hard-faced woman in her white pinafore were enough to strike fear into any kid's heart.'

'Miss Rowbottom came very highly recommended,' he said indignantly. 'She cares as much about the plight of slum children as you or I do.'

'I expect she does,' Matilda retorted. 'But a smile or two wouldn't have hurt her. Good job she didn't see them all yesterday, that's all I can say.'

In fact Matilda's opinion of Miss Rowbottom had improved during the course of the day because she'd found that underneath the frosty appearance was an interesting, intelligent woman. She had come to America as a governess, then moved on to become a teacher in Pittsburgh, but when she'd supported some of her children's fathers in an attempt to get shorter working hours and higher wages, she had found herself out of a job. Having heard that the Reverend Kirkbright was a humanitarian involved with the Abolitionist movement, she came to New York in the hopes he might be able to help her find employment. She had been somewhat surprised to find herself being offered the post as Matron in a new Home for waifs and strays, but as she told Matilda, the idea excited her.

'I can't think of many people who could have coped with what we saw yesterday,' Giles retorted. 'That's exactly why we had to get them cleaned up first. But don't hold that against her, Matty. Not everyone has your strong stomach.'

'I do think she's a good person,' Matilda admitted. 'She'll be a good teacher and I'm sure she'll treat the kids fairly. I just would have liked someone a bit more motherly as Matron.'

They fell into silence, holding on to the sides of the cart as the horse picked its way gingerly along the rutted, muddy lane, jolting them each time the wheels hit a larger rut or hole. The driver was a man called Job, who had escaped from slavery in Virginia and made his way to New York where Kirkbright took him under his wing. He was to be the janitor, odd-job man at the Home. According to Miss Rowbottom, he was a 'pearl' who could do anything from felling trees to washing floors. Matilda had already made up her own mind he was an inspired choice for such a position when she'd seen his big face break into a wide, warm smile at the children's arrival.

It had been a day of taut anxiety. Two adults in charge of eighteen fearful children had not been enough. Some of the children had been sick on the ferry, a combination of the motion and unusually full bellies. One of the older boys had tried to make his escape when he saw the house, convinced it was a prison, and once inside almost all the children had been cowed and uncooperative. Even Matilda had turned pale at the foul language they used, and most of them forgot they could no longer relieve themselves anywhere they chose.

Yet there had been some very good moments too. Little faces wide-eyed with astonishment to see fields, trees, and cows, the way they'd gingerly tried out their beds and asked who else would be sharing it. Their delight to find there was another meal waiting for them on arrival, and a big fire in the room which was to be their playroom. Matilda wondered sadly how long it would take before they would stop behaving like little old men and women, move away from the fire and discover the meaning of play. She had got out a box of building bricks and tried to show the younger ones what they could do with them, but they scratched their little shaven heads and just stared at her. When she showed them a picture-book they just looked at it blankly.

Yet Sidney had been a pillar of strength. He alone seemed delighted with everything, and when any of the others seemed to be getting difficult he stepped in and jollied them along.

But to Matilda one of the saddest aspects of the day was that she wouldn't be involved with the children any longer. She might see them again when they brought another bunch to join them, but that would be only fleetingly. Half of her wished she dared ask Giles if she could go and work at the Home, for that way she could mother them all and watch their progress, yet she couldn't bear to leave Tabitha either, or disappoint Lily by leaving.

As the ferry pulled away from the jetty, Matilda looked back. It was too dark now to see the house, but she could see Job's lantern swaying as he rode up the rutted lane. She offered up a silent prayer that Miss Rowbottom wouldn't turn out to be cruel, that the two girls who were going to help her weren't as dumb as they looked, and that Job would be brave enough to tell the Reverend Kirkbright if he saw anything amiss.

Giles was watching Matilda's face as the ferry got under way, and he was suddenly struck by her beauty. It wasn't the classical, delicate kind, her features were too strong and her colouring too bold for sedate salons and drawing-rooms, but out here on the river with the wind catching at the tendrils of blonde hair escaping from her bonnet, she was perfection. Such a soft, wide mouth, her nose just faintly tilted at the tip, and plump, rosy cheeks. It saddened him to think she would almost certainly end up marrying a working man and that beauty would be worn away with hard toil and child-bearing, her sharp mind dulled by lack of stimulation. For lovely as she was, despite having learned to speak and behave like a lady, there was something about her direct manner and sharp wit which gave her origins away, and no gentleman of means would consider marrying such a girl, however much he desired her.

Giles felt a surge of tenderness for her. She had so many gifts – intelligence, compassion, humour and courage. He knew she hadn't wanted to leave the children tonight, and they hadn't wanted her to go either. All day he'd been astounded by her patience, how she could soothe one child while still keeping a watchful eye on all the others, how she could cheerfully clean up a mess that made him blanch, yet gently explain to the offender why he or she must learn not to do it again. In truth he knew he ought to go straight to Kirkbright tonight and tell him that she should be Matron of the Home, and let Miss Rowbottom just be teacher. Matilda had every talent needed for the job, but he knew he couldn't do it, for he had come to rely on her himself too much, and so had Lily and Tabitha. Besides, he needed her help to get at least another eighteen children out of Five Points.

Lily Milson was sewing in the kitchen the following afternoon but she was watching Matilda out of the corner of her eye. On the face of it the girl was behaving quite normally, kneading the dough for bread on the table, every now and then bending to Tabitha beside her and showing her how to knead her smaller piece properly. But Lily sensed she wasn't quite herself, there were no jokes or laughter, and her voice was subdued. She guessed the cause of it was that Matilda was brooding on those children she'd taken to the Waifs' and Strays' Home.

Lily recalled how emotional she'd been about children when she was Matilda's age, and how she'd longed for the day when she would hold her own baby in her arms. She remembered too how despairing she'd been as the years passed and no man even took an interest in her, let alone wanted to be her sweetheart.

She thought that perhaps this was what was troubling Matilda today, maybe the recent events had reminded her that she had no young man. Possibly she'd suddenly realized that her entire life could be spent caring for other people's children, that she might never find love, get married and have a home of her own.

Thinking on this, Lily felt a stab of guilt that she and Giles relied so heavily on her. Matilda had given up her family to come here to America with them, she had no opportunities to make friends of her own age, and she was probably very lonely.

'Why don't you go to the dance at the church tonight?' she said on an impulse.

Matilda looked up in surprise and wiped a floury hand across her cheek. 'I can't go on my own,' she said.

'You could go with Mrs Arkwright's maid,' Lily said. 'The Italian girl you met at the Bible class.'

'I don't think her mistress would let her,' Matilda said with a shrug.

'I think she will if I ask her,' Lily replied. 'I could take a stroll along to her house now. She's always asking me to drop in one afternoon, today is as good a time as any.'

Matilda smiled. She didn't much like the idea of the dance, but it would be good to see Rosa again for she'd missed the last class. 'Well, if you're sure you won't need me,' she said, a touch of excitement banishing her earlier dejection. 'And you don't mind asking Mrs Arkwright?'

'It will be a pleasure,' Lily said, meaning it. She didn't like the woman one little bit and although it was an unChristian thought, she hoped she would be thoroughly put out by having no one to dress her hair and help her into her vulgar gowns.

Matilda finished kneading the bread while Lily was gone, and put it to rise on the stove, then after tidying the kitchen she sat down with Tabitha to teach her some words. She had devised a game in which Tabitha picked out something in the house, then whatever the first letter of it was, Matilda got her to find other things beginning with the same sound and wrote them down. Tabitha picked 'clock' and Matilda wrote the word and a picture beside it. Soon they had 'candle', 'carrot,' 'couch' and 'cat' too.

The little girl was very quick, she could recognize most letters of the alphabet already, and if Matilda showed her the words from other days, covering up the pictures, she remembered many of them.

They were just going back to the As when Lily came back. 'Rosa's got the evening off,' she said with a beaming smile. 'She'll be along for you at seven. But she has to be back by ten.'

Matilda was so excited she felt like hugging her mistress. 'I'll wear that pretty dress you gave me, the one with the blue flowers,' she said.

'That's a day dress,' Lily said, looking scandalized. 'No, you must wear that rose-pink taffeta one of mine I was going to make over for Tabitha. I'm sure it will fit you.'

Just before seven Matilda came downstairs. She felt she couldn't breathe because Lily had insisted she had to wear stays and pulled them in very tight, but she was prepared to put up with that just for the joy of wearing such a beautiful dress. By her mistress's standards it was dreadfully unfashionable as it had no hoops in the skirt and the bustle was very small, but for Matilda who was used to wearing navy-blue serge every day, it was glorious and made her feel like a princess. She had plaited her hair and coiled it up around her head, fixing a small pink ribbon above each ear. She just hoped her bonnet wouldn't spoil it.

'You look lovely,' Lily said, her small sharp features softening. 'Now, make sure you dance with anyone who asks you and thank them politely afterwards, even if they have stepped on your toes. But don't be too forward, Matty dear, and come straight home afterwards.'

'Perhaps I should go to meet them?' Giles spoke out. It was unthinkable for a lady to be out alone after dark, but he wasn't sure if this applied to servants.

'I'm told that one of the chaperones always finds someone trustworthy to escort girls home,' Lily said. She looked at Matilda and smiled. 'So just mention to one of them that you are Reverend Milson's nursemaid and they'll find you someone.'

At that Rosa knocked on the door, so Matilda slipped her shawl around her shoulders, put on her bonnet and hurriedly left in great excitement.

The dance was a dismal disappointment. There were dozens more men than women, but most of them old enough to be the girls' fathers. The ageing pianist played every tune like a funeral dirge and Matilda felt she was attracting too much attention to herself in her pink taffeta. Everyone else, except a few older women and those who were acting as chaperones, were wearing very ordinary dresses. Even Rosa, who had gasped with envy when she saw it and remarked that her green print cotton looked dowdy beside it, looked a great deal happier later to find she was the one in the right clothes.

Both girls made the best of it and danced with anyone who asked them, but by nine, their feet sore from being trampled on, and weary of being asked questions in halting English, Rosa said she wanted to leave.

'We can't,' Matilda said. 'We have to wait until one of the chaperones finds us someone to walk with us.'

Rosa grimaced. 'I surely can't stand another hour of this,' she said. 'Let's just slip out while no one's looking and go down to Castle Green.'

Matilda knew that the Milsons would be horrified if she did such a thing. The concert hall at Castle Clinton was considered a smart place to go, but the Green surrounding it was reported to be crowded with dubious people at night. It was also too cold to go wandering about. But she didn't want to stay at the dance either, nor did she want her new friend to think her dull and unadventurous.

Rosa must have sensed her wavering. 'Come on, you've gotta see it or you ain't seen nothing. I'll tell one of the chaperones Mrs Arkwright's coachman is here to collect us.'

The moment the girls had left the church hall and Matilda heard the familiar sound of a hurdy-gurdy in the distance, her misgivings left her and excitement took their place. The sound was so evocative of London and the freedom she'd enjoyed before going to work for the Milsons. No harm could come to them in just an hour, and she wanted something jolly to take her mind off those children in New Jersey.

As they turned into the street by the Green the sight that met her eyes thrilled her. It was as good as any street fair in London. Hundreds of people were milling around, hurricane lamps hanging from trees and more on the many stalls made it as light as day, and music was coming from all directions.

Right in the centre there was a carousel, and as the horses pranced sedately up and down and around, the lamps caught the mirrored central pedestal and made a dazzling light show in the darkness. As they joined the jostling crowd the first thing Matilda saw was a big brown bear dancing on a lead, and she clapped her hands with delight.

'Like it?' Rosa said, taking her arms and making her do a polka with her to the sound of a gypsy fiddler.

'It's better than London,' Matilda gasped, breaking away from the dance because people were looking at them. She didn't know where to look first, there were so many stalls selling ice-cream, oysters and fruit, and pretty hair ribbons fluttering in the breeze. 'But I just hope no one recognizes me,' she added.

'Church people don't come down here,' Rosa laughed, nudging her friend to look at a couple of very gaudily dressed women wearing paint on their faces. 'And if there are, they are probably looking for mischief just like us, so they won't be telling.'

'I didn't know New York was like this at night,' Matilda said, stopping to listen for a minute to a man playing the penny whistle. 'I got the idea everyone was kind of serious.'

'Serious! New Yorkers?' Rosa's dark eyes danced. 'You've only met the snooty ones. You should see the Bowery, that's wild at night.'

It occurred to Matilda then that Rosa seemed very worldly for a maid, and it made her feel just a little uneasy, yet after the stuffiness of the dance, it was exhilarating to be in a noisy, carefree crowd.

A little later Matilda was just going to suggest they had an ice-cream, even though it was really too cold, when two gentlemen in silk hats and frock-coats came up to them.

'Good evening, ladies,' the taller of the two said, and raised his hat. 'May we walk with you?'

Rosa giggled. 'Certainly, sir,' she replied, and to Matilda's surprise she winked at her friend and took the man's arm.

Matilda might never have had a young man but she had learnt a great deal about men by observation back in London's streets. Instinct told her these two men had taken her and Rosa for prostitutes.

'No, Rosa,' she said, thinking her friend hadn't realized. But as she spoke the second man stepped in front of her and looked her right in the face. She thought he was around thirty, his face was very flushed with drink, and there was a cold look in his eyes that made her even more nervous.

'Come on,' he said, holding out his arm. 'We both know what we're here for.'

'You are mistaken in why we are here,' she said with all the haughtiness she could muster. 'We just came to look around. Now, if you are a gentleman kindly leave us alone.' She quickly dodged past him and ran to Rosa who was already some distance away with the taller man.

Grabbing her friend's free arm, she hissed in her ear, 'Come away. They think we're gay.'

But to her dismay Rosa only laughed and shrugged her off, turning her face up to her companion and resuming their conversation.

Matilda thought perhaps the word 'gay' wasn't in use in America and she was just opening her mouth to say something coarser, when the other man caught hold of her wrist and yanked her away.

'Come on, blondy,' he said. 'Your pal knows what she's doing and I bet you do too if the price is right.'

Dozens of men had propositioned her in her time selling flowers, it was one of the perils of the job, but Matilda had quickly learnt that once a man actually caught hold of her, actions went a great deal further than words. She shook off his hand, tightened her right one into a fist and punched him in the chin.

He reeled back, more with surprise than hurt. 'Well, you little vixen,' he said in astonishment. 'What saloon did you learn that in?'

If it hadn't been for Rosa, she would have fled immediately. By hitting the man she had attracted attention to herself and the crowd around stopped to watch. Yet still imagining her friend was too innocent to know what was going on, she ran back to her and tried to pull her forcefully away from her escort. But as she caught hold of Rosa by the arm, the man she'd hit came up behind her and this time grabbed her right around the middle, trapping her arms.

'Rosa, they think we are whores,' she yelled.

To Matilda's dismay the gathering crowd let out a cheer and began clapping, perhaps thinking they were watching some kind of street act. But the humiliation of that was nothing compared to the shock of seeing Rosa turn to frown at her in irritation, and suddenly realizing she knew exactly what she was doing.

'Let me go, you oaf,' Matilda screamed out, but her bonnet tipped over her eyes as she struggled to get free and she couldn't see.

She heard a thud and simultaneously she was lurched forward.

'Let the lady go if you know what's good for you,' a deep Irish voice called out. 'Or I'll break your head, so help me.'

The sudden release from the man's hands toppled her, but she recovered her footing, flicked her bonnet back on to her head and turned to see a tall, dark-haired man sparring up to the one who had caught her.

'She's no lady,' he was saying with some indignation. 'And what's it to you anyway?'

'She's my girl, that's what,' the Irishman said and with that threw a punch that laid the man right out on the grass.

Matilda backed away in horror. More people were rushing over to watch and someone among them was bound to know who she was. Rosa and the other man had disappeared.

She moved then, picking up her skirt with both hands, and ran away towards State Street.

'Don't run from me, darlin',' she heard the Irishman call out behind her. 'It ain't safe to be out on yer own. Let me take you's home.'

She faltered at the edge of the Green. The bright lights were behind her now and in front was total darkness. She knew the man was right, it wasn't safe to be alone, and besides, she ought at least to thank him for coming to her rescue.

As he breathlessly caught up with her, and she saw the concern on his face, she suddenly began to cry with shock, covering her face with her hands.

'Oh, me darlin', don't cry,' he said. 'There's folks watching us and they'll be thinkin' I've hurt you.'

He said his name was Flynn O'Reilly, and getting out a handkerchief from his pocket he mopped at her face. 'Now, where are ye staying?' he asked. 'And what were ye thinking of to come out here at night?'

She managed to get out that she was the minister's nursemaid and that she lived in State Street, and that Rosa had let her down, but it was a second or two before she noticed how young and handsome the man was. His hair was black and curly, the lights behind him making it shine like wet seaweed. There wasn't enough light to see the colour of his eyes, only the concern in them, and his teeth were very white.

'I must get home now,' she gasped out. 'Thank you for saving me from that man. I won't ever go there again.'

He lifted her chin with his hand and smiled down at her. 'You must stop shaking before you get home,' he said in a soft and soothing voice. 'Or your mistress will want to know what's happened to you.' With that his arms slid around her and before she could even think of protesting he was holding her tightly against him, stroking her back.

She knew she shouldn't be allowing such familiarity with a total stranger, but it was so good to be held, such a safe, warm feeling, and even though she knew nothing more of him than his name, she didn't want to break away.

'I said you was my girl back there without thinking,' he said against the side of her bonnet. 'But it seems to me now I'm holding you that a good fairy waved her wand tonight.'

He moved her away from him, holding both her elbows, and looked into her eyes. 'My, but you're lovely,' he whispered. 'I just have to kiss you or die.'

Reason told her to run, yet she couldn't, an invisible force seemed to hold her motionless as his mouth came down on hers. She closed her eyes involuntarily, and his lips were warm and so soft, she just gave herself up to them. There were people walking by, perhaps even some who knew her, but in that brief moment of sweetness she didn't care.

'Am I to be told the name of the angel in the pink dress, whose lips taste of honey?' he whispered as he finally drew away.

She knew she ought to laugh, to think of a quick retort, yet she couldn't. 'Matilda Jennings,' she whispered back.

'Well, my little Matilda,' he said with a sigh. 'I'd very much like to persuade you to stay out with me. But I guess you'd be in trouble if I did that, so I'd better walk you home.'

At the door of the house in State Street, he squeezed her hand. 'What day do you have off?' he asked.

'Usually Fridays,' she said, whispering in case the Milsons should hear them and look out.

'Will you meet me then?' he said.

She nodded, hardly able to believe she was doing this.

'I'll be at the Tontine coffee house between two and three in the afternoon,' he said, reaching out to stroke her cheek lightly. 'Now, go on in and keep calm. Don't tell your mistress about your friend. She'll be in deep trouble soon enough without you bringing it down on her.'

He walked away as she put her hand out to turn the door knob. His step was so light she could scarcely hear it, but as she opened the door, he turned and blew her a kiss.

Matilda had no idea how she managed to walk into the parlour, tell her master and mistress she'd enjoyed the dance, then join them in the evening prayers, all without giving anything away.

As she said the Lord's Prayer, her eyes tightly shut, the words 'Forgive us our trespasses, and forgive those who trespass against us' had real meaning for once. She ought to hate Rosa and that terrible bully of a man, yet if it hadn't been for them she wouldn't have met Flynn.

Up in bed later, she whispered his name in the dark and when she relived his kiss she felt as if her whole body was on fire.

'No good will come of it,' she warned herself. Yet to wait six days before she could see him again seemed to be the worst aspect of it.

Chapter Seven

Matilda's heart seemed to be beating absurdly loudly as she made her way to the Tontine coffee house on Friday afternoon. She felt hot all over too, even though it had turned very cold with the sudden onset of autumn. They called it the fall here, but instead of golden leaves swirling around in the strong wind, like she remembered back in Primrose Hill, here there were only bits of rubbish, for there were few trees in this part of New York.

She was wearing a straw boater-style hat which Lily had given her, but now she wondered if she had been wrong to replace the original dark blue ribbon with a bright red one. What if red was too forward a colour?

'It's too late to worry about that now,' she said to herself. 'He'll have to take you as you are.'

She had scarcely thought of anything else but Flynn all week, reminding herself constantly that she had only seen him in darkness, and then only for a few minutes, so he might turn out to be ugly, stupid, or even married. Yet for some strange reason it was the thought of him being married that frightened her the most.

As she passed by the Arkwrights' house she glanced up at the windows. It was one of the smart Federal-style houses, four floors and a fan-shaped window over the front door, and she imagined it to be very elegant inside. She wondered if Rosa was watching her pass by from behind the lace blinds, and feeling ashamed.

Matilda hadn't gone to the Bible class on Wednesday because she couldn't face seeing the girl again. Yet maybe she should have gone, if only to find out why Rosa behaved as she did. Was she so stupid that she imagined that was the way to find a 'gentleman' who would fall in love with her and marry her? Or was it because she needed the money to help out her family? Yet whatever the reason, she shouldn't have taken Matilda along with her, or left her there when everything turned nasty.

But as Matilda turned the corner and saw Flynn waiting outside the Tontine coffee house for her, she forgave Rosa. The first thing that struck her about him was that he was even more handsome than she'd imagined. The second was that he looked very poor.

This surprised her most, for his voice and confident manner had evoked in her mind the image of someone from the upper classes. Even at a distance of some thirty feet she could see his suit had been bought second-hand off a barrow, it was shiny with age and too large for his slender frame. Yet the grey derby hat tilted back on to his dark curls gave him an appealing, rakish air, and the joyful smile that lit up his face as he saw her coming suggested he shared her excitement.

'Matilda!' he exclaimed, opening his arms wide as if intending to hug her there in the street. But then, as if remembering this wasn't the way things were done, he stopped and grinned sheepishly. 'Good afternoon, Miss Jennings,' he said, raising his hat. 'How do you do?'

Matilda giggled. 'Very well, thank you, Mr O'Reilly.'

His eyes were almost navy blue, fanned by long, thick, dark lashes, and his teeth were every bit as white and perfect as they'd appeared in the dark. She thought no man had a right to be so handsome, just looking at him made her feel light-headed.

'Am I really to call you Miss Jennings?' he said. 'In the old country you can call a girl by her Christian name once you've kissed her.'

'You can call me Matty, but you must forget you kissed me,' she said, blushing furiously. 'I wasn't myself after what happened.'

'So who was it I kissed then?' He put his head on one side and made a comic face. 'To be sure, that colleen looked like you.'

His soft Irish lilt, his gentle teasing were as appealing as his face and she had to smile.

'It's a touch cold for walking,' he said, looking up at the grey sky. 'Shall we go and find somewhere warm to have tea?'

She was very glad he didn't suggest going into the Tontine coffee house, it was a place where merchants gathered to auction goods, and to buy and sell shares, and some of them might know the Milsons. She knew they wouldn't approve of her meeting any man on her afternoon off, not unless she'd met him through the church and they knew all about him. But she wasn't going to spoil the day by thinking about such things.

Flynn led her speedily through the narrow streets over to the west side of the island, explaining as they went that he knew a little place with a nice view of the Hudson river. He asked too how long she'd been in America, and if the rest of her family were here too. When she told him that Reverend Milson was a minister at Trinity Church he looked a bit concerned. Imagining this was because he had similar views about clergymen to those she'd once held, she quickly told him Giles Milson wasn't what she'd call a Bible-basher.

The place he took her to was little more than a wooden shack above a warehouse, furnished with rough wood tables and benches. A few men were eating meals, but in the main the clientele were people much like herself and Flynn, young women who could be maids or shop girls with a male companion, all drinking tea. As Flynn was greeted very warmly by a very fat black lady in a red turban, who immediately cleared the table down by the window for them, Matilda imagined he must be a regular visitor.

The view of the river with schooners in full sail, huge steamships, tugs, ferries and fishing boats was so evocative of her father and her childhood that for a moment or two she forgot all about Flynn and just drank it in with nostalgia. The Milsons had made her promise that she would keep well away from the wharves, as they considered them and the men who worked on them dangerous. She had abided by what they said, but at times when she felt homesick it was very tempting to disobey them. Lily could pretend she was back in England by going to church or tea parties with other English women; for Matilda, the docks were a bit of home, the sights, smells and sounds just like London.

Straight ahead across the river was New Jersey, but though she could just make out the ferry landing, the Waifs' and Strays' Home was too far inland to see.

'Are you shy?' Flynn's question made her turn back to him. 'Or are you thinking that this is a terrible place I've brought you to?'

She blushed furiously, suddenly aware she hadn't spoken

since they sat down. 'No, of course not. I'm so sorry to be so rude. I was just enjoying the view of the ships and thinking about some orphans Reverend Milson and I took to a Home in New Jersey last week.'

Tea and doughnuts were brought to them by a small black girl in a ragged dress. She smiled shyly at them, revealing a lack of front teeth, then scuttled away.

'That's just one of Sadie's eleven children,' Flynn said. 'But tell me about these orphans.'

Matilda explained.

'You went into Five Points and took kids out?' He whistled between his teeth. 'Bejesus Matty, that's no place for a girl like you.'

'It's no place for an orphan child either,' she said tartly. 'I shall be going back there too, to round up some more.'

He looked at her in utter horror. 'Does this Reverend Milson have anything between his two ears?' he said, his voice raised in indignation. 'He could be killed in there, and you with him. I once spent over two weeks in that fearful place, and I count myself lucky I got out alive.'

'Reverend Milson has a better brain than any man I've ever met,' she retorted. 'And why should anyone kill us when we are trying to help?'

Flynn shook his head, his navy-blue eyes suddenly doleful. 'Oh Matty,' he sighed. 'You can't know how it is there. When word gets around you are taking babbies away they'll be queuing up to offer you theirs, and demanding money for them too. Those aren't just poor folk in there, they are animals. I know most of them are my countrymen, but Jesus save their souls, they are the scrapings of the barrel. I can't begin to tell you how they live.'

'You don't have to,' she said. 'I came from one of the worst slums in London myself and I know exactly how the people live. It's only luck and the kindness of Reverend Milson that I'm not still there.'

His mouth dropped open in shock. 'But I took you for a country girl,' he said in little more than a whisper.

Matilda wished she'd stopped to think before blurting that out. Even to her ears it sounded like she was a reformed whore. She was just about to rephrase it when she stopped herself. Why should she justify herself to a man who called the poor the scrapings of the barrel?

'I suppose you are descended from the Kings of Ireland?' she said with some sarcasm. 'Most of the Irish in London claim to be.'

'You have a sharp tongue, Matty,' he replied, but his eyes twinkled with amusement. 'Maybe I *am* of royal blood, us Irish have more children than any other race I've ever met, but then there's little else to do in Ireland but grow the potato, cut the peat for our fires and make love.'

She had heard many men use the cruder words for sex, but somehow 'making love' sounded so intimate that she blushed and lowered her eyes from his.

He laughed softly. 'Drink your tea and eat your doughnut,' he said. 'I promise not to embarrass you again today. I come from a very poor family too, twelve of us, and me the third from eldest, with no hope of a shilling, let alone a fortune coming to me. We lived in a croft near Galway, and when the potato failed for two years running, it was hunger that made me walk all the way to Cork to try and find work.'

'How old were you?' she asked.

'About twelve, with nothing in me head but dreams, and rags on me back. Luckily a fisherman there needed a lad to help him and I stayed with him and his wife for two years. He couldn't pay me, but at least I didn't starve. They say fish is good for the brain!' He smiled. 'It must have been, for I worked out for myself that Ireland was no good for me and left soon after.'

She had been wondering how old Flynn was all the way here. His quick, jerky movements, his slender body were all very boyish, but the adult way he spoke suggested he was far older than he looked.

'You came straight to America at fourteen?' she fished. Lily had said it was impolite to ask anyone's age.

'No, first I went to sea as a cabin boy, then I went to England to dig canals. Finally I signed on a ship as a deck hand and arrived here three years ago. I was twenty-two then. A whole ten years since I left Galway.'

Matilda digested this. She had established that he was twenty-five, and he seemed to have no trade. 'And you went to live in Five Points?'

'Not intentionally, few do that,' he said with a shrug. 'Me luck and me money ran out, that's all. But in a way it did me a power of good. I saw what it was like to be right at the bottom of the heap, and I clawed me way out.'

'So what do you work at?' she asked warily. What she'd heard so far didn't look too good. He was too old for her, a wanderer, and it was odd that a working man should have an afternoon free. 'And where do you live?'

He hesitated for a moment as if considering telling a lie.

'I work in a saloon on the Bowery,' he said. 'And I live upstairs. I dare say you won't want to tell your Reverend Milson that!'

Matilda's heart sank. Although she hadn't been to the Bowery she had heard it was a street full of low entertainment which respectable people kept well away from. Added to everything else he'd told her about himself it was patently obvious that he was the kind of man any sensible girl would steer clear of.

Yet he was so handsome and personable, and however poor he might be she could see he was fastidious. His shirt was very worn but it was snowy white, he had shaved, polished his boots, and his fingernails were very clean and cut tidily. He could of course have done this purely for her benefit, but somehow she didn't think so.

'I don't think I can tell the Reverend anything about you,' she said gently.

To her surprise he didn't ask why. He didn't even look hurt, but calmly went on eating his doughnut. 'How old are you, Matty?' he asked after a couple of minutes.

'Seventeen, nearly eighteen.'

He nodded. 'And what do you want from life?' he asked.

The strange question threw her. 'I don't know,' she shrugged. 'So far I haven't ever had any real choice, things have just happened.'

His smile was one of understanding. 'It was like that for me too,' he said. 'But a coupla years ago I got to thinking that it was time I stopped just letting things happen. I was a builder's labourer then, doing back-breaking work for a dollar a day and often sleeping rough on the job because it was better than paying ten cents a night in a flea-pit for a spot on the floor. I talked me way into this job, with the idea that when I'd got enough money to buy some fancy clothes I'd be off down South.'

Matilda had often heard Giles speak heatedly about the Southern states as he'd met many Abolitionists since he'd been in New York. From what she gathered the plantation owners were unspeakably cruel and decadent, and they were either whipping their slaves to death, auctioning off the slaves' children, or throwing great lavish balls and parties that went on for days.

'To do what?' She gave a nervous laugh. 'To buy a few slaves?'

'I hate slavery of any kind,' he said with a grimace. 'But then us Irish have been enslaved by the English for centuries.'

She wasn't sure what he meant by that and she felt it was better not to ask. 'So what would you do there then? Pose as a gentleman?'

'Why not?' He grinned mischievously. 'The greatest gift the Irish have is their blarney. I can ride a horse like a gentleman. I've picked up a few fancy manners in me travels. Dressed well, would anyone doubt me?'

She smiled. Aside from his clothes everything else suggested he had a gentle upbringing, his skin was pale and clear, his fingers were long and slender and his voice was like listening to music. 'No, I don't think they would. They'd take one glance at your handsome face and they'd look no further.'

'So you're thinking I'm handsome then?' He leaned closer to her across the table, his eyes flashing suggestively.

'You know you are,' she grinned. 'But can you read and write, do you know the things gentlemen do?'

'I know more than that "gentleman" you ran into the other night,' he said indignantly. 'I can tell the difference between a nursemaid and a whore for a start. Yes, I can read and write. The priest down in Cork taught me and I have a fine hand.'

'Then there's nothing to stop you,' she said. He sounded so sure of himself she couldn't really doubt he was serious.

He sat back in his chair and looked at her through his long eyelashes. 'You're the first person I've ever told about my plan, Matty, I know most would laugh at me. But then it must be fate that we met, for you and I have a great deal in common. You sound like a lady, even though that coat is threadbare.'

Matty looked down at her coat in surprise. It was the one Dolly had given her the first time they met. She had always considered it very smart.

'My step-mother gave it to me,' she said. 'She's got a tea rooms on the river Thames.'

'Mr Lewinsky sold me this suit off his barrow in Hester Street,' he said, holding out his lapels. 'I paid one dollar fifty cents for it, which was all the money I had at the time. But I don't kid myself I look like a swell in it.'

Matilda was touched by his frankness. 'It's the first coat I ever had,' she said. 'Up till Dolly gave me this one I only had a shawl, even in the middle of winter.'

'Shawls make me think of the women back home,' he said, his eyes suddenly sad. 'They wear them over their heads and somehow it shows they have submitted to poverty. Hats tell a whole different story. I like your one, and what it tells me.'

Matilda giggled. 'Tell me what it says?' she asked.

'I can guess it belonged to your mistress, and you changed the ribbon to a red one because you are a free spirit. Just the jaunty style of it says you have the guts and determination to rise above the station in life which you were born to.'

'I've risen above that already,' she said. 'From flower-girl to nursemaid is a giant leap forward.'

'Maybe, but do you want more than that?' he asked raising one thick dark eyebrow. 'You can't stay a nursemaid, not unless your mistress has another child.'

'But I'm not just a nursemaid, I'm housekeeper too, and I help Reverend Milson with orphaned children.'

He reflected on that for a moment. 'It seems to me, Matty, that your life is just this family,' he said eventually, looking right into her eyes. 'Could it be they have become a replacement for one of your own? Do you ever have a thought which isn't about them or connected with them and their happiness?'

'Of course I do,' she said tartly. Yet as she paused to think of something to put him in his place, she realized that her thoughts were always of the Milsons, it was only since meeting Flynn her mind had moved slightly away from them. 'There's those children in Five Points for one!'

'That's connected to the Reverend,' he reproved her. 'Have you been anywhere in New York aside from their church and messages for them? Have you met any Americans, or immigrants from other countries, and been to their homes? Have you made any friends other than that girl you were with the other night?'

His derisive questions implied he saw her as trapped in a very English middle-class ghetto. Even though she wanted to deny it, she suddenly saw he was very astute. In many ways she could still be in Primrose Hill, her life had scarcely changed at all. She knew very little more about America and its people than when she arrived. The Milsons dictated what she saw, what she did and who she talked to.

'No, I suppose I haven't,' she said, suddenly a little ashamed that she'd failed to notice this for herself. 'But you make it sound like it's bad, like I'm the Milsons' slave. It's not like that at all, I'm very fond of them, and they treat me like part of their family.'

'That's grand,' he smiled, though there was a touch of cynicism in his tone. 'But it wouldn't hurt to expand your cosy little world a little, would it?'

'Don't you think my cosy little world was expanded by seeing Five Points?' she said tartly.

'No. You said you came from a bad place like that yourself so you already knew how low people can sink. How about looking to how high they can climb? Take a walk down Fifth Avenue and peep into some of those mansions. Ask about rich people and discover how they made their wealth.'

She was confused now. He had said he hated slavery, he seemed to despise people with servants, yet he admired the rich. Which side was he on?

'I already know that. Out of poor people. I'm surprised you approve of them.'

'Oh Matty, you misunderstand me.' He wiggled one finger at her. 'It's as big a mistake to think all the rich are wicked as to think all Irish are feckless, lazy devils who'd rather drink themselves stupid than do a day's work. There are of course Irishmen like that, but I know even more who work hard and save their money to send back to Ireland to look after whole families there.'

'Are you one of those?' she asked.

'I work hard,' he said. 'But I don't send money home because Dada would just drink it all away and then go home and hit Mammy. So I saves me money to set meself up for a better life. Dada will drink himself to death before long and maybe by then I'll be doing well enough to bring Mammy over here.'

Matilda was a little startled by such bluntness. Was he a callous man, who would stride through his life taking just what he wanted, without any regard for the suffering all around him, or was he a very perceptive realist who knew he had to accept what couldn't be changed?

They had more tea, and Matilda found herself telling him about how she'd grown up, and about her family. He was so interested, so good at drawing her out, that before long she was describing exactly how she'd ended up with the Milsons and the funnier aspects of suddenly finding herself amongst the middle classes.

'I'm neither fish nor fowl now,' she said thoughtfully. 'I've got all these airs and graces and I don't see myself as one of the poor any more. Yet I know I really am. And if I lost my present position what on earth would I do?'

'That, me darlin', is what you should work out long before you get pushed out their door,' he smiled. 'I've made a study of a few rich people, picking on ones who began with nothing. I've found there was very little luck in any of their stories, the common thread is that they were all fiercely ambitious from an early age.

'Back in England and Ireland you have to first cross the class barrier to make real money. But it's different here, it's a young country, wide open for those with the eye for an opportunity, regardless of background. What people like you and me have to look for is an opening. Then go straight for it.'

When he said he would walk her home because he had to get back to the saloon by half past seven, Matilda was astounded to find it was already half past five and they'd been talking for over three hours. It didn't seem possible that in this time she'd gone from intense excitement at meeting him, to a feeling she should back away, then on to a situation when she didn't want to say goodbye.

'When can we meet again?' he asked once they were outside the tea shop and making their way back towards State Street. 'Is Friday afternoon the only time you can get out?'

She nodded glumly. It was tempting to say she could get out on Wednesday evenings and skip Bible classes, but the Deacon would soon tell Giles she hadn't been there.

'Then I'll meet you at the same place next week,' he said. 'That's if you want to meet me?'

A small inner voice whispered that he wasn't right for her, that all he'd done today was fill her head with airy ideas that had no substance. But as she looked up at him, saw those dark blue eyes, his black curly hair and that mouth she had kissed, she knew that a week was going to seem like a month. All she could do was nod her agreement.

He took her hand as they walked back, and just his skin against hers made her feel weak with longing. She was afraid he would stop to kiss her, but even more afraid he wouldn't.

But he did stop. They had only gone a few more steps when he pulled her into a tiny alley, put his hands on either side of her face and tilted it up to his. He held it there for a few seconds, looking right into her eyes. 'Will you be my sweetheart, Matty?' he asked in a husky whisper. 'For you're the girl of my dreams.'

As his lips came down on hers she knew she was lost, for she was robbed of the will to break away. His tongue gently probed her lips apart and all at once the dank alley and fear of being seen in such a shameless embrace just disappeared. It was like the thrill of standing in the *Druid*'s bows at sunset, watching the waves divide and curl as the ship sliced through them. She felt a yearning deep inside her, a delight in his hard male body pressed against hers. She recognized it to be desire, that emotion that she knew to be so dangerous, yet it felt so right, so beautiful, she didn't care about the danger.

'Oh Matty,' he said softly as he broke away, his lips still kissing her cheeks, nose and eyes. 'A week will be too long to wait.'

That same evening, Lily followed Matilda out into the kitchen after prayers to collect and light their candles to take upstairs. Giles had already retired to bed. 'You were very preoccupied tonight,' she said. 'Did something unusual happen to you this afternoon?'

She noted how quickly Matilda spun round, and the widening of her eyes.

'No, nothing, madam,' she said and reached up for the candles on the shelf.

'Were you with Rosa?' Lily asked, determined to get to the bottom of it.

She had heard a disturbing rumour about the Arkwrights' maid. Apparently she had been seen out late at night on two or three separate occasions, and each time with a different man. It seemed to Lily, knowing that Mrs Arkwright wouldn't allow any servant such freedom, that the girl must be creeping out after she was supposed to have gone to bed. In view of Matilda's distant mood this evening she thought perhaps Rosa might have attempted to entice her to join her.

'No, madam,' Matilda replied. 'I haven't seen Rosa since the night we went to the dance.'

Lily was relieved, she knew Matilda wouldn't lie to her. 'Well, I don't want you to meet her again, Matty,' she said. 'From what I hear the girl is no better than she should be.'

At any other time Matilda would have made no comment to that remark. But after listening to Flynn's views it made her bristle.

'I'm sorry, madam, if this sounds impertinent, but I don't think you have the right to tell me who I can be friends with,' she retorted.

Lily was utterly stunned that Matilda dared answer her back, for a moment she just stared at her in disbelief. 'I beg your pardon!' she said.

'You are probably right about Rosa, and I have no wish to spend any more time with her anyway,' Matilda replied looking straight at her. 'But the decision to be friends with her or not should come from me.'

'Matilda!' Lily exclaimed. 'I can't believe this is you speaking.'

'You and the Reverend have done so much for me and I'm very grateful,' said Matilda, quietly but firmly. 'I've also grown very fond of you both and Tabitha, and I will always do my best for you all. But I really think I should have some sort of life of my own too.'

'Go to bed,' Lily snapped at her, unable to think of anything more appropriate. 'I shall speak to you in the morning. I hope by that time you'll have come to your senses.'

Once Matilda got up to her room the enormity of what she'd said to Lily struck her. She might never have been in service before the Milsons and knew little of what went on in other households, but she knew enough to know that what she'd said was sufficient to get herself dismissed.

'Oh Flynn, what have you done to me?' she whispered to

herself, looking into the small mirror above the chest-of-drawers. In the candlelight her features looked no different to the way they always did. Wide eyes, a small, slightly uptilted nose, and a mouth that she'd always considered far too big. Yet looking more closely she could see defiance in her eyes, her mouth looked wanton, and her chin was jutting out with new determination. She had never considered herself a pretty girl, even though people had often said she was, but tonight she could see for herself there was something arresting about her. Had Flynn done this to her, not only made her look different, but sowed a seed of rebellion inside her that made her challenge her mistress?

She suspected he would applaud her, for he clearly thought no man or woman had a right to control another's life. But after all the Milsons had done for her, wasn't it wicked to suddenly try to change the order of things?

'No, it isn't,' she whispered resolutely. 'You've paid them back for their kindness a thousand-fold by working so hard for them. And it isn't as if you are demanding something preposterous. You won't back down tomorrow. If you do you'll be trapped as a grateful, humble servant for ever.'

She unbraided her hair and ran her fingers through it till it fell on to her shoulders, then picking up the hair-brush the Milsons had given her last year for her birthday, she began to brush it, counting the strokes. By a hundred it looked like spun gold in the candlelight, and the sight pleased her. Unbuttoning the bodice of her dress, she slipped it off her shoulders and looked apprais-ingly at herself. Her shoulders were smooth, her pale skin gleamed in the soft light. In an evening gown she could look as lovely as any grand lady she'd ever seen. Flynn was right, they were alike, they could both pass for quality in the right clothes. But before she was ever to attempt that she had to gain the kind of confidence in herself and her abilities that Flynn had about himself.

Standing up for personal freedom was a start.

'I just don't know what's got into her,' Lily raged to her husband as she got into bed beside him. She had launched into the story as soon as she got into the bedroom, but though she'd hoped her husband would get out of bed and call Matilda downstairs immediately, so far he hadn't moved, or made any comment.

'She's never spoken to me like that before, and I don't understand why you are just lying there as if it's nothing.'

'But she had a point, dearest,' he said with a sigh, closing the book he'd been reading when she came rushing in. He hadn't made any comment during her tirade as he found his wife's face infinitely more interesting when she was angry. Her eyes grew darker, her nostrils flared, and her skin took on a becoming pink hue. In truth he wished she was stirred to anger more often, for mostly she just sulked, which made her so plain and dreary. 'We merely employ her, we don't own her. I think she does have a right to a private life.'

'But she already has a far superior life to most girls in her position,' Lily said, flinging herself down on to the pillows.

'That's true,' he said gently. 'But then she's a superior sort of nursemaid, isn't she? She cooks, cleans, shops, cares for Tabitha and teaches her. We'd be hard pressed to find anyone else who would do all that for two dollars a month. Not to mention how difficult it would be to find someone we could bear to share such a small house with.'

Giles could have used a stronger argument than that, but he knew if he was to say how much he personally depended on Matty, Lily would be even more aggrieved.

'But why did she suddenly come round to this way of thinking?' Lily persisted. 'Something must have occurred today. If she wasn't with the Arkwrights' maid, who was she with?'

'It isn't any of our business,' Giles said wearily. 'Maybe she had made a new friend and for some reason or another doesn't want to tell us about him or her.'

'Him!' Lily exclaimed, sitting bolt upright. 'You think she has a man friend?'

'Lily, calm down,' he said, putting a restraining hand on her arm. 'Just a couple of weeks ago you were saying that you felt guilty because her whole life centred around us. You let her go to the dance because you hoped she might meet a young man. Well, maybe she did. She's a sensible girl, and she'll tell us about him when she's ready.'

'But what are we going to do about her rudeness?' she asked, her voice dropping to a plaintive bleat because she knew her husband had no intention of admonishing the girl. 'We can't have a servant speaking to me as she did.'

'Sleep on it,' he suggested. 'Just think of all the good things there are about her, and weigh them against the bad. That should give us the answer.'

Lily heaved an exasperated sigh and leaned over to blow out the candle. She knew if she did as he suggested she'd merely be indebted to the girl. That was the last thing she wanted to feel.

At six the following morning Matilda was in the kitchen stoking up the stove when she heard Giles's step on the stairs. She broke out in a cold sweat, assuming Lily had insisted he came down either to give her her marching orders, or at least dish out some kind of punishment for her impudence.

He was dressed, and carrying his jacket over his arm. 'Good morning, Matty,' he said in his usual genial tone. 'Is the water hot yet?'

'I d-d-on't know,' she stammered. Then to cover her confusion she turned her back on him and felt the tank on the side of the stove.

'I only want it hot enough to shave, not to boil you in it,' he said.

Matty smiled nervously at his little joke. 'Then it's just right,' she said. 'Shall I take the jug upstairs?'

'No, I don't want to disturb Mrs Milson,' he said. 'I'll use the scullery. I have to go over to New Jersey today. Would you like to come with me and see the children?'

Matilda's heart leapt with excitement, but instantly plummeted again when she thought of her mistress upstairs. 'How can I, sir? You must know Madam's angry with me, and then there's Tabitha.'

He half smiled, his dark eyes twinkling. 'Sometimes a retreat is better than a battle,' he said.

She knew then that Lily had repeated everything to him, and judging by his jovial mood, he was staying neutral.

'I can't apologize because I meant what I said,' she blurted out quickly before she lost her nerve. 'But I am sorry if I sounded ungrateful for all you've both done for me.'

'Matty!' he exclaimed and shook his head. 'As far as I'm concerned no apologies are needed. You made your point last night, now you must just stick to it. Mrs Milson will probably be a little cool for a day or two, but she'll come round eventually. Now, let me have that hot water and perhaps you'd get us both some breakfast. I want to get an early start.'

Matilda's feelings during the long wait to meet Flynn again swung like a pendulum between elation and extreme anxiety, and it wasn't all caused by him.

She was overjoyed to find the Five Points children happy and well, Sidney had greeted her rapturously, showing her how he and a couple of the other bigger boys were helping Job dig the pasture at the back of the Home for vegetables, and he even spoke kindly of Miss Rowbottom, saying she was 'decent enough' to them. All the children had gained weight in the two weeks they'd been there, their faces had lost the gauntness, they had learned to smile and to play.

Miss Rowbottom was winning with them. Though harsh, she wasn't cruel, and she had got all the children into a regular routine in which all of them had to help with the household chores, and the afternoons were set aside for schooling. She admitted that she relied on Sidney a great deal, as the smaller ones looked up to him and followed his lead. Through him they had all accepted her standards of hygiene and none of them seemed inclined to want to run away. But her biggest worry was provisions, the children were all eating heartily now, and supplies were running low. Job's suggestion that they should keep a cow, a few pigs and chickens and grow their own vegetables was a good one, for the children could help with this while learning about farming, and if successful it could eventually make the Home almost self-sufficient. But in the meantime money was needed not just for food, but to implement the Home farm with buying animals, materials to build pens and winter foodstuff.

Giles had promised Miss Rowbottom that this money would be raised by the church, and volunteers brought over to build pens and put up fences, but his main concern was collecting up more children before winter set in. Although Matilda was in total agreement that this was a priority, Flynn's words about the people of Five Points troubled her, and she sensed that the next foray into the slums wasn't going to be as easy as the first. But without telling Giles about Flynn, she couldn't tell him what she feared, and her anxiety increased as he made plans with Dr Kupicha for a second run.

Meanwhile, at home, Lily had been very cool with Matilda. On the evening when they got back from New Jersey she had barely spoken, and on Sunday afternoon when Matilda suggested she took Tabitha out for a walk, for the first time ever Lily asked her suspiciously where she was intending to go, and curtly reminded her to be back within an hour.

From Monday through to Thursday, Matilda was on tenterhooks. Would Giles suddenly choose Friday as the day to go to Five Points, and so cancel her usual afternoon off, and if so how could she let Flynn know she couldn't meet him?

On Thursday morning a letter came from Dolly telling Matilda that her father was recovering from being attacked by two ruffians late one night, and that they'd just got word Luke was in prison for burglary and was almost certain to be transported to Australia. The only really happy note in the letter was that James, Matilda's older brother, had come back to England and had been to visit them. Dolly insisted that she mustn't worry about her father, and that though he might not regain enough strength in his arms to row his boat for a living, he was talking about buying a couple of rowing boats to hire out during the summer.

The letter was dated four months earlier, back in June, so by now her father might have fully recovered, Luke been tried and convicted and sent off to Australia, while James was probably aboard another ship to heaven knows where. Yet the news was very upsetting, and for the first time since saying goodbye to her father and Dolly after their wedding, she gave way to tears.

She had taken her father's advice to 'never look back', but that didn't stop her missing him and thinking about him and Dolly a great deal. Mail took such a long time to come from England, and that always emphasized how far away they were. She wished it wasn't so, she would so much like to ask Dolly's advice about Flynn, to know she could run to them if things went wrong here. She felt so very alone.

Tabitha was her consolation, and on Thursday afternoon when Lily went out to tea with a friend and Giles was off on his business somewhere, they were left alone. It was very cold so they stayed in the kitchen making jam tarts together.

'Tell me about when you were a flower-girl' Tabitha said much later in the afternoon, when the baking was finished, the lamps trimmed and lit and they sat together by the stove in an easy chair.

Her fourth birthday was just a week away, yet she seemed much older, for she was a composed and thoughtful little girl. Matilda had taken to plaiting her hair now it had grown so long, and she wound it round the child's head like a little crown. Although she couldn't be described as pretty, her large dark eyes and the sweetness of her nature endeared her to everyone she met. She never stopped asking questions, and she never forgot anything she was told. It was around a month ago that she'd overheard Matilda speaking about selling flowers, and clearly she'd been waiting for an opportunity to question her further.

'I used to get up very early in the morning and go to the market to buy some,' Matilda explained. 'Then I'd make them up into little posies and go off to sell them to people.'

'That's a nice job,' Tabitha said. 'Could I do that when I'm grown up? I like flowers.'

'It wasn't very nice when it was cold and wet.' Matilda laughed. 'Besides, you'll be able to do something very much better than that because you are clever.'

'But so are you.' Tabitha looked up into Matilda's face and frowned. 'You can do sums, cook things, and you know about everything, just like Papa does. So why did you sell flowers then?'

The child's belief in her was touching, and Matilda's eyes prickled with tears. 'I was very poor, and it's hard to get a good job when you don't have nice clothes. When you are five you'll go to a real school, and you'll learn all sorts of things I don't know. But you won't have to worry about having a job, you'll marry a rich, handsome gentleman, and he'll look after you.'

'I don't want anyone to look after me. I'll be a doctor and make sick people well again.'

Matilda smiled. Dr Kupicha had come for supper earlier in the week and she guessed this was prompted by his visit and because he had shown Tabitha how his stethoscope worked.

'That's a really good thing to want to be, but ladies can't become doctors.'

'Why not? Ladies are kinder, they'd be better at it.'

Matilda thought she had a point. 'Well, men kind of run things,' she said, thinking of men like the Reverend Kirkbright who considered all women were mindless. 'But you're a lucky girl because you have a papa who believes women are just as good as men. I'm sure once you're grown up he'll let you do whatever you want to.'

'Then I shall be a doctor,' Tabitha said with utter conviction.

It was only a few minutes later when her father came in. His face was red-raw from the cold wind and he had an excited glint in his eye. Matilda took his hat and coat and hung them up and added more coal to the parlour fire so he could warm himself in front of it.

'I'll make you some tea,' she said. 'Would you like a couple of Tabby's jam tarts too?'

Tabitha was still in the kitchen, and when he moved in that direction, Matilda assumed he was going to speak to her. But instead he shut the door to the kitchen and turned back to Matilda.

'We're going in tomorrow,' he said. 'We've located ten children, all between three and six, and a baby who's been left with another very young mother. It's this young woman who has helped us, for she's living in the same cellar with them all.'

'Tomorrow!' Matilda's heart plummeted. 'But it's my afternoon off.'

'You can have Sunday off instead,' he said without even looking at her, and went over to the fire to warm his hands. 'We'll get them to Dr Kupicha's by ten or eleven in the morning, on Saturday we'll get them over to New Jersey. I think this time you ought to stay the night with the children because of the young baby. She'll need to be bottle-fed. I'll tell Mrs Milson I left you out at the Home and I'm going out the next day to check everything is all right.'

Matilda suddenly felt angry with him. He was as excited as a schoolboy, and he hadn't for one moment considered that his wife was still cross with her, and this might make her even crosser, or that she might have arranged to do something on her day off. Sunday was an awful day to have off, unless you had family to visit, everything was shut!

Closing her eyes for a moment, she imagined Flynn. She could see his dark blue eyes, picture his thin shoulders hunched up from the cold as he waited. When she didn't turn up he would think she'd had second thoughts about him.

Yet vivid as that image was, and however painful it was to think she might never see him again, the image of a young baby in a cold, damp cellar was stronger.

'Are you all right?' Giles asked. He moved over to her and took her hands. 'Don't you want to come?'

All at once Matilda felt ashamed of herself. Giles was excited, but only because he was burning with desire to help these children. Why would he think of her needs? He didn't even consider his own, only the health and comfort of those children.

'I'm fine, just a bit shocked that you've got it arranged so quickly,' she said, forcing herself to smile. 'Of course I want to come.'

Chapter Eight

Giles and Matilda stopped to look up at the house in Cat Alley before going in. It had been half gutted by a fire during the summer and the upper floors and roof were gone, leaving only the corner brickwork and the chimney stack to show it had once been a three-storey house. But in Five Points that didn't make it uninhabitable; a crude, tent-like structure had been erected over the remaining floor beams with an assortment of old doors and planks. Those upper-floor tenants who hadn't perished in the fire had merely moved in with those on the ground floor.

It was a bitterly cold day, and as they picked their way gingerly over rotten floorboards down the narrow hallway, the wind was coming from all directions through gaping holes in the walls. The residents appeared to still be sleeping, as apart from loud snoring the only other sound was a baby's weak cry coming from the cellar.

'Down here,' Giles said, stopping at the top of the cellar steps to light his lantern. 'I'll warn you now, Matty, it's even worse than the other cellar. That's the only reason no adults have taken it over.'

All at once Matilda realized that Giles didn't tell her everything he did. To know his way round Five Points so well, he had to have been coming here alone on a daily basis, gaining information. She was astounded at his courage – a clerical collar might protect him in some places, but not here, if anything it was likely to single him out as a target. She had always thought him to be a very special kind of man, admired his compassion, dedication and easy-going nature, but until now she hadn't realized he was brave too.

Giles went first, very cautiously, as some of the treads were missing. Matilda picked up her skirt to follow, but she had to breathe through her mouth because the smell was so vile.

'Cissie!' Giles called out once he was down to the bottom. 'It's me, Reverend Milson, with my friend Matty.'

As Matilda reached the bottom she gasped, in spite of telling herself she couldn't be shocked after seeing Rat's Castle, for the floor in front of her was seething with rats, devouring something which could only be a dead animal, or even an infant. The rats barely even turned to look at the lantern, much less scuttle away – clearly the food source was an unusually good one.

Water ran down the walls, it ran in streams round the mounds of debris on the ground and it was icy cold. Tearing her eyes away from the rats, Matilda saw the glint of small pale faces, huddled around a bigger girl at the back of the cellar. Their arms and legs were all entwined like plant roots, and like the rats, most of them didn't even stir at the light. The girl was holding the crying baby to her shoulder, and another was at her breast feeding.

When Matilda saw this girl was even younger than herself, her eyes pricked with tears.

'You've come then,' the girl said in a flat voice. 'I wouldn't have given her me milk if I'd been certain.'

'Which baby is yours then?' Matilda asked.

'This one.' She inclined her head to the one crying on her shoulder. 'Just hope there's enough left for him an' all.'

Matilda was even more moved to think the girl was feeding an orphan child at the expense of her own. 'What are their names?' she asked.

'Pearl and Peter,' she said. 'Pearl's ma was me friend. I always used to say she were a real pearl 'cos she shared everything she got with me. So I called her little 'un that when she died having her. You look after her proper for me, won't yer? I'd keep her meself if I could, but it's hard enough to keep body and soul together with one.'

Matilda had never heard anything so touching. Although it was too dark in there to see the girl clearly, she could make out that both babies were swaddled in blankets, and judging by the lusty sucking from the baby at the girl's breast, and the angry cries of the other, they were both strong enough to survive if help was given now before winter set in. She turned to her master and caught hold of his arm. 'Can't we take Cissie and her baby too?' she whispered imploringly. 'She could help in the Home and feed both of them.'

'We can't take her,' he whispered back. 'The governors of the Home stipulated no one over ten, but we could take the infant if she agrees.'

Matilda moved a couple of steps nearer. 'We could take your baby too, that's if you want us to,' she said gently.

'Take my babby?' Cissie replied, her voice rising with indignation. 'D'you think I'm so low I'd give me son away for the asking? He's mine, and even if I ain't got nothing, I loves him. Now, clear off out of here. I might'a known I couldn't trust a bloody priest, he said he was only taking orphans.'

The light from the lantern quivered, indicating Giles was severely shaken by this verbal onslaught.

'You *can* trust Reverend Milson. He wouldn't separate a baby from its mother unless she was ready to give it up,' Matilda said soothingly, wishing she had the courage to push on through the rats to get closer to the girl. 'We only suggested taking Peter because we thought it would help you.'

'That's right, Cissie,' Giles spoke up. 'We only came for orphans, so if you'll just give us Pearl and wake the other children up, then we'll be off with them.'

Matilda looked down at the squirming rats and shuddered. 'How long will it be before they get her baby if we leave her here?' she muttered to her master.

When he didn't reply she caught hold of his arm. 'Look, sir, I know we don't know anything about her,' she whispered. 'But she's got a big heart or she wouldn't be feeding the other baby. Please, sir! Don't leave her here. Give her and her baby a chance in life too.'

He looked round at Matilda and his face was contorted with anguish, proving he was as moved by the girl's plight as she was. 'Please,' she repeated. 'You can blame me if the governors say anything.'

'How could I blame you for something which is obviously so right?' he replied, then, moving forwards and skirting around the rats, he spoke again to Cissie. 'Would you like to come with us too? I can't promise a permanent home for you and Peter, I'm afraid, but maybe we can keep you for a few weeks. If you'd agree to feed Pearl along with your son, and help at the Home, then perhaps I can find a position for you later.'

Matilda watched the girl's expression. She was frowning, clearly afraid this new offer might be a trick to take her baby.

'Come with us, Cissie. I give you my word of honour no one will try to take Peter from you,' she said. She glanced at the other children now waking at the sound of voices, and saw the way they all instinctively reached out to touch Cissie. 'I'm sure all these others will be much happier with you there too.'

Cissie looked at the children's hands on her, then her eyes went back to Matilda. 'You mean it?' she said incredulously. 'You'd take me and Peter to the same place as them?'

'Yes, of course,' Giles reassured her, though his voice was cracking with uncertainty. 'But first we go to a doctor's house so he can check you all out, let you have a bath, food and clean clothes.'

Her smile was like a sunray lighting up the cellar. She took her baby from her breast, pulled her tattered dress over and fastened it, then, holding a baby on each shoulder, she stood up.

'Come on, you lot,' she said, nudging the pile of children around her. 'We got a home to go to.'

It was not until after nine that same evening that Matilda got to hear Cissie's story. They had gone through the same routine with this bunch of children as the previous one, fed them, bathed them, shaved their heads and dressed them in warm clothes. Both babies were very small, Peter five weeks, Pearl three, but the doctor had pronounced them healthy enough and Cissie capable of continuing to feed them both as long as she took care to eat and drink enough herself.

Her bathing and head shaving were left to last, with Matilda reluctantly supervising. It was easy enough to wash a child, but while she scrubbed away to give a mild lecture on the reasons why cleanliness was so important, although Cissie's thin body was even filthier than the children's, still daubed with dried blood from the recent birth, her engorged breasts were a reminder that young as she was, she was a mother and therefore had a right to be treated as an adult. It was also a poignant reminder of the day Matilda was bathed by Aggie, and she felt deeply for the girl that she should be forced to have her dark hair shaved as the final humiliation.

'It don't matter to me, as long as you give me something to hide me head,' Cissie replied with a disinterested shrug as Matilda tried to voice her sympathy. 'I sure as hell ain't going looking for any men in a while.'

Yet she sneered at herself in the plain dark brown serge dress and made a comment that she wouldn't catch anyone's eye in that. But once she'd put on a mob-cap she seemed cheered, and admitted it felt good to be clean and warm. Matilda thought she might even be a pretty girl once she'd put on some weight and her hair had grown again, for she had wide, green eyes and when she gave one of her rare smiles, they were the dazzling kind.

After Giles had gone home, and the children all been put to bed, Matilda and Cissie went into the kitchen where the two babies were sleeping peacefully, tucked one at each end of a drawer. Matilda had decided to sleep in the armchair, for she was concerned the children might wake during the night and be scared. Cissie gleefully pulled up the straw-filled mattress to the stove and settled down.

'Tell me about yourself, Cissie,' Matilda asked her. So far all she knew was what Cissie had told the doctor, that she thought she was fifteen but didn't know her birth date, she'd been living on the streets since she was about eight, when her mother disappeared. She couldn't tell them if she was born in America, or even what nationality her mother was, but there was a faint Irish inflection to her voice.

'I told you's everything,' the girl replied.

'No, you didn't,' Matilda argued. 'You haven't said who the father of your baby is, or anything about how you feel. Tell me that.'

'I dunno who the father is, I went with a lot of men,' she said in a sullen tone. 'How d'you think I'd feed meself otherwise?'

Matilda blanched. She wondered if she really wanted to know any more. 'Where were you when you had Peter?' she asked. 'Was anyone with you?'

'In that same place you came to,' she said. 'Meg, Pearl's ma, was with me.'

'Were you scared?'

'It were terrible. I thought I was gonna die,' she admitted. 'I didn't care much come the end. But one of the old biddies from upstairs come down and helped. She asked me if I wanted her to get one of the men to throw my babby in the river.'

Matilda gulped.

'They do that all the time round there,' Cissie said quite calmly. 'But I wasn't having none of that because Meg and me was gonna help one another. I loved her, see, we'd been together since we was little 'uns.'

'But you couldn't have brought up your babies in that place, they would both have died the first winter there.'

'We weren't gonna stay there,' she said, giving Matilda a pitying look. 'We used to work the Bowery, see, we had a nice little room an' all. But the landlord threw us out just before I was due, said he didn't want no crying babies there. That's how we ended up in Five Points, there weren't no other place to go and we was too big to please men, know what I mean?'

Matilda nodded.

'Well, we reckoned that if we just had the babbies, then we could take it in turn to mind them while the other worked. Soon as we'd got some money we'd get a place. But we didn't know nothing about birthing, we thought that they just dropped out and you was on your way. It ain't like that.'

Matilda could still remember her own mother's cries when she had her last child, and young as she was it had left an indelible impression on her mind that it was a long, painful process that all too often led to death.

'My mother died in childbirth,' she said, hoping that by sharing her own experiences the girl would open up more. 'I was brought up in a slum too, I was out selling flowers on the street in London when I was ten. If it wasn't for the Reverend, I'd still be there.'

'I thought you was a fine lady,' Cissie said in some surprise.

Matilda laughed softly. 'I wish I was! But go on, you had Peter and then Meg had Pearl, did anyone help her?'

'The same old biddy again. But she was drunk and Meg got weaker and weaker and kept bleeding something awful. The rats came all round when they smelt the blood and I was so scared. I ran out to try and get help, but it was late at night and there weren't anyone sober. I was scared to leave Meg any longer 'cos of the rats and Peter was with her too. When I got back little

Pearl was there, the old biddy had cut the cord and that, but Meg was dying.'

Cissie broke down then, crying her heart out, and Matilda went over to her to comfort her, sensing this was the first time Cissie had allowed herself to grieve.

'I wrapped up the babbies and took them with me to get help again,' she said, tears running down her cheeks. 'I found a policeman in the end, and he came back with me. But it was too late. Meg were dead, and the rats all over her.'

Matilda suddenly got a picture of those rats again and shuddered. She wanted to know who took Meg's corpse away and a great deal more, but Cissie's body was racking with sobs, so she just held her and waited until she grew calmer.

'I told meself I'd never go in that cellar again,' Cissie said at length, drying her eyes on the blanket. 'The police let me stay in their barracks for a coupla nights, but when they turned me out I couldn't get in anywhere and I was scared they'd stick me in The Tombs and take the babbies from me. So when it turned cold and wet that cellar was the only place to go.

'It were those little kids who kept me going,' she went on, thumbing at the room next door. 'They used to bring me things to eat, and cuddle up to me like I was their ma too. That's why when I heard about the Reverend taking that other lot of kids away somewhere good, I made up my mind to find him and get him to take those, and little Pearl too. I never thought he'd take me an' all.'

She pulled back from Matilda, looking right into her eyes. 'But then it was you what made him take me. I owe you for that, miss.'

'You don't owe me anything, my reward is to see you and the babies safe and well,' Matilda rebuked her. 'But if you do feel you owe me something, pay me back by behaving yourself out in New Jersey, no men, no drinking or anything like that, and make yourself useful. I reckon that if you do that, you'll probably get to stay there.'

She laid out what it was like at the Home, about Miss Rowbottom, the two girls and Job that helped her. 'It's a really good place,' she finished up. 'And maybe your life is about to change for the better, just like mine did.'

Cissie took her hand and lifted it to her lips. 'You might say you ain't a lady, but you're a real one to me.' Her green eyes were full of tears. 'Don't you worry none about me. I won't let you down and I won't ever forget you helped me.'

It was only after Cissie had fallen asleep on her mattress and Matilda had turned out the lamp that she gave way to thinking about Flynn. She'd successfully blocked him out of her mind all day, told herself that rescuing waifs was a far better thing to be doing than meeting a young man, yet now, all alone, she could not derive any comfort from that. If it was fate that she couldn't be his sweetheart, why then had she been allowed to fall for him? For she knew she had, her mind, soul and body ached for him.

On Sunday morning Matilda woke very early. It was still dark and she could hear fog horns sounding out in the bay. After church this morning she would have the rest of the day off, but that wasn't a pleasing prospect, she had no idea how she could pass the time all on her own and she knew she'd never get her mind off Flynn. But at least Lily seemed to have forgiven her at last. When she and Giles came in the previous evening Lily had been very solicitous about them being cold and tired. She showed far more interest in the Home too. She thought it might be a good idea to organize a sewing bee to make clothes for the children.

Touched by Lily's enthusiasm, and aware Mrs Kirkbright might very well tell her that they had taken a young woman there too, Giles told her about Cissie and the two babies. As he omitted the cellar and Cissie's previous profession, and leaned more on her kindness in trying to care for her dead friend's baby, along with her own, Lily clearly imagined she was a wronged servant girl who had been turned out by her mistress, and she praised Giles for being so kindly.

Matilda found it almost laughable that her mistress could feel some compassion for an unmarried mother because she imagined her clean and decently dressed, nursing two plump healthy babies, yet if she'd passed by Cissie in her rags begging on the streets she would have rushed past, averting her eyes. But it was good to be able to talk about the Home now without guarding every single word.

As it turned out, rescuing Cissie had been a very good move

for everyone. The children weren't frightened to get on the ferry to New Jersey because she was with them, and only one was sick. Miss Rowbottom was none too pleased at first to have a mother and two babies on her hands, but within a couple of hours she had come round when she saw that the children would do anything Cissie asked. By the time Matilda and Giles left, the new children had mingled so well with the old that apart from the difference between the shaved heads and the ones with an inch of stubble, it was hard to tell them apart.

Matilda lay there wondering how an abandoned child like Cissie could turn into such a loving mother. Giles gave God credit for it, but Matilda thought that was poppycock. From her viewpoint God was an uncaring fellow. He sent disaster to the believers and non-believers equally. He allowed men to grow rich on the sufferings of others, and the evil to prey on the good. He'd even robbed her of the opportunity to see Flynn ever again.

She was laying the table for breakfast just before eight, when she heard the ice man coming up the street. He came at the same time every morning, the wheels of his cart and the slow plodding of his horse over the cobbles distinct from any other merchant's.

By the time she'd got the large bowl from the scullery, he was knocking on the door. She opened it, and to her utmost surprise Flynn was standing there, holding the block of ice in a piece of sacking in his hands.

'Flynn!' she gasped. Her mind switched back to her embittered thoughts earlier today. 'What are you doing here?'

'Looking for you, what else?' he said with a smile. 'I won't go away until you tell me why you didn't meet me on Friday.'

She looked nervously back across the parlour towards the kitchen. Giles or Tabitha could come down any minute. 'The Reverend got me to go back to Five Points with him,' she whispered. 'I couldn't let you know because I didn't know where you lived.'

His smile was as wide as New York Bay. 'That was worth me giving the ice man ten cents to bring this to your door,' he said. 'But just tell me, were you worried you might not see me again?'

'Worried! I was beside myself,' she admitted, then, realizing girls shouldn't be so forward, she slapped her hand over her mouth.

He laughed softly. 'Then you'll meet me this Friday?'

'I could meet you today,' she said, unable to control her delight. 'After church I've got the whole day off.'

His smile was even broader then. 'I'll wait for you along by Castle Clinton. 'But if anything happens another time it's the Black Bull I work at,' he said, putting the ice into her bowl. 'It's not a rough dive, not compared with some up there, but if you daren't come, give a note to an urchin and tell him I'll give him ten cents when he delivers it.'

She could hear her master's step on the stairs. 'I must go,' she said, looking round fearfully.

He caught her two arms and pulled her close to kiss her. The bowl of ice was between them, but even so the brief touch of his warm lips on hers sent her head reeling.

'I'll be there from twelve onwards,' he said as he turned to go down the steps.

Matilda had to close the door hurriedly for fear of Giles seeing him. But as she walked back into the kitchen with the ice she silently apologized to God for having such little faith in His powers.

'A penny for your thoughts,' Giles said to Matilda when he came down the stairs early one morning in February to find her gazing out of the window at the snow-filled street.

'I was just remembering taking Tabitha tobogganing on Primrose Hill last year,' she said. 'Snow was beautiful in England, wasn't it? It's so ugly here.'

'Only this end of New York,' he said, putting a hand on her shoulder and looking out with her. Despite the early hour, dozens of carts had churned up the snow and made it dirty, and though it was still like a thick white blanket on the roof-tops, from down here in the parlour Matilda couldn't see that. 'Further up in Harlem it will be as lovely as in England, and I expect it's a picture out in New Jersey. I don't doubt the children are pestering Miss Rowbottom right now to let them go out in it.'

'When can I go to see them again?' she asked wistfully. She had been only twice since the day they took Cissie, once more with seven new children, then at Christmas for a visit. There was no room for any more children now, but the Reverend Kirkbright was looking to find good people in Pennsylvania and

Connecticut to adopt some of them, to make room for more needy cases.

'When the weather gets better,' he said. 'Sidney and Cissie ask after you every time I visit.'

'Are they really happy?' she asked. Giles had been out there the previous day, checking that the provisions sent had reached them. Over supper last night Giles had talked in general about all the children. But in front of Lily they couldn't really discuss individuals, for fear of letting things slip which would alarm her.

'Yes, they are happy,' Giles smiled. 'Sidney is blossoming into a fine, strong lad, and if I had to pick just one child as an example of how successful our rescue plan has been, it would be him. Miss Rowbottom tells me he's grown three inches since he arrived and he's put on around eighteen pounds. He'll work until he drops alongside Job on the Home farm, and he's an inspiration to the younger children. That lad will go far, he's kind-hearted, canny, and good with his hands. If he doesn't care much for book learning, that doesn't matter.'

'And Cissie?' she asked.

'She's a very impudent girl.' He smiled ruefully. 'But Miss Rowbottom praises her more than she despairs. She's an excellent mother and Pearl and Peter are flourishing. In fact all the children treat her like she's their mother, and that leaves Miss Rowbottom free to do the tasks she's better qualified to do, like teaching and housekeeping.'

He paused.

'There's a "but", isn't there,' Matilda asked anxiously.

'Yes,' he sighed ruefully. 'I sensed signs of rebellion yesterday, Cissie doesn't like taking orders and I think she feels a bit cut off from life and men out there. I think when the babies get bigger and the weather improves, we might find her wanting to leave.'

'But how would she manage with Peter?' Matilda asked.

'That's the real problem,' he sighed deeply as if he'd already spent a great deal of time thinking about it. 'If she comes back to the city she'll be bound to turn back to prostitution. It's the only way she could earn enough money to keep her boy.'

Although Matilda was a little surprised by her master's bluntness, it pleased her to find he had finally grasped the real reason why so many women turned to selling their bodies. Almost everyone of his class believed that such women were low creatures with no morals, but then as Flynn had once pointed out, they had no comprehension of the economics of real poverty.

'Respectable' employment for an unskilled woman meant a sixty-hour week for often less than a dollar a day. It also meant her children must be left alone, often hungry, cold and in danger. Matilda was pretty certain that even she could be tempted into prostitution, however distasteful that idea was, if it meant her children could be warmly clothed, well fed and she had enough money to call a doctor if one of them was sick, all without being away from them for too long.

'There are farmers out in the country desperate for wives,' she said, repeating something Flynn had told her. 'They advertise in the newspaper all the time. Perhaps I could suggest that to Cissie?'

'Have you been reading those and looking for someone?' He laughed and tweaked her cheek with affection. 'You don't have to go to those lengths, Matty, you'd only have to flutter your eyelashes at someone here and they'd come running to be your sweetheart.'

Matilda blushed. Since she had started helping him with the orphaned children, she had gradually become Giles's confidante. It was to her he poured out his dismay at the mainly uncaring society they lived in, with its cruelty, bigotry and snobbishness. He used her as a sounding board when planning a talk to raise money for the Home, he told her of his dreams to see decent, cheap housing built for the working classes, equal rights for women, and slavery abolished. In turn Matilda shared with him her first-hand knowledge of what it was to be poor and disadvantaged. She had opened his middle-class eyes to exactly why the slums were nurseries for criminals, and indeed why so many slum people could never be lured into churches, or their children into schools.

Yet in all this time she was still unable to tell him about Flynn. She didn't understand why this was so. Maybe Giles wouldn't approve that he worked in a saloon, but he kept an open mind about people until he'd met them, and she was sure his only real concern would be that Flynn was an honourable man and capable of taking care of her.

Matilda believed Flynn was, but perhaps that was because she was overwhelmed by the depths of her feelings for him. Merely to say she loved him didn't accurately describe how she felt. It was a passion which roared inside her, demanding more each time they met. More kisses, more touching, more time together, and sometimes that desire grew so strong that she could barely hold back. Sometimes she even blamed Lily and Giles for the way she felt, believing that if she didn't need to hide Flynn away, it wouldn't all feel so desperate.

'There would be no point in me finding a sweetheart,' she retorted. She was just about to add that whatever he was like, Lily would find some fault in him, but she stopped herself just in time. 'I'd never have any time to spend with him,' she said instead, then walked back into the kitchen to cook the breakfast.

Giles stood at the window for a moment or two, puzzling on the sharpness of that last remark. Was it a complaint that she had so little free time? Or something more?

He doubted that Matilda really thought herself ill used, it wasn't in her nature, but added to other things he'd observed in the past few months, he wondered if there was someone she was keeping secret. She always looked flushed when she came in after her afternoon off, and somehow he didn't think looking at the shops, or even meeting up with other maids for tea and gossip, would create such animation. Occasionally she came out with astute social comments about America too, that couldn't have come just from observation or newspapers. But he had never questioned her. Giles believed she was entitled to a private life, and he expected that when she was good and ready, she'd tell him about it.

As Matilda whisked up eggs for breakfast, she was close to tears. She had been seeing Flynn for almost five months now, and though she lived for those precious few hours with him each Friday, sometimes she felt so frustrated she almost wished she'd never met him and churned up all these feelings inside her. It was too cold to go walking, and so the only place they could go was tea rooms. Yet it wasn't enough just to talk and hold hands any longer, they were both desperate to be alone together somewhere they could kiss and hold each other.

All the talking they did just made the differences in their working lives so much more obvious, and the problems insurmountable. Often, lying wide awake in bed, reliving Flynn's passionate kisses, she'd imagine him being in the saloon, pouring out jugs of ale, laughing and joking with his customers. He would still be pouring drinks when she was fast asleep. Then while she was up, cleaning out the grate in the parlour, laying the table for breakfast, and washing and dressing Tabitha, he was still in bed. Even his religion was different to hers, for she knew now he was a Catholic. If he had been able to come to Trinity Church on Sunday, maybe Lily would overlook that he worked in a saloon and let him take her out on Sunday afternoons. But Flynn took his religion seriously, he was proud of being a Catholic, and although one church was the same as another to her, Flynn didn't see it that way.

But then Flynn didn't look at anything in the way others did. He laughed at the middle classes and said they were hypocrites. He thought the poor lacked imagination and daring, and he despised those who had inherited wealth. He took the view that he was entirely unique, a free spirit who could never be shackled to a job he hated, or even to one place.

While Matilda found this attitude to be part of his charm, it also worried her, for when she married she wanted stability and peace of mind. But Flynn would laugh at her when she ventured this opinion. He said life should be an adventure, and that she must trust in his abilities. He said that by the spring he'd have enough money saved to catch a boat to Charleston. As soon as he'd found a job, he'd send for her and they'd be married.

While Matilda was with him, she was always swept away by his belief in himself. She saw herself stepping off the boat, getting married and going to live in a pretty white wooden house, with a porch to sit out on in the evenings, a garden for her to grow fruit and vegetables, a horse for Flynn in the stable.

Yet as soon as she got home, doubts would creep in. Supposing it didn't turn out like that? If Flynn couldn't get the kind of job he wanted, and the riches he expected never materialized? Home might be a tumbledown shack. She might end up having a baby every year like so many other women did, and not enough money coming in to feed them. Flynn might just get so embittered that he'd turn to drinking.

If she had nothing now, then it wouldn't seem such a gamble, but she'd grown used to a warm, comfortable house, good food and security. She told herself daily that she couldn't stay with the Milsons for ever, and that she wanted a life that was all her own. But what of Tabitha? It wouldn't be easy to leave a child she loved so much, and she didn't think Flynn had really grasped how much Giles and Lily meant to her either.

It seemed to Matilda that some of these worries could be eased by just spending more time with Flynn. She had only seen one side of him, a handsome, passionate man who made her laugh, told her stories, and charmed her so she didn't look for faults. But alone in her room at night, she saw how little she really knew about him. His tales about his past were vague, there was no collaboration from a friend or family member. For all she knew he could have run from Ireland or England because he'd been in trouble there. If she could see him working, mixing with other people, or just be out having fun with him, then maybe her doubts would be swept away for ever. But only some sort of miracle would give her that chance.

The miracle came in April just after Easter. Matilda woke one Monday morning to find the sun shining and a definite touch of spring in the air. When she went out into the yard to the privy she noticed green buds on the honeysuckle growing over the walls, and heard birdsong rather than just the customary squawk of seagulls.

She made pancakes for breakfast, and both Giles and Lily seemed to be in an unusually happy mood, teasing Tabitha about how much she ate these days, telling her that if she continued to grow so fast they'd have no clothes to fit her. She thought they must all be affected by spring fever.

Matilda was just about to get up from the table to clear away when Giles said he and his wife had something to tell her.

'We're going to Boston for a holiday,' he said. 'We want you to look after the house for us while we're away, and have a bit of a rest yourself.'

They were going to stay with an old lawyer friend of Giles's from Bath, and they were both clearly very excited at the prospect of seeing a new American city and spending time with people from home.

Matilda hadn't seen Lily so pleased about anything in a long time. The long, bitterly cold winter had worn her down, she'd lost her appetite, she looked pale and drawn, and she had been complaining repeatedly of headaches.

'The Uptons have three children, so Tabitha will have some company too,' she said, her voice suddenly as bright as her eyes. 'I shall have to hurry and get that dress I've been making finished, Matty, we're going on Friday morning.'

It was only then that Matilda realized what this would mean to her. She could see Flynn every afternoon, maybe he'd even get some evenings off too. It was the opportunity she'd been waiting for.

Memories of preparing to come to America came back thick and fast that week as Matilda helped Lily pack. Just like then, she wanted to take far too much, and got herself overwrought worrying about incidentals. Would Tabitha need galoshes, and what ought she to take as a present for her hosts? Would it be warm enough for lighter clothes, would she need her parasol?

They were going on a steam-packet up the coast, but it was interesting to note that Lily didn't appear to be concerned she might suffer from seasickness again, only that her clothes might be too drab for fashionable Boston.

Finally Friday morning arrived, and as Matilda helped them into the cab, she found it hard to restrain herself from showing her joy at their departure.

Going back into the house, she picked up the long list of reminders Lily had left on the kitchen table and laughed aloud. As if she'd forget to lock the door when she went out, or wouldn't remember to turn off the lamps before going to bed!

'They've gone away?' Flynn gasped when Matilda told him her news a few hours later when she met him in the usual place. 'For how long?'

'Ten days in all,' she said, bubbling with excitement. 'The steam-packet gets back at South Pier around six in the evening of the twenty-ninth of April. Oh Flynn, we can have so much time together.'

'You mean they didn't leave you anything to do?' he asked. He always implied the Milsons were slave-drivers.

'No, not really,' she said. 'Of course I'd better do a bit of a spring-clean, otherwise they'll be asking what I did with myself. But Sir said I was to have a holiday too.'

The sun was so warm they sat on Castle Green and talked about all the things they could do. 'I expect I can get a night off tomorrow,' he said. 'I'll take you dancing. Then on Sunday I'll go to early Mass and then we can go to Greenwich Village.'

'We could take a picnic,' she said. 'I'll bake a pie or something tonight.'

'There's so much I want to show you,' he said, his dark blue eyes glinting with excitement. 'We could go over to Staten Island, it's real pretty there, and if the weather stays fine we could take a ferry out to Coney Island where the quality folk go for their holidays.'

That afternoon was the best time they'd ever had together, the only people about were couples much like them, and nursemaids taking their charges out for a walk in the sun. On a seat with a dense hollybush behind them, they could hold hands, steal kisses when no one was looking, and talk without the fear of anyone overhearing them.

'Do you think they've asked anyone to keep an eye on you?' Flynn said a bit later.

She knew exactly what he meant, a spy to see if anyone came in or out of the house. 'I don't think Sir would do that,' she said after a little thought. 'He isn't a sneak by nature.'

'Does that mean I could come in?'

Matilda had anticipated that question, thought about her answer long and hard in the preceding days. She longed to be alone with him, she wanted him in the house with her, but she was scared too that things might get out of hand and they'd end up making love. 'I'm not sure, Flynn,' she said.

He laughed, put his arms round her and kissed her all over her face. 'You think I'll have my wicked way with you?' he said, his eyes dancing. 'To be sure, you ought to know me better than that, Matty. Haven't I always been such a gentleman?'

Matty laughingly agreed he had. 'But then we've never had the chance to be alone before.'

'I could have found somewhere if that's what I wanted from you,' he said, suddenly serious. 'I want to marry you, Matty. And until that ring is safely on your finger and the priest tells me we are man and wife, then I'll hold back my desire.'

'Oh Flynn,' she sighed, holding him tight. 'You make it all sound so wonderful.'

Flynn was in fact a little frightened of such an opportunity to be alone with Matilda, even though he'd thought of little else since he met her. He'd seduced and left several girls in the past, never concerning himself with what happened to them afterwards. But Matty was special, she was the girl he intended to marry and he didn't want anything spoiling the plans he had made for their future.

Night after night he met men and women who'd ruined their chances in life. When they got drunk out came the hard luck stories, babies that came too quickly, no decent place to live, and wages spoken for before they were even earned.

Flynn had no intention of letting that happen to him. When he first met Matty he hadn't got more than a couple of dollars to his name. He was intending to sign up with the crew of a steamer going south, and take his chances when he got there. The tale he'd told her on their first meeting about getting fine clothes first was just a fantasy, a romantic idea, but once he'd told it to her, it took root.

There was something about Matilda that made him believe in himself as he'd never truly done before. She was so quick and smart, hard-working and patient, yet so loving that it made him see what an asset she'd be to him. She was ladylike, she'd learnt the ways of the upper classes, yet she wouldn't run at the first sign of trouble, or baulk at staying somewhere shabby. With her brains and his charm, they could do anything, go anywhere. She was the perfect girl for him and he loved her far, far more than any other he'd met.

He could have taken her up to his room above the saloon on any afternoon they'd met, but for the first time in his life he managed to control his desire. Matty's mind and spirit were far more valuable to him than sexual satisfaction, which he could find anywhere. So he was content to sit in a steamy tea room holding her hand, looking into her beautiful eyes, and talking to her. He also knew that if she saw the way he lived she'd back away.

Five other men slept in there at night, it stank of their sweat and feet, and sometimes they vomited on the floor when they were drunk. But they each gave him a dollar a week to sleep there. He needed that money to secure a future in Charleston.

So he had to be extra cautious now. He had enough money

saved to leave, and though he wanted to make love to her more than life itself, when he sent for her to join him he didn't want her turning up with a child already in her belly. That would dash everything.

He wanted her there fresh and eager, complete with her savings, looking like a lady. That way their future would be assured.

'It will be wonderful. You just wait,' he said, getting up off the bench and pulling her to her feet too. He looked down into her sparkling eyes and knew this was a heaven-sent chance to sweep the last of her doubts away. 'But if I want tomorrow night off, I'll have to work all day. So I'll come and pick you up about seven to go dancing.'

'What should I wear?' she asked, remembering how out of place she'd looked at the church dance.

'You'll outshine any other girl whatever you wear,' he said kissing her again. 'But you looked a treat in that pink dress you had on the night we first met.'

Harry Hall's dance hall on Broadway was packed to capacity, so hot and steamy, condensation was running down the walls in rivulets. Matilda had never seen anything like it, not even when she'd peeped through the door of the penny gaffs back home. There were two or three hundred people at least, most of them dancing, a wide smile on every face. Anything went here, for the musicians in the four-piece band seemed to sense the mood and play accordingly. There had been sedate waltzes earlier in the evening but now they'd moved through polkas, on to wild Irish jigs.

Every nationality was represented, Italians, Germans, Poles and Russians, but Jews and Irish made up the majority and both were equally light on their feet and competing to out-dance each other. Most of the men had shed their jackets now because of the heat, the stiff collars they'd arrived with were now limp, patches of sweat showed on the backs of waistcoats, and carefully slicked-down hair was sticking up in all directions.

The women were mainly very young, aside from a few older Italian ladies brought in as chaperones, who sat on the sidelines gossiping to each other. The girls' average age was seventeen to twenty and they were dressed diversely in everything from a treasured national costume rich with peasant embroidery to calico and hooped satin gowns. Some girls wore a flower in their hair, others ribbons, the German girls had their hair tightly braided, many of the Irish had loose unruly curls, yet pretty or plain they were all in demand as dancing partners as there were two men for every girl.

Matilda knew that what she was seeing was a cross-section of immigrants, bound together in their status as 'greenhorns' and the will to make something of themselves in their adopted country. There was no apathy here, work and bad living conditions forgotten as soon as they walked through the door. Shiny shoes, boiled shirts, newly washed hair and clean fingernails, all showed that they'd come to enjoy themselves and maybe find romance.

The air was thick with cheap scent, cigars and sweat, but there was hope too, and happiness. Matilda drank it all in, thrilled finally to find herself among people she could identify with. But Flynn gave her little time to watch others, he wanted to dance every dance. Her hair she'd taken so long to pin up into a sophisticated style she'd seen in a magazine began to shed its pins and tumble on to her shoulders, and later when the music grew slower, Flynn ran his fingers through it, looking into her eyes with adoration.

'To be sure you're the greatest beauty here tonight,' he whispered, his lips just touching her hot cheek. 'I feel like one of the kings of Ireland, and you are my queen.'

Under dim lights, with no thick outer garments to act as a shield between them, her body felt as if it was on fire and yearning to be closer still to him. He swayed to the music, his hand on her waist, and she closed her eyes and let her body flow with his.

It was almost one in the morning when they got home to State Street.

'Can I stay here just tonight?' Flynn whispered outside the door. 'I'll sleep anywhere, on the kitchen floor if you like. But we have the whole of tomorrow to spend together and it would be a shame if I went home now and then overslept.'

On the previous night Matilda had felt very scared alone in the house, for she'd never spent one night of her life alone before. It would be comforting to have him there. Faced with such a strong argument against sending him home, what little will she had left vanished.

'Just tonight,' she said. 'But you must sleep in the parlour and no coming upstairs or I'll be cross.'

She lit a lamp, stirred the fire back into life while Flynn walked around looking at everything in the room. He felt the frames of pictures, stroked a velvet cushion and fingered the dainty china.

Matilda watched him, suddenly aware that things which had become commonplace to her were new and awe-inspiring to him. It touched her deeply, reminding her of those first few days in the parsonage at Primrose Hill when she had done just what he was doing now.

'How much of this came with you from England?' he asked, picking up a porcelain shepherdess from the mantelpiece.

'All of it apart from the furniture,' she said. 'Why?'

'I was just thinking how much stuff the rich have,' he said thoughtfully. 'I could put everything I own in one small bag.'

'Me too,' she said. 'But the Milsons aren't rich, Flynn, most of the things you see were their wedding presents from relatives.'

'We won't have much when we get married then,' he said. 'My folks couldn't afford to even send a candle.'

His wistful tone surprised her, he never expressed regret about anything in his past life, and only optimism about the future.

'We'll buy everything we want ourselves,' she said, going up to him and slipping her hands round his waist. 'Maybe we'll get rich enough one day so we don't even look at the prices.'

'When I'm with you I can believe that will happen,' he said, drawing her closer and bending to kiss her. 'But right now I have everything I want right here in my arms.'

He had given her kisses that sent her senses reeling a hundred times or more, but now, alone in a warm and cosy room without the possibility of being seen or interrupted, there was nothing to hold back the passion. One kiss led to another, they moved on to the couch, and then slowly sank down on to the rug in front of the fire.

Matilda had never imagined that love-making could be such bliss, or that she'd be so shameless. As his hand crept up under the skirt of her dress and his fingers probed into her, she found herself arching her back against him for more and pulling his shirt out of his pants so she could run her hands over his back.

His skin felt so smooth and warm, and it thrilled her to hear his sighs of pleasure. He knelt up to remove his shirt entirely, and bare-chested, his black curls glimmering in the firelight, he had never looked more handsome.

'We must take this dress off you before it's spoiled,' he whispered, and sitting behind her, kissing her neck he slowly unhooked it, then pulled it off over her head, leaving her in her underclothes and stays.

Matilda gasped as he undid the ribbon on her chemise, exposed her breasts and fondled them. He had touched her there a hundred times before, but through thick serge the sensation was muted, and as his hands cupped and squeezed her breasts she knew she was in danger of going too far.

'We mustn't,' she gasped, trying to cover herself.

'Oh Matty, I won't go the whole way with you,' he murmured against her breast. 'Just let me love you a little.'

The chemise disappeared, and Flynn unfastened her stays, wincing at the cruel marks it had made on her skin. 'Women shouldn't have to wear such things,' he whispered, kissing and licking at the red marks. 'When we're married you'll never wear them again for your body is the most beautiful shape all on its own.'

Finally she was naked, he'd stripped off every last stitch, even her stockings, and Matilda could hardly believe that she could allow a man, even the one she intended to marry, to do such things to her. He kissed and sucked at her breasts, his fingers probed into her, her whole body was on fire and screaming for more.

She stiffened when he removed his pants, but he kissed her deeply and took her hand and placed it on himself. 'I won't go inside you, I promise,' he said. 'Just hold me and pleasure me too.'

It was something of a shock to find that a man's penis could be so hard and so big, but his moan of pleasure as she held it was a joy to hear, she had never expected that two people could give each other such exquisite pleasure.

'Matty, my angel,' he murmured, pushing his fingers hard inside her, and moving his body against hers. 'Hold me tighter, rub me. It's so good.'

*

He carried her upstairs in his arms later and tucked her into her bed. 'I love you, my darlin',' he whispered, kissing her forehead, then her lips.

She moved over in the narrow bed, expecting him to get in beside her. But he moved back towards the door. 'Aren't you coming in with me?' she asked. There was no candle, only the moonlight coming through the window, and although his naked white body was clear enough, she couldn't see his face.

'I don't trust myself in there with you all night,' he said gruffly. 'We must wait until we're married before I can stay in your bed. I'll sleep downstairs.'

He was gone before she could protest, and she lay there, listening to his bare feet padding down the stairs. It had been so heavenly, yet just a bit disappointing that once his seed came out it all ended. She could feel it still on her thigh, dry now, like flour-and-water paste.

She wished Flynn was holding her now, she wanted more touching, more reassurance he really did love her, and that he didn't think she was loose letting him do all that to her. But if he hadn't really loved her he would have gone the whole way, wouldn't he? He wouldn't care if he left her carrying his child.

Her father's words on how a woman could tell if a man truly loved her came back to her then. *'When he knows what's right for her. When he'd row right across the river without thinking how far it was. When he'd give his life willingly for her.'*

Well, Flynn did what was right for her, she didn't think many men would be so restrained. She could believe now that he truly loved her.

The next ten days passed in a flash, and though Flynn had to work most evenings at the saloon, they had all the days together. He didn't stay at State Street again, he said it was too much of a risk, but that made Matilda love him even more because he was so strong-minded and concerned for her reputation with the neighbours.

Even the weather seemed to be in sympathy with them for the sun shone every day. A picnic in Washington Square near Greenwich Village, a ferry-boat ride to Staten Island and a longer one still to see Coney Island and look at the hotels where rich people took their holidays. They paddled in the icy water and chased each other along the deserted sands. Flynn hired an old nag for a few hours, and with Matilda sitting up behind him, clinging to his waist, they explored the open countryside.

'We must fix this in our minds so we can tell our children and grandchildren,' he said reflectively as they made their way back to the ferry later in the afternoon to go home. 'For it will all be changed by then. So many thousands of immigrants are arriving each week now that in thirty years or so there won't be any more room in New York.'

'There isn't any room now,' she said.

'Oh, there is, Matty,' he said, smiling at her ignorance. 'But then I don't suppose you've been much beyond 20th Street, so you wouldn't know how fast things change here. In 1928, just thirteen years ago, Broadway only went as far as 10th Street! Now it's up to 42nd Street. Miles of new streets laid and houses built in a blink of an eye. Now they've finished the Croton aqueduct, water will be piped into millions of homes soon, not just a few thousand like now. Fewer people will die from diseases and the population will rise and rise.'

'But you say there's still room?'

'Yes, loads of it. Beyond the reservoir there's a huge area of ugly wasteland, where rag-pickers and Irish labourers live in shanties. I heard that some of the higher-minded men in the city want to turn that into a vast park, then build houses all around it right up to Harlem at the northern end of the island. Yet at the rate the population is growing it won't take long to fill it, and you can bet these new houses will only be for the rich, and the poorer people will still be ignored and expected to shift for themselves in the old slums. That's mostly why I want to get away. There's so much injustice, I feel stifled by it, and I hope this won't hurt your feelings, Matty, but I hate the strong English influence here more than anything.'

She *was* a little hurt, he was always making disparaging remarks about the English, and even if he did only mean the gentry, they were still her countrymen. But in the days that followed he took her to see so many different places that finally she felt as if she'd stepped out of the little English bubble she'd been in since her arrival in America and saw for herself that it really was a place of great opportunity.

She stared in wonder at the opulent mansions on Fifth Avenue and listened to Flynn's fantastic stories about how the owners made their fortunes. She admired the neat rows of new brownstone houses and wished they could start married life in somewhere so nice. She looked in horror at the rag-pickers' shanty town with the goats and pigs wandering in the mire and felt the injustice as keenly as Flynn when he pointed out that it was Irishmen who had built the aqueduct, dug ditches for water pipes and built the roads and houses, yet while they toiled for the rich, their wages barely kept them from starvation.

'They'll rise up one day and rebel,' Flynn said wryly. 'There's too many of us to keep down for long. But we won't be here to see it. We'll be down South making a new, better life for ourselves.'

He painted word pictures of the vast areas of rich farmland, mountains and forests that lay down there, of the steamboats on the Mississippi, of fur traders who went right out into the wilderness to the West and the Indians who lived out on the great plains. His passion fired her up too, and she vowed to herself that when the Milsons came home she would tell them about Flynn, and prepare them for the day when she would be leaving to start a new life with him.

It was on their last afternoon together that Matilda suddenly discovered Flynn was intending to leave for the South very soon. They were in Hester Street, an area on the East Side which was predominantly Jewish. He stopped to look at a dark green tailcoat with silver buttons, hanging from one of the second-hand clothes stalls. Although it was extraordinarily good-quality cloth and beautifully cut it was marked at only two dollars.

'It was made for you, my boy,' the old man said, and before Flynn could walk away he had it down and was holding it out for him to try.

It fitted as if it was made for him. Matilda laughed and said that if he could find an equally good-fitting pair of pants and riding boots he could easily pass for an Irish lord.

Much to her surprise he said he'd take it and promptly handed over the money. 'That was a bit rash,' she said as they walked away, Flynn carrying the coat wrapped in brown paper. 'You aren't going to find pants to go with it so cheap.'

'I've already got them,' he said with a wide smile. 'And the right boots. I met a young dandy who had big gambling debts, and bought them off him. I wouldn't mind betting that the coat came from the same man, it's his style. So now I'm all set.'

'You say that as if you're about to go and buy a ticket on the boat,' she said teasingly.

'Not this week,' he grinned. 'Next.'

She was stunned. She couldn't believe that he'd up and go so suddenly, especially after all they'd been to one another these past days.

'Don't look like that, darlin',' he said, putting his arm around her. 'It's best I go now.'

'I don't understand,' she said, her eyes filling with tears.

'Do you really think we can go back to waiting for Friday to come round so we can meet and hold hands?' he said, wiping away her tears with his thumb. 'It will be purgatory, Matty.'

Matilda knew exactly what he meant. Since that night in State Street, every time he kissed her she wanted him to fondle her again. She could barely think of anything else and in her heart she knew that if such an opportunity arose again, they wouldn't have stopped just at intimate touches. But for his strong will, not hers, a baby could already be growing inside her.

He pulled her close to him, his forehead touching hers. 'Let me go with your blessing,' he murmured. 'For the sooner I go, the sooner I can send for you and we can be married.'

Tears filled her eyes. It was tough enough only seeing him once a week, but at least she knew he was in the same city. Charleston was over 700 miles away.

'You aren't afraid I will forget you?' he asked, kissing away her tears. 'I'll write just as soon as I get there. Trust me, Matty, and let me go.'

He left her on the corner of State Street an hour or two later – he said he couldn't go into the house one last time because it would break his resolve. Matilda watched him walk away with tears rolling down her cheeks. His jaunty step, the baggy suit, grey derby and his black corkscrew curls were suddenly all so overpoweringly precious to her that she wanted to run to him and beg him to take her with him now.

But she couldn't do that. The Milsons would be home tomorrow, she had beds to air, bread to bake. She owed them more than slipping away like a thief in the night.

May slipped into June, and as the temperature began to soar and it became increasingly difficult to sleep, so Matilda nightly prepared herself to tell the Milsons about Flynn. Yet every morning there seemed to be a good reason for putting it off for another day. When the Milsons first arrived home from their holiday, she couldn't speak out then for she felt they'd suspect Flynn had been in the house during their absence, so she waited. Then Giles was anxious about two children from the Home who had run away after being sent up to Connecticut to prospective adoptive parents and he spent a great deal of time going backwards and forwards to New Jersey, hoping they'd reappear there.

Next the Reverend Kirkbright fell from a horse and broke his leg, so Giles had to take over all the services at the church. Meanwhile, on top of all this, Matilda still hadn't received a letter from Flynn, so without being able to say exactly where he was, or how long it would be before she wanted to leave, she decided to wait a little longer.

Early one morning in mid-July Matilda was just dishing up eggs and bacon for Giles and Tabitha's breakfast when her mistress came downstairs, fully dressed. Matilda was surprised to see her up so early, because ever since the hot weather began she had preferred to have a breakfast tray up in her bedroom where it was cooler.

'Good morning,' Matilda said with a smile. 'Did the smell of the bacon tempt you down?'

To her consternation, Lily blanched, swayed on her feet and then rushed out through the scullery and into the back yard.

Matilda didn't even stop to ask Giles what he thought was wrong, but plonked the two plates of food on the table and ran after her mistress. The privy door was open, Lily's skirts protruding from it, and Matilda could hear her retching.

For a moment or two Matilda just stood there, unsure whether to offer comfort or to withdraw and give the woman some privacy. Lily had a very delicate stomach and was often sick after eating something rich, but Matilda couldn't think of anything she'd eaten on the previous day which might have upset her.

'Can I get you anything?' Matilda called out once the retching seemed to be stopping. 'Or shall I help you back upstairs?'

Lily emerged. Her face was drained of all colour and she held on to the door post for support.

'Sit down out here for a moment,' Matilda said, taking her arm and leading her over to the bench. 'It's too hot to go back in the kitchen.'

'I'm sorry,' Lily said in a weak voice, sinking gratefully on to the bench and looking up at Matilda. 'I was feeling fine when I got up. I intended to go out early to buy some calico to make Tabby a new dress. But as soon as I opened the kitchen door and smelt the bacon, it just came over me.'

In a flash of intuition Matilda knew her mistress was expecting a baby. She had seen Peggie exactly like this when she was carrying George, in her case it was just a faint whiff of fish which made her retch. She'd heard flower-girls discussing early symptoms and around Finders Court such things were bandied around as casually as talk of the weather.

'Could you be having a baby?' Matilda asked gingerly. She knew ladies thought it vulgar to speak of such things. 'I know sickness like that often happens in the early months.'

Lily looked up at her sharply. At first her expression was one of indignation, and a blush coloured her face. But just as Matilda thought she was about to be reprimanded, Lily's eyes widened and a smile lit up her eyes.

'Oh Matty,' she said breathlessly. 'Do you think that's possible?'

Matilda wanted to laugh. It seemed ridiculous that a married woman who already had one child should want confirmation from an unmarried servant. But she managed merely to smile and took her mistress's hand in hers. 'It depends if you've had your monthlies,' she whispered. 'If you haven't, you probably are, but you should see the doctor.'

Before Lily could confirm or deny this, Giles came out, quickly followed by Tabitha, and Matilda went back into the kitchen to eat the breakfast she'd left on the stove.

Yet her appetite vanished the moment she thought what this turn of events could mean to her. However joyful it would be for the Milsons to have another child, it might very well turn out to be yet another chain to keep her here.

Tabitha came running in. 'Mama said she would like tea, toast and a lightly boiled egg,' she said. 'Papa told me to come and help you. That means they want to talk about something they don't want me to know about, doesn't it?'

Matilda was forced to laugh at the little girl's keen intuition. 'Maybe,' she said. 'But it could mean they think it's time you learned something useful, like laying a tray for Mama.'

Lily was none the worse for her sickness, she ate her breakfast in the parlour and then went out to buy the calico, taking Tabitha with her. Giles went off to see the Reverend Kirkbright, and Matilda was left alone to do the daily chores. As she shook the feather mattress from her employers' bed out of the window, she thought Lily's remarkable recovery ruled out a stomach upset. That made her wonder when the baby had started. If it was during their holiday, then she would be around three months already, which meant the baby would be born around Christmas.

'I can't stay that long,' she said aloud as she continued vigorously to shake the mattress. 'Let them find a new nursemaid. I can't stay for another winter in New York without Flynn.'

Chapter Nine

At the end of July the Reverend Kirkbright sent a message round to State Street asking if Matilda could collect two small brothers from a tenement in Mulberry Bend and take them straight out to the Home in New Jersey. Their widowed mother had died from tuberculosis and there was no one else to look after them.

Sad as it was to be given the task of removing two recently orphaned children from the only home they'd ever known, it came as a welcome diversion for Matilda. The confirmation of the pregnancy had thrilled the Milsons, but as Lily was still suffering from bouts of sickness, and very tetchy because of the hot, sticky weather, it had fallen upon Matilda to run the house and care for Tabitha single-handed.

Two days earlier a letter from Flynn finally arrived. This ought to have soothed some of her anxiety and increased her determination to tell the Milsons about him, but it had left her even more confused. Flynn had posted it in Charleston back in May, and at the time of writing he had only just got there. His loving messages were very comforting, his glowing description of Charleston cheering, but in the absence of news of a job, and with no address to write back to, she was left in much the same void as before.

The chance of a day out in New Jersey, to see all the other children and Cissie again, well away from the stink and noise of the city, was almost as good as being offered a holiday. So Matilda put aside her worries and set off to collect the two small boys at eight in the morning with pleasurable anticipation.

Mulberry Bend was almost as notorious a slum area as neighbouring Five Points, but the boys, Arthur and Ronald, aged five and four respectively, were being held on to by a kindly shopkeeper who had been a friend of their mother. They were dear little boys with blond hair and blue eyes, and though poorly dressed, thin and a little dirty, it was clear they had been well loved by their mother. They showed no apprehension whatever at going with Matilda, and by the time she'd got them down to the ferry, the excitement of a boat trip out to the countryside banished the last of their shyness.

Job met her at the ferry with the cart, and to Matilda's delight Sidney was with him. He was sturdy and much taller now, his hair as fiery as her own half-brothers', and his skin freckled from the sun. On the ride back to the Home he regaled Arthur and Ronald with tales about the pigs and chickens they now kept and he promised them they could help him feed them later.

Cissie rushed out to greet Matilda with great warmth, throwing her arms around her and insisting she came at once to see Peter and Pearl. It was surprising enough to see that Cissie had become quite buxom, with rosy cheeks like a farmer's wife, and her short dark hair curling becomingly around her cap, but even better to find that the babies were as fat as butter, placidly sitting up on a blanket under a tree in the meadow behind the Home.

Once Matilda had passed Arthur and Ronald over to Miss Rowbottom for a bath and some dinner, she returned to Cissie, the babies and the other very small children. Sitting down on the grass with them all, Matilda asked Cissie if she still wanted to leave.

Cissie gave one of her dazzling smiles. 'Don't reckon so, I wouldn't mind a night out now and then, or a pal of me own, but,' she paused and waved one arm expansively at the meadow and the children gathered around her, 'I'd have to be crazy to leave all this, wouldn't I?'

Matilda felt a surge of tenderness and admiration for the young mother. Everything had been stacked against her right from her birth, yet from somewhere deep within she'd found the strength of character not only to cope with her dismal lot in life, but also to seize the only opportunity presented to her, and make it work for her. Looking at her now with her shiny dark curls, rosy cheeks and well-rounded body, happily cuddling her son and her friend's baby, no one could possibly guess what hell she'd been through. If the governors of the Home ever wanted just one piece of real evidence that the rescue work in Five Points was worthwhile, Cissie and her babies were living proof.

Matilda took Peter on to her lap, hardly able to believe that this plump, smiling baby was the same bony little scrap she'd washed back at Dr Kupicha's only nine months earlier. He had been bald then but now he had a thatch of light brown hair, two teeth, and his cheeks, arms and fat legs were the colour of honey.

'You would indeed be crazy to want to leave,' she said. 'You can't imagine how hot and stuffy it is in New York, Cissie, it smells so lovely here, and there's always a breeze.'

'I ain't forgotten what it's like, not summer nor winter,' Cissie replied, and a cloud passed over her face as if she wished she could forget. 'But you look a bit peaky to me. What's up? Is your mistress mean to you?'

'No. Of course not.' Matilda half smiled. Lily was often difficult, she tended to forget that servants got tired too, but she wouldn't go so far as to call her mean. For a brief moment she was tempted to confide in Cissie about Flynn, but good as it would be to pour it all out to someone sympathetic, she knew it wouldn't help much. Cissie would probably urge her to catch the next boat to Charleston to look for Flynn, and she certainly wouldn't understand why Matilda was unable to tell her employers about him.

Cissie didn't press her any further about the Milsons, but changed the subject to Miss Rowbottom. She appeared to admire and respect the woman in many areas, but she felt she was too hard on some of the children.

'Don't get me wrong, she ain't cruel or nothin', and she's a good teacher, but she just don't sense when something's up with the kids, not like you and me would,' she said, pulling a face. 'Molly's been sickening for something for a few days now. I said we ought to send Job over to get the doctor, but she told me it was her job to decide such things, and the doctor's time was too valuable to keep dragging him over here for nothing.'

Matilda said she would see Molly before she left, and speak to Miss Rowbottom if she thought there was something wrong.

It was around four when Matilda found Molly lying on her bed in the girls' dormitory and she was immediately alarmed. She didn't think any seven-year-old would choose to stay alone indoors while her friends were outside playing, unless she really was ill, furthermore Molly didn't even lift her head as she came in.

'Hullo, Molly,' she said, sitting beside the child. 'I hear you aren't feeling too well.'

Molly's only response was to cough, an unnatural, hard, dry sound. She seemed to have difficulty in opening her eyes, and when she tried there was yellow matter in them. Her skin felt dry and very hot. Matilda got the child a drink of water and supported her as she drank it, then laid her down again and covered her with a blanket and went back down to find Miss Rowbottom.

She was in the small classroom with five of the older children and she pursed her lips in disapproval at the interruption. 'I thought you'd left some time ago,' she said.

Miss Rowbottom appeared formidable to most people on first meeting. She was a tall, well-built woman with iron-grey hair and the kind of stern, angular face which suggested she lacked compassion and a sense of humour. It didn't help that her voice was loud and harsh too. But Matilda wasn't going to be rebuffed and stated that she'd seen Molly and thought she needed to see the doctor. She offered to call on him as soon as she got back across the river.

'I don't believe that's necessary,' the woman said curtly. 'Molly is always playing ill, she finds it an excellent way to get attention. I looked in on her an hour ago and I saw nothing to be alarmed about.'

'Perhaps her condition has worsened since then,' Matilda said equally curtly. 'I will ask Dr Kupicha to call anyway.'

It was almost a week later before Dr Kupicha called round to State Street. Matilda had answered the door to him, and she stayed in the parlour with the Milsons instead of returning to the kitchen because the doctor said he wanted her to hear what he had to say too.

He had been out visiting patients when Matilda called on him to tell him about Molly, but she had left a message, and he had gone the next morning to see the child. He diagnosed measles and removed her at once to the isolation room, organizing one of the maids to nurse her there. Since then twelve more children had come down with it.

Matilda blanched at this news. Measles wasn't considered a really serious disease like cholera or smallpox, but back in

London she had known it sweep through the tenements like wild fire, claiming the lives of many very young children, and those who survived were often left blind or deaf.

'Measles isn't easily confined,' the doctor said hesitantly, looking hard at Giles. 'The incubation period can be as long as sixteen days, and of course, during that time all the other children would have had some contact with Molly. She is so gravely ill I fear she will die.'

Lily Milson had greeted the doctor when he came in, and asked if he would like some refreshment, but she hadn't said a word while he was explaining why he had called, just carried on with her sewing. But suddenly she dropped it from her hands, looking from the doctor to Matilda in horror, and it was clear she'd suddenly realized that it was Matilda who had alerted him the child was ill after she'd visited the Home.

'Matilda was there. What if she brought it home to Tabitha?' she asked, her voice a frightened squeak.

'That's extremely unlikely,' Dr Kupicha said soothingly, moving over to Lily and laying a reassuring hand on her arm. 'Matilda would have to catch it first before she could pass it on. Besides, you need to be in close contact with an infected person to catch it in the first place.'

Matilda wasn't the least alarmed by what Lily had said. She was more concerned about Molly. 'So how did Molly get it then?' she asked.

Dr Kupicha frowned. 'I was puzzled by that, the Home's isolation is one of its best attributes. But it seems that over a fortnight ago a large family moving out of New York passed by there and stopped to ask if they could buy milk and eggs before continuing their journey. They stayed some little while and Molly was seen playing with their children.'

All at once Lily let out an outraged shriek, the kind she made when she saw a mouse or cockroach. 'You see, you can get it that easily. Matty could have brought it back here.'

Before the doctor could confirm or deny this, Lily leaped up from the couch, and faced Matilda with blazing eyes. 'You went near that sick child, didn't you?' she spat at her. 'You fool! How could you put my child at risk?'

Matilda was reminded of her mistress's callousness when the child died on the ship coming here. She'd made allowances for it that time, after all Lily had been sick herself, but this time she felt angry. 'Of course I went near Molly. How could I judge if she was ill enough to call the doctor otherwise?' she retorted.

'You were only asked to take two children there. Not to poke your nose into sick-rooms,' Lily shouted at her. 'And you didn't tell me anyone was ill when you got back.'

Dr Kupicha stepped in between them. 'If Matilda had measles herself as a child, and most have had it, she couldn't carry the disease,' he said firmly.

Matilda couldn't remember having measles, but she didn't say so. It was embarrassing enough that Dr Kupicha had to find out that her mistress didn't share her husband's compassion for all children in need. She certainly didn't want him to witness one of Lily's hysterical turns.

It was just over a week later that Matilda began to feel ill. It felt like the onset of a cold, her limbs ached and she began coughing. She carried on working and it wasn't until two days later when the light began to hurt her eyes that she realized to her horror she was going down with measles. Afraid to tell Madam because she had been snappy with her ever since the doctor called to speak about the epidemic, she waited until she was alone in the kitchen with Giles, and told him.

'I'm so sorry, sir,' she said in little more than a whisper. 'I know Madam is going to hate me for bringing it into the house. What shall I do?'

The colour drained from his face and he glanced nervously towards the parlour where his wife and Tabitha were. But then he turned back to her and put a comforting hand on her shoulder. 'You can't help it, Matty, it's just one of those things no one could have predicted. But you must go to bed now, you must be feeling terrible. I'll tell Mrs Milson and call the doctor.'

She heard Lily's outraged shriek just as she climbed into bed, but she felt too ill to care what the woman was saying about her. By the next morning the rash had appeared, her skin felt as if it was on fire, and the cough was much worse.

Dr Kupicha called in and advised her to sponge herself down with cool water, but apart from drinks and some medicine to ease the cough, there was nothing more he could do. If he knew her mistress hadn't even been up to see her, he said nothing, and after he'd left Matilda lay crying, feeling utterly abandoned.

It was Giles who came up later. He stayed outside the closed door, but called out saying he'd left her a cool drink and some soup on a tray if she was able to eat it. She understood he could hardly bellow out sympathy through a closed door, and it wouldn't have been proper for him to come into her room, but she still felt very aggrieved that she was being treated like a leper. Yet sick as she felt, her thoughts were mainly of Tabitha and she offered up prayers that she wouldn't catch it too.

She knew she was on the mend on the third day when she woke to find that her skin felt cooler, the rash was fading and the cough looser. When Giles came upstairs as usual to call out and ask how she was, this time he opened the door a crack, and Matilda was able to ask if Tabitha was showing any symptoms.

'No, thank heavens,' he said. 'Her only problem is missing you. She's been playing her mama up in your absence.'

Matilda gave a sigh of relief. On the previous day Giles had called out that both he and his wife remembered having it as children so they weren't at risk of catching it.

'Will that mean Madam will stop being cross with me?' she asked.

Giles didn't answer for a moment, and Matilda guessed he was embarrassed. 'She's turned her anger on me now,' he whispered conspiratorially. 'Yesterday, for some unaccountable reason, Mrs Kirkbright took it upon herself to tell her the grimmer aspects of our orphan rescue scheme. Including some details of Five Points. I'm sure you can imagine how she took that?'

Matilda could. As she hadn't heard any crying or screaming she guessed Lily had gone into one of her famous sulks and accused him of caring more for slum children than his own family.

'Well, perhaps it's best she knows the whole truth, sir,' she said soothingly, turning around in her bed so she could see his face at the door. 'You weren't happy about her not knowing everything. And it's not as if it's something to be ashamed of.'

Giles opened the door a little wider. 'That's true, but I would have preferred to keep it from her while she's in such a delicate condition,' he said. 'She wants me to promise I'll give up the work.'

'You can't do that, sir, it's too important,' she exclaimed, hearing the sorrow in his voice. 'So you must be strong and stick to your principles.'

He didn't answer for a moment and moved away from the door. She guessed he was checking that Lily wasn't within earshot.

'I don't think I can do that, Matty,' he said when he came back. 'You see, when Mrs Milson gets a real bee in her bonnet she can make life impossible. It's lucky in a way you've been up here since all this came out. She's not herself at all.'

Matty wondered if he meant she was just sulking and crying, or if he thought it was something more insidious. But to her mind Madam needed a firm hand and a good talking to.

'You may have a son this time,' she said. 'I don't think he would like to find out in years to come that his father backed away from something which was right and good because of his mother's "delicate condition". Tell her that!'

'Oh Matty,' he sighed again. 'I wish I dared, and had the strength of character to go ahead regardless of what she might say. But I'm torn right now, how can I continue with something which distresses her so badly?'

Matilda didn't feel she was able to comment on that, she was already smarting because her mistress hadn't once come in to see her since she'd been ill. Drinks and water to wash in had been left outside the bedroom door, her slop pail was full, and it seemed to her that anyone who treated another sick person like that didn't deserve any sympathy herself. But she couldn't bring herself to tell her master that.

'You'll have to pray for guidance then,' she said archly.

'Do you think I haven't?' he said, a ghost of a smile appearing on his troubled face. 'Get well soon, Matty, maybe all our troubles will vanish then.'

On the first day Matilda was able to go downstairs for longer than just to use the privy, she noticed immediately that Tabitha was very listless. Her mother said curtly that it was due to the sultry weather, and said she felt listless too because she'd had to cope with everything herself.

Matilda was hurt further by this direct reproach but she made up her mind that even if she still felt weak, the next day she would resume her normal duties.

Lily went out soon after breakfast, making a barbed comment as she left about a mountain of washing waiting to be done, or *had she forgotten she was employed as a servant rather than as a minister's assistant.*

Tabitha sat listlessly in the back yard with her doll all morning, as Matilda sweated over the washing. She showed no interest in trying to help hang out the clothes as she usually did, and she left her midday sandwich untouched. Still feeling weak herself, Matilda laid Tabitha down on the couch in the parlour during the afternoon and sat beside her to read her a story.

It was Giles who came in first at nearly four, just as Matilda was getting frantic, for Tabitha had begun coughing a little and the tell-tale rash had just appeared behind her ears. He blanched as Matilda told him she thought his daughter had the measles, then asked where his wife was.

'I don't know,' Matilda said weakly, struggling not to cry. 'She just said she was going out. I thought she meant only for a couple of hours.'

While Giles ran off to get the doctor, Matilda carried the child up to her bedroom, undressed her and put her to bed, and stayed with her. Frightened and all alone in the house, it seemed to her that Tabitha was growing worse by the minute, all she could do was sponge the child's forehead and try not to think that she was to blame for this.

Giles, the doctor and Lily all came back together. Matilda learned much later that evening that the two men had found Lily walking along Broadway. All three of them came straight up to the bedroom, but when Dr Kupicha immediately asked Matilda about the onset of the child's symptoms, Lily ordered her to go downstairs.

Matilda paced the kitchen floor while she waited, not knowing whether to start preparing the evening meal or not. She had a feeling her mistress would lay into her later, perhaps even dismiss her, but that didn't matter so much, as long as Tabitha recovered.

It was only once Dr Kupicha had left, leaving instructions that the curtains must be kept closed in Tabitha's room, and she must be sponged down every hour and her eyes and ears carefully watched for further infections, that Lily stormed down into the kitchen and viciously turned on Matilda.

'I don't want you going anywhere near my daughter,' she said, her small, sharp features contorted with spite. 'You brought this loathsome disease into the house, and I'll never forgive you for that.'

'I couldn't help it, madam,' Matilda said. 'I didn't know Molly had measles. I only did what anyone would have done, gave her a drink and soothed her.'

'You are treacherous,' Lily yelled at her. 'I know it was you who persuaded the Reverend to go into those places and dig out children. He'd never have thought of it by himself. I thought you were taking nice little children out to New Jersey, not filthy little beggars. But then I might have known. You were one yourself. Water always finds its own level.'

'It was not my idea,' Matilda retorted, wondering if the woman had gone mad, and why Giles wasn't coming down to support her. 'It was Reverend Kirkbright's.'

'Don't you try to wriggle out of it. I know just what you are.' Lily's face was purple with rage now and Matilda was afraid she was going to strike her. 'You're a scheming, ungrateful little minx, you've been plotting with my husband behind my back.'

'Please don't say such things, madam.' Matilda began to cry. 'It's not true and you are only saying it because you're so worried about Tabby. Let's get her better first, then we'll talk about it.'

'You won't go near Tabby ever again,' Lily roared out. 'I shall nurse her entirely myself, I can't trust you anywhere near her. God help you if she doesn't survive, because so help me, I'll kill you.'

She ran away then, back upstairs, leaving Matilda shaken to the core.

It was a few moments before Giles came down, but he had little to comfort her with.

'Don't take it to heart,' he said. 'She's overwrought and distressed. I'm sure by tomorrow she'll have calmed down and forgotten it herself.' He explained then how he and the doctor had found her on Broadway, apparently unaware what time it was. He said she was overtired from doing everything while Matilda was ill, and she wasn't thinking straight.

But Matilda couldn't put it from her mind, in her opinion only a deranged person would say such things. Setting aside the accusation of treachery, plotting with Giles and the snipes at her background, Tabitha could just as easily have picked up the disease at church, or from one of her parents' friends' children, and it was unfair to hold her entirely responsible.

She made a meal nobody wanted to eat, she ironed all the clothes she'd washed that morning, but all the time frightening thoughts kept creeping into her head. If Lily was deranged, and surely she must be to go wandering around the shops all day when she knew her child hadn't been well that morning, how could she look after Tabitha properly? If it wasn't for that she might have packed her few belongings and left the house for good, but she couldn't do so, not without knowing if Tabitha would pull through.

Matilda's misery increased ten-fold in the next three days. At night she could hear Tabitha's harsh, dry cough coming from the next room, and Lily wouldn't relent and let her in to help. The woman stayed in there constantly, day and night, refusing all food even from her husband, and ignoring Matilda's pleas from outside the door. All Matilda could do was deal with the slop bucket and soiled linen left outside the closed door and hope that the next time the doctor or Giles went in they might manage to persuade Lily to see sense.

'I've tried everything,' Giles said wearily late on the third night, as he came down into the kitchen to refill a pitcher with boiled water. 'Dr Kupicha has tried too, but she won't listen to either of us, Tabitha is gravely ill, and I don't believe Mrs Milson's hysterical manner is helping the situation one bit. But what more can I do, Matty? I can't demand she comes out of there and insist you take her place.'

'Oh yes you should,' Matilda said forcefully. 'If I were in your shoes I'd go in there and drag her out. Tabby's your child too, sir. You should do what's best for her, not pussyfoot around when your wife is clearly half out of her mind.'

'That will do, Matilda,' he shouted back in anger. 'I won't have you getting above yourself. Maybe Mrs Milson is right about you. She said today you were intent on taking over this entire house.'

That was the last straw. She'd supported this man through thick and thin and now, when it suited him, he was agreeing with his crazy wife.

'If that's what she thinks then I'll leave,' she snapped back at him, her eyes blazing. 'In case you've forgotten, Reverend

Milson, I've loved Tabby like she was my own for over two years. I'd give my life for her. The only reason I didn't pack my bags after what Mrs bloody Milson said the other night is because I care so much. But don't you worry, I'll be gone in the morning and leave you to cope with that mad woman.'

She ran upstairs then, and left him standing there in the kitchen. Her packing took less than a few minutes, all she had was three dresses, a pair of Sunday shoes, her coat and some underwear. If it hadn't been so late, she would have left right away, but even in her anger she knew a young girl wandering around at the dead of night was likely to be either accosted by someone, or picked up by the police.

Instead she read and re-read Flynn's letter, until her candle burned out. Tomorrow morning she would get the boat to Charleston and look for him. She just hoped the eleven dollars she had saved was enough to get there. He was right after all about the Milsons. She was a fool to think they cared about her, all they cared about was themselves.

At first light the next morning Matilda got up and dressed, then, lifting her bag, she opened her door gingerly. She had no wish to run into either of her employers, she'd spent most of the night crying and now she felt only bitterness towards them.

But as she crept out on to the small landing between her room and Tabitha's she could hear Lily sobbing out prayers and over that the sound of the child's rasping breath. Any sympathy she had retained for the woman was instantly swept away by a surge of intense anger. She didn't think her own nursing skills were any greater than her mistress's, but she did know better than to allow a small sick child to be frightened further by an adult's distress.

Standing there on the landing, she resolved that she must step into the room. She was scared to go against Lily's wishes, but she knew she had no choice. Tabitha's life was in grave danger, and so, squaring her shoulders, she walked in.

The scene that met her eyes proved to her she was right to intervene. The darkened room was stifling hot, the smell of vomit overpowering. Tabitha was swaddled in blankets and a thick eiderdown, and her face was wizened like a little monkey's. Lily was on her knees by the bed, sobbing into the bedcovers, too distraught even to turn her head at the sudden beam of light from the open door and a breath of fresher air.

Side-stepping the woman, Matilda laid her hand on Tabitha's forehead. It was fiery hot, and she instinctively knew that if the child wasn't cooled down immediately she had no chance of survival.

Tapping Lily on the shoulder, she ordered her to get up. 'Go and get that mask you use when you have headaches and get some clean towels,' she added. 'I'm going to prepare a bath for her.'

Running back downstairs, she pulled the tin bath right out into the yard and under the pump to fill it with water. The yard seemed a very inappropriate place to bathe a sick child, but speed was more important than concerning herself with propriety.

She wasn't really surprised to find Lily was still standing in the sick-room when she returned with neither towels nor mask, clearly the woman had lost all leave of her senses, so, grabbing a petticoat of Tabitha's from a chair, she hastily wound it into a roll, and pushing past her mistress, tied it securely around the child's eyes.

'Get the towels if nothing else,' she snapped as she lifted the child up into her arms. 'And hurry.'

As Matilda moved with the child to the door, the woman let out a loud wail and began tugging at the back of her apron. 'Put her down,' she shrieked. 'You are dismissed.'

'I'll leave when Tabby's better,' Matilda retorted through gritted teeth. 'Just get the towels.'

As Matilda swept on down the stairs with the child in her arms, Giles came rushing out of the bedroom, still in his night-shirt.

'What's happened?' he said in alarm.

'Tabby needs to be cooled down, not prayed and sobbed over,' Matilda shot at him, not even pausing for one second. 'And for goodness' sake stop that woman wailing. That won't help.'

Nothing in Matilda's life had been more painful than to see the blindfolded child she loved so fiercely jerk involuntarily at being submerged in the cold water. It felt so cruel, her whole being wanted to cuddle and comfort her. But she knew it was the only way to save her, and she had to keep her nerve.

Giles came running out just in time to see what she was doing.

'Surely not, Matty!' he exclaimed, his previously flushed face blanching. 'Cold water!'

'Trust me,' she implored him. 'She's burning up, and it has to be done. Get towels, and some water for her to drink.'

'You'll feel better soon, Tabby,' she murmured soothingly to the child as she held her down firmly under the water, soaking her hair. 'Just a little while and I'll put you in a clean dry nightgown and then you can go back to bed.'

After a minute or two of submersion Tabitha stopped jerking, and her breathing became less laboured. Giles came running out of the house again with towels, and she got him to hold one out to wrap the child in.

'All better now,' she murmured, cuddling her into her arms. 'Matty's got you safely.'

Dr Kupicha arrived an hour later, summoned by Giles who had run the whole way to his house and breathlessly described what had happened, but by the time the two men got back to State Street, Matilda had Tabitha back in a clean, dry bed, the window open to let in air, and the child was sleeping.

'You did well, Matty,' Dr Kupicha said as he examined the patient. 'The crisis has passed now, and as long as no secondary infection sets in, I think she'll make it.'

'How is Mrs Milson?' Matilda asked. She hadn't seen her since she rushed down the stairs with Tabitha and until now she hadn't given her a moment's thought. But she was so relieved that Tabitha was out of danger she could even bring herself to feel some concern for the woman. 'She said I was dismissed, but I said I was only going once Tabitha was better.'

Dr Kupicha half smiled. In his private opinion Lily Milson was a sad case, a woman so full of anxiety that she could easily slip over the edge into madness. 'I don't think you can take any notice of something said in the heat of the moment,' he said. 'Reverend Milson has put her to bed, and I suggest you both encourage her to stay there for a day or two as she is utterly exhausted. I'm sure I can count on you to look after Tabitha.'

'Of course, I love her,' she said.

The doctor thought that statement summed up the essence of this young nursemaid's character. She was guided by her heart, and it was a great deal larger than most. She deserved a life of her own, children of her own, yet somehow he sensed she would always be helping others to attain their dreams, putting her own on permanent hold.

'I'll pop in to see my little patient again tonight,' he said, as he got up to leave. 'You undoubtedly saved the little one's life today, and I am going to tell Mrs Milson as much, but just remember, Matty, you have a life of your own too, and it isn't necessarily here in this house, with this child.'

Matilda followed him out on to the landing. 'How are Molly and the other children?'

His face clouded over. 'Molly died yesterday,' he said. 'We may lose Ruth too, I fear. But there are no new cases, Pearl and Peter are in robust health. I think we are over the worst of it now.'

Matilda's eyes filled with tears. It seemed so tragic that the two little girls had been rescued from hell, only to die less than a year later from a common childhood disease.

'Matty!'

Matilda had fallen asleep in a chair beside the child's bed, but at the sound of the weak little voice she woke with a start.

'Is it morning yet?' Tabitha asked as Matilda bent over her.

Such a question suggested Tabitha was on the mend because her father had said she hadn't been aware of day or night since becoming ill. Matilda pulled back the thick curtains a crack, and saw the sun was just coming up.

'Yes, it's morning, but still very early,' she said, putting her hand on Tabitha's forehead. It felt naturally warm and moist, yesterday's fever had gone. Her dark eyes were wide open and there was no matter coming from them. 'How are you feeling, my darling?'

'Thirsty,' she said. 'And I want to tinkle.'

Nothing had ever sounded so sweet to Matilda. If it hadn't been quite so early she might have been tempted to rush downstairs to wake the Milsons and give them the good news. She lifted the little girl out of bed and sat her on the chamber-pot, then poured a glass of water from the pitcher.

'I can hold it, I'm not a baby,' Tabitha reproached her as Matilda held it to her lips, and her small hands grasped the glass firmly and drank deeply.

Matilda tidied the bed, shook the pillows, then lifted Tabitha back in.

'Do you think you could eat something?' she asked, astounded that the cough seemed to have gone too.

'Maybe,' she said, frowning as if confused. 'Why were you in that chair?'

Matilda smiled. Clearly Tabitha had no recollection of any of the events of the last few days. 'Because you've been ill, and I stayed in here to watch over you.'

'Where are Mama and Papa?'

'In bed still. But I shall wake them up and tell them you are better very soon. Can I leave you for a minute to go downstairs and find you something to eat?'

Tabitha nodded and reached out for her rag-doll further down the bed. She cuddled her into her arms and smiled at her. 'Have you been ill too, Jenny?'

The clock in the parlour was just striking seven when Matilda heard Giles coming up the stairs to see his daughter. She smiled to herself, imagining his surprise and delight to see Tabitha sitting up in bed eating bread and milk. The door opened a crack, and Giles peeped round. As she had anticipated, he gasped.

'Good morning, Papa,' Tabitha said. 'See, I'm better.'

'Oh Tabby,' he exclaimed, his face breaking into the widest smile. 'Now that's what I call a good start to the day.'

He was still in his flannel night-shirt, his dark curls tousled and a thick growth of stubble on his chin, and as he looked towards Matilda he clearly suddenly became aware of this, and half hid himself behind the door.

'Neither of us care what you look like,' Matilda laughed. 'I'm sure I don't look too grand either.'

Later on, as Matilda caught up with all the jobs left undone in the last few days, she thought how sad it was that Lily wasn't able to express her joy with the same exuberance she and Giles could. She had burst into tears when told the good news, and although she'd got up to go and see her daughter for a short while, she had gone straight back to bed afterwards and had remained there, sobbing into her pillows.

When Dr Kupicha called he'd said she was suffering from shock, and bed was the best place for her. Matilda couldn't help but wonder how she'd cope with tragedy, if good news affected her so badly.

But her own joy sustained her even though she was exhausted and there was still so much work to be done. Her master's gratitude for all she had done more than made up for Lily's stilted apology and the retraction of her dismissal.

'Matty, wake up.'

Matilda woke with a start to find Giles shaking her arm. It was a little over a week since Tabitha's recovery. 'I'm sorry,' she said, imagining she'd overslept. 'Is it very late?'

But she could see it was pitch-dark aside from the lighted candle Giles was holding and he was in his night-clothes. Suddenly realizing he wouldn't come up to her room except in an emergency, she sat up. 'Is Tabby ill again?'

'No, it's Mrs Milson,' he said, his voice shaking. 'I fear she's losing the baby, Matty. I must go and get the doctor immediately.'

Matilda gasped with horror, flung back the covers, and stopping only to grab her shawl, she followed him down the stairs.

Giles had lit two candles in their room, yet even in the dim light Matilda saw the anguish in her mistress's eyes.

Her husband bent over her. 'Matty's here with you now. I'll run all the way there if I don't see a cab. Just hold on.'

Grabbing up his clothes, he disappeared down the stairs. Matilda moved over to her mistress and took her hand. 'Are you losing blood?' she asked gently.

She nodded. 'I woke up with a pain, so I got up and it was all on my night-gown. I'm going to lose the baby, aren't I?'

'Not necessarily,' Matilda said. 'Some women lose blood all the time they are carrying.' This wasn't true, but she hoped Lily would believe it enough to stay calm until the doctor came. 'Let me get you into a clean night-gown.'

As Matilda pulled back the covers she had to stifle a gasp. Lily's night-gown and the sheet beneath her were soaked in blood. Quickly covering her up so she wouldn't see, and moving the candle further from the bed, Matilda found the cloths Lily kept for her monthlies, a clean gown and a sheet, and went back to wash and change her, talking all the while to distract her.

Fortunately Lily was so embarrassed at Matilda washing her in such an intimate place that she kept her face averted and didn't see the bloody night-gown or sheet, but just as Matilda finished she screamed out in pain. Matilda had never felt so helpless as her mistress writhed in agony, veins popped out all over her face and neck, and she arched her back away from the mattress, the screaming gradually changing to a low bellow. Matilda could do nothing more than hold her hands and urge her to stay calm and try not to cry aloud as Tabitha might wake and come down.

The spasm passed and Lily sank back, tears rolling down her cheeks. 'Giles wanted another child so badly,' she whispered hoarsely. 'I'll be letting him down again.'

All the irritation Matilda had ever felt for this woman, the hurt that she had blamed her for the measles, the anger she'd felt when she was intending to leave, even her callousness towards the children at the Home, left her with that plaintive statement. It seemed incredible that Lily would see losing a child as *letting her husband down again*. But for her to say such a thing now, at a time when most women would only be thinking of their own loss, there had to be a root cause, perhaps some incident in the past which deeply troubled her. Maybe it was that too which triggered off the deranged behaviour when Tabby became sick.

Matilda knew Giles really loved his wife, she saw that daily. But perhaps Lily couldn't see it herself. Matilda remembered how cold her parents had been with her before leaving England, the fact that they didn't even come to see the ship sail away. Neglect of children came in many forms, and perhaps lack of interest was the cruellest, for it robbed the child of confidence.

In a sudden flash of insight Matilda saw that all Lily's fears could have sprung from just this. She didn't believe in herself enough to deal with anything unknown, whether that was disease, poverty, or a new country. She even imagined she was unworthy of her husband.

'You haven't let him down,' Matilda said firmly. 'Sir knows as well as I do that things like this are acts of God. He loves you, madam. I never saw a man love his wife so much.'

Lily lost the baby just minutes before Giles and the doctor came in. She asked for the chamber-pot, one last huge pain engulfed her, and as Matilda held her securely in her arms, the four-month foetus slithered out.

Matilda covered the pot quickly and slid it under the bed. It was anger rather than distress that she felt. Here was a couple who believed so strongly in God and his goodness but he had chosen to rob them of a child which would be loved and well cared for. Yet nightly he allowed babies to be born to those without even a roof over their heads, when to them a miscarriage would be a blessing.

A couple of hours later, as Giles and Matilda sat either side of Mrs Milson's bed, they heard Tabitha's feet padding across the landing overhead. 'You go and see to Tabby,' Giles said. 'I know I can count on you not to alarm her. I'll stay and care for my wife.'

It was only then that Matilda cried. She had held back her tears when Giles wept with his wife, seen Dr Kupicha out after taking instructions on how she must be cared for in the next few days, and as she washed and changed her mistress. Lily had fallen asleep, her small face so like Tabitha's, peaceful again now the pain was gone. Yet she knew the physical pain of losing a baby would be nothing to the sadness and heartache which would come once the sleeping draught the doctor had given her wore off.

'Don't cry,' Giles said, and got up from his seat to comfort her. 'You have always been the strong one, don't fail me now.'

'I won't fail you,' she said, wiping her eyes on her apron. 'It's your dammed God who has failed you this time. I wonder how you can serve Him when he rewards you like this.'

'This is how He tests us,' he said, lifting her chin up so he could look right into her eyes. 'But I'll tell you a secret, sometimes I wish I was a non-believer just like you, Matty. It must be a great deal easier to deal with anger when you believe that you alone control your own destiny, than for someone like me who has to bend to God's will.'

She saw the pain in his eyes, and wished there was something she could say to ease it. But there was nothing, only time was going to do that.

Nearly three weeks later Matilda was dusting the parlour when a long-awaited letter from Flynn arrived. Giles and Tabitha were upstairs with Lily, but Matilda didn't give a thought to them and ran straight out to the back yard to read it.

The address at the top was High Oaks, near Charleston.

'My darling one,' he wrote. 'I have a job now as an overseer on a cotton plantation, and a little house for us, so please come on the very next boat and don't delay. The plantation is owned by Mr James Donnelly, another Irishman from Connemara, it's about thirty miles from Charleston, and the most beautiful place you ever saw. Mrs Donnelly has an aunt in the town, and you can stay with her until we can be married which I hope will be just as soon as possible after your arrival. The house is the gate house for the plantation, it's small and bare, but I know you will soon make it a real home for us.

'You might think it strange knowing my opinion of slavery that I took a job on a plantation, but since being here in the South, some of my views that came from ignorance have altered. Mr Donnelly has some thirty slaves, but I assure you he treats them well. But you will see all this for yourself very soon. Write to me as soon as you've booked your passage. I shall be waiting at the dock for the boat to come in, and counting every hour until I can hold you in my arms. I have so much to tell you and show you. Our life together is going to be wonderful, you'll see, your loving Flynn.'

She had to read it twice before she could really take it in. Her first reaction was wild excitement, but it was quickly doused by the knowledge she couldn't possibly make arrangements to leave immediately. Putting the letter in her apron pocket, she went back indoors, but as she continued with the dusting her mind was in a turmoil.

Lily was in a very bad way. Physically she had recovered from the miscarriage, but her mental state was causing great concern to her husband, Matilda and the doctor. She no longer cried, just stayed in her bedroom staring at the ceiling, showing no interest in anything, not her daughter, husband, or even food. If Matilda didn't haul her out of her bed at regular intervals to use the chamber-pot, and to wash her, she suspected the woman would just continue to lie there in her own mess. Dr Kupicha had no real answers, he said there was no medicine which would help, only time and patience.

Patience was something Matilda was running low on. Sad as it was to miscarry, as many as four out of ten babies died within a year of their birth, and amongst the poor the ratio was even higher. She personally knew women who had lost as many as three or four babies, but they mourned, then accepted the tragedy with stoicism, accepting that it was the way things were. Lily hadn't gone the full term with her child, she had been irrational even before this happened, and it seemed to Matilda that there was something more to this than plain grief, perhaps even insanity.

Giles was beside himself with anxiety. Tabitha continually asked why her mama didn't like her any more, and they both looked to Matilda for comfort.

So how could she go to Giles and tell him she was leaving? He could get someone in to do the washing, cleaning and cooking, but would they mother Tabitha, support Giles and understand why Lily couldn't pull herself out of the dark pit she'd slipped into?

She wanted so much to go to Flynn, to shed this heavy burden of responsibility. She wanted passion and love, adventure and fun, to be Mrs O'Reilly and have a little home of her own. She felt bitter that fate appeared to be conspiring against her to prevent it.

Late that afternoon, Giles was up in his study preparing a sermon for Sunday morning, and Matilda and Tabitha were in the kitchen playing their word game, when a thunderstorm began. There was no real warning, other than it had grown hotter and stickier all day – one moment the sun was shining, the next the sky suddenly turned black and down came the rain.

Matilda ran outside to the yard to bring in the washing from the line, and by the time she'd collected the last sheet she was soaked. The lightning came before they'd even closed the door, and it lit up the kitchen brighter than a dozen lamps. Tabitha screamed in terror.

'It can't hurt us,' Matilda said, pulling her into her arms. 'We're quite safe in here.' Then the thunder cracked, so loud it sounded like it was on top of the roof, and the rain lashed down in torrents, shaking the windows.

All at once Matilda remembered that Lily's window was open, and scooping Tabitha up in her arms she ran up the stairs. 'Go in with Papa for a moment,' she said, once up on the landing, and patted the little girl's bottom in the direction of his study. 'I'll just go and check on Mama's window.'

The light in the bedroom was a curious grey-green, with the

rain lashing the open window and the curtains billowing in the wind. Lily was just lying there in bed staring into space – even when another flash of lightning came she didn't so much as blink. Matilda shut the window and mopped up the rain on the floor with a cloth, then she turned back to Lily.

'Don't you hear that?' she asked.

'Hear what?' Lily asked in the same curiously flat voice she'd used ever since the miscarriage.

'The rain, the thunder and lightning,' Matilda said. 'Why don't you get out of bed and come and look, the street's like a river already.'

Lily didn't move or reply, and something snapped inside Matilda. This woman had everything she wanted herself, a loving husband, a lovely child and a secure home. Less than a month ago Matilda had been blamed for bringing disease into the house, not a meal brought to her, or even a kind word, and Lily had even threatened to kill her if Tabitha died. Now she was wallowing in self-pity, frightening her husband and child and expecting Matilda to wait on her hand and foot. And because of this, Matilda was unable to go immediately to the man she loved.

'Stay in that bed if that's what you want to do,' she snarled at her. 'Lie there feeling sorry for yourself for as long as you like. But I'll tell you now, Lily Milson, that if that's what you choose to do, before long you'll be carted off to the mad-house.'

The woman looked at her, her eyes widening in shock to hear Matilda speak so harshly to her. It was the first time she'd reacted to anything anyone had said to her.

'Do you know what the mad-house is like?' Matilda went on, her anger and frustration welling up and spilling over. 'They chain you up, no one washes you or combs your hair, you'll get lice and rats will come in at night and scamper over you. And all you'll hear is the other mad people wailing. Do you like the sound of that?'

There was no reply from Lily, her grey eyes staring in bewilderment. Matilda leaned her forehead against the window and began to cry, for even though she'd spoken out in anger without thinking, she suddenly saw that in her pent-up rage she'd actually predicted what would happen. However much Giles Milson loved his wife, and however hard he tried to conceal that she was going mad, before long someone in his church would get to hear of it, and he'd be forced to put her away. Rich people could find comfortable places with kind doctors, but he was just a poor minister.

She had felt every kind of emotion towards her mistress in the two years she'd worked for her. Admiration, scorn, amusement, envy, irritation, fondness, pity, but she saw now that she'd learnt to love her too, or why would she care what happened to her? She wished she could be detached, she was after all just her servant. But somewhere along the line the woman had got under her skin, and into her heart.

'Don't cry, Matty!'

Matilda spun round at the plaintive plea, and saw Lily was crying herself and holding out her arms to her, just the way Tabitha did. She ran to her, sweeping the small woman up into her arms as if she were a child.

'I'm so sorry, Matty,' Lily sobbed against her shoulder. 'I know I'm behaving so badly. But I can't help it.'

Matilda's anger vanished as suddenly as it had erupted. 'I know,' she said, rocking her mistress backwards and forwards in her arms. 'I wish I could take away the pain inside you and make you see how much you have to live for.'

'Tell me about it,' Lily whispered hoarsely.

'Well, you have the finest husband in the world, he's a good, kind man who wants to put the whole world to rights, and he could if you stood beside him. You have the most adorable child, she's clever, loving and such a credit to you. Both of them love you so much. You have friends who admire your gentleness, and you have me who loves you too, and I'd do anything to make you better.'

'You love me?' she whispered. 'After all the unkind things I've said and done?'

'Yes, I love you,' Matilda whispered back. 'It's because of that I said such dreadful things about the mad-house.'

'I love you too,' Lily croaked. 'You've been my rock, my sister and my friend. You will always have a special place in my heart.'

Matilda had never, ever expected to hear such words from her mistress, and tears poured down her face because she sensed the sincerity in them. As she continued to hold and comfort the woman, she knew that she had truly crossed the line from servant to friend, and that she would never step back over it again. But by crossing that line she also knew she couldn't go and join Flynn just yet.

Chapter Ten

It was New Year of 1845, four months after Lily miscarried her baby, that Matilda finally received a reply from Flynn to her letter explaining why she couldn't come to him immediately.

There had been several letters during the intervening months, happy, loving missives penned whenever he felt the need to pour out his feelings about her, his new position and his life in Charleston. Matilda had sent just as many back, never imagining he would see her delay as anything other than a minor setback. She told him how Lily was progressing, her hopes that by the spring she would be fully recovered, and she assured him she still loved him just as deeply. Yet as she read this angry, bitter letter, she knew all the others would probably be torn up unread, for he seemed to see her decision as an act of betrayal.

> *'You are just their servant, not their daughter. I should be more important, if you loved me as you said you did,'* he wrote. *'I was counting on you, everything I have done was for you. Mr Donnelly wanted a married overseer and now that you haven't arrived it appears to him that I took the position on false pretences. My work is hard, and I need the comfort of a wife to come home to at the end of the long days.'*

She could barely bring herself to read the rest of the letter for he was revealing a side of himself she hadn't known existed. There was no understanding that she had been compelled to stay out of love and compassion for the Milsons, or even sympathy for her mistress. He claimed that back in Ireland such events as losing a child were commonplace and put aside in a day or two, and that Mrs Milson should thank God she had enough to eat, a healthy child, and a roof over her head. When he went on to say that the slave women on the plantation had to work out in the fields with a baby slung on their back and that their children, often younger than Tabitha, had to weed and hoe fields, she knew from his tone he'd not only accepted slavery, but now condoned it. That left her feeling sickened, for she feared he had become what she'd heard the Reverend Kirkbright refer to as 'white trash', one of those men who felt indignant that they were unable to rise in white society, so they took out their spite on the black man.

She could understand his disappointment that she hadn't come. She felt for him that he had to work long hours and then go home to an empty, cold house with no comforts. But the Flynn she had fallen in love with had been a self-sufficient idealist. What had changed him enough to speak of a wife in terms of a housekeeper?

All day she dwelt on both this letter and the previous loving, excited ones in which he'd painted such a rosy picture of the life they were going to share. The more she compared them, the angrier she became, for she suddenly realized that it was this last one, written in rage, which was the true picture of him and his work. In the others he'd just been painting seductively pretty and almost certainly false pictures for her.

She saw too that she had allowed herself to be fooled right from the start. Why hadn't he ever introduced her to anyone he knew? Or insisted that he met the Milsons? Wasn't it most likely that he knew she would then get another slant to his character?

She had believed that by holding back from love-making he was purely protecting her. But now, when she thought about the practised way he'd undressed her and fondled her, she realized he was experienced with women, and knew how to get satisfaction himself without the risk of impregnating her.

All at once that took on sinister tones. He had fired her up, removed all doubt about him from her mind. Wasn't it likely that he was already planning to leave, and knowing she was essential to his future plans, he'd made certain she would be willing to come to him the moment he gave the word?

'He's a confidence trickster, that's what he is,' she thought angrily, remembering the fine jacket with the silver buttons. 'And he wanted to marry me to give him more plausibility.'

She was beyond tears now. When she reached for pen and paper that night she wanted to wound him as deeply as he had her. In a rage she pointed out that she knew what he was. That she couldn't possibly marry a man who had no sympathy for someone losing a child, or live in a cottage owned by a man who made children work in the fields. She said that if he'd written to say he had only a shack for them to live in and no money, but that he had joined one of the underground movements to help slaves escape to the North, she would have jumped on the first boat after Lily was better and worked alongside him. But the thought of him prancing about on a horse whipping Negroes to work harder made her sick to her stomach.

She pointed out that when she married she wanted an equal partnership, not just to be there to cook meals and wash a man's shirts. She could never marry any man who didn't speak the truth.

Folding the letter and sealing it helped her resolve. She wasn't going to allow herself to read it the next day and then soften towards him.

In the days following posting her letter, Matilda found being brave and forthright didn't give her much comfort. New York in January was a grim place, with icy winds sweeping in from the Atlantic, leaden skies and frequent falls of snow which soon turned to black, three-foot-high walls of ice on the sidewalks. The water pump often froze up, vegetables and fruit disappeared from the shops. The plight of the poor was even more noticeable as she trudged out to buy oil for the lamps or something more appetizing than salted pork to eat and saw their children with rags tied around their bare feet, begging just for bread.

Tabitha was five now and she had started at a small school on Broadway after Christmas. But with the child gone from the house between nine and two each day, the days seemed long, alone with just her mistress. Lily had recovered her spirits in as much that she kept herself busy all day sewing, reading and baking, but she was often very withdrawn and rarely went out of the house. Giles on the other hand was very much busier with projects in the parish that included a soup kitchen for the destitute, the opening of a public school, which involved making sure it was attended by all children from the neighbouring tenements, and the Waifs' and Strays' Home in New Jersey. Lily seemed to have accepted now that this was all part of his job, and there had been no further talk of forbidding him to go to places she believed were insanitary or dangerous.

Now that Matilda had much less to do around the home, Giles often asked for her help outside it – at the soup kitchen, persuading reluctant parents to send their children to school, and passing out clothes and blankets donated by good people in the parish. There was no need to go into Five Points to find orphans any longer, word had got around among them about the refuge across the Hudson river and they found their own way to Dr Kupicha's door. As fast as adoptive parents were found for some of the original children, their places were taken by new ones, and now the church was raising money to extend the building.

Cissie was given the position as head nursemaid for the under-fives, a position she delighted in. She had been so very sad when Pearl was adopted by a childless couple in Boston back in November, but by Christmas she had accepted it was for the best, and even asked Miss Rowbottom to teach her to read and write so she could keep in touch with her friend's child. Sidney had been offered a new home twice, but he'd made it quite clear he would run away if he was forced to go. As he was so useful in the home farm and a good influence on the wilder boys, the governors had said he could stay permanently.

Yet even seeing the success of the rescue work, finding fulfilment in helping Giles in new projects, and knowing that she would have always felt a sense of guilt if she had left when Lily was ill, in all these long months Matilda's heart still ached for Flynn. He didn't reply to her angry letter – no apology, no plea for a second chance – and she had to accept that he was never the man she believed him to be, that in reality she'd had a lucky escape. Yet that didn't make the pain any less.

She saw Rosa one day as she walked through Fulton Fishmarket. Her belly was swollen, her dress dirty and her hair matted and as she caught sight of Matilda she darted away. Matilda knew the girl must have expected her to turn away in scorn, but she wouldn't have, not now. Her time with Flynn had made her so much more aware of human frailties, and but for his self-control, she too might have found herself with child. That at least was something she'd always be grateful for.

'What is wrong, Matty?' Giles asked one March morning as they set off to discover why four boys who had been attending school regularly had suddenly stopped coming. It was still so very cold that it seemed to Matilda that she'd imagined how hot New York could be in August. It was indeed a city of extremes – so much wealth, but so much poverty, so colourful and lively, yet dismal and cheerless too. Hope yet despair, sorrow yet joy. Even her own feelings for it ranged from love to loathing.

'There's nothing wrong, sir,' she said, managing to force a bright smile. 'I'm just cold.'

Giles looked sideways at her as they walked along Pearl Street. She wore a grey wool cape with a hood, a cast-off from his wife, and the dress beneath it was grey too. No doubt most people in his social circle would say she was appropriately dressed for her position, but grey didn't suit her character. If he could choose a colour for her it would be bright blue to match her eyes. He'd let that pretty blonde hair loose from its pins, and take her to see something amusing, just to hear her laugh. It seemed months since he'd heard that sound.

'I didn't mean just today, you've been glum for a long while now,' he said. 'I thought you had a sweetheart last year. You used to come home from your afternoons off looking sparkling-eyed and happy. Now you hardly go out, and when you do, you come home looking sad. What happened to him, Matty?'

Matilda gulped. It was too late now to tell him about Flynn, if she told him he was an overseer on a plantation he would find that even harder to stomach than hearing he worked in a saloon.

'There was someone for a while, but he's gone away,' she said simply. 'He didn't turn out to be the kind of man I thought he was.'

Giles didn't reply for some little time, just took her arm and hurried her across the busy street. 'Few of us ever let anyone see ourselves as we really are,' he said at length. 'Sometimes we hide or enhance our real character, or pretend to be someone else, and we all change as circumstances do.'

'You don't,' she said indignantly. 'You are the same now as when I first met you nearly three years ago.'

'I'm not,' he said with a sigh. 'I was naive and rather too fond of myself in those days. I believed my calling made me superior to other men. I know that isn't so now. But other aspects of my character have changed too. I have grown hard to terrible sights. I often doubt my faith. I don't trust the way I once did. And look at you, Matty, you aren't the same girl we picked up in Oxford Street.'

'I'm glad of that,' she smiled. 'She was a little rogue. Did you ever guess that I made out I was more badly hurt than I really was because I thought you might give me a shilling or two?'

He laughed, really laughed, his dark eyes crinkling up and making him look very boyish. 'Thank goodness I didn't offer it, you might have shot off into the crowd and I would never have seen you again! But what I meant was that your needs were so simple then, Matty. Selling enough flowers in a day to buy food was your only goal, you didn't look beyond that.'

'You don't when you're hungry all the time,' she said tartly.

'Well, you aren't hungry now, and haven't been for a long time, so what are your goals now?'

That question was so like the one Flynn had asked on the first day she met him at the Tontine coffee house, only he'd asked her what she wanted out of life. She thought for a moment. 'When I get old I want to look back at my life and know it was a worth-while one.'

'Does that mean you want riches, or position, or to be a good mother to half a dozen children?' he asked, and she sensed he found her reply amusing.

'I think I'd like all of those,' she said with a smile. 'But most of all I want to have made a difference in some other people's lives.' She paused for a moment, knowing she hadn't quite made her point. 'Like persuading you to take Cissie and Peter to the Home, that made a difference in her life.'

'It did indeed, Matty,' he agreed. 'If that is your goal it's the very finest one. So keep it tightly in your head and don't ever let it go. Let me hear you laugh again too, let that man go from your heart if he was wrong for you, and start again. Life is too hard and short to spend much of it sad.'

She knew he was right, but she wished someone could tell her how to push the face of the man she loved out of her mind. She had a feeling that picture was going to stay there for all time.

Fire swept through the financial area around Wall Street later on that year. Fortunately for Matilda and the Milsons it began several streets north of State Street and whipped eastwards towards the docks. But the flames eating up the last of the old Dutch commercial buildings, wooden warehouses and sailors' lodging houses was a terrifying sight, and had the wind turned, the fire could have claimed an even bigger area. The black acrid smoke and thick grey ash filled the air for several days afterwards and struck new terror into Lily's heart. To her it was further proof that New York was the most dangerous place on earth.

'Help me to persuade my husband to go home to England,' she begged Matilda as they battled to clean away the ash which had crept in all over the house. 'I cannot live like this, never knowing when the next disaster will strike.'

Matilda very much wished at that point that they could go home. A recent letter from Dolly had brought news that Lucas's health was fading, and she knew Dolly would never alarm her with such news unless she felt his end was very near.

'I'll try,' she said.

Lily impulsively hugged her, her small face alight with utter faith in her powers of persuasion. 'Oh Matty, just think how good it would be to walk in the countryside, to see apple blossom in the spring and have tea on the lawn in summer. Don't you miss those things too?'

It was a curious thing, but for someone who had raged about Matilda's origins on the night when Tabitha had measles, Lily seemed now to have quite forgotten she came from the slums and had no knowledge of having 'tea on the lawn', or any other English middle-class traditions. Since her miscarriage she had begun to treat Matilda more like a younger sister than servant. She had made her a pretty blue-striped calico dress with pin tucks on the bodice, and sought her company more and more. On several occasions she'd even asked her to stop calling her madam and use Lily instead. Matilda felt a little uneasy about their changing relationship, but it wasn't one-sided, she found she thought of her as a dear friend rather than her mistress. Perhaps it was because she'd discovered for herself what heart-ache felt like, for even if the reasons behind their melancholy were very different, their symptoms were very alike.

'Yes, I miss England,' Matilda agreed. 'I'd give anything to see my father and Dolly again, to go up on Primrose Hill, see the Tower of London and all the other places I liked. But even if the Reverend did agree to go home, I don't think he'd settle for being a country parson, or even take on a parish in a nice part of London. He's too committed now with his work with the poor to give up on them.'

'But why?' Lily stamped her feet with indignation. 'We could have such a happy life in Bath or somewhere like that.'

Matilda smiled in fondness. At times Lily was very like a spoiled child, sunny when everything went her way, sulky when it didn't. 'You know he isn't a man to turn his back on his ideals,' she replied. 'That is the most admirable thing about him, madam, few men are so steadfast in their beliefs.'

Lily pouted. 'What do you know of men?' she said.

'Not much, but enough to know that!' Matilda said. 'It's my opinion that most of them are motivated by greed, lust and adventure, and their poor wives get a great deal less love and attention than you do.'

A few days later, after her mistress had spent almost all day complaining about the shambles left by the fire, and expressing her disgust that a huge mob of rough Irishmen were already squatting on the site in makeshift shanties, Matilda resolved to talk to her master that night.

Lily's anxiety was understandable. Things changed at lightning speed in New York, buildings were torn down and bigger, more spectacular ones took their place instantly. Whole new blocks of houses appeared like magic, and likewise areas which had been the height of fashion just a decade earlier could turn into a slum almost overnight. Cherry Hill had once been the home of notable men like George Washington, but was now a place decent people shunned. The fire, and the subsequent rebuilding needed, would undoubtedly start a mass exodus of their more affluent neighbours to further up town. Their homes would then be rented out and before long the neighbourhood could degenerate into another Cherry Hill. Matilda hoped that even if Giles couldn't be persuaded to return to England, he would at least ask the Reverend Kirkbright if they could move away from here.

She waited until Lily had gone up to bed, made Giles a cup of hot chocolate and then tackled him.

'Go home to England?' he said in some surprise. 'That's unthinkable, Matty. I have pledged myself to this country now, there is still so much to do here.'

Matilda wasn't at all surprised by that response, it was what she had expected, so she went on to explain his wife's fears for this neighbourhood and how she hankered for green fields, gardens and sweet-smelling air.

He nodded in understanding. 'I feel that way myself very often. If it were possible I would try and find us somewhere more agreeable to live. But I am not a rich man, Matty, I have to live where the church places me. My wife knows that too.'

'But can't you see how hard it is for her to think she'll be here for ever?' Matilda pleaded with him. 'Soon the friends she has made around here will move away, it will become noisier and dirtier week by week.'

'I didn't say I intended to stay here for ever,' he said, arching his dark eyebrows in surprise. 'Once I feel I have laid the foundations for a better deal for the poor, I shall move on.'

'Not somewhere even grimmer?' she exclaimed, her eyes widening with horror.

'No,' he laughed. 'You are forgetting I am something of an adventurer, Matty. America is a vast country and I've only seen such a tiny part of it. Right now there are people making their way right across the country to uncharted lands in the West. I'd like to see that too.'

Matilda knew about the people going off in wagon trains to find land in Oregon, and from what she'd heard about the hardships they endured, with everything from high mountains, wide rivers to ford, and hostile Indians, she didn't think her mistress would be overjoyed to join them. When she said this Giles laughed again.

'No, Mrs Milson hasn't the stamina for that,' he said. 'I didn't mean we would join the pioneers. But clergymen are badly needed for missions in the mid-West, and I think maybe she could be happy there, mixing with farming folk, perhaps starting a badly needed school.'

Matilda stared at him in wonder. To her that sounded an ideal solution. 'Have you ever spoken to Mrs Milson about this?'

He shook his head. 'Not yet. It's only recently I began to think about it myself,' he said. 'Many of the immigrants I meet through the church talk to me about their relatives out there, and their plans to join them. I guess they've infected me too with the idea of wide open spaces, and the challenge of building a real community with other like-minded folk from every corner of the world. Do you think Mrs Milson might like that too?'

'I'm sure she would,' she said, imagining her mistress organizing sewing bees and cake sales. 'You should put it to her, maybe if she knew there was something good to look forward to, she wouldn't mind spending another year or two here.'

'And what about you, Matty? Would you come with us?'

'I couldn't let you go on your own,' she laughed, suddenly elated at the idea. 'And I'd like to see all those wonders, we've been in America two years now and the nearest thing I've seen to an Indian is the carved wooden one outside the tobacco store. The only horse I've been on was the one in Coney Island.'

She made the last statement without thinking, and the moment the words were out she blushed.

Giles looked at her intently. 'Did the man who let you down take you to Coney Island?' he said in a soft voice.

For just a second she was going to say she went alone, but if she was going to stay on with the Milsons there was going to come a day when she might let it slip again. 'Yes, sir, when you were in Boston.'

He didn't look shocked, only curious. 'What was his name, Matty? Tell me about him.'

She had always thought she couldn't bring herself even to say Flynn's name again, but all at once she was pouring it all out, how she met him, the Friday afternoons together, and her promise she would join him in Charleston. She was surprised to find how much relief she felt at telling someone.

Giles listened, only asking the odd question now and again.

'It was a good job I didn't go, as it turned out,' she said with a tight little laugh. 'I'd probably be living in some awful little shack and be labelled "white trash" too.'

Giles had taken in all she'd told him, and understood even more about the parts left unsaid. It saddened him to think she hadn't been able to confide in him right from the beginning, and he was deeply touched that her commitment to him and his family was even greater than to the man she loved. And she *had* loved him, still loved him now, he could see that in her face.

'I can think of dozens of reasons why marriage with Flynn might not have been all you hoped for,' he said with deep sympathy. 'Irishmen are a volatile bunch in the main. If you think now that he only revealed a very small part of his true self, I suspect the part he didn't show you wouldn't have pleased you. But I am deeply sorry that you had your dreams dashed, Matty. First love is a very precious thing.'

'I'm getting over it now,' she said, blushing again because she was afraid she'd said too much. 'As my father said when he left me with you at the parsonage, "Never look back."'

'Your father is a wise man,' Giles said in approval. 'But most of us find it very hard not to think wistfully on what is past, or berate ourselves for not acting differently. You have handled this with great dignity, Matty. In time that will be a comfort to you.'

She smiled, her blue eyes suddenly very wide and sparkling. 'You are a comfort to me,' she said. 'If I ever get tempted to fall for another man, I shall make sure he's as much like you as possible.'

It occurred to her later when she was in bed that such a remark could easily be misconstrued. But then she had meant it in the purest way, and she was sure Giles would know that too.

She wanted a man who was as good inside as he was outwardly, who cared about people, rich or poor, valued children and worked hard. An intelligent, well-balanced man who would never lie to her, who thought of his woman as an equal. But she wanted someone with a sense of fun too, who liked to laugh and dance. A man who would make love to her with passion and commitment. A brave man.

Giles was all these things, except of course she had no idea what he'd be like as a lover, or if he could dance.

She giggled, shocked to think she'd even dare think of something so physical in connection with her master. But she had a feeling he would excel in both, he moved gracefully, his eyes smouldered as if he was capable of strong passions. In truth she could find no real fault in him, unless of course it was his blind allegiance to God!

The Sunday before Christmas, the Reverend Kirkbright announced from the pulpit at the morning service that the Milsons would be leaving Trinity Church in the spring for Missouri. The decision to move on had come about suddenly because a minister was urgently needed in the little frontier town of Independence. The present one was old and sick, and the bishop in St Louis who was a friend of the Reverend Kirkbright had asked him to select someone young and dynamic to take his place.

Giles was in his cassock and surplice, and had taken his seat by the choir stalls. Matilda was sitting with Lily and Tabitha in the front row of pews, behind them the church was packed to capacity, and Matilda's heart swelled up with pride as the Reverend Kirkbright spoke of how much Giles Milson had given to the parish in his time with them.

'There can be very few of you here today who haven't had their lives touched by this extraordinary clergyman. He has visited the sick, comforted the bereaved, listened to your troubles and shared your triumphs. But Reverend Milson has left his biggest mark on his care for the poor. Thanks to his compassion and courage, innumerable orphans have been rescued from conditions which few of us here today can even imagine. These children are healthy now, well cared for in the Waifs' and Strays' Home in New Jersey, and many of them have been adopted by good people in other states.'

Remembering the covert way she and Giles had rescued these children, Matilda glanced at Lily to get her reaction at hearing it spoken of openly. But Lily wasn't looking at Darius Kirkbright, only at her husband. Her grey eyes, in which it was usually so hard to see any depth of feeling, were shining, her small face alight with pride. There was no doubt in Matilda's mind that Lily had long since come to terms with Giles's ministry work, wherever that might lead him, and that in future she'd always be at his side.

'Along with this work,' the Reverend Kirkbright went on, 'Reverend Milson has established soup kitchens and got countless children into schools. He told me soon after he arrived in America that he believed that education was the only real weapon in the fight against poverty, and of course he is right. Benevolence to the poor, the distribution of food, fuel and warm clothes eases the suffering, but the real cure *is* education. A man or woman who can read and write can get a better job and in turn better housing. Education banishes ignorance and opens doors in the mind to infinite new opportunities.' The Reverend Kirkbright paused for a moment, his eyes scanning the packed pews beneath his pulpit.

'We are all going to miss Reverend and Mrs Milson, and I'm sure you all join me in wishing them every happiness and success in their new home and church. But it would be a tragedy if after they have left we remembered them only for being kind-hearted, good people. Reverend Milson has left us a wonderful legacy. He has set the wheels in motion for a better, more caring society, and all of us here today must each vow to support and maintain what he so courageously began.

'America is set to be the greatest country in the entire world, but a country, like a house, is only as strong as its foundations. We must all set aside self-interest and work to build these foundations with care for the poor and sick, good schools and housing. We must banish ignorance and intolerance, learn to love our neighbours, regardless of their race or religion. We are all Americans now, wherever we or our parents came from, and as such we must take pride in our new nationality and pull together to make it the greatest nation on earth.'

It was the first time Matilda had ever known the congregation clap in church. It begin with a slight tapping and swelled into a tumultuous roar. A lump came up in her throat and her eyes were damp. She felt in that moment that she might become an American after all.

Chapter Eleven

Early evening sun slanted through a side window, casting a coppery tinge on to Giles Milson's dark curls as he stood at the table looking at the welcoming feast laid out for him and his family. A large, golden-crusted pie, dishes piled high with vegetables, warm, freshly baked bread and a pitcher of milk. After such a long and arduous journey to Independence, Missouri, mere bread and cheese would have been enough to delight him, but such generosity and kindness from his new parishioners seemed to confirm he had made the right decision to move his family here.

Looking at each of them he felt a surge of love and tenderness. Lily with an uncharacteristic sun-burnt face was wiping away happy tears. Tabitha in a decidedly rumpled and grubby pinafore, her dark plaits unravelling, was licking her lips at the sight of the food in front of her, and Matilda, eyes as blue as the summer skies outside, was smiling at the vase of dog daisies in the centre of the table.

'A very special grace is called for tonight,' he said, putting his hands together and closing his eyes. 'Thank you, Lord, for bringing us safely through the long journey to our new home and church, and for the generosity of all those good people who offered us help and hospitality on the way. Our hearts are full of love and gratitude for everyone who welcomed us here today, prepared this house for us and this food on the table. I pray that the happiness we all feel today will stay with us for ever.'

Matilda said a fervent Amen to that. She might not put her trust in God as completely as the Milsons did, but even she was willing to admit that he did seem to have worked a few miracles for this family in the past few months.

They had left New York in April, and it was now July. The 1,200-mile journey had been covered by train, boats and horse and cart. Every mile of it had been thrilling, for none of them had any real conception of how vast America was, or how beautiful.

There had been so many memorable sights – the orchards in full blossom in Pennsylvania, the vastness of Lake Erie, deep forests, wide, fast-flowing rivers and spectacular sunsets over mountain ranges. They had marvelled at the immense flat prairies and the dedication of the people who had sown the seemingly endless miles of wheat and corn.

It had been so good to breathe fresh clean air, to hear leaves rustling and birdsong, and see wild flowers, animals and how folk lived away from the noise and dirt of the cities. They passed through so many picturesque, sleepy little towns with neat little wooden houses and carefully tended gardens. Here and there they saw long tree-lined avenues leading to spectacular mansions, but the further west they went, humble log cabins became more common, and some homes were only made from sods of hard-packed earth. Yet poor as the owners undoubtedly were, they and their children looked healthier and happier than their city counterparts.

Thrilling as the sights on the journey had been, the real joy of it to Matilda was seeing Lily so happy. She had been serene even before they left New York, but once they left the city behind she had become a quite different person.

Suddenly she was chatting, laughing, asking eager questions, and Matilda saw Giles responding to her like a sweetheart. But then leaving New York had set them all free – no more social restraints, dull chores, noise and city dirt, and somehow the wide open spaces seemed to encourage them all to be more open and daring. Giles found great satisfaction in learning to handle the temperamental cart horse and set up camps for the night, Lily in learning to cook on an open fire. For the first time in her life Tabitha was freed from her many petticoats, she could run alongside the cart, swing from branches of trees, paddle in streams and enjoy the simple pleasures that country-bred children took for granted.

What an adventure it had been to sleep out in the open air! Scary sometimes when they heard wolves howling or predatory rustlings in the undergrowth, but exciting too. They lay huddled together round the fire, looking up in wonder at the star-filled sky, and they'd talk about life back in England and in New York and wonder at the changes in all of them.

Matilda didn't think she would ever forget Lily's emotional tears when women, some of whom who could barely speak English, begged her and her family to share a simple meal with them, because a visiting minister meant a blessing on their house. Or the shock they all felt when they came face to face with their first Indians out on the plains in Indiana.

They had come over a hill in their horse and cart, and there they were, riding full pelt towards them. Not almost naked, dirty savages as Matilda at least had imagined Indians to be, but wearing plain buckskins, with long black hair as shiny as tar, riding their sleek horses as if they were one with the animal. Lily had turned pale and clutched Tabitha to her, even Giles confessed later he uttered up some silent prayers, but the Indians ignored them, and rode past without even a glance in their direction.

They learned a couple of days later that they were Cherokees, a tribe which had lived in Georgia until the white man snatched their fertile lands, rounded them up and forced them to walk all the way to the Indian territories west of Missouri. This group they saw were renegades, they'd escaped the round-up and taken the mountains of South Indiana as their new home. They were almost certainly on a hunting trip to take food back to the rest of their group.

But the trip wasn't pleasant or interesting all the time. There was mile after mile of barren, desolate land, there had been heavy rain when they all got soaked to the skin, there were occasions when they ran out of food, and the last leg of the journey had many fraught moments, particularly when a wheel broke miles from anywhere, and Giles had to ride off on the horse to get help, leaving the women stranded on a mere track, with no idea how long it would be before he got back.

Yet it was those bad times which made them laugh later. Matilda had never imagined that Lily was capable of stripping off her boots and stockings, tucking her dress up and wading through mud to collect firewood, or that Giles knew how to fish, or snare a rabbit. Both Giles and Lily had marvelled at Matilda's ingenuity in building fires and finding soft brushwood to make impromptu beds, and her knowledge about carts and horses.

But then she too was surprised that things she'd learnt as a child in Finders Court had stayed with her.

Yet of all the good things which happened in the last few months, the one that meant the most to Matilda happened just before they left New York. The Milsons had called her into the parlour one evening, sat her down, and said she was no longer to think of herself as their servant, but a family friend and in future she was to call them Giles and Lily.

'We insist,' Lily said, smiling at Matilda's embarrassed protest. 'You are coming with us as an equal in a big adventure and it would be ridiculous for you to continue to call us Sir and Madam. In future you will have an allowance, we won't call it wages any longer, and if at any time you wish to leave us, then you are free to do so.'

'Of course we hope that won't happen for some time,' Giles joined in. 'And when it does, we fervently hope it will be because you are to be married.'

At the time Matilda had the idea this kindness was due to her getting the sad news from Dolly that her father had died back in the previous November. All this time she'd clung on to the idea she would one day be able to see him again to tell him all about America and how grateful she was to him for letting her go. There was so much left unsaid, how she valued him making her go to school, things she'd wanted to ask about her mother, that even so far away he was always in her mind, and that she loved him.

Yet later, once they were on their journey, Matilda came to see Giles and Lily's intention to raise her status from servant to friend was so that she could move in the same social circle as themselves, which would enable her to make a far better marriage.

Matilda didn't think she would ever love again, Flynn was still too deeply engraved on her heart and mind. But it was very soothing to know Lily and Giles cared so deeply for her future.

The sound of chairs being pulled out jolted Matilda back to the present.

'What's in the pie, Mama?' Tabitha asked as they sat down.

'I think it's rabbit,' Lily said as she cut the flaky golden crust. 'But whatever it is, Mrs Homberger is an excellent cook, I haven't seen pastry like this since we left England.' She handed out slices of pie, and urged them to help themselves to the vegetables. 'Oh, it's so nice here,' she suddenly burst out. 'I just know we are going to have the happiest future.'

Giles reached for his wife's hand and squeezed it with affection. He was unable to voice how relieved he was that Independence, and the house provided for them by the church, pleased her.

As Independence was the last town in organized territory, and the jumping-off place for the wagon trains going across the great plains to Oregon and the West, Giles had anticipated a wild frontier town with all that entailed.

He had been surprised and delighted, therefore, to find Independence was a remarkably sedate little town, with a solid and permanent community of tradesmen and merchants who supplied the travellers with wagons, oxen to pull them, provisions, equipment and tools for the long, hazardous journey. These people, and the owners of outlying farms, clearly took a great pride in their town. The church, school, small hospital, court room and the minister's house had all been built by many of the menfolk.

One of the good people who had welcomed them today, a burly blacksmith by the name of Solomon, who looked tough enough to rip a man's head from his shoulders, had taken Giles to one side and pointed out that the town could be a wild place come early spring when the wagon trains were preparing to roll, with more than its fair share of drinking, gambling, fornication and fighting. He pointed out that while the travellers themselves were peaceful, industrious, God-fearing families, just like most of the settlers in the area, the scouts, soldiers, professional gamblers, whores and other itinerants could create trouble and disturbance.

Giles had asked if there was any trouble with the Indians. The news that so many of them were being moved out of their ancestral lands in the East to make room for white settlers was a cause of deep concern to him. But back in New York it was hard to separate fact from fiction about this, as land-hungry men in authority would say anything, use any propaganda to justify their actions. He had always suspected that the tales of settlers being murdered in their beds were wildly exaggerated, yet desperate people could do desperate things and he was anxious to learn the truth.

'The redskins ain't ones for towns,' Solomon said. 'I heard tell they meet every wagon train that passes through their land, after food and horses, but the way I sees it, that's fair enough, it is their land. You'll hear a lotta scary talk about 'em, but don't you mind it none. If we leave 'em alone, they'll leave us alone, that's my thinking.'

Giles would also have liked to ask Solomon about this town's views on slavery. Missouri *was* a slave-owning state, yet as Giles had noted, there were no vast plantations here, and he assumed the many Negroes he'd seen were mostly house servants or farm hands. He had heard from the Abolitionist movement back in New York that native-born Missourians, said to be a fiery bunch, were firmly pro-slavery, but the new settlers, particularly the devoutly religious Germans, were vigorously opposed to it.

But perhaps it was wisest to wait and sound people out first. To poke a stick into a hornets' nest wasn't a sensible thing to do, and besides, there was so much else here that delighted him.

After visiting the pretty little white clapboard church, complete with a bell in its steeple, in the centre of Independence Square, the Milsons were then escorted to their new home, and the moment Giles saw it he said a silent prayer of thanks. It was not some makeshift shack-like one like those on the edge of town, or a cabin made from logs, but a two-storey frame-built house right in the centre of the town. It was painted white, and the small front garden was surrounded by a picket fence. There was a wide porch complete with a swinging chair to sit out in on warm evenings, and inside the comfort and space that he'd never dared to hope for: a fair-sized parlour, with doors that opened on to a dining-room, a big kitchen with a stove every bit as good as the one they'd had back in New York, and a pump just outside the back door. Upstairs there were three good-sized bedrooms, and around half an acre of land at the back.

Mrs Homberger, whose husband ran the mail office, had personally overseen the preparation of the house for them. The floor had been scrubbed and polished, sparkling white curtains hung at the windows, the beds were all made in readiness, even the kitchen cupboards had been lined with fresh paper and stocked with basic provisions.

It was a little Spartan compared with the rather over-furnished house in State Street, the furniture well worn, but after the blistering heat outside it was cool, airy and sweet-smelling. Then when Mrs Homberger disappeared, only to return half an hour later with this meal for them, they had all been speechless with surprise. Lily was so touched she burst into tears, forgot her normal coolness with strangers and hugged the woman.

'Will I go to school tomorrow?' Tabitha asked eagerly, her mouth full of pie.

Her mama rebuked her for her bad manners and said she thought getting the house straight was of greater importance than school for the time being.

'We'll have to see about trading the horse and cart for a gig,' Giles said, smiling beatifically. 'We ought to get some chickens and a pig too. We're country folk now, and we've got to learn country ways.'

Lily looked at her husband in horror. 'Pigs smell, Giles,' she said. 'And chickens make such a fearful mess.'

'But they make good eating,' Matilda said, guessing Lily had imagined she was going to lay out the land at the back with flowers and lawn. 'And we'll have to learn to grow vegetables too.'

Giles smiled at his wife's stunned expression. Like Matilda he knew she had visions of an English garden. 'You can have flowers in the front,' he said. 'I'll even order some rose bushes for you, but we'll have to make the land at the back work for us.'

Matilda cynically expected that once they settled down in their new home the old order of mistress and servant would return. She also anticipated that Lily's old ways, along with her fears and phobias, might very well come back if something upset her.

But happily she was wrong on both counts. Whatever miracle had changed Lily into a happy, carefree woman, she remained so. Right from the first day when they got up at dawn, Lily was adamant that all work should be equally divided, and they learned from one another. Matilda had to show Lily how to scrub a floor without turning it into a lake, clean and light the stove and how to work the water pump. But Lily knew a surprising amount about growing vegetables, because as a girl staying with poorer relatives in Bath, she'd helped them. What she didn't know she soon found out by asking local people.

It was terribly hot right through to September, and the school was only open in the mornings as the children's help was needed on the farms. Tabitha was delighted at this arrangement and though only five she was all too eager to pull weeds, and try her hand at digging. Her face and arms turned as brown as a berry from such long periods outside, and she often said she never wanted to go back to a city to live.

Yet however much fun planning and starting a vegetable garden had seemed, Lily and Matilda soon discovered that clearing land, digging, planting and hoeing was back-breaking work. In the evenings they staggered in with aching backs and painful blisters on their hands. But as the first neat rows of seedlings began to grow, the feeling of satisfaction, and the knowledge that come winter they would have their own source of food, more than made up for the effort.

Matilda had imagined too that Lily would get right back into the corsets and hooped skirts she'd abandoned on the way here, but she continued happily to wear the same old simple calico dress and sun-bonnet from Monday to Saturday. She not only learned to tolerate the smell of the two small pigs they bought, but grew fond of them, naming them Cain and Abel. Her dislike of chickens vanished the first time she ate a newly laid egg. But there was still a shadow of the genteel Lily. She almost fainted with shock when a neighbour told her to collect horse droppings from the livery stable to work into the soil. She said that however good it was for the garden she drew the line at being seen walking through the town with a pail of manure. She squeaked with alarm every time a spider or other creepy-crawly came into the house.

It was a completely different way of life to the one in New York. There was no ice man calling each day here, no great variety of food in the store, so they had to make do with what was available. There was no theatre or concerts, or invitations to tea or elegant suppers. But neighbours did call in the evening when the day's work was done, often bringing a batch of cakes, vegetables or fruit, and they sat on the porch, drank lemonade, and shared their experiences and knowledge.

These people were so very different from the brittle society folk and solid merchants the Milsons had rubbed shoulders with in New York. They were plain people, many of German extraction, to whom wealth meant merely a second or third room added to the primitive cabins they'd built themselves, or a real cook stove like the Milsons had.

Most of these people had arrived here after a series of moves, always looking for cheaper and more fertile land, or a start in a new business. Some started out in the North, gradually working their way down, others had come up from the Southern states, or the East coast.

All their lives had been very hard. Most had lost several children in infancy, many were on a second or third marriage because their previous husbands or wives had died. Whether born in America or immigrants, most married into their own nationality. Matilda heard many stories about how the bride had been found for the groom back in Berlin or Hamburg by his parents, the courtship was by letter, and often the first time they met was just shortly before the marriage.

Romantic love as Matilda knew it didn't seem to come into it, marriage was a contract, and if it wasn't joyful, the couple made the best of it. Perhaps the sheer hard work they had to endure and their faith held them together, for church on Sundays was something few of them missed.

Dressed in their best clothes, these devout people flocked into Independence with their many children by foot, horse or cart, often setting off at dawn to do so. They thanked God for their blessings and prayed that they could endure future disasters, but it was also a time for mixing, to gossip and exchange news. The ones who lived a great way off often brought picnics which they shared with others, for making friends was all important to people who lived in isolation. Good neighbours could be counted on at harvest time, to help with building work, and to find good marriage partners for their older sons and daughters.

Matilda and Lily soon discovered for themselves the advantages of encouraging their female neighbours to call. They learned how to make pasta from Angelina from Naples, sauerkraut and spicy sausages from Heidi from Berlin, how to salt pork for the winter from Mrs Homberger, and to make their own soap from lye and animal fats, filtering it through ashes. Tabitha learned to count in German and Italian, and to play dozens of new games with other children.

Lily was glad to teach English to any of the foreign women who asked her for help, and her ladylike manner and sophistication were much admired by women who had never lived in a city.

Giles seemed to grow in every direction during those long summer days. His sermons in church were secondary to his care for his new parishioners. He visited them all in his new gig, often driving fifty miles to outlying farms, he was there to bless a new cabin as the roof was raised, often driving in nails with the other men, he buried the dead and consoled the bereaved, officiated at marriages and baptisms.

There were people with long-established, extensive farms, who perhaps could loosely be called gentry, for their houses were large colonial-style ones, with lush green lawns and paddocks for their horses. Although Giles welcomed them at his church, he kept his distance socially, for these were the slave owners.

Slavery was an inflammatory topic, and while Giles still detested the idea that men, women and children could be owned, and sold on like cattle, he'd also come to see that if he was to serve his new community well he had to calm hot-heads on both sides. By taking a cool, calm look at the situation, he could see for himself that the great majority of slave owners were decent people, and they treated their slaves well. Many of the slaves, fired up by the Abolitionists to run away, found only far greater misery than they'd ever experienced under their former owners.

What concerned Giles much more than the well-fed slaves on the outlying farms was the plight of the people living down by the Missouri river. They were desperately poor, living in conditions as bad as anything he'd seen in New York. They camped in shacks, unfit even for animals, some in holes in the ground covered with a crude roof of wood and sods, and even tents, at risk of being drowned when the river rose in a downpour.

Many of these were Negroes, escaped slaves and freemen, but just as many were white, and like the poor of New York they were considered inferior beings and ignored. They received no medical attention and their many, many children didn't attend school. Most of the crimes committed in the area were hatched in this quarter, just as it was a breeding ground for disease and every imaginable vice. But Giles was at a loss as to how to solve the problem. He had no Reverend Kirkbright or board of governors to back him up here, no funds from the church to alleviate the innocents' suffering.

Most of his preaching on Sundays leaned towards trying to foster a little more Christian charity towards these people. Much of it fell on deaf ears – his parishioners were in the main kindly, but they had little enough themselves. But Giles kept chipping away, doing what he could, and hoped that in time his message would not only be heard, but acted upon.

All through that first summer Matilda looked in wonder at Giles, for happiness simply shone out of him. He let his dark hair grow longer, he didn't care that his clothes were covered in dust, he smiled a great deal, and laughed even more. She found him showing Tabitha how to climb a tree one day, another time he came home late from a wedding and insisted he taught her and Lily the steps of a dance he'd learnt. They didn't need a newspaper, he brought all the news and gossip home, and hardly a day went by without his praising Lily and Matilda for the hard work they did.

Matilda had been warned by many women that the first winter in Missouri was always a testing time for new arrivals, and as the leaves began to fall in October and Tabitha went back to school for the whole day, she watched Lily anxiously. She had come to love their outdoor life during the summer, and Matilda was concerned that now there was much less to do, and no visitors to the porch in the evenings, she might slip back to the way she'd been in New York.

Yet instead of becoming withdrawn when the rain came for days on end, turning the streets into a treacherous swamp of red mud, Lily seemed to grow even happier, turning to preserving fruit and vegetables, making new clothes for Tabitha and even drawing up plans for next year's vegetable planting.

It was quiet in the evenings without visitors calling, but the pot-bellied stove in the parlour and the stove in the kitchen warmed the whole house and Giles would read aloud to the two women as they sewed. As Thanksgiving and Christmas drew nearer Lily made plans for special meals and decorations for the house and church. But even after Christmas when thick snow came and bitterly cold winds seemed to creep in through every window and crack in the floorboards, she had new plans. Twice a week she tramped through the snow to the school-house to help the foreign children learn English, and one day a week she threw an open house for other women to come and sew quilts with her and Matilda.

It was through the quilt-making venture that Matilda finally discovered the root cause of Lily's new contentment. One bitterly cold grey February day they were sitting huddled in front of the stove, both taking apart old dresses to use for patchwork squares. When Matilda saw Lily smiling as she looked at some red printed cotton, she asked about it.

'I don't remember seeing that before. Was it a dress of Tabitha's?'

'No, mine,' Lily said and blushed. 'I brought it all the way from England out of sentimentality.'

'I can't imagine you ever wearing red,' Matilda said in surprise. Lily always wore subdued colours.

'It was given to me by my Aunt Martha, the parson's wife whose children I used to care for. She guessed I was falling for Giles, he was the curate then in their church in Bath and always coming to the parsonage. She had the opinion he was smitten with me too, and she insisted I wore this dress because she claimed the colour would be a signal for him to speak out. I felt very foolish in it, red was much too bold a colour for me, but it worked, he told me I looked beautiful that day and asked if he could court me. A short while after he asked me to marry him.'

Lily rarely spoke of her life before she married Giles, and having met her overbearing parents in Bristol, Matilda surmised that her childhood and girlhood weren't something she wished to recall. But as Lily seemed in the mood for reminiscing, Matilda prompted her to talk about Giles's courtship of her, about his proposal and their wedding.

Lily's sharp comments about the speed with which her father arranged the marriage proved that she was very aware her family were only too glad to be rid of her.

'Father said, "You aren't much of a prize, Lily, you are as plain as a pike-staff, but then a poor curate can hardly be choosy." Mama was just as cruel, she made me wear one of my sisters' wedding dress, even though it was far too big for me. She said they weren't prepared to waste any further money on "frivolities" as whatever I wore I wouldn't turn into a beauty.'

'How horrid of them,' Matilda exclaimed indignantly. Lily wasn't eye-catching, but she had a dainty figure, her skin was good, and she had enviable grace and elegance.

'I didn't care what they said,' Lily laughed. 'I altered the dress myself and the cream satin was very becoming. Besides, Giles was much more handsome and a far nicer man than any of my sisters' husbands. And he was marrying me for love, not money.'

She began to giggle when she moved on to the wedding, and told Matilda how they spent their wedding night in a coaching inn on the road to London. 'I don't know if I should really tell you this, but I wish someone had told me the truth as it would have saved me a great deal of embarrassment,' she said, her pale face growing flushed. 'I didn't know anything about men, Matty, or about the business on the wedding night, and I made the mistake of listening to some advice from Mama. She told me it hurt terribly, and that if I moved around a great deal, it would be over very quickly.'

Matilda was astounded that Lily was prepared to speak of something so personal. She had never referred to sex before, not even obliquely.

'But I misunderstood what she meant. Even before Giles took me in his arms I was moving. He asked me if there were bugs in the bed.'

Matilda laughed heartily. She had a very good idea now of what married love entailed, and she could imagine how disconcerting it would be to get into a bed with someone hopping around.

'Well, you know how I am about such things, just the suggestion was enough to send me flying out of the bed. Giles stripped it all down, and there wasn't one, and he persuaded me back in. But I started it again. Well, the upshot of it was that he eventually got me to explain myself, and when I told him what Mama had said, he laughed and laughed so loudly the people in the next room began banging on the wall.'

Both women went into spasms of helpless giggling, and emboldened by Lily's candour, Matilda felt able to ask jokingly if it was as terrible as her mama had warned her.

'Oh no, Mama was quite wrong,' Lily said, her grey eyes

suddenly dreamy-looking. 'It was the most thrilling thing which ever happened to me.'

Matilda had heard girls back in London say similar things, but they were common girls, not ladies. Lily, with her finicky nature, her slim body and tiny breasts, seemed a very unlikely candidate for passion.

'It's love that makes the difference, I think,' Lily went on. 'Mama only married father because he was wealthy. I suppose then it would be horrid. So mind you marry for love, Matty. Then you'll find out how good it is.'

Matilda was unable to speak, she wasn't exactly embarrassed, just stunned that Lily was being so open.

'Oh dear, perhaps I shouldn't have told you all that,' Lily said, looking flustered by her silence. 'But I thought with you having no mother I ought to pass on what little knowledge I have.'

'I'd always wondered about it,' Matilda said timidly. After her experience with Flynn, she wasn't really one bit afraid of the idea of sex, but she couldn't tell Lily that. 'I'm glad you told me.'

'It's a very important part of married life,' Lily said, keeping her eyes down. 'It can bring such joy to you both. But sadly after Tabitha was born it ended for me. I don't know why, but I became indifferent to that side of marriage for a long time, and it troubled me deeply for it made me a different person.' She paused for a moment, a sudden look of shame on her small face. 'You never knew what I was like before, Matty, you only saw me at my worst. You remember how fussy I was about the smallest things, always worried about dirt and disease? Well, that was all part of it, I suppose because I thought if I wasn't being a proper wife in that way, I had to make up for it by being the best housekeeper, and the perfect parson's wife. Then when Giles said we were going to America I felt pushed into a corner and I became even more troubled. I hated New York, you know, and I began to resent Giles for forcing me to be there. It just grew worse and worse, the only small good part was the time we went to Boston. For a brief time we were happy that way again, and then I found I was expecting another baby.'

She hesitated again, looking down at her lap. 'But I couldn't hold on to that happiness Matty, it slipped away again. You got measles, I found out that Giles had been into all those terrible places with you. Tabitha almost died, and I felt so guilty because

I blamed you. The final blow was when I lost the baby, because I'd pinned all my hopes on that pulling me round again.'

All at once Matilda realized that this intimate confidence went far deeper than just an older woman trying to give a younger woman a little advice. Lily needed to expose what she'd been through, perhaps because she knew it was the only way she could put it behind her for ever. But more than that, it made sense of all those horrible times back in New York. Matilda felt real sympathy now, and complete understanding.

'I wish you'd been able to tell me some of this before,' she said gently, reaching out and taking Lily's hand. 'It must have been so awful for you keeping it all to yourself.'

'I couldn't even speak of it to Giles,' Lily said in a whisper. 'I loved him, but I felt so unworthy of him because I no longer wanted him in that way. I was always afraid too that he would find someone else. I took a great deal of it out on you, Matty, I'm so sorry for that, but sometimes I was jealous of you. That day you told me I'd end up in a lunatic asylum was like having a mirror put up in front of me. I suddenly saw I *was* growing crazy and I knew I had to strive to prevent it.'

'I was so cruel that day,' Matilda said. 'I'm so very ashamed of that.'

'You have no reason to be, you spoke the truth.' Lily shrugged. 'And I can never thank you enough for not leaving me for I could never have got through it without you. Giles told me later about your sweetheart, and I think knowing you cared that much for us all was what helped me turn the corner. The real miracle came though when Giles said we were going to leave New York, somehow in all the excitement my old feelings for him returned.'

All at once Matilda saw what those tender moments she'd witnessed between Lily and Giles on the way here meant, why Lily had begun to laugh and forgot her revulsion at dirt and fear of poverty, why she was so happy and fulfilled now, and why Giles had such a spring in his step, and a sparkle in his eye.

She had often thought when she met poor women who had a baby every year that their husbands were brutes who should abstain from the act that made them. Yet now, after listening to Lily, she understood it wasn't necessarily that way. Maybe they too had found that love-making was the thing which held their marriages together, and gave them far more joy than wealth or possessions.

Matilda felt she ought to say something, for Lily had just bared her soul, but she had no words in her head, only understanding in her heart. She reached out and stroked Lily's cheek. 'I love you, Lily,' she whispered.

Lily smiled and her grey eyes lit up, making her suddenly beautiful. 'I love you too, Matty, far more than I ever loved my sisters. I hope one day you'll meet a good man who will love you as I have been loved. Let's make this quilt for your bottom drawer, shall we?'

Matilda smiled broadly. 'Well, there's no good man on the horizon yet. At least that gives us plenty of time to finish it.'

Lily picked up the red material and smiled. 'We'll put a great deal of this into it. For passion.'

During March people began to flock into Independence and suddenly the small town was a different place. The hotel and rooms above the saloon were soon all taken, and the square and the ground just outside the town were studded with tents and makeshift shelters while the travellers prepared for the trail. From morning till night they could hear Solomon and the other blacksmiths pounding away on their anvils. Hammering, sawing, the sound of horses', oxen's and mules' hooves and hundreds of voices broke the stillness there had been all winter.

Matilda, Lily and Tabitha often broke off from their chores around the house and garden to watch the scouts ride into town. Many were Indians who broke away from their tribes out on the plains to come and offer their assistance to lead the travellers to Oregon and California. They were thrilling to watch, riding effortlessly without saddles, completely at one with their magnificent, spirited horses, their handsome, sculpted bronze faces, beaded buckskins and long black hair sending shivers of delight and fear in equal measure down the women's spines. Other scouts were half-breeds, the offsprings of fur trappers who'd taken an Indian squaw for a wife, and then there were the white scouts, whiskered, tough men who'd spent their whole life adventuring, lone wolves who when they weren't working drank away every penny they'd earned.

Stage-coaches rumbled into town bringing professional gamblers and their women, pedlars and a few ladies who were dressed as elegantly as New York society women but who soon revealed themselves to be anything but ladies. There were men who advertised themselves on their carts as Dr John, Professor Trueman and other such names, who set up stalls to sell their 'miracle' cure-alls. Travelling missionaries came too, often with a piano on the back of their carts, some intending to go all the way to Oregon or California, others intent on saving a few souls from damnation here in Independence.

It was like watching a circus – gentlemen in broad-brimmed hats, ruffled shirts, tailed coats and shiny boots, ladies tripping daintily through the still muddy street holding parasols, pedlars hawking their wares in loud voices, their merchandise as diverse as packets of seeds, hair ribbons and boot laces. Cattle were herded along, mooing dejectedly as if they sensed they had a long trek ahead of them. Carts lumbered in piled high with sacks of flour, sugar and other necessities, while others brought camping stoves, water bottles, blankets, tents and guns. These were mainly driven by men in loud check jackets smoking fat cigars and some said that to buy anything from them was folly.

Yet the travellers themselves were a sober lot, weary-looking women in calico, their men in flannel shirts and corduroy pants. Their tousle-headed children – and there were so many of them – peeped shyly from behind their mothers' skirts.

Matilda, Lily and Tabitha often went into the square where the travellers were gathered after Tabitha had finished school for the afternoon. They watched the finished wagons being packed for the journey and chatted to the womenfolk.

Few of them really wanted to go, they were tearful when they described saying goodbye to their families and friends back where they'd come from. Yet like so many of the settlers here in Independence, this move was just one of a series they'd experienced over the years. They'd usually sold everything for this venture, and the wagon, oxen and provisions for the journey would eat up most of their money. They spoke of their sorrow at leaving a stove, piano or cherished table behind. But their men had insisted on going West, and it was their duty to obey them.

Matilda looked at the many women who were already heavy with child, and wondered how they could think of setting off on such a hazardous journey at such a time. She had heard about the dangerous river crossings, the almost impenetrable mountains and barren deserts with no water or feed for the animals for forty or fifty miles, then there was the ever-present risk of cholera, smallpox and measles which could wipe out half a wagon train. She applauded their courage, and hoped they would find the paradise they expected at the end of the trail, yet she wondered how high a price they would be forced to pay in human life for what looked to her little more than a dream.

The pace of life grew ever more frantic and noisy as April approached. The first of the wagon trains would leave once the spring grass was high enough for grazing for their animals. There were over sixty wagons in just one train, and each day more gathered for later-leaving ones. The talk on the streets and in the stores was all of how high the rivers were, as spring flooding could bog down the wagons, how tall the grass, and how many sacks of flour, sugar and coffee would see the travellers through to their destination.

The missionaries stepped up their open-air services, fiercely insisting that those who hadn't already been baptized should be now to ensure a place in heaven. The saloons grew more crowded nightly, and stories were passed around about men who had gambled away their wagon, oxen and livestock, and didn't know how to tell their wives. Painted ladies no longer kept themselves tucked away, but insolently paraded up and down the main street to the consternation of the regular townfolk. Tobacco-chewing old-timers, some of whom had been at least part of the way along the trail, sat outside the mail office, only too willing to be tempted into telling their often wildly exaggerated tales of skirmishes with Indians, or how they almost faced death during a stampede of buffalo.

While Lily, Matilda and Tabitha grew more excited each day, Giles took it all very calmly. He visited each of the travelling families, prayed with them for their safe journey and blessed them. On many an evening he would do a round of the saloons and hastily set up gambling dens, reminding the men frittering their money away that they had families dependent on them.

On the final Sunday the church was packed to the doors, the local people outnumbered by the travellers, and his sermon was one of admiration for their courage and hope that every one of them would find happiness and prosperity at the end of the trail. He urged them all to keep their faith in God, to be kind to one another and not to neglect their children's education.

'God go with you,' he finished up. 'The people of Independence will be praying for you all.'

Giles, Lily, Matilda and Tabitha all turned out early the next morning to see the wagon train move off. It was raining, and progress was slow as the inexperienced struggled to control their teams of oxen. The wagon-train leader, a heavily whiskered ex-soldier named Will Lessing who had used the trail several times before, rode round on his black horse supervising the departure.

Many of the women looked tearful, looking up at the leaden sky and perhaps seeing it as an omen of what was to come, but the children were excited, running through the rain to one another's wagons, and waving goodbye to the on-lookers.

It was a brave sight to see those seventy or more wagons, mostly pulled by four, sometimes eight oxen, with a cow or mule tethered behind, slowly join the line one by one and set off. Some of the bigger children ran alongside, the smaller ones peeping out of the back of the wagon. Women sat up front with their husbands, often with a baby in their arms, the only protection from the rain a spare piece of canvas draped over their heads. A band of missionaries sang hymns, but their voices were almost drowned by the yelled farewells, the crack of whips, the rumbling of wheels and rain splashing on canvas.

'Most of the wagons are very overloaded,' Giles remarked. They could see cherished tables, chairs, and kitchen stoves on many of them. 'I wonder how many of those well-loved possessions will end up abandoned on the trail.'

'I wonder how those poor women are going to manage looking after their families with no home comforts,' Lily said, wiping away tears from her eyes.

Matilda said nothing. She was too overwhelmed by the courage it took to set out into unknown territory never knowing what perils lay ahead.

Throughout April other smaller trains formed and left, but hurriedly, for unless they set off now in the spring they might get caught out by early autumn snow in the Rockies. But when the last wagon had finally rolled out of town, the itinerant bands of pedlars, gamblers, prostitutes and missionaries left too, leaving Independence suddenly silent and deserted.

Life settled down again in May, and Matilda and Lily worked long hours in the vegetable patch and garden. The two pigs Cain and Abel had been slaughtered and eaten during the winter, and they bought two replacements, along with some more chickens. Lily's roses flowered in June and finally one hot afternoon Matilda experienced having tea in the garden, where a small table had been laid with a pretty cloth and the best china.

'Back home in Bristol Mama did this every warm afternoon,' Lily said with a wide grin as she poured the tea from the dainty bone-china tea pot she'd brought all the way from England. 'Of course the maid brought it out to her, the cakes were on a glass plate and the tea pot was silver. I expect she'd have the vapours if she had to be so near pigs and chickens. She certainly wouldn't call this a lawn either.'

The grass was tough and spiky, not the soft, lush green of home. Wild flowers sprouted up in it, but it had its own kind of beauty, more meadow than lawn.

'She doesn't write to you very often,' Matilda said. She didn't remember Lily getting more than three letters since they left England. 'Does that make you sad?'

'Not really.' Lily gave a little resigned sigh. 'Both she and my father were always so distant, I didn't really expect them to change once I'd gone away. But it would be nice to have news from home more often. You are fortunate that Dolly writes so often to you, Matty.'

'She's such a good woman,' Matilda said with a fond smile. 'She always tells me how much she misses my father, and mentions little things he did or said. And it's a comfort to me to know she's looking out for my brother George too, and to hear he still likes working for the carter. He never learned to read and write, you see, so if it wasn't for Dolly I'd never hear from him.'

'Do you ever want to go back to England?' Lily asked.

'I'd like to see Dolly and George,' she said. 'But there's not really anything else there for me any more, is there?' To her London was all tied up with Lucas, going home would only bring back sorrow that she hadn't seen him one last time.

'That's how I feel now,' Lily said, leaning back in her chair contentedly. 'To think how I used to yearn for England! Now I think I'd be very happy to end my days here.'

Matilda wasn't exactly sure she agreed with that. She was so happy here, yet she was very aware that happiness rested entirely around the Milsons and at some stage she would have to make a life of her own. She was twenty-one now, and at that age most women would be actively looking for a husband, yet her mind wouldn't seem to turn in that direction.

There were a great many more bachelors in the area than single women, and she was well aware that several of them admired her. In church on Sundays she noted their shy smiles, and quite often they used some pretence to call at the house. Two or three of them were nice enough, and if she hadn't known what it was to fall desperately in love, she might well be encouraging them to come courting her. But Flynn had spoiled her for other men – unless they could start her heart racing the moment she saw them, somehow she knew they wouldn't be right.

In truth marriage didn't have the same appeal as it once had. Marrying a settler would mean living in a tiny cabin, working from dawn to dusk with none of the comforts or the stimulating company she had here with the Milsons.

Occasionally she day-dreamed of falling in love and marrying a tradesman or merchant in the town. This dream man looked like Flynn – he was intelligent, articulate, amusing, passionate and kind. She imagined living in a house just like this one, with the Milsons just across the street so she could see them at any time. But she knew that was fantasy. Merchants and tradesmen were invariably old, they treated their wives badly. Men with all the qualities she was looking for were rarer than hen's teeth.

'It's high time you found a sweetheart,' Lily said suddenly, as if she had tuned into her mind. 'Most girls of your age are married with two or three children, and you are the prettiest girl for miles around.' She went on to list every unmarried man she knew, and suggested they should look at them all more closely and invite the more suitable ones to supper.

'Please don't, Lily.' Matilda was instantly alarmed. 'If someone is meant for me, he'll turn up all by himself.'

'That sounds dangerously like a pedlar knocking on the door,' Lily laughed. 'You'd be a great deal safer looking first at ones we know something about.'

Despite Matilda's protests, Lily and Giles went out of their way to find a suitable man for her all through the summer. There was Hans, the six-foot blond son of the Hoffmans who owned the town bakery. He was handsome enough to make most girls swoon, but he couldn't string more than four words together at one time. Then came Johann, his parents were German too and he'd travelled down from Connecticut with the intention of sending for them when his farm was doing well. He could talk, but only about farming, and he was a tobacco chewer too, which made Matilda shudder. And Ernest, appropriately named for he was the most earnest man Matilda had ever met, explained the finer points of animal husbandry in such a stultifying manner that she almost fell asleep. After these three came Michael, Amos and Dieter, all of whom had some conversational skills, were quite presentable, and none of them chewed tobacco in her presence, but they all had that desperate look in their eyes which made Matilda think they would ask anyone to marry them so they could get a home-cooked meal and their washing done for them.

'We'll have to cast our net further afield,' Lily said, when Dieter had been tactfully dismissed after he'd said he didn't think girls should be educated as it just gave them grand ideas.

'How far did you have in mind to cast it?' Giles grinned as he rocked in the chair. 'Shall I go out into the wilderness to search for Matty's true love there? Or would you have me go to the cities and place advertisements in all the papers, listing her special requirements?'

Matilda went into a spasm of helpless laughter. While Lily took all this match-making very seriously, Giles thought it was a huge joke. Often he would rush into the house announcing he'd seen a stranger on the road, and ask if he should interview him as a prospective suitor. The whole business had created so much laughter in the house.

'Don't be silly, dear,' Lily said reprovingly. 'But you could contact your acquaintances in St Louis. Perhaps if you said we were intending to come for a little holiday they'd ask us to stay with them.'

'Lily, not one of them is likely to have anyone I'd consider to be suitable for Matty tucked away,' Giles said. 'They are all either dirt poor, or slave owners. You know how I feel about the latter.'

Giles had found his own way to deal with his conscience about slavery. To openly denounce it as evil from his pulpit would be to court disaster, for feelings ran high on the subject here. During the winter he had gone down river to St Louis and met up with a deeply committed group of Abolitionists who offered help and advice to get runaway slaves up the Missouri river to the Northern states and Canada. There were stiff punishments for helping runaways, but he was prepared to take that risk. Hardly a week passed now without him going off somewhere to arrange safe houses and passages, and to take the food, blankets and clothing other like-minded people passed on to him.

Lily shrugged at Matilda. She supported her husband's views, but she worried it would get him into trouble. The ruffian element of pro-slavers in Missouri were hard men, and they'd think nothing of shooting a man for helping in an escape, even if that man was a minister. The slave catchers were even more brutal, they stood to get as much as a hundred dollars for returning a slave to its rightful owner. They were known to not only torture and maim people who obstructed them, but burn their homes down too.

'Well, I'll just have to think of something else,' she said. 'I'm not giving up.'

'I wish you would,' Matilda laughed. During these summer months she'd often lent a hand when women friends in town had given birth to a new baby, and she'd come to see that marriage was almost never an equal partnership. The men did work hard, but when that work was done they came home for dinner, then went out again to the saloon, played cards with their friends, or slept. Women kept going from early morning till late at night, often survived on just a few hours' sleep, and had the sole responsibility for all the children, the housekeeping and usually tending a vegetable patch and animals. If their husband was a farmer they were even worse off, expected to fit in all this and work alongside him in the fields too, often with a new baby every year. From what Matilda had observed there was precious little tenderness or appreciation either, so if that was marriage, she'd rather avoid it.

'You'll thank me one day,' Lily said, waving a finger at her. 'You'll see!'

During the early part of November Lily became sick. It came

in waves, one moment she was fine, the next she was running out to the privy. As it didn't come in the early mornings neither she nor Matilda suspected she could be having a baby. It was only after spending three or four nights constantly vomiting that Lily consulted the doctor and discovered she was three months pregnant.

She was ecstatic but baffled as to why she hadn't realized it sooner. 'It must be that working so hard I hadn't noticed my monthlies hadn't come,' she said. 'Maybe old age makes you forgetful.'

Matilda showed only delight and excitement to Lily but in secret she was very afraid for her in case she miscarried this one too and lost all the happiness she'd gained. On top of that Lily was thirty-seven. It was ordinary enough for women of that age and far older to have babies, but there was a commonly held theory that mature, less fertile women, who had large gaps between their children, were far more likely to have difficult births.

Backed up by Giles, Matilda insisted she was not to do any more heavy work, and she was to rest every afternoon. The sickness stopped and Lily blossomed, her hair shone, her skin glowed, she was always hungry, and she just laughed at Matilda and Giles when they prevented her lifting a pail of water or logs for the stove. By Christmas her belly was already too big to hide, and though it was customary for ladies to stay indoors or camouflage their expanding shape with cloaks she took great pleasure in her size.

'It's going to be a boy, I know it is,' she would say, her eyes shining with happiness. 'A great big strapping one. It's a good job you haven't found a sweetheart, Matty, I'll need your help with him.'

Matilda stopped being apprehensive in the face of such joy. Not only was it a perfect excuse for giving no more thought to her own future, or her unmarried state, but she loved babies and she could think of nothing more wonderful than Giles and Lily finally getting the son they'd longed for.

She got up extra early to do the chores which had been Lily's, so she wouldn't feel guilty and insist on doing something. She chopped wood with pleasure, scrubbed and polished the floors with new vigour, and constantly tried to think of more appetizing ways to cook the salted pork to please her friend. In the evenings they would sew together, making little flannel night-gowns, jackets and bonnets, and they hurried to finish the big patchwork quilt, just so they could start on a new small one for the baby.

In early January the baby began to kick Lily, and she would often grab Matilda's hand so she could share how it felt. Matilda would put her ear to Lily's belly and listen to his heartbeat, both of them shedding a few emotional tears.

'It wasn't like this when I was carrying Tabitha,' Lily admitted one day. 'It was a lonely business because it wasn't considered proper to mention such things. I was so scared most of the time. I didn't have a friend like you then to talk about it to.'

Giles was every bit as excited as the women, he called the baby Harry, and almost every evening when he came in from his ministry business he would pat Lily's belly and ask how Harry was. Tabitha was thrilled. She made a baby gown for her rag-doll, and practised putting napkins on it, so she could do it for the real baby. But there were times when her endless questions embarrassed her mother.

'How did the baby get in there?' she asked one day.

'God put him in there,' Lily replied.

'But it's a silly place to put a baby, how will he get out?'

It was Matilda who had to intervene and try to explain to the little girl. 'God put him in there when he was very tiny, and he stays in there in the warm until he's big and strong enough to be born.'

'Will he come out of Mama's belly button?' Tabitha asked, determined not to be side-tracked.

'No, further down,' Matilda said. 'When it's springtime I'll take you to see some lambs being born, it's just like that.'

The lambs were born at the same time as the first of the travellers arrived in town to join the next wagon train. Giles drove Matilda and Tabitha out of town to one of the nearby farms and there in a meadow four or five ewes had already given birth to their lambs, and two more were about to. Tabitha watched in horrified fascination as the ewe lay down and slowly ejected her baby.

'It doesn't look like a lamb,' Tabitha cried, seeing what looked to her like a bloody lump of meat emerging. But suddenly the lump was on the grass and the mother sheep began to lick away at the membrane surrounding it, little legs began to kick, and a weak plaintive bleat proved it was a lamb.

'There now,' Matilda said, half laughing, half crying to see the sweet tiny lamb trying to stand on wobbly legs. 'Look, he's already trying to get his mother's milk, isn't he clever?'

Tabitha was only half satisfied, and on the way home she asked dozens more questions, all of which Matilda and Giles found almost impossible to answer honestly.

'The doctor will come and help Mama,' Matilda said finally. 'Her baby will be born at home in her cosy bed. Sheep are different, they don't need any help.'

'I *shall* be a doctor then when I'm grown up,' Tabitha said importantly. 'I'd like to bring lots of babies out. Can I be a doctor?'

Giles and Matilda looked at each other helplessly for a moment. Tabitha was extremely intelligent, her teacher had often said that it was remarkable that a child of seven was outstripping the twelve-year-olds in the class. She read every book she could get her hands on, and delighted in her papa setting her difficult mathematical problems to solve.

'You can be anything you've a mind to,' Giles said eventually. 'Maybe even a doctor.'

'Then I shall be,' she said, folding her arms across her chest. 'And when the doctor comes to help Mama I'll watch, so I know what to do.'

A few days later, while Giles was out and Tabitha at school, Lily and Matilda were doing some baking in the kitchen, when a knock came on the front door. Matilda wiped flour from her hands and went to open it. To her absolute amazement, Cissie and Sidney were standing there on the porch.

'Cissie, Sidney!' she exclaimed, reeling back in shock. 'What on earth are you doing here?'

'Going West to Oregon,' Cissie said with the widest smile and stepped forward to hug Matilda. 'I got your letters and I tried to get someone to write back for me, but the sort of things I wanted to say I couldn't tell Miss Rowbottom.'

'Where's Peter? Oh Sidney, you look so grown up!' Matilda turned to hug him too. There was so much she wanted to know, but the shock at seeing them on the porch drove every bit of sense out of her head.

Lily came forward, smiling shyly. It was only on the trip to Independence that Matilda and Giles had told Lily the entire, unvarnished story of the rescues in Five Points, and the significance of these two leading characters. Telling her the worst of it had made her see how necessary it was. Since then she'd often brought up the subject and indeed said she hoped Cissie and Sidney would master writing well enough to keep in touch with Matilda. Her smile said she was as thrilled as Matilda to find them at her door.

'Matty's forgetting her manners,' Lily said. 'Do come in and perhaps over a cup of tea we can both hear all your news.'

Half an hour later Matilda knew that a year ago Cissie had met John Duncan, a Scotsman who called in at the Waifs' and Strays' Home in New Jersey for help when his horse had grown lame. He was a carpenter, and he'd been on his way to a new house about twenty miles away where he was to build all the windows, staircases and closets. Miss Rowbottom gave him a bed and stabling for his horse for a few nights in return for doing a few odd jobs for her. Cissie and he were instantly attracted, and during the time he was working nearby, he came courting her and finally asked her to marry him.

'He loved Peter right off,' Cissie said, her eyes shining with happiness. 'He don't care about my past either. We got married quick because he got another job where there was a little cabin for us to live in. I carried on working at the Home too, 'cos it weren't that far away, and John used to come over with me to the Home on Sundays and help out. He got fond of Sidney too, and when we got to thinking about going to Oregon, we reckoned we'd better take him along, 'cos he's as sharp as needles, and real good with animals.'

Sidney glowed at this. 'I would have had to leave the Home soon anyway, 'cos I'm twelve now,' he said. 'And John's gonna teach me carpentry too.'

Matilda was still finding it hard to believe that these two people whom she'd cared so much about were really here in the kitchen with her and Lily. Cissie, now eighteen, had grown into a real beauty, just as Matilda had often suspected she might; her long dark curly hair was unruly, escaping from its pins, her sunbonnet shoved back round her neck as if it irritated her. Her green eyes sparkled mischievously, and her body was voluptuously curvy. Sidney was taller than her, his red hair looked as if he'd hacked it short himself. But aside from the hair-cut, he no longer looked like a waif, his shoulders were broad, his arms muscular, he was almost a man.

'Peter's three now, and a fine big boy,' Cissie said. 'He's back at the wagon with John, we didn't think it was polite for all of us to come at once. But how about you all, do you like it down here? How's the Reverend, is he still rescuing orphans?'

Matilda told them a little about their new life and how happy they all were. Cissie looked at Lily's belly and smiled. 'When's your babby due?'

'Next month,' Lily replied. 'About the second or third.'

'I think I've got one on the way an' all.' Cissie grinned. 'But I ain't seen a doctor yet. I hope we get to Oregon before it comes, I know I had Peter in a cellar, so if I can cope with that, I can cope with anything. But I'd rather be in a proper bed.'

Matilda was somewhat surprised when Lily invited Cissie and Sidney to bring Peter and John back for supper later. Her whole outlook had altered since they left New York, but even so Cissie was a little coarse for someone as genteel as Lily. But she meant it, she was smiling at both her and Sidney with real warmth. 'Reverend Milson will be so pleased to see you both again,' she said. 'And we've all got to look at this new husband of yours, Cissie. Tabby will be delighted to have a new little friend in Peter to play with too.'

'Well, bless you, ma'am,' Cissie said. 'We'd sure appreciate it. It's so long since we ate a meal at a table, I'll have to polish up me manners. We'd best go now, what with you doing the baking an' all. Don't want to be getting under your feet.'

That evening was one of the best Matilda could remember. Cissie's irreverent and often caustic observations on some of the people they would be joining on the wagon train had them laughing all evening. It was so good to see how articulate Sidney had become, he described things that had happened to them on the way here so vividly they could all see them. Little Peter, who was very like his mother with silky brown hair and the same mischievous look, took a great liking to Lily and climbed on to her lap for a cuddle, eventually dropping asleep there.

But the best thing for Matilda was discovering that John was a truly good man and perfect for Cissie. He wasn't handsome, his hair was thin and sandy and his skin was pock-marked, but he had an attractive ruggedness, strong features, pale blue eyes and a deep husky voice. He looked tough, with big shoulders and hands like hams, yet his gentleness with both Cissie and Peter revealed a soft centre and generous nature. He told them he was thirty, and that he had left Scotland when he was eighteen for Canada, where he worked first in a logging camp, then for a carpenter where he learned his trade.

'Finding Cissie was the best thing that ever happened to me,' he said without any embarrassment. 'I can get all the work I want, everyone needs a skilled carpenter. But it was an empty, lonely life till she came along. Now I've got a complete family.'

Giles asked him what he intended to do in Oregon.

'Set up a lumber business,' he said. 'I'll build us a little cabin to start with, and maybe do carpentry jobs until we all get on our feet there, but the way I see it there's a fortune to be made in timber, and out in Oregon there's enough trees for the whole of America.'

They had bought a wagon already and Cissie said John had fitted it out better than any one else's. 'We ain't got a lot of stuff like some of those people,' she said, wrinkling her nose. 'They'll be dumping half of it when we gets up in the mountains. But then we don't need much, just a warm bed and plenty of food. John can make everything else we need when we get there. We've hung on to our money for Oregon.'

Giles agreed that this was a very sensible plan. 'I've heard tell the trail is already littered with abandoned stoves, books and trunks of clothes,' he said with a smile. 'And people haven't been using it for that many years either. Imagine what it will be like in another ten!'

'They'll probably have built real roads by then.' John laughed. 'Or there'll be people going along there just for the pickings. That's if the Indians haven't taken it all.'

'Are you scared about the Indians?' Lily ventured. 'I heard only last week that they killed some settlers out on the plains and carried off their two little girls.'

'I heard that too,' John agreed. 'But I'm not going to let that panic me. We've got three Indian scouts on this train, and a leader who speaks a bit of their language, and I trust them to get us through. From what I hear more people die on the way to Oregon through accidents or diseases than from Indian attacks. I reckon the army makes up some of the stories just to justify the terrible things they do to them.'

'I agree,' Giles said, nodding his head. He was totally opposed to the Government's scheme to resettle Indians in other areas the white people had no interest in, and he felt that in time the Indians would retaliate viciously against it. One such move back in 1835 had been christened 'The Trail of Tears'. Fifteen thousand peaceful Cherokees were penned up in stockades in Georgia all summer. Cholera, measles and whooping cough decimated their numbers, then in a 1,000-mile trail to the great plains, which the Government had insisted they settle on, some 4,000 more died. Now it looked as if the white man would claim that land too. Giles wondered how anyone had the audacity to think they could just keep shifting people for their own ends.

'Many of the missionaries create trouble too,' he went on. 'They go out there and try to change these people, make them grow crops, embrace Christianity and become like us. Why should they? It's their country after all and the way they lived was fine and beautiful until the white man poked his nose in.'

John laughed. 'You aren't going to try and convert some of them then?'

'Not me.' Giles smiled. 'Aside from the fact I think they are fine people just as they are, and entitled to their own beliefs and way of life, I have more than enough to do with just the people in Independence and the surrounding area. I have never heard of Indians abandoning their children or of forcing people to work in inhuman conditions, the way white folk do. It seems to me we could learn a great deal from them.'

At this Cissie turned to Lily. 'He's a good 'un, ain't he?' she said. 'I never learned about God and all that till I got to the Home, but I reckon if there is one, He's a lot like him.'

'That's a very lovely thing to say, Cissie,' Lily replied, glowing at the obvious sincerity in the girl's words. 'But you are a good woman too, look at you now, so pretty, so brave and strong, starting out on a big adventure with your new husband, son and young Sidney. You make myself, my husband and Matilda all feel so proud of you.'

In the days that followed, knowing the wagon train would be leaving shortly, Matilda spent as much time as she could with Cissie and Sidney. It gave her so much pleasure to see how much self-assurance they both had, and she came to see that the hardships they'd endured as children gave them an edge over others. They were resourceful, intuitive and imaginative, both sharp-witted and very tough. Matilda heard Cissie one day demanding that they should be up front in the wagon train, and her insistence, perhaps helped by her looks, wore down the wagon master until he agreed.

'But why do you want to be up front so badly?' Matilda asked. She imagined that was the most dangerous place to be.

Cissie looked at her as if she was simple. 'Well, the trail will be smoother, our oxen will get to the good grazing and water first, and we won't get the dust in our eyes when it's dry.'

Matilda hadn't considered that and complimented her on her common sense. 'I should think I have got some,' Cissie said indignantly. 'I had to learn that as a little 'un, didn't I? I ain't got no book learning, but I listens to folk, and I takes it in. I heard a couple of old-timers in the town talking about the positions in the train, and I cottoned on real fast. John wouldn't insist, he's too polite for his own good sometimes. But I ain't. I looks after me own afore others.'

She told Matilda both she and Sidney had got John to teach them to shoot too. 'I ain't going to be like some of them.' She thumbed towards a group of women sitting on the grass sewing. 'They'd be done for if they lost their man, I'm gonna make sure I can do everything, drive the oxen, shoot buffalo and skin 'em too. I never was one for polite lady-like stuff.'

On the morning of the train leaving, Matilda stole quietly out of the house with Tabitha to say one last farewell. John was already up on the front of the wagon, hands on the reins, waiting for the signal to pull out, Sidney and Peter beside him. Cissie was arranging their bed in the back, but as she saw Matilda running through the wagons, she jumped down and ran to her.

'You shouldn't have come,' she said, hugging her fiercely. 'You'll only make me cry.'

'I couldn't let you go without one last hug,' Matilda said. 'Besides, someone's got to do the waving and cheering.'

'I'll get John to write to you as soon as we are settled,' Cissie said, her eyes damp with tears she was trying to hold back. 'If ever you get fed up here, you come to us. You promise?'

Matilda didn't think that was likely. But she promised anyway.

'Look after Mrs Milson,' Cissie said, then, making sure Tabitha wasn't in earshot, she pulled her friend closer and whispered, 'I reckon she's going to have a tough time when the baby comes. She's too big for such a little woman. So you make sure you get the doctor real quick, and not one of those old biddy midwives that think they know everything.'

Matilda gulped. She knew Cissie wouldn't say something so alarming unless she believed it. 'Of course I will,' she said.

Cissie just held her tightly, but a shrill whistle made her jump away. 'That's the signal to go,' she said hurriedly. 'I just gotta say one thing afore we go. I still owes you, Matilda Jennings. I ain't forgotten. You ever find yourself in trouble, or just needing a friend, you come to me. I'll do anything for you. You gave me a life.'

She bent to kiss Tabitha, then turned and ran back to the wagon, jumping up beside her husband as nimbly as a cat.

Matilda and Tabitha ran along beside the wagon as it pulled out of the field, the others following it one by one.

'Go home,' Cissie yelled. 'You make me cry and I'll do for you!'

John blew a kiss and smiled. Little Peter waved excitedly, then Sidney jumped down and ran to Matilda.

'This is for you,' he said, holding out a tiny package wrapped in a piece of brown paper. 'Don't open it till we've gone. Sorry about the spelling, but I ain't much good at letters.'

'I'll treasure it whatever it is,' Matilda said, hugging him tightly for a moment. 'Be good, Sidney, look after Cissie and Peter, and try to write to me now and then. Maybe we'll meet again one day.'

He kissed her cheek and ran off back to the wagon without another word.

Watching the train go was even more moving this time than the previous year, for then her feelings of admiration and fear had been general, directed at people with whom she'd had only a passing acquaintance. But this one was carrying dear friends, and her insides churned with fear for them.

'Shall we run alongside them for a bit?' Tabitha asked.

Matilda looked down at the little girl and wished she had her innocence about what this journey would entail. 'No, we'll go home and see Mama, Cissie won't like us following them.'

'What did Sidney give you?' Tabitha asked, looking curiously at the small package in Matilda's hand.

'I don't know. But I'll wait and open it when we're home,' she said.

Matilda cried when she opened the package. It was six cents, each coin polished and wrapped in a lace-trimmed handkerchief. The note enclosed was brief, but somehow said everything.

'Here is the six cents back you giv me that day. I never knewed you was goin to get me out of that place, otherwise I wood not have took it. Yours always Sidney.'

Chapter Twelve

Lily's labour pains began on 26 April about an hour after Giles had left for the day to visit some outlying farms. She was out the back collecting up the eggs when she felt the first one and sat down on an upturned barrel in surprise.

Matilda was feeding the chickens with Tabitha, but when she saw Lily's expression and the way she was holding her belly, she guessed immediately what it was and rushed over to her.

'Don't fuss,' Lily said. 'It will be hours and hours yet. Don't say anything in front of Tabby either, or she'll start up all her questions and she won't want to go to school.'

By ten, three hours later, with Tabitha safely in school, the pains were every two minutes and strong, but Lily seemed very composed, wandering around the house, just stopping to hold on to a chair or the edge of the table when another one began. Matilda wanted to get the doctor, but Lily didn't agree.

'He'll be out now visiting his sick patients, I'm not ill, and what could he do if he did come? He'd just look at me and say call him again when it gets closer!'

Tabitha came home later, and Lily did her best to disguise that she was now in real pain. Soon afterwards, however, she was forced to go and lie down in the bedroom.

Matilda helped her undress and put on an old night-gown. She also took the precaution of slipping an india-rubber mat under the bottom sheet.

'I wish Giles would come home,' Lily said wistfully as Matilda tried to make her more comfortable by rubbing her back. 'At least he could distract Tabby from coming in here and asking questions.'

Matilda went back into the kitchen and spoke to Tabitha. She explained that her mama would be better left in peace, and that perhaps she should go and play with her friend on Main Street. Then, hearing Lily call out in pain, she decided immediately that action was required and took Tabitha with her to call on Dr Treagar.

'I don't know when he'll be back,' Mrs Treagar said, looking most disturbed. She was a genteel sort of woman, more like Lily in character than any other woman in town. 'He had a long list of patients to see. I'll get him to call on Mrs Milson the instant he gets in. But in the meantime get Mrs Van Buren, she's an excellent midwife.'

Matilda's heart sank at that suggestion. Lily didn't like the Dutch woman, she considered her coarse, loud and too self-opinionated. 'Is there anyone else?' she asked timidly.

'Mrs Van Buren is far more competent than any of the other so-called midwives,' Mrs Treagar said with some indignation. 'And I know she's home because I saw her passing just an hour ago.'

Matilda took Tabitha over to her friend Ruth's house and explained the situation, and Ruth's mother gladly agreed to have her stay the night. 'Mrs Van Buren delivered all my children,' she said when Matilda asked for her opinion on calling her. 'She can be a bit fierce, but she knows what she's doing. Mrs Milson will be safe in her hands.'

By eight that evening Matilda was beside herself with anxiety. Giles still hadn't returned, the doctor hadn't turned up either, and Mrs Van Buren had banished her from the bedroom because she said birthing wasn't a sight for unmarried women.

All she could do was sit in the kitchen, her stomach contracting each time Lily called out in pain. She knew it must be bad, for Lily would never make a scene in front of a stranger unless she was in too much agony to forget who she was.

Mrs Van Buren wasn't very sympathetic either, time and again Matilda heard her snap at Lily with the reminder that she must control herself.

'Matty!' The sudden agonized yell from the bedroom made Matilda jump to her feet and run in.

'I told you to stay out there,' the midwife said, trying to prevent her coming in.

'My friend called me in,' Matilda said firmly, pushing past the woman. 'If she wants me here, here I'll stay.'

She didn't like the midwife any more than Lily did. Apart

from her abrasive personality she had a square, forbidding face, and almost no lips. Her eyes were dark and very cold, reminding Matilda of dead fish.

'Well, get right up the top end of the bed then,' the woman almost spat at her. 'And don't get in my way.'

During the next hour Matilda prayed silently that Giles and the doctor would come. Giles was often later than this when he went on visits, as evenings were the best time to see some of his parishioners. When he'd left this morning everything was so normal there would have been nothing to make him think of cutting his visits short.

Every vein on Lily's face and neck stood out, sweat poured from her, and the pain was now almost continual. Matilda couldn't imagine how anyone could take so much agony and still be breathing.

'You are ready to push now,' Mrs Van Buren said after examining Lily. She came up to the head of the bed and tied a short length of rope around one of the brass rails, putting the end into Lily's hands. 'Pull on that,' she said. 'It helps. It won't be long now, less than an hour I'd say. Now, I'll just put some clean brown paper and towels under you to catch the mess.'

Matilda's knowledge of the events of childbirth were by no means complete, but she did know that once the pushing started it was close to the end. Overheard conversations in Finders Court had revealed some women only pushed three or four times before the baby popped out, so she felt more hopeful.

Lily did cooperate with all the instructions given to her, she stopped yelling out and pushed with all her might and main, but after half an hour of it, Mrs Van Buren began to look worried.

'Run over to the doctor's and see if he's home yet,' she ordered Matilda. 'Say I sent you because I need him.'

Matilda thought by this that the woman didn't know what to do, and considering her earlier confidence, this was frightening. She sped off, only to be told by Mrs Treagar that the doctor still wasn't back.

As Matilda was returning home, Giles was driving his gig back up the street. She ran to him and blurted out what was happening, asking if he'd seen the doctor during the day or if there was another one they could call.

Giles blanched. 'There isn't another doctor in a hundred miles, and no, I haven't seen him. But perhaps Mrs Treagar could give me a list of his patients and I can go and find him.'

But Mrs Treagar had no such list, she said her husband hadn't even mentioned anyone by name that he was calling on. 'He should be back soon as it's getting dark,' she said, picking up their extreme anxiety. 'I'll send him over at once.'

They rushed back to the house and into the bedroom. Mrs Van Buren was kneeling up on the bed, with Lily's two feet pressed against her shoulders. She protested at Giles coming in for it was unheard of for husbands to be present at a birth, but Giles ignored her and took up a position on one side of the bed with Matilda at the other.

The midwife urged Lily to push harder. 'Keep on pushing with each pain,' she bellowed at her.

Matilda and Giles urged her too, but after several more agonized efforts Lily let go of the rope in her hands and clutched at her husband's arm. 'It's not that I'm not trying as she seems to think,' she whispered hoarsely. 'I just can't make the baby come. Ask her if he's moved down at all.'

Giles looked to the midwife. 'Has it?'

Mrs Van Buren shook her head.

Almost all men considered childbirth and the rearing of children as an entirely feminine domain, but not Giles. As a clergyman ministering to both sexes he made it his business to find out about such subjects. He knew that the pushing stage of labour had to be completed within two hours, or the baby would die. Lily might be weak in some areas, but she wanted this baby desperately, and he knew if she said she couldn't push it out, then she couldn't.

'What can we do?' he asked, trying hard not to panic.

'The doctor would cut her stomach, but I can't do that, I don't know how.' Mrs Van Buren's voice rose, showing she too was frightened. 'But I could try using the instruments.'

Giles blanched. He knew she meant forceps, and he knew too that these often caused brain damage to the infant. But he moved closer to the woman, bending to whisper, 'Is the baby still alive?'

She put a metal trumpet to Lily's belly and listened. 'Yes. I can hear his heart,' she said, but just the way she said it suggested it was fading.

'Then get him out however you can,' Giles said in a low, urgent tone. 'What do you need? I'll get it.'

If it hadn't been for the need to hold and comfort Lily, Matilda might have run from the room. She saw the ugly tong-like tool the midwife got from her bag, and the sharp knife needed to cut Lily's flesh, and her stomach heaved. It was Giles who insisted on washing them in hot water, and he who tried to help as the midwife began to use them, Matilda held on to Lily's two hands and urged her to hang on.

Dr Treagar arrived just as Mrs Van Buren had clamped the forceps around the baby's head. From the message he'd got from his wife he must have anticipated what might be needed, because he let himself in, shouted out that he was here and that he was just washing his hands.

The doctor was a small man of nearly sixty, noted for his jovial nature and being a great raconteur, but as he came into the bedroom with his sleeves rolled up above his elbows and an apron over his clothes, he wasted no time on pleasantries and ordered both Giles and Matilda out, telling them to boil more water and get more clean linen. The last thing Matilda saw as she left the room was his grim expression as he took the tongs from the midwife's hands.

Lily cried out only once more, then it went strangely quiet. Giles was praying aloud as he filled kettles and pans, his hands were shaking and his face as white as the clean linen Matilda got from the closet.

The bedroom door opened later and Mrs Van Buren came out. Her apron was soaked in blood and she almost stumbled as she made her way to the stove to get water. Giles lifted the pan for her. 'What news?' he asked.

She avoided his eyes. 'We got the baby out,' she whispered. 'Doctor is just attending to your wife.'

Giles rushed into the bedroom and Matilda tried to follow, but her path was blocked by the midwife. Yet in the second before the door was shut in her face she saw enough to know just how bad things were. The baby had been placed unwrapped on the wash-stand, blue and lifeless. The whole bed was awash with blood, Lily unconscious.

No night had ever seemed so long and desolate. Mrs Van Buren slunk out an hour or so later, silently handing Matilda an armful of bloody linen to put to soak, clearly too distraught even to attempt any kind of explanation. Giles stayed in the bedroom with the doctor.

Owls hooted outside, the wind flapped at the curtains, the wood in the stove spluttered and crackled, but though those were reassuring, normal sounds for the middle of the night, the silence from the bedroom was ominous.

Now and then she would hear the doctor speak in a low voice, and a rustle of covers as if he was checking Lily's progress, then perhaps one or two words, equally low, from Giles, then silence again.

In her terror Matilda turned to prayer, apologizing to God for her lack of faith in Him in the past, but promising that if He spared Lily she would be his servant for ever. 'Take me if you just want another soul,' she begged. 'I'm nothing, of no importance to anyone. But please spare Lily.'

It was five in the morning, dawn just breaking when Giles opened the bedroom door and beckoned her to come in. Right away Matilda knew her prayers had been futile, for his face had no light in it, his eyes dark pools of grief.

'Lily has something to say to you,' he whispered.

The baby was covered now, the blood cleaned up, and the bedlinen as spotless as Lily always insisted on, and although the room was far removed from the one in Finders Court, it held the same pall of approaching death that she remembered when her own mother died.

Lily opened her eyes and lifted one hand weakly as Matilda approached the bed to take hers. 'Are you still my friend?' she asked, her voice faint and croaky.

'How can you ask? Of course I am,' Matilda replied.

'Then can I ask you to promise to take care of Tabitha and Giles for me?' she said, her grey eyes searching Matilda's face for hesitation.

'I promise,' Matilda agreed, her eyes filling with tears. 'But you aren't going anywhere. We'll make you better.'

'No, Matty,' Lily whispered. 'This is the end for me. Kiss Tabitha goodbye for me and try to explain so she'll understand. You've been the best of friends to me. I love you.'

'I love you too,' Matilda said, but Lily's eyes closed again before she could say anything more.

Matilda turned as she went to the door, taking one last look at Lily. She couldn't believe it had come to this. Why Lily, who would have made such a perfect mother to that tiny body on the wash-stand?

It was another hour before Matilda heard Giles sobbing, and the doctor came out into the kitchen. He was grey with exhaustion, his narrow shoulders stooped. 'I'm so very sorry, Miss Jennings, but she's gone,' he said. His brown eyes were bleak, the jovial look he was always noted for wiped out by deep sorrow. 'Mrs Milson was such a fine woman. If only I'd got home sooner, maybe then I could have saved her and the baby with a Caesarean, but I was delivering another infant.'

Matilda could only stare at him blankly, too devastated to speak.

Dr Treagar looked back towards the bedroom at the sound of Giles's sobs. 'He's going to need a great deal of support from all of us for a while. Try and get him to go to bed now. I'll see to getting someone around later on this morning to help with the laying out.'

He left then, the door slamming behind him, and Matilda leaned her head on the table and sobbed. She wanted to keen like the Italian women did when someone died, to wake up the whole town and make them share in her and Giles's grief. Yet she couldn't do that, Lily was a private person and she would want to go quietly in death even as she had in life, a lady to the last.

She got up, wiped her eyes and went into the bedroom. Giles was kneeling on the floor still holding one of Lily's hands. Her small face was at peace now, not a trace of the long and terrible ordeal showing on it. 'I'm so sorry,' Matilda whispered, laying one hand on Giles's shoulder.

He turned on his knees and putting his arms around her waist, sobbed into her middle. Matilda stroked his hair and kept stroking it until his sobs abated.

'You must go to bed,' she said gently. 'Come on, let me help you into Tabby's room.'

He looked up at her, his tear-filled, red-rimmed eyes so pitiful. 'What are we going to do without her, Matty?' he asked.

'I don't know, Giles,' she said truthfully.

*

Matilda washed and laid out both the baby and Lily herself. It was agonizing to find the little boy was every bit as big and sturdy-looking as Lily had always claimed he would be, and as she tenderly dressed him in the embroidered night-gown and bonnet his mother had made so lovingly for him, she felt her heart was breaking.

She dressed Lily in a white night-gown, brushed her hair and arranged it carefully around her shoulders, and tucked the baby into her arms. When she lit candles around the bed, in the soft golden light they looked as if they'd merely fallen asleep together.

Giles brought Tabitha home later after breaking the news to her at her friend's home. She threw herself into Matilda's arms and begged to be told it wasn't true.

'It can't be,' she said, her dark brown eyes wide with disbelief. 'Mama told me that when I got back I could hold the baby.'

Matilda wondered then how Giles could possibly keep his faith in a God that robbed him of his wife and left a child motherless and bewildered. Or how she could hold what was left of this family together and find the words to comfort them.

She took Tabitha into her own bed that night and held the sobbing child in her arms until she fell asleep with exhaustion. Yet Matilda found no such relief, for the silence of the night only brought back vivid images of Lily in agony and the knowledge that the happy life they'd all shared was now shattered.

As there was no other clergyman available, Giles had to officiate at the funeral himself. He said that it would help him, that as minister he could detach himself from his private grief, but for much of the service his quavering voice proved this wasn't so.

When he uttered the final words at the graveside, and tossed the first handful of soil down on to the coffin, his carefully controlled calm broke, and he roared out his pain like an angry animal. It was Solomon the blacksmith, ironically the first man Giles had spoken to when they arrived here two years ago, who led him away and comforted him.

Mrs Homberger had laid on refreshments back at the house for many of the people who came to pay their last respects had come a great distance. Matilda managed to hold her emotions in check long enough to make sure they had food and drink, but her mind was with Giles sitting out on the porch with Tabitha on his lap. Everyone today had offered advice, along with their heart-felt condolences, and although most of them had been through tragedy too, Matilda knew Giles was too wrapped in his own pain to be aware of what they'd said.

A whole month passed slowly with the grief hanging in the air, dark and malevolent. Matilda busied herself with the usual household chores, Tabitha went back to school and on the face of it appeared to be accepting her loss. But Giles was neither accepting nor coping. He hardly went out of the house, he wouldn't eat, and late at night Matilda often heard him crying and pacing the floor. Mostly he was silent, refusing even to talk about what had happened. He would stay slumped in a chair by the stove, his eyes blank and cold.

One evening after Tabitha had gone to bed, Matilda gently suggested he must try to prepare a sermon for the next Sunday's service. His place had been temporarily taken at the church by another minister from St Joseph, a small town further north on the river, but he was anxious to return to his own parish.

'How can I even walk through the church doors again?' Giles shouted at her. 'I don't believe in God any more.'

'That's not true,' she retorted. 'You've been to the church several times and I've heard you praying.'

'I have nothing in my heart but anger,' he snapped at her. 'You once said that you couldn't believe in Him because he takes the good and lets the wicked flourish. I agree with you now. That woman Dr Treagar was helping the night Lily died has twelve children already and she's neglected every one of them. So why not take her instead of Lily? Those other children would be better off away from her.'

Matilda was appalled to hear him say such a thing. 'You don't really mean that, Giles,' she said. 'You'd have been distraught if you knew another woman had died because the doctor was with Lily.'

'I wouldn't, I'd have rejoiced, and I'd gladly sell my soul to the Devil right now if I could have Lily back,' he said.

'Giles!' she exclaimed in horror. 'It sounds to me as if the Devil has already got you.'

'I know you loved Lily,' he said, looking at her sharply. 'So don't you wish someone else had died instead of her?'

Matilda put her hands on her hips and scowled at him. 'Who would I choose? Someone we know? Or would it be a poor slave, a drunken wretch in New York, a Mexican, an Indian because there isn't much value in their lives? There was a time when you cared about every sad and unfortunate soul as much as your own family. Has all that gone?'

'Yes, it has, from now on they can all go to the Devil too,' he retorted.

At this Matilda burst into tears.

'Why cry?' he said scornfully.

'Because it sounds as if I've lost the Giles I admired,' she sobbed, covering her face with her hands. 'That's bad enough, but how would Lily feel if she knew her death had robbed the world of a man who always fought for right, who embraced the whole world with his brotherly love?'

There was silence and after a few moments Matilda peeped through her fingers to see he was crying too, silent tears streaming down his face. 'Oh Giles,' she said, getting up from her chair and running over to him. 'What is going to become of us?'

Giles locked his arms around her middle, leaned his head against her breasts and they cried together. All this time Matilda had suppressed her own grief, but bent over him, her face resting on his dark curls, his arms tightly round her, she let it loose, sobbing until the well of tears ran dry.

'You've soaked my hair,' Giles said a little later, touching it in surprise.

She moved away and found the whole bodice of her dress was wet too. 'You've soaked my dress,' she retorted.

Her first feeling was of embarrassment that she'd let herself go, but this was quickly replaced with unease, for to hold a man the way she'd held Giles wasn't appropriate behaviour, not even under the tragic circumstances.

'I think you chased the Devil out anyway, or maybe drowned him,' he said with a half-smile.

All at once Matilda didn't care about how that smile had been teased out of him, because it was the first since Lily's death. She wiped her eyes on her apron and smiled back.

'Well, that's a blessing,' she said. 'We've got enough to cope with, without Old Nick around.'

As she made coffee for them both she told him in no uncertain manner that he must return to his ministry work for people were depending on him.

'I must take Lily's place at the school too,' she added. 'And we've both got to make this house a home again and a good place for Tabitha to grow up in.'

He nodded in agreement, his eyes still bleak but the anger gone. 'You're right,' he said. 'But then of course you are about most things. I don't really wish someone else died instead of Lily, I guess I just feel cheated that she and I couldn't grow old together with our children.'

Matilda sighed with relief. 'That's better,' she said. 'Now, about that sermon you have to write . . .'

In the following weeks it became clear that Giles was slowly recovering. His tormented crying at night became less frequent and eventually stopped and he went back to his ministry work. He grew calm again, sometimes eating well, now and then even cheerful, but it was like sharing the house with a different man. He was indecisive, often brooding silently, and he searched Matilda out constantly, almost like a child. He wanted her opinion on everything, who he should visit, what he should say, his sermons, even if he needed to take a coat with him in case it rained, and she knew it wasn't right to encourage this dependence on her.

Yet however hard she tried to distance herself from him, she found she couldn't. She did help him organize his time, read through his sermons and advised him on how to deal with parishioners' problems. She made his favourite meals to make him eat more, and often touched him with too much familiarity. If he came in from the rain, she went to take his hat and coat, just as she always had, yet her hands seemed to linger on his shoulders. When he came down the garden to look at the growing vegetables, it was somehow impossible not to touch his arm or hand. If they sat side by side on the couch, she was too aware of his body next to hers.

But it wasn't all one-sided. He tweaked her cheek when he left the house; when he was sitting with Tabitha on his lap listening to her read, he always patted the seat beside them, wanting Matilda to join them. He often turned the handle of the mangle for her, and helped her bring in the washing.

She told herself it was only because they were both so hungry for the affection Lily had given them, and in time they'd both adjust, but sometimes it felt as if there was something more in the air than just mutual grief and kindliness between them.

In September, five months after Lily's death, Tabitha was asked to sleep over at the Bradstocks, friends with several small children who had a small farm just a few miles out of town. Giles arranged to drop her off there in the morning while he was out on his visits, and he would collect her the following day.

That day was terribly hot and sultry, by midday much too hot to work any longer in the garden. Matilda picked some flowers, made them into a little posy surrounded by leaves, just as she used to as a girl, then went over to the churchyard to visit Lily's grave and see the new headstone which had only been erected the day before.

Just the sight of the solidity of the white marble stone and the small stone wall which had been erected around her grave cheered her, for it seemed to say this was Lily's permanent home now, its site under a tree making a fitting place to remember her.

'Here lies Lily Amelia Milson, and her baby son, taken from her loving husband and daughter too soon,' the inscription read.

'GOD IN HIS WISDOM CHOSE HER.
AN ENGLISH ROSE SO FAR FROM HOME.
LET HER GENTLE NATURE TOUCH THE HEARTS
OF ALL WHO SEE THIS STONE.
BORN 1810 IN BRISTOL ENGLAND. DIED 1847
INDEPENDENCE MISSOURI.'

Matilda was surprised by the verse, she had expected Giles to choose something from the Bible. Yet it was so much more personal and touching, and she hoped that in many years to come people would stop and read it, and be as moved by the sentiment as she was.

She sat down on the grass beside the grave, leaned back against the tree and let her mind drift to thoughts of her friend. She had tried this many times before, but she had never got past seeing her that last fateful night, her face contorted in agony, and that was too distressing an image. But this time, perhaps because of the inscription, she could imagine Lily in the garden, smiling as she tended her roses.

She hung on to the comforting image, closing her eyes and remembering how Lily had maintained so many English customs. Tea in the garden, the table laid with an embroidered cloth and her dainty china. Boiled eggs for breakfast, starched napkins tucked into silver rings, and fruit preserve in a little glass pot with its own special spoon.

'I miss you so much, Lily,' she said softly. 'The house seems so empty and bare without you. Remember how we used to laugh and chatter as we did the washing? How we used to inspect the garden every day together? I feel so lonesome without you, I don't think I'll ever find another friend like you.'

She went on to talk about Tabitha and her school work, the animals and how Solomon had given them a little goat called Gertie to rear, but then gradually she moved on to the subject which had been troubling her for some little while.

'I know I promised to look after Giles and Tabby,' she whispered. 'And I will never break that promise, but people are bound to start talking about us soon because I'm an unmarried woman living in his house. What should we do?'

It was so silent in the graveyard, not a breath of wind rustling the leaves, too hot for birds to sing, and the town beyond the fence sleepy in the sunshine.

'Marry him!'

Matilda was startled by this whispered answer. She turned her head to see who it came from. But there was no one there.

She laughed then, assuming she'd imagined it.

'I guess I'm getting a little crazy, hearing voices,' she said aloud. 'Of course that solution has occurred to me, but even if Giles were willing, I couldn't possibly take your place, Lily. Imagine what a terrible minister's wife I'd be, always wanting to interfere, thinking I knew best about everything!'

She sat there for a moment longer and all at once she had the strangest feeling of a presence close by. 'Are you there, Lily?' she asked in a whisper. 'Send me a sign if you are listening!'

All at once she heard the rustle of leaves and she jumped up in shocked surprise. There was no wind to cause it, she couldn't even feel a faint breeze on her cheeks, and the long grass around the edge of the graveyard was still.

'Well, bugger me,' she said, in her shock reverting back to her favourite swear-words from her early London days.

'I should scrub out your mouth with soap and water.' A gruff male voice she didn't recognize came from behind the tree. To her further shock, Giles stepped out from behind it, a wide smile on his face.

'Giles!' she exclaimed, blushing from head to foot. 'How dare you frighten me like that? How long have you been there?' she asked indignantly.

'A bit,' he said, returning to his normal voice. 'I just came to see the headstone before coming home. When I spotted you sitting there I didn't like to interrupt your peace, so I stayed behind the tree. Don't be embarrassed, I talk to her too.'

Mortified that he'd not only listened to what she'd been saying, but tricked her into revealing her innermost thoughts too, Matilda picked up her skirts and fled, jumping over gravestones and rushing towards the gate of the churchyard as if the hounds of hell were after her.

Feeling shamed and foolish, she went right down to the bottom of the garden, behind the pig pen, slumped down on an upturned pail and covering her face with her hands, burst into tears. She heard him coming down the garden, but this time there was nowhere further to run.

He'd abandoned his coat and his clerical collar, and with sweat running down his face he looked more like a farm worker than a minister. 'I'm so sorry, Matty,' he said as he got nearer. 'I didn't think before I whispered to you, I suppose I thought you'd know it was me right off and laugh.'

'But why say that, Giles?' she asked, hardly able to look him in the face.

He leaned down, put one finger under her chin and lifted it. 'Because it's the answer to everything. Will you marry me?'

Matilda gasped with shock. She'd seen so many sides of him in the years she had worked for him – master, clergyman, husband and father – and in all these roles she'd seen his integrity and his deep understanding of people and their needs. Had her words to Lily today troubled him so deeply that he felt he had to offer marriage?

'Don't be ridiculous.' She slapped his hand away from her

chin. 'It's no answer to anything! You have only been widowed for five months, you can't even think of marrying anyone else yet, and besides, you don't love me.'

To her surprise he just laughed, and moved back to lean on the fence of the pig pen. 'Matty, I have always loved you! Not romantic love perhaps, I would have been a poor minister and husband if I had spent my days thinking romantic thoughts about my daughter's nursemaid. But it is love I feel for you, it grew out of admiration, trust and friendship. Isn't it true you held the same feelings for myself and Lily?'

'Well, yes.' She blushed. 'But that's not the right kind of love for marriage.'

He looked at her long and hard for a moment or two. 'Love is love, I don't believe one can claim there are different kinds. Tabitha adores you. We are the best of friends, and in the past we have also been allies in secret schemes. I even know you keep a clean and tidy house and that you cook like a dream. Most couples intending to wed have a great deal less knowledge of one another.'

'But what about desire?' she whispered, blushing furiously.

'Ah yes, desire,' he said, and there was a hint of laughter in his voice. 'Desire, that item which is often the only basis for some couples' attraction. Do I feel it for you?'

He turned for a moment to look at the pigs rooting in their pen, and turned back again wrinkling his nose. 'We could hardly find a less romantic spot to consider such a question. Yet I'm not blind to the fact you are a very pretty woman, and I'd give anything to take you in my arms and kiss you.'

'Sir!' she reproved him, jumping up from her pail. 'It isn't right to say such things.'

'So I'm "Sir" again!' he laughed. 'I should have known you wouldn't think the same way. I take it you don't want to kiss me then?'

His words were like a scythe cutting through the long, tired old grass and revealing the fresh green shoots growing beneath. His dark eyes were looking at her with tenderness, his lips were curved into a sweet smile, and his black curls tumbling around his lean, tanned face suddenly looked so adorable that her fingers itched to reach out and ruffle them. But more than that, she could feel that old familiar tugging sensation inside her.

She knew in that instant that whatever it was that had made her want Flynn was there in Giles too.

'Maybe,' she said cautiously.

'That's a start then,' he said. 'As I recall, when Lily was bent on finding you a sweetheart not one of those men got even a "maybe".'

Stepping forward, he put one hand on either side of her face and held it for a second, just looking at her. Then he kissed her lips. It was the lightest of kisses, yet not an entirely chaste one. 'Was that so terrible?' he asked, his eyes twinkling with mischief.

Matilda ran back into the house feeling totally confused, Giles called out that he was going down to the livery stable to check on his horse. When he returned a couple of hours later he was unusually quiet and made no further reference to anything he'd said earlier.

They ate a cold supper, then when he moved over to his desk to write some notes for his next sermon, she felt he probably regretted everything which had transpired in the afternoon. Unable to speak of it herself, she took some sewing out on to the porch and hoped that someone might come visiting and create a diversion for them.

No one came by, and at dusk Giles came out with a lighted lamp and sat down in a chair next to her. 'It seems to be getting hotter than ever,' Matilda said, casting around for any topic of conversation which would relieve the strained atmosphere. 'I can hardly sew, my fingers are so sticky.'

'It's too dark for you to see clearly, so put it away,' he said, reaching out and taking the work from her lap. 'You work much too hard, Matty. Just sit back in your chair and enjoy the warm, peaceful evening.'

'It seems odd without Tabby,' she said nervously.

'I'm very glad she isn't here,' he said rather gruffly. 'Because I think we need to clear the air.'

'You don't have to say anything,' she said. 'Let's just forget about it.'

'You misunderstand me,' he said, moving his chair sideways so he could see her better. 'I don't intend to retract anything I said earlier, but I do wish I'd put it better.' He paused for a moment as if choosing his words carefully.

'You may think I'm unbalanced by grief, Matty, and that I

asked you to marry me just to solve all our problems. But that isn't so. I've thought about this long and hard. I know it's the right thing to do.'

'I don't see any problems, not ones which need such a drastic step,' she retorted.

'There are, Matty,' he said. 'The main one is that your reputation might be ruined by being alone in this house with me.'

'You don't have to marry me to stop that happening,' Matilda interrupted, somewhat indignantly. 'I could board with someone in town and still look after Tabitha and this house.'

He sighed and looked crestfallen. 'Once again I seem to be putting things badly. Suppose you were in my position, what would you do?'

'I certainly wouldn't rush to marry anyone,' she said. 'I suppose I'd take Tabitha off somewhere for a while, see old friends, sort out my feelings.'

'That's exactly what I'd like to do,' he said. 'Then I'd come right back and try to woo you. But I can't, I am tied to the church, and this house goes with the ministry. So I have no choice but to stay here.'

Matilda was touched by the word 'woo', and she half smiled. 'You could find a better catch to woo than me,' she said.

'Matty, will you stop imagining I am suggesting a marriage of convenience,' he said in exasperation. 'What I tried to make you see this afternoon was that I think we were meant for one another. Not just as friends, or because of our shared love for Tabitha, but as husband and wife with all that entails. You are afraid to look on me as just a man and prospective lover, purely because of the circumstances, but stand back from that, Matty, forget Lily for a moment, and that you were once our servant.'

'I can't,' she said.

'I believe you can,' he insisted, dark eyes flashing. 'Because I have learnt to do it. You are loving, giving, compassionate and you have a fine mind. On top of that you are very beautiful, and I don't believe there's a better catch than you in the whole state.' He reached out and took her hand in his. 'I don't see you as a substitute for Lily, you are so different from her that any comparison would be meaningless. I believe we could have the most wonderfully happy marriage, Matty, we are in tune with one another, we always have been.'

'But how can I step into a dead woman's shoes?' she pleaded with him. 'Especially someone's who meant so much to me. It would be easier to have a marriage of convenience than strive for the kind of bliss you shared with Lily.'

'Our marriage was not blissful, and you know that,' he said, looking at her sternly. 'But for your presence when we first moved to New York, it might well have crumbled. You witnessed the sulking, the hysteria, and no doubt you were quite aware of how unsympathetic I was to her at times. What we had is what most marriages have, some good periods, some bad, and some terrible. I am so very glad that the last two years were so utterly good, for that is the part I look back on now. But in truth, Matty, it was you more than anyone else who brought that Lily back to me. If she could stand here now on the porch she would tell you so herself.'

'But she was my friend.' Matty began to cry. 'I promised I'd take care of you and Tabby, but she wouldn't want – ' She stopped short, unable to say it.

'She wouldn't want you in my bed?' he asked, half smiling. 'But that's just what she did want, Matty, her last words to me were "Marry Matty, Giles, she'll make you happy in every way. And you'll make her happy too."'

Matilda's head jerked up. 'She really said that?'

'Ask the doctor if you doubt me,' he said. 'He heard her too.'

Matilda knew that Giles would never make up such a thing, but even with Lily's approval she still couldn't bring herself to say yes. Her own father had once given her some advice out on the river on the way back from visiting Dolly for that first time. 'Never dally with a grieving man,' he had said. 'They ain't right in the 'ead for some time,' and Lucas, though a simple man in so many ways, had been very wise.

She went off to bed a little later, having changed the subject to talk about Tabitha. But once in bed she couldn't sleep. It was unbearably hot and her mind was in a turmoil. Deep down inside her, however ashamed it made her feel, she wanted Giles. Maybe it was only today that she'd suddenly felt desire for him, but looking back over the years she could see that he had always been more to her than master or friend, she'd just been too naive to see it then. But the fear that she would be living in Lily's shadow frightened her. Could she learn to live with Giles looking sadly over his shoulder? Or would it turn her into a bitter shrew, always trying to prove herself that much better?

She must have fallen asleep eventually, only to wake suddenly at the sound of torrential rain battering down on the roof. She lay there for a while savouring the welcome cool breeze coming through the open window, but a loud crack of thunder, followed immediately by a flash of lightning which lit up the room, made her run to the window to close it. A second brilliant flash of lightning illuminated the whole garden, enough for her to see Gertie the little goat tethered up, and the chickens which she'd forgotten to shoo into the hen-house. Without even stopping to get a wrap, she ran down the stairs and across the kitchen towards the back door.

'Matty!'

Giles's voice came from his bedroom which was on the ground floor.

'I left the goat and hens out,' she yelled back. 'I'm just going to get them in.'

As she opened the door, the force of the wind and rain threw it back violently, almost knocking her over. Giles ran across the kitchen and slammed it shut.

'You can't go out in that,' he said. 'They'll be fine, animals have more sense than us.'

'I must,' she insisted, trying to push past him. 'Gertie will be terrified.'

Giles caught hold of her arms and for a moment they wrestled, Matilda determined to get to the goat, Giles equally determined to stop her. Another blinding flash of lightning lit up the entire kitchen. Matilda shrieked in fright, and suddenly Giles's arms were round her.

'There, there,' he said comfortingly. 'It can't hurt us, and Gertie is on a long chain, she'll get under a bush. As for the chickens, they may be stupid but they are bright enough to go into the hen-house all alone.'

Giles was wearing only a night-shirt, and as he pulled her closer still to him, so the heat and hardness of his body struck through her thin night-gown, and all at once they were kissing.

Passion erupted just as suddenly as the storm had. The windows shook, thunder crashed, lightning flashed and the rain lashed down, mirroring the emotions which had been released.

Arms locked around each other, lips and tongues devouring, their hands explored and fingers caressed.

Giles lifted her up into his arms and shamelessly she wound her legs around his middle, covering his face and neck with more kisses.

'I want you so badly, Matty,' he whispered as he carried her up to her bedroom. 'Is it the same for you?'

'Oh yes,' she sighed, clinging to him even tighter.

The storm howling outside was as frantic, wild and uninhibited as their passion. Night-gowns were tossed aside, two bodies on fire, consumed by their need for one another.

For Matilda it was as if everything in her life so far had been leading up to this moment. She didn't care what tomorrow would bring, his lips on hers, his hands caressing her body, driving her further and further into a spiral of sheer bliss was the only thing that mattered.

As he went to enter her, for just the briefest moment she resisted. But a flash of lighting illuminated his face, and she saw no lust, but such tenderness and caring, that she thrust herself towards him joyfully.

'My darling,' he murmured. 'My precious darling Matty.'

It was like being reborn as they lay still joined together, sticky with perspiration. Whatever had gone before was wiped out by the present. Although she had no real yardstick of previous experience to measure their love-making by, she knew without a doubt that such utter ecstasy was a very special gift. She didn't need Giles to tell her it was new to him too, she could feel it in his kisses, hear it in his contented sighs. They might be damned for tasting it before marriage. The rest of the world might see it as shameful so soon after Lily's death, but Matilda's heart was too full of joy to care about such things.

Giles nuzzled into her breasts and wound his fingers into her long hair. 'Men have often come to me in the past to confide their illicit love for a woman,' he said softly. 'I have listened, sympathized and consoled, and all too often tried to make them break off the liaison. When they failed to do this, I would be bewildered, because you see, Matty, I had no real comprehension of the depths and heights of passion. I understand now though.'

'Are you trying to tell me this will always be an illicit love affair?' she asked teasingly. 'Has the offer of marriage been withdrawn?'

'Of course not, my darling.' He kissed her nose and laughed. 'I think you know what I mean. I didn't intend to bed you until a ring was on your finger. I didn't even think of such things. But now we have taken that step it makes things more complicated because I know I am going to want you by my side every day, every night.'

It was dawn now, still raining just as heavily, but the thunder was more distant and the first rays of daylight had made a dull grey light in the room. He leaned up on one elbow and looked down at her, stroking away tendrils of hair from her face. 'After our conversation last evening I thought that to prevent any talk about us, I could sleep over at Dr Treagar's house for a few months. But this alters everything, Matty. We'll have to get married right away.'

'But we can't do that,' she said, startled by his sudden urgency. 'You know what people will say. I don't care for myself, but it might get to Tabby's ears and I couldn't bear her to think we were betraying her mother's memory.'

Giles slumped down beside her. Clearly he hadn't thought of this. 'What will we do then? I know I won't be able to get through one day without holding you.'

'Nor me,' she agreed. 'But we'll have to learn.'

A loud and violent banging on the front door woke them just before six. Giles pulled on his pants and rushed down to answer it.

Solomon, with a sack protecting his shoulders from the rain, was pacing up and down on the porch. 'I've just heard the river's burst its banks,' he shouted as Giles opened the door. 'I fear the folks down there are drowned. Get someone to ring the church bell. I'm going on down there.'

Giles and Matilda dressed immediately and rushed out of the house minutes later. While Matilda ran across to the stables to get the horse and gig, Giles went to Mr Homberger to ask him to ring the bell and tell everyone who came to the summons to come down and help. As Matilda came out of the stables with the gig, he jumped up on to it, took the reins from her and whipped the horse into a gallop.

As they reached the bluff where goods from the boats were hauled up to bring them into town, they stopped, staring for a moment in horror and disbelief at the sight which met their eyes.

The landing stage was swept away, muddy brown water surged over what had been parched low-lying land the day before. Uprooted trees, parts of homes, tables, stools and household utensils bobbed around on the surface, oxen, horses and pigs were desperately trying to swim to dry land, and even above the still heavy rain they could hear the cries of those waiting to be rescued. Two small children were clinging to the branches of a tree, a woman was desperately trying to tread water, a baby in her arms. A small girl sat screaming on an upturned table that even as they surveyed the scene was floating further downstream. But worse still were the floating bodies, face down, arms spread – healthy men, women and children who had slept so soundly they hadn't even heard the storm, much less the river silently rising until it spilled over and surged through their homes, sweeping them away.

Solomon was already in the water, swimming strongly out to a skiff broken loose from its moorings. He was aboard it in a trice, rowing frantically out towards the woman with the baby, at the same time yelling back for other men to find boats. Two men appeared carrying a canoe between them, and a woman shouted from one shack on slightly higher ground that they could take her boat.

As more and more townsfolk came galloping down on horses and in carts to help with the rescue, Giles took charge. Older women were ordered to go back to open the school-house, collecting as many blankets and dry clothes as they could on the way. Old men were told to commandeer carts and find anything to make stretchers, while he divided the main body of people into groups to search the water's edge for survivors and bodies.

'Get the doctor and then take charge at the school-house,' he ordered Matilda. 'We'll need sheeting for bandages and hot water, and get anyone still at home to provide hot drinks for the survivors.'

Amos Bradstock, the father of the children Tabitha had stayed the night with, came riding into town later on, his horse daubed with mud. His crops, like all the other farmers' in the area, had been destroyed, but he'd ridden in guessing that down by the river things must be bad. His home was safe and he reassured Giles that his wife would continue to take care of Tabitha until the rain had stopped as the road was virtually impassable with mud and fallen trees.

By midday the death count was nine men, fourteen women, and twelve children ranging from thirteen down to a three-week-old baby, and they used the church as a morgue. Some thirty more people were found, almost all of them injured in some way, from broken limbs to severe lacerations, but over thirty souls were still unaccounted for.

Matilda worked flat out, stripping wet clothes off the injured, washing and dressing wounds and trying to comfort them as they waited for news of their husbands, wives, and children. Those who had already discovered members of their families were in the church, sitting in tight little groups, eyes bleak with grief, too deeply shocked to speak.

Many of the women prayed constantly as they tended the injured, provided tea and hot soup. In a moment of cynicism Matilda wondered how some of them could suddenly become so caring, for these flood victims were mostly the same people they normally shunned. They were the ones Giles had always tried to get help for, the scapegoats of the community, accused of every crime, the supposed perpetrators of every epidemic. If they had shown some concern in the past, perhaps these people wouldn't have been forced to live in foul shanties at the river's edge.

She wondered too how the survivors could rebuild their lives. Their few animals were mostly drowned, their rough homes and few possessions gone. One woman had lost her husband and the five youngest of her eight children. When she said grimly that she wished she'd been drowned too, Matilda couldn't blame her.

Yet there were miraculous stories along with the horror. Some people had been swept out of their homes along the river a great way, yet somehow found themselves tossed up on higher ground from which they'd staggered back unhurt. One couple sharing a wooden bed with their two young children had found themselves floating downstream as if in a boat, and the man had managed to catch the branch of a tree and haul them to safety. Solomon picked up a large dog which was swimming, still holding a three-year-old girl up by the back of her night-gown, and apart from a severe case of fright she had no injuries.

But the miracles gave only faint hope to those who waited. As the day progressed and the rain turned to drizzle and finally stopped at six, each time a cart came squelching through the mud it didn't leave its load at the school-house, but went straight to the church.

The men continued searching with lanterns after dark. Matilda went down to the river just after midnight to find Giles and saw the pin-pricks of light on both banks. Now that the rain had ceased it was a warm, clear night, the sky studded with stars, and the moon casting a silver beam right down the river.

Giles spotted the gig and came over to her, and for a few moments they stood in silence watching the lapping water, and listening to the men's whistles and shouts from along the banks.

'It looks so beautiful,' he said wearily. 'But tomorrow when the sun comes up we'll see the full extent of the carnage. The drowned animals will have to be burned or buried, and then the funerals.'

'What will happen to all those homeless people?' she asked, tears filling her eyes. She had fought against crying all day, but now, exhausted and riddled with guilt that they had been making love while this was happening, she was struggling not to break down. 'No one liked them when they lived down here, who will offer them shelter now?'

Giles sighed deeply. 'We will, Matty, and perhaps then others will follow. Maybe a tragedy had to happen to make the townsfolk realize they have to take care of their poor.'

'It makes our problems look very small,' she whispered.

'It does indeed,' he agreed wearily. 'In fact it's solved some of them for us. Tabby must share your room for a while, and I will sleep in the living-room. That way we can take in two families. It isn't the solution I would have sought, but it's the right thing to do.'

'What on earth would Lily have said to that?' she blurted out without thinking.

To her surprise he didn't reprove her, but laughed. 'She would have had fifty fits, Matty, wouldn't she?'

Matty giggled, picturing the horror on her friend's face if Giles had suggested bringing two families into her clean, orderly house. She didn't relish it much herself, just the thought of the cooking, cleaning and washing involved, to say nothing of having unruly children rushing around, was daunting. Yet she was suddenly aware it was the first time they'd managed to laugh about Lily, and perhaps that was a very good sign.

'I think I share her alarm,' Matilda admitted. 'But you are right, Giles, we do have to do it. Alice, the widow with only three children left, is one that must come. You pick the other family.'

They spoke for a few moments about which one it should be, and finally settled on the four Negro children who had lost both parents.

'I probably won't get a chance to say this again for a very long time,' he said, turning to her and touching her cheek. 'But I love you, Matty. When this is all over we will get married, immediately.'

She looked up at him and smiled. He had thick black stubble on his chin, he smelled of river water because he'd waded in and out so many times today. It was too dark to see the dirt she knew was there, just as it was too dark to see the blood and grime on her face and apron. Somehow seeing each other like this made them equals, and even if the events of the previous day hadn't happened, she knew that today's would have made them see what had probably always been there. 'Then I can stand anything,' she said.

'Even seven extra children, and slatternly, grieving Alice?' he asked teasingly.

'You'd better ask your God to give me extra strength,' she said with a smile. 'I think I'm going to need it.'

Chapter Thirteen

Giles and Matilda stood on the porch and waved until the cart with Alice and her three children was out of sight. It was the day after Thanksgiving, and Alice was going off to make a new life for herself in St Louis as a housekeeper for a widower with two children of his own.

'Thank you, Lord, for making it before Christmas,' Giles said, looking skywards, his tone just a little mocking. 'Another month of so many children would have turned me into an old man.'

'Giles!' Matilda exclaimed. 'What happened to your Christian charity?'

They both laughed, for there was no denying the truth, the two months of having seven extra children in the house, and Alice, had been a terrible trial. Alice had been almost out of her mind with grief for some time, and her three remaining children, used to an undisciplined life down on the river, sullenly resented not only the restrictions that came with living in a minister's house, but also having to share it with four Negro children.

The four Hamiltons, aged from two to eight, were easier to cope with than Alice's sullen brood, as they were sunny-natured and surprisingly obedient, but they still had their problems, and as there was no school for Negro children in Independence, Matilda had all four of them home with her all the time. Even Tabitha had been difficult, she resented the visitors who took the attention she had been used to, and didn't want to share her toys and books with them.

The house was too cramped. Washing and cooking for them all was a formidable job, but worst of all was the total lack of privacy. There was no opportunity for Giles and Matilda even to talk privately, much less have any time alone together. It was torture being so close to each other, yet unable to kiss or hold one another. Just the brush of their hands, or eyes locking over the dinner table, was enough to send their pulses racing. Giles would go off out when it got too much to bear, but Matilda had to stay, and quite often she felt like screaming with frustration.

But the Hamilton children had been given a home by a Baptist minister and his wife in Chicago and collected two weeks ago, and Giles had used his connections in the church to find the job for Alice. He sighed with contentment as they went back into the empty house. 'I never knew silence could sound so good,' he said.

Matilda stood for a moment looking around her, suddenly aware how shabby the house had become. The wood floor was scuffed and stained, the walls marked by dirty fingers, every piece of furniture looked worn and scratched. 'I'll have my work cut out to get this back the way it was,' she said wearily. 'And we'll never be able to replace all the things which have been broken and destroyed.'

'We will,' Giles said comfortingly. 'Besides, it will be good for us both to make a new home where everything is ours.'

He was referring to the many treasures of Lily's which had been broken by their guests, and blankets, quilts and cooking pots they'd given away after the flood to those in desperate need.

'I suppose so,' Matilda said. She felt curiously flat, although she'd expected to feel elated now that they had the house back to themselves and full of enthusiasm to sort everything out. But all she really wanted to do now was sleep.

Giles sensed from her tone that something was wrong and looking at her sharply, he suddenly saw she was exhausted. Her eyes were dull, she was pale and thin and her hair had lost its sheen. Even her pinafore was grey instead of the dazzling white it once was. He was immediately contrite, aware she had taken all the hard work of these past few months in her stride, never complaining, always kindly and understanding with the children, even when they were impossible, and now he could see how much it had drained her.

'No work today,' he said, wiggling a reproving finger at her. 'We'll sit down and make plans for our wedding instead. But first a kiss, Matty. I can't promise it will put new life into you, but it will me.'

That kiss was the sweetest ever, wiping out the trials of the past months. They clung to each other, all the passion they'd suppressed for so long welling up and spilling over. Giles picked her up in his arms and made towards her bedroom.

'We shouldn't,' Matty said weakly, yet knowing she had no power to resist.

'We should,' Giles whispered, his lips on her forehead as he climbed the stairs. 'We'll be married in a few short weeks now, but we need one another now.'

It was even better than that first time in the storm, for that had been like the storm itself, wild and frantic, now it was slow and tender. They had made love then in darkness, their hands caressing blindly, only sighs leading them to each other's sensitive places, but now in daylight, Giles explored every inch of her, kissing her in places that made her blush and shut her eyes, yet it was so blissful she couldn't stop him.

She was as eager as he was to have him enter her and this time it didn't hurt at all. Alice had once said early on in her stay here that her husband 'bothered' her almost every night. She said she had wished there was a way to avoid it, but he got 'ornery' if he didn't have his way. Matilda knew Alice's view on married love was common to a great many women, and she fleetingly wondered as she clawed at Giles's back if she was a wicked woman to like it so much.

But then, just as she thought it couldn't possibly get any better, something began happening inside her. It was as though a part of her was swelling up like rising dough, getting hotter and hotter, so intense she thought she'd die from pleasure, then all at once she felt herself kind of overflowing, and the feeling ran right through her body, like shooting stars.

It made her cry out and cling to Giles still tighter, moving with him as if they were one person, and as their lips sought one another's so she felt him spending his seed into her.

There were tears in his eyes as they lay in one another's arms, a sweet torpor enveloping them. 'These past few weeks have made me see just how much I love you,' he whispered. 'I can't tell you what it was like, wanting you so much but being unable to even hold you in my arms.'

'It was the same for me too,' she said, burying her face in his neck and breathing in the smell of him. 'At times I thought I was going mad, so don't you dare leave me now.'

'How could I?' He laughed softly. 'I'm bound to you, body,

heart and soul. But sleep now, my darling, we'll make the wedding plans later.'

Matilda woke to hear Tabitha's voice coming from the kitchen. She sat up with a start, for a moment thinking the child had come home from school and would find them together. But she was alone in the bed, and Giles's laughter burst out from downstairs too, there was a smell of cooking, and it was dark.

She fumbled for the candle by the bed and lit it. To her surprise she was now wearing her night-gown, the clothes Giles had pulled off her so hastily were folded neatly on the chair, and there was no sign of his. Clearly she'd fallen so deeply asleep that she hadn't felt or seen Giles do any of it.

The door opened and Tabitha peeped round. 'Are you feeling better, Matty?' she asked, her big brown eyes full of concern. 'Papa said you were very tired and I wasn't to wake you when I came in from school. We've made fried chicken for supper, would you like some, it's almost ready?'

'I'd love some,' Matilda replied, suddenly so hungry she thought she could eat a horse if it was offered to her. 'Fancy you and your papa making fried chicken all on your own!'

Tabitha came right into the room and jumped up on the bed. 'Papa said we must learn to do more things to make your life easier. He said you'd been worked like a field hand these past few months.'

Matilda smiled. She felt so much better, all the weariness she'd been feeling for so long had just upped and vanished, replaced by joyous anticipation for the future. 'It won't be hard to look after just you two,' she said. 'Not now Alice and her children have gone.'

'I'm so glad they've gone.' Tabitha moved closer and whispered conspiratorially. 'I grew fond of the Hamiltons, they were sweet, but I never liked Alice, she was mean, and her children were even meaner. I felt sorry for them losing their pa and all the other brothers and sisters in the flood, so I had to be nice to them. But being sorry for someone doesn't make you like them, does it?'

Tabitha's opinion was so much like her own, Matilda wanted to laugh. Alice was a dour, cold woman who showed no real appreciation of any kindness shown to her. But at the same time she knew she should instil some of Lily's graciousness into the child.

'We must always support those less fortunate than ourselves, Tabby,' she said reprovingly. 'Even if we don't like them too much. And we must pray that their new life is a happier one.'

Tabitha grimaced, and Matilda doubted she would include that family in her prayers. Then the child beamed at Matilda. 'Papa said tonight's supper is a celebration because you've got a special surprise for me. Is it a puppy?'

'No, it isn't,' Matilda smiled. She guessed Giles was intending to tell her tonight that they were getting married. 'Winter isn't a good time to get a puppy, spring or summer is much better.'

Tabitha frowned. 'So what is it then?'

'It wouldn't be a surprise if I told you, would it?' Matilda laughed. 'So I'd better get up and dressed, hadn't I?'

The fried chicken, black-eyed peas and potatoes were extra specially delicious as Matilda hadn't had to cook them herself and she wolfed the food down appreciatively.

'Don't keep me waiting any longer,' Tabitha said half-way through the meal. 'I can't eat for excitement.'

Giles patted his daughter's flushed face affectionately. 'Would a new mama make you eat?'

Tabitha's dark eyes grew as big as the dinner plates and her mouth fell open in shock.

'Well?' Giles asked. 'Is that an "I'm pleased"?'

Matilda looked at him and smiled. He was forty-one, but he looked so boyish tonight. His eyes were gleaming mischievously, his full lips seemed to be curled into a permanent grin, and his cheeks were rosy.

Tabitha shook her head violently. 'I don't want a new mama. I just want to be here with you and Matty for ever, nobody else.'

'That's a wee bit selfish,' Giles said, pulling a disapproving face. 'Because Papa really wants a new wife.'

'Is she pretty?' Tabitha asked, scowling at him.

'Oh yes, very, and clever too,' Giles said.

Tabitha's face began to crumple and tears filled her eyes. 'No, Papa, you can't get married, what would Matty do? You aren't sending her away, are you?'

Matilda gave Giles a stern look, this teasing had gone on too long.

'No, I'm not sending Matty away,' he said, and tweaked one of Tabitha's pigtails. 'It's Matty I'm going to marry. She'll be your new mama.'

For a moment the little girl just stared at him, then she looked at Matty. 'Is it true?'

Matilda nodded. 'Will I do for a new mama?'

A smile as wide as a slice of water melon tore across the little girl's face, her eyes lighting up like two torches. 'For ever and ever?' she whispered as if she could hardly believe it.

'For ever and ever, if that's what you want,' Matilda said.

Tabitha jumped off her chair, sending it flying back on to the floor, and rushed to Matilda, throwing her arms around her neck. 'That's an even better surprise than a puppy,' she said, her voice squeaky with excitement. 'I asked Mrs Homberger why Papa didn't marry you once, and she said she thought it was a good idea too. Did she tell you to do it?'

Matilda and Giles laughed loudly at that. Mrs Homberger was noted for being the kind of woman who organized everything and everyone. But even she wouldn't have had the cheek to suggest who her minister married.

'No, we made up our minds all on our own,' Giles said.

'Mama will be pleased, I can't wait to tell her,' Tabitha said. 'Last time I talked to her I had a feeling she was worried one of those "Magdalenes" that come in the spring might make you marry her. Mama was always real scared of them.'

Matilda spluttered with laughter. 'Magdalene' was Giles's pet name for a whore. Lily had always been horrified that he often defended them and Tabitha had clearly overheard a conversation about them at some time and got a slightly distorted view of their activities.

Tabitha let go of Matilda and looked at her curiously. 'Why are you laughing?' she asked.

'Just because I'm happy,' Matilda said, grabbing hold of the child and hugging her. 'Shall we go and tell Mama the news together tomorrow and put a very special posy on her grave?'

Tabitha stayed up till late that night with them as they discussed the wedding plans. 'Tomorrow I'll find someone to come in and paint the place,' Giles said, looking around at the grubby walls. 'You two can go and buy some yard goods to make new curtains, and you'd better see about dresses for the wedding too.

But make sure you get someone else to make them up, you haven't got time for sewing now.'

'May I have a red dress?' Tabitha asked.

Matilda looked at Giles, uncertain if Tabitha could abandon her mourning clothes under such circumstances.

'Well, black isn't really appropriate for a wedding, but then neither is red,' he said tactfully. 'I think blue might be just right, with some white lace.'

They made a list of things which were needed, and Giles said they could go and buy them immediately. 'I'll have to go and see if the minister in St Joseph can come to marry us,' he said. 'I'll leave on Monday, that way I'll be back by Saturday, in time to tell everyone in church the following Sunday.'

It was raining hard on Monday morning as Tabitha and Matilda saw Giles off on the river boat to St Joseph. Even though they had been down to the river countless times since the flood, and all signs of it had long since vanished, Matilda still found it impossible to forget that day's terrible destruction.

Most of the surviving members of the families who used to live there had moved away, some back East, others to stake claims further West, only a few had stayed in the town which had robbed them of their loved ones. Those who had remained were mainly ones who had been shown kindness in the town, some of the men had real jobs at last, a couple of the widows had remarried, and several orphans had been adopted by farming families.

But despite everything Giles had tried to do, new families had moved on to the riverside land, and Matilda wondered how they would manage in those hastily built shacks, often with only canvas as roofs, when the winter set in.

Yet the stoic spirit of Americans, whether born here or immigrants, never ceased to amaze her. Fire, flood, failed crops, child deaths, nothing seemed to deter them from their ambitions for long. In the two years they'd been in Independence she had met people who had lost everything over and over again, but still they picked themselves up, moved on and tried again.

'I wonder how Cissie is?' Matilda thought aloud as she and Tabitha rode home in the gig. 'She must be in Oregon by now and had her baby.'

'Maybe we could go and see her one day,' Tabitha said. 'Wouldn't that be fun, you and me and Papa in a wagon!'

'It might be,' Matilda said. Right now she felt even a 2,000-mile journey would sound fun if Giles was beside her. 'But it's an awfully long way, and your papa can't go off and leave his church. So I think we'll just have to rely on letters between us.'

Ironically a letter came the very next day. It was written by John, dated 1 October, and the address given was the Willamette Valley in Oregon. This was unusually fast for mail, and Matty guessed John must have handed it to an army dispatch rider who was making the trip back to Missouri before the winter set in.

Dear Matty. We got here at last, but it was a trying journey and no mistake, specially over the mountains. But we done better than most folks, we didn't have to leave nothing behind, we didn't get sick much and we got here all in one piece. Peter has a little sister now, we called her Susanna and she's a fine healthy baby with her mother's dark hair and loud voice! Peter is real good at minding her and he ain't one bit jealous. We got a parcel of fine land with a stream running through it and I've been felling logs to build our cabin. It ain't so fancy, but it's better than the wagon to live in. Our neighbours are very friendly and kind, some of them came over to help me put the roof on, and the women fussed around Cissie and the new baby. As I thought, there is enough trees here for me to supply timber to the whole of America if I've a mind to. First after the cabin's all done I'm going to set up a saw mill, then come next spring we'll enlarge the cabin and plant fruit trees too. Cissie asks that I tell you it's right pretty countryside and you mustn't forget she'll always have room here for you. Sidney asks to say that he's a crack shot now, and we'll never starve 'cos there ain't a rabbit or deer so quick as him. He's got real good at whittling too on the journey, made Peter some little animals that look real. Best thing we did bringing Sidney along, he's a fine lad, works like a man and tough as old boots.

Give our regards and best wishes to Mr and Mrs Milson, we guess you've all got your hands full with the new baby. Write soon, we ain't got nobody but you to get a letter from. So send us news of what's happening to you all and in the rest of the country. Only way we get news here is if someone comes by that's been some place.

Fond regards, John Duncan.

Cissie had written a line on the bottom. Her round childish writing and the lack of spelling mistakes suggested John had written it out and she'd painstakingly copied it.

Susanna is the sweetest fattest baby and very good. I birthed her in the wagon up in the mountains, but was up next day walking. I think of you all the time, I wish you was here. Love Cissie.

That evening Matilda sat down and wrote a long letter back, even though she knew it would probably be spring before it left the mail office. It was a hard letter to write, for to speak of Lily's death, and then of her new-found happiness with Giles seemed wrong somehow. But in the end she settled for writing it just how it was, for she remembered Cissie was the one person who couldn't be shocked and she would want happiness for those she loved.

She described the blue dress she was having made for her wedding, a fancy one with ruffles around the neck and hem, and a dear little hat with a veil. 'It's taking nine yards of cloth,' she added, still somewhat shocked by such extravagance. 'And Giles said I'll be needing two other dresses and a coat too if I'm not to shame him when we go to St Louis for our wedding trip.'

She sat for a while sucking the end of her pen, wanting to tell Cissie so much more, but hardly daring. 'I love him so completely,' she finally wrote. 'I'm sure you know what I mean.'

Finishing the letter up with messages to Peter and Sidney and then all the news she could think of for John, she added a postscript. 'I'll write again just as soon as I'm Mrs Giles Milson, the minister's wife.'

By Saturday Matilda had run out of things to do. The parlour and kitchen had been given a new coat of paint, new curtains hung at the windows, and she'd sanded and polished the floors till they looked like new. Tabitha was back in her own bedroom, closets were tidied, all shelves were lined with fresh paper, and she'd cut enough wood to last half the winter. If it hadn't been raining hard she would have been down at the river waiting for the boat, but the riverside in the rain wasn't a place she liked to go to, and besides, she told herself, Giles hadn't said for sure that he'd be back on Saturday, only that he hoped to be.

There were no boats on Sundays, and it seemed to be twice as long as a usual Sunday. Dr Treagar, who had often stood in as a lay preacher before Giles came to the town, took the morning service, and he and his wife came over to the house in the afternoon for tea.

'I wanted to tell everyone this morning why Giles went to St Joseph,' he said with a wide grin. 'You see, he told me you were to be married before he went. But I guessed he would want to tell everyone himself, so I buttoned my lip.'

Mrs Treagar and Matilda had become good friends since the flood. Her quiet, refined ways reminded Matilda comfortingly of Lily. As her husband spoke her round, rather plain face lit up. 'I'm so happy for you both, and Tabby,' she said with real warmth. 'We were so afraid Giles would leave Independence after Lily died, but you kept him going and put the soul back into him. We hope you will be blessed with many children and stay here for ever.'

The two women discussed plans for the wedding and Mrs Treagar thought they should use the school-house for a party afterwards. 'I know everyone will want to come,' she said, her brown eyes sparkling with anticipation. 'It's time we had dancing and music again in the town, since the flood it's been so solemn and sad.'

By Monday evening when Giles still hadn't returned, Matilda began to worry. Although she told herself he had probably stayed over to buy new things for their home or because he'd run into old friends, she couldn't rid herself of the feeling something bad had happened. Yet for Tabitha's sake she kept up a cheerful front, going along to the school on Tuesday morning to help the younger children with reading and English, but her heart wasn't entirely in it.

On Wednesday afternoon, Matilda was out in the garden when Sheriff Neilson came riding down the street. As he stopped outside, dismounted and tethered his horse to the picket fence, her heart thudded, afraid he had come to give her bad news. 'Is it the minister?' she called out as she ran towards him. 'Is he hurt?'

Sheriff Neilson was a big man of German descent. Long hours out in all winds and weathers had made his face as brown as an Indian's, and his legs were bowed from riding. He whipped off his hat as he saw her, but his expression was so grim she knew in that instant that Giles was not just hurt, but dead.

'I'm so sorry, Miss Jennings,' he said, twisting his hat in his hands and looking at the ground. 'There ain't no way to tell you this but straight out. The minister was shot up in St Joseph. Seems like he tried to stop a brawl. They just brought his body home for burial.'

She felt her legs go weak beneath her, and the next thing she knew she was back in the house lying on the couch and the Sheriff was dabbing at her face with a wet cloth.

'I'm truly sorry, Miss Jennings,' he said, his brown, weather-beaten face looming over her. 'I knows you've been through so much with him and his family, and a better man never walked. I can't tell you how bad I feel about him leaving Miss Tabitha an orphan and all.'

He left then and went to get Mrs Treagar from across the street. Matilda lay on the couch unable to believe what she'd just heard. It felt like the worst kind of bad dream, and she tried to pinch herself to end it. But as she lay there, looking at the tassels on the tablecloth, the pan holder embroidered by herself with red poppies and the pitcher of milk covered by a beaded piece of muslin, she knew no dream could be so vivid.

'You promised you would never leave me,' she said aloud. 'How could you get yourself shot?'

Mrs Treagar came rushing in, followed by the Sheriff. She enfolded Matilda in her arms and rocked her to her bosom, tears falling on to Matilda's head.

'Oh Matty, it's so terrible,' she croaked. 'Giles was such a good man, with so much before him. How can we tell little Tabitha?'

Death was something Matilda had always accepted. Right from when she was a small child the sight of the undertaker in Finders Court was as common as seeing the knife grinder or the night-soil cart. She'd lost her own mother, a baby sister and Peggie, most families had lost even more of their members. While in Primrose Hill, and back in New York, death continued to strike remorselessly – hardly a week passed without Giles or Lily mentioning someone well known to them dying.

Here in Missouri it was even more commonplace. With so many people so far from medical help, perhaps too poor or ignorant to seek it, even a relatively minor accident or disease could prove fatal. Many women didn't even write to their relatives about a new baby until it was several months old, because they'd lost others in the first weeks and didn't wish to tempt providence.

When Lucas died, Matilda had grieved silently, then put it aside, for that was the way. It wasn't easy to accept Lily's death, because of her close involvement and because of how it affected Giles and Tabitha, yet she had come to terms with it eventually. She had grieved too for all those people who died in the flood, yet once the dead were buried, the remaining relatives comforted and found homes, it too was put aside.

But Giles's death was impossible to accept. Not because she loved him and had intended to spend the rest of her life at his side. Not because he had a daughter who needed him, however much both those reasons hurt her personally. But because he had lived his life for the good of others. Why should a man chosen by God to do his work be shot down by a bullet when his very nature had been a peaceable one, decrying guns and every other weapon of destruction?

As she sobbed into Mrs Treagar's breast, her anger was as great as her sorrow. She cursed the man to hell and back who had taken his life, and she knew if he had been here in Independence she would have picked up the axe and gone to slaughter him too.

It was Mrs Treagar who broke the news to Tabitha when she came in from school, for Matilda couldn't do it. Yet the moment she heard the child's scream of anguish, she rallied herself to run to her and hold her and wept with her, holding nothing back.

'It's not fair!' Tabitha shouted through her tears. 'Mama's gone and baby Harry, now Papa too, and he said you were going to be my new mama!'

'I'll still be your mama,' Matilda said. 'I promise you I'll love you for ever and care for you.' She wanted to say she would never leave her, but she couldn't say that. Giles had said it, and less than two weeks later he was gone.

The pain did not lessen. By day it throbbed remorselessly, at night it became agony. Matilda got through the funeral, saw Giles tucked in beside Lily, comforted Tabitha and received the many people who came to offer their condolences, but inside her was a raw place which showed no sign of healing. Just the mention of his name, touching his clothes, his Bible and his daughter was enough to break open the wound again.

It didn't help knowing the man who had shot him would hang. She was a widow in her heart, but in the eyes of most people and the church Giles set such store by, she was just a family friend, and therefore they didn't imagine her grief was any greater than their own. Dr and Mrs Treagar were the only people who knew of the intended marriage and they hadn't spoken of it to anyone, believing it to be none of their business.

Christmas passed by barely noticed by either Matilda or Tabitha. They turned down the offer of dinner with the Treagars because Matilda knew they were both incapable of even trying to rise out of their grief for the occasion. They didn't even go to church, for to see a visiting minister up in Giles's place in the pulpit would have been too painful, so instead they went for a long walk well away from the town and only returned home when they were too tired to walk another step.

Matilda had never felt so isolated. She could walk down the crowded main street, but it felt as if she was entirely alone, and invisible too. She couldn't sleep at night, she didn't want to eat, look after the house or animals. She did of course, but it was just mechanical, her duties so ingrained in her that she hardly knew she was doing them.

Half-way through January of 1948 when she got a letter from the Dean in St Louis informing her the minister's house must be vacated by the end of the month, fear jolted her enough to realize that the desperate grief she felt wasn't her worst problem.

Suddenly reality hit her smack in the face. She had no money, except the twenty dollars which had been in Giles's pocket at the time of his death, and another eighty dollars she'd found in a cash-box in his desk. Giles had never discussed his financial situation with her – if he had any savings, or an allowance from his family back in England, he'd never told her, and as she wasn't his widow she wasn't entitled to anything anyway. She had seen no will, and though Tabitha would inherit anything he owned, that wouldn't come to her until she was of age. Yet how was she going to continue to look after Tabitha without any money or a home?

In the absence of anyone else to confide in she went to see Dr Treagar. He listened to what she had to say and read the letter from the Dean. His anxious expression didn't give her any comfort.

'Oh dear,' he said, scratching his head. 'How very heartless of the church. I can understand of course that they need the house for a new minister, but knowing Tabitha has lost her last remaining parent I would have expected them to be more sympathetic. I shall write to the Dean myself, Miss Jennings, and explain your situation. They must have some sort of fund for circumstances like this.'

'I don't want charity,' Matilda insisted, trying to pull together some dignity. 'Only a little patience until I can find a job. Could I be a school teacher?'

There had been a time when she imagined school teaching was way beyond her ability, but since moving to Missouri she'd found a great many teachers knew far less than she did. In some small towns the older girls taught the younger ones.

'If we needed a school teacher here in Independence I'd certainly recommend you for the job,' he said. 'But we have a teacher, Matty.'

'Well, in another town then. What about Westport, or Kansas City?' she asked, though she had never been to either place.

The doctor sat back in his chair and studied Matilda for a moment. Both he and his wife were very fond of her, and in his view she would make an admirable teacher. But sadly there was a great deal of prejudice against young single women working for a living and she'd come up against it wherever she went. With an eight-year-old child in tow she was adding to her problems.

'Wouldn't it be wiser to send Tabitha back to her grandparents in England?' he said after a few moments' thought. 'I know you have cared for her right from an infant, and that you love her, but she is going to be a terrible burden for you, my dear.'

'But I promised Lily I would care for her,' Matilda said indignantly. 'You were there, you know that.'

'So I was,' he said. 'But Lily hadn't known Giles would die so soon after her, and she would want the best for her child.'

'How can sending her back there to live with strangers be best for her?' Matilda asked, her tone a little sharp. 'Giles wrote to

Lily's parents when she died and in their reply they didn't offer any help, not even any real sympathy. I met them before we left England and they struck me as cold, mean people, Lily wouldn't want them to take Tabitha on sufferance.'

The doctor nodded. Lily had implied as much in conversation with his wife. 'But from what little I know of Giles's family they wouldn't be the same, would they?' he asked.

'Maybe not,' she said. 'But they won't have received my letter telling them about his death yet. It could be months, even a year before they reply. I have to make some provision for Tabitha now.'

Dr Treagar agreed this was so. 'You can come and stay with us until then, Matty,' he said. 'We'd be very pleased to have you with us, I'm sure you know that both Mrs Treagar and I are very fond of you both.'

His kindness made Matilda's eyes prickle. 'That is so very kind of you, doctor,' she said. 'But I can't even offer you any payment.'

'Do you imagine we'd want any?' he said, reaching to take her hand and squeezing it. 'I would be a poor friend if I turned my back on you and Tabitha now when you most need a little help. So you just pack up all your belongings, and everything that was the Milsons' we'll store it somewhere for the time being.'

'I am indebted to you,' Matilda said in a low voice. 'I promise you I will do everything I can to assist you and Mrs Treagar to help pay for our keep.'

The doctor smiled. He had always assumed Matilda had a similar background to Lily Milson, yet those few words had told him otherwise. Real 'ladies' didn't concern themselves with paying their way, they took, and assumed this was their right.

'I'll write a letter to the Dean this afternoon,' he said, now more determined than ever to get some help for this brave young woman. 'You run along home and start packing.'

It was while packing up their belongings that Matilda found her diary from the previous year. She hadn't touched it since 13 December, two days before she got the news Giles was dead. It made her cry again to read the last few happy entries. '*Alice and the children left'* was underlined, she hadn't dared even allude to what had occurred just after, but she had written that Giles prepared a celebration supper of fried chicken, and that they told Tabitha she was to become her new mama. She'd listed the items they bought at the store and drawn a little sketch of the dress she was going to marry him in, and mentioned her fears that Mrs Abernought wouldn't be able to get it finished in time. Yet Mrs Abernought had worked night and day both on it and the dress for Tabitha, and they had been brought round just two days after Giles was buried. Matilda had never unwrapped the brown paper parcel, but paid the woman for her work and stuffed the parcel unchecked in the closet.

She leafed back through the diary at random, reading little snatches here and there. A bitter complaint about Alice's oldest son Ruben breaking Lily's china tea pot, further back her views on the scavengers who worked their way along the river bank just after the flood water subsided, stealing the remaining belongings of the victims.

Back in February, almost a whole year ago, she'd reported feeling the baby kicking in Lily's belly. It was then that Giles began calling him Harry.

She read again her thoughts after Lily and the baby died. 'I have never known such misery,' she'd put. 'How will I live without my dear friend? It seems like the sun has gone from the sky forever.' She noted that her monthlies came on that day too, for she'd put the little squiggle by the date.

All at once she was jolted. She couldn't remember when she last had a monthly and she began leafing through the diary looking for the tell-tale squiggles. July, August, September, October and November, twenty-eight or twenty-nine days apart each time, but after 21 November there were no more. It should have come again just before Christmas, but even though most of the events at that time were blurred, she knew that wasn't something she would have forgotten, for the soaking and washing of the rags was always an unpleasant chore.

A sick feeling welled up inside her. Today's date was 20 January, it should have come again by now!

'You can't be!' she said aloud. 'It was only twice, God couldn't be that cruel to let a baby start, then kill its father.'

She began to shiver with fear. She pulled a shawl around her and moved over to the stove, and sat hunched up by it, consumed with anxiety.

A month later, now living with the Treagars, Matilda knew for certain she was pregnant. Aside from the missing monthlies she felt sick in the mornings, she couldn't abide the smell of coffee and her breasts were tender. She had worked out the baby would be due around 8 September, and she was terrified.

She couldn't confide in anyone, not even the doctor, for a baby without marriage was a grievous sin and she would be thrown out of the town. She wasn't so concerned about what would be said about her, but to sully people's memory of Giles and Lily was unthinkable. Then there was Tabitha, she would be snatched from her, and if help didn't arrive from her grandparents, she would be put in an orphanage.

Tabitha had adjusted to her father's death. She was often pensive, she would still break into tears suddenly, but she did seem to have come to terms with it, and Matilda knew that was purely because of her. To Tabitha, life hadn't changed so very much. She went to school each day as before, lived in a nice house, was well fed and cared for, cosseted in fact by the Treagars, but it was Matilda's presence which gave her life stability. If that was snatched away it might be one blow too many. She couldn't let that happen.

Cissie was the only person Matilda knew would help her, and the more she thought about her, and Oregon, the more she saw it was the only option open to her.

But could she survive that long, dangerous journey? What if the baby came before she got there? And if she didn't make it, what would become of Tabitha? She couldn't even write to Cissie because the mail only went out when the wagons left in spring. By the time the letter got to her, the baby would be ready to be born.

Yet as the weeks crawled past, and people began arriving in town to make the long journey in spring, Matilda became resolved. Land was free in Oregon, no one but Cissie knew her, and with her help she could pose as a widow and get some kind of work to bring up both the baby and Tabitha. She wasn't going to think about the 'what ifs'. She would make it there.

On 1 March, following a letter arriving from the Dean of St

Louis that morning and enclosing a bank draft for fifty dollars – what he called a 'distress payment' – she resolved to tell the Treagars her plans at supper.

The Treagars' home was one of the best in Independence, a white frame house like the minister's, but larger and with beautiful colonial-style furniture which they'd had made for them while living in Virginia. The dining-room was very elegant, with a highly polished oak table big enough for ten people and velvet drapes such as Matilda had only ever seen in Lily's parents' home in Bristol.

Even though Matilda had insisted she worked while she stayed there, Mrs Treagar had never allowed her to do more than sewing, for she had two maids who did all the housework and a cook who wouldn't allow anyone in her kitchen.

The supper that evening was a particularly good one of roast duck. The doctor's poorer patients usually paid him in kind, the duck being payment for setting a broken leg earlier in the week, and good food always made the doctor happy.

Once the duck had been carved and handed round, Matilda broke her news.

'I've decided that Tabitha and I will take the next wagon train to Oregon to my good friends the Duncans,' she said, hoping her firm tone would prevent either of the Treagars thinking she could be persuaded out of it.

Matilda had met Tabitha from school early in the afternoon and on the way home, stopping off to visit Giles and Lily's grave, she'd put it to the child. Tabitha had become really excited, just the way she was when her parents first told her they were going to Missouri. She had liked Cissie and John very much, the whole idea of travelling in a covered wagon appealed to her. She even laughed when Matilda asked her to promise not to say anything if she heard Matilda telling the Treagars a few little white lies at dinner. She was an astute child, she knew Mrs Treagar was a worrier, and she understood Matilda had to make out the Duncans were richer than they really were, because otherwise she'd try to stop them going.

'If we stay here just waiting to hear from the Milsons in England it might be too late to join a train,' Matilda went on. 'And Tabby doesn't want to go back to England anyway. My friends the

Duncans have a successful lumber business and an extensive farm, Tabby will have the company of their children and the security of a family again.'

'You can't make that long journey without a man,' Mrs Treagar said in horror. 'It isn't safe.'

Matilda had already prepared all her counter-arguments. 'There are a great many women travelling without a man,' she said calmly. 'Most of them are going out to join their husbands who went last year. We shall team up with them. I have worked it all out, I have just about enough money to get a team of oxen, a wagon and provisions for the journey. Once settled out in Oregon I shall take up school teaching.'

Dr Treagar looked at Matilda sharply. He could see she was nowhere near as composed as she sounded, she had two bright red spots of colour on her cheeks and her eyes weren't quite meeting his and this made him a little suspicious. Yet in the two years he'd known her, and from what the Milsons had said about her, he knew she was honest, practical and very hard-working. At the time of the flood he'd witnessed her compassion for others, and her ability to take command of those who might otherwise have just wrung their hands and wailed instead of helping.

But it was after Giles's death that he'd seen the full extent of her courage and pride. Most women in her position, he felt, would have been hysterical, especially as she was clearly deeply in love with him. Yet she hadn't burdened anyone with her troubles, she had cared for Tabitha in the same steady manner she always had, and had held herself with such quiet dignity. He wondered now if her decision to go to Oregon had been made because she was afraid the grandparents would insist on Tabitha being taken from her, and that thought touched his heart. Both Giles and Lily had voiced their affection and admiration for her. Matilda had always been the true mother to the whole family, they would undoubtedly prefer that their daughter stay in her capable hands and in the country they'd grown to love. He didn't think it was his place to try to deter her.

'I think Matty has made up her mind,' he said, giving his wife a warning glance. 'In my view it's a good plan. A fresh start in a land of opportunity.'

He turned then to Tabitha. 'And what do you think about it, Tabby?'

'I want to go very much,' she said earnestly. 'Matty's my mama now and I want to be with her.'

The doctor's heart swelled up. Since Giles's death he had considered suggesting that he and his wife took Tabitha and brought her up as their own, but there was no doubt who the child loved and Giles himself would have chosen love to be a greater priority for his daughter than comfort or wealth.

'Then God go with you,' he said, smiling at them both. 'It's a long, arduous journey, but I don't doubt you will make something of yourselves out there. But my wife and I will miss you very much.'

Matilda offered up a silent prayer of thanksgiving for their approval. She added a plea that her belly would stay flat until she was well away from Independence and that Tabitha would be able to cope with the news then that she was going to have a half-sister or brother come September.

Chapter Fourteen

'I hope that isn't what it looks like!' Dr Treagar exclaimed as he looked down at the wooden box left in his hall. Matilda had packed it with provisions for her journey, but a long object wrapped in a piece of oiled rag was lying across the top.

'It is,' she said, giving him a defiant look. 'And I've learnt how to shoot it.'

'Matty!' he exclaimed with a look of horror. 'Giles would never have approved of firearms.'

'Giles might have changed his mind if he'd known words were no protection against ruffians,' she said tartly. 'Besides, I'm not intending to kill any people with it, not unless they look like they might kill me or Tabby. A rabbit for the pot is all I've got in mind.'

The doctor looked at her sadly. 'You've changed so much since he died, Matty,' he sighed. 'I suppose it was inevitable, but I worry that you are becoming a little – ' He stopped suddenly, afraid of hurting her feelings.

'Go on,' she said, and gave a tight little laugh. 'A little masculine, were you going to say?'

The doctor's high colour became even higher. 'No, tough was the word I intended,' he said. 'Even toting a gun you are far too pretty to be masculine.'

Pretty was too weak a word really, he thought. Even in her plain black mourning dress she was beautiful, and in the past month it had become even more noticeable, despite the sadness in her eyes. Her blonde hair was so shiny, like sun on ripe corn, and her complexion had a new rosy bloom. She had put on a little weight too, maybe due to the good food and rest she'd been getting while she'd been staying here. He wished heartbreak could be cured as easily, he couldn't count the number of times he'd heard her crying late at night.

'Aw, shucks!' she said, in a parody of how one of his maids

from Louisiana spoke. 'You sure do know how to make a girl feel better about herself, doctor.'

He laughed then. Matty always sounded so English, yet just lately, when anyone complimented her she always answered in that mocking Deep South voice.

'So how good a shot are you?' he asked.

She glanced over her shoulder as if to check Mrs Treagar was still out. 'Come outside and I'll show you,' she said.

They went out into the back yard where Tabitha was playing with the puppy the doctor had given her as a going-away present. She'd called him Treacle because he was as black and shiny as the molasses she'd been given recently as a springtime purge.

'Get Treacle out of the way and set up the rocks,' Matilda ordered her. 'I'm going to show the doctor what a crack shot I am.'

Tabitha obediently tied up the puppy and ran down the yard to set up six stones on an upturned pair, then stood aside to watch.

Matilda lifted the gun to her shoulder, squinted down the sights and pulled the trigger. One stone flew off. She reloaded and hit another. In six shots she hit six stones.

'Who on earth taught you?' the doctor asked in amazement. He wasn't much of a shot himself, and he'd certainly never seen a woman handle a gun so well.

'Solomon,' she grinned.

It was mid-April now and she'd spent a great deal of time in the last few weeks practising shooting and reading every pamphlet available on how to survive the trail to Oregon.

'He's also taught me to drive my oxen, and how to change a broken axle and repair a wheel, too. I won't be able to do those things alone, but I know how.'

The doctor shook his head. 'Ladies shouldn't have to do that sort of thing.'

'I was never a lady,' she said dryly. 'Just between ourselves, doctor, 'cos I know you've always been curious about how I came to be with the Milsons, I started out as their nursemaid. Before that I used to sell flowers on the streets of London and I was brought up in the slums. So don't worry about me. The Milsons might have taught me genteel behaviour, but my childhood taught me survival.'

Although the doctor was surprised by such a revelation, it made sense of many puzzling inconsistencies about her that he'd noticed in the past weeks, and he admired her even more for her candour.

'You'll always be a lady to me,' he replied, patting her shoulder with affection. 'Now, shall we get that box of goods round to the wagon before Mrs Treagar sees the gun and has the vapours? Are you really sure you want to sleep in the wagon on your last night?'

'Absolutely sure,' she said with a grin. 'You see, Cissie said I have to get a position right up the front, and if I'm not there tonight someone might just elbow me out.'

'Just smile at Captain Russell and I'm sure you'll get whatever position you want,' he laughed. 'So come on then, I'll take you, Tabby, the dog and that infernal gun along to the square in my gig. I'll bring Mrs Treagar down tomorrow morning to see you off and say goodbye.'

'It's real cosy, isn't it?' Tabitha whispered as they lay cuddled up close together in the wagon, Treacle lying at their feet. It had grown quiet outside, apart from the odd sound of horses neighing and dogs barking, yet there were thirty-five wagons and an average of six people to each one. 'I like it better than a house.'

'We might not like it so much when it rains or it's scorching hot,' Matilda said reflectively. It was a funny thing, but from the first moment Solomon showed her the wagon, she had liked the feel of it, perhaps because she'd never had a home that was only hers before. Solomon had bought it last year from a family who had only gone a couple of hundred miles, then returned to Independence thoroughly disenchanted with the idea of going West, and he asked Matilda for less than half what she would have been asked for a new one.

The previous owners had added lots of extras that she would never have thought of. There were pockets in the canvas to put small items in, the base of the bed was a deep box for more storage, it even had a little table and two stools with foldaway legs for eating meals on, and there was a camping stove on legs too, which Solomon said was the latest thing. Even the water containers hanging all around the wagon were included in the price.

Mrs Treagar had given her an old feather mattress and put in new ticking. Almost everything else they needed like pots, plates and cutlery had come from their old home. The remains of Lily's little treasures and pictures, Giles's Bible, his watch and a few special books he treasured were stored away under the bed along with the sacks of flour, dried beans, rice, molasses, a huge lump of bacon and other essential provisions. They'd kept the good quilts, blankets and bedlinen, but everything else, including the horse and gig, had been sold off to buy the wagon. She'd given away most of Lily's everyday clothes after the flood, but she'd kept the more elegant ones thinking they could be made into things for Tabitha. Baby Harry's layette was packed away too, she felt sure Lily would want the baby to use them.

Twenty-five seedling fruit trees took up the most room, but they were their gift to Cissie and John. They were planted tightly together in a strong tray and wrapped around with sacking to keep the roots moist.

The four oxen had been the biggest expense, and the yokes cost twenty-five dollars, but with luck she could sell them off when she got to Oregon, and she still had thirty dollars left.

'Are you sad to be leaving?' Tabitha asked.

'A bit,' Matilda admitted.

'Because we can't talk to Mama and Papa any more?'

'We can do that wherever we are,' Matilda said. 'I'm sure their spirits will be coming with us to watch over us. And you mustn't worry about no one looking after their grave, Mrs Treagar and Solomon said they'd put flowers on it for us.'

'We had happy times here,' Tabitha said wistfully. 'There were so many nice people. Do you think they'll be nice in Oregon too?'

'I know they will,' Matilda said firmly. 'So go to sleep now, we have an early start in the morning.'

'Chain up, chain up!' Captain Russell's yelling voice woke them at first light.

Matilda wriggled down the bed, looked out the back of the wagon and saw other people were already up and about. She pulled on her dress and rammed a straw bonnet on her head without even combing her hair.

'Quick, Tabby,' she said. 'We can worry about washing and doing our hair later.'

Solomon's training had worked, for she had the oxen yoked and chained well before anyone else. She was just about to climb up on to the driving seat when Captain Russell came riding along on his piebald horse.

'Howdy, Mrs Jennings,' he called out, reining in his horse for a moment. 'I'll let you go second in line as you seem so set on being up front, but if you can't keep up a good pace I'll have to drop you right back.'

He was the main topic of conversation among the women in town for they all thought him very dashing in his army uniform, and were dying to know if he was married. He was at least six foot tall, slim-hipped with long fair hair, bright blue eyes and a droopy moustache. Matilda guessed him to be about thirty, though it was hard to tell as his face was nut-brown and he had crinkles round his eyes from being in the sun. She agreed with the other women that he was an unusually attractive man, but she didn't like his caustic manner, or his unnerving way of studying people silently.

She also knew she was starting out with a big disadvantage. He hadn't wanted her to join his train, he had said it was no place for a lone woman and a child. It was really only Solomon speaking up for her that finally persuaded him to agree. Although he appeared to have come round a little since then, she sensed he was deeply prejudiced against her, and that he would always be waiting for her to make mistakes. On top of this she was terribly afraid that he might have found out more about her in the last few days. She had told him that she was a widow, travelling with her step-daughter to friends in Oregon. Pretending to be a widow was a common precaution for single women to avoid male advances, but if he had learnt about the Milsons in town, and then saw her belly growing larger, who could blame him for thinking the worst of her?

But she was determined not to let such thoughts trouble her today, so she gave him a beaming smile. 'Don't you worry about me not keeping a good pace,' she said. 'I'm in a hurry to get to Oregon.'

Dr Treagar had said the Government were requisitioning army officers to escort wagon trains because their presence would encourage more immigrants out to Oregon. It seemed the Oregon territory was still owned by the British and America wanted it. As they saw it, the more Americans settled on the land, the less likely the British were to hold fast to it. Matilda didn't much care who owned Oregon, or whether the man who would lead her there approved of her. She was just pleased to be under the command of someone who knew a great deal about the territory they were going to cross.

'Make sure you drill your daughter not to jump off the wagon while it's moving,' he said, looking over at Tabitha who was playing with Treacle. 'I don't want to alarm you, ma'am, but I've seen children's legs crushed under wheels. You be careful now.'

'I will,' she agreed. Solomon had already warned her about that.

'Don't be too proud to ask for help if anything goes wrong either,' he said, tipping his hat back on his head and grinning at her. 'Though I guess from what I've seen of you so far that won't come easy!'

She wasn't sure if that was intended as a compliment or sarcasm, but she didn't want to get off on the wrong foot with him. 'I'm not too proud to take advice,' she said, and smiled sweetly. 'I'll bear what you said in mind.'

Matilda and Tabitha were seated up at the front, reins in hands in readiness for the signal to pull away when the Treagars came along in their gig.

'I brought you some ready-cooked food,' Mrs Treagar called out, holding up a basket. 'There's a nice big chicken pie, ham and boiled eggs. That should keep you going for a few days.'

They climbed down from their gig and came over to Matilda. 'There's a box of medicine in there too,' the doctor said with a wide smile. 'Quinine, laudanum, hartshorn for snake bite, citric acid for scurvy, and a mess of other things. I've labelled what they are for. Make sure you wash any cuts or abrasions with boiled salted water, and keep them covered until they heal. If everyone did that I'd be almost out of a job.'

He had already given Matilda a little book about doctoring, and she guessed she was now probably better equipped than most people on the train.

'Make sure you wear gloves and sun-bonnets all the time,'

Mrs Treagar said, looking anxiously up at Tabitha, perhaps noting she hadn't brushed her hair this morning, 'or you'll look like field hands by the time you get there. Write to us, won't you? We'll send any letters for you on to your friends.'

Matilda hadn't heard a word from Giles's family yet. Under the circumstances she hoped she never would.

She jumped down from the wagon and gave Mrs Treagar a hug. Her feelings for this woman during the stay in her home had see-sawed between affection because she reminded her of Lily, gratitude for her generosity, but more often, irritation at her primness and bigoted views. She wouldn't even use the word 'pants' but referred to them as 'nether garments'. To her Indians were all savages, black people needed to be owned by someone as they couldn't look after themselves, and all men, with the exception of her husband, and perhaps clergymen, were to be treated with the utmost caution. Yet now she was leaving, Matilda felt only affection for her.

'I'll never forget how kind you've both been to us,' Matilda said, a lump coming up in her throat. 'I don't know what I would have done without you.'

Mrs Treagar embraced her warmly, whispering that she hoped they could put all the sadness behind them. Then letting her go she took a step back. 'Now, remember to behave like a lady at all times,' she said with her more customary primness. 'You must set a good example to Tabitha. Giles and Lily entrusted her into your care and you must always keep in mind their strong religious convictions and make sure Tabitha reads the Scriptures and says her prayers.'

To Matilda's relief any further lectures were prevented by Captain Russell blowing a whistle to signal they were to start rolling. She kissed the Treagars, watched them hug Tabitha too, then they both leaped up on to the wagon, quickly followed by Treacle.

The inevitable band of missionaries began singing a hymn, banging drums and clattering tambourines, the scouts galloped forward, waving the first wagon to move, and all at once it had started.

Matilda flicked the lead oxen with the tip of her whip, just as Solomon had instructed her, and the oxen dutifully lurched forward, the others following meekly.

As the wheels began to move, Matilda breathed a deep sigh of relief.

'Goodbye!' she yelled, waving back to the Treagars. 'We'll never forget you.'

It was very easy going for the first few hours. The path along the river was worn smooth by previous trains and the oxen plodded along behind the lead wagon needing very little guidance. The spring sunshine felt warm on their faces and aside from the rumbling of wheels, it was quiet and even soothing. Yet however pleasant it was to sit up here beside Tabitha knowing that every mile put the heart-breaking memories further behind them, she was also very aware that from now on their survival and safety depended on her entirely.

When she wrote to Dolly and Lily's and Giles's families to tell them of his death and her promise to take care of Tabitha, it hadn't seemed appropriate to mention that they had intended to be married. Telling them later, and that she found she was expecting his baby, was out of the question, for it might very well have sounded as if she was using him as a scapegoat, knowing he couldn't deny it. Whether they believed her or not, either way they'd be appalled, and they would immediately see her as immoral and an unfit guardian for Tabitha, perhaps taking steps to remove her from her care.

Dolly had written back, the letter arriving just before they left, but her tone had been surprisingly cool. She said she thought Matilda should let the grandparents take responsibility for Tabitha, and that a single woman couldn't bring a child up alone. Although she once again said she would always have room for her should she decide to come home to England, she also pointed out that situations available for women were very limited and she thought America offered more opportunities. She finished up the letter telling her she was feeling very poorly herself, and that as the previous summer's weather had been very poor not many people called at the tea gardens. Overall Matilda felt Dolly was trying to say that she had enough problems of her own to cope with and didn't want to be burdened with anyone else's.

But bigger than her sorrow at knowing she must cut herself off from all old friends, and the fear of what might be ahead of her, was her anxiety about how to break the news of the baby to

Tabitha. Just the thought that she might lose the love and trust of the little girl made her eyes suddenly brim with tears.

'What's wrong?' Tabitha asked in alarm.

'Nothing at all.' Matilda wiped her eyes on her sleeve and did her best to smile. 'I guess it's just after all the preparations, the goodbyes and everything, just sitting up here watching the countryside go by gives me too much time to think about things.'

'Like what?'

It would be easy enough to say she'd had a wave of grief come over her, for they'd both had those so often, but as Matilda glanced sideways at the child she saw Tabitha's dark eyes, so like Giles's, were studying her closely. Right from when she could first speak she had questioned everything, now at eight she couldn't be fobbed off easily, she was too bright. All at once Matilda knew there would never be a right time to tell her the truth, so she might just as well tell her now and get it off her chest.

'I've got a secret, Tabby,' she said. 'It's a very big one, and I haven't been able to tell you before because back in Independence if anyone found out they would think badly of me. I want to tell you. I must tell you because it's very important. But it's going to be very hard to explain it to you.'

Tabitha frowned. 'Have you done something wicked?'

'I don't believe it is, but some people might,' Matilda said. She took a deep breath. 'I'm going to have a baby.'

Tabitha just laughed, her small face lighting up with merriment. 'Don't be silly, Matty. I know you can't have a baby unless you are married.'

Matilda sighed, all at once aware she was going to be forced to explain a great deal more than she'd bargained for. Having been brought up herself in a close, crowded community where adults seldom married legally and bawdy jokes about sex were bandied around even in front of children, from a very early age she'd had a rough idea of adult love and how babies were made. But Tabitha's upbringing had been so very different, there were a great many taboo subjects in genteel society.

'Did you know there is a special kind of cuddle which men and women have that makes babies?' she asked.

Tabitha looked a bit embarrassed. 'Sort of,' she whispered.

'Well, they are supposed to wait until they get married before they do that,' Matilda said. 'But when a couple fall in love they want to do that kind of cuddling, because it's all part of loving one another, and just sometimes they can't stop themselves doing it, even though they aren't married yet.'

Tabitha looked perplexed, but said nothing.

'That's what happened with your papa and me, Tabby. We were planning to be married. If he hadn't been shot we would have been, but before he went off to St Joseph we had that kind of cuddle.'

There was no reply to this, no gasp of horror, nothing.

Matilda waited, fully expecting that once Tabitha had time to consider this, she would turn on her and say she was disgusting.

Yet she didn't. A tear trickled down her cheek and she looked at Matilda with mournful eyes. 'Did Dr Treagar know?'

Matilda shook her head. 'I couldn't tell anyone, not even him, because they would have thought I was a bad woman and said nasty things about your papa. That's why I decided we would go to Cissie's, she's the only person I know who will understand and help.

'But you know I'm not a bad woman, don't you? You know too that your papa was intending for us to get married. We would have loved to have given you a baby sister or brother. You would have liked that too, wouldn't you?'

Tabitha nodded again.

'So does it really matter to you that your papa didn't manage to marry me?'

Everything hung on that one question, and Matilda held her breath waiting for the child to answer.

'No, it doesn't matter to me,' she said with a sigh. 'You are my Matty, just like always, and it will be nice for us to have a little baby. But who will look after you? Mama couldn't do anything much for herself when Harry was coming, and Papa always made all the plans.'

'Widows have to manage by themselves, and so shall I. Cissie will help us in Oregon when the baby is born.'

Suddenly Tabitha's face crumpled. 'Mama died having Harry. What if you do too?'

Transferring the reins to one hand, Matilda slid her arm round the little girl and drew her close to her. 'I'm not going to die,' she said. 'I'm much stronger and younger than your mama. But now we have to talk about the rest of the secret.'

She carefully explained that she had said she was a widow to Captain Russell and that Tabitha was her step-daughter. 'It's not such a big lie,' she said. 'It's how I see us. You are my step-daughter, and I feel like a widow. But I didn't dare say my name was Mrs Milson just in case anyone on this wagon train knew different. So I've got to be Mrs Jennings for now, and you must be Tabitha Jennings. Do you mind that?'

'No.' Tabitha half smiled. 'But what am I going to say if anyone asks about my papa?'

'We'll have to think that one out as we drive along,' Matilda said. 'What would you like him to be?'

'A doctor,' Tabitha said without any hesitation. 'Then I can tell people that's what I'm going to be too. But hadn't you better put mama's wedding ring on your finger? I know Mrs Treagar said you must keep your gloves on, but if you do take them off people will notice you haven't got a ring.'

Matilda was stunned by the little girl's adult observation, and very touched that she wouldn't object to her mother's ring being worn.

'That's a very smart idea,' she said, smiling down at Tabitha. 'And if you really don't mind, I'll get it out when we stop at midday.'

The mild dry weather lasted for eight days. Each night when the wagon train stopped there was good grazing for the beasts and plenty of water as they were following the river, and they were covering some twenty miles each day because the trail was so smooth and flat. Everyone on the train was in high spirits, including the women who had looked so doleful back at the start but had cheered up. Even fording the river brought no problems as the water level was low.

After dark the campfires made a pretty sight, one old man who played the fiddle was very much in demand, and people danced jigs, and sang joyously. For Matilda and Tabitha it was like a holiday, time to talk and laugh together, sharing chores and talking about the future rather than looking back with sadness. When Tabitha happily ran alongside the wagon with Treacle close at her side, or splashed in the river as they filled the water containers, Matilda felt a sense of elation that she was giving her back the childhood she had been in danger of losing for ever.

But on the ninth day the rain came, and suddenly everyone discovered the less attractive side of living out of doors. For Matilda and Tabitha up at the front, the sudden softening of the ground proved no real obstacle, but by the time ten or twelve wagons had passed over it, the later ones were sticking in the churned-up mud and the pace slowed right down.

While Tabitha stayed inside the wagon curled up with a book and Treacle for company, Matilda drove on. Yet even with the india-rubber sheet that Solomon had given her over her head and shoulders, the skirt of her dress and her petticoats still got soaked, and her hands holding the reins were stiff and cold. That night when they made camp they couldn't light the stove as there was no dry wood, and when they climbed into bed after hard bread and cheese, they found the rain had crept in somewhere and made the covers and mattress damp.

'Do you still think it's cosy?' Matilda joked as they lay huddled together for warmth, listening to the sound of the rain beating on the canvas.

'At least we don't have to sleep outside like some people,' Tabitha said. 'Did you know that there's one wagon with nine children in it? Only the little ones and their mama sleep inside.'

One of Tabitha's main delights about the train was the freedom to mix with other people. Back in Independence she went to school, then came home, and there she stayed, going out only by invitation. Here she could join in games of chase alongside the wagons, invite another girl up into the wagon to play with her doll as they rolled along, sometimes she played school with several children, and she was always school mistress because she could read and write very much better than the others. In turn she met these children's parents, and gleaned a great deal of information about their fellow travellers, and she passed it all on to Matilda.

There were five wagons of Mormons going to join the settlement a man called Brigham Jones had founded on a big salt lake. Tabitha said everyone was talking about them because some of the men had two wives. She reported that in one of the families both the wives must be having babies too, for they both had big bellies and sat side by side on the front of the wagon wearing identical grey dresses. 'They aren't wicked people,' she had said earnestly. 'They pray all the time and the ladies call each other "sister". They say they are going to the Promised Land.'

She did think one of the women in one party looked wicked, because she wore a very fancy red dress. Matilda had said tartly that she didn't think she was wicked, just stupid, because by the time she got to Oregon that dress would be in tatters and faded by the sun.

One of the children in another wagon way back in the train was very sick, and another had incurred the injuries Captain Russell had spoken of when he jumped from the wagon and had his foot run over by a wheel. Tabitha had reported that the poor boy was in the most terrible pain and that people were saying he'd have to have it amputated if he got gangrene.

But Tabitha's favourite people on the train were the three scouts. Two were young half-breeds and wore buckskin shirts, the third, Carl, was older, perhaps forty, and looked as if he'd spent his life in the saddle. All three of them had taken a shine to Tabitha too, and often stopped by the wagon to take her for a short ride on their horses. Matilda had been fearful of them at first, especially the half-breeds, but Captain Russell had reassured her that Indians cared for children far better than white folks did, and as she would be seeing a great deal more Indians before they got to Oregon, the scouts' influence on her could only be beneficial.

On the morning of the tenth day, a Sunday, it was sunny again. The Captain said they could stay put for a rest and to give them all time to wash and dry their clothes.

It struck Matilda as she took her washing down to the river that what the Captain meant was that the men could rest. They lay on the grass smoking pipes and playing cards, while their womenfolk were kept even busier than usual, feeding the stock, filling water pots, washing, baking bread, cleaning out the wagons and looking after the children.

She heard at noon that the child who'd been sick almost from the start had passed away. Everything stopped for a brief but very moving funeral service, and Matilda thought she had never seen anything so poignant as the little boy's father trying to burn the child's name into a wooden cross to mark the little grave at the side of the trail.

'There'll be still more of those before we're through,' Captain Russell said to Matilda as he saw her looking back at the boy's mother crying beside the brown mound of earth.

Matilda looked up at him in surprise, his tone was so cold it chilled her.

She had noticed a great many inconsistencies about this man. On the face of it he was a typical soldier, brawny, curt, impatient, and tough on the more helpless men on the train. She didn't mind any of that, it was what she expected of a wagon master. But now and again when he'd stopped to speak to her or Tabby, he sounded and acted like a gentleman. Yet if she looked surprised at anything he said, he immediately covered it up with rough words or sarcasm.

He was so insolent too. Time and again she'd heard him bark out orders to people as if they were imbeciles. He seemed to have no understanding that almost everything was new to the people he was leading. They were farmers, shop-keepers, carpenters, often struggling with large families too. She thought he should be more patient with them and explain things, rather than shout at them.

Now he was showing himself to be callous too!

'Sorry, ma'am,' he said with a faint grin. 'Guess that sounded heartless, I didn't mean it that way. But I look at some of these people and I wonder if they know the real price they'll have to pay for free land in Oregon. If they manage to get past snake bites, measles, cholera and Indians, there's always drowning, frostbite, and just ordinary little accidents that can take them when the poison gets in the blood. I heard tell from a scout that someone's just found gold out in California – if that turns out to be true, afore long there'll be thousands of folk coming this way. God alone knows how many more graves will litter the trail then.'

'It sounds to me as if you don't approve of people trying to better themselves,' she said tartly. She thought he was going out of his way to scare her, but she wasn't going to rise to it.

'Is that what you're trying to do?' he said with a sardonic grin, his blue eyes mocking her. 'Or are you hot-footing it away from something?'

Matilda felt her stomach churn. Had he found out about her?

'My reasons for going to Oregon are my own affair, sir,' she said indignantly.

'Maybe they are anywhere else, but while you're on my train, I'm responsible for you. I don't hold with women travelling alone, it ain't safe.'

'If that's the case then why did you agree I could go?' she said, putting her nose in the air.

He looked at her hard for a moment. She wasn't sure if that was a sneer on his lips or a smile.

'I reckoned you'd set off on your own if I didn't,' he said. 'You've got that determined look about you. Didn't want that on my conscience.'

Matilda riled up. 'You are insufferably insolent,' she said, an expression she'd learnt from Lily. 'Why do you assume a woman on her own is less likely to cope with a long trip than one with a husband? From what I've seen, the women have so much work to do just looking after their men, it surprises me they aren't all flaked out on the ground right now.'

He surprised her by laughing. 'Are all English women as prickly as you?' he asked.

'I dare say they are,' she said. 'And if you'll excuse me now I have things to do.'

Her face was smarting with anger as she walked away. She really didn't know how to cope with him for she'd never met a man like him before. Was it better to ignore him, or try to be nice?

'You can't be nice,' she thought to herself. 'He'll just take that as weakness.'

'It's like we are just standing still,' Tabitha remarked one morning a couple of weeks later. 'Every day it's the same scene, just grass, and grass and grass. Not even a tree to know we're some place different.'

Matilda laughed. The child was right. They'd been travelling along this huge, empty plain with its long waving grass for so long, without anything in the distance to give them the idea they were moving closer to their destination. The vastness of the scene was so scary, nothing out there for hundreds of miles, except of course Indians and buffalo. At night they heard the strangest noises, and it was all to easy to imagine Indians creeping towards them, or savage beasts waiting to pounce.

Attending to the needs of nature was a trial too. Every time a couple of women went off a bit, everyone knew what for – one stood, skirts outstretched, while the other crouched down behind her, it was so undignified. For Matilda it was even worse for she couldn't leave the oxen, so she had to hold it in until they stopped at noon, then had only little Tabitha to shield her.

It was only mid-May but so warm already. They had abandoned their petticoats a few days earlier, but with summer creeping nearer Matilda wondered how much hotter it would get – both their faces were as brown as nuts already.

On the previous day they'd seen a vast herd of buffalo. They had heard them long before they came in sight, a low rumbling noise which got gradually louder as they came nearer, then a rattling sound of their horns and hooves. One of the scouts said there were over 2,000 of them. Matilda had been scared, yet thrilled once they came into sight, such huge shaggy beasts, with big sad eyes. She thought it was terrible that the men killed so many of them, when just two would feed everyone for a couple of days. But she had to admit they were good eating, as tasty as the big steaks she'd had at the Treagars' house, and a nice change from bacon and beans. Some of the women had been appalled when the Captain told them to collect up the buffalo droppings for fuel – Matilda had laughed so much as they prissily sidled up to a pile and holding their nose, shovelled it up with one hand. She had no such qualms; if it burned well, and cooked the meat, she was all for it. And it had burned well, without smoke too, so she was going to make sure she always had a sackful of it hanging beneath the wagon.

'We've got a fair bit more of this grass to come yet,' Matilda said, thinking back to what the Captain had told her yesterday when he dropped off her buffalo meat. 'At least it's easy driving, Tabby, and plenty of fodder for the oxen. It won't be so good once we get to the mountains.'

A shrill shriek from behind them made them turn their heads. To Matilda's horror, riding at full tilt towards them was a group of Indians, about twenty in all, almost naked aside from a bit of buckskin hiding their private parts.

Captain Russell came riding back along the train. 'It's nothing to fear,' he yelled. 'Pull up, keep calm, and don't cock any guns. They are Pawnees and they ain't hostile.'

Matilda felt with her foot under the seat for her gun anyway, and placed it in a position where she could easily reach it if necessary. Her heart was beating very fast, and a sweat was breaking out all over her.

'Aren't they beautiful!' Tabby exclaimed with excitement as the Indians came closer. 'I'm sure the Captain is right when he said they aren't hostile.'

Matilda agreed they were beautiful, but she wasn't convinced they were friendly. They had halted their mounts now, waiting while one of the half-breed scouts rode some fifty yards out to them. They sat tall and proud, black hair and mahogany-coloured skin gleaming in the sun, but their haughty faces gave nothing away.

The scout said no more than a few words to them, then turned and rode back to Captain Russell who nodded as if agreeing to something, then he too turned and went back down the wagon train out of Matilda's sight.

It was some tense half-hour later, with the Indians still waiting like stone statues, before Captain Russell and the scout rode out again to them, this time taking with them a couple of small sacks, a blanket and what looked like a couple of men's calico shirts. The Indians took them, then wheeled round and rode off.

'Roll on,' the Captain yelled. 'The show's over.'

Later he rode alongside Matilda's wagon while Tabitha was taking a nap in the back. 'Were you scared?' he asked, tilting his hat back.

She found it odd that the Captain so often asked her opinion on things that happened on the trail, it seemed like some kind of test.

'No,' she lied. 'Should I have been?'

'Most women are,' he said with a smile. 'I've had women on trains before who have fainted at the sight of them. They think they are all murderous savages just because there's been a few damn-fool stories spread around. That bunch were just checking us out, and the flour and other goods were kind of a payment for letting us pass through their land.'

'Who did you get the goods from?' she said, wondering if they were all supposed to offer something.

'Those who could afford it,' he said with a shrug. 'Some folks have got their wagons so tightly packed with goods they'll never get up the mountains. Glad to see you aren't one of those.'

Again she wasn't sure whether that last remark was praise, or an opener to find out more about her circumstances. She wished she didn't have to analyse every single thing he said to her, it would be nice to have a friendly, open conversation with him.

'My friends in Oregon told me to travel light,' she said airily. 'I heard someone back there has a harpsichord, now that strikes me as plain foolish.'

'Almost as foolish as those who set out knowing they're gonna have a baby on the way,' he said, looking right at her.

She blushed furiously. She didn't know if that remark was a general one, or if he'd noticed the slight swelling of her stomach. But whichever, it wasn't seemly for a man to mention such a condition.

She decided to ignore what he'd said, that was what Lily would have done. But instead of pushing on, or turning back down the train to check on others, he still stayed riding along beside her, less than two feet away. Even though she kept looking firmly ahead at the lead oxen, she sensed he was looking at her and it made her feel most uncomfortable.

'I *do* know,' he said at length.

She glanced at him in alarm. He was grinning at her impudently, his hat tipped back so she had a clear view of his bright blue eyes. 'I can tell when a woman's that way just by the way she walks. So don't deny it, Mrs Jennings.'

'Aren't you a clever devil,' she snapped back at him. 'Where I come from gentlemen do not make such personal remarks.'

He laughed. 'I don't claim to be a gentleman. You might be glad I'm not before the trail's over.'

He rode off then, leaving her quivering with anger.

As May ended so did the good grazing and water. The land they were moving across was dry, rocky and barren apart from sage bush, and so hot during the day that they felt they were being fried alive. The dust the wagon wheels kicked up turned Matilda's black dress grey in minutes each morning, and their lungs felt as if they were full of it. Treacle no longer wanted to go haring off in front of them, but stayed inside the wagon, panting.

As Matilda and Tabitha had only four oxen but many water containers, their beasts didn't suffer as badly from thirst as some on the train, but washing had to be abandoned, and drinking rationed to the bare minimum. Their eyes were sore from the dust, the sun burned their faces, and sometimes Matilda was so tired she dozed off, only to come to with a start as she lurched sideways. Thankfully the oxen were so used to following the wagon in front that they didn't appear to need her guidance. Sometimes they were even too tired to eat at the end of the day, it was a pitiful sight to see them flop down as soon as their yokes were off. Tabitha felt so sorry for them that she rooted around to find clumps of grass to tempt them up again to look for food themselves.

When Chimney Rock was spotted in the distance there was a great deal of rejoicing, as it was known to be a third of the way there. It was an extraordinary sight, to Matilda it resembled a half-buried village with a golden-brown chimney sticking up, only it was some 400 feet high. The Captain informed them it was made of hard clay.

That rock brought home to everyone just how vast the distances were out here, for although they could see it so clearly, it took days to reach it. When they did finally get there, a great many people went closer to write their names on it. But not Matilda. She had already made up her mind to take no risks, there were many snakes around, and even sharp thorns through their boots could cause trouble. Nor did she want anyone to strike up a conversation with her.

She could no longer hide her swelling belly, even with a loose pinafore over her dress her condition was obvious, and much as she ached for another woman to talk to, especially to give her some reassurance about the birthing, she forced herself to stay aloof. She let Tabitha socialize with other families as she prepared the evening meal, but as soon as it was eaten they climbed into the wagon together for the night. Tabitha always fell asleep immediately, and Matilda wished she could too. Exhausted as she was, back aching, hands stiff and sore, sleep didn't come easily, and as she lay there listening to the chatter, laughter and singing all around, her whole being wanted to go out and join in. But lying didn't come easily to her, and she knew if she allowed anyone to get close to her she might very well tell them the truth about her situation and that could be very dangerous.

Her mind was clear now. Tender memories of Giles might catch her short all too often, but making a good life for his two children was her goal and she looked only towards that. Oregon might be a vast place, but gossip could travel as far and as fast as birds. She was never going to do or say anything which might affect her children's standing in society there.

At dusk on 9 June they arrived at Fort Laramie. Matilda breathed a sigh of utter relief at the sight of the crude adobe walls, for they meant two whole days and nights of rest and security. In the past few days there had been many sightings of Sioux, and one morning they found that several horses had been stolen during the night. Since then Matilda had slept with one arm round Tabitha and her other hand on her gun.

Although the fort was a lonely outpost, the army was there to protect them. They could stock up on the provisions they'd run out of, get repairs done to their wagons, and post letters home.

After camping for the night down by the river, Matilda and Tabitha joined in with everyone else to go inside the fort to check out what was available at the stores. Although they had been warned in advance it was used as a trading post by fur trappers to sell their pelts, the stink of the huge piles of raw hides in the centre was disgusting. The prices of supplies were exorbitant too, back in Independence Matilda could buy three sacks of flour for the price of one here, and she was very relieved she didn't need anything that desperately. Worse still though was the dishevelled appearance of the enlisted men. Few had real uniforms, they were dirty and unshaven, and sat around playing cards and gawping at the women travellers. Many of them were so drunk they couldn't stand.

As she hurried out of the fort empty-handed, Captain Russell broke away from talking to another officer and came over to her and Tabitha.

'You didn't buy anything? Wasn't there anything you needed?'

Tabitha saw a child she often played with and skipped off to join her.

'Not so badly I'd pay their prices,' Matilda said with some

indignation. 'As for the stink in there, and those awful dirty, drunken soldiers! I can't believe what I saw!'

He laughed. 'Would you have them shave, polish up their buttons and press their uniforms when they aren't going anywhere?'

She was surprised at his tolerance, she had never seen him dirty or unshaven, even his hair and moustache were always trimmed.

'But the drinking!' she exclaimed. 'What if Indians attacked? How could they fight them off?'

'Don't you worry none about that,' he said, 'Soldiers fight better with liquor inside them. You'd drink too, Mrs Jennings, if you were stuck out here with nothing much to do, missing your home and loved ones.'

'Soldiers would never be allowed to be like that back in England,' she said, suddenly getting a mental picture of Queen Victoria's Horse Guards. 'It's so slovenly.'

'I guess it is,' he said, looking amused. 'But this ain't England, ma'am, it's a big, wild, often cruel country, and it can turn men like that too. I've spent many a year in forts like this one, seen things they never told me about when I was a cadet at West Point. But I can tell you now, I'd rather pick ten men from Fort Laramie to lead into battle than twenty clean and tidy milksops from back in the East.'

Matilda looked at him sharply, noting for the first time how refined his features were, well-defined cheek-bones, an elegant, almost aristocratic nose, shapely lips. That and his words suggested to her that he had indeed been brought up as a gentleman, but that somewhere along the line he'd turned his back on his own class. He was a very unusual man in every way, and her curiosity about him was stirred.

'Are you married, Captain?' she asked. Then, realizing such a direct question would in turn encourage him to ask her equally blunt ones, 'I ask only because it must be difficult to have a home and family when your work takes you away so much,' she added quickly.

'My wife died four years ago, ma'am,' he said crisply, and half turned to look back at the camp down by the river. 'You'd better hurry on back there where the air smells sweeter, Mrs Jennings. Have a good rest, maybe even try a couple of drinks yourself.'

Matilda hurried away, smarting from the rebuff and promising herself she would ignore him completely in future. Later that night she wondered how he thought anyone could have a rest here – it might be sweet-smelling by the river, but it certainly wasn't peaceful.

Some of the men took their cue from the soldiers, broke out bottles of whisky and got very drunk, and the sounds Matilda heard took her straight back to Finders Court: men fighting; and singing, stumbling and cussing, women shouting at them, often quickly followed by loud slaps and the women screaming. Children cried out in alarm, and dogs barked frantically. There were the sounds of love-making too, wagon springs creaking, and heavy breathing.

It struck her that living with the gentle, peaceful Milsons for so long had lulled her into thinking that they were typical of ordinary people. The truth of the matter was that they were very unusual. What she was hearing now was how most people all over the world, regardless of class, education, wealth or poverty, behaved after a few drinks. And if she wanted to make a good life for herself and the children in Oregon she had got to stop yearning for the well-ordered life she had with the Milsons, delve into her own past for the experiences which had shaped her character, and use them and her wits to make one that suited her.

'You seem to be the only one anxious to leave,' Captain Russell said to Matilda on the morning of their departure. She had already yoked up her oxen and she was smearing ointment on a sore place on the foreleg of one of them. Mostly everyone else was still nowhere near ready. 'Why didn't you join us last night?'

The previous day of rest, coupled with everyone being able to replenish their stores in the fort, had led to a big party. The soldiers had joined them, bringing whisky with them. Guitars, fiddles and accordions had been brought out, food shared, and for most of the women it had been a welcome opportunity to put on their best dress and dance. Matilda had let Tabitha join in for a couple of hours but she had stayed in her wagon pretending she was too tired to join in.

'I'm in no condition for dancing and carousing,' she said tartly, putting the lid back on the ointment and wiping her hands on a piece of rag.

He leaned back against one of the wagon wheels and folded his arms. 'You could have just watched,' he said, watching her face. Her eyes were puffy and he suspected she'd spend most of the night crying. 'And talked to the other women. You ain't doing yourself any favours being so chilly.'

She wanted to retort that he'd been chilly himself when she only asked him a simple question. But to do so would imply she cared enough to notice. 'I didn't come on this wagon train to make friends,' she said instead.

'But you'll need them when we get up in the mountains,' he said, tilting his hat back and smirking at her. 'And when your baby comes.'

'I'll manage,' she said. She wanted to get back up on the wagon, she felt vulnerable standing so close to him, but if she moved to do that, she knew he would help her, and she didn't want him touching her.

'Mr Jennings must have been one powerful man,' he said reflectively.

'Why do you say that?' she retorted in alarm.

He gave her a long, cool stare, which seemed to penetrate right inside her. 'Well, ma'am, even after his death and all these miles we've travelled, he's managed to hold your heart so tight that you don't need nobody else. I never had that power over a woman. Tell me about him.'

Matilda's first reaction was to spit out something sarcastic, but as she looked up at the man she saw no ridicule in his blue eyes, only interest.

'He wasn't a tough man in the way you are,' she said with a toss of her head. 'He was a man who cared deeply about people and wanted to end suffering everywhere he found it. Even now I can't understand why the Lord chose to take him when there's so many wicked men in the world.'

The Captain looked hard at her for a moment, his expression one of sympathy. 'Then you must count yourself lucky that you had such a man, even for a short time,' he said with a new softness in his tone. 'I can tell you, ma'am, there sure ain't many out there like him. But from what you've said, I don't think he'd like you to cast yourself off from other people, especially now when you've got so much ahead of you.'

Tears prickled the backs of her eyes, but she was determined she wouldn't cry in front of him. 'Maybe you are right,' she said stiffly.

'I know I am.' He smiled, moving from the wagon wheel and setting his hat straight. 'And it wouldn't hurt to put on another dress, one that don't show up the dust so much. Black holds the heat, you know, and that ain't good for you.'

His concern touched her. She was tired of being sharp and nasty with him, and weary of constantly being on her guard. 'You are a puzzling man,' she said. 'One minute callous and sarcastic, another kind and thoughtful. Tell me what made you like that.'

'Probably the same sort of things that makes you so prickly,' he said, looking down at his feet and shuffling his boots in the sandy earth. 'Death of loved ones, being far from home. You've got little Tabby dependent on you, I've got all this lot.' He waved one hand back at the rest of the wagons. 'Neither of us knows what lies ahead.'

Matilda sensed that he wasn't ready to give her a more detailed explanation, but he'd said enough for her to feel they'd built a bridge between them, even if only a shaky one.

'I'm counting on you knowing what's ahead,' she said teasingly.

He looked up and smiled at her, and this time there was friendship in his eyes.

'I know the ways, and the perils,' he said. 'Don't worry, I'll get you there. So can we call a truce? I'll try not to be sarcastic if you'll stop being so aloof.'

'I'll do my best,' she said with a grin.

After Fort Laramie the going got even harder, rocks caught at the wagon wheels, threatening to turn them over, the dust blew worse than ever and it grew hotter day by day. For days on end there was no water or feed for the animals, and at night when the campfires were lit there was no singing or dancing, just the sound of children crying and laboured breathing from the oxen and horses. The fruit trees were wilting through lack of water, and Matilda found herself dreaming constantly of a hot bath, of starched white sheets on a comfortable bed and cool breezes.

Sometimes they only made around eight miles in a day because the going was so rough. Matilda mostly walked with the lead oxen, leading them, for though it was tiring and hard on her feet, it was better than being constantly thrown around up on the wagon.

Indians came more often now, and presents had to be brought out and laid on a blanket for their inspection before they'd let them move on. The scouts reported war parties further north which made everyone nervous. Two more children died, one of the Mormon women gave birth to a little boy, a man with four children died from a snake bite, and several oxen had to be shot because they were too weak to continue.

Overcome by the heat, Matilda finally dug out another dress, the blue and white one Lily had given her back in London. She had to take the skirt apart to use some of the material to make the bodice larger, and she hoped she wouldn't get very much bigger because nothing else she had would adapt at all.

They were moving into the Black Hills now, and Matilda discovered why the Captain had said she would need friends when her axle broke on a rock. It was all very well knowing the theory of how to change it, but it needed strong men to lift the wagon and fit the spare one.

But people were kind, four men came forward without her even asking, and one of their women took the opportunity to offer her an old dress she'd worn in her last pregnancy. Matilda had to unbend, she made them tea and gave them all the biscuits she'd made the night before.

The day after the broken axle they made camp that night at Willow Springs where there was pasture for the animals. As several of the children on the train were sick, Captain Russell said they would lay up there a whole day to rest which would give the men a chance to go hunting for badly needed fresh meat.

Matilda woke very early the following morning and crept out of the wagon to watch the sun rise. Everyone else was still asleep, the sound of gentle snoring was coming from every direction, even Treacle didn't move from his position under the wagon.

The sky was still very dark, just a pink and yellow glow in the east, and it was deliciously cool. Matilda reached back into the wagon for a towel, thinking that perhaps she could take the opportunity to bathe in the stream, and when her hand touched the gun, she took that too, just in case there were snakes.

As she passed by the ashes from last night's fire in the middle of the circle of wagons, she could feel a little warmth coming from them still, and it reminded her oddly of mornings in New York when she would creep downstairs at dawn to coax the stove into life again and enjoy the tranquillity of being alone while everyone else still slept.

She tiptoed through the wagons on the stream side of the circle, stopping as she saw elk drinking on the far bank, less than forty yards from her. Not wishing to frighten them, she shrank back against a wagon to watch. She had seen these large deer before on the trail, but only at a distance, and she hadn't known that they were even taller than her and that their antlers were so huge. For a moment she just watched, awed by their beauty, expecting that they would sense her presence any moment and run, but perhaps the wind was in the wrong direction because they didn't even lift their heads from the water.

Suddenly she remembered Captain Russell's words last night about the desperate need for the men to go hunting. Hunting parties had not been very successful up till now, for the men on the train were mainly farmers, and few could shoot straight. The thought of killing one of these magnificent animals was abhorrent, but there were many sick children on the train, and Tabitha had informed her she thought many of the families had no food left at all, indeed she'd even suggested giving away the last of their hoarded bacon.

'I'm sorry,' she whispered as she lifted her gun to her shoulder. 'I wouldn't kill you if we didn't need food so badly.' She got the largest one in her sights and fired.

He staggered for a moment as the rest of the herd scattered, then he fell heavily to the ground.

All at once the whole camp awoke, dogs barked, horses whinnied, men came leaping out of wagons and from under them, mostly wearing only their underwear.

'Is it Indians?' someone shouted, and with that, before Matilda had a chance to move or speak, Captain Russell was striding bare-chested through the circle, a pistol in his hand.

'It's nothing to worry about,' Matilda called out. 'I just shot an elk.'

Later, as she told Tabitha how it all came about, they both laughed at the thought of Captain Russell rushing out imagining Indians were about to attack and finding Matilda in her white night-gown, clutching a rifle. But at the moment he came towards her she wanted to hide herself from him and all the other male eyes on her.

The Captain splashed through the stream and bent over the elk to check it.

'Where in tarnation did an English woman learn to shoot like that?' he called back.

Matilda ran away then, back to the wagon to dress herself. She had a strong feeling she would be the sole subject of today's gossip.

At noon Matilda was sitting in the shade of the wagon making some alterations to the dress she'd been given, enjoying the peace which had fallen over the camp in the last hour. Earlier it had been a scene of frantic activity, women washing clothes, airing bedding, children shouting to one another as they fetched water, men hammering and banging as they repaired rock damage to their wagons. Some had taken off their wagon wheels to leave them to soak in the stream, for the dry heat shrank the timber, and if left, it could cause the iron rims to fall off. But it was quiet now, most people resting under the trees by the creek, and there were delicious smells of meat stewing slowly on the many camp stoves.

Tabitha came running back with Treacle and the pair of them flopped down on the ground beside Matilda, panting with the heat. Tabitha's sun-bonnet was dripping wet, just a few days ago one of the scouts told her he kept cool by soaking his hat in water and she'd copied him. Matilda thought it might work with a leather hat, but not with a cotton bonnet.

'Everyone's talking about you down by the creek,' Tabitha said excitedly. 'Mrs Jacobson, she's the one with nine children, said I ought to be real proud of you.'

'I don't really know if you should be, Tabby,' Matilda replied with a smile. 'I thought it was an awful shame to kill such a noble creature.'

'No one else feels that way.' Tabitha grinned. 'Lots of the other people had nothing to eat. Mrs Jacobson said her children went to bed hungry last night, and if the men didn't get something today she didn't know what she was going to do. One of the men said he reckoned they could have been out all day hunting and still come back with nothing.'

Matilda rolled her eyes, she hadn't shot the elk with the intention of saving the men from doing their duty as providers.

'I bet they aren't helping their women instead,' she said dryly. 'Lazy devils!'

'No, they're all talking about you and wondering how an English lady learned to handle a gun like that,' Tabitha said gleefully. 'But I stopped to speak to Mrs Donnier, she's the one whose children are sick. She was making some broth for them with the meat, she said she hoped it might make them better. I told her you knew a whole lot about sick children too, and she asked if you'd come and take a look at them and see if you know what's wrong with them.'

Matilda had been quite enjoying her new-found fame, but at that she turned to the child in horror. 'Oh Tabby, I can't do that,' she said. 'They might have something catching.'

Tabitha looked stunned. 'You sound like Mama,' she said accusingly. 'She was always scared of catching things. I thought you were braver.'

That retort was like having a mug of cold water thrown over Matilda. For not only did she realize how selfish and uncaring she must have sounded, but suddenly after so long she actually understood the primitive instinct behind Lily's fear of disease.

'Your mother, my girl, had a great deal of courage,' she said sharply. 'If she was afraid of disease it wasn't for herself, but you. I can see that now because I don't want to take any risks that might harm you, the baby inside me, or myself for that matter, because I'm the one who has to look out for us.'

'But Mrs Donnier looks so tired and worried,' Tabitha said, her dark eyes welling with tears. 'No one else is helping her, and I was so sure you would.'

Her words were like hearing Giles speak, and immediately Matilda was shamed. She got to her feet and held out her hand to the child. 'You'd better show me the Donniers' wagon then. But mind you keep well away, just in case.'

Even before she got to the wagon Matilda heard the tell-tale dry coughing of measles. Knowing that neither she nor Tabitha was likely to get it a second time made her feel somewhat easier. As the mother came towards her wringing her hands on her apron, Matilda's heart went out to her.

She had that same grey, defeated look that many of the women in Finders Court had, a combination of poverty, too many children, hard work and poor food. She was probably only twenty-four at most, but she looked far older, thin and stooped, with blackened teeth, and even her brown hair was lifeless, like dull wire.

'I sure am beholden to you, Mrs Jennings,' she said. 'I wouldn't have troubled your little girl to fetch you, but she said you might know what ails my children.'

'Their coughing sounds like measles,' Matilda said. 'But let me see them.'

There were five children lying huddled in the bed in the wagon, the youngest just about a year old, the eldest around seven. Matilda crawled in beside them and felt their heads. All of them felt far too hot, and their skin dry, just the way Tabitha had been when she had it. It was hard to see if they had a rash, for the canvas on the wagon made it dark.

'I'm pretty certain it is measles,' Matilda said as she crawled back out. 'Give them plenty to drink. And sponge them down with cool water too, but you must protect their eyes from the light, so tie something round their eyes when you bring them outside.'

She went on to explain about keeping their ears and eyes clean and using boiled salt water, but even as she spoke her heart was sinking. They had almost lost Tabitha, and she'd been in a real house with the doctor calling every day. Worse still, these children had probably had contact with many others in the past two or three weeks, so there would be more children and adults going down with it before long. She realized too that the child who had been sick soon after they set off from Independence had probably been the carrier, yet that mother hadn't told anyone what her child was suffering from, and the two other child deaths that were put down as 'ague' by Captain Russell were most likely measles victims too. She resolved she would have a word with him about that later, but first she felt compelled to help sponge the children down, for their mother looked too exhausted to do it alone.

Over two hours later Matilda went back to her wagon, but although she was tired from fetching water, lifting the children and helping their mother wash soiled covers on the bed, she was too angry to rest.

Mr Donnier hadn't lifted a finger to help. He'd sat in the shade with a group of other men playing cards, the only time he spoke was to ask when his supper would be ready.

Marie Donnier was not the brightest of women, she reminded Matilda of the oxen, plodding along, unaware of anything except what was right in front of her. Like the oxen she would work until she dropped, and doubtless her brutish husband would only take notice when she failed to give him supper.

Marie had said she was married at sixteen, and she'd lost two babies already. They'd lived in Indiana, Ohio and Missouri, she said her husband was never happy in one place for too long.

Captain Russell was talking to a group of men who were rubbing salt into the hide of the elk. When he saw Matilda he broke off and came over to her, grinning fit to bust.

'Howdy, heroine,' he said. 'You've gone from the hermit to the lady everyone wants to talk to, in just a few hours.'

She ignored that remark and laid right into him, accusing him of covering up the two child deaths as ague when it was measles.

'Well, I didn't know,' he said with a look of alarm. 'I ain't no doctor, ma'am. I took the mother's word for it.'

'I take it you know measles is highly infectious?'

'Of course I do,' he said, frowning with anxiety. 'We'll have to move the Donniers' wagon right away from the circle.'

'It's too late for that now,' she said. 'Just as it's too late for poor Marie Donnier to do anything about that useless lump of buffalo dung she's married to.'

He laughed.

'Don't you laugh at me,' she snapped. 'It's bad enough every time we have a rest day seeing the women flogging themselves half to death while the men sit around like lords, but that man didn't even get water to sponge his sick children down. He should be horse-whipped.'

To her surprise he agreed with her. 'You're right, Mrs Jennings. Since taking out wagon trains I've surely seen how unfairly women get treated. There's been many a man I wanted to horsewhip for neglecting his duty as a husband and father. But you tell me what we should do about this measles to prevent it spreading any further.'

Her irritation at him vanished. He was honest enough to admit he didn't know everything, and it felt good to be treated as his equal. 'There isn't much we can do except find out which children have been playing with the Donniers' little ones, and tell those parents not to let them mix with anyone else until they are in the clear,' she said.

He nodded agreement. 'I'll do that now. But you take it easy, ma'am, I shouldn't want to see you get sick too.'

'I've already had measles,' she said. 'And nursed Tabitha through it. I'll be fine. the person I'm worried about is Mrs Donnier. She's worn out already and the chances are some of her children won't survive. You could make that oaf of a man realize his wife needs some help, and some sleep.'

Captain James Russell watched as Matilda walked away. He had been intrigued by her right from the first day she came to him asking to join the wagon train. He was always reluctant to take any woman travelling on her own, for that usually spelled trouble, especially if they were as pretty as Mrs Jennings. On top of that she was English, and the few English women he had taken out West were all a pain in the rump, always complaining or praying, and he didn't know which was worse.

All the time Matilda was making her preparations to leave, he watched her from a distance, and he couldn't help but be impressed. He liked her firm but gentle way with both animals and children, and the way she didn't flutter her eyelashes at any men to get their help, but did everything herself.

Then on the final night in a saloon in Independence he'd heard the story about the English minister who'd first lost his wife in childbirth and then got himself shot. According to what he'd heard, the man was very special, caring for everyone like they were his own, standing up against slavery, supporting the Indians, taking folks into his own home after the flood.

The local men spoke equally warmly of the woman who had come to Independence with him and his wife, and lived with them like a sister. They said she hadn't sent the minister's child back to England but was intending to bring her up herself.

James guessed right away that this woman had to be the English Mrs Jennings he'd agreed to take to Oregon, and he assumed at first she had adopted the role of widow just to prevent anyone taking liberties with her.

It was only a week into the trail that he began to suspect she was carrying a child. He watched her lifting two pails of water one evening, and just the careful way she straightened up reminded him of his wife's movements when she was that way. Belle, like the minister's wife, died in childbirth, while he was off soldiering, and a part of him died too then, because he should have been there.

His initial view was that Mrs Jennings had to be a scheming trollop who had crept into the bed of a grieving man with the sole intention of moving up from poor relation to becoming the minister's wife with all the benefits that would bring her. He thought he would have to watch her very closely to see she didn't set her cap at someone else's husband.

Yet as he watched her, he began to doubt his original opinion. She was no trollop, she had too much dignity and reserve. It was patently clear she loved the little girl, and she was intelligent, very independent, and pretty enough to win any man's heart without guile. When he finally got her to speak of her 'husband', her love for him shone out in the way she praised him.

But yet another facet of her character had revealed itself today. First the shooting of the elk, as food for everyone, not for herself, for she hadn't even demanded the best cuts or the hide, she'd just left the men to the butchering and the dividing up. Then helping Mrs Donnier with her sick children. That was an act of great kindness and courage, for the fear of infectious diseases was even greater on a wagon train than in towns and cities, and few people were prepared to put themselves or their own families at risk.

She certainly wasn't a trollop, he decided as he saw her filling a wash-basin with water by the side of her wagon to wash her hands. She was a woman who followed her heart rather than her head, and God help him, he was falling in love with her.

James knew he created an impression that he was something of a ruffian. He'd found it was a way of hiding his true nature and his past. Being insolent, arrogant, callous and even at times brutish, spared him the attentions of gentlefolk who might wish to draw him into their family circle. There was a bitterness within him he knew he'd got to deal with before he could allow anyone to get close to him again.

In fact James came from one of the best families in Virginia. If he'd married a girl from a similar notable family, his life would have been entirely different. But he had loved Belle, the overseer's daughter on his family plantation since childhood, and when he graduated from West Point he married her.

The entire Russell family turned against him. Belle was 'white trash', so far down the social scale it sent his mother into attacks of the vapours each time her name was mentioned. James was cast out, his old friends shunned him, but he didn't care then, he loved Belle and he thought that would be enough.

But James soon found that being a first-class soldier made no difference if he happened to have the wrong kind of wife. He got all the worst postings and there was no hope of promotion. Belle went with him wherever he was sent, even to the Mexican war, and from what James saw of the wives of the officers who had married the 'right' girl, it made him love Belle still more.

He was glad in many ways that he'd been disowned, for the grim postings and the views of a much larger America all helped him to see that his family's values were warped and that their wealth had been made through human suffering. He began to see how evil slavery really was, he learned to admire and respect the Indians, but these views didn't endear him to his superiors either.

When Belle died in childbirth, he contemplated leaving the army, but knowing he wasn't qualified to do anything else, he stayed. What he excelled at was training enlisted men, and he might have continued along that path indefinitely, but for the Government suddenly deciding that the wagon trains going West needed officers with knowledge of the terrain and of the plains Indians to lead them.

For the most part it suited James. The people who travelled out to Oregon were courageous, decent sorts with open minds, they needed leadership, he liked the adventure and the challenge of getting them there as quickly and safely as possible. For six months of the year he could be his own man without kowtowing to senior officers who for the most part were bumbling fools. He believed he was using his talents to help people, and his country.

He had also believed up until now that he'd buried his heart down in Mexico along with Belle and his stillborn child. But a man couldn't be right about everything.

The first of the Donnier children died that night, the second youngest, a little girl called Clara. Yet even before the little grave could be dug in the morning, her younger brother Tobias passed away too.

Captain Russell decided that they would stay another day at the creek, but as he was holding the simple funeral prayers and trying to find some words of comfort for the grieving Marie, Matilda was in the Donnier wagon minding the other three children.

The sun was so hot that the inside of the wagon was like an oven. The straw-filled mattress was soaked right through, smelling of urine and vomit, and the children were burning up. Matilda knew, just as she had with Tabitha, that their only hope of survival was to get them out of there to somewhere cooler, and quickly. Without waiting for their mother to return she picked up the youngest one, wrapped a length of cotton round her head to protect her eyes, grabbed a quilt and carried her down to the stream. She immersed her in the cold water, holding her there for some five minutes, then tucked her into the quilt under the deep shade of a tree and went back for the next.

She was returning for the third and last child as the Donniers came back. Marie just looked at her with pain-filled eyes, but her husband asked Matilda what she thought she was doing.

'Cooling them down,' she said curtly. He was a big, rough-looking type with unkempt fair hair and black teeth. 'I've bathed the two younger ones and put them in the shade to sleep. I'm just going to take John too.'

'No one takes my little'uns anywhere without my say-so,' he said, blowing out his barrel chest and folding his muscular arms across it. 'You leave them be, Marie will see to 'em.'

'Marie is in no fit state to do anything more,' she said, putting a hand on to his chest to push her way past him. 'If you care anything for your children you'll help, or at least get out of the way.'

'I don't stand that sort of talk from any woman,' he said. 'Clear off out of it.'

'Marie, run down and stay with the other children, give them some water,' she said, looking fiercely at the woman and willing her to do as she was told.

Marie made a timid yelp of fear and ran off.

'Come back here, woman,' Mr Donnier shouted at her, 'or I'll whup you.'

Matilda could not hold back her anger at him any longer. 'You pig,' she hissed at him. 'You have just returned from burying two of your children and you talk of whipping your wife! Have you anything inside that head of yours other than bone? You've lost two children, the other three are seriously ill, what does it take to stir you into some action?'

He clenched his fist and took a step nearer her.

'Hit me and I swear I'll kill you,' she said, and meant it. 'Get into that wagon, get your son out and carry him down to the stream. Now!'

She was aware a crowd was gathering to watch, but getting the child out was all that mattered to her, and he was too heavy for her to carry alone.

'You'll pay for this,' he said through clenched teeth, but he got up into the wagon.

'Cover his eyes before you bring him out,' she shouted.

The man did as he was told, but went to move off the second she was holding the boy in the water.

'Not so fast,' she yelled at him, up to her waist in water. 'You'll clear that filthy straw mattress out, burn it and wash the wagon with vinegar and water, and bring all the dirty covers down here to be washed.'

He disappeared, and Matilda was left holding the coughing, struggling seven-year-old in the water. Marie was sitting beside the two younger ones on the grass, crying hard. The crowd had moved down to watch the proceedings but none of them were coming near for fear of catching the disease.

'Someone help me!' Matilda called out. She could hold John easily enough in the water, even though he was struggling, but she hadn't got the strength to lift him out on to the bank.

No one moved, and her anger rose up and spilled over.

'You lily-livered bunch of arse-wipes!' she screamed at them.

Captain Russell came elbowing his way through the crowd, jumped down into the creek and waded out to her. 'Arse-wipes!'

he whispered to her. 'Now they'll know you aren't a real lady.'

His tone was only teasing and it defused some of her anger. 'I know worse things to call them than that,' she whispered back.

'I do believe you do, Mrs Jennings,' he smiled.

The stony bed of the creek was uneven, and as she held out the child to the Captain her foot slipped, and she wobbled sideways. The Captain caught her with one arm, circling it round her waist. For a moment or two he just held her and the child close to him.

'Are you going to take the boy, or are we going to stay here making a spectacle of ourselves?' she said, only too aware of his hard body so close to hers, and the eyes on them from the bank.

'Just steadying you,' he said. Then, taking the child from her arms, he turned and waded away with him.

The crowd of people began to move away almost as soon as he'd laid the boy beside his brother and sister, and the Captain followed quickly after saying something about getting a dry blanket for them all.

He didn't return with anything dry, so once Matilda had established that all three children were breathing more easily, she left Marie to mind them and made her way back through the middle of the circle of wagons.

To her surprise a large crowd was gathered further along, and she guessed a fight was in progress. Pushing her way through the crowd, she saw it was Captain Russell and Donnier, both stripped to the waist and punching each other. It seemed to her that Donnier, who was heavier, had started out with the advantage, for the Captain had one eye almost closed and blood was trickling down his cheek. But although lighter and thinner he was a fancy mover, dancing around Donnier and hitting out with greater accuracy, and Donnier kept reeling back from the force of his blows.

As she watched, the Captain caught Donnier by the shoulder and drove his fist into the man's stomach like a sledge-hammer. Donnier staggered back and fell over, remaining motionless on the ground.

The Captain calmly went over and picked up a bucket of water. Stopping for a moment to splash some on his own face, he then emptied the entire pail on to the prone man. 'Get up, you dog,' he growled at him. 'Do what you were told, burn the mattress and clean the wagon out. I'll be round later to make sure you've done it.'

Tabitha was already in bed, and Matilda was sitting outside the wagon writing up her diary by the light of a candle in a jar, when the Captain came past, doing his rounds before turning in himself.

'Still up?' he said. 'I thought you'd have been tucked up hours ago after all the ruckus today.'

She had washed all Marie's bedding and hung it up to dry, then stayed with the woman by the stream with the children until it was cooler, when they'd carried them back to the wagon, which was now clean and smelling strongly of vinegar.

'I guess I had to write down my thoughts about that dreadful man,' she said. 'Poor Marie, I hope he doesn't take it out on her.'

'He won't dare while I'm around,' he said, squatting down beside her. 'What puzzles me is why a woman would choose a man like that in the first place.'

'She told me her parents picked him for her. They thought as he was big and strong he'd work on their farm and be good to them all. But her father died just a few months after the wedding, and her mother quickly followed him. Donnier let the farm go to ruin, then sold the land and insisted they move on. It's been like that ever since for her.'

'I wish I had a dollar for every time I've heard similar stories,' he said, shaking his head. 'It's an unfair world, that's for sure. I sure am glad I wasn't born a woman.'

His sympathetic tone surprised her. She had expected him to claim Marie was at fault.

'The awful thing is that there is no way out for her,' Matilda said, looking up at the Captain with concerned eyes. 'Her life is hell with him, but if she left him how could she manage to bring up her children?'

'How are you going to bring up yours?' he asked.

Although a week ago she would have bristled at that question, she sensed now that he meant it kindly.

'I'm not made of the same stuff as Marie,' she said. 'I was making my own living right from a child. I can't say I know how I'm going to do it just now, but I'll find a way.'

She caught him looking at her intently. She expected that he would say she must find herself a husband, and she was ready to snap at him if he did.

'I believe you will find a way,' he said, taking her by surprise. 'A woman who can shoot straight, drive a wagon, nurse a stranger's children and still be a picture to look at, sure ain't gonna come to much grief.'

'Well, thankee kindly, sir, for that pretty compliment,' she said in her mock Southern accent. 'I do believe you are a gentleman after all.'

They both laughed and something warm and sweet ran between them.

'Goodnight, ma'am,' he said, getting up and lifting his hat to her. 'Sleep tight tonight.'

Chapter Fifteen

Matilda waved goodbye as ten wagons forked off from the main party to go north to Whitmans' Mission in Oregon's Walla Walla Valley, part of her wishing she was with them.

It was September now, the birth of her child imminent, and the Mission was only a relatively short distance away. But Narcissa and Marcus Whitman, who had founded the Mission, and eleven other people had been massacred by the Cayuse Indians last year, and many others taken as hostages. Those who had decided to go there had relatives and friends in the area and they believed that the army would protect them from any further hostilities. Captain Russell agreed this was probably correct, and that the new people at the Mission would offer Matilda shelter and care, but in his opinion it was far more sensible for her to press on to The Dalles by the Columbia river. Although it meant a much longer journey now, it was a well-established town and she would be safer there if bad weather came and she couldn't make it all the way to her friends in the Willamette Valley.

Knowing James's advice was always sound, Matilda was following it, but she was so very weary of travelling.

Since leaving Willow Springs nearly three months ago she had been through hell. So many of the animals had died through exhaustion and days without water or feed. Wagon wheels broke as the sun dried out the timber. Many families had been forced to abandon their wagons, continuing on foot and carrying what little they had left on their backs. Stinging, choking dust got into their eyes and lungs, hunger, thirst and exhaustion weakened everyone. By day they were roasted by the sun, at night they were frozen. Both climbing up mountains and coming down the other side was gruelling. Often the wagons had to be emptied and hauled up, the oxen coaxed along on dangerous ledges where one wrong step could lead to certain death. There was an ever-present fear of the animals stampeding too, for crazed with thirst, if they smelled water in the distance they would bolt towards it. There had been so many deaths on the train that Matilda could no longer recall all the names, or even the places where those people had been buried.

Measles had claimed a further five victims, although the three remaining Donnier children had survived. Marie Donnier was pregnant again, looking so frail that Matilda doubted she would live to see the child born. Eight men, women and children had died from cholera, but fortunately this vicious killer which could have easily wiped out the entire company had remained localized in only two wagons. Two men drowned as they forded the Snake river, swept away by the fierce current before anyone could throw them a line. Countless gruesome accidents included a child crushed by a wagon wheel, and a woman who had tripped on a mountain pass and broken her back in the fall over rocks. A man had disappeared on a hunting trip and although the scouts found his horse wandering alone a day later, they'd been unable to find him or his body.

They had seen the wonders of the hot springs, water pumping up from the bowels of the earth hot enough to boil a hog, marvelled at the beauty of the mountains and valleys, and seen sunsets so incredible they brought tears to the eyes. But Matilda cared little for scenery now, all she wanted was rest.

Her limbs were hard with muscle, her hands callused and ugly, and every bone in her body ached. At night she cut up and hemmed napkins out of an old flannel petticoat, and whenever she looked at the baby clothes so carefully made by Lily for her child, she prayed that she would have an easier time and that her baby would be born strong and healthy. She was terrified of the prospect of giving birth in the wagon, yet hoping almost nightly that the pains would come, just so she could get it over and be released from the torment of such a swollen, awkward body.

There had been times when but for Tabitha she might have been tempted to throw herself down a mountainside or into one of the fast-flowing rivers to end the misery. She asked herself why she was struggling so hard – once the baby was born things would be even tougher for her. But each time such dark thoughts came to her, she would look at Tabitha's trusting little face and remember her promise to Lily.

Yet for all the hardships and suffering, there had been joy too. Never before had she felt such personal freedom – the restraints of being a servant, and of trying to keep up the image of a lady, were gone. She could speak her mind, and often did, no longer hiding behind delicate euphemisms. She had earned herself a reputation as being as physically tough and self-reliant as a man, yet she felt she was also equally admired for her intelligence, knowledge and kindness. Even though she hadn't set out to make friends, she had won them anyway. She felt the regard her fellow travellers had for her now that she was so near her time – her water containers were always miraculously filled, she found little gifts of berries, soup, meat and biscuits left outside her wagon, and on the toughest parts of the trail, someone always came to help her.

But of all the friendships forged, the one with Captain James Russell was the strongest. It seemed odd sometimes that a man who had irritated her so much at first could become a valued friend, but then he had hidden his concern for her behind so much sarcasm and insolence, and hadn't allowed her to see the real man beneath.

He might be intolerant of bigotry and stupidity, yet he did have a keen understanding of human frailties. His opinions on the plight of the poor and oppressed were so like Giles's. He also had an irrepressible sense of humour, and he was every bit as curious about people as she was. She had found him to be a well-rounded man, tough, yet with an underlying tenderness towards the weak. He was highly intelligent and well-educated, but had the ability to converse with those less able too. He was a natural leader, commanding respect and admiration.

Most nights he would stop by to see her and Tabitha, and their conversations were open and easy. He told her one night about his childhood in Virginia, of a father who rated a man only by his wealth and the number of slaves he owned, and a mother who was more interested in parties and balls and the latest fashions from France than her own children.

'I was raised with the stick in one hand, the Bible in the other,' he said with a wicked grin one night. 'Neither did anything for me. I often get to wondering if there could be another way of life for me, something between soldiering or running a plantation. I sure don't like either much, both mean bullying someone. But that's all I know.'

When he told her about his wife Belle, how his family disowned him, and how Belle died in childbirth, Matilda understood then about the bitterness inside him, and why he had turned his back on the class he had been born into.

She had told him about her childhood in London, and his interest in a life so far removed from his own was so intense that she found herself vividly describing common London scenes to make him laugh. She did tell him how she came to America as a nursemaid, but as he didn't press her about her 'husband' or how she ended up in Missouri, she had left that part of her history blank.

Once they got to The Dalles some families would build rafts to take the wagons down the Columbia river towards Portland, others would take the longer but safer route around Mount Hood. Their journey's end was almost in sight, yet she had a sickening feeling the worst was yet to come before she saw Cissie and her family.

A few days after parting company with the people who had gone to Whitman's Mission they made camp for the night in a beautiful spot. It was a wide, flower-filled mountain meadow, surrounded by huge fir trees, with a small stream running through the centre. The animals had been let loose to graze and the children were making the most of the late afternoon sun, playing leap-frog and chase as their mothers prepared the evening meal.

Matilda made a rabbit stew with dumplings flavoured with wild sage on her camp stove. She had shot the jack rabbit herself the previous day and its skin was pegged out to dry, ready to join the many others she'd shot during the trip, to be sewn together later for a bedcover. While the stew was simmering she hauled out the mattress from the wagon to give it a good shake and an airing. Tabitha was off with the other children, and Treacle lying down under the wagon for a snooze.

Captain Russell came striding along a little later. He had clearly been for a dip in the stream as his fair hair was wet and he was wearing a clean shirt. 'That smells good,' he said, bending to sniff the stew pot appreciatively.

'Stay and have some with us,' she said, prodding the dumplings. One of the German women had taught her to make these and they were Tabitha's favourite. 'It's almost ready and there's more than enough for three.'

He smiled, his blue eyes crinkling up with pleasure. 'That would be real nice,' he said. 'But I didn't come by looking for food, I came to say that when we reach The Dalles, I've got it fixed so you can go down river on the first canoe with Carl, we'll get your wagon on a raft after you've gone.'

'Thank you, Captain,' she said softly, looking up at him through her lashes. The scout Carl had an Indian wife who belonged to one of the tribes who lived along the Columbia river. She guessed the Captain had arranged this for her knowing Carl could get help for her if the baby should come suddenly. Touched as she was by his concern for her, she didn't think he should be singling her out for such preferential treatment. But before she could voice this, Tabitha came running up and the Captain opened his arms to catch her, spinning her round in his arms and making her squeal with laughter.

'More, Captain,' she shouted gleefully as he put her down.

'If you can manage to call me James,' he said.

Tabitha was dizzy and she reeled around trying to look at him straight. 'Matty said I mustn't be familiar,' she said.

The Captain burst out laughing. 'Letting someone whizz you around seems pretty familiar to me,' he said.

Matilda laughed with them. She felt happy tonight. The weather was good, there was good grazing and plenty of water, and the rabbit stew was the best she'd made yet. She couldn't see how she could object to Tabitha calling a man by his Christian name when he'd proved himself to be such a good friend.

'Wash your hands, the pair of you,' she said, pointing to the pail. 'Then sit right down, it's ready now.'

It was a very jolly evening. The Captain told them a great many funny stories about strange characters he'd met on previous wagon trains, and Matilda in turn told him ones of people she'd known back in London. Tabitha giggled at all the stories, and later, when they joined everyone else on the train around the big campfire, and Mr Ferguson got out his accordion to play a few jigs, she led the dancing with the Captain as her partner.

Matilda sat on a camping stool and just watched everyone

enjoying themselves. The firelight softened even the plainest of faces, warmth and good food mellowed even the crustiest of them. She observed too how dramatically the long journey had changed them all: women who had started out fat and pale were now brown-faced and lean, once neat dresses and sun-bonnets were now ragged and faded. Men who had been pompous and arrogant back at the beginning were gentler, seemingly weak ones had risen to become assertive. The trail had tested everyone, death and serious injuries had affected almost every family, marriages had been shaken, former beliefs shot to pieces, and there were few that hadn't come to see how ill-equipped they were, both mentally and physically, for such a trip. Children had grown wild, and the close contact with other families often made them question their parents' authority and codes of behaviour.

Yet overall, Matilda thought everyone had benefited in some way. They had all learnt new skills and endurance, faced disaster with courage, and the deep friendships formed along the way had enriched their lives. Yet it was the women who had gained the most, she thought. Back home they had been passive, bending to their menfolk's will, quietly caring for their families and seldom voicing an opinion about anything. Gradually on the journey their resourcefulness, ingenuity and natural patience had given them new status, and they'd risen to become men's equals, with a voice of their own. Matilda very much hoped they would hold on to this liberation when the trail ended and they found themselves back in settled homes. She knew she wasn't going to be subservient to anyone ever again.

She woke during the night with a stomach ache, and thought it was because she'd eaten so much. It went away after a few seconds, but just as she was dropping off to sleep again, it returned.

Through the round drawstring hole at the back of the wagon she could see the stars twinkling in a black velvet sky, but a faint orange glow from the campfire's dying embers suggested dawn was a long way off.

As she held her belly and tried to rub away the pain, all at once she realized it had nothing to do with eating too much, but was because the baby was on its way.

Her first reaction was dismay. The Captain had said over supper that he thought Carl could get them to Oregon City by river within two weeks and she'd hoped the baby would wait until then.

But as she lay there waiting to see if a third pain came, listening to sounds of owls hooting, the wind in the firs and Tabitha snuffling softly in her sleep beside her, all at once it felt right to have her child here. No place could be more beautiful, she knew she had only to call out and people would come running to help. Her son or daughter would be a true American, the spirit of this brave and splendid country would enter him or her at the moment of birth.

'Come quickly, my little one,' she whispered in the darkness, smoothing her round hard belly tenderly. 'I'm waiting for you.'

She lay there calmly all night. The pains grew ever stronger and more frequent until they were almost continuous, but she concentrated on watching the patch of sky through the back of the wagon, waiting for it to lighten before waking Tabitha.

She felt Giles and Lily's comforting presence, and she reached out and pulled over the quilt she and Lily had made together for comfort, remembering how Lily said, 'Let's put in lots of red for passion' that day in the kitchen.

As the sky gradually lightened, and the colours in the quilt became more vivid, so each one seemed to have some important significance. Green for the fields back in England, purple for the violets she'd once sold in London, orange the colour of her brother's hair and blue-grey for the Atlantic they'd crossed to find a new life. Yellow for the cornfields they'd passed on the way to Missouri, turquoise for the skies over them most of the way here. Pink for the dress she'd worn that first night she met Flynn, white for the night-gown she'd been wearing when Giles took her in his arms in the kitchen the night of the storm.

As it got lighter still she saw Lily's and her own characters sewn into the quilt too. Lily had used tones of the same colours in her squares, to give a quiet, muted effect, just the way she lived her life. Matilda had put red against yellow, purple against orange, bold and commanding.

All at once the sun rose to peep into the back of the wagon, falling on to Tabitha's face. With her normally straight dark hair tousled, and her cheeks rosy with sleep, she looked far more like Giles than Lily, and even through her pain Matilda felt her heart swell with love for her.

'Tabitha, wake up!' she said, gently stroking her face.

The child woke instantly and sat up sharply, rubbing her eyes. 'I dreamed about Mama and Papa. They were here with us. Did I cry out?'

'No, I woke you because I need you to get Mrs Jacobson. You see, the baby has started to come.' Another pain came, even stronger, and it was all she could do not to cry out. 'Just put on your clothes and go and get her. I'm sure she'll let you stay there with her children till I've got the baby to show you.'

The child turned to her, eyes narrowing with suspicion, and Matilda remembered then that the last time she'd sent her away to stay with another child her mother had died while she was gone. 'I'm going to be fine,' she said, forcing a wide, cheerful smile. 'I think the baby will come very soon. Now, run along because I really need Mrs Jacobson.'

Tabitha wriggled off the bed and dressed in just a couple of seconds, sitting down on the back of the wagon to put her boots on. 'I shan't stay away,' she said, looking back over her shoulder and frowning at Matilda. 'I'm coming back to wait outside. I want to be the first to hold my little brother.'

Matilda tried to get up once Tabitha had run off. She had put everything that was needed in a wooden box and tucked it down at the head of the bed. She managed to roll over to get on her hands and knees, but then another pain came and she had to stay in that position.

She was still struggling to get the box out when Mrs Jacobson arrived. She was a big, stout woman in her early forties, with iron-grey hair, and she wheezed as she climbed up into the wagon.

'What in tarnation are you doing, Mrs Jennings?' she asked, finding herself presented with Matilda's rear view. 'That's no position to have a baby in!'

Matilda managed to rasp out her explanation and the woman climbed right in, yanked the box out and laid Matilda down again. She lifted up her night-gown, laid gentle hands on her belly just as another pain came, and nodded.

'He's in a hurry, I'd say,' she said knowledgeably. 'So we'd better get ready for him. I've never delivered one on me knees afore, but there's a first time for everything.'

The woman was very confident, and quick. In no time she'd laid the india-rubber sheet under Matilda, a cotton sheet, then thick brown paper, and found a pail for the afterbirth. She had brought with her string and a tin with browned flour in it, which she said was for the baby's cord. She laid this with a knife and a clean white sheet to wrap the baby in on the wooden box and placed it by the bed.

'I've just got to go and get someone to boil up some hot water,' she said. 'If you feel the urge to push before I get back, go ahead.'

She was hardly out of the wagon before another pain came, and it was so violent Matilda cried out. But even as the white-hot pain engulfed her, she remembered Tabitha might be right outside, and she bit into the pillow instead.

Pain after pain came, each one stronger to the point where she felt she would surely die. She felt fluid running out of her and began to cry, but suddenly Mrs Jacobson was back and she wriggled up beside her and laid a cool hand on her forehead.

'You haven't had an accident,' she said softly. 'That's just your water's breaking. I bet with the next pain you'll want to push.'

She was right. The sensation came and there was no ignoring it, for she could almost feel the baby urging her to help him out. She pushed so hard she was grunting like a pig, and the older woman got right in front of her on her knees, took her two feet and held them up against her shoulders.

'With the next one bear down hard on me,' she ordered her. 'Give it everything you've got, and then some. Remember my knees aren't what they were.'

Another pain came and Matilda did as she was told, pushing so hard she was afraid she'd push Mrs Jacobson right out of the wagon. But she remained as sturdy as a rock, and encouraged her all the way.

'I can see the top of his head clearly,' she said, her voice rising with excitement. 'He's got dark hair. Now, think only of him and push him out.'

Matilda took a deep breath as the next pain came, then held it in and gradually released it as she pushed, her hands gripping the side of the bed.

'That's it, he's coming,' Mrs Jacobson said gleefully. 'You're a tough one and no mistake, he'll be here before anyone even wakes up.'

The sun was coming right in through the back of the wagon now and the thought flashed through Matilda's mind that anyone walking past would view the whole thing. But she didn't care, all she was concentrating on was bracing herself for the next pain and delivering him quickly.

She pushed again with every ounce of strength and it felt as if she was being torn apart.

'His head's here now,' Mrs Jacobson crowed. 'Don't push any more, honey, just pant and let him come of his own accord.'

Matilda rallied herself enough to prop herself up on her elbows. To her amazement there was his little head covered in dark hair sticking out between her legs. Another pain came and she panted, sliding down again on to the bed as she felt a warm, slippery, fluid sensation.

'It's a little girl!' Mrs Jacobson yelled in excitement. 'I could have sworn it would be a boy, but that shows how much I know!'

Matilda reared up again to see her baby in the older woman's hands. She was dark red, plump and glistening in the early morning light. For a moment her stillness frightened Matilda, and she was just about to ask what was wrong with her when a loud, angry cry burst out, and she kicked out her little legs with some indignation.

'Bless her,' Mrs Jacobson laughed. 'A little fighter, just like her mother.'

Placing the baby on Matilda's belly, she explained she was 'just dealing with the necessary'. Matilda neither knew nor cared what that meant. The pain had gone, she had a strong, healthy daughter. She would call her Amelia, Lily's second name, the sun was shining, in a few weeks she'd be with Cissie. All was right with the world.

'She's made of stern stuff, that one,' Mrs Jacobson informed Captain Russell an hour later. 'Never made a peep, except to cry with joy when she took her baby in her arms. I hadn't even got the water boiled up. But I don't know why I'm telling you all this. I expect you're just like my man and think having a baby is like shelling peas.'

'I know it isn't,' he said, looking towards the Jennings' wagon and wishing he had the right to go in there and tell her how proud he was of her. 'I just thank the Lord she was spared the suffering most women have. She's had more than her share already.'

For a moment the two of them just stood there smiling at one another. Until this moment they'd passed no more than a few dozen words with one another on the journey, with nothing more in common than that they both wanted to get to Oregon quickly and safely. Mrs Jacobson was plain, fat and prematurely old from farming and bearing nine children, and her only ambition was that her children should have a better life than the one allotted to her.

He was ruggedly handsome, lean and tough, born into wealth he'd walked away from. He took each day as it came, and he had no ambitions for he'd seen too many die without fulfilling theirs. But they were now linked by shared admiration and his affection for Matilda, and he was euphoric that she'd come through the perils of childbirth safely.

'Go and see her,' Mrs Jacobson said, suddenly aware that the Captain's eyes were misty. 'Seems to me that you two loners have a lot in common.'

James stood at the back of the wagon, his hat in his hand. Matilda was lying propped up by pillows, the baby in the crook of her arm. Her blonde hair was loose, falling over her white night-gown and the baby's head like a bolt of gold satin.

Over the years he'd seen many women just after they'd given birth, officers' and men's wives, relatives, and on wagon trains. But never before had he seen such serenity in a woman's face, or felt such a surge of utter tenderness.

'Well done,' he said, suddenly shy in the face of such beauty. 'I just came to offer my congratulations. I hear you managed like you always do, practically all on your own!'

She smiled, and her eyes were as blue as the sky above. 'That's not true. I couldn't have managed without Mrs Jacobson.'

'She's like a dog with four tails,' he said. 'You'd think after nine of her own she'd have nothing left to say on the subject. But she's off now, informing everyone. I guess we'd better lay over for a day and let everyone rejoice.'

'I don't think anyone will do that but me and Tabby,' she said.

'You're wrong there,' he said, hauling himself up on to the

back of the wagon. 'You've won yourself quite a little place in a great many hearts. Don't know quite how you do it when you call folks arse-wipes and the like, but seems you have. Now, can I have a look at the little 'un?'

She nodded and turned the baby round in her arms.

James didn't want just to look, he wanted to hold the baby himself. He got up into the wagon and crawled on his knees right up to Matilda, taking her baby in his two hands.

'As pretty as her mother,' he said, holding her up and kissing her nose. 'My wish for you is that you won't be so hoity-toity!'

Matilda giggled. It was so funny seeing such a tough-looking man holding a tiny baby. 'Oh, she'll be that,' she said. 'I shall train her from the start, and to shoot straight too.'

He smiled, perched on the edge of the bed, his knees sticking up awkwardly, and cradled the baby in his arms, looking carefully at her. Her skin was darker than her mother's and her hair as black as night. 'She doesn't favour you,' he said, smoothing her hair tenderly. 'I guess she takes after her pa.'

'I hope she inherits his nature too rather than mine.'

James half turned towards Matilda, saw the tears in her eyes, and still holding the baby with one arm, with his free hand patted hers.

'There'll never be a better time to tell you that I know who he was,' he said in little more than a whisper. 'Don't worry, no one knows but me, and from what I heard he was an even finer man than you let on. I'm only telling you now because I reckon you need someone to share that secret with right now and maybe talk about him. Am I right?'

He saw her face stiffen momentarily, then gradually soften, and a large tear rolled unchecked down her cheek.

'We were to be married. He went to St Joseph just to find a minister and he got shot.'

'That's what I heard,' he nodded. 'I'm so sorry I tried to rile you back at the start of the trail, I guess I was just an arse-wipe too. But you got a friend in me, any time you need one. You got all my respect.'

'Thank you, James,' she whispered.

'What, no Captain?' he said in mock horror.

'You can't go on calling someone Captain when they know all

your secrets,' she said, wiping her eyes on her sleeve. 'And you'd better give me back my baby and clear off, before folks start wondering about us.'

Two weeks later, as the Indian guide held the canoe steady on the banks of the Columbia river, James gave Tabitha a kiss and helped her into it. 'Be good, look after Matty, and God bless,' he said.

It was raining hard, he could see the river was rising, and he couldn't bear to think about the danger ahead in the Cascade rapids. But Matilda was adamant she must press on to her friend's home, or be forced to spend the whole winter in The Dalles, and Carl had hand-picked the guide because he was the most experienced man in the territory.

James turned to Matilda then. She looked so small and frail under the india-rubber cape, her eyes were full of fear, yet she was still forcing a smile.

'Thank you for everything, James,' she said shyly, looking down at the baby tucked beneath the cape. 'I really don't know what we would have done without you. We're going to miss you.'

James moved forward, kissed first the top of the baby's head, then Matilda's cheek. There was so much he wanted to say, but he was choked by emotion and the words he'd rehearsed last night just wouldn't come.

'I'll miss you too,' was all he managed to get out, cursing himself for losing his nerve now. 'Trust White Bear. He may not speak English but he's a good man, and no one knows the river as good as he does.'

'Write to me?' she said, looking right into his eyes and lifting her free hand to touch his cheek.

James nodded. But as he glanced around him he saw all the others who had come to see Matilda off. They had said their farewells under the shelter of the trees, and he knew he couldn't delay her any longer. 'Good luck,' he croaked, and taking her arm, helped her into the canoe, bending down to arrange her cape snugly round her. He turned then to Tabitha. 'I'll take good care of Treacle,' he said. 'He'll be on the raft with your wagon, guarding all your things.'

He thought it strange that he could manage to reassure a child about a dog, but that he couldn't tell her mother that he'd fallen in love with her.

White Bear leaped nimbly into the canoe, picked up his paddle, pushed off, and the canoe moved swiftly out into mid-stream.

Behind James a chorus of goodbyes came from the other members of the wagon train. Some ran along the bank waving and shouting out last-minute messages.

James just stood there, watching the little craft skimming through the water. His heart was as heavy as the sky overhead.

At four on a misty and chilly autumn afternoon four weeks later, Matilda was driving the wagon up a narrow, badly rutted muddy track. To both her right and left were meadows of tall waving grass, to her left the ground sloped down to a small brook. Ahead of her she could see a small log cabin and behind it dense woodland. The leaves were falling fast now, the ground covered in a blanket of red, gold, orange and yellow, and there was a smell of woodsmoke in the air. Nothing had ever looked more beautiful.

'Is that Cissie's house?' Tabitha said, holding baby Amelia tight to her chest.

'Well, it said "Duncan" on the board down there,' Matilda said with a chuckle. 'And it surely feels like we must be at the end of the trail.'

These last weeks had been a further test of her endurance. White Bear was an experienced guide, but it had rained constantly, the rapids were terrifying, and between being scared out of her wits, soaked to the skin and using all her ingenuity to keep little Amelia and Tabitha safe and dry, Matilda could only pray that they wouldn't be drowned so near to their journey's end.

At night they camped out in a crude makeshift tent in dense forest. Insects bit them, they heard wolves howling, imagined bears setting about them, and each time the baby woke yelling for more food White Bear would peer into the tent. By day Matilda knew this was out of concern for her and both her children, but in the darkness his silent movements and unintelligible language brought on panic and she wished she had defied James and insisted Treacle came with them. Tabitha caught a bad cold, turning hot then cold with fever, but still smiled bravely as if they were on a Sunday school picnic.

After so many terrifying patches of white water, long climbs down over rocks, with little Amelia strapped to a board on her back like an Indian papoose, Matilda ached all over for a bath, dry clothes, a warm bed, a cup of hot, sweet tea, and another English-speaking adult to reassure her it would soon be over. Only grim determination and the knowledge that if she broke down they would be lost, kept her going.

But they made it to Oregon City. The minister and his wife there took them in and at last she could have a real bath, dry napkins properly, feed Amelia in comfort, and pamper Tabitha as they waited for the wagon, oxen and Treacle to come down on a raft.

Autumn came in with a vengeance, bringing endless rain and cold winds, but safe in a real house, sitting by a fire, with the baby safe in her arms and Tabitha glowing with health beside her, Matilda could only thank God for getting them there.

It was still raining hard when the wagon arrived and many of their belongings had been damaged by river water, but Treacle's delight to see them again was so very cheering. Matilda had only the sketchiest of maps to the Duncans' house, drawn by the minister, only Treacle as a protector, but her old enthusiasm and optimism were back. The rain had finally stopped, the countryside was beautiful, and even the oxen seemed to sense they were nearly there, picking up a little speed.

'There's someone up there,' Tabitha exclaimed suddenly. 'He's got red hair. Is it Sidney?'

As the boy began to move towards them, Matilda laughed. 'It is,' she said, waving her hand at him. He faltered, peering at them and shielding his eyes from the afternoon sun. 'It's me, Sidney,' she yelled at the top of her voice. 'Matty!'

'Matty!' he yelled back with a tone of disbelief, then ran back to the cabin like a hare, screaming out for Cissie. The moment she appeared in the doorway with a baby on her hip, he turned again to run back down the path towards Matilda.

No reunion was ever sweeter than the moment Sidney held up his arms to help her down and she fell into them laughing and crying at the same time. He was firing questions at her that she couldn't yet answer, and all at once Cissie flew down the hill, her child jiggling on her hip.

She stopped short by the oxen, looking up at Tabitha holding the baby in her arms. 'A baby!' she said incredulously.

Matilda nodded and reached up to take Amelia from Tabitha.

'Where's Giles?' Cissie asked.

'He was killed, Cissie,' she said, hardly able to get the words out. 'Just after my last letter. Before we could even get married. I had to come to you. You were the only person I knew would understand. I couldn't warn you, a letter would have taken as long as me to get here. Is it all right?'

Cissie just gaped at her in shock for a moment. Suddenly her green eyes brimmed with tears, and shifting her own plump little dark-haired girl more firmly on to her hip, she held out her free arm for Matilda. 'All right?' she whispered hoarsely. I'd have been madder than a hornet if you hadn't come to me. You just come on in, all of you's, and tell me all about it.'

The log cabin was just one main room with Cissie and John's bed in a curtained-off area, and a smaller bed and a cot at the far end, but after the wagon it felt like a mansion. There were two small windows, a plank floor, a table and benches, and a real stove. Cissie proudly informed them that John had made the furniture, and they were the only people around to have real glass windows and a stove. He was at the place where he was building his sawmill, Peter was with him, and they would be back around seven o'clock for supper.

'It's so lovely,' Matilda said, suddenly feeling very awkward about arriving here unannounced. She could see that the bright rag rugs and the curtains were Cissie's handiwork, her appearance too was much more matronly, with her dark curly hair pulled back tightly into a bun. Now that Cissie had become respectable she might just have developed a prudish nature too!

Cissie seemed to sense her friend's anxiety, so instead of questioning her further, she suggested Sidney should take Tabitha outside to unyoke the oxen, sat Susanna on the floor with some wood blocks, took Amelia from her mother's arms, quickly changed her napkin and tucked her into a wooden box to sleep.

It was some time later over tea and thick slices of freshly made fruit loaf that Matilda gradually found herself able to explain what had happened since she last wrote, before Giles was killed.

'I can't tell you how terrible it was when he was killed, and then I found I was carrying his child,' she blurted out. 'I couldn't stay in Independence, I'm sure you know how it would have been. But I can see how you're fixed here, Cissie, just say if you want us to go. I only came because there was no one else to turn to.'

Cissie stood up, putting her hands on her hips with that familiar defiant expression in her green eyes. 'Now look here, Matty,' she said. 'Don't you go thinking I've got all stuck up, I'm still the same old Cissie even if I've got a wedding ring on me finger now, and a house of me own. I ain't never going to forget who the person was that helped me out of that cellar. I owe you, and now's my chance to pay you back. So don't you go talking about moving on. You and yours is staying here, for as long as you need us.'

By the time John came in, supper, a big pot of chicken stew, was on the table, and Cissie had moved Susanna's cot close to the bed Sidney shared with Peter, got the mattress out of the wagon, and made up a bed for Matilda and Tabitha on the floor. She said John would soon make another real bed, and they'd all be snug as bugs over the winter.

John's welcome was every bit as warm as Cissie's. He was terribly shocked to hear of Giles's death, even more so to find Matilda had a baby, but he quickly recovered and his words echoed his wife's.

'If it wasn't for you and the Reverend,' he said, reaching out to pat her hand reassuringly, 'I doubt Peter would have survived, and I wouldn't have met Cissie. So I'm glad to be able to take care of you and your children, Matty. Besides, Cissie and me love company. I really appreciate those fruit trees too, I can't believe not one died on the way.'

'I thought I was going to sometimes,' Matilda admitted with a chuckle. 'But I guess the trees didn't have to do anything other than guzzle up the water.'

Over supper they compared horror stories about their trips, all laughing at them now they were well behind them. It warmed Matilda's heart to see how happy John and Cissie were together, and how Sidney was as important to them as Peter and Susanna. He spooned food into the little girl's mouth as he ate his own, and it was he who changed her napkin and put her to bed in her cot.

'We'd have found it very hard when we first got here without him,' John said, smiling fondly as the boy tucked Susanna under a quilt. 'Cissie couldn't do much with the baby always in her arms. He chopped trees down with me, chained them up behind the oxen to haul them here, and worked like two grown men. Now I'm out at the sawmill getting that going, he does almost everything around here. I just hope he never wants to leave us.'

Sidney's head jerked up at that last statement and he grinned sheepishly. 'Nothing would make me leave you,' he said. 'You're my family now.'

Matilda's last thoughts as she drifted off to sleep that night with Tabitha and Amelia beside her were about Sidney's remark. She too felt as if she was with family. It was a good, safe feeling, as if nothing could ever hurt her again.

The next morning after John had gone off to the sawmill, and Sidney had taken Peter and Tabitha out to feed the animals, Matilda was sitting by the stove feeding Amelia while Cissie began to clear away the breakfast things.

'Tell me more about this Captain Russell?' Cissie suddenly asked.

'I told you everything about him last night,' Matilda replied in some surprise.

'No you didn't,' Cissie retorted. 'You said who he was, and that he was kind to you, but it sounded to me as if he were a bit more than a wagon master.'

Matilda giggled. Cissie had changed beyond recognition since her early days at the Home, yet even sober clothes and her dark hair tucked under a cap couldn't quite eradicate the street girl within her. There had always been her rather sly sideways glances, the ribald comments, the flash of mischief in her green eyes. To a certain extent it had still been apparent in Independence, but so muted that only someone who knew her well would notice it.

Now there was nothing to distinguish her from any other wife and mother. She was plump, and gently spoken, and her grey dress, spotless apron and the way her dark curly hair was restrained all spoke of complete respectability. Yet that last incisive remark about Captain Russell proved she hadn't quite forgotten her roots.

'Oh Cissie!' Matilda exclaimed. 'I was hardly likely to think of any man in *that* way in my situation. I just liked him. He became a real friend.'

Cissie rolled her eyes impatiently. 'You ain't talkin' to one of them Bible-punchers now,' she said. 'It's me you're talkin' to! You took a fancy to him, I know you did, and from what you've said he was sweet on you an' all.'

Matilda blushed, but knowing Cissie wouldn't let the subject drop she told her a bit more about him, including that he was the only one on the wagon train who knew she wasn't a widow.

'Well, how did you leave it then?' Cissie asked, sitting down at the still uncleared table and looking hard at her friend. 'Did he say he would look you up?'

Matilda shook her head. 'When we parted at The Dalles, he kissed all of us and wished us well. I asked him to write. He nodded. That was all.'

Cissie smiled. 'That's good enough. He'll turn up one day.'

Matilda laughed, she thought her friend was getting carried away. 'Of course he won't. He's got better things to do than look up a woman like me with two children in tow.'

Cissie could only smile knowingly at her friend. Her time as a prostitute had taught her a great deal about men. From everything Matty had told her she guessed this Captain Russell had fallen for her. She wondered if Matty had any real idea how truly lovely she was, not just her looks, though her blonde hair, pretty face and blue eyes would be enough for most men, it was what came from within that was her biggest asset.

In Cissie's view, Matty had an intriguing blend of innocence and earthy sensuality. She looked prissy and demure in her shapeless shabby dress, her hair all braided neatly, until she spoke and fixed people with that direct unwavering look that said she was afraid of nobody. It wouldn't take any man long to see her strong will, courage or kindliness, especially one as smart as Captain Russell sounded.

'Take my word for it, he'll turn up,' she repeated.

Amelia had fallen asleep at Matilda's breast. She gently lifted her away, buttoned up her dress, and then wrapping her in a shawl laid her down in her box.

'I can't love another man,' she said with a sigh. 'There's nothing left inside me now.'

Cissie heard the truth in that statement and saw the depth of sadness in her friend's eyes. She got up and went over to her, laying one hand on her shoulder. 'You might think that now, but it won't be that way for ever,' she said softly. 'Six months' time everything will be different.'

On 1 April 1849, Matilda stood at the door of the cabin sniffing the good earthy smell of spring, and those words of Cissie's when she'd first arrived six months earlier came back to her sharply. Cissie was right, everything was different now. She might still not want a man to love – Amelia, Tabitha and Cissie's family were quite enough for her. But she knew the time had come when she must think of her future.

A pale green haze of new leaves was on the trees, the grass was growing again, and the stream was heavily swollen from ice melting in the mountains. The winter had been very mild here compared with New York. There hadn't even been frost, just a great deal of rain, and she had heard men could grow corn all year round. The sow had produced fourteen piglets the other day, and the cow had two calves, and Tabitha was so entranced with them it was hard to drag her away. They would never starve here, the rivers were full of fish, there were rabbits, hares and deer everywhere, and so many different berries to pick they were spoilt for choice.

She loved it here, the beauty of the scenery, the cosiness of the cabin, the feeling of security in sharing a home with Cissie and John, and the happiness of watching the children playing together. Tabitha was nine now and shadow to fourteen-year-old Sidney. She'd become quite the little tomboy, choosing to wear a pair of boy's dungarees instead of a dress. Amelia was almost sitting up on her own now, and she liked nothing better than to be lying on a blanket near Susanna and Peter so she could watch them.

By day Matilda worked alongside Cissie, digging, planting vegetables, washing, cleaning and baking. By night they mended and made clothes for the children, as John worked away making something. He'd made a bed for Matilda and Tabitha, a fine pine one with the wood as smooth as a piece of satin. Amelia had moved on into Susanna's cot, when her father made her a bed of her own. He'd made a swing chair for out on the porch, and a cherrywood dressing table for Cissie which was as fine as anything Matilda had ever seen back in New York. Almost every day he talked of enlarging the cabin and making real bedrooms, his way of telling her he expected her to stay for ever.

On top of all this contentment there was the joy she got from Amelia. She was such a happy, contented baby, full of smiles and baby chatter. Often late at night Matilda would hang over the cot, just watching her sleeping. Her eyelashes were black, thick and long, like fans on her plump rosy cheeks, her eyes were dark blue, and her hair had remained as dark as Giles's and curly like his too. But even as she looked at her, Matilda knew Giles would want more for both her and Tabitha than growing up half wild in a log cabin.

Both Lily and Giles had often spoken of Tabitha's future. It had been their intention to find a good school for her once she got to eleven. Lily would perhaps have been content for her to learn lady-like pursuits and marry well, but Giles had wanted much more. Tabitha was very intelligent, her old ambition of becoming a doctor had never left her, even on the wagon train she'd mentioned it often. Matilda didn't think the medical profession allowed women to become doctors – if they did she'd never heard of one – but she did know that even to try for such a career meant getting the right education first.

'How on earth are you going to find the money for that?' she said aloud.

A letter had eventually arrived from the Milsons in England, sent on from the Treagars in Independence. Matilda had been shocked that a father replying to the news of his son's tragic death could show so little sorrow or compassion. He barely mentioned Giles, saying only that it had come as a tremendous shock that their son should end his days 'gunned down in a frontier town'. He dismissed Matilda's request to become Tabitha's guardian as 'kindly meant, he was sure, but inappropriate', and said that he believed there was an orphanage for children of clergy in New England which would be an ideal home for her, where she would have the benefit of a good,

Christian education. He suggested Matilda get in touch with the local Dean to this end. There was no mention that he or any of his family intended to keep in touch with Tabitha, or even any offer of financial aid. He ended the letter curtly saying he hoped Matilda would soon find a new position.

That last cold line said everything, a reminder she was a lowly servant and that she could keep her place. It was also confirmation that he was a stupid man as well as heartless, because he preferred to think his grand-daughter would be better cared for in an orphanage than with someone who had loved her since babyhood.

Matilda burned the letter without ever telling Tabitha it had arrived. In her view it was better for the child to believe any reply was lost, or even that her grandparents were dead, than to know the truth. As nothing came from the Woodberrys, Lily's parents, she had to assume they cared even less.

Yet her anger at these people was tinged with relief, at least they hadn't snatched Tabitha away from her. But a little voice at the back of her mind kept warning her too that Mr Milson might very well have written to the Dean himself and stated his wishes. That might cause trouble at a later date.

It was all this and more that Matilda thought about as she made her way down to the stream to collect some water. She knew Cissie and John loved having her and the children here, they claimed the work she did was worth far more than the food they ate, and this was probably true, but just the same she couldn't stay with them indefinitely, it wasn't right.

But what could she do to make herself independent? She had forty dollars, that was all, and that had come from the sale of the oxen. She might be able to claim a parcel of land, but how would she build a cabin and buy seeds for crops, tools and animals with so little? Her idea of being a teacher had been dashed some time ago when she made inquiries in Portland. Such jobs went to spinsters, and paid so little they had to live with their families. No one would take her on as a maid, housekeeper or for any other domestic job because she had children.

'You've been strange all day,' Cissie said in an accusing tone as they were preparing the supper. 'What's wrong?'

Although Cissie could read no more than the simplest words,

Matilda had found her to be very astute. John had once lovingly said, 'She knows how many beans make five,' and she did. She did everything by instinct – cooking, raising her children and growing crops – and her instinct served her far better than those who studied books. But her greatest talent was with people, she could tell just by the look of someone if she could trust them or not. She sensed even the best-hid anxiety or secret.

Knowing she wouldn't rest until she'd dug it out of her, Matilda told her what was on her mind.

'I love being here with you, Cissie,' she finished up, terribly afraid she might have offended her friend. 'But I can't stay for ever.'

Cissie surprised her by agreeing. 'I loved it at the Waifs' and Strays' Home,' she said. 'Just after you've had a baby you want nothing more than security and to be fed. But I got to want something more, a home of my own, a man. Maybe we ought to look around for a husband for you.'

Matilda riled up. 'Finding a man to look after me and the girls isn't an answer to me,' she snapped. 'I want a life of my own.'

'Whatcha gonna do then?' Cissie retorted, putting her hands on her hips, eyes flashing with irritation. 'Sell flowers on the street again?'

'I doubt anyone in Oregon would buy flowers,' Matilda said, putting her nose in the air. 'From what I've seen of your neighbours they are too dull to want a little beauty in their lives.'

'That ain't fair, and it ain't true neither,' Cissie snapped back. 'You know city folks only buy flowers to cover up the stink under their noses, so don't you get all high and mighty with me.'

Matilda was ashamed then, she knew Cissie thought she was implying she was dull too. 'I'm sorry,' she said. 'There's nothing wrong with anyone around here, least of all you. I guess I'm just getting nasty because I don't know what to do. How can I earn enough money to get my children a good education?'

Cissie shrugged. 'To me giving them good food and loving them is enough,' she said with a look of bewilderment in her eyes. 'I don't know nothing about education.'

'You've done all right without it,' Matilda said soothingly. 'But things are changing, Cissie, by the time our children are grown up it will be necessary for everyone. Don't you worry about Peter and Susanna?'

'They can go to the little school near the sawmill when they're old enough,' Cissie said stubbornly. 'And their pa and me can teach them everything else they need to know.'

Matilda fell silent then, she knew Cissie hoped her children would never go near a city, that they'd stay here, and eventually in the fullness of time take over the sawmill. She couldn't sneer at her simple ambitions, Cissie knew the dangers in cities, and perhaps she imagined education would make them too curious about the world beyond these mountains and pine forests. Yet while she understood Cissie and knew she and John had worked so hard to create this safe haven for their children, it was their haven and dream, not hers.

Chapter Sixteen

One afternoon around the middle of May, Matilda and Cissie were just collecting the dry washing from the clothes-line when John came riding up the lane in a fury, his horse steaming with perspiration from being ridden so hard.

'What's wrong?' Cissie called out, dropping the clean washing into the basket and running to him.

John worked long hours at his sawmill and he rarely came home before six-thirty in the evenings, so Matilda immediately imagined the worst, that he'd heard hostile Indians were heading this way. She looked nervously towards the cabin where the children were playing on the porch.

'Gold!' John yelled as he leaped off his horse. 'They've found gold out in California, bucket-loads of it.'

Matilda laughed, mostly in relief that it wasn't Indians, but also because it was unusual to see staid, sensible John in such a lather. Yet as she looked to Cissie, she saw alarm in her face at such uncharacteristic behaviour.

'Is that the reason you've left the sawmill, you great oaf?' she yelled at him. 'Don't you know any better than to believe in fairy-tales?'

'It ain't a fairy-tale,' John said indignantly. 'It's true, Cissie, and half the men in town are already preparing to go and get some.'

'Well, they're knuckle-heads,' Cissie retorted. 'Whoever heard of gold lying around waiting to be picked up!'

Matilda decided to keep out of it, although she guessed it had to be true as Captain Russell had spoken of the rumour a year ago, so she continued to get the washing in. John went off to tether his horse under a tree, he was clearly deflated to find himself in trouble rather than bringing joy and excitement. By the time he'd given the horse water and rubbed him down, Cissie and Matilda were back in the cabin folding the washing ready for ironing.

Cissie started in on him again the moment he came in, admonishing him for leaving his work early because he might have missed some customers.

'No one wanted timber today,' he said, shrugging his shoulders. 'You can't imagine how it is, Cissie, everyone's going crazy. Everyone's looking for a way to get to California.'

'I'm surprised you haven't yoked up a couple of oxen and gone yourself,' Cissie said tartly. 'Or were you intending to go on that poor horse you've already whipped half to death?'

'Did I ever say I wanted to go?' he asked, catching hold of Cissie to hug her. 'Would I leave my darling and my little 'uns for a bag of gold?'

His tone was teasing and Cissie's anger faded as suddenly as it had reared up. She responded to his hug and giggled. 'Well, why did you come home in such a hurry?'

'Because I thought you might like a ride down there to see all the men rushing into the store to get provisions and tools,' he said. 'I've never seen anything like it.'

Over coffee they discussed it further and finally decided it was much too late to go now, but they'd go first thing in the morning instead. Cissie had a great many jars of jam and preserves left from the previous autumn she could take in to sell, and by morning there would be at least a dozen freshly laid eggs too.

'Maybe I could sell my wagon to someone,' Matilda said thoughtfully. It had been laid up at the sawmill ever since she arrived and until now she hadn't imagined anyone would ever want to buy it.

'I'm sure you could,' John agreed, his grin stretching from ear to ear. 'Horses and mules are fetching a high price. I wish I had a couple of spare ones to sell.'

They talked of nothing else but gold all evening, John listing people they knew who were preparing to leave, and the gossip he'd heard about each of them.

'Jonas Ridley's wife is hopping mad,' he said. 'They said she reckoned she would take up with another man if he left.'

Cissie snorted with laughter at this for Mrs Ridley was a plain, fat woman with five children and known to be a terrible nag. 'I don't reckon she'll find many wanting to hop into Jonas's boots,' she said.

Matilda told them how Captain Russell had predicted that folk would go crazy if the whisper was true, and that in his opinion the smart people would let the fools rush off to start mining and they'd sit back and think of ways to provide goods or services to make a more certain fortune.

John looked thoughtful at this. 'Maybe I could supply timber for pit props and the like,' he said.

'You aren't going off and leaving me,' Cissie said quickly.

John smiled at her anxious expression. 'I'll never leave you,' he said. 'This is my home and here I'll stay. I'm gonna be one of those smart folk like Matty's captain talked of, I'll figure out a way to make a few bucks out of this gold without ever leaving Oregon.'

It was those words of John's which stayed in Matilda's head long after they'd all turned in for the night. She couldn't for the life of her see how John could organize any business with miners from such a great distance away. She thought only the man on the spot would get orders for timber, tools, building work and the like.

Oregon City *had* gone crazy, just as John had reported, and it was clearly extremely infectious, for although the men who were jostling, pushing and even fighting each other to buy picks, shovels and firearms at the stores came mainly from cabins up in the mountains and outlying farms, even the steady, sober residents who had established homes and businesses in town for some years appeared to be caught up in the madness. Anyone who had anything remotely appropriate to sell was out offering it. The blacksmith had a large sign outside his forge reminding people to get their shoes shod before they left, at the clothing store a table had been set up outside with piles of flannel work-shirts and pants for sale. Brisk business was being done by horse and mule traders, the general store had long since run out of tents, and a missionary was standing on a wooden box proclaiming to deaf ears that chasing gold was the road to ruin.

The saloon was packed to the doors, women stood around in groups twittering, many as wild-eyed and excited as their men who were intending to leave them, others crying pitifully and clutching babies to their breasts as if convinced their world was about to end.

After being in town for an hour or two Matilda was no longer so sure which side of the fence she was on. Although it did seem crazy for these men who had struggled across America to claim land, then worked so hard to clear it and grow crops, to suddenly up and leave, expecting their women and children to cope alone, she sympathized with them. Farming was a laborious way to make money, for most it would be years before they could make enough to move their families on from a shack to a real house, and perhaps too they even missed the excitement and adventure they'd experienced on the trail coming out here.

She too felt that yearning for sudden riches – a nugget or two of gold would be enough to start a small business, become independent, and maybe realize those dreams she had for her children.

By midday she had sold her wagon for sixty dollars to four men who intended to start the 630-odd-mile trek to San Francisco the very next day. If she was going she'd take the quicker sea route, and be first in line to stake a claim, but she didn't voice this, just in case it made them change their minds about buying the wagon.

Yet on the way home Matilda didn't dare admit she understood this rush to the gold fields for fear of coming between Cissie and John. She sensed that whatever John said, he was very tempted to go. Like her, he'd probably worked out for himself that only timber merchants there would get the orders. Clearly Cissie suspected he was torn because she kept up a barrage of scorn for the men who were abandoning their families.

Matilda thought her friend's insecurity was understandable. She had been abandoned as a child, and until she met and fell in love with John she'd never dared look ahead even one day. Now she had what she saw as a perfect life, and she wasn't going to allow anything to threaten it.

The children and Cissie were all worn out after their long day out, and after they'd gone to bed and John was smoking his pipe on the porch, Matilda slipped out to join him. An idea had come to her during the ride home, but she didn't want to raise it in Cissie's hearing.

'You could do with an agent in San Francisco,' she said in a low voice, hoping Cissie wouldn't overhear her. 'Someone you could trust to take orders for timber, and perhaps collect the money for you.'

John looked at her in some surprise, clearly he hadn't realized her mind was also on California. 'That thought came to me too. But I can't find anyone without going there,' he said. 'Even if Cissie was agreeable for me to go, who would look after the sawmill? Sidney's a good lad, but he isn't experienced enough to handle it alone. I guess I'll just have to wait a while until someone approaches me to supply them down there.'

Unlike his wife's, John Duncan's appearance hadn't changed since Matilda first met him in Independence. His beard was a little bushier, his sandy hair a touch thinner, but he still looked what he was, a sober, hard-working, muscular man. Yet in the last six months Matilda had come to see that he was more than just one of life's plodders, he was smart, ambitious and far-sighted. While most of the pioneers looked only to their immediate needs – rich, fertile land, a gentle climate, an abundance of wildlife and enough raw materials to build snug little cabins – he saw way beyond that.

He had often voiced a fear that scenically beautiful Oregon with its mountains, forests and wide rivers could easily be spoiled if someone didn't make a stand soon to prevent haphazard building by ruthless speculators. But to be able to have a voice in this place he'd come to love, to get the carefully laid-out towns he envisaged, with fine houses, schools and hospitals, he knew he needed to make his sawmill the most successful in the area, or no one would listen to him.

Matilda took a deep breath. 'I could go for you,' she blurted out. 'I know I don't know anything about timber, but you could give me samples to show around. I could go and see all the builders and carpenters and find out where they get their supplies from. You'd only need a few big orders to start with, then when they saw the timber was good, and you were reliable, you'd be bound to get all the repeat business.'

John turned to stare at her, his eyes almost popping out of his head in surprise that a woman could think of such a thing.

'You couldn't do that,' he said in a shocked tone.

'Why not?' she shrugged. 'Because I'm a woman? I drove a wagon two thousand miles on my own. I was selling flowers on the streets from a child and I'm a mean bargainer. I've got to find some sort of work soon so I can look after my children, so why not work for you so all of us could benefit?'

'Cissie wouldn't like it,' he said, shaking his head.

'Do you mean she wouldn't like me working for you, or that she'd object to looking after my children while I'm gone?' she asked.

'Of course Cissie wouldn't mind looking after the children,' he said quickly. 'She just wouldn't want you to go away, she'd be afraid for you. It could be dangerous down there for a woman alone.'

'But she knows I'll have to go somewhere, sometime,' Matilda said evenly. 'Better for me to do something which would help you two get rich than me getting a job in a store or something. Anyway, I can't see that going to California would be any more dangerous than coming out alone on the trail here.'

'I don't know what to say,' he said, frowning and scratching his head. 'I thought you were like Cissie, thinking they were all fools rushing off down there.'

'I do think the folk who believe they'll find bucket-loads of gold just lying about are fools,' she laughed. 'But what we saw today must be going on all over America and there'll be millions of those fools trekking out there. Just imagine John, every one of those men will need wood for something, whether it's for houses, carts, or just plain old stuff to burn on their fires. I don't know if there are forests in California like there are here, but you can bet your boots that if someone jumps in and has a supply of ready-cut timber ready to build with shipped straight down to the nearest port, they are going to buy it rather than taking time off to find a closer supply.'

John leaned his elbows on his knees and covered his face with his hands. Matilda guessed he was so stunned at her idea that he couldn't think straight.

'Think about it for the next day or two,' she urged him as she got to her feet to go back inside. 'I could do it, I know I could. I'd take a boat because it's quicker that way. Get you orders and come back fast. You could give me a percentage on them. I hate the idea of leaving Tabitha and Amelia even for a couple of days, but if it worked out real good, who knows, I might be able to move on down there and take them with me.'

She left him then to mull it over.

Early on Sunday morning two days later, as Matilda was down at the stream filling up the water pails, John came down to join her. He had said nothing more about her idea, and she knew he hadn't spoken of it to Cissie because her fiery friend would have had something to say on the subject.

'I think your idea could work,' he said, taking one of the full pails from her. 'I'm going to put it to Cissie this morning.'

Matty looked up at him. He looked tired, with circles beneath his eyes, obviously he hadn't been sleeping very well, but he had a look of determination too, and she knew he'd thought it through carefully. 'Shall I disappear for a bit?' she asked.

'That's a good idea,' he said and grinned. 'Better still, take the children with you.'

Matilda grinned back, she guessed he intended to soften Cissie up with love-making. 'I'll give you two hours,' she said. 'Don't forget to impress on Cissie that it could mean making enough money to eventually build a house in town.'

Much as Cissie loved her little cabin, she was a city girl at heart and missed seeing people every day. Matilda thought that would be her scheme's best selling point.

Matilda packed Amelia and Susanna into the little cart John had made for them and with Sidney pulling it behind him, Tabitha and Peter giving it the odd push to help over rough ground, and Treacle running excitedly around them, they set off along the well-trodden path up through the woods behind the cabin.

'Why did Uncle John want us to go out?' Tabitha asked almost as soon as they'd left. Although she was delighted to have a break from the usual chores she was too bright not to think there was something suspicious about it.

'Because he wants to talk something over with Cissie,' Matilda replied. She realized then she must tell Tabitha about it before they got back, and bring her round to the idea.

She waited until they'd got right up to a little glade half a mile from the cabin. Sidney had strung a length of rope from a tree there the previous summer and he leaped on it eagerly with Peter begging him to help him swing on it too. Leaving Amelia in the cart, she lifted Susanna out to play on the soft, lush grass, and put a blanket down to sit on.

'Come and sit with me for a minute,' she said to Tabitha. 'I've got something to tell you.'

It was very reminiscent of the day she told Tabitha about her expected baby. Like then, the child made no real protest, but her eyes were mournful.

'I wouldn't leave either of you if there was a better alternative,' Matilda said. 'But I have to make some money to make a real home for you and Amelia. Maybe Aunt Cissie will refuse – you see, she'll be frightened of me going to California on my own. But sooner or later I have to do something. It isn't right for us to depend on Aunt Cissie and Uncle John for ever.'

'Can't I come with you?' Tabitha asked in a small voice.

Matilda shook her head. 'I don't know what it will be like there. It might be tough enough for me to find somewhere to stay without having a child with me. I shall come back just as soon as I've got some orders for Uncle John. The longest part will be the boat rides either way.'

'Auntie Cissie said the other day that you ought to find yourself a husband.'

The prim tone of Tabitha's voice and her pursed lips were a sudden and sharp reminder of Lily.

'Is that what you'd like?' Matilda asked.

'Not unless it was Captain Russell,' Tabitha replied. She half smiled then, and Matilda saw she wasn't angry, only a bit sad.

'Well, Captain Russell hasn't come a-calling, so I reckon we have to forget him,' Matilda said regretfully. It had surprised her how often she thought about him, and she was very disappointed he hadn't come to find her, as he'd become such a dear friend. But as he hadn't even written, clearly he'd forgotten her. 'Anyway, I'm not going to marry someone just so they'll take care of us. I reckon I can do that myself.'

Tabitha asked a great many questions, most of which Matilda couldn't answer, all she could do was explain again that Aunt Cissie might not let her go anyway. 'But if I do go, you must promise me you won't worry, and that you'll look after Amelia.'

'Of course I'll look after my sister, but I might not be able to help worrying.'

Matilda hugged her tightly. 'You must always remember that

I love you. I know I'm not your real mother, but I think of you as my real daughter, just like Amelia. We've been through such a lot together, Tabby, and you are so very precious to me.'

'I love you too, Matty,' Tabitha said, reaching out and touching Matilda's face tenderly.

'I wouldn't go so far if there was any other choice,' Matilda explained. 'But if you still want to be a doctor, I've got to find the money to send you to a school.'

'Sidney won't like you going either,' Tabitha said, looking over to where he was swinging Peter on the rope. 'He loves you too.'

'I think he'll understand,' Matilda said. 'He had such a hard time as a little boy that he knows people have to do things they don't always want to, just to get by.'

Tabitha sighed. 'I know you are only going for me and Amelia,' she said in a tight little voice. 'But that won't help when I'm missing you.'

Matilda held the little girl tightly and bit back tears. Tabitha had been through so much, but she took it all without complaint. Silently she vowed to herself that come what may, she'd give the child what she deserved.

Two weeks later Matilda waved goodbye to her friends and children from the deck of a small tramp-steamer bound for San Francisco. She had two changes of clothing, timber samples and price lists from John in a carpet-bag, but her heart felt as if it were being torn from her. John held Susanna in his arms, Amelia was in Cissie's, Tabitha and Peter were standing either side of Sidney, and they were all waving frantically, but she knew that except for the three youngest who couldn't know the significance of the parting, each one of them was offering up silent prayers for her safety, success and speedy return.

At first Cissie had been horrified at the suggested plan, her weeping protests centred mainly on her fears for her friend, but eventually as she began to see the logic of the idea, she came round. It was she who insisted Matilda must look like a lady of quality if she was to be successful and suggested they went through the box of Lily's clothes and press them into service. Matilda was now wearing Lily's dark green wool cloak trimmed with velvet and the matching bonnet. Beneath it was a dark grey dress with a lace collar. The hooped petticoat felt uncomfortable and restricting, and without Cissie's insistence she would have left it off, but she supposed it was a small price to pay for the elegant figure she cut in the looking-glass.

The children's faces became a blur as the steamer picked up speed, all Matilda could make out now was Sidney's red hair and Tabitha's bright green bonnet. 'I love you all,' she whispered to herself, wiping her damp eyes. 'Be good and keep safe till I get back.'

It was night as the steamer approached San Francisco two weeks later. They had made excellent time as the weather had been good, but the journey had been very tedious for Matilda. She'd felt obliged to stay in her tiny cabin most of the time as she was the only female passenger on a boat stuffed to capacity with prospective gold miners. In the main they'd behaved in a disgusting fashion, more like excited little boys than grown men. When they weren't drinking themselves stupid or playing cards, they were being sick or fighting. The crew of the boat were every bit as bad – the original crew, all but two members of it, had jumped ship the last time they called in San Francisco, in search of gold like everyone else. The Captain told Matilda in confidence he expected the new crew to do likewise, all he could hope for was that there would be old sailors who were tired of California, ready when he got there to sign on to get home. He had told Matilda in no uncertain terms that San Francisco was no place for a lady, a town of tents, brawls, whores and gamblers, where the streets were mud, the air thick with foul language, and perversion of every kind was on public display.

Yet as they sailed into the small port Matilda was thrilled by the view. Some 300 ships lay at anchor, and behind them rose what looked like a huge, shimmering, golden amphitheatre. What she was seeing was in fact thousands of tents. They stretched from the waterfront right up on to the surrounding hills, the gold colouring from the candles and lanterns lit in each tent. As they sailed in closer, a hum above the sound of the waves and wind gradually became louder and louder until it became a ferment of music and shouting.

She stood back in alarm as her fellow passengers, many of them drunk, fought their way on to the launch boat. The Captain took her elbow and urged her to stay aboard till the morning for her own safety. She agreed gratefully, suddenly very aware of just how vulnerable a lone woman could be.

The noise from the town didn't let up until almost dawn. It was far worse than anything she'd ever heard back in Finders Court for the music, laughter and rough raised voices were often peppered with gun shots too. It crossed her mind she could always sail straight back again to Oregon, but to come so far and not inspect this town thoroughly seemed so very cowardly.

Cold, damp mist hung in the air as she was rowed to the jetty early the next morning. She clutched her cape tighter round her, and told herself that her first priority must be to find somewhere safe to stay and leave her bag. But as she moved to climb out of the boat, she found herself being hauled out bodily by a fierce-looking man in a coonskin cap and buckskins, a rifle over his shoulder, and terror gripped at her insides.

She was surrounded by men, the like of whom she'd never seen before. Brown, red, yellow and white faces, all gawping at her, pistols and knives stuck in their belts, and the smell coming from them made her feel faint.

'Don't be afeared,' the man in the coonskin cap said in a gruff voice. 'They ain't wanting to hurt you none, or rob you, they just ain't seen a lady in a while.'

She thanked him in a whisper and scuttled off, carpet-bag in hand, her heart thumping as loudly as the hammers she could hear ringing out all over the town.

Picking her way through heaps of merchandise just dumped on the dirt street, and avoiding teamsters who drove their carts at full pelt regardless of the throngs of men in their path, she reached the comparative safety of an ironmongery store. Stunned by the utter mayhem all around her, she paused.

What she could see, hear and smell was like London's docks, New York's markets, Independence just before the wagons rolled out of town, and perhaps Fort Laramie thrown in too. The noise and frantic pace were incredible. An auctioneer in a black frock-coat and top hat was standing on a box gabbling away so fast she couldn't make out what he was offering. Before him a crowd of men waved fistfuls of notes. Men were rolling casks, others hauling huge wooden crates. Mules, horses, and even baskets of live chickens added their voices to the din. Every nationality she had ever heard of was here. Mexicans with droopy moustaches in sombreros, mingled with Negroes, Indians and Chinese. Slender, dusky-skinned men argued with burly white men, she saw the gold-braided uniforms of ships' captains, the dark blue of the American army, and red flannel shirts of working men. Fleeting words of English wafted to her as she stood there, Scottish accents, Irish, Australian, but there were far more foreign languages. She had been warned that there were few women here, but she could see no more than perhaps four or five, among perhaps 600 men.

Taking a deep breath and telling herself they were all just people, with wives and children back home, she lifted her bag again and set off in the direction she hoped was the town's centre. The amount of quite valuable merchandise just left in the streets – a crate of cigars, a bundle of shovels, and many other such things – struck her as very odd as she walked. If this town was all the Captain had claimed it to be, why weren't they stolen? In London or New York they would be.

After a ten-minute walk through streets lined with wood-framed shacks covered in canvas, the ground beneath her feet a bog of rubbish and human effluent, she came to a plaza. Aside from an old adobe-built Custom House, the other buildings around the plaza were quite imposing wooden ones. As they were named the Alhambra, El Dorado, Veranda and the Bella Union, and a great many people were going into them, she assumed they were hotels, and hurried across to the Bella Union which looked the nicest.

But as she walked through the doors, to her astonishment she found it was a gambling hall, one great long room, made even longer in appearance by mirrors on the far end, and along the sides, tables for faro, roulette and monte. It wasn't even ten in the morning yet, but most of the tables were taken, a man played a harp sitting up on a raised platform in one corner, and the candles in the crystal chandelier were all lit.

She stayed for a moment or two, astounded by the sight. The men playing the games wore rough work clothes, knives and guns in their belts just like down on the wharf, but there were elegant women in beautiful satin gowns dealing cards, bankers in stiff collars and frock-coats with oiled moustaches.On the floor was fine matting, there were oil paintings on the silk-covered walls, and palms in tubs too.

She was soon to see that every building in the plaza was a gambling hall, and stopping to speak to a young lad with a friendly face, who was sweeping the steps outside the El Dorado, she heard that they were open all day and night, even on a Sunday. He told her men often played with nuggets of gold which were weighed by the banker before they began to play, but usually the gamblers left with nothing in their pockets.

When she asked him about hotels he directed her to a nearby street which he said was lined with them. She was puzzled however when she reached it, for it seemed to be only restaurants, dingy ones at that, with grand names like the Astor House, Delmonico's, Revere House and George Washington. The lad had been so adamant that they were hotels she assumed they must have rooms at the back, so going into the Astor House she inquired.

'A dollar a night, ma'am,' a swarthy waiter in a soiled apron replied. He jerked his thumb at a tier of narrow bunks lining the wall. 'Ladies up the other end.'

She found it hard to believe anyone would pay a dollar for a bed in full view of diners, but several were still occupied, the dirty blankets pulled over the sleepers' heads.

Out of sheer curiosity she went 'up the other end', but the only difference between this and the male end was that the bunks were even narrower and shorter, but a flimsy curtain had been added which could presumably be hitched across the front of the bunk.

It wasn't even a wooden or brick building, just canvas stretched over wooden lathes and a dirt floor. Her curiosity didn't go so far as asking if there was a wash-room, or even a privy. She was pretty certain such refinements were unheard of in this town.

As the morning wore on she became frightened that she would never find a decent place to stay. People were using anything and any place for some sort of shelter. She saw a rotten boat turned upside down and a crude hole cut for a door, several packing cases with men curled up in them like dogs in a kennel, even tepee-like tents, canvas wrapped around a few poles. As she walked further out of town, up on the hills, she saw close up the tented city which had looked so enchanting from the boat. It wasn't pretty close-up, even though jokers had put up signs with names like 'Happy, Pleasant and Contented Valley', for there were rotting animal carcasses lying around, tattered shirts left drying on prickly shrubs, filthy, unshaven men sprawled around in a drunken stupor.

Going back into the town she tried everywhere. There were so many saloons she couldn't count them, but the only rooms they had were for 'their girls'. She saw desperate-looking gambling shacks, an opium den, and countless brothels with frowzy-looking women in low-cut dresses urging the men in. She was shown one tiny canvas walled cubicle in one place, and such was her desperation that she was on the point of agreeing to take it, despite the filthy bare mattress, when she heard a man vomiting in the cubicle next to it. She fled from there, with the sound of the owner's ribald laughter ringing in her ears.

From time to time she caught glimpses of ordinary-looking ladies scurrying into stores, some smartly dressed, some in the calico dresses and sun-bonnets she'd grown so used to seeing on the wagon train. It cheered her to know there were regular folk here in this crazy town too, but their hurried, nervous manner reminded her of frightened deer and it was a further reminder that this town was not for ladies.

Most of the women on the streets were clearly prostitutes, some flashily dressed in gaudy silk gowns and fancy bonnets, but many more as bedraggled as the whores in New York. Like the men, they appeared to come from every corner of the world.

None of the streets were paved, there weren't even any sidewalks. She saw people emptying slop buckets and rubbish straight out into them. A dead mule abandoned there was so rotten that even the stray dogs ignored it. The stench was overpowering, far worse than anything she'd ever encountered in either London or New York. All she could be glad of was that the weather was good – she imagined that in the rain most streets would be impassable.

Yet for all the horror, and however despondent she was at finding nowhere to stay, there was an infectious, raw excitement in the air, very like being at a fairground. The men who were saddling up mules and horses to go on up to the mountains had a look of joyful expectancy on their faces. There was a frantically busy pace in the many small stores which sold everything from picks and shovels to camping stoves and blankets, and long queues outside the banks as men deposited gold dust, nuggets and money. She knew with absolute certainty that if she could find a bed, this town could be her own private goldmine. Several times she had stopped to ask people if they knew of anywhere to stay, and in the conversations she struck up she heard that all building materials, especially timber, were in very short supply, and prices of every single commodity were vastly inflated. To take her mind off the weight of her bag, and her aching feet, she mentally adjusted the price list John had given her, using local prices.

Finally, in desperation, she turned to the church. It was one of the oldest buildings in town, made of adobe and painted white, with a strong Mexican influence. It didn't matter that it was Roman Catholic, as a person who only considered God as a last resort, she didn't care about denominations.

Half an hour later as she left, she was more inclined to believe in God, at least for today. Not only had the priest, Father Sanchez, who had been inside, commiserated with her on her plight and prayed with her for her success in the town, but he'd given her a letter of introduction to some personal friends of his, Mr and Mrs Slocum, in Montgomery Street.

Mr Henry Slocum was a city alderman. Father Sanchez had said he was behind the idea for filling in tide lands along the cove and constructing a new wharf. Matilda had already been up Montgomery Street once today, for it was only around thirty yards from the waterfront, and found it to be one of the older and smarter streets in the town and the centre for banking and finance. She was determined she was going to charm Mr Slocum and his wife into taking her in as a paying guest, for aside from her own personal comfort, they might very well be interested in John's timber too.

She straightened her bonnet outside number eight and flicked the dust from the bottom of her cape, then, taking a deep breath, she walked up the two steps and rapped on the door knocker.

It was one of the best houses she'd seen in the town, a wooden-framed, shingled three-storey, well built and maintained with demure cream lace at the windows. A young Mexican maid answered the door.

'Father Sanchez asked me to call on Mr Slocum,' she said. She held out his note. 'This will explain everything to him.'

The maid's dark eyes scanned Matilda briefly, perhaps not entirely understanding what she'd said, but in halting English she asked her to come in and indicated she was to wait in the hall.

After the noise, dirt and confusion in the street, Slocum's house was almost church-like in its peace and cleanliness. The floor was waxed, a marble-topped side table held a glass dome with a stuffed bird, and a collection of black framed cameos hung on the wall.

To her left, just beyond the staircase, was the door through which the maid had entered, and from behind it she heard the murmur of a male voice. Matilda looked down at her gloves, they were light grey kid, and she regretted putting them on so early this morning for now they were stained from carrying the suitcase. But she couldn't remove them, the man would take one look at her rough callused hands and know she wasn't a real lady.

The door opened and the maid came out.

'Meester Slocum will see you now,' she said, bobbing a curtsey. Matilda stifled a giggle, no one had ever curtsied to her before. Leaving her suitcase in the hall, she swept into the room and smiled brightly.

'How very good of you to see me, Mr Slocum,' she said in just the way Lily would approach Giles's smarter parishioners. 'I do hope you won't consider it an imposition.'

Mr Slocum was a small, fat man, perhaps in his thirties, the lack of hair on his head in marked contrast to his bushy black beard, and he had a slight cast in one eye. He was standing by the fireplace, but she thought he had been working at his desk under the window when the maid interrupted him as there were a great number of papers and charts lying on it.

'It is always a pleasure to meet a lady in this town, there are so very few of them,' he said with a smile. 'Father Sanchez informs me in his note that you are a widow, Mrs Jennings, and you have come to San Francisco on business, but have been unable to find anywhere to stay. May I inquire what business are you engaged in?'

'Timber,' she said. 'I am acting as an agent for my brother-in-law's sawmill back in Oregon. But I've had a terrible time today. I tried several of the hotels to try and find a room, but I'm afraid they weren't what they advertised. I called on Father Sanchez in utter despair.'

He sympathized with her, asked her to sit down and take coffee with him, then went on to say his wife was visiting friends, but she'd be back soon.

It was such a relief to sit down, and she folded her hands on her lap so he couldn't see her stained gloves.

'San Francisco is not a place for a woman alone,' he said, looking at her intently, perhaps trying to guess how old she was. 'I find it surprising your brother-in-law sent you.'

'It was purely my idea and he took some persuading,' she said with a wide smile. 'You see, Mr Slocum, I have been left with two children, and I am not prepared to accept charity, not even from family. Mr Duncan couldn't leave his business at present, so it seemed to me that I should repay his kindness to me by helping him. Of course when I set out I had no idea how hard it would be to find accommodation.'

'Are you English, Mrs Jennings?' he asked. He had a very short neck, and when he moved his head, his body followed too in a most disconcerting manner.

'Yes I am, from London,' she said. 'I came over in 1843, and after two years in New York as a lady's companion I moved to Missouri where I married Mr Jennings, a widower with one small daughter. Sadly he died in December of '47, so myself and Tabitha his daughter joined a wagon train in the spring to see my sister in Oregon. My baby was born on the journey.'

She had changed nursemaid to lady's companion as it sounded better, just as Cissie being her sister did too. She could see Mr Slocum was both touched and impressed, exactly as she had intended. His face softened, and as the maid came in with a tray of coffee, she knew he was thinking he should help her.

'I am so sorry to hear about your husband, was he a farmer?' he asked, once the maid had left.

'No, a doctor,' she said. 'Tabitha wishes to follow in his footsteps too.'

'It seems ambition is common in your family,' he said, and his smile was warmer now. 'I am an ambitious man myself and I admire that quality in others. But Mrs Jennings, San Francisco is a dangerous place now that gold has been found. We have convicts swarming over from Australia, desperate Mexicans,

Chinese, all the very lowest class of person from this country and Europe, and many of them criminals. Every night someone is killed here, there is no police force, if the army was to come they'd only desert to the goldfields. I fear for your safety, my dear.'

'That is very sweet of you,' she said with a gentle smile. He was an odd-looking man, but he had a good deep voice and he was obviously a real gentleman. 'But once I find a safe place to stay, I won't be wandering about at night, or attracting any undue attention to myself. I would consider it a great favour if you could put me in touch with someone who would take me as a paying guest, just for as long as it takes to fill my order book and get a passage home.'

He silently drank his coffee, his one good eye staying right on her. Matilda was willing him to invite her here. She didn't care if he offered her a bed in the kitchen in return for some housekeeping duties. Anything would be better than having to trudge around those filthy streets again.

He put his cup down and sighed. 'Well, Mrs Jennings, I never could resist a lady in distress, and I know my wife Alicia would be glad of some feminine company,' he said. 'You must stay here with us, and perhaps in a day or two we can talk about your timber too.'

'Are you sure?' she asked, tempted to jump up and kiss him. She didn't care that he had a funny eye and no neck, she was overwhelmed by his generosity. 'That really is too kind of you!'

'Not at all, Mrs Jennings,' he said with a smile. 'We have plenty of room in our house, and it will be delightful to have someone new and interesting to talk to.'

It seemed to Matilda that Henry Slocum must be starved of company, for he kept her talking for quite some time, and told her a great deal more about himself and the town. He came from Virginia, where he studied architecture, but he had spent some years in South America before arriving here. He and his wife had no children, which he laughingly called a 'mixed blessing', adding that San Francisco wasn't a suitable place for them. Matilda got the impression from odd things he said that he was something of a maverick, who slotted himself into places where he could rise to a position of authority, possibly making a living out of town-planning schemes.

He spoke with some anxiety about fire being an ever-present danger in the town, and the need for something more than the volunteer fire fighters they had now. He wanted the streets graded and new houses to be built from brick. The lack of sanitation concerned him greatly.

Yet he showed no dismay about the wildness of the town at all. 'Yes, we need a police force,' he said. 'People get themselves shot every day here, both the innocent and the rogues. Just the other day a bullet meant for someone else brushed past my coat and singed it. In fights knives are invariably pulled. But there is no theft to speak of, these rough people have their own code. Should someone try to steal another man's property he is dealt with swiftly and mercilessly. You could have left your bag down on the waterfront, Mrs Jennings, and I could guarantee it would still be there now untouched. Likewise up in the hills, if a man stakes a claim, no one will try to take it from him.'

That at least made sense of the merchandise left in the streets, but Matilda wasn't so sure a place in which you could be shot or stabbed, but not robbed, could be said to have a high moral tone.

At seven that evening as Matilda changed for dinner, she was so excited by her good luck she could hardly fasten the buttons on her dress. Alicia Slocum had been a little chilly, but considering her husband had sprung a house guest on her the moment she came in, giving her no chance to consider whether she wanted a stranger in her home, that wasn't so surprising.

Alicia was a very elegant woman, tall, with lustrous, rather bulbous eyes and thick chestnut hair. Matilda got the impression she thought herself better than anyone else, she had a disconcerting way of looking down her long, thin nose, and merely nodding rather than attempting to strike up a real conversation. But as Matilda intended to be out all day anyway, she wasn't going to let that bother her. The room she'd been given was splendid. A big brass bed with lace-trimmed sheets, mahogany furniture, even an odd-looking kind of couch in front of the window which Alicia had called a chaise longue.

The bay with its many ships at anchor was just forty or so

yards from her window, and now at sunset it looked so beautiful. Even better, there was a china hip bath decorated with pink flowers in the closet adjoining the room, and Maria the Mexican maid had come up unasked and filled it with hot water for her.

Nothing could compare with the delight of stripping off her clothes and getting into that hot water, it took her right back to the first bath she had after the nightmare trip down the Columbia. On the boat coming here she had been lucky if she could get a jugful of water to wash in, and washing her hair was out of the question. She wallowed in it luxuriously, promising herself she would make so much money that one day she could have a bath every single day.

Her hands bothered her though, they really did look appalling – one fingernail was missing, ripped off back on the wagon train when she caught it in the folding legs of the table, and it hadn't regrown. There were scars, calluses and brown liver-spots, even the goose-grease she'd been putting on them every night on the boat hadn't improved them.

Cissie had suggested she wore Lily's lacy gloves, even indoors, and that had seemed a good idea, but did ladies wear gloves while they were eating dinner? Somehow she didn't think so.

When she got out of the bath she found Maria had unpacked her clothes, pressed her two dresses and hung them up in the closet. She decided she would keep the gloves on at all times – she might be considered odd, if no one else did, but that was better than having her hands stared at.

'You can't make a silk purse out of a sow's ear.' Matilda was reminded many times in the ensuing days of the phrase her father had so often used. By day, going about in the town she felt confident. Being bold, female and English gave her a distinct advantage, businessmen agreed to see her even when they were busy. John had given her enough information about his timber to speak knowledgeably, and her fast arithmetic impressed these men, so she got the orders she wanted.

But each evening back at the Slocum house, she was only too aware of her shortcomings, and she felt as though she was being put through slow torture. Time and again she was tempted to fake a headache to excuse herself from having dinner with them and their many guests, but she couldn't do that. She sensed Mr Slocum hadn't invited her to stay purely from kindness, rather that in this male-dominated town she was something of a trophy which he wanted to display. Perhaps too as timber was such a valuable commodity, he wanted to keep her right where he could see her.

Maybe if she'd been brave enough to confide in Alicia right away that she wasn't accustomed to mixing with society folk, the woman might have made things easier for her, but by saying her late husband was a doctor, she had inadvertently set a trap for herself.

She had believed the Milsons had trained her well enough to mix with anyone, but she was wrong. Their ways were country ways, their food was plain, and there was never any wine. The Slocums served fancy food she had no idea how to tackle, their guests seemed to bring out the worst in her, and she soon discovered her clothes were all wrong too.

The first night here had been humiliating, though in fairness to the Slocums it was her own fault, not theirs. Unused to wine being served, when she saw her full glass she thought she must drink it or they'd consider her odd. The guest that night was Jose de Galvez, a swarthy, black-eyed man with an oiled moustache and large sparkling white teeth, who paid her far too much attention. Matilda gathered, before the wine took effect and made her head swim, that the Slocums had met him and his family when they were living in South America. Jose had a large cattle ranch there, and he had come to San Francisco to make some deals for his beef.

'Henry he tell me you drove a wagon all alone from Missouri to Oregon,' he said with a heavy Spanish accent. 'That ees remarkable, Mrs Jennings. Weren't you afraid?'

'No,' she said. 'There were sixty or more wagons with me, being exhausted was the worse thing, but then of course I was pregnant.'

The moment that word came out she knew she'd made her first drastic mistake. No lady ever used it, they wouldn't even speak of 'a delicate condition' in mixed company.

Maybe if she'd stopped right there it wouldn't have been so bad, but she tried to justify herself. 'I'm sorry, I know one isn't supposed to use that word. I can't think why, it's the right one.

But then in America you can't even say "pants", can you? It's sit-me-downs, nether garments or even unmentionables.'

Alicia's bulbous eyes nearly popped out of her head. Henry blushed and Jose smirked.

'Of course, Mrs Jennings is English,' Alicia simpered to Jose. 'I do believe the English enjoy teasing us Americans.'

Alicia's remark, along with the stimulating effect of the wine, made Matilda forget the lessons Lily had taught her about sticking to light, frothy conversation at the dinner table. She brought up the subject of slavery, the plight of the poor in New York, and when Jose and Henry made patronizing remarks about their wives, she couldn't let them pass by.

First Henry said something about Alicia's head being too stuffed with gossip to take in anything about world affairs, then Jose laughingly said his wife was so lacking even in knowledge of her own people's history that she had thought Spain must be a town somewhere in South America.

'Do you ever take your wife travelling with you?' Matilda asked Jose, suddenly seeing a mental picture of a lonely Spanish woman left all alone on a ranch while her husband travelled the world.

'Oh no, my dear Mrs Jennings,' he replied, rolling his dark eyes. 'Rosita stay home with our children always, she has no interest in other places.'

'How would you know if you never take her anywhere?' she asked.

He looked at Henry as if for support.

'South American women are very different from Europeans, Mrs Jennings,' Henry said feebly. 'They like to stay at home.'

Matilda chortled with laughter. 'I wish I'd got a dollar for every time I heard that statement on the wagon train,' she said. 'They would say it about German women, Dutch, Indian squaws, French and Americans. It's rubbish, women are basically the same everywhere, just as men are. Given half a chance, all women would welcome seeing new places.'

'I'm not so sure that's true, Mrs Jennings,' Alicia piped up, her face a little flushed. 'Very few women have chosen to come with their men to San Francisco.'

Dressed for dinner in a coffee and cream lace gown and her chestnut hair swept up into a coif on top of her head, Alicia was a handsome woman. Matilda had been fooled by her looks, imagining her to be intelligent and strong-willed, but that foolish remark proved she was neither.

'Their men didn't offer their women the chance to come here, any more than Mr Galvez offered it to Rosita,' Matilda retorted. 'They just took off from their homes with scarcely a thought for their wives and children. Judging by the amount of saloons and gambling dens I saw here this morning, most will slink back with less than they came with. And as I also saw plenty of evidence of prostitution, I dare say they'll take a few nasty diseases home too.'

It was then she realized she had drunk too much and she was being rude, not amusing. 'I'm sorry,' she said, blushing at her outburst. 'I just get cross when I think of what some women have to bear.'

'You are quite a leetle firebrand,' Jose said with a smirk. 'You should go far in your business.'

She managed to get through the rest of the meal without disgracing herself further, but when the men retired to Henry's study for a cigar she tried to explain herself to Alicia and asked if she didn't get angry when men made such foolish remarks about women.

'Angry?' Alicia exclaimed, raising one perfectly arched eyebrow. 'Why should it make me angry? Men don't wish their wives to interest themselves in anything outside their homes because it's their way of protecting us from unpleasantness.'

'It isn't,' Matilda retorted. 'It's their way of keeping us down. In my opinion most women have far more common sense than men and if they'd only stand up for themselves, learn about things outside their home, they could use their influence to make this a better, fairer world.'

'It's fair enough to me as it is,' Alicia said. 'As long as I have a husband to look after me and pay my housekeeping and dressmaker's bills, I'm perfectly happy.'

'I can't really believe that's all you care about,' Matilda said, her eyes widening with shock. 'Don't you ever look at the filthy streets in this town and think of putting pressure on your husband and his friends to get something done about them? Don't you worry that all these men in the town have deserted their wives and children to come looking for gold? Are your dressmaking bills more important than that?'

'Well, I can see you don't spend money on dressmakers,' Alicia replied, looking pointedly at Matilda's dark blue velvet dress. 'But if you can take your mind off business or our dirty streets for an hour or two while you are here, I'd be happy to introduce you to my French dressmaker. She instinctively knows what is right for one.'

Matilda was stopped short. She had thought that Lily's dress was perfection and that it would take her anywhere. She knew Lily had had it for several years, but that meant nothing to a girl who had once owned only one shabby dress. But worse than having her dress sneered at was the knowledge Alicia had seen through her pose as a 'lady'. She was probably angry at her husband for inviting her to stay, irritated that Matilda set herself above other women by taking an interest in business, and jealous because she was both pretty and outspoken. Sniping at her dress was an attempt to shake her confidence.

'Clothes don't mean a thing to me,' Matilda said airily. 'I have always thought women who follow fashion are rather like sheep. I am far more concerned with important things, like my children's future. This dress is a few years old, but it's good enough for this town.'

She got a twinge of pleasure at seeing Alicia's supercilious smile fade, but almost immediately she felt ashamed, after all she was only a guest, and an uninvited one at that.

'I think I'd better go to bed now,' she said awkwardly. 'I can't thank you enough for your hospitality. You really are so kind.' She rushed off to her room then, and once there gave way to tears. It wasn't clever to set Alicia against her, she was missing her children dreadfully, and if she didn't get any orders for John, it would all be for nothing.

But she did get the orders. Nine days later, only one man out of over thirty she'd seen had turned her down. Henry had given her a huge order for the planking he needed for his wharf, and he said if the first shipment was good quality and came within four months, he'd give John a regular contract. This helped to keep up her spirits when she had to put on her velvet dress night after night, and saw Alicia's sneers. It helped her to refrain from saying anything subversive to the Slocums' dinner guests, no matter how much they riled her. It soothed the ache of missing her children, and she found she could escape from the tedious evenings by letting her mind slip away to imagining Cissie's and John's pleasure when she came back with a full order book.

Yet being here alone, away from her friends and children, had taught her a great deal, and perhaps the most valuable lesson of all was that she must accept herself as she really was. She remembered how she'd once told Flynn she was neither fish nor fowl, and she saw it was even truer now than it had been then. She didn't have the background, or the frivolous softness to pose as a real lady. She also knew she had lost the docility she once had, so she could never step back and become anyone's servant again.

But she had proved she had a head for business by her full order book. She also knew now she had the nerve, brains and ambition to reach any goal she set herself.

Sadly, she knew that she had gone as far as it was possible to go on John's account. He couldn't physically cope with any more work than she'd already got him. While he was going to be delighted with her, once the timber was felled, sawn and shipped down here, the buyers would then deal directly with him for repeat orders and she'd be obsolete.

Matilda knew John would want to continue giving her commission on all accounts she'd opened. But after a taste of business, she wanted more than just living on her commission in a remote cabin. She wanted something that was all her own. A business which she could build, perhaps to pass on to her children and grandchildren.

Each day as she went around San Francisco she studied the town and its people carefully. The horror she'd felt on her first day here had left her once she discovered more about it. Two years ago the population of San Francisco was just some 800. It had little to recommend it, with its chilly mists and sparse vegetation, other than its safe harbour. But since gold was discovered in the surrounding hills, that population had soared to well over 25,000, with hundreds more arriving every day, by sea and across land from the East. She'd heard tell that in one week alone some 600 vessels lay out in the bay, and the captains were unable to sail away as their crews had deserted them.

The gold-seekers didn't stay in San Francisco, they brought their equipment and provisions then hastily left for the mountains. But they came back to sell their gold, have some fun and spend their money. When the fall came and it was too wet and cold in the mountains, they returned again. The whole town's prosperity was built on just this, which was why no one was anxious to calm the madness, or clean up the seedier side of it. Gold was the only export from the town. Everything the ever-increasing population needed, from food, drink and clothes to equipment and machinery was imported and sold on at a vast profit.

One day she watched a man standing on top of Telegraph Hill sending semaphore messages with flags. Henry had told her it was this man's job to spot ships coming into the bay, then alert businessmen about what sort of ship it was and the cargo it was carrying, so that they could be first at the wharf to meet it and offer a price for the entire cargo. The auctioneer she'd seen on her first day was one of many, and even an absolute novice bystander could make a swift and handsome profit by bidding for a crate of cigars, silk handkerchiefs, shovels or pails, then hawking them off around the town.

Captain Russell had been so very astute when he said the smart people wouldn't go mining. Each day as she walked around the town, Matilda saw the bankers from the casinos, the restaurant owners, the builders and even fishermen with great wads of money. And she wondered what she could supply to this town that someone else hadn't already thought of.

Nothing came to her. Someone had thought of everything, there was even a man making and selling chocolate, women offering to wash shirts for five dollars each. The only thing she'd noticed was missing were flowers. But even if it were possible to ship flowers here before they wilted, who would buy them? Certainly not the miners.

On Matilda's ninth day in town, it was after five when she got back to Montgomery Street, and when Alicia opened the door to her with red-rimmed eyes, instead of Maria, she guessed immediately that the maid had left.

Matilda wasn't too surprised by this, she'd heard Alicia laying into Maria countless times, and often seen slap marks on the girl's face. A young, pretty girl could go straight to any of the casinos and get well-paid work immediately; if she wanted a husband she could take her pick from hundreds of eligible men.

'I'm so glad you've come home. Maria has left me,' Alicia blurted out, breaking into fresh tears. 'I don't know what I'm going to do. You can't get a maid anywhere in this town.'

Matilda groaned inwardly. Alicia was stupid, vain, and far too self-righteous, and although she had tried very hard to find something she liked about her, she hadn't yet discovered it. Yet remembering that but for Henry's kindness in taking her in she might have been forced to sleep in a canvas cubicle, she knew she must comfort and console his wife.

'How awful for you,' she said, putting her arm round the woman and taking her into the parlour and sitting her down. She poured her some brandy, and sat down by her to listen.

As Alicia sobbed out how well they had treated the girl, giving her food to take home for her family, old clothes and even an entire day off now and again, and she couldn't understand why she'd gone, Matilda had to bite her tongue not to say perhaps the girl didn't feel appreciated.

Instead she offered the idea that maybe someone had made the girl a better offer. At that Alicia suddenly sat up straight and blew her nose.

'I know all the quality people in this town,' she said archly. 'Not one of them would stoop to poaching one's maid. It just isn't done.'

'Well then, perhaps she's gone to work at something else,' Matilda replied. She wished now she'd thanked Maria personally for bringing up her bath water. Two flights of stairs was a long distance to carry several pails of water. She of all people knew how heavy they were.

'What could she do? She doesn't even speak good English,' Alicia snapped, full of indignation. 'There's something very peculiar about this,' she went on. 'When I said she was being foolish running out on me, she muttered something to the effect that she could get paid ten times for doing the same as she did here. Do you know, Mrs Jennings, that I paid her four dollars a week? No one would pay more than that for a maid.'

Four dollars a week was very good wages for a maid. Matilda

had only got two dollars a month. But then everything was overpriced in this town.

'She even said something nasty about Mr Slocum,' Alicia went on. 'She said he was mean and implied he didn't give her something he'd promised. I tried to find out what it was, but she pretended not to understand. What do you make of that!'

Matilda hesitated, that sounded very much like complaints other flower-girls had aired about the men in their life. 'I expect he promised to get her an extra day off or something,' she said quickly. 'Then he forgot about it.'

Could Henry have been having his way with Maria, she wondered. Men had been known to promise the moon for just that. She knew countless girls who'd never got what they were promised.

It was feasible. Maria had slept down in a little room at the back of the kitchen. Henry always seemed to stay up long after Alicia retired to bed. One night when Matilda couldn't sleep she'd heard Henry's footsteps coming up the stairs just as the clock down in the parlour struck two. Had he been in Maria's room?

Then there was the remark about getting paid ten times more for doing what she did here. She couldn't get forty dollars a week as a maid anywhere, but she could as a prostitute. If Maria had been submitting to her master's lust on top of all her real work, she probably did think she might as well join the women who got paid well for it.

Matilda was horrified to think a man in Henry's position would do such a thing, but even more worried about Maria. Unable to say anything to Alicia, she offered to make some tea.

As she entered the kitchen she groaned. It was in the most appalling mess, with the previous evening's plates, pots and pans still unwashed on the table, along with the breakfast things.

Exactly how this house was run hadn't ever concerned her, she always went out straight after breakfast, and stayed out as long as she could. But she did know another woman came in daily to prepare and cook the evening meal, as Alicia had boasted she was lucky to get her, for she was the best cook in San Francisco. Clearly Maria had decided to stop work after last night's dinner, and only served breakfast this morning just to avoid a scene with her master before he left for his office.

Matilda's first thoughts were that she should get out of this house as soon as possible. But if she did that Henry might cancel his order for timber. He could even persuade others to do so too. There was no point in her being righteous about him and Maria, she could be wrong. Besides, Henry had shown her great kindness, and if she was to start a business in this town, she would need his support.

She made the tea and took it back to Alicia, who was now lying down on the couch.

'Maria didn't wash up before she left,' Matilda reported, though she was sure Alicia already knew that. 'I'll do it now. You stay where you are and rest.'

Predictable Alicia gave her a watery smile. 'Oh Mrs Jennings, I can't let you do that.'

'I've had a little experience of washing up,' Matilda said lightheartedly. 'You don't want to lose your cook, do you? She'll be off too if she comes in to see that lot.'

It took her over an hour to put the kitchen straight. By the time she got back to the parlour, Alicia had composed herself with the aid of another brandy.

'It's fortunate we have no guests tonight,' she said, yawning and lying back on the cushions. 'Mr Slocum has a business meeting so he won't be in either. So it will be just us for dinner. I shan't dress, I'm feeling too weary, so don't feel you have to either, my dear. Cook will be in any minute so I'll just pop down to speak to her. Maybe she'll know someone who can take Maria's place.'

That evening seemed interminable. Alicia had no conversational skills, she would ask a question, but then as Matilda answered it, she would look away, or say something else, entirely unrelated. By the end of the evening Matilda was even beginning to feel sympathetic towards Henry. While she disapproved of him seducing the maid, she could understand perfectly why he might take a mistress, and indeed why he'd invited her to stay, knowing very little about her. His wife was just so empty-headed and utterly dull, almost anyone would make a welcome diversion.

'You've been very kind having me as your guest,' Matilda said, just before she made her excuses to go to bed. 'But I think

I must see if I can get a boat home tomorrow. I have a full order book now, and I'm missing my children terribly.'

She saw pleasure creep into the woman's bulbous eyes, but predictably she pretended to be distraught.

'Oh no, you can't go just yet,' she said, holding out her hands to take Matilda's. 'It has been so nice to have another woman to talk to, and you have been so kind to me today.'

'A little washing up was nothing,' Matilda replied. 'Especially after you'd looked after me so well. But I hope we will see one another again soon. I expect I shall be back. Hopefully someone will have built a real hotel by then and I won't have to impose on kind people like yourselves.'

Next morning Matilda came downstairs to find Henry standing over the kitchen stove with a look of bewilderment on his face.

'I put some water on for coffee some time ago,' he said. 'But it won't boil.'

Matilda wanted to laugh, but she didn't dare. 'It has to be raked out and lit each day,' she said. 'Don't worry, I'll do it.'

It took her only a few moments to see to it, Henry stood there looking at her in wonderment as she lit twists of paper and then fed in small pieces of wood.

'You are a marvel,' he said once she had a good blaze going. 'Where on earth did you learn to do that?'

'As a child in London,' she said with a smile. 'We had no maid in our family. It proved a very useful talent on the wagon train, you have to learn to make a fire even when it's raining.'

Alicia was still in bed and Matilda thought she'd probably stayed there purposely, so she offered to make the breakfast, and as she whisked up some eggs, she told Henry she was intending to see if there was a boat to Oregon leaving today.

'First Maria, and now you,' he exclaimed in some alarm. 'I do hope you aren't leaving for the same reason.'

That remark suggested he blamed his wife for Maria's hasty departure. There was certainly no guilt in his eyes, only a look of concern.

'There's no connection, I assure you,' she said, suddenly feeling a lot easier being alone with him. 'I've got all the orders I need now and I miss my children too much to stay any longer.'

'I tend to forget you have a family,' he said. 'Last night I heard there is a boat leaving at four this afternoon. If you really are set on going I'll take you down there after breakfast and make sure you get a decent cabin.'

Matilda thanked him and they chatted quite comfortably about the children, and Oregon, while they waited for the stove to get hot. After a breakfast of scrambled eggs, ham and coffee, which they ate in the kitchen, Matilda took a tray upstairs to Alicia, and said her goodbyes. She was so relieved to be leaving that she even kissed the woman with some warmth.

'What a lovely morning,' Henry said as they left the house a little later.

There was no mist for once, the sun rising up in a clear blue sky, and before them the bay with its many ships looked enchanting.

'It is, isn't it,' Matilda agreed, smiling at him. He was wearing a silk top hat and a dark grey tail-coat, and he cut quite an imposing figure, even carrying her carpet-bag. 'If I wasn't so overjoyed at the prospect of seeing my children again, I could almost be sad to go.'

'I should have said this first thing this morning,' he said a little hesitantly. 'I was appalled Mrs Slocum allowed you to clean up the kitchen for her yesterday. I regret to say she can be rather presumptuous, and not a little disagreeable.'

'I didn't mind tidying the kitchen at all,' she said, sensing that he was trying to tell her his marriage was not an entirely happy one. Wanting him to feel she sympathized with him, she put her hand on his arm. 'Mrs Slocum and I have such different backgrounds and interests I'm afraid we were destined never to be real friends. But I was very grateful for your hospitality, and I do hope I haven't offended either of you. I'm afraid I am a little outspoken.'

'You did not offend me in any way,' he said, looking sideways at her. 'I found you to be an interesting, stimulating guest, and I very much admire your business acumen.'

'Well thank you, sir,' she smiled, fluttering her eyelashes just a little. 'I would really like to start a business of my own here. I sincerely hope I could count on your advice and knowledge if and when I do.'

'My dear Mrs Jennings,' he said. 'I would consider it an honour to help in any way I can. I believe you are a very rare bird, not only beautiful, warm and amusing, but with a fine brain tucked away under that pretty hair. You could do well in this town.'

Henry said goodbye after arranging her passage home and inspecting her cabin. A short while later Matilda left the boat for one last look around the town and to buy some small presents for the children.

She had finished her shopping within an hour and was on her way back to the boat when she stopped to look in the window of a cigar store, amused by a display of stuffed racoons, each with a large cigar in its mouth. Suddenly she saw reflected in the glass a young girl passing on the other side of the narrow street. Just the way she appeared to glide, rather than walk, reminded her of Maria.

She turned abruptly. This girl was wearing a stylish bright yellow dress and a straw bonnet, but her glossy black hair and golden skin were most definitely Mexican.

Maybe if the girl hadn't looked across at Matilda, and paused for just a second, a look of alarm on her face, Matilda would have thought she was mistaken, but with that the girl suddenly broke into a run, rushed up a flight of wooden stairs at the side of a chandlery and disappeared.

Without stopping to think, Matilda darted after her.

The steps led to a wooden veranda, which went round the back of the upper floor of the building. There were several chairs and tables, and two doors. Matilda knocked on the first one.

It was only as she waited that she questioned why she was chasing the girl. They had established no rapport in her stay at the Slocums', and Maria was bound to see her as an enemy. Was it really any of her business why she left?

However, it wasn't Maria who opened the door, but an old woman dressed entirely in black with a mantilla of black lace over her white hair.

'I just saw Maria come in here,' Matilda said. 'Could I speak to her for a moment?'

'What business do you have with her?' the old lady asked. She had a tinge of a foreign accent, though Matilda couldn't identify it, her eyes were bright blue and very sharp, and they seemed to bore right into her.

'No real business at all,' Matilda said. 'I was a guest at the house where she was working and I was concerned about why she left so suddenly. I have left that house now too, but when I spotted her just now I just wanted to be certain she was all right.'

'Why would you care about a Mexican maid?' the woman said scornfully, looking her up and down.

Matilda riled up. 'I'd like to think I could spare a thought for anyone who had been ill treated, whatever their position or nationality,' she snapped back.

To her utmost surprise the woman smiled. She had only two teeth left in her mouth, and smiling should have made her look older still, but instead she suddenly looked years younger.

'You must be the English woman everyone is talking about,' she said. She cocked her head on one side and looked quizzically at Matilda. 'You are every bit as pretty as they said, but that green cape and bonnet doesn't do much for you.'

The woman might be old, and her face as crumpled as an ageing apple, yet there was something very attractive about both her and her voice. Even her personal remark had a note of humour about it.

'I didn't wear it for any other reason than to keep warm,' Matilda retorted. 'Now, may I speak to Maria for a moment?'

'Would you like to step inside?' the old lady asked, opening the door wider to reveal a small hall decorated in dark red and gold. 'I wouldn't normally ask a lady like yourself in, but since you are concerned about Maria, I feel it would be better for you not to be on public display up here on my veranda.'

In a sudden flash of intuition Matilda realized that this place had to be a brothel and the woman the madam.

'You do know what this house is?' the woman said before she could back away. She smiled as if amused by Matilda's shock.

The smile was a challenge to Matilda. She was too proud to admit she'd blundered up here without realizing. She was also curious.

'Oh yes,' she said as boldly as she could manage. It was after all the middle of the day and she couldn't see that she could come to any harm in broad daylight. 'But I can only stay a few minutes as I am booked on to a boat leaving soon.'

The old woman left the front door wide open and led the way through another door. Matilda followed, fully expecting squalor, but instead she found herself in a large and very luxurious room. It was gloomy, for the light from windows overlooking the street below was muted with heavy lace curtains, stale cigar smoke mingling with the smell of fresh polish. The walls were deep gold, the many couches dark red, and a chandelier hung from the ceiling.

For a second she thought she had jumped to the wrong conclusion about the nature of the place, until she turned and saw a painting of an almost naked woman reclining on a bed, hanging over the fireplace.

A tinkling laugh from the old lady startled her. 'My dear! Your face is a picture. I am *so* sorry, you said you knew what this house was.'

'I did,' Matilda said with more confidence than she felt. 'But I have never been in a brothel before.'

'A brothel!' the woman exclaimed with some indignation. 'This, my dear, is a parlour house.'

Cissie had used that term occasionally and from what Matilda remembered it meant the 'girls' were high-class whores, operating in a place which was something like a fancy gentlemen's club, where the members had a few drinks, danced and ate a good supper. Cissie of course had never got anywhere near such refined surroundings, but her view was that this was the top branch of the tree.

'I'm afraid I wouldn't know the distinction,' Matilda said. She was very nervous now, wondering if she ought to run for the open door. 'Perhaps you ought to enlighten me?'

The woman showed absolutely no sign of embarrassment as she explained. It seemed it was much as Cissie had said, only the woman claimed that not all men came looking to buy the company of a girl, rather that they saw it as a congenial place to meet and make friends, to talk in comfortable surroundings. She called her girls 'her boarders', just as if they were merely guests, there to make the place more decorative.

It was the woman's cultured voice and her gracious demeanour which calmed Matilda. She still felt it would be wiser to go, for if it got about in the town that she'd been in here, people might deduce she was like the girls who worked here. But she did want to talk to Maria, and she also found the old lady quite compelling.

Perhaps the old lady realized her predicament because she touched her arm very gently.

'You are quite safe. We are closed now. There are no men on the premises, only myself and my boarders, and most of them are still sleeping. Have some tea with me, and I'll call Maria. I have never ever entrapped a girl to work for me yet, and I certainly would not start with you.'

She picked up a small bell and rang it. A door opened at the far side of the room and a tall, thin Negress in a maid's uniform complete with starched apron and cap came in. 'Ah, Dolores. Will you bring a tray of tea for my guest and myself,' she asked, 'and tell Maria I wish to see her.'

'Where are you from?' Matilda asked once she had been invited to sit down. 'You have a very interesting accent.'

'Russia.' The woman smiled. 'But I was sent to England as a young girl, and I have lived in France for many years too, so I guess my accent comes from all three. I left England over fifty years ago, but the memories of it are indelible.'

Matilda guessed that made her in her late sixties. She wished she dared ask what made her open a parlour house. 'We haven't introduced ourselves. I'm Matilda Jennings,' she said.

'I'm Contessa Alexandra Petroika. I am known as "the Russian woman" by those who fear me, "the Contessa" by those who admire me, but "Miss Zandra" to my girls.'

Matilda gave a little start at this. One night at dinner Alicia had made a curiously oblique remark about 'the Russian woman', and Henry had quickly turned the conversation in another direction. Now she understood why.

Maria came sidling in, she looked very alarmed at seeing Matilda and moved to turn back.

'Don't be afraid, I haven't come from Mrs Slocum,' Matilda assured her, then speaking slowly and clearly, she explained. 'I am just worried about you. I would like to know why you left your job and came here. I promise I won't tell Mrs Slocum where you are.'

She hadn't really studied Maria back in the house, noting a pretty face beneath her starched cap but little else. She was in reality dramatically beautiful, with golden skin, lustrous hair, and such large, expressive black eyes.

'She bad woman,' Maria said with a toss of her head. 'Always slap me, work, work, work.'

Matilda sighed, she could imagine this was true. 'And Mr Slocum?'

'He not bad man,' she said. 'But I tell him geeve me five dollars each time he come to me, and he say yes Maria, but he stop geeving me money because he say he love me.'

Matilda gulped. Even taking into consideration that Maria spoke poor English, she was clearly admitting she had instigated this arrangement. The look of pique on her lovely face was chilling. Matilda looked to the Contessa, not really knowing what to ask next.

'I think Mrs Jennings wishes to know if you are happy to work here,' the Contessa said.

Maria's face broke into a smile. 'Oh yes. Good food and no hard work.'

'Will you tell Mrs Jennings why you came here to work rather than find another job as a maid?'

Maria pulled a face. 'I not like to clean and wash dishes. I want beeg money and pretty dress. I go now?'

The Contessa nodded and Marie left immediately without so much as a backward glance at Matilda.

The Contessa raised one eyebrow. 'Did that satisfy you?' she asked as she poured the tea. 'I'm sure you must have wished to question her further, but her lack of English makes it impossible to hold a real conversation with her, or even see the real girl underneath.'

'I saw and heard enough,' Matilda said sadly.

The Contessa shrugged. 'You are shocked, maybe even disappointed, to find Maria is just a mercenary little baggage. I expect you either imagined Mrs Slocum treated her as a slave, or that her husband forced his attentions on her and she was compelled to submit to keep her position, maybe both?'

'I think Mrs Slocum was too hard on her, yet I couldn't really believe that of her husband,' she said.

'I suspect the truth of the matter was that Maria took that position with the sole purpose of entrapping Henry,' the woman said with a shrug. 'He has a cold, childless marriage, and such men are easy prey. Maria and his wife are much the same inside. Money is what they both want.'

Matilda was startled by her using the familiar term of 'Henry', and by her incisive view of his marriage. This woman was becoming more interesting by the moment.

She handed Matilda her tea, the dainty bone china was decorated with small green leaves, and to Matilda it was an untimely reminder of Lily. Her views of love and marriage had been so idealistic, she would have been shocked to the core to think many women didn't share them.

'Now Maria has come to me,' the Contessa went on. 'I agreed I would give her a try, but I doubt she will be here for long. I do not like that coldness in my boarders, even as beautiful as she is. But maybe she can change. She has had a very hard life.'

'You make it sound as if you were running a school for young ladies,' Matilda burst out. Her feelings were muddled. She didn't know who to be angry with, Maria, Alicia or Henry, or even herself for pushing her nose into something which didn't concern her. The Contessa was the only person she could take it out on. 'But you are training them only as whores. You make money from them, you corrupt them.'

'Not I,' the Contessa said, pursing her lips. 'The girls who come to me are not virgins. They come of their own free will, and it is usually a far better life than the one they have often come from. My parlour is select, outside that door there is a steep slope downwards to brothels which deal with the fast trade, then down again to the cribs and hog ranches. Finally the street-walker who doesn't even have a bed. My girls all know this, here they have a real chance to live well and save their money. I tell them all they must plan for their futures, some listen and take note, some do not. But I cannot help that.'

Matilda was even more confused now. Maria's cold statement about Henry proved she knew exactly what she was doing. She knew too from Cissie, Flynn and Giles that many girls deliberately chose their life because it made them more money than anything else. But however many reasons she'd heard for women turning to prostitution, it still appalled her.

'But it's terrible that they have to sell their bodies to make a living!' she said.

'I agree with you,' the Contessa said, turning in her seat to look right at Matilda. 'At least in principle. My heart bleeds for the ones who have no choice in the matter. There are young girls ravaged by their masters and family members, many who do it from hunger, or to care for sick children, and those who have been forced, or even sold into it. I wish there was some kind of decent employment they could take up.

'But let me put you straight, Mrs Jennings. Not all girls who become whores are sad little victims. That is a myth, put about by self-righteous, men-hating women like your Mrs Slocum. Girls come to me for a variety of reasons, and there's surprisingly few who are really desperate. I have boarders who arrived here in California looking for adventure, just like the men. I have ones who are just plain lazy and who do not want to get a job where they have to work hard. I have ones who think they might find a husband, others who just count the money they earn, and others who just do it because they adore sex. Do you think this place would be any fun for the men who come here if all the girls were reluctant? Every night is a party here, the pianist plays, my girls dance and often sing. If it weren't so I wouldn't be so successful.'

'But the men,' Matilda protested.

The Contessa laughed. 'You have only been here in this town for a few days, Mrs Jennings, but from what I've heard you have created quite a stir. Why? Because you are young and pretty, and I'm told very entertaining.'

'What have I got to do with it?' Matilda asked. She was surprised this woman knew so much about her.

'Because you, my dear, are exactly what most men want in a woman. I don't mean that every man you've met in town is lusting after you, far from it. For most of them who have left their wives and sweethearts thousands of miles away, it is enough just to see someone like you and admire you. But there are other men who need something a little more substantial than a smile or a chat. I fill that need.'

'But this town is full of prostitutes,' Matilda argued. 'You may have the "gentlemen" in here, but what about the rest?'

'All men have the same need, whether they be gentlemen, sailors, soldiers or gold miners,' she said with a shrug. 'When a man has spent weeks up to his waist in icy water, his tent blown away by the wind up in the mountains, and only the dream of great riches to keep him going, he needs a break now and then.

Just holding a soft, warm female body in his arms for a few hours gives him the will to go on.'

'You make prostitution sound almost holy,' Matilda said scornfully. 'It's not, it's grubby and demeaning.'

The Contessa gave her an arch look. 'Not always,' she said. 'It can be tender, funny, relaxing, stimulating, and just plain exciting. Young men often learn to become great lovers through whores and in turn take that experience home to delight their wives. A man doesn't have to pretend to be something he isn't with a whore. In my time I've heard a great many men's secrets, and sent them away feeling cleansed. I have known men who but for the affection shown to them by whores might have ended their lives by their own hand. Is that all grubby and demeaning?'

'No, I suppose that isn't,' Matilda said reluctantly. 'But when I was in London as a girl I saw a terrible side to it, girls selling themselves on street corners just for a few shillings to buy a meal. I wish there was some way those girls could be given a chance in life, before they end up in some back alley riddled with disease.'

'You have a kind heart,' the Contessa said, reaching out to pat her hand. 'You truly care about people, rather than just morality. I admire that.'

Matilda thought she'd stayed long enough. She could see the woman's point. She even rather admired her for being so honest.

'I'd better go,' she said. 'I've got a boat to catch later. I can rest easier now I know the truth about Maria and Mr Slocum, that's all I came for.'

'Don't rush off unless you really must,' the Contessa said, her small lined face alight with real interest. 'You see, I've heard so much about you from my gentlemen, what you looked like, how clever you are at sums. I heard tell you are a widow, with small children. I'd love to know your whole story!'

'You learned all that in here?' Matilda gasped. 'Are you saying the men I've been doing business with are your "gentlemen"?'

The Contessa laughed. 'Of course, my dear. Many of my best customers are pillars of society. But just like the gold prospectors, they like a little fun too. That surprises you?'

Matilda nodded. It was hard to imagine any of the serious, rather dull men she'd sold timber to whooping it up in here at nights and talking about her to this extraordinary woman.

'If their wives were a little warmer, less concerned with propriety, I'd have no customers.' The woman gave a wry smirk. 'The women they are married to are as much whores as my girls, only they trade their bodies reluctantly for being looked after. But enough of that, I don't often get the chance to have a good chin-wag with another woman. Do tell me how you came to America and why.'

Matilda wasn't aloof by nature and since leaving Oregon she had often felt very lonely, and wished for another woman to talk openly to. Maybe she started out telling the Contessa about herself more from politeness than anything else, but the woman was so interested, so good at drawing her out, that before long she found herself telling her the entire story, concealing nothing.

'I expect you are shocked I'm not really a widow,' she said somewhat shamefacedly as she finished up with arriving at Cissie's in Oregon. She was a little bewildered by why she'd revealed so much, yet she felt better for it.

'Not one bit,' the older woman said with a shake of her head. 'All I think is how very plucky you are. But I'll give you a word of advice now for the future. Saying your husband was a doctor isn't too smart, it could be checked. And you might just run into someone who met you back in Independence or New York.'

'But I can't change what I said now,' Matilda said in alarm. 'Well, not here in this town, too many people have heard that.'

'Almost everyone in this town is living a lie,' she said with a sniff. 'Don't you worry too much about that. But if you should come back here one day, if I were you I'd refuse to say anything more on the subject. Eventually it will be forgotten and instead you will be something of a mystery.'

Matilda smiled. 'Like you, I suspect?'

The Contessa gave her youthful, toothless smile. 'Yes, I'm something of a mystery. From what I can see we have a great deal in common, Mrs Jennings.'

'Call me Matty,' Matilda said. 'I'm more comfortable with that, especially now you know all about me.'

'And me with Zandra,' she said. 'And if you do come back again, Matty, and I really hope you will, you must call on me.' She paused and laughed. 'Now, don't you go thinking I want you for one of my boarders, nothing is further from my mind. I just like you, my dear.'

Matilda impulsively reached out and took her hand. 'I like you too,' she said. She was glad she'd stuck her nose into Maria's business, for she would never have met this fascinating woman otherwise. How Cissie was going to love this story!

'You must keep in touch with me,' Zandra said with a smile. 'I'd love to hear about your home and children, and how your business grows. I can pass on the gossip from down here, and perhaps new gentlemen in town that might want timber.'

Matilda liked that idea very much. She took out a pen, wrote down her address and handed it over.

Zandra wrote hers down too. 'One more word of advice,' she said as she handed it over. 'Use a little of that money you have made here for some new clothes. Blue is your colour, Matty, not grey and green. I believe if one surrounds oneself with the right colours, one's path in life suddenly becomes clear.'

As Matty got up to go she felt the oddest sensation of regret. Not at speaking so openly, more that she hadn't met this woman when she first arrived and had time to get to know her better. Everyone who had been important in her life so far she'd met by pure chance, and she had the strangest feeling that Zandra was one of those. Maybe Zandra knew it too, for she stood up, took Matilda's two hands and drew her closer to kiss her cheeks.

'*Au revoir,*' she said softly. 'People use that as a goodbye in France. But the literal meaning is "till we meet again".'

Chapter Seventeen

Matilda spotted Sidney's unmistakable red hair amongst the crowd of people on the waterfront at Portland long before the boat came close enough for her to make out his face. She was surprised he was there because she wasn't expected to return today, but delighted because it meant she wouldn't have to try to get a ferry ride up to Oregon City.

She waved frantically. Sidney waved back, but for such an excitable, exuberant lad his return wave seemed rather muted. She would have expected him to jump up and down and yell out a greeting too, especially if he'd come all the way here on the off-chance of a boat coming in from California.

But as she got nearer to the waterfront she sensed something was wrong. Just the way he stood, shoulders slumped, hands in pockets, spelled out despondency. She thought maybe he'd fallen out with John and Cissie, and perhaps he'd come down here hoping to catch her and tell her his side of the story before returning home.

The boat docked and Matilda was the first of the six passengers to jump off, not even waiting for help from one of the crew. But although Sidney rushed towards her, there was no excited cry of welcome home, he just flew at her, throwing his arms around her.

'What's wrong, Sidney?' she asked. But he just held her tighter, his slender body quivering and his face buried in her shoulder.

'John's dead.'

She heard what he'd said, but she didn't believe her own ears. She grabbed him forcefully by the waist and pushed him away from her so she could see his face.

He was fighting to hold back tears, but his red-rimmed eyes and ghostly white face proved he'd been crying constantly for some time.

'Dead!' she exclaimed, a cold chill sweeping over her, even though it was a very hot afternoon. 'How could he die?'

'He was crushed by a load of timber,' he blurted out. 'Oh Matty, it's so terrible. I dunno if I can even tell you it all.'

Severely shaken as she was, she took his hand, and ignoring the curious stares of people watching them, led him round the side of a shed and sat him down on a packing case lying there. Sitting down beside him, she drew him close in her arms and insisted he tell her the whole story right away.

'It were ten days ago,' he said with a gasping sob. 'We got back to the sawmill with a load of trees on the cart, it was about five in the afternoon and tipping down with rain. John sent me off to fetch Bill Wilder, to help us unload it. I couldn't find Bill straightaway, and so I reckon John must have got tired of waiting and got up on the cart to start unchaining the trees. He must have slipped in the wet, fell right down on the ground, and the trees toppled down on top of him. When I got back with Bill, we saw all the timber on the ground, but we couldn't see John anywhere. Then I saw one of his boots sticking out.'

Sidney broke down, sobbing like a child. It was some minutes before Matilda could calm him enough to get the rest of the story. They couldn't lift the trees, they were too heavy, so they yoked up the oxen to pull them off, one by one. Finally they reached John, but he was already dead.

'It ain't fair,' Sidney sobbed. 'John loved his trees, he wanted to plant as many new ones as he cut down. If all the men hadn't gone rushing off to California there might have been a way we could have got them off him quicker. But it took too long.'

Matilda broke down then too, clinging to Sidney in anguish. It was so unjust that a man who worked as hard as John should die in such an awful way. She could hardly bear to ask how Cissie was. She just knew her friend would think her own life had ended too.

'We took him home on the cart and buried him a coupla days after,' Sidney said at length. 'It were terrible, Matty, you not there an' all. It's even worse now, Cissie's just all in pieces, she can't do nuthin' for herself no more. Peter keeps asking where John is, I can't make him understand.'

'What about Tabby and Amelia?' Matilda asked, a sudden fear clutching at her heart.

'They's fine,' Sidney said in a flat tone. 'Tabby's been real good with 'Melia and Susanna, but she wants you so bad 'cos she's scared about Cissie being the way she is. I've been telling them all everything would be all right once you got back, so when I heard yesterday that a boat was on its way, I just comed down here, hoping you'd be on it.'

Matilda felt as if all her blood was being slowly drained from her body. She'd spent the entire two-week voyage home thinking of little else but John's glee when he saw her order book. John was a man who should have lived to be ninety, he was fit and strong, and so full of life. Cissie and Sidney had depended on him completely for he was the one with an education, a craft, foresight and wisdom. Even she had come to lean on him.

'I miss him so much,' Sidney whispered, his eyes brimming with fresh tears. 'He was like a pa to me, and I don't know what to do without him.'

Matilda hugged him tightly for a moment. There was nothing she could say which would take away his hurt. To say he had to be a man now and take John's place wasn't appropriate, even though she guessed that was what he'd been trying to do.

'You've got me,' she whispered back. 'Now let's go home.'

Cissie was just sitting by the stove staring into space when they got back to the cabin. She looked at Matilda as if she was seeing a stranger, and even when Matilda rushed to embrace her, she didn't respond. Sidney said she'd hardly moved from that spot since she buried John, and when she made rare utterances, it seemed she was talking to him.

She was as grubby and untidy as the cabin, her hair like a bird's nest, the buttons on her dress all askew. Her once plump cheeks were sunken, there was no light in her green eyes and her skin was grey.

Tabitha had rushed down the lane as soon as she heard the cart coming and had thrown herself into Matilda's arms, sobbing out her view of everything that had happened. She had composed herself now, sitting on her bed holding the wriggling Amelia on her lap and restraining Susanna from rushing across the cabin to climb on Matilda while she was embracing Cissie. 'Why is she like that, Matty?' she said, her tone rather cold and stilted.

'It's just shock,' Matilda said, suddenly aware that she must try to hide her own feelings for the sake of the children. 'She's sort of gone somewhere else in her mind for a short while. But now I'm back to look after you all, she'll soon get better.'

But even as Matilda made that seemingly confident statement, she wasn't so sure her presence would effect an immediate recovery. John hadn't just been Cissie's beloved husband. He'd banished her memories of her tainted childhood, lifted her into respectability, and given her the sort of life she would never have been able even to imagine back in her time in Five Points. Every single item in the cabin he'd built for them was a reminder of him – the furniture carved by his loving hands, the fruit trees outside tenderly planted by him. Even the bed they shared still held an indentation of his body. Each time Susanna tried to climb on her knee, Cissie would see John's blue eyes looking back at her. And the dreams they had woven together for their future hung in the air to taunt her.

Matilda suspected Cissie's mind had slipped back to that cold, damp cellar in New York. For in her grieving and confused state, John's death must signal that everything good had ended, and she would sink back to where she came from.

'I tried to do everything Aunt Cissie used to do,' Tabitha said, her voice quivering. 'But I couldn't manage all of it.'

Matilda took one look at the little girl's haunted face, saw the dark circles beneath her eyes and her red and swollen hands, and her heart went out to her. With the best will in the world, a nine-year-old couldn't cope with a baby, a toddler and a six-year-old, as well as trying to make meals, feed animals and do the washing and cleaning.

'You did very well, Tabby. I'm proud of you,' she said. 'Now let me take Amelia from you. Did you really say she can crawl now?'

After being away for so long her whole being longed to be alone with her baby, to cuddle her and examine her closely. But she couldn't single her out for special attention when Susanna, Peter and Tabitha needed her so much more. She could see Amelia had grown, she had more hair, and two more teeth. As she put her down on the cabin floor, the sight of her wriggling fat little bottom, the cheeky face turned around to make sure her mother was watching, made her want to laugh, yet she couldn't laugh at a time like this, not even at her own baby.

'I'm scared of Aunt Cissie now,' Tabitha confided later that evening as Matilda took all the children down to the brook to wash them. They needed a real bath, but it was a warm evening and with so many pressing things needing to be done, Matilda had decided a quick dip in the brook would do for now.

'Scared of Cissie!' she exclaimed, thinking it was better to make light of it than try to explain. 'You'll be telling me you're scared of me next.'

'Well, she should remember she's a mama,' Tabitha said, pursing her mouth in a way that reminded Matilda sharply of Lily. 'She doesn't even hold Susanna any more.'

'Even mamas can get sick sometimes,' Matilda replied, wondering if Tabitha was remembering her own mother acting strangely. She tucked up the skirt of her dress, peeled off Susanna's clothes, then waded in to wash her. Susanna squealed with laughter because the water was cold, and after all the misery it sounded like music to Matilda's ears.

She looked back at the other children. Tabitha was undressing Amelia on her lap, Peter sitting beside her, taking off his boots. She just wished she could make them laugh too. 'But this mama doesn't get sick, and after you're all clean I'm going to make you pancakes for supper. I might even read a story too.'

But however reassuring Matilda was trying to sound, she was frightened as well. Susanna might be only two and a half but she was only too aware something was badly wrong. She had grown out of babyhood into a little girl in Matilda's absence, but disturbed by the sudden change of atmosphere in her home she had reverted back to wetting herself, and Sidney said she often sat on the porch just sadly rocking herself.

Peter wasn't eating, Sidney reported he'd been crying in his sleep, and several times he had found him just waiting in the lane, pitifully hoping his father would return. It didn't matter too much that all of them were dirty, or even that they'd only eaten the scantiest of meals in the last nine days, but to be suddenly deprived of love and affection was very serious.

Sidney's grief was almost too painful to consider. This family was everything to him, he saw the little ones as his brothers and sisters, John had been father, teacher and his idol. At his side he'd begun to learn a craft, to be a man. But at only fourteen he was still only a boy, he needed reassurance that this was still his home, that the love he'd been shown by this family would never be withdrawn.

Even faithful, affectionate Treacle seemed cowed and scared. He had slunk around Matilda's skirts when she got out of the cart with Sidney, but his tail barely wagged and his ears were laid back. He had always shadowed Tabitha wherever she went, but now he was keeping his distance from everyone, lying up on the porch looking mournfully at them.

Yet overall it was Tabitha who concerned Matilda most. She had been through so much before they got to Oregon. She had become so settled and happy here in the cabin, but now, once again, death had thrown her back to a state of uncertainty.

In the days that followed Matilda's anxiety grew. On that first night she had believed that once she got the cabin straight, the children to bed, Cissie bathed and her hair washed, Cissie would sense she was safe again, and begin to respond again to her family.

But there was no improvement. Each morning when Matilda got up, Cissie would be awake already, silently staring at the ceiling, and it was clear she'd slept very little. She would get up and get dressed when Matilda told her to, but immediately slumped down into the chair where she would stay all day, only moving when she needed to go to the privy, or if Matilda ordered her out on to the porch.

She had all of Matilda's sympathy, for she knew what it was to have her heart torn apart. She remembered only too well all those long, long nights after Giles was killed, wondering why she had to be singled out for such cruelty. She knew too that feeling of hopelessness, the desire just to lie down and die herself. But she had rallied herself to take care of Tabitha, and she couldn't understand why someone as strong as Cissie could shut out her children.

She tried everything to make her respond, coaxed, cajoled and sometimes even snapped at her, but it seemed her friend was deaf to everything. Nothing affected her, not Susanna screaming, Amelia trying to haul herself up by pulling at her skirts, or Peter demanding something. Matilda began to think if fire broke out in the cabin she would do nothing.

Her skin grew greyer, there was no shine on her curly hair, the impertinent grin which was once so much part of her character never showed itself. She answered questions with a nod or a shake of her head, rarely uttering a word, and she would take just a few spoonfuls of food before pushing it away.

As time went on Matilda found herself exhausted with trying to do all the household chores, looking after the children and tending the crops, milking the cow and feeding the animals. She kept telling herself that Cissie had managed while she'd been away, but Sidney and John had always seen to the animals, chopped wood and shot or trapped meat for their meals, and now she had to do that too. Sidney tried to do all he could to help, but he had to go down to the sawmill every day, just to make certain that nothing was stolen and to try to sell the timber in stock, so mostly she had to struggle through it alone.

The children wanted Cissie's attention, and when they couldn't get it, they played Matilda up. Tabitha did her best to help, but she grew angry when things went wrong. One day when Amelia crawled right out of the cabin and into a puddle of water, she picked her up and smacked her out of pure frustration as she'd only just dressed her in a clean dress. Another time she tried to chop wood for the stove, and unable to do it, she hurled the axe down, narrowly missing Peter's foot. Matilda shouted at her on both occasions, and Tabitha ran off into the woods crying. Matilda felt like doing the same herself, but she couldn't, someone had to stay and do the mountain of work, and care for the little ones.

The future worried her even more than the present. John had invested everything he had in his sawmill, and if Cissie didn't recover soon and decide what should be done with it, the trade John had built up would be lost and the mill would become worthless. They wouldn't starve, she and Sidney could shoot rabbits and deer, and there were enough vegetables to live on, but it was going to be grim when winter came without money to buy oil for the lamps, foodstuffs for the animals and provisions like flour, sugar and rice.

Each time she looked at those timber orders she became even more frustrated. If they could be filled and shipped down to San Francisco the profit would solve all the immediate problems. Sidney did have a surprising amount of knowledge about timber, but he couldn't do it alone, and while Cissie was locked in grief,

Matilda couldn't find out how much money John had left, find men to help, or safely leave the children to go into town to get some advice.

Two long weeks passed with it growing hotter each day. Although the endless sunshine made washing and drying clothes so much easier, Amelia and Susanna grew tetchy, and it meant the crops and fruit trees had to be watered too. Often Matilda had to leave this chore until dark when the children were asleep, and one night she stumbled over a stone and fell headlong into the brook.

She was surprised rather than hurt, but as she hauled herself out in the dark, dripping wet, and caught her foot in her dress, ripping it, she was suddenly very angry, as that meant yet another chore for her to tackle. As she stamped back up to the cabin and saw Cissie sitting out on the porch, the usual far-away look in her eyes, her anger and frustration rose up and spilled over.

'That's right, you just sit there like you're waiting for the parson to call. Don't worry yourself that I'm doing all the work, wearing myself out and nearly drowned in that fucking brook,' she burst out. 'You just carry on feeling sorry for yourself. Stupid bloody Matilda will sort everything out for you.'

She had never ever used that terrible swear word before, it was a remnant of Finders Court she'd buried, but perhaps by using it she had inadvertently called up the violence of that place too. Some primitive reflex action made her leap up and strike Cissie hard across the face.

'Get up off your arse and do something,' she yelled at her. 'I'd care for you if you was sick, but I'm buggered if I'll wait on a bloody ghost. 'Cos that's what you are, Cissie my girl, a fucking ghost, with no guts, no heart and no soul no longer.'

Cissie looked up at her in utter surprise, her hand moving tentatively towards her burning cheek. 'I didn't know you knew such bad words,' she said.

To hear Cissie speak a whole sentence was such a shock that Matilda reeled back, suddenly aware that in her anger she'd reverted right back to what she once was, a guttersnipe from Finders Court. Yet she couldn't apologize, she was seething with rage.

'I know far worse than that,' she growled at the girl. 'And if you don't come out of that bloody trance you've been in, you'll hear them.'

'No one hits me and gets away with it,' Cissie replied, leaping out of her seat and springing at Matilda, fingers poised to scratch her.

Matilda nimbly side-stepped her, and Cissie fell forward off the step of the porch on to the hard ground beneath it, landing flat on her face.

All at once Matilda came to her senses, horrified by what she'd said and done. She jumped down and bent over to pick Cissie up. But to her surprise Cissie rolled over, caught hold of her by the knees and pulled her down to the ground, pummelling her with her fists and screaming out abuse. Treacle came haring out from the bushes, barking furiously and pulling at both the women's clothes, not knowing who to attack or defend.

It was Sidney who stopped it, he came running out, wearing only his pants, jumped down and pulled them apart.

'What's going on?' he exclaimed. 'Have you both gone off your heads?'

Matilda was lying on the ground, flat on her back, her wet torn dress sticking to her. Cissie was standing by Sidney, panting as furiously as Treacle who looked from one to the other in bewilderment. Above her was Sidney, his bare chest very white, and his red hair shining like a torch with the light of the porch lantern behind it. But it was his shocked expression which made her see the funny side of what had just occurred. His eyes were like mill-stones, his mouth hanging open.

Her laugh was just a tinkle at first, but it gradually grew into a loud guffaw which she couldn't stop. She rolled on the ground, holding her sides, and laughed until she began to cry.

'She's gone off her head. She swore at me, and hit me,' she heard Cissie exclaim. 'What's up with her, Sid?'

'I dunno,' he replied. 'But at least she's got you speaking again, Cis. I reckon we'd better get her inside.'

Matilda veered between laughter and tears constantly as the pair of them took her in, sat her down and kept peering anxiously at her face. It was some time before she was able to voice what she was thinking.

'I shouldn't have sworn at you, Cissie,' she said eventually. 'And it was terrible that I hit you. I'm sorry for that. But at least

I seem to have stuck an arrow up your backside. It's the first time you've shown the old Cissie is still at home.'

It was Sidney who laughed then, long and hard, as he made a pot of coffee.

Cissie looked round at the sleeping children and put a finger to her lips. 'You'll wake them, Sid. Stop laughing and tell me what's so funny.'

That night Matilda was too exhausted to believe Cissie had really snapped out of it. When she woke the next morning to the sound of the stove being raked, and opened one eye to see it was Cissie in her night-gown, with a shawl around her shoulders, she could hardly believe her eyes.

She crept out of bed, for she didn't want to wake the children yet, and slid her arm around Cissie. 'How do you feel today?' she asked.

'Confused,' Cissie said with a sigh, and laid her head on Matilda's shoulder. 'I know John is dead and buried. But I don't understand how we came to be fighting. What was it about?'

'Me losing patience,' Matilda said. 'Sit down and I'll explain.'

Cissie smiled weakly as Matilda told her what had sparked off their fight. But as she went on to speak of the frustration she had felt, Cissie looked bewildered. 'You mean I've been crazy? Not even looking after the children?'

Matilda made light of it. 'You were shocked, you couldn't help it, Cissie. Lily was like it for a time after she lost her baby. I was just as cruel to her too.'

'It's all kind of blank,' Cissie whispered. 'I remember Sidney and Bill Wilder coming back with John on the cart. I washed him and laid him out myself. I remember the minister coming out here too, and the funeral service at the church. But I can't remember coming home afterwards, or anything else. When did you come back, then?'

Matilda told her a little about that. 'None of that matters now,' she said gently. 'I guess you've been in a kind of sleep. But you've woken up now, and the children are going to be so very pleased.'

It wasn't an instant recovery, Cissie was confused, sometimes weepy, sometimes silent, now and again talking so much Matilda wished she'd shut up. But she gradually began picking up the pieces of her life, she cuddled the children, made bread, swept the cabin, and hoed down the weeds between the rows of vegetables.

Sometimes she wanted to talk about John all the time, at others she couldn't bear to speak his name. She told Matilda one day that she felt she couldn't live without him, the next she retracted that and said she had to for her children's sake.

The day she finally asked about the sawmill, Matilda knew she really was recovering. At last she was able to speak about the orders for San Francisco, and her belief they should try to fill as many of them as possible.

'But how can we?' Cissie said, her green eyes wide with surprise and shock.

'I'll tell you,' Matilda replied and launched into the plan she'd been working on in the last week.

Sidney had told her that several men had made inquiries about whether the sawmill would be coming up for sale. Clearly they thought they could get it at a very low price because they knew Cissie couldn't run it herself.

'But if we can hire someone to run it for you, and get those orders filled, it will be worth so much more,' Matilda said.

Cissie looked doubtful. 'Why not just sell it now? If you offered the buyer those orders they'd be bound to give me more money, and it would save us a lot of trouble.'

'But John stood to make over four thousand dollars' profit from them,' Matilda replied. 'That's after deducting all the shipping costs and my commission too. I doubt if you'd even get a buyer to pay one thousand for the business, even with these orders, because they'd be scared they wouldn't get paid for the timber.'

'Well, we might not get paid either,' Cissie said doubtfully.

'Oh yes we will,' Matilda assured her. 'Leave that to me.'

'But how am I going to pay a man to run it?' Cissie asked. 'I don't know how much money John had in the bank, but it can't be more than a couple of hundred dollars. Besides, one man couldn't do the job alone.'

Matilda had already thought of this. 'We go to the bank and tell them everything, then we'll ask to borrow the money.'

'No one lends money to women,' Cissie said despondently.

Matilda grinned. 'They will when they've heard me out!'

Jacob Weinburg, owner of Oregon City Bank, had anticipated that Mrs Duncan would call on him before long to discuss her late husband's business affairs. But he hadn't expected her to come accompanied by Mrs Jennings, who not only claimed to be Duncan's agent, but had drawn up a plan to keep the business going.

Weinburg held the opinion that women had no place in business, but almost as soon as Mrs Jennings began speaking he had to concede that she was not only the most attractive woman he'd seen since he left Boston some years earlier, but remarkably intelligent, and very resourceful.

'You say you went to San Francisco and placed all these orders yourself?' he said, leafing through the order book she'd handed to him.

'Of course,' she said, looking him straight in the eye. 'I've already told you, Mr Weinburg, I was acting as an agent for Mr Duncan. I was returning with these orders when he was killed, and I believe I have a duty to him and Mrs Duncan, to see them filled, delivered, and payment collected.'

Weinburg had been in banking all his life, just like his father before him. He was fifty-five, slightly built, with a sallow complexion and a rather prominent nose, and he knew that but for his wealth and position he might never have found a wife.

Yet as he looked at Mrs Jennings, and remembered he'd heard she too was a widow like her friend, and had come alone with her children to Oregon, he couldn't help but wonder why such a lovely lady hadn't remarried. She could surely have the pick of any man in the territory. Her eyes were the clearest blue he'd ever seen, and although much of her hair was tucked beneath her bonnet, it was pure blonde and very pretty.

He dragged his eyes away from her to look at Mrs Duncan. He'd met her on two or three occasions before, the last, sadly, at her husband's funeral. She too was a pretty woman, and it saddened him to see how thin and gaunt she looked now. He had very much admired John Duncan, indeed he had expected the enterprising man to rise to become one of Oregon City's leading citizens in a few years. Perhaps he shouldn't dismiss his widow and her friend without a fair hearing.

Matilda sensed that this ugly little banker was taken by her looks rather than by what she'd said so far, but as she now had his attention, she launched first into how she'd taken the boat to San Francisco with the sole intention of making money, and then on to her plan to fill the orders.

'If Mrs Duncan can offer high enough wages, we can get the orders shipped in time,' she said firmly. 'All we want from you is to meet that wages bill until I return from California with the money.'

As she expected, he brought up the possibility of people refusing to pay.

Matilda leaned forward on his desk and looked hard at him. 'That town is absolutely desperate for every single commodity you can think of,' she said. 'Timber and other building materials are at the top of the list. If the men don't collect the timber and pay me at the wharf, I shall get it auctioned then and there.'

She gave him a brief but vivid description of the auctions on the waterfront, and how men waited for ships to come in, ready to buy the entire cargo.

'The real fortunes in that town aren't made from mining gold,' she said. 'This order,' she said, pulling out the one from Henry, 'is from Alderman Slocum who is planning to build a new wharf. I lodged with him and his wife while I was there, and I can tell you, Mr Weinburg, men who are intent on building wharves, gambling halls and hotels are not going to pass up the chance of someone else snapping up the timber they ordered.'

Moving on then, she told him it was their plan to hire a man, offering him eighty dollars a week on the understanding he got the timber felled, sawn and delivered to the ship by 10 September. To make sure he did this they would offer him a bonus of 300 dollars on completion. She said that whoever took up the offer would have to take on men to help and pay them from his money.

Weinburg nodded. 'That is an extremely good offer for anyone,' he said. 'But you couldn't keep up those kinds of wages after this shipment is completed. How were you intending to manage the sawmill then?'

'I haven't decided about the future yet,' Cissie said. Throughout all this she had remained silent, knowing Matilda could explain it far better than her. 'We may offer it for sale, the price would depend on the size of the orders Mrs Jennings brings back with her.'

'So you were intending to get more?' he exclaimed.

'Of course,' Matilda said. 'And look around for any other business opportunity while I am there. We are both widows, Mr Weinburg, with small children dependent on us. We didn't make that long hazardous journey here to Oregon to just hang up our sun-bonnets and grow a few vegetables.'

Jacob Weinburg was rarely amused by his customers, but Mrs Jennings made him want not only to laugh, but applaud her. She would go far, she had too much determination to fail.

He looked towards Cissie, addressing his remarks to her. 'Well, Mrs Duncan, go ahead and hire your man. Your husband left a balance in his account of four hundred and twenty-three dollars, and when that is used up I will continue to let you make drawings each week until the shipment is made and the costs met. I shall need to draw up a document to this end. Perhaps you can come in again next week to sign it.'

Cissie and Matilda looked at each other and smiled.

'Thank you so much, Mr Weinburg,' Cissie said, her face suddenly flushed and animated.

'It was a pleasure doing business with you,' Matilda said, reaching out to shake his hand. 'I hope we can do more in the future.'

Before leaving town, Matilda went into the office of the *Oregon Spectator* and placed an advertisement for a man experienced with timber. As they drove the cart home later, Cissie began chattering just the way she used to. 'Wasn't Weinburg ugly!' she exclaimed. 'Imagine having to share a bed with him!'

'I'd rather not,' Matilda said.

'Did you notice he had hairs coming out of his ears?' Cissie went on. 'And his teeth were all brown – ugh.'

'I kept looking at his hands, they were so white and smooth. Good job I kept my gloves on, he probably wouldn't have wanted to shake my hand if he'd seen them.' Matilda laughed. 'But you must be getting better if you imagine sharing a bed with someone.'

'That's what I miss most,' Cissie said sadly. 'What do you miss most about Giles?'

Matilda thought for a moment. 'His smile,' she said. 'Even

when I first went to work for him and Lily, I liked that most. His mouth used to kind of tremble slightly, his eyes would twinkle, then it spread right across his face. It always made me smile too.'

'You don't miss the you-know-what then?'

Matilda giggled. 'We only did it twice, Cissie. Can you miss something you did so little of?'

'We didn't do it so much after Susanna,' Cissie said thoughtfully. 'We was scared to because we didn't want another baby before we'd got on our feet, and anyway we were always too tired. I think the last time was that Sunday when he told me about you going to San Francisco.'

'I wished I'd never gone, not when Sidney met me at Portland and told me he was dead,' Matilda said.

'It would have happened even if you'd been here,' Cissie sighed. 'John really liked you, Matty. He said he really missed you one night and I got jealous. Wasn't that silly, because I missed you too.'

'Not really.' Matilda reached out and took her friend's hand to squeeze it. 'If I'd been living with Giles and you came to live there too, I expect I'd have got fed up sometimes. I think you were really remarkable that you took me in, and cared for my children.'

'I love them as if they were mine, they never annoy me. But it's going to be hard when you have to go back to San Francisco,' Cissie said with a sigh. 'Still, maybe it will be good for both of us. We can't cling together for ever, can we?'

'Maybe we can't cling, but we'll be friends for ever,' Matilda said, feeling a lump come up in her throat. 'I haven't even told you all about San Francisco yet, maybe if you decide to sell the sawmill we could all move there. After the children are in bed tonight I'll tell you all about it.'

The night sky was bright with stars, the warm breeze was scented with pine, and the moon hung over the huge oak tree like a lantern, lighting up the tinkling brook, when Matilda, Cissie and Sidney moved out on to the porch later that evening. From behind the cabin an owl hooted, everything was so peaceful and so very different to San Francisco, yet it was the perfect time and place for Matilda to tell them about it.

Their eyes widened as she described the scene on the

waterfront when she first arrived, they gasped about the casinos, grimaced at the canvas restaurants with bunks for a dollar a night, and the filth in the streets. But as she warmed up she found her stories about the dinner parties became very funny, and her spirited impersonation of the auctioneers, the rough drunken miners, and the prostitutes in the streets made them alternately gasp with amazement and roar with laughter.

It all seemed so long ago now, she could hardly remember the fear she'd felt on her arrival at the port, or that humiliating embarrassment at the Slocums' dinner parties, only the good memories were really clear. By sharing it all with her friends, hearing their laughter and seeing their shining eyes, she felt she'd given them something to think on other than John and all the shattered dreams lying around them.

Three days later, on Friday, five men were waiting outside the mill when Matilda arrived there with Sidney in the cart, all of whom had seen the advertisement in the newspaper. Cissie had declined to come with them, she laughingly said she would only choose the most handsome one, and anyway Matilda had the business head.

Of the five men Matilda had no real choice but to select the one she liked least, for he was the only one who had the physical strength, the real knowledge of timber, and enough greed to get the job done in time.

Hamish MacPherson was a Scot, like John, but that was the only similarity. He was a giant of a man, at least six feet three, with forearms like tree trunks. His black hair was long and greasy, his teeth were rotten, he smelled as if he'd never taken a bath in his life, and he chewed tobacco too. Each time he opened his mouth he spat out a disgusting brown stream.

He listened to what had to be done very carefully, stopping Matilda now and then to make a point or two clear. She thought he was a very sly man, his eyes never met hers, and she had a feeling his mind was on working out some kind of fiddle.

'You're really gonna pay me eighty dollars a week?' he asked finally.

'Of course, that's what I promised,' she said, taking a step back from him because his smell was making her faint. 'But you must understand that you will have to find men to help you, and pay them yourself. And you won't get the bonus I offered until the timber is all on the ship.'

'I reckon I can get the help,' he said, scratching under his arm pit and revealing he was lousy as well as dirty. 'I been working on a logging camp up in Canada and most of the men I was working with have come down here, intending to go on to California for the gold. A few weeks longer won't bother them too much, specially if I'm the boss.'

'You will be *their* boss, but I shall be yours,' she said crisply, giving him a stern look. 'I was Mr Duncan's agent and I am handling everything for his widow. I shall be here every day, and if you fall behind, our contract will be cancelled immediately.'

'I ain't a shirker,' he said, looking a little hurt. 'I'll get the timber on that boat for you, come hell or high water. Got anywhere I can sleep? I ain't got fixed up with a place yet.'

The thought of having him sleeping at the mill was horrifying, but under the circumstances she had no choice but to offer him the shed where her wagon had once been.

'Just make sure you don't start a fire,' she warned him. 'Now, we'd better go through the orders so you know exactly what timber is needed.'

Cissie looked very apprehensive when Matilda described MacPherson. Sidney went into a sulk because she said she intended to come in with him every day too.

'But why?' he asked. 'I can see to everything. You should be here.'

'I'm not going to be there to supervise you,' she said quickly, afraid she might have hurt his feelings. 'I'll need you to check each order as it's completed to make sure it's the right thickness and length. I'm just going to be there to watch MacPherson. I know his sort, I bet he's already thinking of selling off timber on the side. And we don't want him finding out who any of the orders are for, or getting an inkling of how much profit we'll be making. Or he'll be off to California getting his own orders. You'd be no match for a blackguard like him!'

'And you reckon you can deal with the man?' Cissie said with a saucy grin. 'If he's as big as you've said, you won't be tall enough to kick him in the balls if he plays you up.'

'There's more ways to keep a man under control than kicking

him in the balls,' Matilda laughed. 'You always seem to forget that I grew up amongst his kind. Now, are you going to be able to cope here without me?'

'I reckon so,' Cissie said, picking Amelia up off the floor and cuddling her. 'But I think Sidney ought to build me a little pen, so I can put this one in it to play sometimes. She crawls so fast I need eyes in the back of my head and it ain't fair to make Tabitha and Peter stand over her all the time.'

Sidney cheered up then, delighted to find he was really needed. 'I'll make something tomorrow,' he said.

MacPherson proved to be far more efficient than Matilda expected. When she and Sidney arrived the next morning he had three equally rough-looking men with him, one of whom was already yoking the oxen up to the cart. MacPherson said they were going out to the forest straight away to fell the timber. He said they would camp out and stay there until they'd felled all the trees necessary.

'Better that way, won't waste so much time,' he said, spitting out a stream of tobacco and narrowly missing the hem of Matilda's dress. 'Once we're nearly done I'll come back with one load and start on the sawing, then they can bring the rest back in relays.'

'How long will this be?' she asked.

He shrugged. 'Two weeks maybe. Keep me money till then. Ain't nuthin' to spend it on out there.'

Matilda lived in a permanent state of anxiety for the next two weeks. Although MacPherson had been advanced no money, he had the cart, the oxen and John's felling equipment. She had no way of knowing exactly where he and his men were, so she couldn't ride out to check how they were doing, and there was nothing to keep her at the sawmill each day.

Suppose they hadn't really gone out to the forest, but had gone instead in the cart to California? By the time she found out it would be too late to hire another man.

She took out all her nervous energy back at the cabin, chopping enough wood to last right through the winter, and digging over a piece of ground which John and Cissie hadn't yet touched, ready to plant more fruit trees. Often at night she would look at her hands and sigh. They'd looked better when she arrived back from San Francisco, a few weeks of no rough work had softened them, but now they were awful again, and she didn't think anything would improve them.

Seventeen days after MacPherson left, Sidney came galloping home one evening to report MacPherson and one of his men had come in that afternoon with the first load. They had unloaded it, and the other man had turned around and taken the cart back for a second load.

'I sure don't like the look of the man, he's an animal,' Sidney said, breathless from the ride home. 'But he's a worker and no mistake. Said they'd been felling from first light till dusk.'

Matilda felt like falling down on her knees to offer a prayer of thanks. 'Let's just hope he's as good at the rest of the job,' she said. 'But I'll come with you tomorrow to see.'

If Matilda had thought work on the land back at the cabin was gruelling, she was soon to find running a sawmill was even more so. MacPherson and his assistant never let up on the sawing regardless of how hot it was. The saw buzzed, wood chips flew, the dust got right into her chest, even when she escaped up to the tiny office above the wood shed, it followed her. But she rarely stopped to rest, for there were so many small jobs she could do while Sidney helped the men. She swept and shovelled up the sawdust and chips, for that could be sold later to the paper mill further along the river. Bark and small off-cuts could be used for fires, and the larger off-cuts stored to be sold to carpenters.

As the sawn planks gradually piled up, she and Sidney carried them between them to start the piles for each customer. Mostly the orders were for pine planking, but there were also some for oak and ash, and she soon learned to tell the difference.

Meanwhile the other two men kept returning with further loads, dumping it and going on back for more. It was Matilda who led the oxen down to the river to let them drink and graze before the next load, and she wondered at their gentle docility when they were treated so callously by the men.

At the end of each day she often envied the men when she saw them run off to the river to swim and wash their grimy, sawdust-covered bodies before going along to the saloon. Their lives might be hard, but they were uncomplicated by domestic problems. From what little she learned of the men from Sidney, they had been moving between jobs like this for years, the wages they earned all spent in saloons and brothels, none of them had ever stayed in one place long enough to marry. Sidney said their conversations with one another were all about the gold in California, where they believed they would strike it rich, and never need to work again.

Their arrogance amused her. They all knew she had been to San Francisco, yet not one of them had asked her for advice, or even her opinion about the place, because she was a woman. If they had, she might have advised them to delay going until early spring, for if they arrived in the fall, it would be too wet and cold to pan for gold. As it was, she thought it would serve them right when their money ran out and the only shelter they had was a tent. But at least that lust for gold was making them work hard.

It was as she arranged the shipping of the timber and booked her own passage with it for the morning of 12 September that Zandra came back into Matilda's mind. Half the orders were completed now, well before time, and in all that had happened since she returned from San Francisco she hadn't had time even to think about her, much less to sit down and write a letter. That visit to the parlour house was the one story she'd omitted to tell Cissie and Sidney. It didn't seem appropriate after John's death, Cissie didn't need reminders of her past at such a difficult time.

But she had liked the woman very much, and Zandra had offered to help her find accommodation. She might even have some ideas about a business Matilda could run with Cissie to support the children. Her friend was on the mend now, she was gaining weight, her old energy was back, and even though she still lapsed into mournful tears sometimes, on many an occasion she'd expressed a wish to live somewhere with a bit of life and colour.

Knowing there was a boat sailing to San Francisco at the end of the week, which would be carrying mail, Matilda sat down in the sawmill office and wrote several letters, first to all her customers advising them of the shipping date. She stated that she would be sailing with the timber and that she expected it to be collected and paid for at the wharf on docking. Then she wrote to Zandra.

It was the first week in September when Zandra's maid Dolores came in with two letters from the mail office. Zandra was feeling very disconsolate as both her knees were badly swollen and she had been unable even to walk down the stairs, much less make it to the mail office. Joining the line of men waiting patiently for news from home was one of her little pleasures, it was here she often overheard the most interesting gossip. Men who couldn't read themselves often asked her to read their letters to them, and it gave her a chance to touch the very pulse of the bustling little town.

But when Dolores handed her the mail, she forgot her aching knees, that the doctor had said she must accept old age graciously, and that the parlour mirrors hadn't been polished as she liked to see them. The first letter was from a lawyer friend, Charles Dubrette, in New Orleans. He had decided to come out to California to see what was going on there himself, by sea to Panama and then overland to the Pacific, and should be arriving around the end of September. The other letter was from Matilda.

Zandra was delighted by Charles's letter, she was very fond of him, but even more by Matilda's, for everything in it proved she was right in her feelings about the girl.

Contessa Alexandra Petroika had always preferred men's company to women's. Never in her entire life could she remember ever opening up to any woman as she had to Matilda, or particularly wanting friendship with her own sex. Her relationship with her 'boarders' was akin to that of a schoolmistress with her children. She taught them how to behave, how to dress, scolded them when they misbehaved and looked after them when they were sick. But they rarely touched her emotions.

Yet there was something about Matilda which had touched her, and she'd thought about her a great deal since that one, rather brief meeting. She thought perhaps it was because she recognized a very similar character to her own: a good-hearted, feisty woman who looked life right in the eye and refused to be brought down by either tragedy or misfortune.

Now as she read Matilda's letter she saw she'd had more misfortune with her friend's husband dying, yet nowhere in the letter was there any self-pity. Zandra guessed that Matilda had taken the entire burden of looking after her friend and her children on to her own shoulders, and she knew too how hard it must have been for a woman to organize getting that timber felled and ready to ship. Most would just have covered their faces with their apron and wept.

Zandra read between the lines of the letter and recognized that same indomitable spirit which had driven her to Paris at a similar age, where, penniless, with nothing but her wits and her looks, she'd risen to become the most fêted and influential courtesan in the city.

She could have stayed in her beloved Paris, accepted any one of many offers of marriage to ensure she would be cared for in her old age. But her pride wouldn't allow her to do that, these men had been lovers and friends for many years, and she wanted to remain in their hearts as she was when she was young and beautiful. So at forty-five, twenty-two years ago, she packed her bags and slipped out of Paris to take a chance on America.

She opened her first 'parlour house' in New Orleans. It took her entire savings to get a house in the right location, to pay for the lavish decorations and elegant furnishings. Her 'boarders', as the girls were known, were selected equally carefully, not just for their looks, but for their warmth and personality. She opened with a grand soirée, inviting only the richest men in town, and laying on champagne, fine wines and superb food. She recouped the cost in just the first few weeks, for her gentlemen soon discovered an evening in her sophisticated 'parlour' was not only the best fun in town, but utterly discreet.

Twenty years later, at sixty-five, Zandra was growing tired, and she felt it was time to retire. She had one last glittering party, said her goodbyes, sold up and moved to Charleston, taking Dolores her maid with her. She might have stayed there for ever but for hearing a whisper that a carpenter had found some gold near Sacramento. In the early spring of the following year she booked a passage for herself and Dolores on a ship sailing right around the Horn, just to take a look.

It certainly wasn't a desire for gold which prompted this hazardous trip by sea. Zandra had enough money to see out her days in luxury, but her curiosity and her adventuring spirit made her want to discover if there was any truth in the rumour, and if so, to be an observer of the madness which would surely follow.

Zandra arrived in San Francisco in June, to find the tiny port almost deserted. She heard that on 12 May, just a month earlier,

Sam Brannan, a Mormon Elder and editor of the *California Star*, after returning from Sacramento to investigate the rumours, had marched down Montgomery Street waving a whiskey bottle full of gold dust and announced the American river was full of gold. Almost every able-bodied man had taken off to get some for themselves.

Zandra found herself unexpectedly marooned in the dreary little town. Ships sailed in every day, bringing in more and more gold-hungry men, but they couldn't sail away again, for their crews deserted to find riches too.

After the sophisticated life she was used to, she viewed the cluster of primitive adobe dwellings which made up the town with utter horror. But as she couldn't leave, experience told her to make the best of it, and she bought a piece of land and erected a tent as temporary accommodation. Dolores, who had shared so much with her in the past, accepted it, if not with pleasure, with resignation. With persistence, bribery and endless cajoling, Zandra managed to get herself a shingle and timber place built. It was two storeys, consisting of a spacious and by anyone's standards in the town luxurious apartment above for herself, and beneath it two stores which she intended to offer for rent.

By the fall, when the rain came and men began returning from the mountains, their pockets full of gold, entrepreneurs began arriving in their thousands. Gambling halls cropped up like mushrooms around the plaza, canvas-walled saloons and restaurants were put up in the blinking of an eye. Zandra was offered three times the amount she had expected for her two stores. She looked at her apartment with new eyes and decided to come out of retirement and back into the parlour house business.

Zandra's parlour was very busy the evening after she'd received Matilda's letter. The candles in the chandelier cast a subdued but twinkling light over the room, the pianist played everything from spirited polkas to gentle Mozart, and her twelve girls, in gaily coloured satin gowns with carefully coiffured hair, mingled with her gentlemen.

As always, she greeted the men personally at the door, took their hats and then got one of her girls to bring them drinks. She refused entry to anyone who wasn't smartly dressed, or the worse for drink. Guns and knives were confiscated and kept in her locked drawer until the owners left.

Zandra's role was to make sure no man was ignored by her girls, and that strangers in town were introduced to regulars. While her doorman discreetly watched out for potential trouble-makers, Dolores escorted gentlemen to the three boudoirs at the back of the house, and it was into her hands that the money was slipped. Later Dolores would go back to the room to change the bed linen.

Although Zandra was unable to provide the French champagne and the superb suppers she'd offered back in New Orleans, or even facilities for gentlemen wishing to stay all night with the girl they'd chosen, she had kept her high standards of hygiene, and cared for her girls. She insisted they bathed each day, she introduced them to the European-style wax pessaries which prevented pregnancy, and kept them vigilant for any symptom of disease. They were well fed and paid, receiving half the sum paid for their personal services.

Most madams here and in other towns provided fancy dresses and lingerie but then charged exorbitant prices for them, keeping their girls constantly in debt to them. They turned a blind eye to rough stuff from the gentlemen, kept the girls virtually prisoners, some even encouraged the use of opiates to make them more docile. But Zandra only charged the real cost of the clothes, any man treating a girl badly was thrown out and never allowed in again, and she gave her girls freedom. For she had learned long ago that by treating them well, their happiness was reflected in their work.

But tonight Zandra's heart wasn't in it. Her knees were throbbing, the smoke from the men's cigars were making her eyes sting, and she felt drained of all energy.

'I'm too old for this now,' she thought as she watched Maria smiling seductively up at the man she was dancing with. 'I think it's almost time to retire for good.'

'That's yer lot, ma'am,' MacPherson called out to Matilda during the afternoon of 6 September. 'All the orders completed ready to go down to Portland tomorrow.'

She was up in the office above the wood sheds sorting out old customer orders of John's. MacPherson's voice carried through the open window, and she rushed down the narrow ladder to see for herself.

MacPherson was lounging against one pile of timber, as always chewing tobacco. Sidney was standing on another pile, fastening a rope around it.

Few things had ever looked so beautiful to her as those neat stacks, each with the owner's name chalked on it, stretching from one side of the yard to the other. She didn't need to ask if Sidney had checked it all, not one cracked plank got past his sharp eyes, and he wouldn't have allowed MacPherson to call her unless he was satisfied.

'Well done, Mr MacPherson,' she said. 'You've done a grand job. I just hope there aren't any problems getting it down to the ship and loaded.'

'There won't be, ma'am,' he said. 'And we've got a few days to spare anyway. I just hopes you gets your money the other end. From what I've heard there's a lot of rogues down there.'

Matilda suppressed a smile. The men down in San Francisco would be pussycats next to MacPherson. After half the orders were completed he'd started getting above himself, she'd come in early one morning to find him loading another man's cart with some of their timber, clearly intending to pocket the cash. When she ordered him to unload it, he swore at her and claimed it was his timber, as he'd felled it. She pointed out that all timber once it had been brought into the yard was Mrs Duncan's property, and if he didn't obey her she would call the sheriff. He backed down then, but she suspected he'd previously pocketed money for other loads she didn't know about.

He had argued about everything in the past week, claimed he was left with nothing after paying his men, that she was the hardest woman he'd ever met, and that Sidney was a jumped-up little snot. But none of that mattered now the job was done.

'Can I have me bonus now?' he asked. 'I got some things I got to see to.'

'Certainly not,' she said, guessing he was intending to be on the boat leaving for San Francisco tonight. 'The deal was you get the bonus once it's on the ship.'

He scowled at her, spat noisily on the ground and walked away.

'It's all ready for shipping,' Matilda said gleefully as she came into the cabin at dusk with Sidney. Cissie was bathing Amelia and Susanna in the washing tub, Tabitha was laying the table for supper, and Peter playing with Treacle on the floor. 'And to celebrate we've all got presents.'

'It's all done!' Cissie exclaimed, scooping Amelia out of the tub and wrapping her in a towel. 'Already!'

'We have to thank the nasty MacPherson for that,' Matilda laughed, and put some brown paper packages on Tabitha's bed. 'Now, who wants to have their present first?'

'Where did you get money for presents?' Cissie asked suspiciously.

'I did have some left from the sale of my wagon,' Matilda said, a little hurt by her friend's tone. Just lately Cissie had begun to act as if she was her servant, and she didn't like it. 'I haven't stooped to selling any of *your* timber, if that's what you think.'

Cissie didn't apologize, but then she rarely did, any more than she gave Matilda much credit for sorting out her husband's affairs.

Matilda had brought little rag dolls for Susanna and Amelia. Peter had a lead soldier and Tabitha a book on medicine. Sidney had already opened his present of a new woollen shirt on the way home.

'Come on then, open yours,' Matilda urged Cissie, taking Amelia from her arms. 'And make any more nasty remarks and I'll take it back.'

'I haven't had a present since I first met John,' Cissie said, suddenly looking tearful. 'He brought me some red woolly gloves.'

As she opened the parcel she gasped with pleasure. It was an emerald-green wool dress, with tiny pearl buttons down the bodice.

She held it up to herself and her eyes welled over. 'Oh Matty, it's beautiful and my favourite colour. Where did you get it?'

'I had it made for you,' Matilda replied, 'at a dressmaker's in town. I took the measurements of your Sunday dress to her. So you'd better try it on and see if it fits.'

'What's in those parcels then?' Cissie asked, looking down at the two lying on the bed.

'The small one is Amelia's birthday present. I'm not going to tell you what it is, you'll have to wait till the day after tomorrow. The other one is the dress I was going to marry Giles in. I got it altered. I thought I'd need something a bit more fashionable to wear in case I run into Alicia Slocum again.'

'Let's try them together,' Cissie said.

The children laughed and clapped as they tried on their dresses. Cissie's was a little loose as she was still much thinner than she once was, but she looked lovely in it. Matilda's blue wedding dress had been altered to give it a lower neckline and an elegant bustle and it now fitted her to perfection, accentuating her small waist.

'Don't we look a pair of grand ladies!' Cissie said, mincing around the cabin with one hand on her hip. 'If I'd had this back in my days in New York I'd have been able to work in a parlour house at least.'

Matilda put a finger to her lips to remind her the children were listening. Tabitha rarely missed anything and was likely to ask her what she meant.

It struck Matilda last thing that night before she fell asleep that it was the first reference to her past that Cissie had made since she arrived here in Oregon eleven months ago. Was it just the dress, or had Cissie been thinking about it a great deal?

In San Francisco, a month later in early October, Matilda stood on the waterfront watching the cart carrying the last of the timber trundle away. Her reticule fastened firmly to her wrist was stuffed with banker's drafts and although it was raining heavily, she was glowing with pleasure.

She could have sold four times as much. As each stack was lowered on to the lighters which carried it to the waterfront, men had come up to her again and again to ask if she had any timber to spare. But the owner of each of the loads had been far too eager for that, they'd all been waiting to meet the ship, and they paid her and carted the timber away speedily. After all the trials and hard work of the past weeks she was almost disappointed she wasn't left with just one load to auction off. She knew with utter certainty she would have got a great deal more money for it that way.

It was a heady feeling to have succeeded in a man's world, to see admiration on the faces of men who a few months earlier had seemed almost scornful of her ability to deliver. They would all give her new orders, most certainly of three or four times the size, but it wouldn't be her filling them – Cissie had made it plain before she left that she wanted to sell the mill.

On the long voyage down here Matilda had churned the question as to why Cissie wanted to get shot of it over and over in her mind. At first it had seemed that she wanted to cut free from painful memories of John, but now Matilda wasn't so sure.

It seemed more likely, after weighing up the way Cissie had shown no real appreciation for her efforts, and the way she often treated her like a poor relation, that maybe she didn't want Matilda running the sawmill because she felt she would be relegated to a role of housekeeper.

On their last evening together Cissie had suddenly announced that she wanted to sell the cabin and the land, to move into the town and open up a small shop. Matilda hadn't liked to point out that a shop owner needed to be able to read and write well, nor had she liked to ask if Cissie was trying to tell her to find a home of her own.

But she wasn't going to ponder on Cissie any more for now. It was nearly five in the evening, so she was going straight to Zandra's parlour to see her and find out if she had managed to arrange a room for her.

As she made her way to Kearny Street she could hardly believe the amount of new buildings since she was last here. Several hotels, which looked like the real thing, more saloons, shops, restaurants and houses had jumped up on all available lots like mushrooms. But the rain made the street like a quagmire and she had to pick up her skirts and do what everyone else was doing, hop from one strategically placed crate, box or plank to another.

Dolores the maid opened the door to her and ushered her through the main room to Zandra's sitting-room, telling her as she went that her mistress's legs were in a bad way.

Matilda was very curious about the maid. She was a very plain woman, with a severe expression, but from the affectionate manner in which Zandra had mentioned her several times in the letter which came just before Matilda left Oregon, it was clear she was more than just a maid to her. That was just another thing Matilda would like to find out about.

'My dear, how lovely to see you again,' Zandra said, and struggled to get up from her chair. 'I can't tell you how good it was to hear you were coming. I've already heard from one of my sources that your customers were all lined up as the ship came in. You must be so pleased to see the last of timber for a while.'

Her sitting-room was unexpectedly beautiful, very small but decorated in cream and blue, with dainty furniture which looked French. There were many books and small pictures but it wasn't cluttered with ornaments as was the fashion. Matilda felt by looking at it she was seeing another side of this interesting old woman, at heart very feminine and cultured.

When Zandra grimaced with pain Matilda nudged her back into her chair. 'It's good to see you again too, but not to see you poorly. What's wrong with your legs, can I get you anything for them?'

'It's just old age, and I have to accept that,' Zandra smiled. 'Now, tell me about your friend, how tragic that her husband was killed.'

Matilda told her a little about how Cissie and the children had been when she got home, and how getting the timber orders filled and shipped had seemed to be so important if Cissie was to sell the sawmill. She laughed as she described the panic she'd been in for fear she couldn't get it all done in time.

'But where will this leave you if she does sell up?' Zandra asked.

'I don't rightly know,' Matilda replied, frowning because Zandra was voicing the niggling worry she'd been hearing in her own head. 'It's odd really because Cissie talks about my children in the same way she does about hers, like she can't imagine life without them around her. But she doesn't ever ask if I've got any plans, sometimes I think she imagines I just have to fit in with her.'

'Two women in one house rarely works,' Zandra said in sympathy. 'Especially when they are both strong characters. But what is it you'd like to do?'

'Well, when I last saw you I was thinking about finding some business of my own down here. But then I never imagined anything happening to John. I did suggest to Cissie that we all move down here, and for a time she seemed to like that idea, but

I think she's changed her mind now. That makes it difficult for me, I suppose I'd just assumed she would look after the children while I supported us all. Of course I could get some land of my own up there, but I'd never make much money and it's such a hard life for a woman on her own.'

Zandra leaned forward and to Matilda's surprise she took her right hand in hers, and peeled off her lace glove.

'No, don't look at them,' Matilda cried out, trying to snatch her hand away, but Zandra held it tight and ran her finger over the calluses and scars. What with the digging, chopping wood and splinters from the sawmill, they were even worse than they'd been a few months earlier.

Zandra tutted. 'They say everything about your life up there,' she said softly. 'You must find a way to use your fine brain to make a living rather than labouring as you have so clearly been doing. If you continue like this you will be old before your time.'

'I was born to hard work,' Matilda said.

'I was born into the nobility,' Zandra retorted. 'But one doesn't necessarily have to accept that the position one was born into is the only one for you. Tell me what you want most from your life.'

Matilda was startled for a moment. That question had been fired at her twice before, first by Flynn, then by Giles, both formative characters in her life. She had a strong feeling that this woman was going to have an equally great sway on her future.

'To see Tabitha and Amelia have a good education.'

'Why?'

'So they don't feel they have to marry the first man that asks them, so they can choose to be doctors, teachers or lawyers if that's what they want.'

'So they can be accepted in the right social circles is what you really mean, isn't it?'

'I suppose so,' Matilda said, feeling a little embarrassed.

'Don't be bashful with me, my dear,' Zandra said with a half-smile. 'You are right to want something better for your children, but the kind of education you want for them is expensive. You will never earn enough with a parcel of land in Oregon. You will have to think bigger than that.'

'I know,' Matilda said sorrowfully. 'Most of the way here I was thinking about it. I could maybe twist Cissie's arm to make her keep the sawmill, and get enough orders for timber while I'm here to make it really pay, but even if Cissie agreed to it, the work, the organizing is so hard, I don't think I could do it for very long.'

Zandra nodded. 'That's because it's not right for you. For one thing you have to rely on getting male help for it all, for another, unless you could get Cissie to agree to a real partnership, the profits won't go to you, but to her. You would get no joy from it, only get worn down with the hard work. And you and Cissie would soon fall out. What you've got to dream up is some scheme that is all yours. Something you can put your soul into, and will make a great deal of money at.'

'I've already tried to think of something, but I can't,' Matilda said, pulling a face. 'I know there is something here in San Francisco, something right under my nose, but I can't put my finger on it.'

'I've booked a room for you in a new hotel close to here,' Zandra said. 'Now, tonight when you are tucked up in bed, you must first think of all the places, shops and businesses that you ever admired, or felt some affinity with in your life. Then once you've got a mental list of those, go through each of them and try to imagine them here, and if they'd be successful. Once you've done that, think of all the talents you have, and ask yourself if they would slot into such a scheme.'

'I'll probably come up with an idea I can't afford,' Matilda joked.

'How much money you have doesn't matter. If you get a good enough idea there are always people who will back you,' the older woman said with a knowing smile. 'But you should leave now, my dear. My gentlemen will start arriving soon and I don't want you to run into any of them. Come and see me again in the morning.'

Matilda left soon after with the directions to the hotel Zandra had given her in her hand. It was dark now, raining even more heavily, and a strong wind was coming in from the sea. She stood for a moment or two under a canopy of the shop below the parlour house entranced by the sight in the street, for she hadn't seen it at night before. Lanterns burned above every saloon, their lights glistening in the puddles and bouncing off shop windows. Music was coming from every direction, including the piano from upstairs in Zandra's parlour, Irish jigs played on fiddles, penny whistles, a harp and a guitar. Along with the music was loud laughter, the clink of glasses and the sound of hobnailed boots stomping on a wooden floor. Further along the street were two tents for gambling, the bright lights inside silhouetting the players at the tables, reminding her of a shadow theatre. The air was full of tantalizing smells of food – fried onions, bacon, steak and many more which she couldn't identify.

But it was the variety of people darting here and there to get out of the rain that was even more fascinating. Gentlemen in top hats, sharp-looking men in derbys and natty suits, army officers in uniform, a sprinkling of sailors, Chinese, Negroes, and grubby-looking miners in tattered clothing. Girls too were in every doorway, inviting the men inside, their satin dresses catching the gleam of the lanterns and every man's eye. So maybe the street was filthy, but it was the most exciting sight ever. She knew this was where she really wanted to be.

The hotel was small and so new it still smelled of wood and fresh paint, and the owners, Mr and Mrs Geiger, a German couple, greeted her warmly. They said in halting English that their guests were only respectable business people, and that they changed the sheets after each guest, and provided a dinner each evening too.

Sheets, whether changed or not, were something of a luxury, and although Matilda's room was tiny, and the walls were only thin partitions, the bed was clean, there were hooks behind the door to hang her clothes, and there was a wash-stand with a bowl and pitcher of water, along with a chamber-pot beneath the bed.

After a surprisingly good dinner of roast pork, sharing a large table with a couple from Santa Fe who said they were in town to buy land, and two commercial travellers from St Louis, Matilda went to bed. She was very tired, the voyage here had been rough, and the excitement of what lay ahead of her had prevented her from sleeping very well.

She did what Zandra had advised, and as memories of many fascinating businesses in London came into her head, she sat up, relit her candle, and taking a note-pad from her carpet-bag, made a list.

There was the sweet shop in Oxford Street she had always stopped to look at. She could see right now the hundreds of jars on the shelves, see the lady inside weighing them up and tipping them into paper cones. There was a hat shop too, that had always caught her eye, and a shoe shop which grand ladies swept into while their carriages waited outside.

She had always liked the look of an ale house in the Strand. The smell of cigars wafted out with the sound of male laughter. There was the pie shop in Fleet Street, and the doll shop in Regent Street. The printer's in Fetter Lane had always fascinated her with its pungent smell of ink and the man who picked out little metal letters and slotted them into rows. She'd always rather fancied the undertaker's in Hampstead too, there was something peaceful about the flowers in the window and the purple satin surrounding them, not to mention the fine hearse pulled by four black horses.

The more select second-hand clothes shop in Rosemary Lane was good, so was the marine shop where the scavengers took their day's findings to sell, the sausage shop and the cheese stand in the market. She could remember admiring dozens of book shops down Charing Cross Road. And flower shops, too – she had loved so many of those.

Theatres of course, they had to go down, not that she'd ever been into any of the gilded palaces she'd admired. And that place in the Haymarket, the one where all the toffs took the gay girls.

She paused as a vivid picture of the last one came into her mind. At night they had flaming torches alight outside, a man in red livery opened the doors for customers, and a burst of exciting music always wafted out. They had shows on in there, dancing girls, performing dogs, jugglers and fire-eaters, sometimes prize fighters too. Once the doorman had allowed her to take some rosebuds in there to sell, and she'd been so spellbound by the act up on the central stage, a lady contortionist, that she didn't approach anyone to sell her flowers.

When she had filled right down the left-hand side of the page with ideas, she went back down them crossing out ones she couldn't imagine working in here in San Francisco. Only two, the hat shop and ladies' shoes, were definite mistakes, she wasn't sure about the book shop. At the moment she doubted anyone read, but maybe they would if books were available. Nor was she sure about the marine shop. Was there any market for second-hand nails or bits of wood? A doll shop could work, most of the men who came here had children, but then would they buy a doll when they were living in such primitive conditions?

The next column was for her talents. Reading and arithmetic, selling, she could shoot straight, drive a wagon, cook, clean, and look after people.

Digging the pencil into her cheek, she studied that short list and thought it sounded dull. She could make people laugh, she was good at giving orders, she was a happy person, quick-witted and pretty, so she put all those down too.

Finally the last list: how those talents would slot into the ones on the first column. At first glance the only one where they wouldn't fit was the undertaker's. Being happy and making people laugh was not an asset in that business, so she crossed it out.

Sweets she could do, but would it make enough money? There were more than enough ale houses and saloons already. And pie shops too, even if none of them was as lovely as the one she remembered in London. Second-hand clothes were a possibility, but where would she go to acquire them? Besides, she couldn't bear the thought of lice. Flowers were lovely, but who would buy them here, even if she managed to find a supplier?

A printer's was a good idea, she didn't think there was one already, but she knew nothing about printing, so that was out. So were theatres a good idea, but she doubted her talents stretched to that, and it would cost a fortune to build.

Only one thing was left. The fun house in the Haymarket.

She blew the candle out then and lay down, but a bubble of excitement ran up through her veins and seemed to burst, sending out thousands more. That was it, the one thing this town needed. There were enough ordinary saloons to get every man in California drunk for a week, brothels galore, dozens of casinos to relieve them of their hard-earned money. But although eating, drinking, gambling and sex had been taken care of, there just wasn't any harmless entertainment.

She could run a place like that, she knew she could. Dancing girls, clowns, jugglers and fire-eaters could be advertised for in other cities. There were musicians in town already, she'd heard them playing on street corners for a few cents thrown in a hat. A few pretty girls to act as waitresses could be found easily enough. Maybe girls to dance with the men customers too.

'But it would be so expensive to set up,' she thought. 'It would need to be big, solidly built in a prominent place, with luxurious fittings so it attracted the rich people. Would anyone lend me that kind of money?'

She fell asleep imagining herself in a velvet gown with diamonds around her neck, mingling with her customers as dancing girls performed on her stage.

Next morning Matilda rushed into Zandra's sitting-room without waiting for Dolores to announce her. 'I've got the idea!' she said.

Zandra had both legs up on a low stool to ease the swelling, but she forgot her discomfort at the sight of Matilda's flushed face and sparkling eyes. 'Come and tell me about it then,' she said. 'Bring us tea, Dolores. If any of the girls want me they'll have to wait until later.'

'What about a fun palace?' Matilda asked, and promptly went into a spirited and visual description of it. 'Dancing girls, snake-charmers, fire-eaters, every night a different show. Something for everyone, and the show is included in the price of the drinks. A place a man could take his wife, or his sweetheart, somewhere he wouldn't lose all his earnings, or get so drunk he couldn't stand up.'

Zandra's bright smile made her bring out the crude sketches she'd made of how the interior should be: a central stage, so the customers could wander around, a small dance floor, a long bar along one side. She said she thought it should be further up on the hill, so that people could see the lights outside for miles around.

'What do you think?' she said as she finished up.

Zandra's small lined face broke into another smile and she clapped her hands. 'I think it's a truly wonderful idea,' she said, her voice full of warmth. 'I've seen places something like it in both London and Paris, but it would go down even better here because we have such a diversity of nationalities.'

'We could have special nights for different countries,' Matilda said excitedly. 'Mexican, French and German. The waiters and waitresses could dress up for it.' She paused and pulled a face. 'But it's going to cost a fortune.'

'Yes,' Zandra said thoughtfully. 'But from my experience the bigger and more splendid the project, the easier it is to borrow the money or get backers. This is an exciting project, Matty, like you said, it's what the town needs.'

'When you say "backers", does that mean it wouldn't be my business?' Matilda asked, suddenly nervous that she'd said so much. 'I mean, this is my idea. I don't want anyone stealing it.'

Zandra looked at her for a moment, a wry smile pulling at her mouth. 'You are just like me at the same age. Impetuous, suspicious, and wanting to keep control.'

'I didn't mean to sound suspicious of you, Zandra,' Matilda said quickly. 'But you see, I don't know how to go about any of this. I'd be afraid of speaking to the wrong person and getting led up a blind alley and robbed.'

'It just so happens that my lawyer, Charles Dubrette, will be arriving in the next day or two,' Zandra said thoughtfully. 'I think you should have a word with him about it. As for backers, they just put money into a business and they take back their money with a share of the profits as they come in. They are often invited to be backers because they have some useful skill or knowledge, but they don't usually take an active part in the running of it. For instance, you could invite me to become one. Or Henry Slocum, he's an architect, remember.'

'I shouldn't think he'd want to be one,' Matilda giggled.

'I think you are wrong there, I believe he'd be really enthusiastic and useful. Just as I would.'

'Would you really?' Matilda asked.

'Do you mean would I be enthusiastic or useful?'

'You've been useful already,' Matilda replied. 'I meant enthusiastic.'

'Oh yes,' she said with twinkling eyes. 'It's the sort of scheme I wished I'd dreamed up myself. Now, have you given any thought to what you'd call it?'

Matilda blushed and giggled. 'Yes, but I don't know if it's right.'

'Try me.'

'Well, I thought of Matilda's Fun Palace at first, but it doesn't trip off the tongue does it?'

Zandra tried saying it. 'No,' she agreed. ' "Matilda's" is too long a name.'

'So how about London Lil's?'

Zandra clapped her hands again. 'Perfect,' she said. 'Cosmopolitan, snappy, just vulgar enough for this town. It kind of sums up your idea. But why Lil?'

'I was just looking for a name that began with "L" and of course Lily came up because that was Tabitha's mother's name.'

'A good omen to name it after someone you were fond of,' Zandra said. 'Right, so we've made a start, you have a concept and a name. Next comes costings, before you can even approach backers.'

'I wouldn't know how to start that,' Matilda said.

'Nor I,' Zandra said ruefully. 'But Charles will! I can make inquiries for you about vacant lots. If, as you suggested, you choose somewhere up on the hills it will be far cheaper than down here. I reckon you could buy one for around six hundred dollars right now. But the way things are going here in town I reckon by next year that would be doubled.'

'All I've got is nine hundred dollars,' Matilda sighed, thinking of her commission on the timber. 'And I won't get that until I get back home. The other three hundred won't go very far, will it? Especially if I've got to find a home for me and the children too.'

'Ah, the children,' Zandra said thoughtfully. 'Now that, my dear, is going to be your biggest dilemma.'

'What do you mean?' Matilda frowned.

'This town is no place for children right now,' Zandra said, shaking her head. 'It's a filthy place, disease is rife, and it's full of violence. My advice to you is to leave them where they are, for they will be safe with Cissie.'

'But I can't just leave them!' Matilda's voice rose to a squeak of indignation. 'Amelia is just a baby. She had her first birthday just before I left. I'd hardly ever be able to see her if she is six hundred miles away. And Tabitha would think I was deserting her.'

Zandra sighed. 'My dear, you have to think that one through yourself. You have a brilliant idea which I believe could make you a fortune, more than enough to pay for that education you want for your daughters. In a couple of years you might very well have enough to build a house somewhere nearer here, hire a good nursemaid, in fact a whole household of servants.'

'A couple of years!' Matilda exclaimed. 'I missed Amelia starting to crawl while I was away, and two more teeth. I'd miss her entire babyhood if I was away from her that long.'

'I know, but opportunity rarely knocks more than once,' Zandra said sagely. 'This place is a boom town now, everything is wide open for those with guts and imagination. But it won't stay that way, pretty soon the cheap land will all be snapped up, just as the gold will be. If you are going to take a gamble with London Lil's you have to do it now while the odds are all in your favour. What you must consider is if the sacrifice of leaving your children now is better for them in the long term, by being able to provide for their future.'

Matilda's eyes filled up with tears. She tried to bite them back, but she couldn't. She'd woken up this morning full of joy and excitement, imagining not only her glorious fun palace but having an apartment upstairs for her and the children, Cissie and Sidney too if they wanted to come.

In her excitement she'd chosen to blank out what the town was like. Zandra was right, it was no place for children. However lovely the apartment was, every night the noise from below would prevent them sleeping. There was no school for Tabitha to go to, no fields or woods to play in. Every day they would see the base side of human nature, drinking, gambling, opium dens, fighting and indeed murder.

She could protect them from all that evil back in Oregon. But as Zandra had pointed out, she would never be able to give them a good education, and she would have to spend the rest of her life tilling land. Before long Tabitha and Amelia's hands would grow as rough and horny as hers, they'd almost certainly marry farmers and even her grandchildren would have the same hard life.

Zandra saw the tears trickle down Matilda's cheeks and her heart went out to her, for she knew exactly what was going through the girl's mind.

'I know just how you feel, Matty,' she said. 'It's a terrible choice to have to make. All I can suggest is that you try to think on which is the greater good.'

*

Matilda left about an hour later feeling wretched. Zandra had been so very kind, for a woman who had no children of her own she seemed to have a remarkable grasp of what it was like for a mother to be separated from her children. Men were lucky, she thought, they could go out into the world, do what they wanted to, and still retain their children's love.

That was what frightened her the most. Deep down she knew she could leave them, just so long as Cissie was prepared to care for them. She'd proved that by coming here twice. It was just that terrible fear they would ultimately reject her. Could they possibly understand that she was going away for their benefit?

She thought Tabitha would. If Cissie did move into the town Tabitha would be able to go to school there, she'd make friends of her own age, and she would almost certainly be far happier there than she would here. But it was different for Amelia. She was just one, too young truly to know which of the two women who'd brought her up so far was her mother. In two years' time, without Matilda's presence, Cissie would be the one most important to her. Could she bear that?

Thinking deeply, she wandered up the hill to where Zandra had said a piece of land was coming up for sale. It belonged to a Mexican who had big gambling debts to pay, and Zandra had said no one had shown any interest in it yet because it was some way out of town.

Matilda found it easily, lying beyond the last huddle of tents. A simple fence made from a single strand of wire tacked to a few posts marked it, a few goats were tethered on the sparse grass.

Slipping under the wire, she walked to the centre of the lot, then turned to look back at the bay below. Yesterday's rain had cleared overnight and the chilly mist she'd woken to this morning had lifted. It was an awe-inspiring view – turquoise-blue sea, green hills on the far side of the bay, hundreds of ships lying at anchor, sails flapping in the breeze to dry. Seagulls and pelicans were flying overhead, swooping now and then to catch a fish. Yet from where she stood she could barely hear any noise from the town, the air was fresh and sweet-smelling, but in just a few minutes' walk down the hill you could be back amongst the filth, stink and racket.

It felt so right, as though it belonged to her already. She thought people were being very short-sighted not grabbing the high ground now as it was obvious to her that before long there would be no room for building down below. If she were rich, this was where she'd build a house, and she could bet it wouldn't be long before others came round to her way of thinking.

'Take the chance and buy it,' she whispered to herself. 'Even if you can't bear to leave the children you can sell it in a year at a good profit.'

Chapter Eighteen

'You want paying?' Cissie exclaimed, her eyes cold as a January morning. She gathered up the pile of banker's drafts on the table protectively, almost as if she expected Matilda to steal them. 'I thought you collected this for me?'

Matilda was taken aback by this sudden hostility. Just a few minutes before Cissie had been whooping with joy that she'd brought back still more orders for timber from San Francisco.

'Of course I collected it to help you,' she said, thinking Cissie was confused. 'I don't mean I want anything from the new orders, that was just to help you sell the mill. But I do want the commission that John promised me on the first lot.'

It was November, the passage home had been very rough, and she and Sidney had got soaked to the skin by heavy rain on the cart ride home from Portland. But as she came through the door of the cabin, Cissie had given her an emotional welcome, peeled off her wet clothes for her, and wrapped her in a warm blanket. They couldn't talk seriously about the trip over supper because the children were so excited, and it was only once they'd finally gone to bed that Matilda had been able to get out all the banker's drafts, show Cissie the orders, and catch up on all the news.

There were two men both keen to buy the sawmill, but Mr Weinburg had advised Cissie to wait until Matilda returned before fixing a price. Just a few days ago a family from Connecticut had arrived in Oregon and they were anxious to buy the land and cabin.

It was all smiles and excitement until Matilda told Cissie about the lot of land she wanted to buy and suggested that when they went to the bank in the morning, Cissie could get Mr Weinburg to give her a draft for 600 dollars to send down to Charles Dubrette to buy it on her behalf.

'I don't know how you can ask for it now John is dead,' Cissie went on, her face white and spiteful. 'It's taking food out of my children's mouths.'

'Cissie!' Matilda exclaimed. 'How can you say such a thing? It's you who is trying to do that to *my* children! I earned that money, without my efforts you'd have nothing worth selling at the sawmill. I can't believe you can be so mean-spirited, John would turn in his grave.'

'That's right, bring him up to hurt me again,' Cissie retorted angrily. 'We took you in, fed you and looked after you, and we never asked for a cent. Now you want paying!'

Matilda was both exasperated and deeply hurt by this. 'I worked like a demon around this place,' she said. 'You claimed I more than earned my keep. Besides, even before we went to the bank to get help, I explained the final figure you would get once the expenses, shipping costs and my commission were deducted. You stand to make so much from selling the mill and this place that you can live in comfort for the rest of your life without doing a hand's turn. So how can you begrudge me what I was promised? What am I supposed to live on?'

'I'll keep you,' Cissie said.

At this Matilda felt like screaming. She wondered if Cissie had gone crazy again. Yet Sidney had reported she had been especially cheerful and energetic while Matilda was away. He said on several occasions she'd got all dressed up in her new dress and, taking the children with her, had driven the horse and cart into town. This was something she had never done before, not even when John was alive.

'Cissie! Only a minute ago you reminded me how long I've been here without paying a cent. Now you say you want to keep me! Am I supposed to be your slave?'

Cissie's head suddenly slumped down, and she burst into tears.

Matilda ignored her, too angry even to consider soothing her. When Sidney came out from behind the curtained-off room he shared with Peter, rubbing his eyes wearily, she looked to him for an explanation, guessing their raised voices had woken him.

'She's scared, Matty,' he said, putting a protective hand on Cissie's bent shoulder. 'She don't understand just how much money there is, she ain't never handled more than ten dollars in her life. John used to sort everything out for her, and then you took over after he died. I don't understand it either, I just trusts you, but Cissie's too scared you might go away and leave her all on her own to think straight.'

Matilda was chastened by this explanation. She had assumed Cissie understood money even if she couldn't read or write very well. She got up and went round the table and put a hand on Cissie's heaving shoulders. 'Is Sidney right?' she asked.

A faint nod confirmed it and Matilda's anger left her. 'But why didn't you tell me this before? If you had, I would have explained everything to you really carefully.'

Cissie turned in her seat and without lifting her head reached out blindly for her friend. 'Because I'm dumb,' she sobbed. 'John knew how I was and he took care of everything, then after he died I couldn't tell you so I just left you to do it. But once you'd gone away and first there was men wanting to buy the mill, and then that family came to ask about buying the cabin, it all got too much for me. When you said about buying that land, I kind of panicked and said the first thing that came into my head that might stop you from going.'

'You aren't dumb at all. Look at all the stuff you've learnt since I first met you! You can cook now, sew, look after animals and grow things,' Matilda said, holding her to her and rocking her. 'And if you can count up to ten dollars you can count to hundreds and even thousands. Tomorrow I'll show you how easy it is, and we'll talk through everything about the future. There's no need to be scared.'

Later, when Matilda was in bed, listening to the wind howling around the cabin and reflecting on Cissie's problem, she realized that many of the sharp remarks her friend had made in the past ought to have been a pointer to what was wrong. It had to be very scary not to be able to read or understand figures, especially when from a small child you'd learnt never to trust anyone. Banker's drafts to Cissie must be just bits of paper with meaningless scribble on. Perhaps if she'd been handed a bag full of dollar bills, she would have been able to relate to them better.

She understood now why Cissie had blown hot and cold about coming to San Francisco too. How could she make a rational decision about whether to sell the mill and the cabin when she had no idea of their true value, or indeed whether that money would last long enough to give her and her children some security?

The heavy rain of the previous day had stopped the following morning and as soon as they'd had their breakfast, and the children had gone out to feed the animals, Matilda first plonked Amelia in her pen to play, then tore pages out of a note-book and wrote '$10' on ten of them. 'That makes a hundred dollars,' she said, putting the wodge into Cissie's hands. 'I haven't got enough pieces of paper to show you exactly what a huge pile of money those banker's drafts mean, so I'll just put crosses on this piece of paper to show you in hundreds.'

She covered the paper in crosses, counting aloud as she did it.

Cissie gasped when the page was full.

'Right, that's the total, give or take a few dollars,' Matilda said. 'Now I'll cross out nine of them for my commission, and you'll see how much is left.'

'I've got all that left?' Cissie's eyes widened with surprise. 'It's an awful lot!'

'It is, Cissie,' Matilda agreed. 'Far more than John could have made in years selling timber around here.' She crossed out a few more crosses. 'That's roughly what will be taken away by the bank to pay what you borrowed from them, the wages and shipping costs, but you are still left with all this. Almost four thousand dollars.'

She went on to explain in simple terms that if it was all put into a bank and left there, Cissie would get interest on it too, so it would grow. 'Once the sawmill is sold and that money goes in there too, you'll have enough to live on from the interest alone as long as you don't get extravagant. But I'm going to teach you some arithmetic so you can jot down everything you spend and add it up yourself. Then you'll know no one is cheating you.'

Matilda moved on then to explain why she wanted to buy the piece of land in San Francisco. 'Even if I don't do anything with it, just leave it sitting there for a year or so, it will increase in value. That's called an investment. It's much the same as putting money in the bank and getting interest on it. But I've got an idea of something to do on it which would make me even more.'

She described her fun palace in detail, and how people she'd spoken to down there thought she'd make a fortune, as long as she jumped in now while the gold was still pouring into the town.

'There was a place like that in the Bowery,' Cissie said, her face animated with excitement. 'All the toffs used to go in there. It was packed every night. You gotta do it, Matty, it's a great idea.'

'But there's a big problem,' Matilda said, her lips trembling because every time she even thought about it she felt she could never do it. She glanced out of the window to check the children weren't about to come in. 'I can't see how I can take Tabitha and Amelia with me, not at the moment. It's a filthy, dangerous place and I can't expose them to it. Maybe in a year or so it will be more civilized, but right now it's not safe.'

'Well, leave them with me,' Cissie said without any hesitation.

'How can I do that?' Matilda sighed. 'You've got enough to do with your own.'

'Tabby's worth her weight in gold,' Cissie said with a shrug. 'I can't imagine how I'd cope without her help anyway. But it ain't just that, Matty, I love both her and 'Melia as if they were me own.'

'I know you do,' Matilda replied. 'But I love them so much I don't know if I can bear to leave them, not even with you. Besides, you said you were frightened of being alone without me.'

Cissie gave her a long, hard look. 'I won't be scared once I really understand the money. Specially if I can go and live in town, 'cos there'll be people around I can ask things. Anyways, from what you've said about San Francisco, I guess Tabby and 'Melia will be happier staying here than down there. But that ain't really the point, is it? You've gone and set your heart on doing this, ain't you?'

Matilda nodded. 'It's burning inside me, I can hardly think of anything else. The mother in me tells me I should stay here, get some land and be satisfied with just that. But I know I'm not cut out for farming, Cissie.'

'You'll be a bad mother to them if you ain't happy,' Cissie said evenly. 'I reckon you gotta do it. If you don't, well, you'll always be wishing you had. Anyways, it ain't like you's goin' for ever. If you're the boss you can come home anytime you please.'

Matilda heard Tabitha approaching, talking to Peter. She put her finger to her lips.

'We'll talk about it more tonight,' she said warningly. 'Now, why don't we drive into town and show Mr Weinburg that money.'

'I'll tell him to give you your lot,' Cissie said, and held out her arms for a hug. 'I sure am sorry that I said those mean things, Matty. You're the best pal anyone could ever have, and I truly never want to lose you.'

It was almost Christmas, just a few days after Tabitha's tenth birthday, when Matilda got a letter from Charles Dubrette telling her the land in San Francisco was now legally hers.

Cissie's future was settled now. The mill had been sold at an excellent price and Sidney had been given a job there with the new owners. After getting a very good offer for the cabin, land and livestock from the family from Connecticut, Cissie had found a little house in Oregon City to move into after Christmas, so both Tabitha and Peter could start school in January. It would be easier for Sidney living so close to his work too, and he was taking great pride in the fact he would be man of the house now. Matilda had of course been intending to help with the move and stay on with Cissie for some time in the town, perhaps until the spring, but this letter from Dubrette meant she'd have to go much sooner.

He had costed the whole project – the building, a well to be dug, furniture, equipment, and the initial stock of drink – to be around 5,500 dollars. He went on to say that if Matilda still wanted to proceed, he considered her stake, the land itself, should be counted at 1,500, for the moment the building went up, that would be its true value. With four other people each putting in 1,000, she could remain the largest shareholder.

He said that he would like to be one of these shareholders himself, as would Zandra, Henry Slocum and a friend of Henry's, Simeon Greenstater. If Matilda was agreeable to this, he would like her to come to San Francisco as soon as possible so that the legal documents could be signed, architectural plans approved and the building work commence immediately. He pointed out that each of the four shareholders would be bringing their expertise into the project. Henry was an architect, Greenstater a builder, Zandra and himself would act in an advisory capacity in the areas of the business they knew well.

Her first reaction to this letter was to panic. Five and a half thousand dollars was an enormous sum of money – up here in Oregon it would build several streets of houses – and she hadn't expected Dubrette to start moving so quickly. But if Henry believed in it enough to put money into it, and draw up the plans, it must be a good idea, for he was no fool. She didn't know Greenstater, but Henry had brought him into it, so he must be okay too, and he had the expertise to build it.

After much deep thought, she couldn't see what she had to lose. The land would still be hers, even if the place burned down. If Greenstater, Henry, Zandra and Dubrette, all astute business people, were prepared to back her idea with their money, what possible reason could she have for declining it?

Matilda had met Dubrette, the elegant, white-haired lawyer, at Zandra's, and she had been very taken with him. Although he had the manner and the slow drawl of a Southern gentleman, Zandra had said he made his money from his law practice, not inherited wealth. Matilda liked his sense of humour and the fact he didn't share the normal male view that women were all silly, weak creatures incapable of running a business. Even the speed with which he had organized all this proved his belief in it.

When Matilda explained to Cissie what the letter contained, she was excited at first, but this changed to dejection when Matilda explained she would have to go soon after Christmas.

'I truly don't mind you going,' she insisted. 'I'm as hot as mustard for it. I guess I'm just scared that once you start mixing with those nobs you won't want me as a pal no longer.'

That last remark tore at Matilda's heart. In reality Cissie was a match for almost anyone, but because of her background and lack of education she always felt inferior. No amount of telling her that she was admired by just about everyone who met her would convince her otherwise.

'You will always be my best and dearest friend,' Matilda said quietly. 'I shan't change through mixing with a few nobs. Neither will I ever forget that without you and John caring for me and my children when I most needed help this opportunity would never have come my way.'

Cissie brightened up a little then, and went on to say it was all the more reason to make this Christmas extra special as it would be the last in the cabin.

'We will have a wonderful Christmas,' Matilda said, hugging her friend 'And I won't go to San Francisco until after you are settled in the new house.'

Christmas Day was magical. She and Cissie had decorated the cabin with holly and mistletoe, tied up with red ribbons, and hung gingerbread men and candy canes on more ribbon around the windows. The smell of the roast goose mingled deliciously with the cinnamon, oranges, lemons and cloves they'd put in the pot of mulled wine warming on the stove.

The shrieks of delight as the older children opened their stockings was the happiest sound of all – they had expected nothing more than the usual meagre amount of candy and fruit they'd been used to. This year the stockings were stuffed with extras, sugared mice, toffees in little tins, Tabitha had pretty hair ribbons, a necklace, a diary, Peter had more lead soldiers, a top and whip.

There were bigger presents for everyone too. Sidney had new pants and a tweed jacket, Tabitha the red dress she'd always wanted. There was a small cart for Peter, a real china doll for Susanna, and for Amelia a wooden horse she could push along. Matilda had bought Cissie a new bonnet trimmed with fur, and Cissie had bought her a pretty lace-trimmed night-gown. Treacle had a new blanket to sleep on.

But even while Matilda's heart was almost bursting with happiness and excitement for the future, and delight in the new prosperity which had come to Cissie, deep down within her she felt twinges of sorrow because she knew today was the end of an era.

The children and Cissie would have a far more comfortable, easier life in the town. They could attend school, go to church, and make friends with other families. Sidney had a real job, and their new shingled house was like a palace compared with the cabin, with a staircase up to the bedrooms, a water pump right outside the back door, and a cellar where food could be kept cool in the summer.

But this cabin and the land outside with its dozens of young fruit trees and neat rows of carefully tended vegetables was the dream which had kept Cissie, John and Sidney going in their long trek from New Jersey, and gave them the strength and determination to see it fulfilled. For Matilda and Tabitha it had been a sanctuary, where the love and kindness shown to them had healed their heartbreak.

Peter, Susanna and Amelia were too young to appreciate what these crude wooden walls represented to the older members of their families. While both Cissie and Matilda never wanted them to experience any of the hardships and deprivations they'd lived through, they hoped the spirit of this place would be retained in their minds through to adulthood.

'Do you like your new house?' Matilda whispered to Tabitha, sitting down beside her on the bed she was sharing with Susanna. The younger child was already fast asleep, as was Amelia in her little cot.

The shutters were tightly closed against the stiff wind outside, and the candle cast a soft golden light round the room. Yesterday they had celebrated the New Year of 1850, and Matilda was leaving for San Francisco in the morning. This was her last chance to discover if Tabitha had any fears about her leaving.

Two old friends of John's had helped them with the move three days earlier, taking all the furniture on a big farm cart. They had kept a few chickens and put them in a pen out in the yard behind the new house, and Sidney had dug up an apple and a pear tree to grow here as a lasting reminder of their life at the cabin.

A pot-bellied stove downstairs kept the whole house warm, the cook stove too was far bigger and better than the old one. Matilda and Cissie had made curtains for the parlour windows, and it was Cissie's intention to spend a little of her money on a carpet and a couch too.

'I love the house,' Tabitha said, her dark eyes looking right into Matilda's blue ones. 'It's so snug and it will be very pretty when everything's done. Cissie said today that we'll make a real garden with grass and flowers, because I told her about Mama liking to have tea in the garden in summer.'

It pleased Matilda to find Tabitha remembered so much about her mother, especially the quintessential Englishness of her. Cissie's influence was very much American, and although

Matilda tried to keep up many English customs, and indeed to make all the children speak correct English, sometimes she felt the girl's heritage was in danger of being lost for ever.

'Is there anything you don't like then?' Matilda asked, smoothing the child's hair back from her forehead.

'Only that you won't be here,' Tabitha said with a little sigh. 'But perhaps I won't mind so much once I'm at school.'

A lump came up in Matilda's throat. 'You do understand why I'm going?'

Tabitha nodded. 'To make lots of money for us.'

'It's not only money,' Matilda said gently, knowing she owed this child absolute truth. 'I want to do this thing too because it's a chance for me to prove myself. For some people, just earning enough to feed and clothe themselves and their children isn't enough. It's called ambition. Your father's ambition was to stamp out poverty, and free slaves. Uncle John wanted to see this town be a fine place with paved streets, a hospital, and even parks for people to walk in. Your ambition is to be a doctor, and I hope you never lose that.'

'I won't,' Tabitha said. 'I want to be one even more than ever.'

'I don't think my ambition is quite so honourable as that, or your Papa's and Uncle John's,' Matilda smiled. 'But it will give some people work, it will make the people who come in there happy, and I hope it will make enough money for you and Amelia to have the kind of life your Mama and Papa would have wanted for you.'

'I think you are very brave,' Tabitha said, smiling weakly. 'Aunt Cissie said men rule this world and you will show other women that they can run businesses too.'

Matilda smiled at that. Over the last few weeks she and Cissie had spent long hours together not just on simple arithmetic but reading and writing too. Cissie could write a whole shopping list now, and add up a list of figures. Many times Matilda had caught her looking at the reading books Matilda had bought last summer to teach Peter. She seemed determined to master it, perhaps she even hoped she could run a business one day too.

'Whatever I'm doing down there in California, I will always be thinking about you and Amelia and missing you,' she said, her voice cracking because it hurt so much to know this was the last night she'd tuck them into bed and kiss them goodnight. 'I shall write to you every week and you must write back telling me everything. I'll come home as often as I can. But it's going to be hard for a while because there will be so much to do.'

Tabitha nodded. 'I know, Aunt Cissie explained to me that a big restaurant would take a long time to sort out.'

Matilda was just about to say there was no restaurant when she stopped herself. At no time had she actually told Tabitha, or Sidney for that matter, just what the place would be, only that it was a business venture.

She kissed the child goodnight and went downstairs. Cissie was sitting at the kitchen table copying out a list of words Matilda had given her to learn. Shutting the door behind her, Matilda sat down beside her friend.

'Why did you tell Tabby it was a restaurant?' she asked in a quiet voice.

'Did you tell her different?' Cissie replied, giving Matilda a sharp look.

Matilda shook her head.

'Why?'

'Because I didn't like to.'

Cissie shrugged. 'That's 'xactly why I said it was a restaurant. It sure wouldn't be too smart to let her go off around the town telling folks her mother owned some sort of hurdy-gurdy place.'

Matilda thought for a moment before replying. Hurdy-gurdy places were only one or two steps up from brothels. The girls employed there danced with men for a few cents a dance. But quite often the girls did sell their bodies too.

'But you know it's not going to be like that,' she said eventually.

Cissie grinned impishly. 'Sure I do, but God-fearing folk round here have only got to get a sniff of liquor and hear talk of dancing girls and they'll stick their noses in the air. I reckon it's best Tabby believes it's a restaurant, we don't want no one being mean to her, do we?'

Sudden fear clutched at Matilda's insides. 'San Francisco is so different to here, Cissie. It's so wild and free from hypocrisy that it makes you forget how narrow-minded the rest of the world is. When I dreamed this up I didn't think anyone would think it was shameful.'

Cissie smiled at her worried expression and patted her hand. 'Neither did I, but then we come from places where folk liked a bit of liquor and dancin'. We ain't got that kind of stuff in our heads. If I get to be a hundred I'll still be wanting folks to have a bit of fun. But I was in the store before Christmas and I heard a couple of ladies gossiping about that French woman that runs the saloon. I kinda knew they'd say the same kind of things about you.'

'Perhaps I shouldn't be doing it,' Matilda said, for the first time thrown into doubt. 'I don't suppose Giles would like it.'

'Giles is dead, God rest him,' Cissie said flatly. 'I know he were a good man, but he didn't get to leave nuthin' for you, or his girls. If'n you ain't had so much wits and courage, you mighta ended up in bad trouble, Tabby in some orphanage.'

'I know that, but – '

Cissie cut her short. 'Those wits of yourn is what's left me so comfortable, too. So what I'm sayin' is go on off and do it. San Francisco sure is a far way from here, and if we makes out it's a bit more proper than it really is, who's to know?'

Matilda had to smile. As John had always remarked, Cissie knew how many beans made five!

Matilda looked round the table at her four co-shareholders and felt a surge of gleeful excitement. She thought they made a formidable team. Charles Dubrette with his elegant Southern charm and his extensive knowledge of the law, portly Alderman Henry Slocum who had a finger right on the pulse of this town, and knew how to get things done. The Contessa, privy to just about every businessman's secrets in town, and Simeon Greenstater who had made a personal fortune building houses in Philadelphia.

Matilda had already studied the architect's plans Henry had drawn up, and she was astounded how he'd taken her rough, tentative sketches and with his own knowledge of structural work come up with a plan for a building which was practical, attractive, and could be built quickly and cheaply, while pleasing everyone involved.

It was to be a long, low, two-storey brick-built place, with a wide veranda right along the front. The entire ground floor, but for several small rooms at the back, was to be the saloon, with an open staircase going up to a gallery, beyond which was Matilda's private apartment.

Simeon had suggested using the iron-frame style of building favoured in New York. It was quickly assembled, strong and fire-resistant. Simeon wasn't an easy man to like. He was brash, tough, and shouted people down when he didn't agree with him. His loud checked suit, florid colouring, the stink of the oily pomade on his hair and his habit of talking without taking his large cigar out of his mouth were all irritating, yet his knowledge of building was vast. Henry said that when he gave a date for a building to be finished, it could be relied on. He wasn't given to skimping on sub-standard materials, and the men he employed respected him.

They were holding this meeting in Zandra's parlour, but she now half-jokingly called it the boardroom, for while Matilda had been away, Zandra had finally decided to retire from her old business. Her boarders had all gone, mostly to a new parlour house further along the street. Their dormitory-style rooms were empty, Matilda was sleeping in one of the three boudoirs where they once took their gentlemen, and Dolores the maid had another one. After a few weeks of rest Zandra's legs were much better, she was bright-eyed and enthusiastic about the new project and said it had given her a new lease of life.

'Shall we get on with the business in hand?' Charles asked, looking to each of them in turn. 'I'm sure you will all be pleased to know that Mrs Jennings has approved the plans of the building and each of you as her co-shareholders, and is anxious that we start work without delay. Mrs Jennings would like to address you all at this point.'

They all looked to her.

'First of all I'd like to welcome you all aboard London Lil's,' she said, her voice cracking with nerves, even though she'd rehearsed this little speech many times. 'I hope we will not only be co-shareholders, but friends, and along with making a great deal of money, we'll enjoy ourselves too.

'As I believe Charles has already informed you, I have insisted on having a clause written into our agreements that should anyone wish to sell their share in the business at any time, a meeting like this one will be called, and that share offered first to me. This is, as I'm sure you'll understand, to ensure I do not lose control of the business. But likewise, should I wish to retire at some future date, my share will be offered to all of you before any outsider is approached. While Charles will be handling the legal side of the business for us, I intend to appoint an independent accountant to look after the books. These of course will be open to all of you for inspection.'

She then went on to outline in more detail her plans for the interior decor and equipment needed and suggested they invite tenders for the supply of glassware, beer and spirits from companies Zandra had previous experience with. She had already explained her idea of the central stage, the long bar and a small dance area to Henry, and he had completed detailed sketches which he passed around for their approval. Matilda pointed out that she would require a wage from the business as once it opened she would be working there constantly, and had to provide for her children, but she also pointed out that each of them would be paid for any services they rendered on submission of a bill.

For over two hours they discussed varying aspects of the business, from the interior decoration to specialist tradesmen who would need to be called in, and agreed they would have a further meeting each Friday evening to discuss the work in progress.

'I think that covers just about everything,' Matilda said finally, smiling round at them. 'Except that I'd like you all to drop the Mrs Jennings title, at least in private. I'm Matty to all of you.'

Zandra rang the bell and Dolores came in with a bottle of champagne and glasses for a toast.

'To London Lil's,' Charles said, raising his glass. 'May she become a beacon of light, fun and happiness in this town.'

'To London Lil's,' they all repeated, and clinked their glasses.

Everything in San Francisco moved fast, but it was nothing short of miraculous how quickly the building went up. One day there was nothing but a piece of scrubby land, the next the trenches for the foundations were dug. There was a slight delay waiting for the iron frame to arrive by sea, and watching men haul the large heavy pieces up the hill on carts was nerve-racking, as to Matilda at least it seemed impossible to imagine anyone being able to figure out how it all slotted together.

But Simeon and Henry knew exactly what they were doing, and in no time at all their labourers had assembled it and riveted it together. It stood up above the town like a huge, ugly brown cage, creating a great deal of both laughter and suspicion. But then the bricklayers began work, and each day it began to look just a little more like Henry's drawings. Fortunately the weather all through February and March remained mild, with very little rain, and the miners who'd come down from the mountains for a break from the freezing conditions up there were glad of a few weeks' work. By mid-March Matilda was able to climb up a ladder to view the shell of her private apartment, and the view of the bay from what would be her parlour window. Although there was no roof at that stage, only timber, it was exciting enough to help ease the pain she felt at being away from her children.

Tabitha wrote every week, and mostly there was a page from Cissie too, proving she was taking her lessons seriously. Amelia had begun to walk, as long as she had something to hold on to, she had several more teeth, and liked to feed herself now, making a fearful mess. Sidney wasn't very happy at the sawmill. Cissie called the owner an 'arse-wipe' because instead of teaching the lad new skills, he treated him like a labourer, fetching and carrying, but never trusting him to plane or saw timber. She said she was now going to church, because it was a good excuse to buy a pretty hat.

Reading between the lines, it was clear Cissie was very much happier. Moving to town had relieved her of so much hard work and anxiety, and there were less painful reminders of John. She had time to make friends with other women, she was financially secure, and she felt safer knowing she had neighbours close by. Although she said in every letter that she missed Matilda terribly, there was no hint of real loneliness.

Tabitha's letters were full of all the little details of their life together that Cissie's never touched on. Treacle had fathered a litter of puppies with a bitch further along their street. She said they were so sweet she wanted to have all of them, but the owners of the bitch were cross with Cissie for letting Treacle wander around the town, so Sidney had built him a kennel in the garden and repaired the fence. Peter was getting on very well at school, he was the best reader of his age and he had a friend called Tom. She described how Susanna would look at a book and pretend to read it, but it was often upside down. She kept insisting she was a big girl now and that she thought she ought to go to school too. But of all the things which pleased Matilda in Tabitha's letters, her obvious contentment in her new life was the best. She spoke about the shops, watching the blacksmith, walking along the river bank, her teacher at school and new things she'd learnt, and it was clear she felt happy and confident.

The days just weren't long enough for Matilda. From early morning till late at night she was busy choosing furnishings, seeing commercial travellers' samples of everything from glasses and oil lamps to chairs, sitting in at auditions with entertainers, looking out for the right staff to help her run the place. There were terrible panics when things ordered didn't turn up, anger when inferior items were substituted, and frustration when Henry or Simeon said part of the building work wasn't right.

Henry and Simeon hardly left the site. They always seemed to be arguing over some small detail, the carving on the banisters going up to the gallery, the design on the glazed doors, the exact length of the bar, and the height of the mirrors behind it.

The whole stage was built, then had to come down again because it wasn't supported strongly enough. The men who came to dig the well had three false tries before they finally found water. And when the glazier arrived to fit the windows, a young apprentice fell out of the first-floor window and broke his arm. Every day seemed to be fraught with anxiety, and although Zandra reminded Matilda again and again that she had four other partners, and they shared the problems and could solve them together, Matilda still felt responsible for everything that went wrong.

Yet however full her life was, however exciting the future looked, missing her children was something which never went away, and she often felt stabs of terrible guilt because she knew she hadn't come here entirely for their benefit. This knowledge left her with an inner feeling of worthlessness as a mother, and as a result she plunged herself into working even harder, to justify herself.

It was Zandra who pointed this out to her one evening in early April when their grand opening was only a week away.

The exterior of London Lil's was complete, except for the sign which would be placed over the doors just a day before the opening. It sat proudly up on the hill, reminiscent of the grand plantation houses in the Southern states. Painted white, with green tiles on the roof, and the veranda balustrade and window-frames a glossy red, it could be seen clearly for miles.

Inside, the central stage was yet to have its final coats of varnish, but the walls had already had a coat of paint, and the artist who had been commissioned to reproduce street scenes of London, copied from a book of sketches Zandra had lent, was hard at work.

A long bar with mirrors behind ran along the entire right-hand side of the main room, this too was waiting for varnish. The left-hand side was to be the dance floor. A wide staircase led up from the back on to a narrow gallery which would give a better view of the shows on the stage for those booking a table in advance, and also give Matilda a place from which to view the entire lower floor. Two small rooms were up here too, intended for private poker games. A further door led to Matilda's apartment, four rooms and a small kitchen. The back of the building was taken up with store-rooms, a large kitchen, wash-room and changing room for performers, and a few smaller rooms intended for staff. A large cellar ran right under the building, and the privies were up a small path.

'Put those books down, come over here and put your feet up,' Zandra ordered Matilda as for yet another evening she had found her friend squinting at the accounts books by candlelight with a worried expression on her face.

'I can't, I haven't got time,' Matilda said in a weary voice. 'We've spent well over the budget and I need to get the exact figure to give to Charles tomorrow.'

The building costs were just over 3,000 dollars, all of which had been paid, but the stock, equipment, furniture and all the incidentals came to well over another 1,500, and a great many of these bills were still outstanding.

Zandra just laughed, came over to the table, snapped the books shut, snatched the pencil from Matilda's hand and pointed to the couch by the fire.

'Charles won't care. We all know it's over budget, but the first week we're open will take care of that. I want to talk to you.'

When Zandra used that imperious tone everyone obeyed her, including Matilda. Reluctantly she moved to the couch.

'Shoes off, feet up!' Zandra said sharply. 'And I've poured you a glass of brandy.'

Matilda picked up the large goblet from the side table and sipped it cautiously. She had developed a taste for it since Zandra introduced her to it, but she still had a feeling hard liquor was dangerous.

'In the last few weeks you have never stopped,' Zandra said. 'You can't go on working at that pace, Matty, you'll get sick, and then where will we be?'

'I won't get sick, I'm as strong as a horse,' Matilda retorted.

'I used to say that,' Zandra smiled. 'But then we are very alike in many ways. Working till you are on the point of collapse is a good way of avoiding one's problems and heartaches. But I assure you, if you do collapse, they'll come bounding up to hit you in the face.'

'I don't have any problems,' Matilda said indignantly. 'Other than worrying about whether everything will be finished in time, and whether the dancing girls will turn up for the opening.'

'You do, you feel you are a bad mother.'

That bald statement made Matilda's head jerk up in surprise.

'I'm right of course, so don't deny it,' Zandra said, waving one hand at Matilda. 'I can't possibly say anything to make you believe this isn't so, but I can tell you I know how you feel, and that you've got to come to terms with your decision to leave your children. If you don't, then you will become more and more unhappy, and when that happens to a woman the consequences can be disastrous.'

Matilda looked at the brandy glass in her hand and wondered if Zandra meant she might get to like that too much.

'Yes, that's one way you could go,' Zandra said, raising an eyebrow. 'There's allowing the wrong men into your life, spending more than you earn, even resorting to opiates. I know because I've been down all those roads.'

Matilda was on the point of retorting that she wasn't that big a fool, but she stopped herself, remembering Zandra had said she knew how she felt.

The bond between her and Zandra had grown steadily strong in the past weeks. She no longer noticed that Zandra was old, wrinkled, with bad legs and few teeth, what she saw now was just a dear friend, someone she could trust, a woman who like herself had to have come through a great deal of personal suffering to be as knowledgeable and understanding as she was.

'Did you leave a child?' she said in little more than a whisper.

Zandra nodded.

'Can you tell me about it?'

Zandra sighed. 'I have never told anyone this before, Matty. So you must promise that even if we fall out one day it will remain a secret between us.'

'Of course,' Matilda replied.

'I was seduced at seventeen by our coachman. My father horse-whipped him, and sent me off in disgrace to live with my aunt in Somerset,' she said quickly as if by telling it fast she wouldn't be able to feel the pain of it again now.

'When I realized I was carrying a child I knew I could expect no help from my family, so I slipped off one night and made my way to Bath. I had been there once or twice before, and it appeared such a jolly place I suppose I thought someone there would help me. Someone did. I met a very distinguished gentleman, who seemed smitten with me. He had a big country estate, and when I told him my situation he said he would take care of everything.' She winced and faltered. Clearly even rattling it out didn't stop it hurting.

'That care meant he had his way with me at any time, in any manner he chose, right up until my son Piers was born. Then he gave me an ultimatum. I was to have my "brat" as he called him farmed out, which he would pay for, and stay with him in luxury, or I was to get out immediately. Needless to say I left, unwisely taking a few of his valuables with me.'

Matilda half smiled. 'I would have done too.'

Zandra shrugged. 'He got some men to trace me, I had just settled in a little cottage, and they took everything away, not just what belonged to him, but my jewellery, and most of my clothes too. Suddenly for the first time in my life I was absolutely destitute. Alone with a baby I was looking after by instinct alone, for I certainly had no experience of caring for a child.'

She stopped again, her eyes brimming with tears.

'I can't bear to tell you about what happened to me in that terrible year, Matty. Suffice it to say I suffered every kind of humiliation. I was hungry, dirty and desperate. Then, fearing my son would die of starvation, I finally wrote to my father and begged him to help me.'

'Don't tell me he turned you away?' Matilda exclaimed.

'He refused to see me himself, but he sent me a little money and said I was to go and see his lawyer in London. It was there I had the proposition put to me. A friend of my father's, another extremely wealthy man, was desperate for a son and heir. His wife had carried five until the seventh month, then each of them had been stillborn. They were willing to take Piers and bring him up as their own. I knew these people well, Matty, and I knew them to be kind and honourable. Anyway, the deal was that I was to hand Piers over to the lawyer and would be given two hundred pounds on the understanding I left the country and never came back.'

She paused, and gave Matilda a defiant look. 'I agreed. I chose to go to Paris because I spoke fluent French. The money I'd been given set me up to enter the only profession I had any qualifications for. I kept my end of the bargain and never went back.'

Matilda moved over to kneel in front of Zandra. 'I'm so sorry,' she whispered.

Zandra shrugged and dabbed at her eyes. 'I don't regret giving my son away, if I had refused I doubt he would even have seen his second birthday. But what I do regret is taking that two hundred pounds,' she said. 'That's my guilt, Matty. Even some fifty years later it still eats away at me.'

'I don't think you had much choice,' she said.

'I did,' Zandra said. 'I could have handed him over and walked away, but I took it because I knew without money behind me I'd die in the gutter.

'Now, you chose to come here and leave your children with Cissie, no one forced you. And like me you have to live with that decision. It's different for you, you haven't given them away and walked out of their life for good, you certainly haven't taken money for them, and I know you'll be paying for their keep. But I know it troubles you deeply just the same. However, you must find a way of forgiving yourself, Matty, because if you don't you'll become hard and ruthless, just like me.'

'I don't think you are hard or ruthless,' Matilda said, and she stroked the older woman's face tenderly. 'Maybe that was my first impression but it soon left.'

'My first impression of you was a woman with a big heart,' Zandra said softly. 'That impression has remained in place, just make sure it stays there.'

On opening night the flaming torches outside London Lil's were lit at eight and the band struck up a merry jig as the doors were opened. The huge crowd which had been gradually gathering in the past hour burst in like a flood.

There were those who had said no one would want to walk up the steep hill for a drink, not even if dancing girls and fire-eaters were thrown in, but they did walk up the hill, rode horses and mules and drove carts and carriages – everyone wanted to take a look.

Dolores had arranged Matilda's hair into fat curls on the top of her head, and she could hardly believe that the sophisticated woman staring back at her in the looking-glass was really her. Her dress was a present from Zandra, an old dress of her own, but taken apart and remade by the dressmaker who had once made her girls' gowns. It was blue velvet, indecently low cut over her bosom, or so she thought, but Zandra insisted that she couldn't look like a school marm, and besides, it was the latest fashion in Paris. She'd dyed some elbow-length lace gloves to match, and beneath her dress, holding up her stockings, were red garters, a present Charles had given her. He'd laughed at her shocked expression when she opened the box. He said she might be proper and demure on the outside, but he knew she had a wicked streak and she was to wear them for luck. Somehow just putting them on made her feel reckless and naughty, and she liked the feeling.

'Here's to a night to remember,' Charles said, bringing over a bottle of champagne to the table on the balcony where she was sitting with Henry, Simeon and Zandra. 'Just look at that crowd!'

Men stood at the bar six deep, jostling and pushing to get a drink, elsewhere every inch of space was taken, and their faces all held similar expressions of wonder at the decor.

'There's a great many women,' Matilda said in some surprise. At a quick count she estimated there might be as many as fifty, and most of them very well dressed. She had expected all the prostitutes in town to come. No doubt they'd heard that the owner of this place had trawled around among them to find waitresses, and wanted to see for themselves if their friends were in fact merely operating their old business from here. They would be disappointed to find this wasn't so. Matilda had interviewed over forty girls and women, of whom she'd taken on only ten, for various roles. Each one of these had confided in her they wanted to take a step up in life, and she'd offered them the chance to prove it. She didn't doubt some would fall by the wayside, that a pretty dress, a clean bed, food and wages wouldn't be enough for the greedier ones. But as she'd told them, they'd be back out on the streets if that was their choice.

'Who are all the women, Henry? Do you know any of them?'

'Some of them are actually wives,' Henry said with a grin, his one good eye on her and the other wavering uncertainly round the room. 'I'm astounded to see some of them, but I guess they felt they had to unbend tonight at least, and see if there's any truth in the rumour that this isn't a bordello.'

All the partners had stuck fast to the idea that London Lil's would never stoop to the lowest kind of entertainment seen elsewhere in the town. It was important that they made a niche for themselves as a place for good, clean fun, where men could bring their wives and sweethearts without fear of fights, crudeness or profanity to embarrass them. Women were to be encouraged to come in, for single women were beginning to arrive in the town, and both Matilda and Zandra felt it was important that they should have somewhere to go where they could make friends and meet young men in safety.

'Is Alicia coming later?' Matilda asked with some trepidation. She had seen Alicia several times in the past few months, but the woman was always very cool with her, and had never extended any invitations to her home. Henry had confided in Matilda on several occasions that Alicia disapproved of his new venture, particularly because Zandra was involved.

His smile faded. 'No, she's playing ill,' he said. 'I half expected she would find some excuse not to come. She has so many ways of making me feel guilty, and this is her favourite one.'

'Poor Henry,' she said in sympathy. She had grown very fond of this man in the past couple of months. His enthusiasm for their project and his belief in her had helped her through many bad patches.

His smile came back. 'I'll doubtless have more fun without her,' he said. 'And when she sees how much money we'll make she'll be left with egg on her face.'

A roll of the drums signalled the show was ready to start. Two of the barmen rushed forward to move the people around the dressing-room door back, and to hang up a piece of rope on either side, making a clear passageway for the dancers. Immediately all faces turned expectantly towards the dressing-room door.

The music began, the changing-room door opened and out came six dancers, bright satin dresses held up to reveal frilly petticoats, black stockings and button boots. With wide, provocative smiles they ran up the steps on to the stage, formed a circle, and began the dance.

This was Zandra's pet project. Although she had left Paris a great many years ago, she corresponded with old friends there, and through them she had heard of this dance the cancan, which had started there in the 1830s and symbolized all the naughtiness of Paris. Zandra had left no stone unturned to get it right, she'd had sheet music, theatre billboards, sketches of the costumes sent to her, and details of how the dance was choreographed. She had herself found a little troupe of dancing girls and schooled them here every afternoon. Until now, none of the partners, not even Matilda, had been allowed to see it.

The crowd roared their approval, clapped their hands and stamped their feet, almost drowning the music from the band. Matilda was as enthralled as any of her customers, leaning forward on to the balustrade and watching as the girls whirled around swirling their skirts, giving tantalizing glimpses of shapely legs as they did their high kicks. It was not a highly polished performance, they were not in step, often their movements were clumsy, but the girls were enjoying themselves, and as Zandra was probably the only person in the whole place who had ever been to Paris, it didn't matter one bit.

Zandra's words at their first meeting about the miners' need for something feminine in their hard lives came back to her. They were looking up at these girls as if they were goddesses, their smiles warm and their eyes sparkling. For a short time they could forget that they had to go up into those mountains again, that some of their number would die of disease and accidents, and that even those who survived might not go home with riches. Maybe a glimpse of soft, white flesh above stocking tops would remind them of their wives at home, and even hasten their efforts to make their fortune and go back. At least this place wasn't robbing the men, neither were the girls for sale. Maybe it wasn't exactly proper, not in the black and white way Lily saw things, but it wasn't, and it never would, become an evil place, that much Matilda promised herself.

After the cancan girls came jugglers, then a contortionist who was billed as 'The Man With No Bones'. Grown men squealed with disbelief as he went through a series of amazing feats, placing his feet behind his head and bending over backwards until his hands touched the floor, then walking crab-like across the stage.

After the show, the band struck up again. This was the point when Matilda had been afraid people would leave for the saloons where the drinks were cheaper. But they didn't go. Maybe they wanted to see the second show later, and were afraid they wouldn't get in again, but they stayed, bought more drinks, and people began to dance.

It was three in the morning when the doors were finally shut, the night's takings locked in the safe, and the oil lamps extinguished. The varnished wood floor was awash with beer, spittoons overflowing, and the smell of cigars and human sweat overpowering. But it had been the most glorious evening, and Matilda knew in her heart that from now on it would be packed every night.

Zandra was still sitting up at a table on the balcony, she was staying here tonight because it was so late. As Matilda turned from locking and bolting the door, the old lady looked down at her and smiled.

'You, my dear, have made history tonight,' she said.

'Why's that?' Matilda asked, hobbling up the stairs because her new boots were pinching.

'The first woman to open a place of entertainment. A young and pretty woman at that. You sent those men back to their tents dancing. I bet you'll be the name on everyone's lips tomorrow and for weeks to come.'

'I just hope we can keep on getting good performers,' Matilda said wearily. 'Those poor dancing girls must have been exhausted by the time they did the last show.'

'They'll soon be queuing up at your door to appear here,' Zandra laughed. 'Why, in a few months they'll have heard of you in cities like New York and New Orleans. Musicians, dancers, singers and tumblers will be taking the next boat, wagon train or mule to get here. Soon you'll have to charge admission, the acts will be so good.'

'I hope so,' Matilda said. 'But right now all I care about is my bed. Are you coming?'

She took the old lady's arm and helped her up, Zandra had drunk a great many brandies tonight, and even if her brain was still functioning, Matilda wasn't sure her legs would be.

'Can you recognize that smell?' Zandra said, leaning on the younger woman.

'Yes, beer, cigars and sweat,' Matilda laughed.

'No, it's not just that, my dear,' she said. 'It's the smell of success. Breathe it in good and hard now. And don't ever forget what it smells like.'

Chapter Nineteen

San Francisco 1852

From the parlour window of her apartment Matilda watched a steady stream of people coming up the hill for an evening's entertainment at London Lil's.

'Do you ever get scared that your luck can't hold out much longer?' she asked Zandra who was sitting in an armchair, her feet up on a stool.

'At my age it hardly matters,' the older woman chuckled. 'But you mustn't allow such thoughts to creep into your mind, Matty. You've made a huge success of this place, you have money behind you now. Even if the very worst happened and the building burned down tonight, you could start some other venture.'

London Lil's had been open for two years now, and it was everything they'd hoped for, and more. Charles Dubrette had gone back to his law practice in New Orleans, Simeon Greenstater was involved in building work in Sacramento, even Henry Slocum's visits to London Lil's were only social calls, but all the shareholders were delighted with the continuing excellent returns on their investment.

Most nights it was packed to capacity, many of the staff they'd opened with were still with them, and as Zandra had predicted, the fame of the place had spread so far that entertainers found their way to the door. They had expected that during the spring and summer when the miners returned *en masse* to the mountains, it would grow much quieter, but this hadn't happened, for every new day brought more gold seekers in on ships, wagon trains and stage-coaches.

In just these two years the town had quadrupled in size, and tents had been replaced by real buildings. The waterfront area was quite different now. What had once been beach was now filled in with rock and rubble from Telegraph Hill, with buildings erected on the site, and new streets too. Wharves had been built so that goods could be unloaded directly from the ships, instead of the old system of using lighter-boats to ferry them in.

Some of the streets were now planked, and sidewalks built too, and much-needed organization of the town had taken place. The lawyers and bankers had Montgomery Street, clothing and dry goods were in Sacramento Street, and slaughter yards were banned from the centre of town. The French Adelphi Theatre had opened in 1850, along with a Chinese theatre too. The Germans and Jews had started schools recently and there was a new Roman Catholic Church, St Francis.

Most of these refinements had come about as respectable wives and sweethearts arrived in town to join their men. There was an ice-cream parlour now, a milliner's and a gown shop, one could see a play by Shakespeare, or go to a concert.

London Lil's was no longer in splendid isolation up on the hill. As Matilda had anticipated, gradually all the land in front of it had been bought, and wealthier people had built houses here away from the hubbub and stink of the harbour. Most people Matilda had met when she first came here had moved away from the centre of the town now. The Slocums had sold their house in Montgomery Street to a lawyer, and moved to a far grander place out by the old Mission.

There was finally some attempt to curb the worst excesses of the town. Gambling houses were banned from opening on Sundays, and prostitutes no longer enjoyed the same deference to their profession as they received in the early years. But the lack of law and order was still a serious problem. Almost every night someone was murdered, shootings and stabbings were so common that people rarely remarked on them. Disease was rife too, cholera, smallpox and yellow fever all took their terrible toll especially in the hideously squalid part they called Sydney Town where the Australians, all rumoured to be ex-convicts, lived along with the rest of the city's disreputable folk.

The mention of fire made Matilda turn away from the window in alarm. 'Don't say that, Zandra,' she said. Fire was the biggest danger in the town. With buildings of wood and canvas, a knocked-over candle, oil lamp, or just a carelessly thrown cigar butt could start a fire that would turn into an inferno within minutes. Hardly a week passed without something burning down, often whole streets.

Zandra's old parlour, the two shops beneath and the buildings all around it had gone this way just a few weeks ago. Fortunately Zandra had sold her property a year before and moved into Matilda's apartment temporarily because her legs had became badly swollen again, so she hadn't suffered financially, but fifteen people had perished in that fire, two of them girls who once worked for her.

'You've taken every precaution against it,' Zandra said soothingly. She was always impressed by the vigilant way Matilda checked around the building every night before retiring, and insisted that water and sand buckets were placed around the saloon. 'Besides, this place is well built, and it's not too close to anyone else. So what else can go wrong?'

Matilda shrugged. 'Well, you know how my life has been so far, I've had more ups and downs than the well bucket.'

'Maybe you've had your share already then,' Zandra chuckled. 'Your children are fine, you are fast becoming a wealthy woman, you are young, beautiful and smart, think on that instead of anticipating trouble.'

Matilda smiled. Zandra had become so very dear to her since she'd moved in. It was intended to be only a short stay, just until she could get a little place built nearby, but they soon found it to be a mutually comfortable, pleasant arrangement which had become permanent. Zandra couldn't manage stairs very well, so mostly she stayed in the apartment and played mother to Matilda, cooking meals, sewing and reading. Dolores, her maid, had come too, taking one of the rooms at the back of the building downstairs, and she did everything from the cleaning to dressing their hair. This left Matilda free to concentrate solely on her work, but she had Zandra for company when she wanted it.

'This young, beautiful and smart woman ought to go downstairs now,' she smiled, hearing the band striking up. 'Do you need anything before I go?'

'I'm perfectly capable of getting out of this chair,' Zandra reproved her. 'Just go down and have a good evening.'

Matilda's eyes swept around the parlour before she left the room. As always it gave her a rush of pleasure: cream lace curtains at the windows, maroon velvet couches, a thick carpet on the floor and an exquisite rosewood French bureau which Zandra had given her – never in her wildest dreams had she imagined having such an elegant home.

When she'd gone back to Cissie's house last October she had been rather disturbed to find that the bare wooden floors and simple furniture which had always seemed so homely before now looked primitive after the sophistication she had become accustomed to through Zandra's influence. She wanted to suggest that Cissie varnished the floor, or that some rugs would make it look less austere, but she didn't dare, for fiery Cissie would no doubt tell her she was getting above herself.

As Matilda walked along the gallery, as always she stopped to look down at the crowd below, and as usual many of the men smiled up at her. This was another source of pleasure to her, for she knew that even if she wasn't accepted by the likes of Alicia Slocum and the other society women, she was very much admired by their men, and by her customers. Back home her emerald-green, off-the-shoulder silk dress would raise disapproving eyebrows. Even Cissie would be shocked at the amount of exposed flesh. But by becoming 'London Lil' she had stopped attempting to sound, and behave like an American 'lady'. When she stopped to think about it, she had adopted a persona which was an amalgamation of London street girl, hard-bitten business woman and adventuring pioneer, with more than a touch of the glamour and elegance she'd picked up from Zandra.

Beneath her silk petticoats she had a little pistol tucked into her red garter. It might be pretty with its mother-of-pearl stock, but on many an occasion when things had turned rough in here she'd whipped it out, fully prepared to use it. Indeed, just so her customers knew it wasn't an empty threat and that she could shoot straight, she had once taken part in a shooting contest and won.

In the same way she hid her hands beneath lace gloves, she had learned, too, to hide her feelings. She knew her staff and customers saw her as tough and impervious, a woman who never resorted to feminine tears, but she often wondered what they would make of her if they saw her late at night alone in her room.

She did cry often. For her children she missed so badly. For those blissful short months after she'd arrived at Cissie and John's, when her days were spent loving and playing with them without any real anxiety for the future. She cried for Giles too, and the happiness which could have been theirs if he hadn't been shot. Still, after all this time, her heart and her body ached for him. She wondered if that would ever leave her.

Yet apart from all those she missed and still grieved for, there was much here in San Francisco which saddened her too. So many of the men who had left their wives and children in search of gold died out here, from gun shots, accidents and disease. How were their women faring without a man? Were some of them tempted into prostitution just to feed their children?

This town was full of whores, though the names dreamed up to make their occupation seem less sordid almost amused her: ladies of the night, soiled doves, fair but frail, painted ladies, street-walkers. For the few who were young and pretty enough to get into a select parlour house, it might be a pleasant enough way to make a living. But the truth of the matter was that for most girls and women who chose to enter the profession, it was a slippery slope down to degradation and eventual untimely death.

In these last two years Matilda had learned that there were travelling whores who went up into the mountains to earn their money. In a hastily erected tent they would take on as many as sixty men every night. In the further far-flung mining towns there were the hog farms too, a row of dirty little shacks with a woman in each, and they worked round the clock to satisfy the men's needs. Worse still, Chinese girls, some as young as nine or ten, were being shipped over here, often sold by their families because a girl child was of no value. Their life was the very worst, kept in what was little more than a cage, half-starved, doped on opium to keep them quiet, and never receiving a cent from their hundreds of customers. Matilda had heard to her horror that when the owners knew these young girls were too diseased to attract any sort of buyer, they were administered poison, and their emaciated bodies were then dumped into the bay.

Matilda could do nothing about any of this, particularly for the Chinese girls. To most Americans this race were not even considered to be human, fit only to work as coolies on road gangs, at best as servants, lower still than Negroes who at least spoke English. So when she tried to rouse people's sympathy she met a wall of indifference. All too often she had seen groups of miners catch hold of a Chinese man and cut off his pigtail to humiliate him, then beat him to a pulp, and this was considered good sport! It was hardly surprising the Chinese stayed in their little part of the town and rarely ventured out of it, and that in itself perpetuated the myth that they were to be feared.

Yet she was determined that she would do something to get these evils stamped out. So far all she'd been able to do was rescue a few girls from the streets and offer them proper employment.

She looked down at Mary Callaghan elbowing her way through a group of men carrying a tray of drinks. With her red ringlets, a sprinkling of freckles across her upturned nose, and her bright smile she looked like a girl fresh from a farm in Idaho. Yet six months ago she was better known as 'Adobe Moll', living in an adobe cabin on the river bank in Sacramento, taking on all the fresh young men stepping off the boats in search of gold.

It was just by chance that Matilda met her. She was on the way down to the mail office early one morning when she saw the girl staggering across a vacant lot towards her. She looked as if she'd been rolled in mud, her dress was filthy, the bodice ripped open, her face swollen and cut. Instinctively Matilda asked if she could help, and how she had got her injuries.

'What's it to you?' the girl replied defiantly.

Matilda said that she wasn't able to walk past anyone who looked hurt. At this the girl slumped down on the ground and burst into tears. She said she'd left Sacramento to try to make a new start here a few days ago. Last night a man had approached her and said he'd like to look after her.

'I knew what he meant all right,' she said angrily. 'I told him I didn't need no pimp, I could look after myself. It were a bit later when these two fancy women came up to me, first I thought they was going to get rough 'cos I was working their patch, but they seemed real friendly and bought me a gin. Next thing I know they said they was going up to London Lil's and did I want to come too. I never got there though, they led me over there.' She pointed back across the vacant lot. 'He was there waiting, weren't he. The geezer I met earlier. He hit me and kept hitting me till I passed out. When I come to, I found he'd robbed me too, so I just stayed there all night hurtin'. I don't know what I'm gonna do now. I ain't got no money and he said if I tried to work in this town he'd kill me.'

Matilda couldn't help herself, she just put her arms round the girl and hugged her. 'He won't kill you,' she said. 'I'll see to that. Now, come on home with me and let me clean you up.'

'I ain't working in no brothel,' the girl said, recoiling from her embrace. 'That's how I got this way, letting a woman who said she'd look after me take me back to her place.'

'Is that what you think I am? A brothel keeper?' Matilda exclaimed.

'Ain't you then?'

'No, I am not,' Matilda said indignantly. 'What made you think I was?'

'A regular lady wouldn't speak to the likes of me,' the girl said.

'I guess I'm not that regular,' Matilda said, and laughed. 'I own London Lil's.'

The girl just stared. 'You ain't! They says the woman up there is as hard as rock-face.'

'Do they now,' Matilda replied with a wry smile. 'And why's that?'

''Cos she won't allow no fancy girls doing business in there.'

'That's true, I don't,' Matilda said. 'But that doesn't stop me from taking a girl in to clean her up.'

Matilda was reminded of the day she bathed Cissie as she prepared a bath in the wash-room for Mary, for the two girls had a great deal in common. Mary was every bit as saucy as Cissie and her story just as tragic. She had come out to California on a wagon train in '48 with her widowed father and two younger sisters. One sister died of thirst in the Nevada desert, later her father accidentally shot himself while cleaning his gun, and died a couple of weeks later from the infected wound. Mary made it through heavy snow in the mountains to Sacramento, but her last sister died soon after they arrived. Mary was just thirteen when the brothel owner sold her virginity to the highest bidder.

Matilda found her a dress to wear while her own was washed and mended, but it wasn't until the next day that she offered

Mary a job as a waitress and a room at the back of the saloon, on the understanding she was to turn away from prostitution for good.

Almost all the girls who worked for her had been whores, and she had no illusions that they'd all abandoned it for good. She paid good wages, but if for some reason they left, she guessed they'd be back to their old habits quickly. As Zandra had said, girls got into the profession for any number of reasons, and greed and laziness were two powerful ones. But Mary was different, the joy on her face when Matilda offered her the job was deeply moving. When she said she never wanted a man even to touch her again, she meant it, and now six months later she was the most hard-working and conscientious girl in the place, and fast becoming a friend rather than a mere employee.

Matilda moved on downstairs as the evening's entertainment got under way. Tonight there were dancing girls, a tenor from Italy and a lady contortionist, and as usual the place was packed. Matilda moved around through the crowd, greeting regulars, introducing herself to those in for the first time, and watching for trouble. She had grown adept at sensing danger signals, often she could look at someone as they came through the door and know that were spoiling for a fight.

There had been some terrible fights in here on occasions, tables and chairs flung at the mirrors, bottles smashed and innocent people hurt as onlookers joined in the fray. Usually it was over a woman, for there were still so few in proportion to the men – at the last count she had heard there were eighty men to every woman.

The dancing girls returned briefly at the end of the show, and Matilda was just about to go back up to the gallery to keep watch from there when she sensed someone staring at her.

Mary had recently laughingly claimed that she had another pair of eyes hidden under her hair, and it was true she could sense something going on even behind her back. She turned, and to her utmost surprise Captain James Russell was standing just inside the door, looking right at her as if he couldn't believe what he was seeing.

Her first instinctive reaction was to run and hide. She had thought about this man so often in the first few months in Oregon, and she would have welcomed him calling at the cabin at any time. But he hadn't called, or even written her a letter, and all she could think in the first moment of recognition was that this was the man who knew all her secrets.

But she couldn't run, she was penned in on all directions, and anyway he was moving towards her.

'Is it really you, Matty?' he asked, and his deep voice brought back so many sweet memories of the wagon train. 'I can't believe it. Oh, Matty!'

The surprise, joy and utter disbelief in his face was almost too much to take. She felt as if she'd been winded, her stays were suddenly too tight, her heart pounding. The desire to hide had gone, it was wonderful to see him again.

'Why, Captain Russell!' she said, trying very hard to regain her composure. 'What on earth are you doing in San Francisco?'

He came nearer still. His fair hair was cut shorter now, barely reaching his collar, his moustache trimmed to a thin line, he was wearing a dark green coat over riding breeches and long shiny brown boots. He looked like the gentleman she knew him to be, but the leanness of his body, the lines around his eyes from squinting into the sun for long hours hadn't changed. Applause for the show erupted all around them, and if he did answer her question, she didn't catch it.

His hand came snaking through the people surrounding them. 'Come with me so we can talk,' he said, grabbing her wrist.

He led her towards the door, clearly intending they should go out on to the veranda, but Matilda stopped him. However stunned she was to see him, it was a chilly evening, and besides, she needed to keep watching her customers.

'No, come upstairs on the balcony,' she insisted, and turning away, left him to follow her.

He raised one eyebrow as she sat down at the table marked reserved, but Matilda didn't inform him that it was her table, or even that she owned this place.

He just sat there for a few moments looking at her almost as if he was seeing a ghost. 'What a thrill,' he exclaimed eventually, his bright blue eyes even more sparkly than she remembered. 'I'm sorry to keep repeating myself but it's just so amazing. You see, when I was told London Lil's was the best place in town, that name instantly made me think of you.' He paused as if to steady himself and put his two hands to his temples. 'It was so strange. I got this sudden vivid picture of you telling me about London. I think even if I'd been told it was the worst saloon in town I'd still have come, for the name alone. All the way up the hill I was thinking about you. Then I walked in and there you were.'

His delight in seeing her was very touching. It brought home what good friends they had been, and indeed reminded her that if she hadn't been pregnant it could possibly have grown into something more. Yet it still stung that he hadn't written to her as he said he would.

'I'm surprised you even remembered me,' she said starchily. 'You must meet so many women on the wagon trains.'

'Not like you,' he said with a smile. Just the way his full lips curved made her feel uncomfortably aware of how much time she'd spent thinking about him when she first got to Cissie's. 'I was so disappointed when you didn't reply to my letter, but I thought maybe you had married.'

'Letter! I didn't get a letter,' she exclaimed. 'When did you send it?'

'That first Christmas after we parted. I stayed on at The Dalles for some weeks, organizing the rest of the party down the Columbia. I planned to come and see you later in the spring, but as I got no reply, and then I was posted back to Fort Laramie, the chance was lost.'

She didn't know whether to believe this or not. She had after all received other letters sent on from Independence. If they could get to her from such a long way off, why should his letter fail to reach her?

'So what are you doing here?' she asked. He sounded as different as he looked, a real gentleman now, not the rough, tough man he'd appeared to be on the trail. 'Have you left the army?'

He shook his head. 'No. I stuck with it. I'm on my way to a new posting in New Mexico territory. But tell me about you, Matty. How are Tabitha and Amelia? Do you live here now?'

Nothing had ever been so hard as to admit her children were still in Oregon with Cissie. She saw his eyes grow cold and he seemed to move back a little from her.

'And you took a job here?' he said in a scandalized tone.

'This is my place, Captain Russell,' she said in a haughty manner. 'I am London Lil, I own it.'

She beckoned to Mary over the balcony while he reflected on this. Suddenly she needed a drink, and quickly.

Mary came. Matilda ordered a brandy for herself and whiskey for him. Mary looked curiously at the handsome stranger but at a sharp glance from Matilda she shot away again.

'How, why?' he asked once Mary had gone. He looked bewildered. 'I thought you'd get land and turn to farming.'

Matilda explained as quickly and concisely as possible. 'I'm not cut out to farm,' she said. 'I wish I could bring the girls here, but it's not a safe place for children as I'm sure you've seen. They are very happy with Cissie, the money I send keeps them very comfortably. I miss them a great deal, but I go home as often as possible.'

He didn't say anything for some time. Mary returned with their drinks and he sipped his reflectively. 'Amelia must be four now, and Tabitha twelve,' he said at length, and it was clear that he was recalling many memories of all of them. 'I had always imagined you tucked into a little cabin, perhaps even married with another baby too. But then you always were a surprising woman.'

'Tell me why men always consider that getting married and having babies is the answer to any woman's prayer,' she said, tossing her head in defiance. He was making her feel she ought to apologize for the way she'd turned out, and she didn't like that. 'If I'd come in here and discovered this was your place I'd say "How marvellous", "What a clever man you are". I wouldn't say I expected you to be back in Virginia cutting sugar cane, with a parcel of children around you. I never met one man in Oregon I even liked enough to hold his hand, much less marry. I'm working to give my children a future, and giving work to dozens of people. Is that so bad?'

'As bristly as ever,' he smiled. 'Still as English and twice as beautiful! I have to admit, Matty, that your gown becomes you far more than the widow's weeds you wore on the trail. If I haven't been able to express my admiration for this place, it's only because I am so overwhelmed by seeing you again.'

Appeased, Matilda relaxed a little, telling him that it had all really come about through John's business, then his death. He questioned her closely about the timber deals, clearly impressed by this, and went on to say how so many of his old friends had been caught up with gold fever, and how men he knew back in the East were hoping to build a rail road right across America to here before long.

'I've heard that too,' she said. Henry Slocum was anxious to get involved with this scheme and just lately he rarely talked about anything else. 'I just wish people back in the East could be warned before they set out that few of them will make a fortune from gold. I've seen more men leave the town penniless than ones with loaded wallets.'

'I don't much care about the crazy people who chase dreams,' he said. 'My fear is chiefly for the Indians. There is bad trouble brewing, so far there have been only minor skirmishes with the settlers, but the Indians are far from happy now so many people are trailing across their lands. We are introducing diseases that they have no resistance to. The herds of bison they rely on for survival are being decimated. If we lay train tracks across their hunting grounds and bring millions more people, they will rise up and we will see bloodshed so terrible I cannot bear to think of it.'

She was very pleased to find he'd retained his support for the Indians, most men she'd met in this town would gladly see them wiped out. 'That will make it very difficult for you then, James,' she said in sympathy. 'For I suppose as an army officer, you will have to lead men out to fight them?'

He nodded, and looked ashamed. 'What else can I do? I have to take orders. But I don't like it, Matty. I've learnt to admire and understand the Indians, there is much in their culture which is preferable to our own. I think it would be possible for white settlers to live peaceably alongside the Indians, if it was handled with sensitivity on both sides. But the vast majority of men in government are fools, or greedy speculators interested in nothing more than lining their own pockets.'

'Can't you take a middle road and speak up for Indian rights, while still protecting the settlers?' she asked.

'There doesn't appear to be a middle road anywhere in life,' he said with great sadness. 'You of all people must know that, Matty.'

She knew exactly what he meant. By opening a place like

London Lil's she had ostracized herself from society. Yet had she chosen to stay in Oregon living what most people perceived as a 'decent' life, she would be no nearer it either.

'Someone long ago once asked me what I wished for from life,' she said. 'My reply was, that by the time I died I wanted to have felt I had made a difference, for the good, in someone else's. It's still my wish, and that's my middle road, Captain.'

He smiled. 'That's a good wish,' he said. 'And I'm glad to see you haven't lost an ounce of the integrity and courage that you displayed so admirably on the trail. Now, I see there are people dancing down there – is London Lil herself allowed to dance?'

'I see no reason why not, Captain,' she laughed. 'It will probably be the talk of the town tomorrow, but such things never bothered me before.'

'If you call me Captain one more time I might just give them even more to talk about,' he said with twinkling eyes. 'You have been warned!'

Matilda had never danced with a man since the night with Flynn in New York when the Milsons were away in Boston. But the moment James held out his arms to her all the excitement and wonder of that night came back to her. Lily had schooled her back in Missouri, just in case the opportunity of a real dance ever arose, but two women holding each other and giggling as they tried to hum a tune and keep in step was nothing like being in the arms of a real live man.

Her eyes couldn't even see over his shoulder and he held her so tightly she could only follow the movements of his body with her own. But then the dance floor was so tightly packed that these movements weren't fast or intricate, and soon she was closing her eyes, listening only to the music and luxuriating in the delight of being held by strong male arms.

She suspected the band moved on to play slow numbers just for them, for the fast jigs were more popular with the customers. With so few women to dance with, men often danced together. Indeed, part of the attraction of London Lil's was the ridiculous performances put on by some men. She'd seen men don a sunbonnet and apron and adopt a simpering manner with their partners. When the cancan was played there were higher kicks from men than ever were seen from the dancing girls on stage.

But tonight she was oblivious to all but James's hand on her waist, his cheek resting against her hair, and his lean body moving at one with hers. Somewhere along the line he let go of her right hand and let his come to rest on her shoulder, gently stroking the bare skin with the tips of his fingers. She felt the stirring of desire deep inside her, and she wished she was taller just so that his cheek could be against hers.

A small voice whispered inside her head that she was making a spectacle of herself, but she ignored it. James was an old and very dear friend, why shouldn't she dance with him? Fate had brought him back to her, and there was absolutely nothing to prevent them becoming sweethearts if that's what they wanted. She knew then that was exactly what she wanted. In all this time in San Francisco, countless men had tried to woo her, but she'd given them all short shrift. Not one had ever made her feel dizzy and excited, and she'd begun to think that no man could. Until now.

Other men tried to cut in, but James ignored them, whirling her away with a little chuckle. She kept her eyes shut because tonight she didn't want to see curious stares or smiles. All she wanted was this state of bliss to last for ever.

They were stopped by the band suddenly switching from the sad refrain of 'Fair Annie' to the frenzied rhythm of 'Oh Susanna' and Matilda realized the second show of the evening was about to commence.

'Did you have a good time?'

Matilda stiffened with shock at hearing Zandra's voice as she stepped into the apartment some hours later.

'Yes, it was lovely,' she replied, lifting the oil lamp a little higher so she could see to bolt the door. She guessed by Zandra's question that Mary had popped up to tell her she had gone out with a man.

'Well, come in here and tell me all about it,' Zandra called out. 'I haven't been able to sleep because I was consumed with curiosity about who you were with. Mary said she'd never seen him before, but she thought he must be an old friend.'

Matilda went into Zandra's bedroom and put the lamp down on the wash-stand. Her friend had made this room very attractive. Above her brass bed, drapes of blue dyed muslin were fixed to a central crown, and the quilt she'd made herself was all in different shades of blue. Propped up among pillows trimmed with lace, wearing a snowy-white night-gown and cap, she looked every inch a Contessa.

Sitting down on the bed, Matilda explained who the stranger was, and how after dancing with her, he had asked her to go down to the Bella Union in the plaza to play the tables.

'He said he wasn't a gambling man, but that I'd bring him luck,' Matilda giggled. 'And I must have done, he won two hundred dollars. Then we had some supper at a new place called Georgie's. Then he brought me home.'

Zandra smiled. She wondered if Matilda had been kissed, her skin and eyes were glowing with a light that didn't only come from the lamp. She recalled her friend's stories about this man who led her wagon train, and there had been a hint she'd been disappointed he didn't write or come to search her out at Cissie's place. 'And will you be seeing him again?' she asked.

'He's taking me riding tomorrow,' Matilda said, leaning forward, her face suddenly anxious. 'What on earth will I wear?'

'I doubt if he'll care if you ride in your chemise,' Zandra said tartly. 'Not judging by the enraptured look on your face.'

Matilda giggled. 'You can't imagine how good it was to see him again, Zandra. I liked him so much then, but I was pregnant and I couldn't even begin to think of anything romantic. But it's different now, isn't it?'

'It certainly is, and it's high time you let a man into your life,' Zandra said. 'Now, about what you can wear tomorrow. I do have a riding habit in my closet. You're welcome to wear that, I'm sure it will fit you. Unfortunately it's bottle-green, not your colour, but I have a silk scarf you can wear which will lift it.'

'Why do you have a riding habit?' Matilda asked. Zandra never wore anything other than black, but when she moved in with her she brought four trunks of gowns and other clothes, some dating back forty years. But a riding habit seemed a very unlikely thing for her to own.

'Because, my little innocent, I wasn't always a frail old lady, I used to ride well and I loved it. So I kept the habit for old times' sake.'

Matilda suddenly realized how late it was. 'I'd better go and leave you to sleep,' she said. 'Would you like anything before I go?'

'No, my dear,' she said. 'It's good to see you happy. You have a lovely time tomorrow and don't worry about downstairs. They'll cope without you.'

'Will I do?' Matilda said, twisting this way and that in front of Zandra's cheval looking glass. The riding habit could have been made for her, the close-fitting velvet jacket was flattering and the skirt was divided like men's pants, yet standing up it had the appearance of a normal long skirt. To top it off was a pert little pill-box hat with a veil and feather.

Zandra knotted a scarf lariat-style around her neck. It was cream with green spots and instantly reflected a more flattering tone on to Matilda's face.

'Do? You look adorable,' Zandra said. 'Now, don't get yourself thrown, it's undignified, not to mention painful. If he wants to career off at a gallop, resist the temptation to copy him. I suspect your riding experience is limited to cart horses.'

'It is,' Matilda giggled, suddenly feeling as if she was sixteen again instead of twenty-six. 'But I didn't tell James that.'

'I doubt he's setting out to test you,' Zandra said with a wicked grin. 'You'll soon know if he has if he turns up with a huge stallion for you.'

Clearly Zandra was right, for although James rode up the hill at eleven in the morning on a fine black stallion, he'd brought a docile grey mare for her which looked at Matilda's slight figure almost with relief.

'You look splendid,' James said with a smile. 'I take it by that outfit you go riding a great deal?'

Matilda wasn't going to admit her habit was borrowed, or blurt out that she thought he looked splendid too. He was wearing his uniform and it suited him far better than civilian clothes, giving him that slightly rakish look she'd admired when they first met. But she wasn't going to flatter him, or admit she didn't normally ride, so she just laughed, and before he could even dismount to help her, she put one foot in the stirrups and leaped up into the saddle.

'I didn't think you'd have much use for a lady's saddle,' he said, grinning broadly. 'Which is just as well because the livery stables didn't have one.'

They took the path going away from the town, right out to

beyond the last buildings, and then on to rough ground along the crest of the hills going south. It was a beautiful morning without any of the customary mist, and as there had been little rain recently it was easy going.

They rode for perhaps an hour, chatting easily, very much the way they used to on the trail. Last night they'd talked about current things, the town and her business, but now he wanted to know everything about Tabitha and Amelia. It became increasingly clear to her that she and her children had left a vivid and permanent mark in his memory, and this thrilled her.

'And what of your step-mother and brothers back in England?' he asked.

'I only received one letter from Dolly after I got to Oregon,' Matilda said sadly. 'She didn't sound herself then, all she said was that she was very tired. I guess she must have died soon after and there was no one to let me know. I often wonder about my brothers, where they are, what they are doing. But I guess I'll never find out now. What about your family, James, have you seen them at all?'

'I kinda made the peace with them when I was back in Virginia for a while,' he said with a wry smirk. 'I can't say I like them any better, but I guess getting older has made me more tolerant.'

He didn't elaborate on this, and reined in his horse to stop and look at a fine view of the bay. As usual it was full of ships, and in the bright spring sunshine it looked idyllic.

'This would be a fine place to build a house,' he said reflectively. 'I could sit by a window every day and never get tired of that view.'

'Would you want to settle here then if you left the army?' she asked, her heart suddenly skipping a beat.

'I used to think I would before they found gold and the whole place turned crazy,' he said, looking at her and smiling. 'I love the mild climate and the ocean, but I don't think I'd want to live so close to all those vagabonds and thieves down there in the town.'

'What a ridiculous sweeping statement!' she exclaimed indignantly. 'Mostly they are just adventurers.'

'Like you?' he said, raising one bushy fair eyebrow, his lips bent into a sneer.

'Yes, like me,' she retorted. 'It's my kind of town, I love its courage, its lack of hypocrisy, it's a far more honest place than any other I've lived in.'

He shook his head at her. 'It may seem that way now, Matty, but when the matrons, the ministers and law and order arrive you may very well find yourself on the wrong side of the fence.'

'That's ridiculous too,' she snapped. 'My place is the most popular in town.'

'I know, a great many people have told me so,' he said. 'They say everyone loves it, right from the most influential businessman down to the poorest miner and stevedore.'

His tone wasn't sarcastic, so Matilda told him how it was. 'It's really worked, James. I planned on a good, clean fun place where men could take their wives and sweethearts, something different and good. I've done it too, it's a landmark, the nearest thing this town has to an institution. I can't tell you how many of the town's leading businessmen have tried to persuade me to let them buy a share in it.'

'But tell me, Matty,' James said, looking at her curiously, 'do you get invited to the homes of those businessmen? Do their wives receive you?'

'I haven't got time for such things,' she snapped.

'Then perhaps that's just as well,' he said in a quiet voice. 'Because if you had more time you might notice that your engagement book was rather empty.'

That remark was the last thing she wanted to hear, for it was something she knew, but chose to ignore. Smarting with humiliation, she dug her heels into the mare's side, but instead of the horse taking it as a signal merely to move on, she took off at a gallop.

A gentle canter was one thing, but Matilda had no experience of riding at speed. She bobbed up and down in the saddle, holding on for grim death, in fear of being thrown, and not having the least idea how to slow the mare down, she tried to pretend she was enjoying it.

She must have gone a couple of miles before she heard James's horse's hooves right behind her. 'Whoa!' he called out, and galloping up alongside her, he reached over and pulled on her reins, bringing the mare to a halt. 'Why do you do everything at a gallop when you've hardly learnt to canter?' he asked, grinning at her.

Realizing he knew perfectly well she wasn't an experienced horsewoman added to her embarrassment. She released her right foot from the stirrup to dismount, but as she cocked her leg up, she realized too late that she should have taken the left foot out too, and she slithered down the horse's flank, only to fall on to the ground, with her foot still caught in the stirrup.

James jumped off his horse and came rushing round to her, but instead of showing some concern, all he did was laugh. She managed to wriggle her foot out eventually, but only after exposing her entire leg to his eyes.

'You arse-wipe!' she screamed at him, jumping up to slap his grinning face. He dodged back from her, and her hand merely caught his arm. Maddened still further, she lunged at him to pummel his chest.

He caught hold of her two elbows and jerked her towards him, and suddenly he was kissing her. She struggled momentarily, but the warmth and softness of his lips made her yield, all fight in her gone. It was over five years since Giles had kissed her that last time as he left for St Joseph. But as James's arms slid round her, pressing his entire body into hers, all those feelings of desire and passion she'd worked so hard on forgetting came back like a flood.

His tongue was flickering into her mouth, his hands were caressing her back, drawing her ever closer to him, till the buttons on his uniform dug into her breasts. She felt that old familiar hot surge inside her, and in that moment, if he had pushed her down on to the grass and taken her, she wouldn't have resisted.

It was he who broke away first, still holding her tightly but burying his head into her shoulder. 'I shouldn't have done that, Matty. I'm so sorry.'

She hadn't for one moment expected an apology, and lifted his head up between her two hands so she could see his face. His expression was almost childlike, his mouth quivering, his eyes so soft, and she'd seen the same look just once before. It was the morning when Amelia was born and he'd climbed into her wagon to congratulate her. That day she'd seen it as just compassion, but somehow she knew it wasn't that now, it was something far deeper. 'Well, I'm not sorry,' she said, smiling at him. 'I liked it very much.'

'So did I,' he whispered in a curiously strained voice. 'But then I spent most of the time on the trail, and afterwards, imagining kissing you. If only I'd had the courage to do it then.'

'I don't remember you lacking courage,' she said. 'But things were different then, I was preoccupied with just getting to Oregon before my baby was born, and afterwards I was in no fit state to think of romance.'

He took her hands away from his face and stepped back. He looked so troubled, his expression made her think of Treacle when he knew he'd done something wrong. She thought maybe he felt guilty that he hadn't come looking for her.

'What is it, James?' she asked softly. 'I can see there is something you want to say. So just tell me. I don't believe it's too late for us.'

He didn't reply, and his face became contorted as if in pain.

'Tell me,' she insisted.

'I can't, Matty,' he said. 'It *is* too late.'

It was as if the sun had suddenly gone behind a cloud. She couldn't reply for a moment for a lump had come up in her throat which felt as if it might choke her.

'You're married now, aren't you?' she finally got out.

He nodded, looking at the ground.

For a moment she couldn't speak. Instinct told her he had been in love with her, and if his kiss was anything to go by, he still was. Last night had been so very beautiful, so many times they'd just looked at one another and began to laugh about nothing. She had gone to bed hugging the thought of him to herself, so sure that she was on the very brink of something wonderful.

'Why didn't you tell me this last night?' she said, her voice shaking. 'Why take me out, then ask me to come out riding with you today? Why, James?'

'I was so thrilled to see you again,' he said, still hanging his head and looking at her through his lashes. 'All those feelings I had for you came back, within minutes it was just the way we used to be. I guess I just wanted to hang on to that for a little longer. If I'd told you immediately then suddenly it would have been polite, neutral conversation, and I couldn't bear that.'

'You mean I wouldn't have danced with you,' she said, sadly

thinking of that blissful feeling of being held close in his arms, for that was the point when she knew she'd stepped over the line from friendship to something more.

'I didn't plan any of it,' he said with a touch of anger. 'Whatever you might think of me please bear that in mind. It was just so good to be with you again, to hear about the children, how you got here, all the important things. But the longer we talked, the more difficult it became to tell you. Because all I could think of was that I should have ridden down to the Willamette Valley, found you and asked you to marry me.'

Matilda closed her eyes for a moment, she was remembering the way he'd tenderly tucked her into the canoe, and the sadness in his eyes as White Bear pushed off from the bank. She knew he was telling her the truth about his feelings, and in truth she was just as much to blame because she hadn't seen it then.

'What are you thinking?' he asked.

Matilda sighed deeply. 'How sad this is,' she said honestly.

'I was going to tell you today,' he said, looking right into her eyes. 'I wasn't going to creep away like a thief in the night if that's what you are thinking. But just tell me one thing, Matty. Did you care for me on the trail?

'You know I did,' she said indignantly. 'I never allowed myself to think of you in *that* way because of my situation, but you were a dear friend.'

'And later, once you got to the Duncans' place, did you spare any thoughts for me?'

'Yes,' she admitted. 'I was hoping you'd turn up. Tabitha and I often spoke about you.'

'That doesn't sound like the feelings I had for you,' he said, reaching out and running his forefinger across her lips, his eyes scanning her face. 'That's also partly why I felt no real necessity to tell you immediately that I'd married. You see, you weren't quite the same Matty I knew. You seemed so sophisticated and worldly. I thought we could renew our friendship, laugh about old times, and I would forget how much you'd once meant to me. But when you took off just now at a gallop, and then fell off the mare, it reminded me so much of the old Matty, headstrong, independent and so utterly beguiling. I just forgot myself.'

'We'd better go back now,' she said, feeling that she might just break her own rule and cry in public.

'No, not yet,' he said, catching hold of her arm as she turned back to her mare. 'I can't just let you go again, you kissed me as if you wanted me. We can't leave it like that.'

She knew as she looked into those vivid blue eyes that she should deny any feelings, brush him off as if he was just one of many would-be lovers. But she couldn't.

'I do want you,' she said simply. 'But if you are married then there can be nothing between us. We must go back now, and try to forget the past.'

They rode back to town slowly, and James told her that he was due to take command at a fort in New Mexico. She wondered who he had married – his more gentlemanly manner and speech, and his earlier, rather prudish remarks suggested he'd found someone of his own class. But he didn't speak of her, not even mentioning her name, and Matilda wasn't going to ask.

James dismounted outside London Lil's and came over to Matilda to help her down.

'May I call on you if I come through here again?' he asked. 'Just as a friend.'

As he put his hands on her waist to lift her down she wanted to kiss him long and hard to give him something more than friendship to remember her by, but she resisted the temptation.

'Of course, James,' she said, trying to sound casual. 'You will always be welcome.'

'Give my love to Tabitha when you write to her,' he said. 'Tell her I hadn't forgotten her, and send a kiss to Amelia.'

All she could do was nod. Somehow it said a great deal about the man that his last words should be for her children.

Zandra was sitting up by the parlour window as Matilda came in. Her old wrinkled face was alight with excitement, clearly she'd taken a good look at the Captain before he rode off, and liked what she saw.

Matilda threw her hat on a chair, and slumped down opposite Zandra. 'He's married,' was all she could say.

Zandra didn't make any comment for a while. She could feel the deep sorrow in her friend, see the hurt and bewilderment clouding her eyes. To Zandra marriage meant very little, her whole life had been spent with men who were committed elsewhere, and she'd been glad of that because she'd had their love, and still kept her freedom to do exactly as she pleased.

But she knew Matilda wasn't ready for her more cynical views, she was in the sway of passion, ripe for love, and to her this was another body blow. 'I'm so sorry, Matty,' she said in sympathy. 'He looked so dashing and handsome, and I can imagine how disappointed you are.'

'Disappointment doesn't cover it,' Matilda burst out. 'I'm hopping mad, I wish he'd got himself killed out on a campaign, anything that would have prevented him from coming back into my life.'

Zandra nodded. It was a great many years since any man had stirred her emotions as Matty's clearly were. But she remembered how it felt.

'You don't wish he'd been killed, and in a while you'll be glad you saw him again, for he was a good friend when you needed one,' she said soothingly. 'Why don't you book a passage home next month to see the children? It will be quieter once the men go back to the mountains for the summer. I'm perfectly capable of looking after things with Mary's help while you are gone.'

Matilda nodded, her eyes brimming with tears. 'If only I'd been away and never seen him,' she said. 'Why is fate so cruel sometimes, Zandra?'

'If I knew that I'd be the wisest woman in the world,' the older woman said with a smile. 'But I have learnt these things are sent to test us, and for every sad or terrible thing which happens we grow a little stronger.'

Matilda didn't speak for some time. She was just staring out of the window, deep in thought. But eventually she turned back to Zandra. 'What would you do about James, if you were in my shoes?' she asked.

Zandra thought for a minute, torn between the truth and a more noble lie. Yet she couldn't lie to her friend, she knew she would see through it.

'I'd rush down into the town and find him,' she said. 'I'd tell him I wanted him as a lover regardless of him having a wife. I'd snatch every bit of happiness I could without any thought of the consequences.' She paused and looked right into Matilda's tear-filled eyes. 'But I have the soul of a whore, Matty. I was never the marrying kind, and I had very little integrity when I was your age.'

Captain Russell tightened up the straps of his saddlebags, then leaped gracefully up on to his horse. It was dark now, and he had intended to stay one more night in town before leaving at first light in the morning. But he knew if he did he would only go back to Matty, and if he did that he'd be lost.

He could see London Lil's so clearly up on the hill, the bright lanterns all along the front of it were like a welcoming beacon, and so very tempting. He had spent the last six hours drinking whiskey, yet he was still sober, but perhaps that was because his drinking companions had kept bringing up Matilda's name.

She was fast becoming something of a legend. He had heard about her deals with timber, and her friendship with the madam of a parlour house whom she now had living with her. He'd heard too about the whores she'd taken from the streets and given honest work. One man had said she was known to have given two failed miners their passage home and vowed she'd shoot them if she heard they'd stayed in town and left their wives and children alone for another winter.

He knew she paid her staff good wages, and she treated them well. Yet she was also said to be as cold as ice if anyone stole from her, or if her girls were found to be offering themselves for payment with her customers. The men he'd spoken to didn't understand the reasoning behind that, they seemed to think she was foolish not taking a cut in such arrangements, nor did they really understand why she spoke out against slavery, or sympathized with the plight of the Chinese, Negroes and Mexicans who were treated as inferiors by everyone else.

These men thought her views peculiar at best, subversive even because she was giving other women ideas that they shouldn't accept male dominance. But they still admired her. Her place was one of warmth on a cold night, of honesty in an increasingly dishonest town, of clean fun when everything else was diseased.

It had been so hard for him not to speak of what he knew of her. The pictures in his mind of her nursing those children through measles, of her leading her oxen along mountain passes with her belly swollen with child, and her dirt-smeared face as she bent over a cooking pot, were all so vivid, so poignant, he so much wanted to share them with someone.

He couldn't tell men who were speaking longingly of her beauty that he'd once caught a glimpse of her naked, bathing in the river Platte. Her belly was just a gentle curve then, skin rosy from the cold water, her breasts full and her legs so long and shapely. Nor could he say how many times he'd watched her brushing her hair by the campfire, that it looked like shimmering gold, cascading down on to her slim shoulders, in a way that brought a lump to his throat just remembering.

One of the men had remarked on how she always wore gloves, even when she was collecting dirty glasses. James knew why, he'd dressed her hand for her when her nail was torn off on the trail. He'd blanched at them himself, for no woman as young and beautiful as her should have the callused hands of a farm worker.

Yet he'd been unable to make any comment about her, for fear that if he did the floodgates would be opened and he'd be unable to hold back not only on his own knowledge of her, but that he loved her.

As he rode out of town along the rutted road towards New Mexico in the darkness, tears filled his eyes. His wedding to Evelyn, the only daughter of Colonel Harding, had taken place last September back in Virginia. She was an ideal officer's wife, a gracious hostess, accomplished, pretty, amusing company, and she understood that a soldier had to spend much of his working life away from home. While James had been aware that he didn't love her passionately as he had Belle, or Matilda, he had told himself a marriage based on firm foundations of similar backgrounds and compatibility had a far greater chance of success and that in time true love would grow from it.

Until yesterday he was entirely contented. He was at peace with himself, and the marriage had partially healed the rift between him and his own family, for they approved of Evelyn. Promotion could come to him soon, and hopefully children too.

But finding Matilda again had blown that peace of mind away. When he got no reply to his letter to her four years ago, he had convinced himself that any feelings she had for him were purely sisterly, and that she hadn't replied because she was embarrassed and perhaps shocked by his admission of love. Even the look of fright on her face when she first saw him in the saloon seemed to bear that out. It had been a relief when she said she didn't get the letter. He really thought he was over her, and that he could spend an enjoyable evening with her without looking back over his shoulder, and any ghosts would be laid to rest for all time.

But he was wrong. Her face, the sound of her voice, the way she moved, even the flashes of fire in her eyes when she spoke of things she cared deeply about, brought everything back. He had lain awake comparing her with Evelyn, and in a moment of pure cynicism tried to see them as horses. Evelyn came to his mind as a pretty, dainty little Arab mare, while Matty was a strong, sleek hunter. The dainty Arab might be a joy to look at, but it couldn't cope with rough terrain, jump hedges and ditches as a hunter could.

This morning when he saw the elegant woman in the green riding habit waiting for him outside London Lil's, she was so far removed from the old Matty that for a while he thought he had his head back on straight again. But then she had to take offence at what he'd said and go galloping off, and all at once, there she was again, the headstrong, impulsive, so utterly adorable Matty, and he just had to kiss her.

That one kiss had opened up the old scar so wide he knew it wasn't ever going to heal again. She should have been his, every nerve ending in his body screamed it at him. He should have followed his heart and gone to find her, whatever the cost. Now he would have to live with regret for the rest of his life.

'Damn you, Matty,' he exclaimed aloud, glancing back over his shoulder. The lights of San Francisco were blurred now, just a golden haze against the dark velvety sky. For a moment, he was tempted to turn back, but he resisted the impulse, dug his spurs into the horse's flanks and broke into a canter.

Chapter Twenty

Matilda arrived back from Oregon in late July, and rushed up to see Zandra. She had pink cheeks from the invigorating sea voyage, a sprinkling of freckles on her nose, and she looked rested and bright-eyed.

Zandra had been dozing in her chair, but as Matilda bounded in she woke, her face breaking into a wide, toothless smile. 'My dear, what a lovely surprise. I didn't think you'd be back for another couple of days.'

'The new steamers are so very fast. It's not like the old days,' Matilda said, going over to give the old lady a hug. 'How have you been?'

'Fine, better still now you are back. I missed you terribly,' Zandra said, clutching Matilda's hand and squeezing it. 'And you look splendid, even if I don't approve of young ladies exposing their faces to the sun. Come and sit down and tell me all about your holiday.'

'It was just so lovely,' Matilda sighed. 'Tabby has become quite the young lady, and so clever – why, she leaves me standing the things she knows about! You'll remember that a while back she wrote to say an English minister called Reverend Glover was giving her extra coaching? Well, I met him and his wife while I was up there, and they've both become very fond of Tabby. The Reverend asked me if I'd consider allowing her to leave school, which he believes is holding her back, and let her board with him and his wife, so he can act as her tutor.'

'Is that a good idea?' Zandra looked doubtful. 'She's a great help to Cissie, isn't she?'

'Yes, she is,' Matilda agreed. 'But Cissie was the first to say that she thought it was too great an opportunity for Tabby to turn down. The Glovers haven't any children of their own, and Tabby would get the kind of education which would prepare her for college or university. Do you know, the Reverend is even teaching her Latin! I think it's what Giles would have wanted for her, and besides, Tabby can slip home to Cissie any time she feels like it.'

'And Amelia?' Zandra asked.

'Oh, she's just the sweetest thing you ever saw,' Matilda said rapturously. 'Cheeks like rosy apples, long black lashes, and her hair is so curly now. Tabitha is quite jealous of it, hers is as straight as a poker. But don't get me talking about her or I'll bore you to death. I kept talking about her to a woman on the boat coming home. I think she was quite glad to see the back of me.'

Zandra laughed. 'So how are Cissie and her children?'

'Peter thinks he's such a big tough man now he's nine.' Matilda smiled fondly. 'I adore him, you know, every freckle on his face, his wide grin, the way he hangs on every word I say. I always feel he's part my little boy because I rescued him from that cellar, and gave him his first bath, but I have to be careful I don't make too much of him or Susanna will get jealous. She's a real girlie girl, all playing house and nursing her dollies, but she can be a little madam too – when she has a tantrum, the whole town hears it!' She paused for a moment, smiling at the memories. 'Oh, and I almost forgot,' she added. 'Cissie has an admirer!'

'Really! Do tell,' Zandra exclaimed. Although she'd never met Cissie she felt she knew her well from all that Matilda had told her.

Matilda wrinkled her nose. 'His name is Arnold Biggleswortth and he owns a small printer's, but he's a bit pompous to my mind. He's already asked Cissie to marry him. I'm a bit scared he might be after her money.'

'Has she accepted his proposal?'

'Not yet, she's happy the way she is, alone with the children. But he escorts her to church and takes her for walks, so it's some company for her, and the children like him, especially Tabitha. So she might yet marry him.'

'You haven't mentioned Sidney!'

'Well, that's the surprise. You'll be meeting him yourself soon, he's coming here to work for me in September.'

'How wonderful,' Zandra exclaimed. 'But how did this come about? I thought he and Cissie were inseparable.'

Matilda grimaced. 'They are, almost. That's part of the reason he's coming. Folk are talking about him living with Cissie. He's seventeen now, and it's got around he isn't her true brother, well, you know what folk are like! On top of that he hates it at the mill, and I guess he wants to see a bit more of America too. Oregon City is lovely, but it's not very exciting for a young man.'

Zandra nodded. 'From what you've told me about him I'm sure he'll be a great help to you here. I can't wait to meet him.'

Matilda went on to say how they'd had lots of picnics, long walks and taken the ferry down to Portland a couple of times. 'It was so blissful,' she said wistfully. 'Cissie's made the garden real nice with a lawn and flower-beds. Sidney's built the little ones a play-house out there too. It was tough to leave them again though.'

'You could go back, you've made enough money to open a shop or do almost anything you wanted,' Zandra reminded her.

Matilda looked at her glumly. 'I really wouldn't fit in there any more, I'm too citified. Much as I loved being with the children, sometimes in the evenings I thought I'd go mad with boredom. Cissie only talks about the children and the people from church, I suppose she was always like that but I never noticed before.' She paused, a sudden look of excitement spreading across her face. 'I almost forgot, I got a letter from Tabitha's aunt back in England!'

'On which side of her family?' Zandra knew all the family history.

'One of Lily's sisters, the youngest one called Beth. Let me get it and read it to you.' She ran off to get it out of the bag she'd left in the hall.

'It's from an address in Bristol,' she said. 'But it's dated January of last year, so I suppose it was hanging around in Independence for some time before anyone sent it on to Oregon City.'

Dear Miss Jennings, she read. *I have no doubt you will be surprised to hear from me so long after my brother-in-law's death, but it was only a few weeks ago that I learned about the tragedy, while clearing out some papers at my old family home following my father's death. I found your letter dated January of 1848 to my parents at the bottom of a desk drawer in his study.*

I may of course be mistaken but I suspect my father didn't reply to this, because he was in very bad health then. He certainly didn't tell either myself or any of the rest of the family about your letter.

If he didn't reply you must have thought very badly of us, so I beg you to accept our apologies, and also our deep sorrow that such a fine, deeply committed clergyman should meet his death in such a terrible way.

As a mother of two small children, I thought your offer to continue to take care of Tabitha was extremely kind. I was only just married when my sister and her husband came to stay at our house in Bristol before leaving for America, but I remember your devotion to Tabitha being remarked upon then.

After discovering your letter I paid a visit to the Milsons in Bath, assuming they would have taken responsibility for Tabitha. I found that Mrs Milson had died two years ago and Mr Milson told me in no uncertain manner that he had corresponded with you and suggested you place his grand-daughter in an orphanage.

What must you have thought of us relatives? No reply from my father, and such a cold-hearted one from Mr Milson. I do recall in all of my sister's letters home, especially after she moved to Missouri, that she spoke highly of you and said she counted you as a dear friend, so I am sure you will have acted in Tabitha's best interests, but I cannot imagine how even with the best intentions a single woman would be able to take care of a child, it certainly would prove impossible in England.

Since discovering the letter, I have been consumed with anxiety about my niece, and indeed how you have fared since Reverend Milson's death. I ask that you write back and let me know what the outcome was, and if Tabitha is no longer with you, please let me know the name and address of the orphanage she was sent to so I can contact her.

With best wishes, Beth Hardacre.

'My goodness,' Zandra said, looking startled. 'Is it possible a father could read such sad news and just shove it in a drawer without telling anyone its contents?'

'It has to be true, or why would she write now?' Matilda replied with a shrug. 'She sounds so nice, doesn't she? I remember Lily saying she was ten years younger than herself, so she'd be around thirty-three now, I think.

'I've written to her now and said Tabitha is safe and well, and wants to be a doctor. I also said I never told Tabby about the cold letter I received from Mr Milson because it would have hurt her.

What I couldn't say was that I was living and working down here and that Tabitha has a little sister.'

Zandra looked concerned. 'Did you show Tabby this letter from her aunt?'

'No. She has no idea her grandfather was so uncaring, and I thought I'd wait and see how her Aunt Beth responds first before speaking of it.'

Zandra nodded. 'I think that was wise. It wouldn't be advisable to build up the child's hopes, after all once the woman knows Tabby is in good hands she may take no further interest. But speaking of letters, there is one for you in your room. I think it might be from your Captain.'

The speed at which Matilda ran out of the room proved to Zandra that even a holiday in Oregon with her children hadn't put the man out of her mind.

Matilda snatched up the letter and with trembling hands unsealed it.

> *Dearest Matty,* she read. *I have penned a dozen letters to you before this one, and each has been torn up because I said things I have no right to say. So I will stick to what is safe and say how pleased I am of your success in San Francisco, no one deserves it more than you. I wish you and the children every future happiness.*
>
> *I want, too, to apologize for not telling you about my marriage right at the outset. In my joy at finding you again after so long, and indeed in realizing what a grave mistake I had made in not coming to find you back in Oregon, I wasn't thinking clearly.*
>
> *All I can ask is that I can still count on you as a friend.*
>
> *Yours forever, James.*

Matilda read the letter again and again. She could hear the words he hadn't written down, feel all the emotions he'd felt as he penned it. He might have made a good marriage with someone who was a far more suitable partner than she could ever be, yet it was her he really loved.

But knowing that wasn't any comfort. She loved him too, going away had made it even more obvious to her, for she'd thought and dreamed about him all the time. She had only to close her eyes and remember his kiss, and she felt her stomach tighten with the need for him. He had every quality she wanted in a man, strength, intelligence, daring and tenderness. She loved the way he looked, moved, spoke, she couldn't think of one thing she didn't like about him.

But while talking it over with Cissie, she had seen for herself that even if James had been free, love alone wouldn't have been enough for lifelong happiness. A woman who owned a saloon wasn't a suitable wife for an officer, it would have blocked any promotion and ostracized him from society. The chances were he'd be posted permanently to somewhere remote like Fort Laramie. Would she have been prepared to give up all she had and go and live somewhere like that with him?

Matilda sighed deeply, looking around her bedroom. It was as beautiful as the parlour, imported paper with delicate pink scrolling on the walls, heavy velvet drapes at the window and a view of the bay that lifted her spirits every morning when she looked out. The ornate bedstead had come from one of Zandra's boudoirs, with a new thick feather mattress and a white lace and satin counterpane. She had real closets for her many clothes, her water jug was filled with hot water every morning by Dolores, and if she was too tired at night to hang up her gowns, Dolores did that too.

A Chinese man came to collect the laundry and brought it back in a day or two, washed, starched and ironed. Even her hair was arranged by Dolores every evening, she didn't cook a meal, sew on a button or clean her own boots.

It would be bliss to make love with James here in her clean, sweet-smelling bed, but how would she feel if she had to wash his shirts herself in the river, contend with sharing a makeshift shack with snakes, insects and rodents? Would being with the man she loved make that bearable?

Yet there was no point in dwelling on what-ifs. James was married, and even if he didn't love his wife as much as her, she couldn't have him. What she ought to be doing was thanking God for all she had, instead of dwelling on what was missing.

It was some time before Matilda returned to the parlour. She didn't say a word but slumped despondently down on the settee. Zandra looked up at her red-rimmed eyes and knew she'd been crying her heart out.

'Do you want to tell me about his letter?' she asked.

'There's nothing to say,' Matilda sighed, and a tear trickled down her cheek. 'He's married, and that's all there is to it. I've got to try to forget him.'

It was just a few months later on New Year's Day of 1853 that Zandra died. She had been feeling poorly since well before Christmas, and she stayed in bed most of the time. On Christmas Day she and Matilda exchanged presents, and she managed to come downstairs for the turkey dinner with all the staff, but immediately after she went back to bed again.

Matilda looked in on her just after they'd let off some Chinese crackers to welcome the New Year in. Zandra was sleeping peacefully, her two hands folded on the crisp white sheets, and when Matilda kissed her cheek and wished her a happy New Year she didn't even stir. The next morning Matilda went in soon after eight, only to find her dear friend had passed away in the night.

Matilda sat and cried with her for some time, unable to believe those eyes would never open again, and that wrinkled face couldn't break into even one more youthful smile. She felt as if she'd lost her mother, only it was worse than when she lost her real one, for she hadn't known her the way she'd known Zandra.

To many she was just an old madam, a grand one because of her title, but still tarnished by her profession. Yet to Matilda she had been an education and inspiration. She knew seventy-two was a ripe old age, that Zandra had been lucky she'd kept all her faculties along with her keen sense of humour and died without pain or distress. But that didn't soothe Matilda's grief, or stop her thinking what a void would be left in her life.

She would never again be able to curl up on Zandra's bed and share the gossip of the town, or read Tabby and Cissie's letters to her. Zandra would never meet her children as they'd hoped. No more heart-to-heart talks about men and love, no one to share her joys and triumphs with. No one to reassure her that in time she would forget James.

It was Sidney she turned to for consolation. From the moment he arrived in September, he and Zandra had become firm friends. It was Zandra who helped him adjust to life in a busy city, who told him of the pitfalls for an unwary young man, where to buy the right clothes so he looked gentlemanly, yet tough enough to be taken seriously. She told him about women too, to stay away from gambling, and to be wary of drink. He idolized her, nicknamed her Grandma, kept her plied with brandy and often brought her home chocolates. He was perhaps the only other person apart from Matilda and Dolores who had got through that sophisticated façade and found the real woman beneath.

Matilda laid Zandra out with Dolores, who was equally inconsolable, dressing her in a scarlet silk night-gown and negligee which Matilda found carefully packed away in tissue paper as if it had some sentimental value. She chose the three barmen Zandra had liked best as pall bearers, along with Sidney, and they carried her coffin on their shoulders down California Street Hill to St Francis for the funeral.

The small church was as packed that afternoon as London Lil's on Saturday nights. Many of the men had come straight down from the mountains to pay their last respects, still daubed with mud they'd had no time to clean off. There were sailors from the ships, soldiers, draymen, stevedores and carpenters, along with a great many merchants and town dignitaries. It was odd to see Zandra's old 'boarders' and many street girls she'd befriended dressed soberly and without their face paint. When Matilda said a few words about what the Contessa had meant to her personally, a great many of the assembled congregation had swimming eyes. As her coffin was carried out for the burial, the organist played a spirited Russian folksong, and after the burial everyone went back to London Lil's, where the drinks were on the house.

That evening was the first that Matilda had ever been drunk. She never had more than three drinks in one night, it was a rule she'd made for herself when they first opened, and she'd stuck to it. But that night she put all her rules aside.

Henry Slocum stood beside Sidney and watched as she danced with one man after the other. He sensed that the young lad was distressed by Matilda's unusual behaviour. 'This is exactly how Zandra would have wanted her send-off to be,' he said, trying to soothe him. 'She wasn't one for mournful farewells.'

Sidney's new position as Matilda's general assistant, and Zandra's influence, had given the young man a polished appearance. With his red hair, pale lashes and freckles he could not be described as handsome, but he was tall, and muscular from the heavy work at the mill, and his tawny eyes and ready smiles were very attractive. Zandra had overseen his hair being cut well, picked him out a dark green jacket and a vest beneath embroidered with gold thread, as well as teaching him to tie a neck-tie with style. He looked and sounded like a young gentleman and he had such inner confidence that most people who met him assumed he was.

'I think I ought to take Matty up to bed, sir.' Sidney frowned. 'Zandra might appreciate a jolly send-off, but I ain't so sure Matty will be best pleased if she's the talk of the town tomorrow.'

'Leave her be, son,' Henry said, laying one hand on the lad's arm. 'She's with friends tonight and she needs to let her hair down. I never knew her give a jot for what folks said about her.'

Sidney had downed more drinks himself than he should have done, and Henry's last remark incensed him because he knew it wasn't true. 'That's just where you are wrong,' he burst out. 'She cares a great deal, but then no one in this town knows her like I do.'

Henry raised an eyebrow. He had no idea where Sidney fitted into Matilda's past, last September she had just introduced him as her new assistant. 'Really! I would have thought you much too young to think you know her better than an old pal like me.'

The older man's slightly mocking reply incensed Sidney even more. 'You've known her a couple of years, that's all. I was eight when she rescued me and a parcel of other kids from the worst slum in New York,' he blurted out. 'She was the first person I ever trusted and I'd surely lay down my life for her.'

Henry had taken quite a few drinks himself, he too had lost a very dear friend today. But at this surprising outburst, he suddenly sobered up. 'She rescued you? Well, son, that is an intriguing statement. I admire Matty more than any other woman I've ever met, and I'd love to hear more about her.'

Sidney was glad to have the man's ear. Ever since he came to work at London Lil's he had been irritated that people saw Matilda as tough and chilly, he'd even heard it said by some that the only thing she loved was money. 'Well, just don't ever let on I told you,' he said. 'She'd have me hung, drawn and quartered.'

Launching into a graphic description of how and where he met Matilda, he explained how she and the Reverend Milson planned and executed the rescue and started the Waifs' and

Strays' Home in New Jersey. 'But for her we'd all be dead by now,' he ended up. 'But keep it to yourself. She don't like to talk about the Reverend any more, it's all too sad that first his wife died and then he got shot later. You all think she's as tough as mule hide, but she ain't. She's one loving lady.'

Henry moved on later to talk to someone else, but Sidney had opened up an unexpected and new, very appealing view of Matilda. As a worldly and astute man he guessed that the Reverend Milson had to be the father of Matilda's child, but as she hadn't taken his name he couldn't have got around to marrying her before he got shot. But rather than being shocked, he found it touched him deeply.

Around an hour later Sidney saw Matilda fall flat on her back while attempting to do the cancan, revealing her legs in the most improper manner. He pushed his way through the other dancers and pulled her up from the floor. 'Come on, Matty, it's time to go to bed,' he said.

'Don't be a spoilsport, Sid,' she said, but her words were hopelessly slurred.

Sidney took no notice and put his shoulder to her middle, hoisted her up on to his shoulder and carried her upstairs. He laid her on her bed and unbuttoned her boots. He was just about to put the counterpane over her and creep out when she suddenly lurched towards the drawer beside her bed.

'What is it you want?' he asked.

'Look in there,' she said, pointing to the drawer. 'I've still got them, and your note.'

Puzzled, Sidney moved forward and opened the drawer. 'In the wooden box,' she said. 'Open it!'

He did as he was told, and saw the lace handkerchief he'd given her in Independence. He unrolled it and the six cents were still inside, and his childish, badly spelt note.

'You kept them!' he exclaimed, a lump coming up into his throat.

''Course I did,' she said, slumping back on to her pillows. 'They mean the world to me. I kept them in my pocket even going down the Columbia river in the canoe. When it's my turn to die I want them in the coffin with me.'

Sidney was overcome with emotion. He had spoken of his first meeting with Matilda tonight because it was the most important milestone in his life. Yet he hadn't known it meant a great deal to her too. He leaned forward and kissed her cheek. 'You ain't gonna die for a long time yet,' he whispered. 'And I love you.'

'You go and find someone your own age to love,' she said with a giggle, but she caught hold of his hand and kissed it. 'And don't remind me how drunk I was in the morning.'

One morning in March Matilda found the daffodil bulbs she planted in tubs during the fall had finally opened in the sunshine on the veranda. Flowers were rare in this town, the pace was too fast, people too intransigent to think of planting a garden. Just the sight of them brought tears to her eyes, and a nostalgic whiff of England, but at the same time their bright colouring seemed to suggest it was time she put aside her sorrow at Zandra's death and looked to the future.

Just a couple of weeks earlier she'd heard from Charles Dubrette that Zandra had left the bulk of her estate to her. Not only her share of London Lil's, but some $12,000 and her considerable collection of jewellery. It seemed Zandra must have anticipated her end was near, for in the previous September she had sent a letter to Charles asking that when her time came he was to tell Matilda that she thought of her as a daughter, that she loved her dearly and wished to thank her for enriching her last few years.

Matilda had always been well aware that it was Zandra's encouragement, knowledge and contacts which had set her on the road to success; without this astute woman behind her she would never have dared to aim so high. Yet now, through Zandra's legacy, her life had taken a further upturn, and the possibilities open to her were almost limitless.

But rather than thinking of investments or new business projects, she often found herself day-dreaming about returning to England. The ten years she'd been away had almost certainly eradicated most of the pointers to her real background. With money behind her and a carefully planned story, she was fairly certain she could blend in with the middle classes. Tabitha's thirteenth birthday had been just before Christmas, the perfect age for her to attend one of those elegant schools for young ladies. Amelia would benefit as well from a private governess. Maybe too she could stop hankering after James in a country where there were no reminders of him.

This day-dream had been partly brought about by Beth Hardacre when she replied to Matilda's letter last summer. While she was clearly very relieved that her niece was safe and being brought up carefully, she had expressed a desire to help with Tabitha's future. Her husband Charles Hardacre was a doctor himself, and though Beth pointed out that most medical men were totally opposed to women entering the profession, she said Charles was an enlightened man who believed this view must change in time. Altogether it was a delightful letter, which seemed to suggest that Lily hadn't been the only person in her family to have a kind and caring nature.

Matilda intended to go home to Oregon soon, to tell Tabitha about her aunt and uncle, and discuss her future education with the Reverend Glover. He was a kind, good man, and since Tabitha had gone to board with him and his wife, he'd sent Matilda monthly reports on her progress. He was the best person to give advice about Tabby, because he really knew what she was capable of. Perhaps then the path ahead of her would become clearer.

As Matilda stood out on the veranda a group of men came riding by on mules. They cheerfully called out to her, saying they were off back to the mountains and would see her again in the fall.

She watched them ride down into the town, and hoped they would strike lucky, because the word now was that gold was becoming very hard to find, especially for prospectors like these who panned in the mountain streams. But then, times were getting harder for everyone, not just gold seekers.

Back in the early years when California relied solely on imported food and every other commodity, merchants made huge profits. But in the last eighteen months farms and factories had sprung up locally, providing the communities' needs directly and squeezing out the middle men. There was a flour mill too, and a much larger fishing industry.

There were no more quick fortunes to be made by buying and selling plots of land, and in speculative businesses bankruptcies were becoming ever more common. Skilled men like carpenters, stevedores, builders and teamsters could no longer command the excessively high wages they had demanded back in 1850 and '51, and there were so many unskilled men and women looking for work that supply well exceeded demand for their labour.

Matilda expected that her profits, too, would drop this year, and she doubted they would ever return to the high of her first two years. She had bought Simeon Greenstater's and Charles Dubrette's shares in the business not long before Zandra died, so she owned all but the one-fifth interest that Henry Slocum still retained. On Charles Dubrette's advice she kept her savings in the bank in Oregon City, and her cash in her safe, for there was a distinct possibility that some of the banks here might fold in the near future.

Yet while she knew she must keep a close eye on her own business and adapt to the changes all around her, Matilda's real concern lay with the poor.

Rowdy, mucky and lawless as San Francisco had been back in the early years, there had been no real poverty or hunger then. Men might lose everything at the gambling tables, but they helped one another and there was plenty of work for those who needed it. But it was different now, starving men and women begged in the streets, just as they had in New York. There was little help for the destitute, charities like the Ladies Relief and the YMCA could only help a tiny minority. As for medical help for the poor, that was almost non-existent. Conditions were so terrible in the Marine Hospital that few would even attempt to go there, people with infectious diseases were sent to the Pest House, and few came out of there alive.

As she went back indoors she thought how much luck this city had brought her, and that perhaps it was time she put something back into it.

During the afternoon Matilda was sitting at her desk in the parlour writing her weekly letters to Tabitha and Cissie when Dolores came in.

'You should be out in the sunshine, ma'am,' she said reproachfully. 'You's spend way too much time indoors, it ain't good for you.'

Matilda smiled. Dolores was something of an enigma. She was the perfect servant, competent, loyal and entirely trustworthy, and since Zandra's death she had transferred all the care and devotion which she had lavished on her old mistress to Matilda.

But although she fussed around her like a mother hen, constantly urging her to eat more and work less, Matilda still hadn't managed to break through the black woman's reserve and discover her real feelings about anything.

Zandra had told her that Dolores had turned up at her parlour house in New Orleans over twenty years ago, when she was around thirteen or so. She was in rags, half-starved, and her whole body scarred from a recent beating. She said she'd run away from the plantation she'd been born on when her mother was sold by her master. It appeared that she'd been raped too, but Dolores never confirmed or denied this. Zandra bathed, fed and clothed her, intending to pass her on to one of the organizations who helped runaway slaves, but the girl begged her to let her stay as a maid.

Zandra had said she'd never met any girl who was so willing to learn, within two or three years she'd become an accomplished hairdresser and needlewoman, but it was her utter loyalty to her new mistress which endeared her to her the most. So Zandra kept her with her, through retirement, then on to San Francisco. She often remarked that in over twenty years, Dolores had never shown any emotion about anything and never told her anything personal.

Matilda thought Zandra would have been very touched to see how Dolores reacted to her death. She stayed in her room with her body for the whole two days before the burial, wailing pitifully. Yet once that was over, she reverted back to her old dignified manner and asked Matilda if she could stay on as her maid.

'Perhaps you're right,' Matilda said, glancing out of the window and thinking how inviting the sunshine looked. 'Maybe I'll go for a walk.'

Dolores beamed. She was an exceptionally plain woman, tall and thin with sharp cheek-bones and a wide, splayed-out nose. Her usual expression was severe enough to daunt most people, and it was only when she gave one of her rare smiles that one got a glimpse of the kindness within her. 'Good girl,' she said, as if Matilda were a child. Then walking over to the window she touched the velvet drapes and frowned at them. 'I'll get these down while you're gone and give them a good brushing,' she said.

Matilda put on her sturdiest boots and her plainest bonnet and slung her old grey cape round her shoulders. She glanced in the looking-glass and winced at her appearance. Her complexion looked muddy and what little hair that showed beneath the bonnet was dull. She thought Dolores was right, she did spend too much time indoors. She'd hardly been out at all since Zandra died.

As she walked through the closed saloon Sidney was stocking up the bar for the evening. Since Zandra's death, for propriety's sake, he had moved into Dolores' old room down behind the saloon, and Dolores had taken his room upstairs.

'I'm going for a walk,' she called out. 'I'll see you at supper-time.'

They always had supper together in the kitchen upstairs. With Zandra gone, and Sidney living downstairs, it was their way of maintaining a family life and getting a chance to talk over any problems about the business.

'Don't go too far, it's going to rain later,' Sidney called back.

Matilda smiled at his remark in disbelief as she walked down California Street Hill. There wasn't a cloud in the sky, and it was almost too warm for a cape. A young couple ran past her hand-in-hand, their boots clattering on the planking, and she guessed they were making for the open space at the top of the hill. In summer it was a favourite place for courting couples, with the splendid view and the soft, sweet-smelling grass. She guessed that the warm sun had tempted them to go looking for a secluded place to make love.

She turned for a moment to watch them running up the hill. Their backviews reminded her of herself and Flynn. They looked very poor, the girl's bonnet was misshapen, her shawl and dress very shabby. The lad had a grey derby hat just like Flynn wore, and similar ill-fitting clothes.

As she walked on she remembered the way Flynn had made her feel, the churning stomach, the sleepless nights wondering what he was doing, all those dreams which came to nothing. It was odd that a love which was once so momentous, so all-consuming, and so very painful when it ended, could become something she looked back on with a smile. But then perhaps that was because in time she'd come to see she had had a lucky escape. Yet Flynn was her first love, and he would always have a small place in her heart. She hoped he managed to achieve some of his big plans.

Her thoughts turned to James some time later, once she was on the coastal path which led to the Presidio, the old adobe fort and mission built by the Spaniards some seventy-odd years ago, perhaps because he'd had been staying out at the fort the time she'd last seen him. She wished she could put him out of her mind, or at least find that her memories of him had turned to pleasant nostalgia, without the regrets and the heart ache. But he still gripped her heart, even after all these months. So often she remembered how Zandra had said she would have gone after him, and settled for being his mistress. Perhaps that's what she should have done.

But it was too late now for regrets, he was far away in New Mexico, and she must keep her father's advice to 'never look back' firmly in her head. She looked around her as she walked, the sea was sparkling, the breeze soft and warm, the dirt and hubbub of the town seemed a hundred miles away, the only sound that of sea birds. The salty air was exhilarating, for the first time in months she felt tranquil, and perhaps this meant she was on the mend at last, and that some new interest was about to present itself.

A few carts and people on horses passed her as she walked on to the Presidio, and she planned when she reached there to take another route back into town. There were some black clouds gathering on the horizon, but she paid them no attention.

One man in a light gig called out to her and asked if she wanted a ride back as there was a storm coming, but as he looked a disreputable sort of fellow and anyway she was enjoying her walk, she turned down the offer and continued.

About a mile on, the sun suddenly vanished. Looking up, she saw the entire sky had grown black, and alarmed, she immediately turned back. It was a common occurrence in San Francisco for cold, thick mist suddenly to swirl in from the sea, but this was more than that, and within just a few seconds the first drops of rain began to fall.

All at once there was not one person in sight, not a walker, cart or rider, and as the raindrops became heavier and faster, the path quickly turned to mud. Matilda regretted turning down the man's offer of a ride, for he was right, it was a storm, not a shower, all light was fading fast, and she had some three or four miles to go before she'd reach any kind of shelter.

Picking up her skirts, she began to run, but as the rain got heavier and heavier, so the path turned to a bog, and she was slipping and sliding. Her cape was drenched, her felt bonnet was sodden, and her boots were letting in water.

She battled on, head down, but a wind had sprung up now, too, slowing her down even more, and as it worked its way through her wet clothes she found herself shivering with cold. But it was the ever deepening gloom which worried her the most, she had imagined it was only around four o'clock, but maybe it was far later than that, and it really wasn't safe for a woman to be out alone in the dark.

It became more and more difficult to walk. The slippery ground and the dark made it so treacherous. She stumbled several times and, afraid she might twist her ankle and then be unable to walk at all, she slowed right down, picking her way cautiously.

As the darkness grew deeper Matilda became really scared, cursing herself for not listening to Sidney's warning. She couldn't even be sure she was on the real path. What if she had veered off it and was going towards the cliff edge! She couldn't hear the sea, but then the rain was coming down so hard she doubted she'd even hear a cannon firing.

On and on she went, at a snail's pace, growing more frightened and cold by the minute. She had an awful feeling she might very well be going round and round in circles.

Then, suddenly, she could hear something above the drumming of the rain. She stopped, peering ahead of her into the darkness her ears pricked up.

It was horses' hooves she could hear, and the jingling of spurs, a great many of them, and they were coming towards her. No sound had ever felt sweeter, for she guessed it had to be soldiers on the way to the Presidio.

She stood her ground in the middle of what she hoped was the pathway to wait for them to get nearer. It crossed her mind that in the darkness, and her so wet and bedraggled, they might ignore her and ride by. But she gritted her teeth and got ready to call out.

All at once she could see them, at least the dark shapes of men on horseback.

Picking up her sodden skirts, she moved towards them. 'Please help me. I've lost my way in the dark,' she yelled out.

There was no response, no single rider breaking ranks to come to her, they just kept on coming towards her, and now they were so close she could see the leaders, faces beneath their down-turned hats, tired, drawn and cold from a long ride.

Instinct made her move back when she saw they were going to pass without stopping. For a moment she stared in disbelief as the first ten or so men rode by without even looking at her. Anger welled up inside her, for she knew that by tomorrow night these same men would be coming into London Lil's to see the show. How dare they ignore a woman calling out for help on a lonely isolated path!

'Help me, please!' she yelled out again, trying to run alongside them. 'I'm lost, cold and wet. Are you just going to leave me out here to perish?'

She heard a couple of them laugh and that made her even more angry.

'You leave me out here and none of you will ever set foot in London Lil's,' she screamed at the top of her voice. 'And I shall make a formal complaint to your commanding officer.'

But still they rode on. 'Call yourselves men!' she screamed. 'Lily-livered bastards, the lot of you. I hope you all die of the pox.'

Then suddenly one man at the back of the company broke ranks and rode up to her. 'Well, at last we have a gentleman,' she said.

'And what is a *lady* doing out here on a dark wet night?' he retorted.

She felt like she'd been struck by lightning, for even though it was too dark to see the man's face, his voice was so very familiar, and the sarcastic tone.

'James!' she gasped. 'Is it really you?'

'None other,' he replied, leaping from his horse. 'I do declare, ma'am, you turn up in the most unlikely places.'

It crossed her mind that she might be delirious. Why should a man who meant so much to her suddenly appear just when she needed help? Yet it wasn't wishful thinking, he was here, the rest of his company heading on towards the fort.

She vaguely heard him call out to his men and say something

about taking her home, but she was so stunned he could have been speaking another language.

'What are you doing here?' she managed to gasp out as the last of the riders went by. Her legs felt weak, she was so cold her teeth were chattering like castanets, and yet her heart was thumping like a bass drum.

'I've got a new posting in Benicia,' he said. 'But why are you out here? You're soaked right through.'

'I was out walking when the storm began,' she managed to get out, then her legs buckled under her.

James caught her in his arms before she reached the ground. 'What is it? Are you sick too?'

'No, I'm not sick,' she managed to get out. 'I guess I'm just overcome with shock at you coming to my rescue. I was beginning to think I'd be out here all night, unable to find the way home. But I'm absolutely fine now you are here.'

He held her tightly against him. He was as wet as her, and smelled strongly of horse, but nothing on earth had ever smelled so good. 'Oh Matty,' he murmured. 'This has to be fate! When I knew I'd be passing through San Francisco I promised myself I would keep well away from you.' His voice quivered with emotion. 'But here we are again, like it was meant to be. How can either of us fight that?'

She looked up. His hat was tipped back, his face shining with rain water. She had seen him like this so often on the trail, and it felt as if they had moved back a few years to that time when their friendship had been the one thing which made the trip bearable.

'There's no place I'd rather be,' she whispered. 'I'm not going to fight it.'

His lips came down on hers. They were as cold and wet as her own, but his tongue parted her lips, and the unexpected warmth, the joy of being safe and in his arms, fired up all that desire which had lain dormant for so long. The kiss went on and on, growing in intensity as they clung together. The rain came down in sheets, the wind whistled around them, but they were oblivious to everything but one another.

He lifted her off her feet and took her off the path under the shelter of a large tree, still kissing her. 'I thought you were lost to me,' he murmured, burying his face into her neck. 'These months have been slow torture, I can't believe you are flesh and blood. Tell me it isn't just a dream!'

She reached up and held his face between her two hands, looking into his eyes. It was too dark to see their colour, but she could see the passion and love in them. In that instant she didn't care if he had a wife at home. She had known him first, he was hers by rights. Nothing mattered but the moment, not the children up in Oregon, Sidney and Dolores growing frantic at home because she hadn't come back. Not his commanding officer in the Presidio, or his grand family back in Virginia. She wanted James, body and soul, and tomorrow could take care of itself.

'Take me,' she whispered and before he could make any protest, she kissed him again, and undulated her body against his. She heard a faint moan as his hands reached underneath her cape and he fumbled with cold fingers to unbutton the front of her gown. But as his hand found her breast, he let out a sigh of ecstasy.

It was frantic, crude and rough, yet somehow it was far sweeter than making love in a warm and comfortable bed. Two cold bodies warming to each other's touch, the shock of skin on skin, mouths clinging to one another, fingers searching out sensitive places, and the rain and the darkness enveloping them.

As he bent to kiss her breasts, Matilda held her face up to the rain, delighting in the extremes of the cold on her face and his warm mouth nuzzling her. His hands were under her skirts now, his fingers lingering on the soft flesh on her inner thighs. Nothing had felt more sensual, or so delightfully wicked, and her fingers were reaching for the buttons on his pants, desperate to please him too.

He gasped as she released his penis and held it lovingly in her hand. He pushed his fingers deep inside her, making her moan and writhe against him.

'I love you, Matty,' he whispered as he lifted her on to him, and all at once he was sliding into her, and it felt so good she screamed out his name.

His fingers dug deep into her bottom, holding her up and moving her in time with him, and all the time his mouth never left hers, kissing her with such passion she felt she was melting into him.

He stopped suddenly, and she realized he was withdrawing to protect her from pregnancy. She loved him even more then that he could think of her at such a moment, when that danger hadn't even crossed her mind. He spent his seed against her belly, holding on to her, and still probing deeply into her with his fingers to give her pleasure. The last thing she heard as she gave herself up to the bliss of the climax was his whisper that he would love her for ever.

'I'm so wet,' was the only thing she could manage to gasp out as she leaned back against the tree to catch her breath. She could hardly believe she'd been so abandoned, or so careless about being spotted by a passer-by.

'Wet maybe, but never more beautiful,' he replied, showering her face with kisses as he tried to fasten her gown again. 'But I must get you home before you catch a chill.'

They stood looking at each other for a moment, strangely nervous now, knowing they'd passed the point of no return. Matilda reached up and ran her fingers down the line of his cheek-bones. 'We're probably going to regret this tomorrow,' she whispered. 'But I don't regret it now.'

'Nor me,' he said, and she knew he was smiling. 'But come now, up on my horse, and home. I will regret it if you end up with a fever.'

He lifted her bodily into the saddle, then mounted behind her, his slim hips sliding in so close to her buttocks that it felt as if they were one. With his arms around her, his chin on her shoulder, and his moustache tickling her cheek, the dark ride home wasn't frightening any longer, or even cold.

He told her about the posting in Benicia. It was a military post around thirty miles or so away, south-east of San Francisco. Its situation was convenient should any trouble occur here, in Stockton or Sacramento. Matilda couldn't ask if his wife would be joining him there, to bring her name up now would only spoil the moment. Maybe tomorrow they could talk of such things. As they jogged along he rubbed his cheek against hers, and told her that not a day had passed when he didn't think of her, and that he'd begun to believe she'd cast a spell over him.

'My little English witch,' he chuckled as the lights of the town came into view. 'But if this is a magic spell, I sure don't want anyone breaking it.'

James secured his horse to the rail outside London Lil's. Through the windows they could see only a handful of customers, for it was early yet, and the heavy rain would probably deter all but the most determined drinkers tonight.

As they walked in, both sopping wet, Sidney rushed out from behind the bar. 'Where have you been, Matty?' he exclaimed, his usually jolly face etched with anxiety. 'Are you hurt? What happened? Who is this?'

Matilda quickly explained where she was when the rain started and how the Captain and his men had come by and rescued her.

'You will remember me speaking of Captain Russell,' she went on. 'You know, the captain who was in charge of my wagon train. Wasn't it strange that it was he who came along? I thought I'd never see him again.'

Even as she made this explanation, she knew it must sound entirely improbable. As a young lad Sidney had loved to hear about this man. Under any other circumstances he would have greeted James with wild enthusiasm. But he was a man now, he saw himself as Matilda's protector. He had almost certainly overheard her talking about James to Cissie on her last visit to Oregon, and who could blame him for thinking this meeting was planned?

'Have you been posted here, sir?' he asked with a touch of starch in his voice.

'No. I'm on my way to Benicia,' James replied. He glanced down at the ever-growing puddles around both their feet. 'But let's talk later, Sidney, Matty will get a chill if she doesn't get into a hot bath quickly, she'd been out in the rain for a long time before I came along.'

'Of course,' Sidney said quickly, taking Matty's dripping hat and cape from her. 'Dolores is still holding our supper,' he said. 'I couldn't eat, I was so worried. You should have said where you were going. I didn't even know in which direction to look for you. I sent one of the boys up to Mr Slocum's place thinking you might be there.'

'I'm so sorry,' Matilda said, blushing under Sidney's close scrutiny. She didn't think he was mature enough to know her burning cheeks were the result of passion rather than the wind and rain, but just the same she was anxious to get away from him. 'Now, do you think you can rustle up some dry clothes for the Captain? After rescuing me the least we can do is dry him off too, and feed him.'

Sidney led James off to the wash-room at the back of the saloon, and Matilda went on upstairs, her wet skirts leaving a trail behind her.

'Oh my Lord!' Dolores exclaimed as Matilda came in.

'I'm fine, only wet,' Matilda said firmly, anxious not to get a long lecture from her maid, however kindly meant. She explained how she'd been caught in the rain, and that the Captain had brought her back. 'I'll just have a bath and get changed,' she said. 'Sidney's seeing to the Captain. Is there enough supper for him too?'

'Sure, I made a whole mess of fried chicken,' Dolores said, putting both her big hands on Matilda's shoulders and nudging her into her bedroom, where she grabbed a blanket from the closet. 'Now, off with those wet duds, and wrap yourself in this until the bath's ready. I'll make you some hot brandy to kill the chill.'

Once Dolores had gone off to the kitchen for hot water, Matilda quickly stripped off her wet and muddy clothes. Once wrapped in the blanket, she looked at herself in the looking-glass and grinned at her bedraggled appearance. Her hair was plastered to her head, yet she had bright pink cheeks and sparkling eyes. She didn't look or feel the least bit poorly, the apartment was so very warm, and the smell of the fried chicken was making her mouth water.

'You ought to be ashamed of yourself,' she whispered at her reflection. But she didn't, she felt elated, giddy and fizzy inside. All she hoped was that over supper she and James would be able to act naturally and not give Sidney or Dolores any reason to suspect there was something going on.

Even that made her smile. Dolores had spent her entire adult life in a parlour house and like Zandra she would be hard to fool. Yet all the same Matilda had a position to maintain, and so she must act with the utmost propriety. If one word of this got outside, women like Alicia Slocum would go into a feeding frenzy. She didn't much care for herself, but there was James to consider, and her girls. She wanted to bring Amelia down here to live before long, and it wouldn't do for her to hear that her mother had a lover.

When Matilda went back into the parlour, bathed and dressed in a pink gown, her still damp hair tied back with a ribbon, James and Sidney were sitting by the fire waiting for her, chatting as if they'd known each other all their lives. James was wearing a red flannel shirt and a pair of worn work pants which belonged to Albert, one of the other waiters. He was wearing no shoes, only a pair of thick socks. His damp fair hair was steaming a little as it dried.

'Are you feeling all right?' Sidney asked, jumping to his feet.

'Never better,' she replied, trying hard not to catch James's eyes. The hot brandy laced with honey and lemon that Dolores had dosed her with had gone straight to her head, making her feel even more giggly and girlish. 'And what about you, James?'

'Your maid is one bossy woman,' he laughed. 'She snatched my uniform to dry it, wouldn't even let me have my boots back. Maybe she doesn't know soldiers are used to wearing wet boots.'

Matilda smiled. Normally she and Sidney ate their supper in the kitchen, but while she'd been bathing, Dolores had laid the table in here with the best lace cloth and Zandra's silver. While this could be purely because of James's rank and class, she thought not, it was far more likely her maid knew perfectly well this was the man she'd been mooning over for so long, and had decided for herself that she was going to encourage him.

'I got Albert to rub the Captain's horse down, give him some oats and put him in the shed out the back,' Sidney said. 'The rain's so heavy he'd best stay here tonight. I reckon parts of the town will be flooded by now.'

At that Dolores pushed open the door and came in with a large tray piled high with food.

'You all sit right down at the table now,' she said.

None of them needed prompting. The dishes of fried chicken, roasted potatoes and several different vegetables all looked and smelled delicious and they were all very hungry.

'This fried chicken is the best I've ever eaten,' James said, smiling up at Dolores as she came back into the room later with more potatoes. 'It puts me in mind of the meals back home.'

Dolores didn't acknowledge this compliment but added another piece of chicken to his plate, then quickly left the room.

'Did I say something wrong?' James asked, looking at Matilda.

'Not at all,' she said with a smile. 'Dolores is a woman of few words, giving you another piece of chicken is her way of showing her appreciation. I've got used to her now, but when she first came here with Zandra I found her quite intimidating.'

'I can imagine,' he said. 'I heard the Contessa brought her from New Orleans, was she a slave?'

'Not Zandra's, she was appalled by slavery,' Matilda said, then went on to tell the story.

'I suppose if Dolores had been less plain she would have pressed her into some other kind of service!' he replied with some sarcasm.

Matilda bristled. 'Don't you ever make those kind of remarks about Zandra,' she snapped. 'She never "pressed" anyone into service, as you like to call it. Just the fact that Dolores chose to stay looking after her when she was old and frail proves the high esteem she had for her. Zandra left her five hundred dollars in her will, so she clearly cared for her too.'

'I'm sorry,' he said, looking a little sheepish. 'I guess I'm just like everyone else, and find it difficult to imagine a woman owning a parlour house having a heart.'

'It was a pity to you didn't get to meet her,' Sidney piped up, wanting to smooth the waters. 'She was one lovely lady, Captain Russell, you'd have liked her the way we did, but tell us about your new posting.'

James repeated what he'd already told Matilda. 'Benicia is one of the better postings because it's a newly built fort. Unfortunately, the temptation for some of the enlisted men to desert will be even greater here, so close to this city of sin and gold, than anywhere else,' he said with a sigh. 'Especially as for the most part there will nothing to do all day but drill.'

'Won't you be fighting Indians?' Sidney asked.

James smiled at the naive view that this was all soldiers did, and shook his head. 'We're only here to keep law and order in the gold-mining towns,' he said. 'Trouble can brew up like a spark in dry straw, our job is just to quell it.'

After asking a few questions about army life, Sidney reluctantly went back down to the saloon. Matilda and James moved back to the couch in front of the fire while Dolores cleared the table.

'Don't you have to go downstairs tonight?' he asked once

Dolores had left the room and Matilda handed him a brandy.

'I should, but I won't,' she said. 'I don't want to leave you alone up here and you can't come down with me without any boots.'

'I don't mind being alone,' he said, stroking her cheek with one finger. 'By rights I should be up at the fort with my men, not lying around here in comfort. I'll have to get back very early in the morning to lead them to Benicia.'

Matilda hadn't realized he was moving on so quickly. 'I thought you'd have a couple of days here,' she said sadly.

He drew her into his arms. 'I guess this is as good a time as any to talk about how things are,' he said. 'I don't know where we can go from here, Matty. Evelyn's joining me soon in Benicia.'

Matilda's heart plummeted. While his wife was right over the other side of America in Virginia she imagined she could forget about her. 'Are you trying to tell me that this is all we get?' she asked softly.

He tilted her face up to his and looked into her eyes. 'How can I say that, Matty? I wish I could say it was a terrible mistake and this is where it has to end, but I can't. It sure doesn't feel like a mistake, it feels like the rightest thing I've ever done.'

'But how can we have anything more, James?' she asked gently, suddenly so very aware of how precarious this love affair would be. 'How can I be in your life when Evelyn is with you at the fort? Maybe I could bear you having a wife if she was far away. But not here, so close.'

He said nothing for a little while. She could see a tic twitching under his eye, and knew he had something he wanted to share with her, but felt he couldn't say.

'What is it? Come on tell me, we can't have secrets now.'

'She doesn't want to come,' he blurted out suddenly. 'It was her father who insisted she must.'

Matty frowned. 'But why doesn't she? Surely every wife wants to be with her husband.'

He hung his head, she thought he looked embarrassed.

'The truth of the matter is that Evelyn expected that her father would immediately push me up through the ranks once we were married,' he said in a rush. 'She thought I'd get a posting in Washington and saw herself in a smart house, entertaining fellow officers and their wives. She was shocked when her father packed her off to join me in New Mexico, her plan was to stay at home in Virginia.' James paused and leaned forward to give the fire a poke. 'The sad thing about this is that Evelyn was as mistaken about her father as she was about me. He's of the old school, like me, believes in real soldiering, not sitting behind a desk somewhere. He knew my real talents lay in training raw recruits. He also believes a woman who marries a soldier should take what comes with the job.'

'Well, so she should,' Matilda said stoutly.

James gave a mirthless little laugh. 'Can you begin to imagine, Matty, what it's like to have a wife with you who is determined to hate everything sight unseen? She was a spoiled, pampered child, Matty, she has no spirit of adventure, no desire to broaden her horizons, and she has never learnt that sometimes life has to be a compromise.'

Matilda noted that James had carefully chosen every word he'd said about her, he was too gallant to be openly disloyal. She thought the plain truth was that Evelyn had married James believing she could manipulate him and her father to get exactly what she wanted, and that real love had never come into it.

If this was true, then she need have no guilty conscience about taking Evelyn's husband as a lover. It still meant that they had no real future together. It would always be an illicit relationship which they would have to hide. But however painful and difficult that might be, it had to be far less agonizing than cutting him out of her life.

'I can't say goodbye,' she said, leaning into his chest. 'So there's nothing for it but for us to be lovers in secret. That is, if you can find a way to come and see me now and then?'

'I can find a hundred and one excuses to come into San Francisco, if you still want me,' he said, with a voice husky with emotion. 'Maybe you could even organize regular riots so I've got good reasons.'

Matilda giggled. 'There will be a riot if you don't come.'

A little while later Dolores knocked on the door to say she had made up the bed for the Captain in Zandra's old room and asked if they needed anything more this evening.

Matilda thanked her and said there was nothing more they needed. James smirked as the door closed behind the maid but made no comment.

'I don't think I'll ever be entirely comfortable with having a servant,' Matilda said thoughtfully. 'You see, I was a very nosy one, and knew absolutely everything about the Milsons. I don't like the idea that Dolores knows everything about me.'

'I've never thought about it in that way,' he replied with a smile. 'But then I was surrounded by servants right from birth. The way Dolores fussed about my wet clothes was almost like going home again.'

'And they must have been slaves?'

'Yes,' he said, a shadow flitting across his face. 'Of course I didn't understand the significance of that until I was about eleven. My father stopped me playing with the children around that time. Up till then I thought we were just one big family, black or white. Indeed, I much preferred the black people, they were far nicer to me than my own folks.' He paused for a moment, a troubled look in his eyes. 'That's another cloud on the horizon,' he said after a few moments. 'If the Southern States are ever to join the Union they will have to agree to abolish slavery. But I can't see them doing that, and I can only see it ending in civil war.'

Matilda didn't see why this should trouble him unduly, and said so.

'You are forgetting I am a Southerner,' he said with a sigh. 'How could I lead my men against my own people?'

Any further deep conversation was halted as the band struck up downstairs. James jumped as the lamps began to tinkle with the vibration, and Matilda laughed. 'Our peace is over now,' she said. 'In an hour or two we won't even be able to hear ourselves speak.'

'Then kiss me again instead,' he said.

The kisses earlier had been savage, a thirst that had to be quenched, the whole act had been a primitive urge which had no finesse or delicacy. But now it was time to tease, please and explore each other. James made a nest of cushions in front of the fire and laid her down on it, pulling the ribbon from her hair and running his fingers through it. He whispered endearments, his eyes full of tenderness, he said again that fate must have planned for them to be together. Between kisses, garments were removed slowly, piece by piece, and tossed aside.

Matilda looked down at him as he hooked her breasts out

from the confines of her chemise to suck at them, and she trembled with pleasure. As his shirt came off and that hard golden-brown chest which she'd so often admired on the trail touched her nipples for the first time, it was so erotic she felt faint with desire.

It was she who removed his pants, running her hands down his muscular thighs, stroking his hard buttocks, delighting in the soft gold hair on his legs. His penis was far bigger than either Flynn's or Giles's, as upright as a sabre, yet so warm and smooth to the touch.

James stroked her body as if tuning a musical instrument, waiting for the moment when the pitch and tone were perfect. Every kiss heightened the sensuality of his probing fingers, he licked and sucked at her naked flesh as if he was feasting on her, and when he finally entered her, Matilda's senses were already spiralling out of control, lost in the wonder of loving and being loved.

They moved together like one person, her legs clenched around his waist, bodies wet with perspiration, making sucking noises as they touched. She wanted him deeper and deeper inside her, she clawed at his back and buttocks, and then at last it happened again, that glorious eruption inside her, and she could only cling to him, murmuring his name over and over again.

An hour or two later, James sat back on his haunches and smiled down at Matilda naked on the pile of cushions.

'Why are you smiling?' she asked. 'Do I look funny?'

'You look wanton,' he said. 'But not funny, unless I count your reluctance to move to a comfortable bed as amusing.'

'Well, Dolores might have come out of her room to see if we wanted anything,' she said.

'I don't think even fire would drag Dolores out of her room tonight,' he said. 'She knew you had designs on me.'

'She knew no such thing,' Matilda retorted, pulling out a cushion and throwing it at him.

'Good servants are mind-readers,' he said. 'She probably knew too that you needed some good loving.' He had never known a woman as abandoned in love-making as Matilda had been, and yet he knew it hadn't come from experience. She was also the most beautiful woman he'd ever made love to, his heart ached just to look at her.

He felt he could drown in the depths of those blue eyes, her lips were so soft and full, her skin like cream satin. The scent of her hair made him think of that sweet-smelling sage out on the prairies, and her body was perfection. Breasts still as firm and uptilted as they'd been that day he glimpsed her naked in the river, her tiny waist emphasizing the curves of her hips, and such a pert, rounded bottom. Most women of twenty-six had begun to lose teeth, yet hers were still as white and even as a child's.

'It was good loving,' she said with a smile, and just the way she looked at him made him tremble and want her again.

He lay down beside her and pulled her into his arms, burying his nostrils in her hair and breathing in that cool, clean scent. There was so much he wanted to say to her. That Evelyn didn't like love-making, she just endured it. That she was so empty-headed that an hour or two alone with her seemed endless. All she thought about was her appearance, always preening in front of a looking-glass, and she was insufferably rude to servants too. But he could say none of these things, even if it would make Matty understand why he had been unfaithful to his wife.

He'd already committed the greatest act of disloyalty, it wasn't right to talk about Evelyn's failings too. She couldn't really help being the way she was, she was just a typical product of her class and upbringing.

'I could leave the army, run off with you and your children to England,' he whispered, as the idea came to him. 'We could make out that we married on the wagon train, that Amelia is my daughter. I could find some work there, and we could have other children.'

She half smiled. 'You couldn't leave the army,' she said, tweaking his nose. 'It's what you love. You would hate England, it's cold and rainy, and just as full of bigots as America. In time you'd come to hate me for taking you there.'

'But what else is there?' he said.

'What we've got right here.'

Right now it seemed enough for him. He could stand being out soldiering for months on end, as long as he always had her to come back to. But he guessed that once Evelyn joined him, every evening in her company would seem like eternity.

'But I have no right to expect you to just wait until I can come to you. It could be months, maybe even years sometimes.'

'It doesn't matter, James. I'll wait,' she said, her eyes wide and honest. 'I'd rather have just a few hours of your time now and then than have you for ever, knowing I spoiled your life and career. You could get to be a general one day, you might be able to help put this country to rights. I'll be happy to watch you do that.'

James leaned up on one elbow and looked down at her. 'But you are worth so much more than that.'

'While I'm waiting for you I won't be idle,' she said. 'I do have a life of my own, and a business to run.'

He admired her more than ever at those brave words. She was a truly independent woman and she wasn't going to wilt in a corner while he was away.

'That's more like it,' he teased. 'For a moment I believed you had only the highest of ideals. The truth is, you want me out of the way, there *is* an element of self-interest!'

'Of course,' she said with a sly grin. 'Now we've straightened that out, perhaps we can talk about something else.'

'I have to go now,' James whispered just as dawn broke. 'I don't want to go, Matty, but I must.'

They crept into her bed once Matilda was convinced Dolores was fast asleep, but they hadn't slept for more than a brief few minutes the whole night. They'd made love, talked, and made love again and again. Matilda was exhausted, but still she reached out for her wrap.

'Don't get up,' he said. 'I'll let myself out.'

'I have to,' she replied. 'I need to bolt the saloon door again after you.' She pulled the drapes back a little and peered out. 'At least it's stopped raining. I'll go and get your clothes.'

His uniform was hanging up, dry and brushed free of mud. His boots stood beside the table, polished by Dolores as if he was due on the parade ground. The sight of them made Matilda want to cry, for she wished it was she who had done these things for him. But she opened the larder door and took out the remains of a meat pie, and wrapped it in paper. She hadn't made that either, but at least it was she instead of Dolores who was offering it.

James dressed very quickly, too quickly she thought, and she guessed this was something she'd just have to get used to. She hoped she could control her tears until after he'd gone.

'Can't you stay just for a cup of coffee?' she said, as he fastened on his belt and adjusted his holster. He shook his head, but smiled as she held out the parcel with the pie.

'Now, don't you stand waving at the door,' he warned her as they went out into the passageway. 'You'll give the game away dressed like that!'

Matilda looked down at herself. In her hurry to get up she hadn't thought how delicate the wrap was, and she might as well have been naked. It seemed odd that last night she hadn't minded James looking at her body, but now in the morning light she was embarrassed. She took her coat from the closet and put that on over it. James laughed softly.

'The memory of your beautiful body will stay with me for ever, however many clothes you wear in the future,' he said, and coming closer he took her in his arms.

'I love you, Matty,' he said softly. 'I'll be back to see you again as soon as possible.'

For a moment he held her silently, and Matilda sensed he was giving in to a moment of despair, just the way she was. It was always going to be like this, for them there would never be ordinary, husband-and-wifely moments of tedium. It was always going to be nerve-racking urgency. That might seem thrilling now, but for how long? How long could two people stand living on a knife edge?

Their last tender kiss was almost too painful, she could sense he was as reluctant to leave as she was to see him go. 'I love you too,' she said, clinging to him and breathing in the faint horsy smell of his uniform.

She let him out the back way, pointing out where his horse was stabled, staying for a while watching as he saddled him up. Then she bolted the door and ran upstairs to watch him ride away.

His horse was frisky, prancing up on his hind legs for a moment before making the steep descent down the hill. Matilda thought she had never seen anyone look so gallant or handsome as he turned to wave one last time. His hat was tilted to one side, his boots and spurs glinted in the early morning light, and the tears she'd tried to suppress came trickling out.

Tired as she was, she couldn't fall asleep. Her bed smelled of him, and she buried her nose in it and cried again. She had thought Giles's love-making was wonderful, but James's had taken her to even higher levels. Now she understood what Cissie had meant about missing it, even now when her body was weary and even a little sore, she still wanted more.

She woke later to the sound of Dolores coming in with two pails of hot water for her bath and was surprised to find it was nearly ten. Dolores only said good morning, filled the bath behind her dressing screen, then left.

Matilda got out of bed, and was just stripping off her nightgown when Dolores came back in with a tin jug in her hand, its contents smelled of herbs. 'You'll need this, ma'am,' she said.

Matilda took it from her hands, imagining perhaps it was for her hair. But floating in the fluid inside was an india-rubber ball-shaped thing with a nozzle. 'What is it?' she asked, looking at the maid in puzzlement.

'A douche,' Dolores said, her face devoid of any emotion. 'You don't want no babies, do you?'

Matilda blushed scarlet.

'Don't you go looking like that,' Dolores said, her face suddenly softer. 'Miss Zandra always told me I'd got to look out for you after she was gone. I knows you loves that man, but he ain't yours, so you do what I tells you, and wash inside and out. Then you'll be safe.'

'Safe!' Matilda whispered later as she dressed. She supposed being able to protect yourself from pregnancy should make a woman feel safe, but she thought some magic potion against falling in love would be safer still.

Chapter Twenty-one

'I sure wish I was coming with you,' James said, wistfully looking up at Matilda. Dolores was at her feet pinning up the hem of a new gown she'd made for her mistress to wear home to Oregon.

He wasn't wearing his uniform, just a checked shirt and a pair of old pants. His hair needed a cut, it was touching his shoulders, but when he was with Matilda he liked to forget about the army.

'Don't be silly,' Matilda said, but her tone was tender because she wished it were possible too. 'How would you stand being with two prattling women and a parcel of kids?'

It was July of 1855, yet though it was over two years since they first became lovers, in reality their love affair amounted to just a few days and nights together, with still no hope for any future. Back in May of 1853, just a few months after they had become lovers, Evelyn arrived in Benicia to set up home in the officers' quarters.

All through the summer James stayed out at the fort. He didn't write or send any messages, but miserable and forlorn as Matilda felt, she believed he was doing the right thing in staying away from her and trying to make a success of his marriage. But news of him did filter down to her through soldiers coming into London Lil's. They made crude jokes about 'The Southern Belle', who changed her clothes four or five times a day, whipped a maid for not being able to dress her hair as she liked it, and had fallen out with all the other officers' wives. It was only right at the end of the year James came to see her, and only then because he and his troops were ordered into the city to keep order at a controversial public hanging.

When James called at London Lil's she was deeply shocked by his changed appearance. His eyes were dull, deep frown lines had furrowed into his forehead, even his customary sarcasm and wit seemed to have left him. After a couple of drinks he eventually admitted his marriage was floundering.

He said Evelyn was incensed by the lack of comfort in the officers' quarters, the other officers' wives being so unfriendly, and she bitterly resented being forced to live amongst uncouth enlisted men, miles away from any form of civilized entertainment. He said she kept threatening to go home to Virginia unless he got what she called a 'decent posting'.

James insisted that the other wives had been very kind to her at first, they'd arranged little parties, offered to help her make her quarters more homely, but Evelyn was so rude to all of them that they eventually gave up and ignored her.

Matilda found herself in an impossible situation. While she loved James, and indeed couldn't help but secretly hope his marriage would fail so completely that Evelyn would take herself off permanently, she also felt sorry for Evelyn. It had to be very hard for any wife so far away from her family and friends, especially when she was left alone at the fort for weeks on end while James was off in Sacramento or Stockton. She felt guilty too when James admitted he was impatient and harsh with Evelyn because of wishing he could be with her.

At that time, the only honourable thing to do was to tell James it was over between them for good. She said she had found she couldn't spend her life wishing for something which could never be, and that he must forget her, and try harder to be a kind and considerate husband. It was so painful watching him ride away. Her heart felt as if it had been torn out, but she thought she'd said and done the right thing for all three of them.

But when spring came, Evelyn made good her threat and left for the East on a stage-coach. Her last words to James were that unless he got a posting in Boston or Washington, she would stay at her family home in Virginia permanently. When James wrote to Matilda to tell her this, any sympathy or concern she'd had for the woman left her. It was quite clear Evelyn didn't love James, she probably never had, all she cared about was herself and having the kind of busy social life she believed an officer's wife was entitled to.

So Matilda welcomed him back into her life wholeheartedly, and since then they had grabbed every moment they could together. At times it was like riding on an emotional see-saw. While together it was wonderful, so much passion, happiness, love and laughter, yet as soon as he'd gone back to Benicia

Matilda was often plunged into despair, tormenting herself with thoughts of Evelyn finding a way to bring her husband to heel, of them making love together when the time came to go home on leave. What might happen if they had a child together?

Jealousy struck her so often, for while she knew she held James's heart, his wife had his name and the dignity of marriage. They could never be seen in public together, dining in restaurants, as partners at a ball or dinner party. While no one would care if an army officer visited a brothel almost every night, a love affair with someone as well known as herself would mean certain disgrace. Their social life was limited to supper upstairs at London Lil's with only family and a few trusted friends.

Tomorrow James was going to Kansas City. Trouble kept erupting there between Abolitionists and pro-slavers and his role was to quieten things down. Matilda was going home to Oregon. Tonight might be the last time together for months or even years before they could see one another again. But neither of them was voicing that fear, they spoke of trivial things, because that way they could keep the lid on their emotions.

Dolores got up from the floor and stood back to check the hem of the dress. 'It's straight now, ma'am,' she said. 'Take it off and I'll get it sewn up right away.'

Matilda left the parlour to slip out of the dress, and hastily put on her old one before returning. It seemed a foolish thing to do when James saw her without clothes more often than he did with them, but in front of Dolores she always kept up a ladylike demeanour.

'This will be the last visit home with Tabby there,' she said as she came back into the room, determined to keep the conversation light. 'I can't imagine how I'm going to cope when she goes to Boston. It's so very far away and I don't suppose I'll get to see her much.'

Tabitha was fifteen and a half now. For the last two years she had continued to board and have private tuition with the Reverend and Mrs Glover, but in September the Glovers were going to a new ministry in Connecticut. The Reverend had suggested it would be an ideal opportunity for Tabitha to start at the Boston Academy for Young Ladies too, as she could travel across country with them to Boston, and she would be close enough to visit them during holidays.

While Matilda was fearful of Tabitha going so far away, and boarding at a school in a strange city where she knew no one, she knew the Reverend was right in saying she needed such an opportunity to round out her education to prepare her for university. Along with all the academic subjects she was so good at, she would also learn to play the piano, to dance and paint. It was a chance to make friends with similarly-minded young ladies from good homes, and the tutors would guide her towards a career in medicine.

'It's so long since I've seen Tabby I can't possibly imagine her all grown up,' James said with a smile. 'I still see her in my mind's eye with pigtails and a doll in her arms. But if this is the last time you'll see her for a while, it's probably a very good time to bring Amelia back with you. Have you made up your mind about that yet?'

Bringing Amelia down here to live had been on Matilda's mind for the last couple of years, in fact ever since Tabby went to board with the Glovers. Cissie had protested then, saying she was still such a baby, but things had changed since. In a recent letter Cissie had said she intended to marry Arnold later in the year. Matilda was sure they'd want children of their own, and it would be a better start to married life with only Peter and Susanna to care for.

'Yes, I'm going to,' she said, sitting down beside him. 'It's time she was with me, isn't it?'

James turned to her and put his arms around her, resting his cheek on her hair. 'Yes, it is. If she's anything like you in nature she'll weather the little barbs that might be thrown at her. And better for her to come here while she's still little than wait until later. I think it might be better though if you find somewhere else to live with her. Living over a noisy saloon isn't the best place on earth to bring up a child.'

Matilda reached up and stroked his cheek. She loved him for a great many reasons, his strength, courage and strong will, his intelligence, sense of humour and his passion, but it was his innate kindliness which she loved most of all. She saw brutes every night in her bar, they treated their wives with disdain, their mistresses with callousness, but James had never been like that. He had tried his best with Evelyn, and would continue to support her whatever she threw at him. She heard stories about him from some of his men too, and it was clear by the way they spoke of him that he was respected and admired, but never feared.

James cared about people in the same way Giles had, he hated injustice and intolerance, believed the weak should be protected. While Giles went into battle armed only with his belief in God, James had his sword and gun, but at heart he was every bit as peaceable as Giles, motivated only by loyalty to his country.

There was a great deal of talk about England's war with the Russians in the Crimea. When Matilda read in the newspapers about the casualties and the terrible conditions over there it had brought home to her what being a soldier really meant. She fervently hoped that James was wrong in saying the Indians would rise up in force before long, and that the ongoing arguments between the North and South could be settled without bloodshed.

'It's not that rowdy in the saloon these days,' she said with a sigh. This year there had been financial panic in the city, for the gold had finally run out. Up in the mountains whole towns were deserted, machinery, picks and shovels left to rot where they were dropped. Here in the city, scores of shops, restaurants, saloons and gambling places lay empty, and hundreds of people were thrown out of work. Every day saw more people leaving to return home to take up farming or work in factories. London Lil's was surviving only because it was so well known and she had the cash reserves to keep it going until better times came.

James had suggested she sold up and moved away too. But she had a gut feeling this was where she belonged. Maybe when she returned from Oregon with Amelia she would put her energies into something new, but she couldn't even think that far ahead right now, not when she knew James couldn't be part of that new life.

Perhaps he sensed she was a little pensive, for he suggested going up for a walk on the hills. Matilda agreed readily, she didn't want sad thoughts dominating the precious time they had left together.

She was out of breath when they got to the top of the hill and she stopped to look at the view of the city. She remembered when she first came up here in '49 there had been only a cluster of permanent buildings hugging the waterfront, now the city spread right around the bay. Gone were the wood and canvas buildings she remembered being so much part of the scene in the early years, new regulations meant all building work had to be made of brick. She could barely recall now just how desperate it had been before the streets were planked, or a real sewage system laid. Now there were even gas lights in some places, and a horse-drawn omnibus service.

There were now dozens of churches, all well attended, schools, a real prison instead of the old hulk anchored out in the bay she distantly remembered, yet it was still a wild, lawless place. She supposed it always would be with its volatile brew of diverse nationalities and cultures, and now that the gold had gone, many of the more desperate, villainous element who had no money to leave the city would find new ways to make a living here. She suspected that even if they brought in a strong police force, however many sober-minded people tried to stop the gambling, vice and corruption, built churches, schools and middle-class homes, it would never quite lose its unique and colourful character. She hoped not, for that was what she loved about it.

'Did I ever tell you that it was something you said that made me come here in the first place?' she said thoughtfully.

'Me!'

'Yes, you were talking about the rumour that there was gold in California and you said the smart people wouldn't go searching for it but make their money from supplying those who did with whatever they needed.'

'I always was a smart arse,' he grinned.

'You were, weren't you?' she laughed. 'Remember that day you said you knew I was carrying a child? I was so mad with you.'

'It was you getting so uppity which made me love you,' he said. 'If only I'd been braver and told you how I felt, maybe our lives would have turned out very differently.'

'I wasn't ready for love then,' she said ruefully.

He was silent for a moment, standing with his arms around her waist looking out to sea. 'There had to be a purpose for us finding one another again hundreds of miles away from where we last parted,' he said at length. 'Surely it wasn't just chance?'

'I'd like to think so, but from what I've seen, there is no sense or reason in fate,' she said. 'Look at Giles and John! Giles hated violence but he got shot. Poor John crushed by the timber he loved!'

'Maybe that was all part of the plan, terrible though it was,' he said. 'If not for Giles's death we wouldn't have met, and John's was responsible for guiding us to meet again. But I've no intention of leaving everything to fate, what we have is too precious for that. There is divorce, there is life without the army.'

While divorce was growing very common in California, Matilda wasn't so sure it was as easy in other states. Nor was she convinced a gentleman from one of the best families in Virginia, a graduate of West Point, could turn his back on everything he'd been brought up to believe in. She turned to kiss him. 'Don't be too hasty, James, you love the army, so don't throw that away carelessly. Give it more time.'

His head slumped down on to her shoulder. 'Time will only make it worse. I can't bear Evelyn,' he whispered. 'I know perhaps that's not a very gallant thing to say about the woman I vowed to love and cherish, but I have to tell you, Matty, it's important that you know.

'Within days of our wedding I knew it was the worst mistake I'd ever made, she is so shallow, utterly self-centred, just another empty-headed Southern Belle. I caught her whipping her maid with my belt one evening, just because she didn't like the way she'd arranged her hair. She would fly into a tantrum if her bath was too hot or too cold, I couldn't even see that she was pretty any more the way I once did, just the sound of her voice grated on my ears. You can't imagine what hell it is to have to live with someone you feel that way about. I felt like I'd been shut into a prison. But while I didn't know where you were, I could try to live with Evelyn. Once I met you again, it became impossible.'

This was the first time he'd spoken so openly about her, and it shocked Matilda to think he'd kept all this bottled up within him for so long out of loyalty.

'Don't, James,' she whispered, holding him tightly. 'You mustn't say such terrible things about her.'

He lifted his head and caught hold of her two elbows, his eyes so hard and desperate. 'I should have known better, Matty, because I knew what real love was like. I loved Belle with my whole heart, and I thought I would die too when she did. I got a second chance when I met you, all the feelings were the same, but like a fool I let you slip away, perhaps because I was afraid that you'd reject me.

'When I met Evelyn I was never taken with her as I was you or Belle, but she set her cap at me, and I'm ashamed to admit that I went along with it just because she was the Colonel's daughter. We didn't even have a real courtship, Matty, I saw her only when I was home on leave, at dinner parties and dances. In between these times I was out on the plains with my men, and I fooled myself into believing I loved her because of who she was and what it would do for my career.'

'I don't believe you were as cold-blooded as that, James,' she said. 'You did what any sensible man would do, picked a wife who had all the right credentials. If you hadn't met up with me again it would probably have worked out fine. Few people marry for love, they have children together and they learn to rub along.'

'I don't think I can ever rub along with her,' he said wearily.

'You've got to try to,' she said. 'Other men do, they bury themselves in their work. You are fortunate that yours will take you away a great deal.'

'Let's hope it will always bring me to you.'

Matilda bit back tears. She wanted so much more than stolen moments. She wanted him with her every day, to have his children, to love and be loved openly without shame or deceit. Her business was no longer important to her, she would gladly wash his shirts in a stream and cook over an open fire. But she couldn't tell him that now, for he might throw away his career and lose everything. She had to keep him stable, love and cherish him so he could keep his faith in his ideals. It was the only way.

Instead she held him and kissed him until he lowered her down on the grass and made love to her. As he thrust himself into her with the skirts of her dress billowing around them in the breeze she was reminded of couples she'd seen as a girl in London parks. She had always imagined the women were whores, but perhaps they were just women like her, blotting out reality for a few brief moments.

The next morning as Matilda stood on the deck of the steamer waving goodbye to Sidney on the wharf, tears trickled down her cheeks. James had left at first light after a whole night of love-making. They had drunk wine with their supper, gone down to the saloon and drunk champagne as they watched the show, for once they didn't care who saw them together. Henry Slocum had joined them later, and Matilda had danced with both men as recklessly as she had the night of Zandra's funeral. Then later James had taken her back upstairs, undressed her, unpinned her hair, and loved her with such fury she lost all sense of time and place.

But she had to think of the future now, and face that James might never be part of it. She had the holiday with Cissie and the children to look forward to, and all the excitement of bringing Amelia back with her. Last night Henry had suggested the houses being built at South Park would be ideal for her, it was a fashionable area, close to the best school, and above all a safe place to bring up a child. Maybe she'd even sell her share in London Lil's, stay home and be a full-time mother.

'Mama, Mama!' Amelia shrieked, breaking free from Cissie's restraining hand and running towards her mother as she came down the gangplank of the ferry to Oregon City.

Matilda dropped her valise and scooped her up into her arms, tears of joy welling up in her eyes. 'My darling,' she murmured as she showered kisses on her little face. 'It's so good to see you!'

'Why are you crying?' Amelia asked, her plump fingers wiping away the tears on her mother's face. 'Aunt Cissie said you'd be very happy to see how big I've grown.'

'So I am,' Matilda replied. 'I'm the happiest lady in the whole world.'

Cissie, Susanna and Peter all rushed to hug her too, all of them talking at once. Cissie was trying to tell her she and Arnold had set their wedding for next month, Peter asking about Sidney, Susanna demanding that she admired her new dress and Amelia shouting out that they had made a special cake for her, and that Tabitha would be coming to see her later.

'One at a time,' Matilda exclaimed, laughing as she put Amelia down so she could hug and kiss each one of them in turn. 'We've got lots of time.'

It was a warm, sunny afternoon, and as they walked home, the two little girls each holding her hands, Peter and Cissie carrying the valise between them, Matilda felt the tingly glow of anticipation she always experienced on visits here. This evening and all tomorrow it would be mayhem, each one of the family bombarding her with their most important news, and each one vying for her undivided attention. But slowly, as they got used to her being there again, it would quieten down, and bit by bit, she would piece together the progress each of the children had made, and hear from Cissie all the funny stories, the local gossip, the triumphs and disasters. Then the best times would come, the serenity of being one with them again, to be able to relax, listen and observe. To feel like a real mother again as she hung out washing, prepared vegetables for dinner, and played with the children. Time to renew her friendship with Cissie, to talk about all those ordinary things old friends needed to share. To love and be loved.

She glanced down at Amelia, and smiled with pure delight. At first glance she didn't resemble either her or Giles. Her hair was dark and curly like Giles's, but her eyes a very dark blue, and her skin prone to freckles. Yet she had her mother's determined chin and she was a very pretty little girl. At only six and a half it was too soon to know if she was going to be as smart as Tabitha, she certainly didn't have the same serious nature – as she skipped along beside her she was singing a little song, and each time she saw someone she knew she called out to inform them her mama had come home.

Susanna was a smaller replica of Cissie. Identical dark curly hair, and the same wide mouth. But she had John's blue eyes and his quiet, diligent nature, never happier than when she was making something with her hands, be it pastry, sewing dolls' dresses or drawing, the sort of child adults admired and other children trusted.

It was hardly surprising that no one had ever guessed twelve-year-old Peter wasn't John's real son because he'd grown quite like him. He had brown eyes, but the dark hair he'd had as a baby had lightened to a pale sandy brown. He also had the same stalwart look. Yet he had Cissie's fire – in several letters this year she had reported that he got into fights at school, led other boys into mischief, tore his clothes climbing trees and was always missing when she needed him. But there was always a touch of pride in her words, she was glad he was a real boy. Sometimes when Matilda looked at Peter she felt almost jealous he belonged to Cissie. She loved Susanna too but she didn't have the fierce feeling about her. She supposed it was only because Peter was the lynch-pin from the past, all tied up with the memories of Giles and New York, almost like the foundation stone of their family.

'You haven't been listening to a word I've been saying!'

Matilda was so engrossed in her thoughts and looking at the children that Cissie's indignant remark startled her. 'I'm sorry, Cissie,' she said. 'I was too busy admiring our brood. What did you say?'

'That I got the house painted, look, isn't it smart?'

Matilda looked ahead and gasped in surprise. Every time she came home to Oregon she found herself amazed at how the city had grown, how much cleaner and prettier it was than San Francisco, and at the pride the residents took in their homes and businesses. But Cissie's rather drab little house now stood out as the smartest in the row. Not only had the clapboard been painted white, and the front door dark green, but the narrow strip of ground in front of it had been enclosed by a small picket fence and a few shrubs had been planted.

'It looks as elegant as you, Cissie,' she said with a smile, for her friend was wearing a fashionable green sateen gown with cream ruffles at the neck. She wouldn't have looked out of place in one of the big eastern cities. 'Now, what brought that on? Could it have anything to do with you about to become Mrs Bigglesworth?'

Cissie giggled. 'Arnold built the fence himself. I think he wanted to prove he was as good as John. Once he'd painted it white it showed the house up, so I got a man to do it. I keep making excuses to go out, just so I can admire it.'

As Matilda had expected, that evening was riotous. Treacle gave her a rapturous welcome, all licks, wagging tail and yaps of pleasure, and the children fought for her attention, each trying to outdo the others. Between being dragged from room to room to admire every new item, school books being shoved into her hands, questions fired at her and every triviality which had happened in the last year being brought up, she couldn't possibly talk to Cissie about anything adult. Tabitha had arrived at six, and though her presence calmed the younger ones down a little, she too was very giggly and excited, desperate to talk to Matilda alone about the plans to go to Boston.

Tabitha was now taller than Matilda, with a slender, boyish figure. Although she had Giles's expressive dark eyes and Lily's small features, she wasn't really like either of them. Matilda knew many people thought her plain, and this irritated her. In her view Tabby had the delicate beauty of a shy, unobtrusive violet. But even if her looks never became more striking, or her body more shapely, her keen mind, her warmth and patience would see her through.

It was only when all the children were finally in bed and the house became silent that the two women were able to talk.

'Arnold and I had planned to get married in October,' Cissie said. 'His two brothers will be arriving from Ohio then. But I insisted we brought it forward so you could be there.'

'Are you sure he's right for you?' Matilda asked, after listening to all the wedding plans. 'You haven't once told me you love him!'

'I surely don't feel about him the way I did about John,' she said ruefully. 'But he's a good man, Matty, and I've been a widow too long. I'm twenty-seven now, my chances are running out and I need a man, I'm sure you know what I mean?'

Matilda nodded. Cissie missed love-making.

'He loves me though,' Cissie grinned wickedly. 'He can't wait to bed me!'

Matilda thought that almost every man in Oregon would want to bed her friend, and she wasn't sure that just because Arnold did too was sufficiently good reason to marry him, but then Cissie had been walking out with him for years now, so she must know what she was doing.

She moved on to tell her about her plans to take Amelia back with her. 'I know you love her, Cissie, and you've been her real mother to all intents and purpose. But she should be with me now.'

Cissie's eyes instantly filled up with tears, but to Matilda's surprise she didn't launch into an argument. 'You're right, she should be with you,' she said, looking bleak. 'I sure don't know how I'm gonna get by without her, I love her just the same as my own, sometimes I even forgets she ain't mine. But I guess it's better you take her now than later, Arnold's been saying that for some time.'

It was after one in the morning when they went up to bed but as Matilda got into bed, she suddenly felt sad. She had always thought of this little house as home, Cissie like a sister, Peter and Susanna as dear to her as Tabitha and Amelia.

But first Tabitha had gone off to the Glovers, soon she'd be moving to Boston, and Amelia was coming back to San Francisco to live with her and Sidney. She had a feeling that once Cissie was married, this house would become very much Arnold's home, and she and the other children would not be so welcome any more. She had smarted when Cissie had said he thought it was time she took Amelia away, he had no right to air his opinions on an agreement made between two close friends. But then it appeared he had strong opinions about everything, and it seemed Cissie went along with most of them.

Matilda hadn't ever taken to him. He was a man with a very narrow view of life, bound by the confines of his work and religion. His mother was German, his father English, from Lancashire, and they'd met and married as young immigrants and adopted the Puritan way of life when they moved to Pennsylvania. Arnold had held forth one evening last year on how scrupulously clean his mother kept their house, despite having four children, and how hard his father had to work, almost as if he believed Cissie and Matilda had been born into a life of luxury.

While Matilda didn't believe Cissie should tell Arnold everything about her early life, she thought her friend was laying up problems for herself by allowing him to believe she shared all his narrow views. She was after all a fiery and fun-loving woman, and to spend the rest of her days denying her true self would be a living death.

One bright sunny morning, two weeks into the holiday, Matilda and Peter waved goodbye to Cissie, Arnold and the two little girls as they set off in Arnold's gig to visit some friends of his. These friends had come out from Pennsylvania like Arnold, but they'd been given land some twenty-five miles away, and he'd only seen them once since they first arrived in Oregon. He'd got word they had had a new daughter recently, and he hoped to persuade them to come to his wedding. As it was a fifty-mile round trip, he and Cissie intended to stay overnight with them.

As this family had only young daughters, Peter wasn't very enthusiastic to go with them, so Matilda had suggested he stayed with her, and they would take a trip on the ferry to Portland to look at the ships.

'Have a lovely time,' Matilda called out as they set off. Cissie looked very pretty sitting up beside Arnold in a green and white print dress and a matching sun-bonnet. The two little girls were in the back with a picnic basket, Amelia in blue, Susanna in pink, both with starched white pinafores over their dresses. 'You two behave yourselves,' Matilda added as the girls blew kisses at her. 'I'll miss you.'

Her anxiety about the impending marriage had faded now. Arnold was staid and opinionated, but in the last two weeks she'd come to see there was another side to him too. The break-through had come on her first Sunday afternoon here when she'd seen the stout little man with his stiff collar and Sunday suit romping with Amelia and Susanna out in the garden. There was no pretence in his delight at playing with them, he clearly was a man who liked children, and these ones especially. Later that same day she'd caught a glimpse of him and Cissie kissing passionately in the parlour, and she'd decided that maybe she'd misjudged him.

Since then the man had surprised her many times, he helped with washing up when he came for a meal, he read books to the children, and he had a very close relationship with Peter, and Tabitha too. Maybe he was a little stuffy in that he disapproved of liquor, and women in business, but he was kindly, he clearly adored Cissie, and he would take good care of her and her children.

Matilda glanced sideways at Peter, he was watching the gig's departure very intently. 'Are you really sure you don't want to go too?' she asked, ruffling his sandy hair with her hand. 'You could run after them if you've changed your mind.'

Peter grinned. 'It will be more fun with you, Aunt Matty,' he said, his brown eyes twinkling with mischief. 'I bet you'll let me go swimming!'

Matilda smiled affectionately. Arnold didn't approve of boys swimming in the river, she suspected this was purely because he couldn't swim himself. Somehow she doubted he'd ever climbed a tree, torn his pants in rough play, or had a fight. She personally thought boys had to do these things if they weren't to grow up to become cissies.

Peter certainly wasn't a cissy; since Sidney left for San Francisco, he had taken it upon himself to be the man of the house – he chopped all the wood, lit the fires, and shot rabbits and ducks for the table. He also helped out the owners of the grocery shops after school, delivering orders, filling up shelves, and the money he earned was always handed over to Cissie.

'We'll see about swimming,' she said. 'Maybe we could take a towel just in case. If nobody's watching I might even have a paddle.'

Peter was excellent company, old enough for her not to flap every time he disappeared out of view, young enough to view the ships and the port with tremendous excitement. In many ways he was like Sidney in nature, the same exuberance, the interest in everything and anything, but then Sidney had been a formative influence since his birth. Yet Peter was a great deal smarter, he read extensively, and had a good head for figures. Matilda thought she ought to speak to Cissie when she got back about sending him to a better school too, for she thought he'd outgrown the little one here in Oregon City.

During the day Peter confided in her that he wanted to be a soldier. Knowing Cissie would never want him in the enlisted ranks with all those rough men, Matilda said he must work hard at school then, and maybe he could go to West Point and become an officer. She made a note mentally to ask James about this when she saw him again.

It was almost dark when they got home that evening, and it was strange to have the house all to themselves. They decided that the next day they would collect Tabitha from the Glovers and go for a long walk right up along the river, and if they found anywhere secluded enough, she might even have a dip in the water too.

Arnold and Cissie arrived home late the following evening, both the girls fast asleep in the back of the gig, and they didn't even wake when Arnold lifted them out and carried them up to their beds. Arnold left after a light supper, and Cissie launched into an account of the trip and Arnold's friends, Martha and Egon.

'Their cabin was horrid,' she said, pulling a disgusted face. 'Just a dirt floor, and no windows, they haven't even got a stove. I surely didn't want to spend even one night there, but it was too late to set off for home.'

This amused Matilda. Cissie had become remarkably ladylike in the past few years. She had made a concerted effort to speak better, and she was forever studying a book on manners. 'Don't tell me you've got above yourself!' she teased her.

Cissie grinned. 'It wasn't so much the cabin really, it was the way they were, kind of lazy and not caring enough to try and make it nice,' she explained. 'Egon's not a real farmer, back home he ran a dry goods store. As for Martha, well, I felt real sorry for her with a new baby and four others all under six, she looked so weary and sickly, I don't reckon she had enough milk for the baby, it kept crying all the time. Thank goodness we took a lot of food with us, they had hardly a thing to eat but beans and rice. The children were so dirty too!'

The scene Cissie was describing reminded Matilda of ones from her own childhood, and she guessed by the anxiety in her friend's eyes that she too had been reminded how lucky she had been to have married a resourceful man like John.

'I did what I could,' she went on. 'But Matty, there was so much needed doing, the little ones' dirty napkins were just left in a pail, the pots and pans all needed a good scouring, the chickens kept coming in the cabin, and that poor wailing baby! I could see Arnold wished we'd never gone, and Susanna just kept looking at me as if to say "When are we going?"'

'I bet your home looks pretty good now, doesn't it?' Matilda said.

'Oh Matty, it does,' Cissie said, running her fingers through her hair distractedly. 'I can't wait to get in my own bed. We slept on the floor last night, but I couldn't sleep for thinking what might be running about in there. I haven't thought about that cellar in years, but it all came back to me in the dark.'

Matilda saw that Cissie had been deeply affected by visiting Martha and Egon. For the next two days she kept washing clothes, scrubbing the floor and polishing windows, as if her life depended on it. Even Arnold seemed subdued when he called round the following evening, he said Egon had always seemed so strong and energetic when he was back in Pennsylvania, and he couldn't understand why he'd changed so much.

On the third night after returning home, Amelia called out in the early hours of the morning saying she had bad tummy ache. Matilda went in to her and sat her on the chamber-pot, and was perturbed to see her stools were very loose. As she went straight back to sleep afterwards, Matilda thought it was only a mild upset, and went back to bed herself.

Early next morning Susanna went rushing out to the privy, holding her stomach, only to scream out for her mother a few seconds later. She hadn't been able to get there in time and she was distressed at messing herself. This was followed a while later by Amelia crying out from upstairs that she too had had an accident.

As both children kept complaining of pains in their stomachs, they were put to bed, but it was only later in the day when Cissie complained of a kind of rumbling in her stomach, and aches in her legs, that Matilda went for the doctor. He was out on calls, but his wife promised he would come as soon as he got back. As she returned to the house Cissie informed her Amelia had been sick.

In the four hours before the doctor finally came, it became clear to Matilda that both the girls and Cissie had something far more than an ordinary stomach upset. Cissie had a bout of diarrhoea just like the children. All three of them were very thirsty and all had pains in both stomach and legs. But Amelia was by far the worst, she had brought up all the food in her stomach, now there was just thin, colourless fluid coming up, and the same from her bottom. She cried pitifully and lay scrunched up in the bed, unable to straighten her legs.

Cissie had tried to stay up and help with the children, but as each time a cramp came she was doubled up, Matilda made her go to bed. As a precautionary measure she told Peter to stay downstairs.

Dr Shrieber apologized profusely in his thick German accent for calling so late, listened to Matilda's description of the symptoms carefully, then followed her upstairs to see the patients.

Matilda had never met this man before, but she had heard

from both Cissie and Tabitha that the big blond man with steely blue eyes was considered to be one of the finest doctors in the whole territory.

He examined Amelia first, taking her pulse and gently feeling her stomach and legs. As he tucked the bedding up round her again, and moved on to examine Susanna, Matilda thought he had gone very pale, but as the light from the lantern was a little dim, she hoped she was imagining this.

The jovial way he greeted Cissie, and said they'd all been eating too much and would be better in a day or two allayed her fears. It wasn't until he was downstairs again that Matilda saw his expression was very grim.

'It isn't eating too much, is it?' she said.

He shook his head. 'No, I vish it vere just that, Mrs Jennings. I fear it is cholera,' he said in a strong accent.

She gasped, and clutched at the kitchen table for support. She knew only too well that this terrible disease rarely left any survivors. No one knew what caused it, and there was no treatment for it other than a few drops of laudanum and keeping the patient warm.

'I am so sorry, Mrs Jennings,' he said, his eyes soft with sympathy. 'Have you any symptoms?'

She shook her head. 'No, nor Peter, as yet. We stayed behind when Mr Bigglesworth and Mrs Duncan went to visit some friends. Maybe they caught this there? Have you heard if Mr Bigglesworth is ill too?'

'No, but I vill investigate that. You must keep Peter vell away from the sick room,' he said, dabbing at his perspiring face with a handkerchief.

'What about Tabitha?' she asked, fear clutching at her insides. 'She's been here too.'

Tabitha had been in and out on most days during her holiday, but mostly only for short periods because of her studies.

'I vill call on the Glovers too, and ask that they keep her at home for the time being,' he said. 'I advise you move Mrs Duncan into the room with the children, please soak a sheet in vinegar and hang it over the door. You must take care yourself, Mrs Jennings. Vash your hands after touching the patients, all soiled bedding must be boiled and chamber-pots and other vessels scoured. Until this disease has run its course you and Peter must not go out, and I vill place a sign on the front door to keep visitors away.'

Matilda suddenly felt very faint as the enormity of what he was saying slowly sank in. If he was right and this was cholera, then within a few days Amelia, Susanna and Cissie could all be dead.

She looked up at this big German for whom the whole city had the greatest respect, saw the deep concern in his eyes and knew he was unlikely to be wrong. She wanted to scream at him, tell him it was unfair, but she controlled herself and asked what she could do to try to save them.

'Keep them warm, much to drink, brandy too is helpful, I will return with a bottle for you later and some laudanum. Give the children two or three drops, Mrs Duncan can have up to ten. I vill call again to see you.'

'Come up here, Matty,' Cissie called out after the doctor had gone. Matilda went up hesitantly, afraid her friend was going to read what was wrong in her eyes. Cissie looked so small in the big bed John had made so lovingly. Her hands were tweaking at the quilt, her face very white. 'I know what it is,' she said, her green eyes wide with fear. 'I saw it on the wagon train. I could kill Arnold for taking us to that place. But I guess he couldn't know we'd catch something like this.'

'Of course he couldn't, and you are all going to be all right,' Matilda said, moving closer to her friend and taking her hand. 'I'll look after you.'

'If you've got any sense you'll clear off now,' Cissie said sharply. 'I've never known anyone survive cholera. The only good thing about it is that it's usually a quick death.'

'We'll have no defeatist talk of dying,' Matilda said fiercely. 'I won't have it. And neither am I going away, we can fight this, Cissie, but you have to work at it. First I'm going down to Peter to explain what's wrong, then I'm coming back up here to move you in with the girls.'

She dragged Tabitha's narrow bed into the girls' room and made it up for Cissie, between the two children's. An hour or two later Susanna was vomiting, just like Amelia, and both girls were crying out with pain.

Matilda barely noticed the sun come up again in the morning, for by then Cissie was vomiting, and between cries of pain the three demanded water. But as fast as Matilda could get it down them, laced with brandy and laudanum, it was being ejected. She tore up sheets, pillow-cases and towels to use as napkins, but almost as quickly as she tucked a clean one round their bottoms, they were soaked again in that curiously white fluid like rice water.

At daybreak she ran downstairs to empty and scour the vomit bowls, and to put the napkins to boil on the stove, ordering Peter not to touch anything, but to keep the stove going with fuel. She didn't know which was worse, to see the terror in his still healthy eyes, or the resignation in the ones upstairs.

Dr Shrieber called later that morning to say Arnold was ill too, and he'd moved him into isolation into an outhouse at the boarding-house where he lived. Matilda didn't ask if anyone was nursing him, she knew only too well no one other than the doctor would dare go near him. It was terrible to think that a man who had been eagerly anticipating his marriage just a couple of days ago would die alone.

'Did he send any message for Cissie?' she asked.

The doctor nodded. 'That he loves her, and is praying for her recovery. He said please do not tell her he is ill too.'

'What about Tabitha?' she asked.

'She is very vell. She wanted to come and help you nurse Mrs Duncan and the children,' he said with a faint smile. 'Of course I said she couldn't. She asked me to tell you she is praying for you all.'

All that day and again through the night Matilda slogged away, soothing, giving drinks, holding vomit bowls, washing and changing her patients, and running up and down stairs during the brief lulls to rinse the boiled napkins and set a newly filled pail to boil. Peter called out to her to ask what he could do, but hanging the washing on the line, chopping new wood for the stove and bringing in fresh water from the pump were the only things she could allow him to do.

But despite all her efforts and prayers, by the morning Amelia had sunk into the final stage of the illness that the doctor had described to her. She just lay there, almost lifeless, her face blue in colour, her eyes sunken, her breathing short and laborious, her skin cold and clammy and with almost no discernible pulse. Matilda knew then that the end would come very soon.

It was so hard to control her feelings. She felt utter rage that her only child was to be taken from her. Guilt that she'd gone away to make money. Such deep remorse that they'd had so little time together. But she had to control them, she couldn't let her child sense anything more than her love for her in her last hours on earth.

Sitting by the child and whispering endearments, she saw Cissie watching her silently. Her face was drawn with the pain of her cramps, but she didn't utter a sound, and Matilda knew her friend was grieving with her, for she'd been Amelia's mother too.

Susanna was equally silent, it looked as if she too was fast approaching the last stage, for her eyes were beginning to sink like Amelia's. In some strange way, the scene reminded Matilda of her first meeting with Cissie. There were no rats here, it was a warm, pleasant room, but perhaps it was that Cissie appeared to be guarding the two children, just as she had all those little ones in the cellar.

'John and I will look after her,' Cissie said, her voice little more than a whisper. 'I'll tell Lily and Giles too what a fine job you did with Tabby. We'll all be looking down on you and watching over you.'

Matilda turned to her friend, wanting to say she was being maudlin, and she would hear no more of it, but Cissie's expression prevented it. It was the same one she'd had that day in the cellar as she bravely fed baby Pearl at the expense of her own child. Noble, honest, and expecting nothing for herself.

Amelia died some ten minutes later. Her breathing got weaker and weaker and finally dwindled to a halt. Matilda stroked her little blue face, ran her fingers through her tousled curls, and wanted to scream out her pain, but she couldn't. Susanna was sinking fast too, it wasn't right to let her know her little playmate had slipped away.

So she silently shut Amelia's eyes, got up and moved to Susanna's bed. It was her turn to be comforted.

Susanna hung on for another three hours. Matilda moved her bed closer to her mother's so she could hold her hand and just sat there, talking to them both as if this was any night when she tucked the children into bed.

She spoke of the cabin, of the animals and the fruit trees, of bathing in the stream and walks in the woods. She told them that Tabitha would become a doctor, and that Peter would be a fine officer in the cavalry, and that all the happiest moments in her own life had been spent with them.

Cissie reared up as Susanna stopped breathing, and Matilda caught hold of her, afraid she was going to try to get out of bed. 'I'm so sorry,' she whispered, hugging her friend tightly.

They held each other for a few moments, wordlessly drawing comfort from their mutual loss. They had become friends through Matilda rescuing Cissie and Peter, but it was the two smallest children that had made them like sisters – both born in wagons, so close in age, permanent reminders of the two good men they'd loved and lost. And as the girls had played together, shared everything, both women had found solace in believing that they'd inherited all the talents of their two fathers and had golden futures ahead of them.

'You shouldn't be hugging me,' Cissie said, slumping back down on the bed again. 'If you catch up with me in heaven, I'll have you for being so reckless.'

There was a ghost of her old impudent smile, but her face too was turning blue, and her eyes were sinking. 'Can I ask you to take care of Peter?' she whispered.

'You don't have to ask. Of course I will,' Matilda replied, struggling to hold her tears back. 'I'll make sure he becomes everything you wanted in your son.'

'Tell him all about me when he's a man,' she croaked. 'Tell him how much I loved him.'

'What will I do without you, Cissie?' Matilda asked.

Cissie just looked at her and a tear trickled out from one eye.

'Go and find other girls like me to save,' she whispered. 'I'll be watching to see you do.'

Matilda lit a lamp as it grew dark and watched as Cissie's face turned from blue to purple, and her hands became dark and sodden-looking like a washerwoman's. She opened her eyes only once more and looked at Matilda. 'Saddest thing is, I never found out what it would be like with Arnold,' she croaked. 'Tell him I love him, and I wished I'd let him do it just once.'

Her breathing gave up after that, as if she'd used her last air for that one last ribald remark. Matilda closed her eyes, kissed her forehead, then covered her face with the sheet.

'I love you, Cissie Duncan,' she whispered. 'Go straight to John with a child in each hand. Don't you worry none about Peter, he'll be my boy now.'

She kissed the girls and covered them too. She lit a candle by each of their beds, then, taking the lamp, she pulled aside the vinegar-soaked curtain and went downstairs.

It was just on eleven at night, and Peter was curled up with Treacle on his blanket on the kitchen floor, fast asleep. Treacle looked up at her with mournful eyes, and his tail thumped on the floor in greeting.

'Stay with him for now,' she whispered to the dog. 'I'll see to you both in a minute.'

Taking the last pan of hot water from the stove, she took it outside, stripped off her clothes and scrubbed herself from head to foot with lye soap, until her skin was a deep red, before returning to the kitchen. Tomorrow after the bodies had been taken away she would have to boil her clothes. The bedding and the mattresses would all have to be burnt, the rooms scrubbed out. Yet she still had no way of knowing whether she and Peter might yet get the disease. Wrapping herself in a tablecloth, she went back upstairs to find a clean night-gown, and only then when she was certain she'd taken every conceivable precaution did she go back downstairs to wake Peter.

She sat looking at him sleeping for some time. There were tracks of tear stains on his honey-coloured cheeks, a sprinkling of freckles on his nose, and it brought home to her what he'd been through these last two days, imprisoned down here in solitude, apart from Treacle, listening to sounds of retching and groaning, and seeing countless piles of soiled napkins and sheets boiled up on the stove. He'd been a man, keeping the stove going, hanging out the washing, and looking after himself without complaint, but he was only twelve, still a child, and now she had to wake him and tell him his mother and sisters were dead.

Twice she'd had to give similar terrible news to Tabitha, but that wouldn't make it any easier to find the right words for Peter. It seemed such a short while ago that John had been killed and she'd comforted him. She remembered how he used to wait in the lane still vainly hoping it was all a mistake and John would come riding home.

How could she possibly speak calmly when she was in so

much pain at her own child's death? How could she tell him that they would find happiness again soon, when her heart felt it had been wrenched out of her and she wished for her own death?

Just the way he was lying curled up round Treacle suggested that he knew there was going to be no miraculous recovery. It was tempting to let him sleep a little longer, but she was dropping with exhaustion herself after two days and nights without rest, and she couldn't take the risk that he might wake again in the night to come up and investigate why it was so quiet.

'Peter,' she called softly. 'Peter, wake up!'

He sat up and rubbed his eyes. 'Are they better?' he said in little more than a whisper.

Matilda shook her head. 'No, Peter, they died a little while ago, I'm afraid. I'm so sorry.'

She had vowed to herself she wouldn't touch him just in case it was possible to pass the disease on that way. But she couldn't help herself when his face crumpled, she had to go to him and hold him.

'Your mama said I was to tell you she loved you, and that you must be my boy now,' she said, holding him tightly against her chest and trying very hard not to cry herself. 'She was so very brave, Peter, just like she always was, and Susanna and Amelia slipped away without knowing anything.'

Cissie had always been so proud that Peter never cried even as a small boy. She claimed that even when she smacked him he laughed. But he cried now, long and hard, burying his face in Matilda's breast, sobbing out that he hoped he'd catch the disease too because he didn't want to live without his mother and sisters.

'I know how you feel,' she whispered back. 'I loved them too, just as much as I loved Amelia. But wishing for death too is an insult to their memory, Peter.'

She made them both some hot milk and put a measure of brandy in each. 'We both think we've lost everyone we love tonight. But we mustn't forget we've still got one another. There's Tabitha and Sidney too. I'm going to take you back to San Francisco to see Sidney in a little while. We will build a new life for ourselves there together.'

'Why, Aunt Matty?' he asked, his face devoid of colour, brown eyes utterly bleak. 'Why did Mama and the girls have to die? It's not fair.'

She couldn't tell him that life wasn't fair, that all over America, and the whole world too, people died suddenly with no sense to it. All she could do was murmur the kind of things Giles would have said, that God wanted Cissie and the girls to live with Him and the angels because they were extra special. She doubted he believed it, any more than she did, but the words did have a comforting ring.

Taking his hand, she led him up to his bed later, and lay down beside him, cradling him in her arms. The brandy worked quickly on him and after a while his sobbing turned to snores, but no such oblivion came to Matilda.

She knew everyone had to face such tragedy. Even as a small girl she could recall the neighbours talking about the children they'd buried, the fires which had taken other family members, and diseases which could run through a tenement like the rats. But what she couldn't understand was why fate singled her out for such cruelty, so often.

Arnold died just a few hours after Cissie and the funeral service held the following day was for all of them. Cissie and the children were buried alongside John, and Arnold close by.

It was so painful to see Tabitha for the first time since the deaths, standing between the Reverend and Mrs Glover in a severe black dress and bonnet. Few other people had come out of fear of the disease, and Matilda had been told by the doctor she must not embrace Tabitha until all danger had passed.

Tabitha's eyes mirrored everything Matilda felt. Deep dark pools of sorrow and disbelief. They stood some ten feet from one another, both silently yearning to reach out for the other, knowing that the words they would exchange later could never soothe as a cuddle could.

Matilda held Peter's hand tightly as the coffins were lowered into the graves, and thought of Cissie's courage in that cellar when he was born, and made a silent pledge to her friends that she would always love and protect him.

After the grave had been covered over, Matilda beckoned for Tabitha to come and speak to her, and they moved over to the side of the churchyard, still keeping a few feet of distance between them.

'What will happen now, Matty?' Tabitha asked, tears running down her cheeks.

'I'm going to take Peter back with me, but I want you to stay with the Reverend,' Matilda said firmly, even though her whole being wanted to take her last remaining child away too. 'You must do everything we planned, Cissie would be so angry if you didn't become a doctor because of this.'

'But you are the only one I have left now,' Tabitha wept. 'I want to be with you.'

'I want you with me too,' Matilda said, distressed by the child's grief. 'But when your mother and father entrusted me with you, I made a promise that I would always do the right thing for you. I know taking you back to San Francisco isn't that.'

'Are you sure?' Tabitha asked, her dark eyes full of doubt.

Matilda nodded. She had thought this through very carefully. While Tabitha might enjoy San Francisco for a holiday, at a time when she wasn't grieving, to take her there now would be the worst possible thing, for she would hate it. The noise, the dirt and rowdiness would all appal her, she would have no friends, be a virtual prisoner in the apartment, and she would soon bitterly regret that she'd turned down the chance to go to Boston.

'The Reverend and Mrs Glover love you,' she said soothingly. 'All your friends are here, it's a peaceful, lovely place and a life you know and trust. If in a few weeks you still feel you desperately want to be with me, then maybe we can change our minds. But try it first.'

'You aren't going straight away, are you?' Tabitha said with a look of alarm.

Matilda shook her head. 'Do you think I'd go before I could hug you again? Of course not, Tabby! I'm going to stay until I've sorted out Cissie's house and everything. I need time to visit Amelia's grave too, reconcile myself and say my goodbyes to her.'

A look of deep concern crossed the girl's face and she instinctively took a step nearer Matilda.

'I was forgetting,' she said, then stopped mid-sentence and blushed.

Matilda understood what had gone through her mind. 'I have

always loved you, Tabby, as if you were born to me. To me you are my daughter, and nothing will ever change that. But Amelia was so very special too, she was your father's and my child, the very reason we had to flee all these thousands of miles to find safety here in Oregon. Your sister too, the baby that bound us two even closer together. And now she's been taken from us, that's another very good reason why you must never lose sight of your ambitions.'

'Poor Matty,' Tabitha whispered. 'I was feeling so sorry for myself I didn't think about your pain.'

Matilda felt a surge of love for this child-woman who had her father's ability to slip into another's shoes. 'No one will ever replace Amelia,' she said in a low voice, trying very hard not to cry again. 'But I have you, Peter and Sidney. And when I look at you, Tabby, I see Giles and Lily too. That is so very comforting.'

'I love you, Matty,' Tabitha said, and as fresh tears rolled down her cheeks she looked just the way she had at six or seven.

'I love you too, my darling,' Matilda replied, her arms aching to hold the child. 'Now, go on back with the Glovers, and I'll see you in a day or two once we know this terrible disease has run its course.'

A few days later as Matilda was burning the mattresses in the garden, Dr Shrieber came by to tell her he had paid a visit out to the farm where Arnold and Cissie had visited, only to find the whole family dead. As Peter and Matilda were still healthy, despite close contact with those struck down, he didn't think it could be a contagious disease like smallpox. He had a theory it might come from drinking water that had been contaminated with sewage, and he intended to study other cases to see if he could prove this was the cause of the disease.

Matilda thought he was a good man and wished him success in his studies, but her heart was too full of pain to discuss theories about the cause of her child's death. She had left Amelia here thinking it was a safe place, but in the end it proved just as dangerous as anywhere else.

All she wanted now was to take Peter and Treacle, and leave Oregon City for ever.

Chapter Twenty-two

'You can't go on grievin' this way, ma'am,' Dolores said, as yet again for the fifth morning running she found her mistress had ignored both her breakfast and bath and was still lying in bed at noon. 'Now, git yourself out of that bed!'

Matilda opened one bloodshot eye. Her breath was sour from the brandy she'd drunk the night before, and it made her feel nauseous. 'Go away and leave me alone,' she snapped. 'It's no business of yours what I do!'

'Well, is that so?' Dolores put her hands on her hips and glowered at Matilda. 'It sure seems like my business when my mistress is behaving like a fool. I knows you are hurtin', heaven knows it's a terrible, wicked thing that happened. But you ain't the first person to bury folks you loved, and you go on like this, it will be me burying you.'

'How dare you speak to me like that,' Matilda exclaimed.

''Cos I'm an uppity nigger, or so I've been told a thousand times,' Dolores said, her jet-black eyes rolling with impatience. 'Miss Zandra, she told me to look out fer you, and that's just what I'm gonna do, even if I have to take a belt to your back to make you see sense.'

Matilda had coped well enough with the voyage back to San Francisco. She had managed to break the terrible news to Sidney and to find a good school for Peter. But then, when that was done, she woke one morning to see how utterly empty her life was now, and she couldn't bear it.

Since Amelia's birth everything she'd done had been with her and Tabitha's future in mind, now suddenly she had no purpose. She had looked upon Cissie and Susanna as her family, and Oregon as home, but there was nothing left there now. Tabitha was with the Glovers, and James was gone too.

Looking back, all she could see was a row of tombstones, every one of them engraved with the name of someone she had loved dearly. Having fine clothes, money in the bank, and a successful business meant nothing to her without a goal to work towards. She was twenty-nine, too old and cynical to believe there might be something good around the next corner, yet too young to accept her life was now on the downward slide.

This feeling of melancholia grew worse each day. She didn't want to eat, to talk to anyone, or do anything. Both Peter and Sidney looked at her in bewilderment, and it made her feel so guilty to see them leaning on one another to gain the comfort she should have been giving them.

She began taking little nips of brandy during the day to make herself feel better, and that seemed to work at first, but before long she was drinking whole glasses, staying up in the apartment alone for longer and longer periods, and ignoring what was going on downstairs. Finally she had withdrawn from everything, the business, staff, Sidney and Peter. She didn't even bother to get dressed, but began drinking the minute she woke, and continued till she eventually found a state of oblivion.

'If you're so dammed clever, you tell me how to get over this,' Matilda spat at Dolores.

'You think of someone worse off than yourself,' Dolores shot back. 'Miss Zandra left you her money because she thought you'd do something good with it. If she knew you was drinking it away she'd come back and haunt you. And there's the Captain too. What will he think of you if he comes back and finds you like this?'

Even though Matilda's mind was confused, in so much as she had no idea what day it was, or how long she'd been holed up in the apartment, her maid's scornful words cut a clear path through the fog. 'He's never coming back,' she said plaintively. 'He's gone, just like everyone else.'

Dolores winced at this uncharacteristic display of self-pity. She thought her mistress looked and smelled worse than a street girl, and decided she needed to take a stronger line. Grabbing hold of Matilda's shoulders, she shook her like a mop. 'That man will be back,' she shouted at her. 'I never knew a man love a woman so much. And you've got Sidney, Peter and Miss Tabitha to think about.'

Matilda pushed her away and cringed back across the bed, frightened by this assault. 'They aren't my children,' she retorted.

'Maybe's they wasn't born to you,' Dolores replied. 'But you's the nearest thing they got to a mammy now, and they is hurtin' because you ain't behavin' like one. There's girls down in the saloon that would lay down their life for you because you gave them a chance to get off the streets. You is somebody, Miss Matilda, folks round here respect you, and I ain't gonna let you lose that respect neither. So you'll get in that bath right now. Or else!'

Matilda could only stare at Dolores, profoundly stunned that this woman who rarely spoke, and never offered an opinion about anything, should launch into her with such ferocity. She needed a drink, but she had a feeling that if she attempted to get one Dolores would make good her threat and beat her. Unable to see any alternative, she got out of bed, but the minute her feet were on the ground Dolores snatched at the hem of her nightgown and pulled it off over her head, leaving her naked.

'Get in!' she said in a voice that couldn't be ignored, pointing to the filled bath in the corner. 'And I'm gonna wash your hair too, it surely looks an' stinks like a rat's nest.'

An hour later Matilda was bathed and her hair washed. Now as her hair dried by the open window, Dolores had forced her hands into a bowl filled with some kind of warm oil. Indignant as she was that she should be treated like a feeble-minded child, it was also soothing to be cared for. The sunshine coming through the window, the lavender fragrance on her clean skin, was making her feel a little less dejected.

The cleaning up in Oregon, and the endless washing in strong lye had made Matilda's hands look the way they'd been when she first came to San Francisco, but she'd had no heart to do anything about them, or even cover them with her usual gloves.

'It sure is shockin' to see a lady's hand this way,' Dolores tutted. 'I never did see worse, not even on a field hand.'

'I'm not a lady, Dolores,' she said weakly. 'I never was, and I never will be.'

'Is that so! Well, you is my mistress, so that makes you one,' Dolores retorted sharply. 'I can make these better, I can do your hair real pretty, and I guess I can make you eat again and hide the liquor. But I can't make you smile none, only you's can do that. You better start thinking of something to make those pretty lips curl up again, and the light come back in your eyes.'

It was the woman's tone which amused Matilda. Half-angry, half-loving. The way she'd so often been with Tabitha in the past.

'That's better,' Dolores said in appreciation as her mistress smiled. 'You sure are one handsome woman when you smile.'

'Do you really believe the Captain will come back?' Matilda asked a little later, as Dolores wound her hair up in curls. She guessed the woman knew a great deal about men from her time with Zandra, and anyway there was no one else she could confide in about James.

'I knows he will,' Dolores said stoutly. 'He ain't the kind of man to give up. Reckon if he knew about your sadness, he'd have got here already, if'n he had to walk clean across the country with Indian arrows in his back. You two were meant for one another, that's for certain.'

'But he's married, Dolores!'

'So?' Dolores paused in her hairdressing and put her hands on her hips, glowering into the mirror at her mistress. 'The way I sees it, you got his heart. That surely counts for more than a ring on your finger.'

'Have you ever loved a man?' Matilda asked, all at once curious about this plain, tall woman who had devoted almost all of her life to Zandra.

Dolores shook her head. 'I was used by some, back afore I found my way to Miss Zandra. What I saw there of men fair put me off for good. But that don't stop me knowing what it's like for you and the Captain, just as I knows how you feels about losing your little girl. Reckon one kind of love is much like another when all's done. I loved Miss Zandra, I thought my heart would wither when she died. But now I got you to love and take care of, and I sure ain't gonna let you fall apart.'

A lump came up in Matilda's throat and her eyes prickled. In a few rough words this usually inarticulate woman had managed to convey a very simple but profound message. All Matilda had to do to recover was to transfer the love she felt for Cissie, Amelia and Susanna to someone or something else.

'I very much appreciate that,' she said softly, catching hold of the black woman's hand. 'You've made me feel much better. Thank you.'

During the afternoon Matilda went downstairs. She was wearing a black mourning gown, but Dolores had insisted on softening the severity of it today by attaching a cream lace collar to it. She felt a little shaky, but she'd decided that a walk would do her far more good than allowing herself to brood up in the apartment.

Sidney was alone in the saloon, checking the stock. His smile was tentative, and it reminded her she'd treated him very callously in the past few weeks.

'Come here a minute, Sidney,' she said.

He wiped his hands on a cloth and hurried over to her. 'What is it?'

'Just a hug,' she said, opening her arms and drawing him into them. 'And to say I'm sorry I've been so wicked.'

He hugged her back and she could feel him quivering with emotion. 'You don't have to say sorry to me,' he whispered. 'And you ain't wicked, Matty, only grievin', it takes us all different ways.'

'I do have to say I'm sorry,' she said. 'I was so wrapped up in my troubles I forgot how bad it is for you too. You spent much more time with Cissie than I did, and the girls. I'm ashamed I didn't think about that and look after you better.'

'I'm a man now. I can get by without being looked after,' he said, but he sighed as if this wasn't strictly true. 'What scared me most was thinking I'd lost you too.'

'You'll always have me,' she said, lifting his chin up and kissing his cheek. 'I reckon I went a bit crazy for a time, but I think I'm on the mend now. I'm going out to get something for our supper, we've got to hold on to what's left of our family.'

He smiled shyly, tawny eyes glinting with tears, and he stroked her cheek lovingly. 'You look real pretty again, Matty. I like to see you that way.'

'I think I like it better too,' she said with a smile. 'If Peter comes back from school before I do, give him a hug from me, and tell him I won't be long.'

She bought steak for supper, fresh vegetables and fruit, then wandered along Market Street, just looking around her. It was a very long time since she'd been down here, Dolores normally shopped for food, and when Matilda went out she usually stuck to the smarter streets.

Before she went back to Oregon there had been a great deal of talk about what the financial panic had done to the city, but perhaps she had been too preoccupied to notice just how bad it was. But she was seeing it now, and it shocked her.

There were so many shops boarded up, once prosperous businesses lying empty, and many, many more people begging in the streets. Her heart contracted with pity at the dozens of hollow-eyed, ragged children, but when she saw a woman with a baby in her arms stoop to snatch up a turnip dropped in the gutter, and hide it under her shawl, she felt ashamed that she'd failed to notice before how bad things had become.

Right from the start of the Gold Rush, this city had always been one where people conducted their social lives on the streets. Working men gathered on corners to discuss boxing or fire engines, young Christians on the steps of the churches. Courting couples favoured Stockton Street, while the middle classes chose Montgomery Street. The plaza was a meeting place for everyone, while small boys flew kites and played baseball, businessmen held impromptu meetings, and the elderly sat and watched.

Maybe this very public way of living had sprung purely from the lack of space in living accommodation, and the need for most of the population to eat in restaurants, but it had remained that way, even when housing was improved.

Everything about the city enhanced the feeling of intimacy. By day the narrow streets were cluttered with goods, buggies, carts and teamsters ploughed their way through, forcing people physically close to each other. At night the gaming halls, theatres, saloons and other places of entertainment filled the streets with music, light and mirth. Even though the Chinese, Italians and many other different nationalities all had their own areas of the town, these were all closely connected and used as thoroughfares by everyone. Matilda had often thought it was like a living theatre, with a dozen different plays going on at any one time. Any excuse brought on a parade, music from a dozen different sources assaulted the ears. It wasn't the least bit unusual to hear an Italian tenor singing opera, a group of Spanish gypsies dancing the flamenco, or Negro minstrels singing all in one street. But today, though she could still hear spirited music, laughter from cafés, saloons and restaurants, and there was just as much traffic and people thronging the streets, she could feel despondency in the air.

She saw men wandering aimlessly, perhaps hoping to stumble across some work. Women looked anxious, pausing before displays of foodstuffs as if mentally juggling a very tight budget. The shop keeper's cries sounded desperate rather than jovial, even the many stray dogs rooting in gutters looked thinner than she ever remembered.

But what concerned her most was the sheer numbers of girls and very young women meandering around, when once they would have been working in private houses as servants, or in the shops. She felt they had probably come to San Francisco in the last two or three years when it was booming, but now had lost their positions. It seemed such a short while ago that Alicia Slocum complained there were no servants to be had anywhere. Even last year there had still been signs in many shop windows offering employment inside, but those signs were gone now, and she knew only too well what line of work these girls might turn to in desperation if nothing else turned up.

Thinking on this, she walked towards Sydney Town, the notorious slum area around the base of Telegraph Hill. Although only about eight blocks in all, it was packed with brothels, gaming houses, saloons and low dance halls. It had always been home to the very lowest and most desperate characters and a hotbed of crime and murder, but in the past year, politicians, would-be social reformers and newspaper men had taken to calling it the Barbary Coast and claimed it stood with Seven Dials in London and Five Points in New York for its filth and depravity.

Matilda had always laughed at the idea of San Francisco's red light district being compared to the two monstrous places she had explored personally, and considered that the people who made such claims were over-reacting. To her Sydney Town had a gaiety and even sophistication which the other two lacked. Yet today, perhaps because she was more receptive, she saw these people were right, it was every bit as bad.

She could smell the stink of filth and poverty, sense the disease and corruption lurking in the dark alleys, just as she had in London and New York. Even now in broad daylight, prostitutes were out doing business in their hundreds, blatantly displaying their breasts in low-cut satin gowns, some even sat in shop windows wearing only underwear. As she passed alleyways she had to avert her eyes to avoid seeing hurried coupling between whores and sailors. There were many wretched men and women with the tell-tale glazed eyes of opium users, and countless drunks who lay where they had fallen, insensible to their surroundings.

All at once she understood why the upper-middle classes of the city were constantly demanding that this area should be razed to the ground. Yet sadly that would never happen, not while liquor licences continued to be a major source of income to the city, and indeed businessmen received exorbitant rents for their properties here.

Having seen enough to sicken her, she turned homeward, trying to turn her mind to more pleasant things, yet a small voice inside her head kept reminding her that while she lived and ran a business in this town, she couldn't close her eyes and ears to what was going on in certain parts of it.

A few nights later, at the end of September, Matilda sat up on the balcony overlooking the saloon. She was feeling very much better now. She'd stopped drinking, and she had begun to pick up the reins of the business again, filling her days with work so she had no time to lapse into self-pity. Every evening she shared a supper with Peter and Sidney, and they were all beginning to be able to speak of Cissie and the little girls again, which she saw as a good sign they were on the road to recovery.

Tonight she had expected a quiet evening because it was raining hard, yet it was surprisingly busy. Aside from regular customers, the merchants and tradespeople who lived close by, there were a great many sailors. One group was from a Russian ship that had sailed in this afternoon, the other was from South America, and this crew was a mixture of Americans, Germans and Irish. Sailors had a habit of making London Lil's their first call in the evenings, then once they'd had a few drinks and watched the show, they moved on downtown for the rest of the night for more heavy drinking and to find women.

When two unaccompanied girls came in a little later, Matilda smiled as every male head swivelled round to look at them. The female population might have increased in the past few years, but there still weren't nearly enough young, pretty and single women to go round. One of these girls was a Mexican, the other a Negro. It struck her that they seemed very nervous, she thought perhaps they'd never dared go into a saloon before.

Sidney came haring up the stairs to her. 'Shall I warn them off?' he asked, inclining his head towards the girls.

'What on earth for?' she exclaimed. The girls wore plain, well-worn calico dresses and heavy boots, they didn't look one bit like street girls. 'I expect they are maids and they've got the night off together and want a bit of fun for a change.'

'I don't think so, Matty,' he said, frowning. 'I saw the Mexican one down on Kearny Street the other night.'

'Maybe you did, but that doesn't mean she's a whore,' Matilda retorted. 'Besides, I've never banned street girls from having a drink in here, only for soliciting. It's so wet outside, and they are entitled to a bit of friendly company like anyone else. Give them a free drink, I'll watch them, and if they get up to anything, I'll mark their cards for them.'

She saw Sidney get the girls drinks, then they disappeared into the crowd. The show started a few minutes later, and Matilda forgot about them because she was too busy scrutinizing the dancing girls. She thought their costumes looked decidedly shabby, and their routine lacked sparkle. They had been appearing here twice a week for over two years, and their complacency showed. She would have to have a word with them about it later.

But the jugglers who followed them were excellent, slick and polished. She thought she would compliment them later, and offer them a regular spot.

The dancers came on again to end the show, and Matilda got up, ready to go down and speak to them before they left. As she started down the stairs, a sudden movement near the doors caught her eye. Pausing to look over the banister, she saw the Negro girl had collapsed on to the floor, and her Mexican friend was rushing out of the door.

She ran the rest of the way. 'Let me get through,' she said, pushing the men who were crowded round the girl out of the way.

'The darky's just had one too many,' someone called out. 'Chuck her outside, the rain will soon sober her up.'

Matilda bristled at that remark, even after twelve years in America the callous attitude to Negroes still riled her. She knelt down beside the girl and put her hand on her forehead, which was very hot.

'Bring me some smelling-salts,' she called out to Sidney, who had elbowed his way through the crowd. 'And some water.'

The smelling-salts brought the girl round, she recoiled from the smell and opened her eyes. Her straw bonnet had slipped off to reveal close-cropped curly hair, like a boy's. She was very young too, perhaps only fourteen, and terribly thin. Her coal-black eyes looked too big for her face, and very frightened.

'It's okay, I guess you just fainted,' Matilda said, bending down close so the girl could hear her over the noise of the music. 'Try sitting up and taking a drink.'

She slid one arm under the girl's back and helped her to sit up. Her dress felt clammy, but whether that was from the rain outside, or from a fever, she couldn't tell. 'Can you tell me your name?' she asked.

'Fern,' the girl said, but her face contorted suddenly with pain, and she involuntarily clutched at Matilda's forearm.

'Where does it hurt?' Matilda asked.

The girl put her hand on her stomach.

With the horror of cholera still so fresh in her mind, Matilda might have backed away, but she was on her knees so that wasn't possible. 'I'll take you somewhere quiet to lie down,' she said.

It was as she and Sidney helped her on to her feet that Matilda noticed an ominous bloodstain on the back of the girl's skirt. Thinking it might just be a very bad monthly, and not wishing to embarrass the girl, she said nothing, and putting her arm around her to give her some support she led her out the back to one of the spare rooms, laid her down on the bed and lit a lamp.

As she put the glass back in place and the light grew brighter, she saw the girl was crying silently, and Matilda instinctively sensed that the tears came from something more than pain or embarrassment.

Her broad flat nose and thick lips prevented her from being described as pretty, but her angular cheek-bones, huge eyes, and the sheen on her dark skin was very striking.

'You are bleeding, my dear,' Matilda said, sitting down beside her. 'Is it your monthly?'

The girl turned her head away from Matilda and covered her face with her hands, drawing up her knees towards her chest. Although Matilda recognized this as a childlike defensive stance, it also revealed the bloodstain again, and it had spread to a patch some four or five inches across. She looked at it for a moment and decided it was far too much for a mere monthly.

'I am trying to help you,' she said more firmly. 'But I can't do that if you won't talk to me. Are you losing a baby?'

There was a tiny little whimper, and the girl covered her head as if expecting a blow. 'I had to do it,' she whispered. 'It was the only way.'

Matilda wasn't sure if the girl was trying to say she'd been raped, or if she was admitting to having had an abortion. 'I don't know much about things like this,' she said gently. 'But my maid will, so I'm going to get her. Now, just you lie quietly. I won't be long.'

Dolores listened while Matilda explained what had happened. She made no comment but immediately disappeared into her room, coming back with a covered basket, which she handed to her, and two old towels from the linen closet.

'You go on down,' she said. 'Master Peter's sound asleep. I'll just get some hot water and rags.'

'Do you think she's done something to try and get rid of the baby?' Matilda said fearfully.

Dolores nodded, her proud face very grim.

Matilda saw yet another side of Dolores in the hours that followed – kindly, soothing with not a word of reproach to Fern, or even shock when the girl admitted she had pushed a meat skewer up inside her. She stripped the girl of her clothes with Matilda's help, made no comment about the weals from a recent beating on her back, or the marks on her wrists and ankles as if she'd been shackled. She washed her all over as though she was a helpless baby, and rubbed the girl's lower back each time a pain came.

Matilda might have helped with Lily's miscarriage, and at the birth of her stillborn child, yet those experiences didn't make the sight of so much blood and the girl's pain any less terrifying.

'Should I call a doctor?' she asked Dolores fearfully.

Dolores gave her a contemptuous look. 'What doctor would come to a black girl?'

Matilda looked from Dolores to Fern and wanted to cry for both of them. What sort of a country was she in that women were refused medical aid because of the colour of their skin?

The noise from the saloon grew louder as the evening wore on, and Fern's pains became almost continual. She wondered how someone so young could be so stoic, for the only sounds she made were little whimpers. Matilda could only collect up the soiled pads of cloth, fetch more water, and pray that the girl would survive.

Finally the band stopped playing and they heard everyone leaving as the saloon closed. It was now so quiet Matilda even heard Sidney locking the doors, but he didn't attempt to come in or even call at the door, perhaps guessing at what was going on. Only he, Mary and Albert slept in these downstairs rooms now, and Matilda thought he'd probably made the others stay away.

Finally Fern screamed out for the only time that night, and passed a bloody mass on to the brown paper Dolores had slid beneath her.

'It's all over now,' Matilda said soothingly, hoping this was the case, while Dolores quickly removed the brown paper and its contents. She wiped the girl's face and neck with a cool cloth. 'You're safe with us, we're going to take care of you.'

Fern seemed to relax a little, the veins which had sprung up on her face and neck during her ordeal slowly receding. She turned her head slightly towards Matilda, her eyes full of tears. 'Why did you help me?' she asked in a whisper.

'Why? Because you needed it of course,' Matilda replied. 'Now, suppose you tell me why you came into my saloon when you'd just done something like this to yourself?'

'Anna, my friend, said gin would surely make it work. Anyways, I didn't have anywhere else to go and it was raining.'

'A fine friend she turned out to be, she disappeared when you fainted,' Matilda said tartly.

Dolores came back then with a fresh bowl of hot water and began washing Fern again. 'You's ain't gonna be going nowhere for some time,' she said sharply. 'So you'd better be tellin' us where you come from.'

Fern looked anxiously from one woman's face to the other.

'Just tell the truth,' Matilda said gently. 'We aren't going to tell anyone, we're your friends.'

She was just fourteen. Her mother was a housekeeper to a family in Philadelphia, and Fern had acted as a kitchen maid for them from the age of seven. A year ago she travelled out to California with nine other girls under the supervision of a Negro woman called Mrs Honeymead, who said she could get them all good well-paid jobs as maids. What she found at the other end of the long journey was a waterfront brothel.

Matilda was somewhat surprised when Dolores told Fern that was enough for one night. She put a clean night-gown on her, dosed her with some medicine, and said she was to go to sleep, but she'd be checking on her during the night.

Sidney, Mary and Albert were sitting drinking coffee in the saloon, and they all looked up anxiously.

'The girl's poorly,' Matilda said. 'But she's sleeping now, you all go to bed. I'll explain in the morning.'

As soon as she and Dolores got back upstairs, Matilda asked her why she'd stopped Fern so sharply.

Dolores gave her a withering look. 'I didn't want her gettin' no bad dreams about that place,' she said. 'She's bin through enough tonight.'

'You know the brothel then?'

'I sure do,' Dolores replied shaking her head. 'Its called Girlie Town and just about the worst place any girl could end up in. They gits little girls, niggers and Chinese mostly, and the beasts they let in on 'em ain't even worthy of being called men.'

Matilda listened in horror as Dolores went on to say that she'd heard many of the girls were chained up. 'You saw those marks on her,' she said. 'That's how men like to take their pleasure down there. And that Mrs Honeymead! She's one evil woman, I heard tell she's from Haiti, they say she casts spells to ruin folk who cross her.'

It was astounding how much Dolores knew. Mrs Honeymead was a procuress and worked for a man called Gilbert Green, known as Big Gee. He owned a great many melodeon places down on 'the Coast', where for ten cents, a man could watch a woman performing with a donkey, or be raped by a man invited up from the audience.

'All the girls who works for him get there like Fern,' Dolores said. 'Little innocents miles from home. In a couple of years he's brutalized them so bad they don't care what he makes them do no more.'

'I can't believe none of this has come to my ears before,' Matilda said indignantly.

'It weren't happening when you first come,' Dolores replied. 'Back then the mining men just wanted a woman and that was that. But there ain't no money in gold no more, so the bad men soon see a new way to make money and this is what we got.'

'But how do you know about it?'

'I's a nigger,' she said, shrugging her shoulders. 'Other niggers they tell me. I been called too, to fix up girls like Fern.'

'You mean you've helped them get rid of babies?' Matilda exclaimed, deeply shocked.

'Don't you go looking like that,' Dolores said, her eyes narrowing. 'There ain't nuthin' worse than a child to be born when it ain't wanted, all they got in front of them is misery. Better for someone like me to do it than one of those dirty old crones who don't care if she butchers them.'

Dolores often slipped out at odd times, but Matilda had always imagined that the messages left for her in the bar which prompted her, had something to do with her church. But the rights or wrongs of what Dolores did weren't something Matilda wanted to discuss now. 'But Fern said she had nowhere to go. Do you think this man, Big Gee, threw her out?'

'He ain't one for throwing girls out, not when they's as young and fresh as her. I reckon she escaped, and if that's the case he'll come looking for her.'

Matilda found she couldn't sleep that night for Dolores had put so many horrible pictures in her mind. Twice she got up and went downstairs to check on Fern, but thankfully she was sound asleep. She wondered what on earth she could do with the girl once she was better. She didn't need any more waitresses, and even if she had if Dolores was right and this Big Gee came looking for Fern, she'd be right back where she started.

Yet Cissie's words just before she died, about saving girls like her, kept niggling at Matilda. She had to do something more than patch the girl up and send her on her way.

Fern was very much better in the morning. She had no fever, and Dolores said the amount of blood she was losing was just normal, so she didn't think there would be further complications. For safety's sake, Matilda got Sidney to carry the girl up to Zandra's old room; so many people had seen her collapse in the saloon, and it wouldn't take Big Gee long to hear of it.

'If anyone asks about her, tell them I let her lie down for a while, then sent her on her way,' she told Sidney. 'Don't let anyone know she's still here.'

Sidney looked very worried. 'I've heard about Big Gee,' he said. 'He ain't one to mess with, Matty.'

'Would you like to see Fern go back to that life?'

'Well, no,' he said, looking a little sheepish.

'I didn't think so,' she smiled. 'You always did have a soft heart. So we have to protect her, don't we?'

Matilda went in to see Fern later, and sat down on the edge of the bed.

'Tell me how you got away,' she asked.

Fern looked even younger than her fourteen years as she lay in the big bed, her huge brown eyes full of fear. 'Miz Honeymead kept us locked up all the time,' she said. 'Only time we got out was when she came to take us to a man, and we got locked in there too. But the day afore yesterday, she was taking me back from a man when Big Gee he came by. He was real mad about sommat, and she shoved me in a room and went away with him. I s'pose she was so rattled she forgot about lockin' me up. I took the chance and run fer it. I ain't never seen no place 'cept the ones I got locked in, but I went on down to the kitchen, hid behind a door till the woman in there turned away, and I ran out the back door and climbed up over the wall.'

'This was the day before yesterday?' Matilda asked to clarify it.

Fern nodded. 'It were in the morning, and all I had on was a shift. I come to a kind of yard behind a saloon, and that's where I met Anna. She was just sitting out there having a rest. Anyways, I tole her I was runnin'. She said I wouldn't get far with no clothes, and she took me up to her room to hide me. I stayed there all that day, and the night. I got to tell her I was carrying a child and she said best to get rid of it, or I'd be heapin' more misery on me. I only knowed the way I heared Miz Honeymead did it to the girls, so that's what I done.'

Matilda's stomach turned over at the mental picture of such a young girl doing something so barbaric to herself.

'I thought it would come right away,' Fern said in a matter-of-fact manner. 'It hurt some, but that was all. I guess Anna got scared 'bout hiding me too, 'cos she gave me a frock and boots, and tole me to get out of "the Coast" and wait up by London Lil's for her. She said she would try and get me some money and meet me again. It started into rain while I was waitin', and I didn't feel so good then, but she come and met me, and that's how I come to be in your place.'

Suddenly Matilda understood. Anna had probably heard she was sympathetic to young street girls, maybe she even hoped that by sending Fern to wait by her place, she would see the girl and take her in. Clearly Anna had a heart, she had to come to check out what had happened to her new friend, and who could blame her for disappearing once she felt she would be in safe hands?

'Please don't send me back to Miz Honeymead!' Fern said suddenly, her eyes pleading with Matilda. 'I'll do the dishes, scrub the floors, whatever you say.'

'I certainly won't send you back there.' Matilda caught hold of the girl's two hands and squeezed them. 'But I can't keep you here for ever, Fern, however much I'd like to, I don't need any more help. But I promise I'll find somewhere safe for you when you are better.'

She let Dolores talk to Fern later, and through her maid she discovered that the girl had been subjected to sex with dozens of men in one day. Mrs Honeymead had advertised Fern to her 'gentlemen' as a little 'hell cat', claiming she was so ferocious she had to be kept chained up. Fern had been trained to buck and struggle and to spit at the men. If she didn't put up a good enough show she was beaten and starved.

Such utter depravity sickened Matilda, she couldn't possibly imagine what kind of man could enjoy such horrible sport. But Dolores said darkly that far worse than that went on down in 'the Coast'.

Two nights later, Matilda was down in the saloon with Henry Slocum. It was a quiet night because there was no show, only the band playing. Matilda had been asking Henry what could be done about people procuring very young girls and keeping them virtual prisoners. His answer wasn't encouraging, he thought it would be the hardest thing in the world to prove because while they were only using Mexicans, Chinese and Negroes, their word would hardly be taken over a white man's.

They had moved on to talk about the city in general, Henry telling her that Mr Meigg, a fellow alderman and famous for building the 1,600-foot-long Meigg's Wharf, had run off after using city funds to support his own precarious business deals. He was just saying that the man was reported to be in Peru, building roads, when the doors of the saloon crashed open and in came a very big man in a loud black and white checked jacket and a black derby hat. Just the size of the man, well over six foot, and his irate expression, told Matilda immediately it was the infamous Big Gee.

His size alone was enough to make Matilda quake, and just the way he looked told her he was exceptionally dangerous. A big square face, the colour of raw liver, with black stubble on his chin and mean pale, eyes. The kind of man who looked like he would enjoy killing or maiming anyone who crossed him.

Clearly the man had learned a great deal about Matilda, for he strode right up to her, elbowing Henry out of the way.

'I hear you're harbouring one of my gals,' he said, looking menacingly at her. 'I want her back, right now.'

'Excuse me, I don't know what you are talking about,' Matilda retorted. 'I'm not harbouring anyone.'

'Now then,' Henry said. 'I don't know who you are, or what your business with Mrs Jennings is, but that's no way to speak to a lady.'

The big man gave Henry a scathing look and pushed him roughly aside as if he were an irritating insect. Henry, perhaps thinking he could help better by not interfering further, backed away.

Matilda had always supposed no one would dare hurt her in her own saloon, but she sensed this man would have no scruples about attacking anyone, man, woman or child, wherever they happened to be. Close up he was even more formidable – so very ugly, with black hairs sticking out of his large nose, and the few teeth he had left rotten, but it was his eyes that scared her most, for they were pale blue, and they had a mad look in them, like a rabid dog's.

'Don't you go messin' with me,' he snarled at her. 'I got ways of sortin' out folk who stick their noses in my business. Get the girl now.'

The band was still playing merrily, but everyone in the bar had fallen silent, and the tension was palpable. Matilda could see he had a gun tucked into his belt, his jacket gaped open enough to see the shiny stock. She had no doubt he would not hesitate to use it.

She felt sick with fear. She didn't dare order anyone to go and get help, for he would surely round on the first person who moved. All she could do was try to talk him round.

'I'm sorry I don't know your name,' she said, trying to defuse the situation with a little charm. 'And I can't imagine how you came to think I was keeping one of your girls here. I'm not in the brothel business, the only girls here are my waitresses.'

'The name is Gilbert Green,' he said with a sneer, as if just the sound of that name would send her running for cover. 'I know all about you, I makes it my business to know everything about folk in this town. So if you don't want any trouble, just get her.'

Scared as Matilda was, she had her position to maintain, and she wasn't going to allow anyone to think they could talk to her like that.

'Will you kindly leave, sir,' she said, drawing herself up as tall as she could, but even so she was barely to his shoulder. 'Like I said, you are mistaken. And I don't like people making threats to me.'

He scowled at her, and he did move, but back towards the door which led to the rooms where Sidney slept. Clearly he'd heard this was where Fern had been taken.

'You are welcome to look in there,' she said. Sidney was moving towards them and she shot him a warning glance to stay away. 'Here. I'll show you myself.'

She moved in front of the man, unlocked the outer door and led him from one small room to the other. 'You see!' she said triumphantly. 'They are just rooms where my staff sleep, nothing more.'

'But you took her in here,' he said as they came back to the door. 'I know you did.'

Every pore in her skin seemed to be opening up in fright. She could feel sweat on her face, her chest and even down her back. 'A young Negro girl did faint in the bar the other night,' she said, as if only just remembering. 'Yes, I did bring her in here at the time, just until she recovered, but she left at closing time. I haven't seen her since.'

He appeared to believe her and as he began to walk away, Matilda felt a surge of relief. But he stopped suddenly at the foot of the stairs and looked up at the doors on the balcony.

'What's up there?'

At that Matilda panicked. Not only was Fern in her apartment, Peter and Dolores were there too.

Before she could think of anything to deter him, he was up the stairs taking them two at a time. All she could do was chase after him.

She let him look into the first rooms, which were private gaming rooms, and there was no one in either, hoping that someone downstairs would have the sense to run and get help. But if anyone did move, she didn't hear them, and he was now approaching her apartment door.

He tried to turn the knob, but it was locked. He turned back to her, a leering evil grin on his face. 'Open this,' he ordered her.

'I will not,' she said indignantly. 'That's my apartment.'

'Then I'll break the dammed door down,' he said.

Just the thought of him grabbing Fern out of bed and dragging her back to that brothel while she was still losing so much blood made Matilda's legs almost buckle under her, for it would be like signing the girl's death warrant. She knew too that Dolores would fight like a grizzly bear to protect Fern, and the man might very well turn his gun on her. Peter was in there too, and if he heard anything going on he'd be up to see about it.

As he turned to put his shoulder to the door, Matilda bent down, lifted her skirt and pulled her small pistol from her garter.

'Come away from that door,' she called out. 'Or so help me, I'll kill you.'

She hadn't had any cause to threaten anyone with her gun in two years, but out of habit she always had it on her, loaded, and she had kept up her target practice.

The band suddenly stopped playing, the saloon instantly as quiet as a church, all eyes turned up to the scene on the balcony.

It was the sudden hush, more than her words, which made him turn, but as he saw the small gun he laughed derisively. 'You couldn't hit an elephant with that,' he said.

Matilda was terrified. The hand holding the gun was shaking, she might not be able to pull the trigger if it was necessary. But she couldn't let the man get the better of her. She'd got to stand her ground and prevent him from opening that door.

'Don't tempt me to prove you wrong,' she said, her voice quivering as much as her hands. 'Just come away from that door, now.'

As he moved away just slightly, then braced himself to run at the door, Matilda knew that bluff wasn't going to be enough.

She aimed the gun at his shoulder, and pulled the trigger.

In the silent room the retort sounded like a cannon. The big man turned around, staggered towards her, and then fell face down just three feet from her. There on the back of his checked jacket was a clear hole, the material around it black and smoking.

Matilda was stunned. She had aimed at his shoulder, intending to wing him, nothing more, but he must have turned slightly as she fired. She stood transfixed with horror, the smoking gun still in her hand.

All at once the silence was broken, someone cheered, others stamped their feet and clapped. But it was the sound of feet racing up the stairs behind her which brought her back to reality. Sidney reached her first, clasping her in his arms. Alfred, the other barman, went over to the prone man, rolled him over on to his back, and removing his gun from his belt, fired one shot at the door of the private gaming room.

'Why did he do that?' Matilda asked weakly. The balcony seemed to be swaying and there was so much smoke she could hardly see. It felt like some strange dream, yet she knew it wasn't.

'So we can say Big Gee fired at you first,' Sidney whispered.

'Is he dead?' she asked looking down at the man lying on the floor, Henry Slocum leaning over him.

'Not yet,' Henry said, his face as white as parchment. 'But I guess he soon will be. Don't you worry none, Matty. We'll deal with it.'

Dolores came rushing out of the apartment door, quickly followed by Peter who was wearing only a night-shirt and they both gasped to see the man's body on the landing.

'Go back inside,' Matilda managed to say. 'It's all over now.'

The last thing Matilda heard as Dolores ushered Peter back in was the boy's excited voice, 'Do you reckon Aunt Matty killed him?'

If Matilda had ever doubted the loyalty and admiration her staff and customers had for her, in the next few days such doubts were swept away. To a man they backed Sidney and Henry's tale to the police of how Big Gee came into the bar threatening her, and how she'd drawn her gun as he went up the stairs just to try to prevent him entering her apartment. He'd turned, seen her gun, drawn his, and fired, missing her by inches, and she'd fired her own as a last resort as he once again attempted to break down her door.

The police, hardly efficient at any time, were happy to accept this story. Gilbert Green was hated and feared by hundreds of people and his death, a few hours after the shooting, was a cause for merriment and pleasure, not sadness.

Matilda was so deeply shocked that for a couple of days she found it almost impossible to go into the bar. While she had no misgivings about the man's death – he was after all an evil brute – it stunned her to think that she was capable of killing another human being. She'd done a great many things in her time, but killing, even if it had turned out to be for the public good, was too much for her to cope with.

She was also rather perturbed to find that overnight she had become a heroine. While it was pleasant enough to be called a gutsy lady, and gain the respect of men who had previously thought she was a mere figure-head at London Lil's, she knew her actions had propelled her rather too quickly towards having to make a public stand against the atrocities happening daily in the city.

On the third night after the event she braced herself to go downstairs again. Staying upstairs would only serve to fan more outrageous tales about her, and she knew she must appear calm and in control. The bar was crowded – Sidney had joked at supper-time that perhaps she ought to shoot someone every month as it was good for business. As she made her way through the throng, stopping to speak to regulars as she always did, many men called out words of praise.

Jack Skillern, an ex-gold miner who had used the gold he found to open a boot store, came up to her and kissed her cheek.

'What's that for, Jack?' she laughed. She was fond of this scrawny little man, he'd been here on opening night and been a regular ever since.

'It ain't just from me,' he said, looking bashful, 'but from all the boys. See, we're all right proud of you. You was real brave. Most of us would turn tail and run if Big Gee came our way.'

'Well, thank you, Jack,' she said, and kissed him on his cheek too. 'And perhaps you can tell them all how much I appreciate them all standing by me. I was very touched by that, I didn't know I had so many friends.'

'You got a lot more than you know, ma'am,' he said. 'See, we think of London Lil's as our special place. You always give us a good welcome, it's friendly and happy here. All us boys would do anything for you's.'

She just looked at him for a moment, a lump coming up in her throat. This funny little man had made a fortune from gold, lost it on the tables, and made another. Finally he'd had the sense to hold on to a little to open his store. He was like so many of her customers, noisy braggarts, feckless, improvident, warm-hearted and very dear to her. His few words of praise meant more to her than anything.

'You and the other boys must have a drink on the house,' she said. 'I'll tell Sidney right now.'

Big Gee was hardly buried when Mrs Honeymead was arrested, charged with procuring girls for prostitution, and Matilda was asked by the prosecution lawyer to come with him to speak to some of the girls left in the brothel, to encourage them to come forward as witnesses.

It was raining hard the morning Mr Rodrigious took her in his buggy to meet the girls. He was a small, wiry South American, with oiled black hair and a droopy moustache, who spoke faultless English. He told her on the ride to the brothel that he had been educated in Boston, and he hoped one day to go to England as he believed British law to be the best in the world.

'You may find the conditions the remaining girls are in very distressing,' he said as he halted his buggy in Kearny Street. 'Most of the girls vanished at the time of Mrs Honeymead's arrest. What we have left is those too sick, confused, or even too feeble-minded to run. I took them in food and water, but they wouldn't come out of their rooms, not while I was there.'

As they made their way along a winding, narrow, putrid-smelling alley, Matilda was reminded of that excursion into Rat's Castle so long ago. Above the door standing at the end of the alley was a sign, 'Girlie Town', and either side of it were lurid painted pictures of naked girls. The windows above were all blacked out and barred and even in daylight a sense of evil sent shivers down her spine.

Mr Rodrigious opened the door with a key, then looked back at her, as if expecting her to falter.

'I'm fine,' she said. 'And I want to see everything. Not just what you think is fit for a lady to see.'

The lawyer paused in the hall to light an oil lamp, as due to the covered windows everything was in darkness, and absolutely silent. Downstairs there was little to surprise her: a fair-sized saloon at the front with shabby plush couches, and a small bar which looked as if it had been ransacked just recently. Beyond that was a kitchen, notable only in that it was filthy, with piles of unwashed dishes and the table covered in mouse droppings. She pulled back the curtain on the door, and saw the yard and the wall over which Fern had made her escape. Mrs Honeymead's rooms were next to the kitchen, an over-furnished parlour and a bedroom adjoining it, remarkable only in that it was surprisingly homely and well cleaned.

Then they went upstairs. There were six small rooms here, bare of furniture but for a central iron bed in each. There were no blankets or sheets, just dirty mattresses which even in the dim light from the lamp could be seen to be spotted with blood and other sickening stains.

'These are the rooms the girls were taken to by Mrs Honeymead,' Mr Rodrigious said, moving his light closer to the head of the bed so she could see the leather restraints still hanging there. He cast the light on to the walls to show her splatters of blood. 'One can only guess at the horrors endured in these rooms.'

As they went up a further flight of stairs, Matilda could hear faint moaning.

The lawyer turned to her and spoke in a low voice. 'You may wonder why they prefer to stay up here once you have seen their rooms. My conclusion was that they feel safer with what they know.'

Around a small central landing, on which lay an empty tray, presumably once holding the food the lawyer had taken them, and an empty pitcher, there were a dozen narrow doors, each with an open grille in it. Matilda looked through one and instantly recoiled from the smell of excrement.

'They've eaten the food I brought them, but their slop pails haven't been emptied since Mrs Honeymead's arrest,' Mr Rodrigious said, putting his hands over his nose. 'I haven't succeeded in getting anyone to come in here and see to anything.'

Matilda opened the door nearest to her, and taking the lamp from his hand, she walked in. A small girl was curled up on the floor like a dog. As she was caught in the beam of light she let out a yelp of terror and tried to back away into the corner.

The windowless room was more like a cage, less than three feet wide, approximately five feet long, the ceiling so low a man would need to stoop to go in. Not one stick of furniture, only a blanket on the floor and the stinking pail.

The girl was no more than ten and Chinese, her only covering a ragged stained shift. She wrapped her skinny arms around her legs, and her eyes darted fearfully between Matilda and the man in the doorway.

'I've come to help you,' Matilda said, moving closer to her. She reached out to caress the girl's forehead. 'That man wants to help too. He won't harm you.'

There was no response, and Matilda guessed she didn't understand English. 'Friend,' she said, taking one of the girl's small hands between hers and rubbing it.

'There is another Chinese girl, two Mexicans and four Negroes,' Mr Rodrigious said from behind her. 'I can translate Spanish, but I'm afraid I don't know any Chinese.'

As Matilda saw each girl, so her anger and indignation at Mrs Honeymead and the men who had used these girls grew. Just the way they had stayed cowed in their own cages, instead of seeking comfort from the others, showed how terrified they were. One of the black girls had the most fearful wounds from a recent beating, and both the Mexicans looked near death, they were so still and silent on their blankets.

They were in a far worse state than the children in Five Points, for lack of food and clothes were easily rectified. But these girls had been imprisoned in the dark, subjected to untold cruelty and perversions, and it would take a great deal more than a hot bath and a few good meals to mend their broken spirits.

Mr Rodrigious stood out on the landing as she spoke to each of the girls. She felt he was a good man at heart, but even further out of his depth than she was.

'We have to get them out of here,' she said as she rejoined him. One of the youngest black girls seemed to understand she was there to help and had come nearer to her, slipping her hand into hers. 'They are all sick, half starved, and heaven knows where their minds are.'

Mr Rodrigious looked dismayed. 'But there's nowhere to take them to,' he said. 'The orphanage won't take girls like these.'

Matilda flared up with anger at his stupidity. 'Surely you can see that before they can be questioned about what went on here, they have to be nursed back to health.'

'But who will do that?' he said, his sallow face blanching. 'They could be harbouring any number of serious diseases.'

He was right in that, and much as she wanted to scoop them all up and take them to her own place, that would be foolhardy.

She thought fast. 'I'll do the nursing,' she said. 'And if there isn't anywhere else to take them, then it will have to be here, downstairs in the saloon. But you'll have to find a doctor prepared to come and examine them.'

'No doctor I know would come here,' he said, and he moved towards the stairs as if he intended to run off.

It was a sudden clear picture of Cissie, Amelia and Susanna lying in their beds dying that suddenly clarified Matilda's mind. Nothing could have saved them, and nothing would ever wipe out the pain of losing them. But she could and would save these children, whatever it took.

She stepped in front of him, barring the stairs. 'Look here, Mr Rodrigious, when you came to me asking for help, I believed that was because you had a kind heart and a caring nature. One of the biggest hurdles these girls will have to face is learning to trust men again. You can assist in that by doing something for them right now,' she said fiercely.

'But I don't know any doctors likely to come!'

'Go to Henry Slocum, he'll know someone, tell him I insisted.

And I want some clean mattresses brought here, sheets, blankets, food and a couple of women to clean the kitchen, I'll pay whatever it costs.'

'I don't know about this,' he said, backing away from her. 'My instructions were merely to get you to help in bringing witnesses forward, not to turn the place into a hospital.'

'There won't be any witnesses left alive unless you do help,' she snapped at him. 'I'm not asking you to roll up your sleeves and do any dirty work, only to care enough for eight children that you'll act on their behalf.'

He was now twitching with agitation, and she saw he was weak rather than heartless.

'Two of those girls are the same race as yourself,' she said, intent on driving her message home. 'How would you feel if one of your daughters was lured away from home on the promise of a good job, only to find later that she'd died in a brothel for want of one man getting her help?'

He sighed deeply and pulled at his moustache. 'Okay. I'll do what I can, Mrs Jennings. But I must warn you, I think you are being overly emotional and foolhardy.'

'Better foolhardy than a coward,' she said in a determined manner. 'Now, go on downstairs while I explain to this little one that I'll be back.'

She knelt down in front of the little black girl and smoothed her face gently. 'I'm going to take care of all of you,' she said gently. 'But first I have to go out and get some things for you. But I'll be back very soon with food and other things. Don't be scared when you hear noises downstairs, it will only be me coming back with some kind ladies. Can you try and tell the other girls that too?'

Three hours later, Matilda was ready to bring the girls downstairs.

It occurred to her as Mr Rodrigious drove her back to London Lil's that using the saloon as a dormitory wasn't practical. If men came hammering on the door and windows at night, the girls would become even more distressed. So she'd decided to use Mrs Honeymead's parlour and bedroom, which at least had a semblance of comfort, and windows that weren't barred and blacked out. She asked Dolores to come with her too.

Two women were brought to her, one Irish and the other Negro, and although they seemed apprehensive, once Matilda had explained the position, and offered them extra money, they soon had the stove lit and pails of water heating, and the sound of scrubbing and the smell of soap filled the lower part of the house.

Dolores took soup and bread up to the girls while downstairs Matilda stripped out surplus furniture and anything which might be a reminder of Mrs Honeymead. When the mattresses and bedding were delivered, she made up beds on the floor.

The two women had made an excellent job of the kitchen. The last task Matilda gave them before paying them off was to bring in two tin baths from outside and fill them with hot water.

Then she and Dolores went upstairs to get the girls.

Dolores had already stated that she believed one of the Negro girls was beyond help, her entire body area was covered in bruises and she thought that she had internal injures too, both the Mexicans were too weak to take more then a few spoonfuls of soup, and the little Chinese girl Matilda had seen first was so fearful of her she had to leave the soup and bread on the floor and walk away.

'We'll jist have to carry the weakest ones,' Dolores said as they reached the top landing. 'Maybe the others will follow.'

Matilda went into each of the rooms to greet the girls before moving them. The small black one who had held her hand before came eagerly enough, and the first Chinese girl shuffled a couple of feet in her direction. Picking this one up in her arms, she was astounded to find she weighed around the same as Amelia, and holding her tightly she went back into each of the other rooms again.

'We're coming back for you,' she said. 'We won't be long.'

Dolores carried the very badly injured black girl, crooning gently to her as they made their way down the stairs. A padding of bare feet behind them made them pause – the little black girl was following them cautiously.

'Come on then,' Matilda nodded to her. 'There's nothing to fear.'

While Matilda put the Chinese girl straight into the bath, Dolores felt her girl was too badly hurt even to sit up, so she laid her on the kitchen table and began to strip off her bloodstained shift. 'Come and look at this,' she whispered.

Matilda moved nearer, but the shock of what she saw made her nauseous. The girl's ribs were sticking out through her skin at odd angles, hardly an inch of her body was left unbruised, and as Dolores parted the girl's stick-thin legs she saw her vagina was torn and swollen.

It took a long time to get each of the girls clean and into their new beds. Every movement had to be slow and gentle so as not to frighten them further, and they couldn't even discover the girls' names to make it easier to communicate with them. Matilda followed Dolores' lead by chatting gently about nothing in particular, in a crooning manner, for they seemed to find that soothing.

But then the doctor arrived, and the moment he walked into the room with Matilda, they all began to wail, except for the badly injured one who didn't seem to be aware of anything.

'He's not a bad man,' Matilda said firmly. She knew Polish Dr Wilinsky slightly, as he sometimes came to the saloon. 'He's a doctor, and he's come to make you well.' But her words did nothing to calm their fears.

Matilda sensed Dr Wilinsky was only there under duress, and his examination of them was neither thorough nor particularly sympathetic. It was at that moment that she truly began to believe women should be allowed to practise medicine, if only to girls and women who had been abused by men.

Outside the parlour half an hour later, the doctor told Matilda he held out no hope for the badly injured Negro, as he thought her broken rib had punctured her lung, but suggested they bound her ribs firmly with a bandage to ease the pain and gave her laudanum. Of the others, he thought that rest, good food and tender care would bring them round, as he didn't think any of them were suffering from anything infectious.

She was just about to admonish the slight man for his lack of interest, when he suddenly said he would write a full report to Mr Rodrigious, and he was prepared to stand up in court to see Mrs Honeymead hang for what she'd done to these girls.

'Well, thank you, doctor,' she said, glad she hadn't laid into him after all.

'I didn't want to come,' he admitted, having the grace to look bashful. 'I'm just like most folk, I guess, but you have shamed me, Mrs Jennings. Now, what will you do with the girls when they are better?'

'I don't know right now,' she said with a sigh. 'But I believe every grown man and woman in this city ought to join me in trying to put a stop to this kind of bestiality.'

'You will have my support,' he said to her surprise. 'Especially if you can think of a way of rehabilitating these girls, so they can forget what they've learnt in this place.'

A week later, back at London Lil's, Dolores was packing a big basket with fried chicken, a flagon of soup and some of her home-made bread, ready to go down and relieve Matilda for the night, when Sidney came rushing into the kitchen.

'Captain Russell's down in the saloon,' he said breathlessly.

'Lord above!' Dolores exclaimed, her expression a mixture of both delight and apprehension, for like Sidney she realized he couldn't possibly know about the tragic deaths in Oregon. He'd only left in July, it was now early October, and if he'd spent the past few weeks travelling from Kansas, he couldn't have got Matty's letter.

'I guess we'll have to tell him before he sees her,' Sidney said. 'But I surely don't want to.'

Dolores patted the lad's shoulder in understanding. 'Bring him up, Sidney,' she said. 'Master Peter's in his room doing his homework, I'll jist make sure he stays there and we'll tell the Captain together.'

Downstairs in the bar James was puzzled. First, Sidney hadn't greeted him with his usual warmth, but hurried off saying he had to have a word with Dolores. Then he'd turned towards Mary and Albert, but they seemed to be going out of their way to serve customers at the other end of the bar. Could it be that Matilda had found a new man?

But as Sidney came back downstairs looking strained and asked him if he'd like to step up for a chat with him and Dolores, James suddenly felt frightened that something had happened to her.

He voiced that fear as he was ushered into the parlour.

'A great deal has happened to her since you were last here,' Sidney said. 'That's what we need to tell you before you see her.'

Dolores came in, poured him a glass of whiskey, then launched into the story.

'Amelia, Cissie and Susanna all dead?' he whispered in horror. 'Oh no! And she's brought Peter here?'

Dolores nodded. 'She sure sunk down pretty low for a time, Captain, and no mistake, but she gone and picked herself up again now.'

'But what about Tabitha?' he asked. All colour had left his face, and he slumped back in a chair as if the deaths were his own family.

Dolores explained that she'd stayed with the Reverend Glover, and that now she was in Boston at school.

'So that was Treacle who came to greet me outside?' James said in a hushed tone. 'I thought he was remarkably like him, and wondered why he was making a fuss of me. So she brought him back here too?'

'Well, Tabby couldn't take him to Boston,' Sidney explained. 'And it cheered Peter to have him come. But I've got more to tell you yet.'

Sidney went on to tell him about Fern, Gilbert Green, the shooting, and finally what was going on down at Girlie Town.

James looked stunned, and confused, but he managed to get out a few questions.

'Fern's better now,' Dolores said. 'She's still here, helping out a bit. But Miz Matilda, she'm putting everything she's got into gettin' those girls well again. One died, never stood a chance poor little thing, but Miz Matilda sure ain't gonna give up on the others, she's talking all sorts of nonsense, 'bout opening a place for girls like that. You gotta talk some sense into her pretty little head, Captain!'

James was so deeply shocked by the deaths of Cissie and the two little girls that he could hardly take anything more in.

'Are you in agreement with Dolores?' he asked Sidney after a moment's thought.

'No, I ain't.' Sidney looked at Dolores and smiled. 'Dolores is just afraid for Matty. It's not that she don't like the idea of a girls' home, she's worked just as hard as Matty with those girls, and without her help I dare say some more of them would have died. But Dolores wants her mistress to be a lady and she don't think this is what real ladies do.'

James had to laugh at that. 'Well, that's true, they sit in their carriages and twirl their parasols, but I don't think any of us can see Matty doing that.'

Dolores scowled at him. 'You knows what I mean, sir,' she exclaimed. 'She's the talk of the city now, famous as that English nurse, Florence Nightingale. She'll be thirty soon, and if she don't mend her ways she'll never find a respectable man to marry her, all she'll have is a parcel of children who don't belong to her, all her money will be gone, and she'll be all alone.'

James knew a maternal speech when he heard one and he smiled fondly at Dolores. 'Why, you've become her mammy,' he exclaimed. 'So she won't ever be alone, you'll be there.'

'That's the truth,' Dolores said, wiggling a finger at him. 'And if I'd been her mammy when she first got entangled with you I'd have sent you packing. Don't s'pose you can give us some good news, like your wife's bin carried off with a fever or kicked by her horse.'

'Dolores!' Sidney said in a horrified tone.

'That's okay, Sidney,' James chuckled. 'You see, down South it's fine for a mammy to air such views, when her darlin's future is at stake. But I'm sorry to disappoint you, by all accounts Evelyn's in the rudest of health. Happy because I'm posted so far off.'

Although Sidney didn't hold with married men having mistresses in general, he admired the Captain so much he allowed himself to overlook this one flaw.

'Here, in San Francisco?' he asked.

'At the Presidio, no less,' James said with a smile. 'Not for long, I suspect, they'll have us out chasing renegade Indians and guarding mail coaches. But here for a while.'

Dolores stood up. 'I guess I'd better be gettin' down to Miz Matilda,' she said. 'She'll be a-wondrin' what's keeping me. I'm sure glad to see you, sir. Maybe with you here Miss Matilda will get better still. See, she's still grievin' badly for her baby, I reckons that's why she got so all fired up 'bout these girls.'

'I'll come with you to carry that basket,' he said. 'And I'll bring Matty home too.'

'You can't go in there,' Dolores said in some alarm. 'Miz Matilda don't allow no men in, those girls get so scared.'

'Then I'll wait outside.' He grinned. 'It will be like old times seeing your mistress caring for folk. I guess that's what made me love her in the first place.'

Chapter Twenty-three

Matilda leaned up on one elbow to watch James sleeping beside her. She thought he was handsome in any light, with or without his uniform, travel-stained or on parade. But lying here next to her in a sheltered hollow, by the beach at Santa Cruz, with sunshine playing on his fair hair, and his features relaxed, he looked much younger than his thirty-six years.

It was January of 1856, and three months since he came back to San Francisco. Next week he would be going back to Kansas with his company, and she had no idea when she'd see him again. But they had shared so much happiness in the past months that she wasn't going to let anything spoil these last few days in Santa Cruz together.

They had ridden here on the coastal path, and they were staying in a little beach cabin which they'd rented from a man in the fishing village. They woke each morning to the sound of rolling waves and the shriek of sea birds, and they had spent their days riding, walking and making love. For two days now they hadn't seen another soul, and if Matilda could have just one wish, it would be that they could stay here for ever.

There was nothing here to remind her of Amelia. Back in San Francisco there were Peter and Sidney, and so often when they talked about the past Amelia's little face sprang into her mind and just stayed there. Not that she needed reminders to recall every last thing about her, but at least here she could control the memories, savouring the sweet ones, pushing the nasty ones of her death away.

She was so glad she'd helped Fern now, and that it had led to finding the other girls. It would never make up for losing Amelia, but doing something worthwhile had soothed the heart ache. As Dolores had said that day when she was angry, she did have Tabitha, Peter and Sidney. Tabitha was very happy at her new school and doing well. Peter had made friends in San Francisco and seemed more settled. As for Sidney, well, sometimes she wondered what on earth she would do without him.

Rolling over, she sat up, looking towards the sea just a couple of hundred yards away. It was turquoise, the sky above clear and blue with just a few wispy white clouds, the sun as warm as a spring day back in England.

She smiled at the thought, for her memory seemed to be playing tricks on her these days. Why was it that when she thought of England she visualized trees in blossom, the scarlet coats of the Beefeaters in the Tower of London bright against the ancient grey walls, and the Thames sparkling in sunshine? She knew that in reality if she was to be transported back there now in January, the wind would be biting cold, the streets awash with filth, and the people every bit as ragged and forlorn as when she left thirteen years ago. Yet she sometimes yearned to go back there.

She knew such thoughts were foolish, everyone she cared about was here in America, and besides, after this holiday she was going to open the Jennings Bureau, an employment agency for young ladies.

There were many in San Francisco who believed she was crazy to consider such a venture during a financial crisis, but she believed they were all short-sighted. People were still flocking to California, attracted by its gentle climate, and they were a steadier, sturdier bunch than those who'd come during the gold rush. A great many of these would need servants, nurse-maids, seamstresses and shop assistants, and she was going to supply them. At Christmas she had made Sidney manager of London Lil's, to leave her free to concentrate fully on this new project.

The idea had come to her during the time she was nursing the sick girls from the brothel. As they recovered physically, she saw the only way to heal their mental scars and to prevent them ever being drawn back into a life of vice was to find some way of training them for some kind of decent employment. But none of them was old enough for that, and at first she had tried to induce some of the more upstanding people in the community to take a girl into their own home and care for her until she was thirteen or so. This had failed miserably – no one, it seemed, had a big enough heart to take on such damaged girls. But some of the more charitable of them had offered her donations to help with the girls' upkeep.

It had been her old friend Henry Slocum who had suggested that she take these donations and set up a trust fund. He said if she were able to find and equip a house to take these girls to herself, and care for them until they were old enough to work, he would personally see that the city council gave her funds to help. She could then appeal to the public for more donations to meet the rest of the costs.

Back in late November Matilda had found such a house in Folsom Street, at a low rent. The owners had gone to South America but were undecided about selling it. She set up the Jennings Trust, and started it off by paying the first year's rent herself, then began persuading people to donate funds, clothes, furniture and equipment.

The girls' spirits rose dramatically as soon as they were moved out of the old brothel building with its terrible memories. Although that first week in December the new house was scantily furnished and chilly, the day they moved in was the first time Matilda had heard real laughter from any of them.

Fern had proved to be invaluable. Matilda had kept her at London Lil's after she recovered, and while Dolores was down at the brothel nursing, Fern took over her old jobs. She was also an ideal go-between down in Girlie Town for Matilda, as the much younger ones there trusted her, knowing she had been there too. It was she who managed to get them to talk, sitting in with an interpreter for both the Chinese and Mexican girls. Mr Rodrigious got his statements, and Mrs Honeymead was convicted of procuring and sentenced to hard labour for ten years.

Now Fern was at the house with the other girls. Although she was old enough at fourteen to work, both Matilda and Dolores felt she was made of the right stuff to train to become housekeeper eventually.

For now Dolores was in charge at the house, having taken up residence in the front room. Each one of the girls knew that behind her stern front lay a kind and understanding woman, but they'd learnt since then that she was vigilant, nobody's fool and very tough. She had high standards of hygiene she expected them all to follow, they had to eat what they were given or they got nothing else, and she made it quite clear that even when they were well enough to go outdoors, it would be with her, not by themselves.

Matilda had let the girls know that although this was to be a safe home for them for as long as they needed it, they were there to learn too. They were to share the chores, the Mexicans and Chinese had to learn to speak English. All of them would learn to read and write, sewing, cooking and other housekeeping skills.

James stirred beside her, his hand coming up to caress her back. 'I must have dropped off,' he said. 'That wasn't very gentlemanly of me.'

Matilda turned to him and kissed his nose. 'Perhaps you should try sleeping at night,' she giggled.

'What were you thinking about?' he asked, sitting up beside her. 'I hope it wasn't something sad.'

'Not at all,' she said. James coming back was the best kind of medicine for her heart ache. He had let her talk and cry about Cissie and the girls, but he'd also given her a great deal to laugh about too, and often that was better than sympathy. 'Though I suppose I was kind of wondering if the Jennings Bureau will ever have any clients.'

'Of course it will,' he said firmly. 'It might take a while to get going, but I'm sure a year from now it will be a roaring success, just as your lumber business and London Lil's were.'

'My first advertisement will be in the *Alta Chronicle* next week,' she said thoughtfully. 'They promised they would write an article about it too. But I'm afraid I might get dozens of women wanting work, but no work to offer them. I'll look pretty silly if that happens, won't I?'

'Have faith,' he said.

'That's what Giles always said about everything,'

'Did it work?'

'Some of the time,' she said with a smile. 'But if it didn't, he just used to turn it around and claim God had refused for a reason. I often wonder if when he got to the Pearly Gates he was cross that he'd been called too early.'

James looked up to the sky and cupped his hands round his

mouth. 'If you're listening, Giles, make sure it works for Matty,' he called out.

Matilda giggled. 'I think he's looking after Tabitha, in her last letter she said she was top of her class.'

'Peter's bright too,' James said. 'He was speaking about a mathematical problem to me the last time I called around, I couldn't even begin to think how to work it out, but he knew. He's such a nice lad, most thirteen-year-olds are so awkward, and after all he's been through in the past six months one would expect him to be difficult.'

'I'm very pleased at how well he's settled down with me and at his new school,' she said. 'But I'm not sure he's quite stable yet. Remember how he reacted when I explained about his mother's estate?'

James nodded. Cissie had left some 8,000 dollars. When Matilda tried to explain to Peter that it would be invested for him until he came of age, he had flown into a rage, saying he didn't want blood money, and that Matilda was to write back to the Oregon lawyers and tell them it was to go to poor families who really needed it. 'I suppose to a young boy, money like that must seem like being paid off for his mother's death,' he said. 'But he'll think differently in a few years' time.'

'I suppose so,' Matilda agreed. 'But what shocked me that day was how angry he was, I guess he'd been holding it in inside him all that time, and I never knew until it all came spurting out. Since then he often talks about death to me, about how other boys in his class lost someone close to them. I can't bear to think he's brooding on who will be the next person to go. Just six months ago the only things he was interested in was climbing trees and going swimming.'

'The death of someone close to you is often an awakening experience,' James said. 'I've known young soldiers who thought of nothing but drinking and carousing, until one of their close friends got killed. Suddenly they see how fragile life is, and they grow up fast.'

'Perhaps that's why I feel so old then,' Matilda said. 'I keep telling myself thirty isn't so old, but when I look back at all those who have died younger than me, it seems a great age.'

He pushed back her bonnet and peered at her hair. 'There's not a silver hair amongst the gold yet,' he joked. Then, forcing her to open her mouth, he looked in there too. 'And all your teeth are still there!'

'No they aren't.' She laughed. 'I got Sidney to pull out one that was hurting back last year.'

'He did that for you?' James pulled a mock-horrified face.

'Well, it was either him or going to the barber's shop,' Matilda retorted. 'I'd sooner have pain at the hands of someone I trust, than a stranger.'

'Just thinking about pulling teeth makes my legs ache,' James said, and jumped up, pulling her up after him. 'I'll race you down to the sea.'

Matilda ran as fast as she could, but burdened by her long skirt and petticoats, she couldn't keep up with him. When he got to the sea, he turned and held out his arms, and she ran to him knowing he was going to twirl her round just the way he once did Tabitha.

'I love you so much,' he said, once he'd put her down, and she clung to him, dizzy and panting. 'If we don't get a chance to be together again for a long time, I shall carry the memory of what you looked like today in my heart.'

'How do I look?' she asked breathlessly.

'Tousled,' he said, tucking the strands of hair that had come loose under her bonnet. 'Your eyes are bright and beautiful like the sky, your cheeks like two ripe peaches, and you have sand all over your dress. I think I'm seeing how you were when you sold flowers.'

'I didn't wear fancy clothes like this then.' She laughed, looking down at her fine wool dress and matching cloak trimmed with velvet. 'I had only one ragged dress, a shawl and a mob-cap.'

'Tell me what you used to shout out to sell your flowers,' he asked, taking her hand and walking back up the deserted beach.

Matilda giggled and cleared her throat. 'Lov-erly fresh violets, only a tanner a bunch,' she yelled at the top of her lungs in her best Cockney accent. 'Come on, sir, treat the little lady and put a smile on'er face.'

'I'll take the whole basket,' James said.

'Gor blimey, guv, that's mighty generous of you. That's six bob to you.'

James pulled some notes from his pocket. 'I've only got dollars it seems,' he said.

'Fair enough, guv,' she said, snatching them. 'Shame I ain't got no change to give you.' With that she ran off laughing to their cabin.

On their last afternoon it was still bright, but a little chilly. James made a big fire indoors and one out on the sand, and they sat out on the porch watching the sun go down, listening to the waves breaking on the shore. As the sun slowly dipped into the sea, the flames of the campfire brought back poignant memories of the wagon train for both of them. They clasped hands and stared into the flames, both only too well aware that the time they had left together was fast running out.

Matilda had learned never to ask questions about Evelyn, for all answers hurt, however carefully James worded them. She tried only to remember that she held his heart. Tonight she didn't envy Evelyn one bit, she might live in a grand house, and bear the title of Mrs Russell, but as a married woman, afternoon tea with other ladies in the same circumstances was all the gaiety she could expect. Parties or balls were out of the question without her husband to escort her, and she could never take up any kind of work, other than something for a charity. Her life had to be so very dreary.

'I have put forward Peter's name for West Point,' James said suddenly. 'Should anything happen to me, I mean before he's old enough to go, as his guardian you must contact them yourself and of course remind them of me. I said his parents were old friends of mine.'

It was the 'should anything happen to me' which sent shivers down her spine. Each time James went away she always tried to imagine him training raw recruits, or just sitting up on his horse, leading his company across endless empty plains. But the Indians were rising up against the white man now, hardly a week went past without a new story of massacres, scalpings and hostages taken, somewhere in the Mid-West or down in Texas and Arizona. She knew too that the trouble in Kansas could grow into something very serious. The 'Free Soilers', as the people who had settled there on free land were known, were all totally opposed to slavery, but neighbouring Missouri was still a slave-owning state and its people wanted the freedom to take their slaves anywhere in the West, and they were prepared to do anything to uphold what they considered their right.

'Not that I'm anticipating an untimely death.' James laughed softly. 'But it's best to discuss all eventualities, just in case.'

'In that case, if something happens to me, will you make sure Peter does get to West Point?' she said, keeping her tone light.

'Of course I will,' he said, squeezing her hand. 'And I'll keep in touch with Tabitha, no one will be prouder than me when I see MD after her name.'

'I wonder if she really will make it,' Matilda said. 'Henry Slocum said the other day that there's only about a dozen fully qualified lady doctors in the country. He was telling me about an English lady called Elizabeth Blackwell who was the first lady to get a medical degree here, back in 1851. She went back to England and applied for a job in a hospital. She signed her name E. Blackwell MD, and they took her on, thinking she was a man. But they pushed her out pretty quickly when they found out, so she came back here to work.'

'But things are improving all the time,' James said. 'Today a dozen lady doctors, tomorrow hundreds of them. You can get a divorce easily in California, right now. Soon it will be just as common in Virginia, and I'll be one of them.'

She turned sideways to look at James. It wasn't the first time he'd spoken of divorce, but it was the first time he'd stated he intended to do it. His eyes met hers, grave and unwavering, and she knew he meant it. 'Whatever the cost?' she asked.

'Whatever,' he replied. 'And will you promise to marry me the minute I'm free, whatever the cost to you?'

'Yes, I promise,' she said, nodding.

'Then you must do something now to prove it,' he said, with laughter in his voice.

'Whatever you say.'

He looked at her appraisingly for a moment, his blue eyes twinkling and one side of his mouth twisted up a little, the way it always did when he had mischief on his mind.

'You must come and have a dip in the sea with me.'

'But it will be icy!' she exclaimed in horror. Now the sun had vanished it was cold, only the bonfire and the shelter of the porch were allowing them to stay outside.

'If you don't, I can't take your promises seriously.'

Without a second thought Matilda began unbuttoning her dress; off it came, then her petticoats, stays and stockings, right down to her chemise. James began to undress too, casting his jacket, shirt and pants back into the house until he was left with his long underpants.

'Those too,' Matilda said, pointing at them.

'Then you must take off your chemise,' he grinned. He waited until she was stark naked, then tossed one of her red garters back at her. 'Just wear that,' he said. 'Then I'll keep it in my pocket till the day we marry.'

She laughed, even though the wind was already chilling her, and pulled it up her leg on to her thigh.

'Ready?' he said, then took her hand and they ran down the beach and straight into the water.

It was so cold it took her breath away. But when he dived in she had to follow, and as she inched forward it was like a slow torture feeling the cold creep up her warm skin.

'Right down till only your head is out the water,' he shouted at her. 'If you don't, I'll push you under.'

There was nothing for it but to do it. She bent her knees, bobbed down just long enough for him to see her, then rushed out of the water.

He ran after her as she raced back up the beach, picked her up in his arms and hugged her. 'You are the bravest woman I ever met,' he said, covering her face with salty kisses.

Carrying her squirming in his arms, he took her into the house, kicked the door shut and grabbed a blanket from the bed to wrap round them both. He made her laugh as he forced her to shuffle around the room with him as he collected pillows, cushions and more blankets to place in front of the fire.

'Do you know what I'm going to do to you now, Mrs Jennings?' he asked, rubbing his wet hair against her face.

'I suspect, sir, that you are intending to have your evil way with me,' she said in a high indignant squeak.

'How right you are, my dear,' he said, lifting her up and then lowering her down on to the blankets. 'There's no point in calling out for help, there's no one around for miles.'

'Then I guess I'll just have to submit,' she said, screwing up her eyes. 'Just do it quickly, that's all I ask.'

He began by kissing her right foot, right up her leg until he reached the garter, then he caught hold of it with his teeth and pulled it down her leg. It had left drops of sea water on her skin, and slowly he went up it again, licking each one away. Then he moved to her left foot and worked up that leg, going right up her stomach to her breast.

Nothing had ever been quite so erotic, her skin was tingling from the cold sea, and when he took her nipple in his warm mouth, she wanted him then and there. But it was clear James had every intention of making her wait. He moved to her fingertips, sucking those, and slowly worked his way back up her arm, towards her breast again, then the other one, until she felt she couldn't stand it another moment. Then he moved down her middle to her belly, and with his face pressing into the soft flesh there, he probed inside her until she found herself begging him to fuck her.

'Fuck you?' he said, lifting his head from her belly, his face a picture of mock indignation. 'Ladies don't use such language!'

His seeming reluctance to enter her made her even more desperate, she was writhing against his fingers, pushing them harder still into her. He knelt between her legs, pushing them further apart and smiling as he watched her moving against him. Then all at once he moved down towards her sex, opening it wide with his fingers, his tongue ready to lick her there. She was shocked, but she wanted him so much she didn't care what he did any longer.

But the feeling when his tongue lapped over her was so wonderful, she forgot herself and her ideas of decency, and just gave herself up to the utter bliss. Her arm nearest the fire was terribly hot, the other cold, steam was coming off his wet hair, but she was drifting off into a world where physical discomfort couldn't touch her.

Her orgasm came all too soon, sending her off into a whirlpool of ecstasy. She heard herself screaming out his name, yet the voice didn't appear to be coming from her own vocal chords.

All at once she was aware of him again, his mouth covering hers, and the sea-like smell of her on his lips. 'Now I'm going to fuck you,' he murmured. 'For hours and hours.'

She thought they had risen to the greatest possible heights of passion many times before, but he took her a stage further still. He rolled over on to his back and made her ride on him that way, kneading her breasts so hard that at times it hurt. But then he turned her over on to her stomach, and entered her from behind, tenderly whispering endearments into her ears, and kissing her neck, until she had a second orgasm. Then he turned her over again and carried on, kissing her with such fire she felt consumed by it.

When he finally came he cried out her name, and tears ran down his cheeks. She held his hard, sweaty body tight to her and gloried in the moment, knowing she had to hold it for ever in her mind, just in case it never happened again.

That night as they lay in each other's arms listening to the sea and the wind, she wished she could put into words what she felt for him. Love encompassed so many different degrees of emotion. She'd felt it for her father, for Giles and Lily, for Tabitha, Cissie and her children, and Sidney too. There was the love she'd felt for Amelia, distinct from the others, yet the same too. Then of course the romantic love, for Flynn, Giles, and now James. With each one it had seemed nothing could be stronger or more intense, yet looking back the passion she felt for Flynn was nothing compared with Giles, and her feelings for James far surpassed both previous experiences. Poets spoke of wishing to die if they couldn't have their beloved, but she felt such a sentiment was feeble. Love was enriching, it should be carried in one's heart with pride, even if the loved one should die or be torn from you.

Yet she knew it was easy to think such noble thoughts while safe in her lover's arms, knowing his heart and mind were in tune with hers. Maybe that pride could crumble without constant reassurance, or if they should be kept apart for too long.

There was still enough glow from the fire to see his face, he was looking back at her, almost as if his mind was reading hers and agreeing with every thought. A long, lean face, each line giving a clue as to how he made his living. The small ones at the corners of his eyes, from squinting into the sun, the small scars, all from various battles he never would relate. She had noted on the wagon train that he frowned at incompetence, and those frown lines on his forehead were far deeper now. Then there was the way he stuck his chin out with determination, the thin line beneath his lips showed he'd lost none of that.

'I love you,' she whispered. 'I can't tell you how much.'

'One of these days when we're together for ever, I wonder if we'll still be scanning each other's faces and trying to read one another's mind,' he said.

'Maybe we won't need to then,' she whispered.

He took her in his arms and held her tightly, and she knew he was crying silently.

A week later Dolores came back to the apartment at London Lil's to see Matilda and found her sitting looking at a daguerreotype of James with tears running down her cheeks.

'Now, what's all this?' Dolores said. 'You is supposed to be the woman who never cries!'

Matilda smiled weakly. 'That's just a myth,' she retorted.

'You jist get that picture taken?' Dolores asked curiously, taking it from her hand. 'Mighty clever what some folks can do, ain't it? I can't figure out how they can make a picture of someone come on a piece of paper.'

'Nor me, Dolores,' Matilda sighed. 'We both had one taken, but I looked as stern in my one as James does in his.'

'Sure looks like he's got a poker up his nether regions.' Dolores chuckled. 'But he's a fine-lookin' man and no mistake.'

'That's all I've got to remember him by for a while,' Matilda said wistfully. She thought of how James had tucked her picture into a little leather case along with her red garter and a lock of her hair. He said he was going to keep it in his pocket for ever.

'No, it ain't all you got. You got a head full of happy memories,' Dolores snapped at her. 'That's more than some folks got.'

Dolores always had a knack of pointing out the real truth.

'You're right, of course,' Matilda said, putting the picture down. 'I'm forgetting myself. How's things down at the house?'

'Jist fine,' the maid said. 'Little Mai Ling learnt a whole sentence yesterday. She said, "Me no likee corn." I guess that's a start and she sure understood when I said she'd eat it and like it.'

Matilda really smiled at that, Dolores didn't stand for anyone refusing to eat anything she cooked. 'How's Bessie?' she asked. Bessie was the youngest black girl. At the time they found the girls at the brothel, she appeared the least distressed, but since then she had had many very bad nightmares when she woke screaming. She continually wet her bed, and on one occasion had smeared excrement on the walls of the room she shared with three other girls.

'I reckon she's gittin' to settle down,' Dolores said. 'I took her in bed one night after she woke screaming, and she never wet. So's I've bin lettin' her sleep with me since.'

'But she's got to learn to sleep alone sometime,' Matilda said.

'She's just a babby,' Dolores said, proving she was a great deal more maternal than she made herself out to be. 'Anyway, what I come up here for is to tell you one of Mrs Slocum's friends gave us one of them new-fangled sewing machines. I tried and tried, but I can't make it work.'

'I'll come later and take a look at it,' Matilda said. She was thrilled by such a present, for if the girls could learn to sew on it, that would be another useful skill.

'You come now,' Dolores said in her most commanding voice. 'There ain't no sense in you sittin' up here moping, and the girls all want to see you. Fern, she's been practising the letters you taught her over and over, I's mighty sick of hearing that slate squeaking when she cleans it.'

Matilda had to agree. Dolores was right, she would only mope if she stayed here.

The house in Folsom Street was cosy, if not elegant. As all the furniture had been donated, it ranged from a roughly hewn bench seat, which filled an unwary hand with splinters, to a once grand mahogany table, with much of its varnish worn away, and a shabby, overstuffed couch. Dolores had the front room as her bedroom, and that was as bare as a monk's cell – an iron bed, a wash-stand and little else. At the back was a large kitchen and living-room, kept warm by a cook stove. A scullery beyond housed a boiler to heat up water for bathing and washing, and when the fire under this was lit too, the heat was enough to roast a pig.

There were two bedrooms apiece on the two upper floors, but the girls slept four in a room, two in a bed, on the lower floor. The beds themselves ranged from a simple wooden one strung with rope, to a fancy brass one with real springs, and two old iron ones. But donations of rag rugs, biblical pictures and many brightly coloured quilts gave the rooms a cheerful, snug character.

When Dolores and Matilda arrived at the house, the girls were all in the kitchen. Mai Ling and Suzy, the two Chinese, were sitting on a bench playing cat's cradle with a bit of string, Maria and Angelina, the Mexicans, were huddled by the stove, and the three Negro girls, Bessie, Ruth, and Dora, were seated at the table while Fern imparted her knowledge of letters to them.

At the older women's arrival, Bessie rushed to greet them and Fern's face broke into the widest of smiles, but the others only nodded to acknowledge their presence. Matilda had found this coolness one of the most difficult things to get used to, for she'd always been used to exuberant children, who flung their arms around her in greeting. But Dolores, a mine of information on almost any subject, assured her that she'd won their trust because they didn't hide themselves, and besides, they were always asking when she was coming again.

'One of you's can make some tea for Miz Jennings,' Dolores said. 'I reckon it's Ruth's turn, and Dora, you show Miz Jennings the cookies we made.'

Matilda found it hard to believe that these girls were the same cowed, sad little creatures she'd found in those terrible cells in the brothel. They had all gained weight, Bessie and Dora were even growing fat. Mai Ling, Suzy, Angelina and Maria's black hair had begun to shine again, and their skin had a golden glow. Ruth, the third black girl, was the only one who still gave Matilda real cause for concern, for even though she'd gained weight, her dark eyes still had a haunted look, and she cringed each time someone made a sudden movement near her.

They all wore similar striped calico dresses, some pink, some blue, for the owner of one of the dry goods stores in Market Street had given them two bolts of cloth. Matilda had got the dresses made up by two seamstresses. When Matilda took them out in a little crocodile to have a walk, they could easily pass for girls from a private school, and though some of the neighbours had initially been hostile to having such girls living in the same street as them, now they never excited anything more than a curious glance.

Matilda spoke to each of the girls in turn, Mai Ling and Suzy smiled shyly, but their lack of English prevented them from saying much more than yes or no. Maria and Angelina were learning fast, and they both thanked her for the hair ribbons she'd left for them on her last visit. But Bessie, Dora and Fern had a great deal to say, about the cookies they'd baked, about Fern's letters, and the sewing-machine, for Fern had seen one working when she was back home in Philadelphia, and she'd described to them what it did.

'Well, we must get it working now,' Matilda said. 'I've never used one but I'm sure if we all put our heads together, we can make it sew. Where is it, Dolores?'

'In my room, ma'am,' Dolores replied.

All the girls trooped behind her as Matilda went to look, and when she gasped in surprise because she recognized it as the latest model, Fern clapped her hands in excitement. Opening the little drawer in the stand, she found an instruction book with diagrams as to how to thread it, and realized Dolores hadn't known it had to have two lots of cotton thread, one above and one beneath.

Within minutes she had it threaded and Dolores brought her an oddment of cotton to try sewing on. Following the instructions, Matilda clamped the little foot down on the material and began turning the handle. As a clear row of neat stitches came out the other end, Dolores proclaimed it was a miracle.

One by one, they all had a try, and as Matilda looked at all the enthralled faces around her, she suddenly saw that the real miracle of this machine wasn't just that it would save time sewing by hand, but that it had brought them all together with a common interest, as nothing else previously had.

Later on, while the girls were still taking turns on the machine, Matilda sat down to talk to Dolores. 'We could use that machine to make money for this house,' she said excitedly. 'We could start out by making simple things like aprons, but we could progress in time to dresses and shirts, couldn't we?'

Dolores, who was a very able needlewoman already, grinned broadly. 'We sure could, ma'am, I reckon we could make a heap of money that way. Specially flannel shirts for workin' men. They ain't too fussy about the fit, as long as they is strong. It will teach the girls sommat useful too.'

By March Matilda was seriously worried about the viability of the Jennings Employment Bureau. Many girls had come to the small office she rented in Montgomery Street, following her advertisements in the *Alta Chronicle*, but few prospective employers came forward, and when she couldn't find work for the girls immediately, they soon lost interest and disappeared. But she refused to give up, and each morning she trekked round the city calling on all businesses and wealthy households personally, haranguing the owners at least to hear her out before dismissing her out of hand. She pointed out that although they could have dozens of applicants for a position by just hanging a notice on their doors, it was time-consuming for them to have to interview girls, take up references and dredge through hopelessly unsuitable candidates. For just a small fee, she would find exactly the right kind of girl for them, check her references and make sure she knew exactly what was required of her. She promised that if the girl proved unsatisfactory after a month's trial, she would find a replacement free of charge.

Slowly the tide began to turn during late spring as the financial crisis began to abate. First she got a contract to supply a dozen girls to a new candy-making business, a bakery wanted two more staff, a whole spate of people contacted her wanting maids and kitchen hands, and there were half a dozen vacancies in a fish-canning factory.

It was hard work. Most of the girls who came to her were illiterate, they might be bright and willing, but often they were dirty, hungry and with only the ragged clothes they stood up in. Matilda lost count of how many she ordered down to the bath-house or for whom she had to find a respectable dress and pair of boots before she could even think of sending them to work. She often sent such girls to stay at Folsom Street for a couple of days before they took up positions as maids, so Dolores could drill them on the sort of tasks that would be expected of them.

Yet gradually it began to work, girls were being placed in decent employment, and as word got around the city that she could be relied on, so more positions were offered. But one of the most heartening things to come out of it was support from some of the more benevolent ladies in San Francisco's society. They sent parcels of clothing, unwanted lengths of calico and flannel, and in a few cases offers of accommodation for homeless girls.

Meanwhile, back in Folsom Street, several new girls had come to the house seeking refuge, and Dolores took them in, nursed them back to health, and got them to help with the shirt-making. This had proved to be a real source of income. Dolores cut the patterns and the cloth, the girls willingly took turns at the machine, others sewed on buttons, made buttonholes and pressed the finished articles, and a men's clothing store in Market Street bought them as fast as they could make them.

At the end of each long day Matilda was so exhausted that she fell asleep instantly. She still insisted on having supper with Sidney and Peter each evening so they maintained their links as a family, but the meal was often brought ready-made at the bake-house as she had little time to cook herself. She knew the bureau was running at a loss, but it was only a small one, and she could afford it. The house in Folsom Street was just keeping its head above water with the funds from the city council, donations and the shirt-making business. Tired as she often was, however bleak it sometimes seemed with James and Tabitha so far away, she had never felt more fulfilled. Sidney was running London Lil's every bit as well as she had, he was growing in confidence each day, helped by what she saw as the start of a love affair with Mary, and Peter was happy too, both at school and at home.

If the number of girls she could help seemed very small in comparison to the huge numbers finding their way daily into the sewers of the 'Barbary Coast', at least she felt she was doing something. She remembered how she had once told Giles her ambition was purely to think she made a difference in some people's lives, and she was achieving that. She intended to do a great deal more before she was finished.

Chapter Twenty-four

1861

Sidney came bounding into the parlour one May morning waving a letter and grinning broadly. 'It's from the Captain,' he said. 'Maybe he'll make some sense of what's going on.'

Just under a month ago, on 12 April, General Beauregard had ordered his rebels from the South to open fire on the Union troops at Fort Sumpter in Charleston harbour. The only casualty was a Confederate horse, but even so war had been declared between the North and the South, and no one could talk of anything else.

Matilda opened the letter quickly, but once she'd seen James was still writing from Fort Leavenworth where he'd been based for the last five years, she looked up at Sidney. 'He's still in Kansas,' she said.

The troubles between anti-slavery Free Soilers from New England and pro-slave Southerners from just across the border in Missouri had finally escalated into a war in May of 1856. A mob of pro-slavers sacked the Free Soil town of Lawrence in Kansas territory, blew up the Free State Hotel, burned the Governor's house, and tossed the presses of the local newspaper into the river. John Brown, a fiery Abolitionist, retaliated by rushing into Pottawatomie Creek, a pro-slavery settlement, where he slaughtered five men in cold blood. Brown was hanged, but by the end of the year over 200 people had been killed in what had come to be known as 'Bleeding Kansas'.

Sidney looked disappointed. 'I thought the Captain would be in the thick of it,' he said.

Matilda half smiled at Sidney's naiveté. He took little interest in politics, only the more sensational news attracted his attention.

'The trouble in Kansas is what started all this,' she said. 'And it's still a hotbed of guerrilla warfare. I had hoped Mr Lincoln could cool things down once he became President last year, but now eleven Southern states have seceded because they can't agree on the slavery issue, and have formed the Confederacy, I suppose all-out war is the only option.'

Sidney looked baffled. 'Maybe the Captain's letter will explain it so I can understand,' he said. Both he and Peter idolized James, and they soundly believed his views were more accurate than those they read in the newspapers. 'I guess I'd better leave you to read it.'

Matilda smiled, knowing he really wanted her to read it now and tell her its contents. She would tell him later, for over the past few years he'd become her closest friend and there were no secrets between them. Her little street urchin had grown into a fine man and she was very proud of him. A sparkling sense of humour, kind heart and lack of conceit were the things most people liked him for, but he was nobody's fool. He ran London Lil's efficiently, he was tough enough to deal with the most difficult customers, and his early life had made him so wily he was always one step ahead of most people.

He was twenty-six now. His distinctive red hair and beard, along with added weight and muscle, had earned him the nick-name of Big Red, but marrying Mary Callaghan two years ago had given him an extra dimension of calm and stability. Matilda had been overjoyed at their union, for Mary's harsh earlier life, and the years she and Sidney had spent working together made them ideal partners. They delighted in their own little home a few blocks away, and were now eagerly awaiting the birth of their first child.

'I'll come down and tell you all his news in a while,' Matilda said. 'What's Peter doing this morning?'

'Still champing at the bit to enlist,' Sidney said with a wide grin. 'But I gave him a clout earlier, and said he was to clean out the cellar and not be such a fool.'

Matilda frowned. Peter had lost none of his enthusiasm for being a soldier, and he had been eagerly waiting to hear if he had been accepted at West Point. But the moment he'd heard about the war, he suddenly didn't care about being an officer, he just wanted to go off and fight immediately.

Peter had always had a special place in Matilda's heart, but since Cissie died he had become even dearer to her. While Sidney had always felt like a younger brother, she thought of Peter as her son. She often felt that she had transferred all the love she felt for Amelia, Cissie and Susanna to him on their deaths; caring for him and watching him grow from boy to man had fulfilled a deep need in her. He had such a sunny disposition, all the warmth and fire Cissie had, but was so bright and quick. He was her clown when she needed cheering, her companion and helpmate. Since his schooling had ended last fall when he became eighteen, he had filled in the time waiting to hear from West Point by working for her. He did the book-keeping, painted the whole outside of London Lil's, and ran messages for her in connection with her girls.

Apart from her reluctance for him to leave her, and the terrible fear he could be killed, Matilda hated the idea of him enlisting. She had done her best to bring him up as a gentleman, and the thought of him mixing with hard-drinking, uncouth desperadoes made her feel quite ill.

Sidney had no such desire to enlist. He wasn't patriotic, he said his only allegiance was to those he loved, and he saw no sense in fighting for something he didn't understand. He doted on Peter too, and he was every bit as anxious as Matilda to prevent him leaving home.

'I guess we can't chain him up to stop him going,' Sidney said, his brow furrowed with a deep frown. 'I'll do my best to talk him out of it.'

'Maybe James has said something about Peter in this letter,' she said. 'I wouldn't mind him going quite so much if he could join his regiment.'

'I'll leave you to read it then,' Sidney replied. 'Meanwhile I'll keep him working in the cellar.'

Once Sidney had gone, Matilda settled down to read the letter.

Nothing had worked out as they had planned. After their brief holiday in Santa Cruz, James returned to Fort Leavenworth in Kansas, and on his first leave went home to Virginia and asked Evelyn for a divorce, but she refused point-blank. She didn't care that they had a marriage in name only, that there would never be children, or even that he said he was in love with another woman. All she cared about was that no scandal should touch her.

James told her that she must consider herself deserted in that case, because he was never coming back to her, and this was something he'd stuck to. He would have resigned his commission there and then too, but the situation in Kansas was volatile, and the innocent settlers so desperately in need of protection, he felt he must hang on until it was resolved.

In the last five years, and despite the 2,000 miles between them, they had managed to spend some time together. Matilda had travelled to Denver to meet him three times. Last year she'd gone all the way to Ohio to see Tabitha when she started at Clevedon Medical College and met up with James there too. In all this time they had clung to the belief it would only be a few months before James could break free from the army and come to her, but once the news of the war reached Matilda, she knew he would never resign during a crisis.

My darling,' she read. *'I write this letter with a heavy heart, knowing that in all probability, by the time you receive it, we will be at war. Over the years I have sent so many letters apologizing for letting you down, but in this one I cannot even offer words of hope for our shared future, because things look so terribly grave.*

I haven't even got the conviction that this is a war which has to be fought, for the forces bringing it about are as muddled as my own feelings. If it were simply a matter of the morality of slavery then I would be glad to gallop in rattling my sabre, for you know my long-held views on that. But in fact it is merely a clash of an elite minority.

Most Northern people are not wealthy or politically powerful, neither do they care enough about slavery to go to war over it. Likewise in the South most whites are poor farmers and not decision-makers. The Northern elites want economic expansion, free land, free labour, a free market, a high protective tariff for manufacturers and a Bank of the United States. The Southern elites oppose all that, they see Lincoln and the Republicans stopping their pleasant and prosperous way of life.

My feelings are torn in both directions. I am after all a Virginian, and even if I deplore some of the traditions, these are my people I am being asked to wage war against. Maybe if I could believe I was to fight on the side of right, I could put aside personal loyalties. But I know all too well that slavery isn't the real issue and even if the war does finally set them all free, the problems won't be over, for there is enormous prejudice against the black man, and there are very few who believe he should have the same rights as white men.

In truth Negroes often receive worse treatment in the North than they do in the South because of ignorance and fear. In New York a black man cannot vote unless he owns two hundred and fifty dollars in property. That rule doesn't apply to whites. But then I do not need to tell you such things, dear Matty, for you have always been a champion of the poor and the oppressed regardless of the colour of their skin, gender, or religion.

It is being said that the Union Army can easily overthrow the Confederacy, they claim we have more wealth, weapons, roads and railways, and a strong navy, while the Southern states are almost bankrupt, and the cotton their only real asset. This is all very true. But I know that in any battle the strongest opponent is the one who truly believes in his cause. The South have strong leaders, and utter conviction that their cause is one of honour, and I believe they will fight to the death to uphold it.

Today I heard that young men are pouring in all over the country to recruit for the Union, just as they are here in Kansas. Few of them are really inspired by glory, the ideals, nor the flags and bugles, only the thirteen dollars a month, and perhaps the adventure. They firmly believe it will all be over in ninety days.

Knowing Southerners as I do, I doubt the rebels can be subdued so quickly. I wonder too how we can hope that our men will remain steadfast to a cause when they experience what war really means, they'll find living conditions far worse than those they left behind in the slums of the cities, the rations poor and death a real possibility.

But enough of this my love, for you do not want to hear such pessimistic thoughts. One certainty has come out of this situation, and that is if I have to fight against my old neighbours and friends, I will never be able to return to Virginia again when this is over. I shall leave the army for good then, and come back to you for always. So pray as I do that it will be a short battle, with few casualties.

I have your picture close to my heart, I kiss it each night and morning. Write soon with all your cheering news of your girls, and tell Sidney I will be back to be godfather to his child as I promised, though I can't say when just yet. I have a feeling young Peter will be desperate to join up, for he is as hot-blooded as I was at the same age. If you cannot persuade him out of it, at least make sure he comes here and joins my regiment, for perhaps then I can try and keep him safe for you.

Remember that I love you, my darling. My body might be here in Kansas and my mind on war, but my heart is with you and will be for ever.

Yours always, James.

Matilda wiped away the tears coursing down her cheeks, folded his letter and tucked it into the bodice of her dress. She bit into her bottom lip to prevent herself crying any more and tried to cheer herself as she had often done before by simply looking at the view from her window.

It was a beautiful May morning, with warm sunshine and the lightest of breezes, and the view of the bay over the rooftops was as beautiful and peaceful as ever, busy with ships and fishing boats. But even as she admired it, she was reminded that everything which was good about this city she'd come to love had only been achieved by long, hard battles to fight the evil within it.

She thought back to the days of the Vigilantes. Sam Brannan, the man who first proclaimed the gold in the American river, had organized a band of men to take the city's lawlessness into their own hands. In the absence of a strong police force, they had targeted the gamblers, arsonists, street ruffians, ballot-box stuffers, crooked politicians and real and suspected criminals. Some they hanged, others got a good beating, and many more were banished from the city. In their heyday of the mid-'50s, they had 4,000 infantrymen armed with muskets and thirty cannons, and they operated with military discipline from Fort Gunnybags, their headquarters in Sacramento Street. Matilda could still vividly recall the excitement in the city in the summer of '56 when the Vigilantes demanded that the authorities should hand over to them two murderers called Cora and Casey, and took them to Fort Gunnybags for trial. They were found guilty and hanged from the second-floor windows.

The Vigilantes had disbanded later that same year. Maybe their organization had been flawed, but they had moved the city out of the old boom-town era, shown the worst of the rascals that their presence would not be tolerated, and created the beginnings of a civilized, real city. Later, in '59, silver strikes in the Comstock Lode brought welcome new prosperity to the city, but there was none of the madness Matilda remembered in the times of the gold.

Yet there was still so much more that needed to be done. Maybe for the vast majority of its citizens San Francisco was becoming a clean and ordered place, with pleasant suburbs, good schools, colleges, theatres and libraries, yet the 'Barbary Coast' and all its obscenities were still thriving. It would remain that way too, for most people turned a blind eye as long as it didn't touch their lives and brought extra revenue to the city.

Sometimes Matilda felt that the task she'd set herself to help girls escape from prostitution, and keep away from it, was like trying to empty a huge bath of water with only a thimble. Over the last five years she and Dolores had been instrumental in getting only five brothel keepers prosecuted for procuring under-age girls. They had rescued a total of thirty-three children, and given temporary care and shelter to over 200 girls. But that was only skimming across the surface of a morass filled with unfortunates they could never reach.

Of the first eight girls to come to Folsom Street, Fern was still with her, acting as housekeeper in a working girls' boarding-house Matilda had founded. Mai Ling had married the owner of a restaurant, Suzy was a maid for a wealthy family in Rincon Hill. Maria and Angelina worked as seamstresses, Dora and Bessie were both in service. All of them dropped in to see Matilda and Dolores from time to time, and offered friendship and encouragement to the new girls they found there.

Ruth was the only casualty of those first few girls. That haunted look had never left her, and shortly after taking a job as a kitchen maid, her body had been washed up on the beach. As the police could find no signs of violence it was believed she had taken her own life.

Of the other girls Matilda had given shelter to, around sixty per cent were still in the same employment she'd found them, thirty per cent had either married, flitted from job to job, become reunited with family, or moved away to another city. She believed that about five per cent of the total number might have been drawn back into prostitution, for she had never seen or heard from them since.

It wasn't possible to keep track of the girls helped by the employment bureau. Unless they returned to her at some stage, they had no real reason to keep in touch. But as they were mostly capable, smart girls who had friends and family she doubted many of them had fallen by the wayside.

The Jennings Bureau made a small profit now, but it was never intended as a money-making scheme anyway. She had found work for over 2,000 girls, and perhaps managed to influence some businessmen into thinking females had equal brainpower to men, and even treating employees fairly. But she couldn't sit back now, war in its way was yet another opportunity, and if she didn't use it, someone else would.

Thinking about this, she got a note-pad and pencil from her desk. What did an army need?

She made a list. Food, weapons, ammunition, uniforms, tents, horses, hospitals and nurses. She frowned at the images the last two threw up. She had no doubt that Tabitha would feel compelled to break off from her studies to nurse. Her desire to be a doctor had always been tempered by the need to help the sick rather than based on personal advancement or glory – in that she was very like her father. Should she write to her now and tell her she must stay at the college?

'You'll do no such thing,' she said aloud. 'She's twenty-one, the same age you were when Lily died, and if she wants to help the wounded, then she should not be prevented.'

Tabitha had gone to England to visit her aunt and uncle when she finished at school. Matilda had held hopes that her relatives might be able to help her get into a university there to take a degree in medicine. But sadly the English medical profession was still firmly against women joining their ranks, and her doctor uncle had recommended she go to the medical college in Ohio because there was no such prejudice there. Yet the trip to England had given Tabitha a great deal, she had got to meet her remaining relatives and discovered a great deal more about her mother as a young girl. It had also made her see she was an American now, and it was to this country that she owed her allegiance.

Matilda looked at her list again. She would go and see Henry Slocum later, he would know how people had to go about getting government contracts, he might even know of any local businessmen putting in tenders. They'd need extra staff, and with so many men rushing off to join up, there would be vacancies women might be able to fill. If she had to wait for James until this war was over, she might as well do something to help with it.

Matilda often regretted that she had always followed Dolores' instructions for avoiding pregnancy. She was thirty-five now, and by the time James came back to her, maybe it would be too late to have a child. Often the girls she and Dolores helped had a baby, and each time she held one in her arms, she yearned desperately for her own. It was a feeling that never went away entirely, just as she would never be free of the pain of losing Amelia.

It was like a tidal wave that came unexpectedly. She would flounder in it, sometimes become so deeply immersed she thought she'd drown. Then it would go away again, and she'd allow herself to think it was gone for good. But it never was.

Dolores always seemed to know when it struck her. She would reach out for her hand and squeeze it, rarely saying anything. Matilda often wondered how Dolores knew these things, but then she was a truly remarkable woman in all ways.

Matilda drove herself up to Rincon Hill later to see Henry. As she left, Treacle jumped up beside her in the gig. He was growing old now, his black fur tinged with grey, and mostly he lay in the sunshine sleeping, but he loved rides in the gig as much as she did. She thought perhaps it was because he remembered their wagon, and it pleased her to think an animal could be nostalgic, just like a human.

Few things had given her as much pleasure as buying the gig. She loved the red and black wheels, the smell of the red leather upholstery, and the sense of freedom it gave her. Star, the chestnut mare, was calm and gentle, yet she liked nothing better than a good fast gallop on a clear road.

Henry's house was an imposing one, double-fronted with pointed gables and five balustraded steps up to the front door. Matilda drove into the drive and ordered Treacle to stay with the gig, and as so often when she came here, she reflected on how odd it was that Henry, the first person to help her in San Francisco, had remained her staunch friend, while Alicia was still as distant.

Alicia seemed content at last, she had her bridge afternoons, and her endless dinner parties, and now and again she stirred herself with some charity work. Even after Henry became a partner in London Lil's, and Alicia benefited from the profits they made, she still couldn't bring herself to admit to having a share in a saloon, and would never dream of inviting Matilda to one of her smart parties. Yet she did collect up parcels of clothing for Matilda's girls, and she did persuade her snobby friends to use the Jennings Bureau when they wanted domestic help. And she didn't mind Matilda calling on her husband.

'It's good to see you, Matty,' Henry said with great warmth as the maid showed her into his study. 'Funny that you should come by today, I was just thinking about you.'

'Something nice I hope,' she laughed. 'With all the talk of war, I could do with a lift.'

'My thoughts of you are always nice ones,' he said gallantly, and complimented her on her pink silk dress and bonnet. 'I don't understand why when all my other friends are growing grey and lined, you seem to have found the secret of eternal youth,' he said.

'You are an old flatterer,' she smiled. She didn't know how old Henry was, but she guessed he must be sixty, and his once dark beard and the frill of hair around his bald head had gone snow-white in the past few years. He was very fat now, like a round barrel, but his mind was as sharp as ever. 'But I'll get straight to the point about why I called. I want to discuss government contracts for the war.'

He laughed, and offered her a seat. 'Surely you aren't thinking of moving into gun-running!'

Matilda told him what she'd been thinking about. 'I just want to steal a march on others,' she admitted. 'It struck me that uniforms must be required, and foodstuffs too. I want jobs for my girls.'

Henry said he thought the uniforms would all be made in the East, and he doubted it would be practical to supply food owing to the vast distance. 'But I'll keep my nose to the ground, and there will be vacancies with so many men enlisting,' he said, then went on to ask about James.

One of the most comforting things about her friendship with Henry was that he truly cared about her happiness. In their early years as partners he had introduced her to many men he hoped would be prospective husbands. He had given that up once he saw James was the man she wanted, and perhaps because of his own loveless marriage, he sincerely hoped that one day they'd find permanent happiness together.

Matilda told him about James's letter and confided his dilemma at being forced to fight against his own people.

'There will be many in his position, I fear,' Henry said with a sigh. 'I come from the South too, remember, my loyalties are divided as well.'

'Surely you don't approve of slavery, Henry?' she said in horror.

He shrugged. 'I was brought up to it, Matty. Our slaves were treated well, I had a black mammy, played with slave children. It isn't all like *Uncle Tom's Cabin*, you know, Harriet Beecher Stowe has a great deal to answer for in painting such a slanted picture. I wonder what will happen to the slaves when they are all set free – few have any experience of anything but growing cotton.'

'People can learn other trades,' Matilda said indignantly.

'But you are forgetting how many there are of them.' Henry shrugged. 'If they all rush to the cities, who will feed them, and give them somewhere to live? Many will die of cold if they go up North, white men will be fearful that they will become cheap labour. I can see so many problems ahead. Lincoln himself doesn't have the answers.'

'So will you be involved in gun-running to the South?' Matilda sniped.

'No, I won't,' he said quietly. 'Not to North or South. I'll sit on the fence and watch the two sides fight it out. Later, when it is over, I guess I'll be one of those who tries to put the country back together again.'

Matilda felt a little chastened, his voice was one of reason. 'I'm sorry, Henry, I don't know why I'm getting so worked up, it's not my fight either.'

'It doesn't have to be,' he said, leaning forward and putting one hand on her arm. 'There will be enough hot-heads without us joining them. I heard today that my three nephews have rushed to enlist down in Georgia. They will be in my prayers, along with James, and Peter too if he joins. Meanwhile people like you and me, Matty, have to keep the wheels turning here.'

After leaving Henry's house, Matilda went straight down to Folsom Street, taking a box of clothes Alicia had given her.

As she walked in through the front door she heard Dolores raging in the kitchen.

'I don't care if your breasts are sore,' she shouted. 'That babby needs milk or he will die. Stop whining, girl, and go and get him.'

Over the years, many girls had come to them pregnant, and their babies were born in the house. It was always very difficult to find such girls jobs, usually they ended up answering advertisements from widowed farmers out in the territories. Yet many of these arranged marriages had worked well, as for most of the girls a home and a husband was all they wanted.

But Matilda had known from the first time she met Polly, the girl Dolores was shouting at, that she was trouble, She could see it in her calculating blue eyes and, her insolent stance, and hear it in her whining voice. Yet she couldn't turn her away.

Fern had found her late one night crouched down in a doorway, heavily pregnant. She was just fourteen, and she'd turned to prostitution when she'd been thrown out of her job as kitchen maid because her mistress found she was pregnant. She had been living on the streets since March, she was filthy, lousy, half starved, and Dolores believed she had the pox. Her belly was huge, her legs and arms like sticks, and her eyes sunken into her head. Dolores had to cut off her hair because it was too matted to get at the lice. She looked worse than any of the children in Five Points.

Matilda walked into the kitchen to find Polly slouched in a chair. Dolores was standing over her, so angry that the veins in her forehead were all popping out.

Polly's baby had been born eight days ago. Dolores delivered him and even gave up her own bed so the new mother could have peace and quiet for the laying in. Polly called him Abraham, after the President, and one of the other girls, laughing, said it was a good name, as he was as long, thin and ugly as Lincoln. He was around six pounds at birth, but he looked sickly, and clearly this was why Dolores was so angry now.

Matilda had hoped that she was wrong about Polly, but unfortunately she'd turned out to be far worse than any other girl they'd ever had under their roof. She resented being asked to do anything, she insulted all the Negro girls, and kept boasting that back home in Indiana her father owned the biggest farm for 300 miles. She stole hair ribbons and other of the girls' little treasures, and wouldn't accept any of the rules of the house. Dolores said she slipped out one night and came home later with two dollars, which she must have got from a man.

She didn't look pitiful now, three months after her arrival. Her blonde hair was growing again, she had a rosy bloom to her skin, and her limbs had filled out. In a blue print dress she looked well cared for and pretty.

'I'll get baby,' Matilda said, hoping to calm everything down. She remembered her own breasts had been very sore at first, and she had heard since that most fair-skinned women reacted this way.

Abraham wasn't crying, just lying there quietly, and she knew it was this passive silence which worried Dolores more than anything. She picked him up and found his napkin, night-gown and the bedding beneath him were sodden. Clearly he hadn't been changed all day, even though there was a pile of clean napkins and gowns on the dresser.

Matilda took him through to the kitchen, laid him on a towel on the table, and quickly stripped him. His tiny bottom was fiery red.

'When did you last change him?' she asked Polly.

'Not an hour since,' Polly said sulkily.

'That's a lie,' Matilda said, trying not to get angry herself. 'His bottom is red and sore. I don't believe you have changed him once today. Now, this won't do, Polly. Babies are helpless, and he's too small yet to even cry loud enough to tell you how uncomfortable he is.'

'Why don't one of the niggers see to him then?'

Matilda rounded on her. 'We don't use that hateful word in this house,' she said. 'The other girls in this house are guests, just like you, they are not here to look after you, or your baby. And if you can't show some respect for me, Miss Dolores and the other girls, then you'll be off to the poor-house.'

Dolores was rolling her eyes. Her expression said, 'Let her go there now. I've had enough of her.'

Matilda put some ointment on the baby's bottom, making Polly stand up so she could see how it was done, and then put a clean napkin and gown on him. 'Now you'll feed him,' she said, handing him over.

'I can't, it hurts,' she insisted.

'There's a great deal that hurts about motherhood,' Matilda said crisply. 'Now, sit down and feed him, stop thinking about yourself.'

As Polly unbuttoned her dress, Matilda could see her nipples were a bit sore, but not so bad she couldn't manage five minutes on each breast. She informed Polly of this, and went back into the front room to change the linen on the crib. As she bent down to pick something off the floor, she saw Polly had thrown bloody pads under the bed, and the chamber-pot was almost full.

Such slutty ways infuriated her, but she decided to wait until the baby was fed before saying anything, and returned to the kitchen. She noted that Polly barely looked at her baby as she fed him, her eyes were staring off into the distance, cold and indifferent.

Dolores made them all some tea, and after the baby was fed, Matilda took him and explained to Polly she must wash and dry her nipples, then put some ointment on each of them after each feed. 'Now go into your room, collect up those pads and the chamber-pot and deal with them,' she said. 'Fatal diseases are spread by filth. I won't have it in this house.'

'But she's the maid, ain't she?' Polly pointed to Dolores. 'She does all that.'

Matilda's temper flared up. 'Miss Dolores is the housekeeper here. She may have emptied your pot and cleaned away other things when you were too weak to do it yourself, but you are quite capable of looking after yourself now. So do it!'

Polly reluctantly did as she was told. Matilda cuddled the baby till he'd gone back to sleep and then went and tucked him into the crib. As she came back into the kitchen, Polly was slouched down in the chair again and clearly had every intention of staying there.

The success of this house depended on all the girls pulling their weight. Matilda certainly didn't expect Polly to scrub floors so soon after having a baby, but she was perfectly capable of doing a little mending or peeling potatoes for supper.

'This won't do, Polly,' Matilda said, as Dolores busied herself with some washing up in the scullery. 'You were in a bad way when Fern brought you here, if she hadn't, you might have died out there on the streets. So tell me why you seem to be going out of your way to be difficult with everyone.'

It was unfortunate that the other five girls in the house all chose that moment to arrive home from a walk. Hearing her voice they halted in the hall, not knowing quite what to do.

''Cos you all thinks you are better than me,' Polly retorted, pale blue eyes as cold as ice. 'Look at you fer a start, all done up in silk. What do you know about having a baby all on your own, or having no money? I've heard all about you on the streets, a heart like a stone they say, and you makes money out of girls like me.'

Matilda knew the last part of the charge against her was a rumour put about by brothel owners to deter girls going to her. She didn't care about that. But the first part really riled her.

'I know a great deal about having a baby all on my own,' she said, suddenly not caring that the other girls would hear her. 'I had mine on a wagon train, and when the baby was as young as Abraham I went down the Columbia river in a canoe with her. I didn't have a kind person like Dolores to take care of me. I had to sleep in a tent in the rain, to try and dry napkins somehow. My nipples were much sorer than yours too. But I still fed her, whenever she needed it.'

'I suppose she's off in some fancy boarding-school now,' Polly sneered.

'I wish she were,' Matilda said, her blood rising. 'She's dead, Polly. She died of cholera, along with my best friend and her little girl too. She was just six and there's not a day passes when I don't grieve for her.'

There was a gasp from the hallway, and Dolores moved across the kitchen to shoo the girls upstairs.

'You are a little gutter-snipe,' Matilda went on, her voice gradually rising with anger. 'A rude, ungrateful, dirty wretch. But I'll tell you one thing, I'm going to turn you into a real mother, and a decent human being, however long it takes me. My friend who died was a prostitute too when I first met her. I found her in a New York cellar full of rats with her new baby. She was far worse off than you, but once she was given a chance she took it, and made something of herself. The night she died she made me promise I would help other girls like her. That's why I started this house, for her. Because I loved her.'

'So!' Polly spat out. 'You make a fair packet out of it. I don't see you giving anything away. You ride round in your fancy cart and you've got that boy running your messages.'

The implication that Peter was some sort of paramour riled Matilda even more. 'That boy is my friend's son, the baby born in a cellar. Along with promising my friend to care for girls like you, I also promised to take care of him. You don't know anything about my life, you wretch, but I can tell you I've had just as much hardship as you. So, I wear a silk dress and have a fancy carriage, but then I used my brains to earn the money for it. Any woman can sell her body, that doesn't take brain or skill, all you have to do is open your legs and take the money. Maybe you had no choice once you were on the street, but you have a choice now.'

She paused, panting with rage.

'What is it to be, the poor-house and back on the street? Or buckle down here and fit in with everyone else?'

'I can't stand the niggers,' Polly said defiantly.

That was the last straw and Matilda smacked her hard across the face. 'You aren't fit to walk in their shadow,' she roared out. 'God gave them black skin because they come from a hot country where they need protection from the sun, inside they are just the same as you or me. But they have one thing you don't have, and that's a mind, because each one of them wants a better life than the one they were born to. Now get back to your room. I don't suppose any of them want to be near you either. I shall be back tomorrow morning, and God help you if I haven't found some improvement in your attitude.'

The girl ran out, a look of terror on her face. All at once Matilda's anger left her, leaving nothing but shame she'd reacted so violently. She slumped down on a chair, put her head on the table and burst into tears.

She didn't hear Dolores come back in, just felt a warm hand on the back of her neck. 'Don't cry about her, she's just trash,' Dolores said softly.

'No she's not,' Matilda sniffed. 'She's just a kid who's been brought up all wrong. She doesn't know about love because no one's ever given her any.'

'You's got too much love sometimes.' Dolores pulled Matilda

round and cradled her against her bony chest. 'Some people they just born bad. You can't fight that.'

'I've got to try,' Matilda sobbed. 'I shouldn't have smacked her.'

'Sometimes a kiss will do it, sometimes a smack does, either way you done your best. I don't reckon you'll crack that one, she's too tough. But I loves you for tryin'.'

Matilda looked up, and for the first time noticed that Dolores was turning into an old woman. Her crinkly hair was streaked with white, she had lines on her face. It shocked her, and reminded her that in all the time they'd been together, for all the things they'd shared, she still knew so little about her friend, not even her exact age.

'I've never even asked you if you want to be here,' she said, all at once ashamed that she had never really considered what Dolores might want. All she ever did was make plans and expect that Dolores would go along with them. 'You aren't so young any more, and this place must be too much for you. But I could get someone else to run it, and you could come back to my apartment and have an easier time.'

Dolores gave a rich belly laugh. 'What would I do with myself up there now?' she said. 'These girls is like the children I never had. Only way you's gonna get me outta here is when the good Lord comes a-callin' for me.'

'Even when some of them are nasty like Polly?'

'You buy a dozen eggs and one is broken,' Dolores said with a resigned sigh. 'But you can still use that broken one if you's quick. Maybe you gotta whip it up some, but you sure as hell don't throw it out.'

'Reckon I whipped her up enough?' Matilda whispered.

'Maybe, time will tell. Now, you dry those pretty eyes and go and see the other girls. Reckon what they heard you say will be all around town by tomorrow, it won't do your reputation much good when folk hear you've got a heart after all.'

Matilda laughed. The legend of her being hard was one she enjoyed. It was a darn sight better than being taken for a sucker.

Matilda failed with Polly. Just two weeks later, while Dolores was out, the girl slipped out of the house in Folsom Street taking the housekeeping money Dolores kept in a tin with her, and leaving Abraham behind. Two days later, they received a report she had been seen boarding a stage-coach to Denver. Matilda guessed she was intending to try her luck in the brothels there. Although she was saddened by the failure, she wasn't really surprised. Polly had a heart of stone.

It was tough having to make the decision to turn Abraham over to the Foundling Home, but as Dolores pointed out, 'We ain't in the business of minding babies, Miz Matilda. And I ain't gonna stand by and watch you git attached to him. You've got to be ready to have babies of your own when Captain James comes home!'

It was that thought alone which gave her a shred of comfort when she woke one morning to find Peter had gone too, leaving her a note to say he was going out to Kansas to join James's regiment. 'Don't worry about me, Aunt Matty,' he wrote almost as an afterthought. 'James and me will lick the rebels and be back in no time.'

A year later, on Sunday, 6 April 1862, James was woken by bright sunshine coming into his tent, checked his watch and found it was just after six. He had been here, with 42,000 troops under General U. S. Grant, in wooded ravines on the west side of the Tennessee river near Pittsburg Landing for almost a month, waiting for General Buell and his Army of the Ohio to join them. The plan was to plunge into the heart of Mississippi, routing out the rebels.

Not for the first time James wished he'd chosen some other career than soldiering. Here he was in the middle of a war, dying to get on with it and then go home, but instead he had to wait upon decisions from generals who seemed more preoccupied with their image and convoluted strategy than getting out in the field and fighting. Eight out of ten of his men were green farmers' boys and he suspected that however hard he trained them they would never acquire the killer instinct of real soldiers. He was very glad he hadn't been at the first humiliating defeat at Bull Run. When he'd heard it described as the 'Greatest Skedaddle', he'd blushed with shame that the Union men had run from battle. It was no wonder Confederates were laughing up their sleeves at them.

At least back in Kansas he'd felt a sense of real purpose.

Civilians had to be protected, and those murderous Missourian ruffians who burned their cabins and laid waste their crops, all in the name of secession for their state, had to be hunted down and punished. Under Brigadier General Nathaniel Lyon, a fearless man he much admired, he'd seen the kind of action he believed in. But even that had ended in failure, they had chased those men over 200 miles across Missouri to Wilson Creek, only for Lyon to be killed and the Union army driven back to St Louis.

Now he was here in Tennessee just waiting, while the rebels were just twenty-two miles away in Corinth. While the generals argued among themselves and kept stalling, the Confederates gained time to enlist more men, organize themselves better, and became more confident.

It was rumoured that even Lincoln himself had written to General Buell, saying that 'Delay is ruining us.' In some regiments the men drank and fought among themselves, many had run off home believing their wives, children and farms needed them far more than their country. James couldn't blame them either, there had been times when he'd looked longingly westwards.

But perhaps now that General Grant appeared to be running the show, things would move. Grant had already won two important victories, at Fort Henry on the Tennessee and Fort Donelson on the Cumberland. Within a week he'd won Nashville and the Confederates had been forced out of Kentucky.

James picked up the letter to Matilda he'd begun writing the night before and read it through. She was with him always, in his head. He went to sleep thinking of her, woke to find she was the first thing which popped into his mind. He often wondered if other men loved as deeply as he did. It was loving her which kept him sane and gave him purpose. He could while away long hours in the saddle imagining how and where they would live when the war was over. His plan was to buy a farm somewhere in California where he could breed horses, nothing fancy, just a nice comfortable house with a big shady veranda, an English-style garden for her, complete with rose beds, and paddocks beyond. He hoped it wouldn't be too late for children of their own, but if it was, maybe they'd adopt some. He liked to imagine Sidney, Peter and Tabitha coming for holidays, later on bringing their husbands, wives and children. He thought he would get hold of an old covered wagon and make it into a play-house. The children would love it, and sometimes he'd take Matty out to it and make love to her there, under that old patchwork quilt she had which meant so much to her.

He pulled himself up sharply and tucked the letter away, remembering he had to go out and see his men. Many of them were suffering from dysentery, or, as they liked to call it 'The Tennessee two-step'. He paused by his tent, heartened by the sight in front of him. It had rained earlier, and the now bright sunshine was glinting on the trees surrounding the camp like thousands of diamonds. A smell of fresh coffee wafted to his nostrils, and the men were all busy either cleaning and polishing their muskets, or brushing their jackets. It was just like it was a Sunday back home.

He wondered if the rebels were similarly occupied. Their commander, Albert Johnston, was in James's opinion the ablest soldier in the Confederacy. If he were in Johnston's boots, he'd launch an attack now, before Buell's troops arrived to swell the Union's numbers. He'd voiced this opinion only yesterday to General Grant, but it had fallen on deaf ears.

James spotted Peter Duncan across the camp, sitting on a log, polishing his boots. His cap was pushed back on his head, and he was engrossed in his task. Peter had turned up unannounced at Fort Leavenworth last summer on a mail coach, his young, fresh face so full of eagerness that James hadn't the heart to take him to task for slipping off without saying a proper goodbye to his aunt.

It was fortunate that James had just arrived back from Missouri. If he hadn't been there, Peter could very well have been marched off immediately with the rest of the raw recruits to Tennessee and the battle at Fort Henry, and been killed, even before Matilda knew where he was. But as it was, James was able to take him under his wing and give him some basic training and a taste of combat in Missouri before the march down here.

James couldn't be seen to be singling the lad out for special treatment, but Peter expected none, nor had he told anyone of his connection with the Captain. James thought he had the makings of a fine soldier. He didn't complain, he was a crack shot, and popular with the other men. James just hoped he could stand up to heavy fire, for he hadn't been tested in that yet.

At half past nine the peace and tranquillity of the camp was shattered by gunfire and that distinctive rebel yell, half-shout, half-foxhound frenzied yelp. James had heard it many times before, but he still found it sent a curious tingling sensation down his spine. As the men rushed to pick up their weapons, fasten buttons and even put boots on, James felt some pleasure in knowing he had second-guessed General Johnston, and that they would now see some action, but angry that he'd been ignored by his own general who surely should have received some warning the Confederates had marched out of Corinth overnight.

As the ripping, roaring sound of gunfire and cannons came ever closer, James leaped on to his horse and led his men to thickets that grew along a winding sunken road. The rebels would reach it before long, and if he and his men could just hold their position there until the reinforcements arrived, they had a chance.

The rebels came much sooner than he expected, a bad sign as it meant the troops further down the line hadn't been able to hold them. A Union cannon fired on them and three men fell, but the rest just stepped right over them, blasting away to left and right with their rifles.

'Hold your fire till they're right up to us,' James urged his men lying shoulder to shoulder in the undergrowth. 'It's just like shootin' squirrels,' he added for the benefit of the many who had never faced a human target before.

He could see how scared many of his men were, but he hoped he'd trained them well enough not to run when things got tough. The rebels' aim would be to force them back to the river, and if they succeeded they'd slaughter them all there. He had to hold this road, at least until he received further orders from Grant.

Cannon fired again, blasting trees and even rocks, and now the rebels were close enough to fire on. James galloped down the line, firing through the bushes as he went, galvanizing his men into action.

The rebels were falling thick and fast, but still more came from up behind. His men were shooting well, holding their position, and James checked quickly to see where Peter was.

It was a relief to see he'd found a better spot than most, with a fallen tree in front of him for protection, and two regular soldiers either side of him. He was shooting like a seasoned professional, but as he turned on his side to reload, and saw James behind him, he grinned wickedly.

'Keep your head down, Private,' James ordered him, then levelled his pistol at some stragglers who were breaking through the bushes towards Peter and shot them in quick succession before riding on.

It was the worst and bloodiest battle James had ever been engaged in. Again and again as he rode along, he swiped out with his sabre as rebels who had made it through the lines tried to unhorse him. But more kept coming, relentlessly, like maddened demons, and the roar of cannon and dropping shells was so loud he couldn't even hear his own shouted commands or the crack of his pistol.

He left his men later to go and reconnoitre what was going on in a peach orchard nearby where he could hear even heavier fighting. He saw Union men lying flat on their bellies, firing as the rebels came that way, a snow-storm of soft pink petals floating down on both the living and the dead.

Later he was to hear from another officer that many of the men under his command had fled in terror. James blanched, but pointed out that he'd seen Confederates running too.

Later that afternoon as James and his men still clung tenaciously to their fragile position, they heard that Johnston, the rebel leader, had been killed and command had passed to Beauregard. Yet James could take no pleasure in that, Johnston was a good man.

Darkness finally fell, but although James's men and others along the sunken road on into a place they christened the Hornets' Nest had held their position, the rest of the army had fallen back two miles. When morning came they would surely be defeated. Word got to them that some 5,000 of their men were cowering down by the bluff at the river's edge, some had even tried to swim the river to safety.

Peter was unhurt, but badly shaken by the day's events. When James last saw him that evening he was writing a letter for an illiterate comrade, his hands trembling so badly he could barely hold his pencil. He gave James a tentative smile, then bent his head over the letter as if he feared James might see fear in his eyes and despise him.

James despised himself at that moment, wishing he'd never filled the lad's head with tales of valour in battle. Perhaps then Peter would be safe in a university somewhere, forging a career for himself that was about life, not death. Just outside the camp, wounded men lay among the dead, calling out for help, but there was no system in place for gathering or caring for them in the field. He had never felt so impotent.

It began to rain later, and wounded men who had been crying out for water were suddenly silenced.

'Reckon God heard their pleas,' someone in the camp called out, and this was followed by a burst of embarrassed laughter. When lightning flashed later, James saw wild hogs feeding on the dead.

He lay down under a tree to try to get a couple of hours' sleep, covered his ears to block out the screams of the wounded, and tried to imagine that he was riding along the beach at Santa Cruz with Matilda, and that the only sound he could hear was the sea. He thought he heard a bugle call in the distance, but told himself that was fantasy too.

But the bugle wasn't imaginary, it was Buell's Army of the Ohio arriving with 25,000 reinforcements.

'We licked them after all, sir,' Peter said, grinning up at James the following evening.

With the fresh troops they had attacked the rebels at dawn. During the day they had seen the rebels fall back twice, only to counter-attack, but finally in the late afternoon they had retreated to Corinth, firing as they went.

James looked down from his horse and smiled at Peter. He wanted to jump down and hug the lad, for his face was black with gunpowder, eyes shining with the light of victory. He had the singe of a bullet through the top of his cap, and mud up to his waist. Time and time again today James had seen Peter boldly standing alone, firing relentlessly with no thought to his personal safety. Another time he'd seen him walking backwards, dragging another wounded man to shelter, firing as he went. He had proved himself to be a man today, but in James's eyes he was still very much the child Matilda loved. But though another enlisted man could hug a comrade, as the boy's captain he had to remain aloof in the sight of others.

'Yes, we licked them,' James agreed. 'And you fought well and bravely, Private Duncan. I'm so very proud to have you under my command.'

'What now, sir?' Peter asked, reaching up to stroke James's horse. 'Do we go after them?'

James sighed. Peter was a true soldier, his blood was up and he wanted more. He'd been just the same once, yet now he'd gladly walk away from it.

'We have the worst task ahead of us yet,' he said gently. 'The dead have to be buried. Not just our men either, but theirs too.'

The ground was littered with corpses. James had walked around the battle-grounds earlier and sometimes it was difficult to put his foot down on solid earth. The pond in the cherry orchard was red with the blood of the wounded who had crawled to drink there. There was the terrible job of searching through men's pockets for trinkets and letters to be sent home to their loved ones. Then the burials.

Peter sighed. James knew why, he wanted more fighting.

For just one moment James was tempted to remind the boy that he had to keep safe for Matty because she surely couldn't bear any further tragedy in her life. But just as he couldn't hug the boy, so they couldn't speak openly of the ties that bound them together.

'They are going to call this the Battle of Shiloh,' James said instead, reaching down and affectionately straightening the boy's cap. 'Did you see that little whitewashed church some of the men fought by?'

Peter nodded.

'That's what it is called, "Shiloh". It's a Hebrew word and it means a place of peace. Let's hope all the men we have to bury here will find it.'

Chapter Twenty-five

1863

'Water,' Private Newton croaked out as Matilda passed his bed.

'Of course,' she said, going over to his side. This young soldier had a very bad head wound, and as she slid her hand gently under his neck to lift him enough so he could drink from the glass, she saw the bandage and pillow were soaked through with blood again.

'Slowly,' she warned him as he gulped at the water. 'Not too much at one time.'

He was no more than seventeen at most, but so many boys had lied about their age to enlist. A pretty boy with soft brown eyes, framed by thick dark lashes, and what little hair showed beneath his bandages was blond and curly. But he had a deathly pallor and she knew he wasn't going to last the day.

'Would you like me to write to your mother for you?' she asked. 'I've got a moment now if you feel up to telling me what you want to say to her.'

The expression in his eyes was one of gratitude, but anxiety because he knew that by the time the letter reached home he would be dead.

'Just tell her I did the best I could,' he said weakly. 'Say my brothers must take my place now, and be good to her.'

Matilda took out a pad of paper and pencil from her apron pocket and hurriedly wrote down his words. She would add her own message later, telling his mother what a fine soldier he had been and how bravely he died. Each time she wrote one of these letters for someone, she hoped and prayed that if James, Peter or Sidney was lying in a hospital bed somewhere, another nurse like her would take time to jot down their last messages.

'Shall I tell her you love her?' she whispered, squeezing the hand that had reached out for hers.

'Yes,' he whispered, a tear trickling down his cheek. 'Say I'm not in any pain too, I don't want her to fret.'

Matilda couldn't count the number of men who had told their family back home that gallant lie. War was hideous in its destruction and cruelty, yet it threw up the best and bravest of emotions.

Matilda would never have thought of becoming a nurse but for Tabitha. She had arrived here at The Lodge hospital in Washington last November, seven months ago.

Almost as soon as the war got under way, London Lil's became very quiet as the young men rushed off to enlist, and it also became much harder to find entertainers as they disappeared off to the busier Eastern cities. Matilda kept herself busy with the agency and her girls in Folsom Street, but after the Battle of Shiloh, James was promoted to brigadier, and Peter to corporal, and she knew that nothing short of serious injury was going to bring them back before the end of the war.

Then the draft came in, and Sidney, Albert and her other barmen all had to go, so Matilda shut London Lil's down. Sidney and Mary's baby, Elizabeth Rose, was a year old at that time, and as Mary was expecting a second child, Matilda got them to move into the upstairs apartment with her for the company and to save on expenses.

But Matilda was fidgety. The days were long enough, but the evenings without the saloon open seemed interminable. She felt cut off from the rest of the country, for apart from fund-raising rallies, and the sudden departure of so many young men because of the draft, San Francisco was scarcely touched by the war. She wanted something useful and interesting to do, but she didn't know what.

Then out of the blue came the telegraph message from Tabitha begging her to join her in Washington to nurse.

Her first reaction was one of horror. She didn't believe she had the stomach for that kind of war work. But once she sat down and thought about it, the idea began to develop some appeal. It would be wonderful to see Tabitha again, and she might even get to see James, Peter and Sidney too. In a moment of pure recklessness, she sent a return telegraph message and said she was on her way.

Once she'd sent it, doubts set in. Could she really nurse the wounded? Wasn't she too old and set in her ways to start taking orders from others? But she was sure Tabitha must have had excellent reasons for asking her to go. Dolores would look after the girls, and Mary and her children, with Fern's help. And she had a reliable and trustworthy woman already running the Jennings Bureau. She wasn't needed here.

It wasn't until she arrived in Washington that she discovered the reason behind Tabitha's request. All Union hospitals were organized by the Federal Sanitary Commission, but Dorothea Dix, the woman in charge of all the nurses, who was greatly influenced by Florence Nightingale's nursing out in the Crimea, would accept no women under thirty, for fear younger ones might be looking for romance.

Tabitha was frantic to use her medical knowledge to ease the suffering of the thousands of casualties, but knowing the Commission would turn her down when they saw her age was only twenty-two on her application, she went straight to Washington to see Miss Dix personally. Perhaps the indomitable woman who had claimed 'all nurses should be plain looking', found Tabitha plain enough, or maybe she was wise enough to recognize that a girl prepared to postpone her medical studies until the war was over was dedicated, for she didn't dismiss her out of hand. She said she would be prepared to take Tabitha, if she could find another older woman to join her and act as her chaperone.

Once Matilda was on the stage-coach heading across the mountains, she felt exhilarated rather than fearful. She was looking forward to being back in the mainstream again, to talking to people who could give her more insight into how the war was progressing, and hearing their opinions on it, for she knew James and Peter held a great deal back in their letters.

But by the time she had alighted from the first of the trains which would take her across to the east coast, she was dismayed by the views of her fellow passengers. A few were fiercely patriotic, most showed great sympathy for the bereaved, but the vast majority, whether from the North or the South, proved themselves to be alarmingly against the abolition of slavery.

She spoke to avid supporters of the Union who were horrified that freed and runaway slaves were flocking to the army and to the North to find shelter. When she asked what their solution to this problem was, they said they should stay on the plantations where they belonged. She spoke to a Southerner from Charleston who was furious that the Union were enlisting Negroes to fight his people. 'It ain't never right for a nigger to be given a gun to shoot fight white folk,' was how he put it.

She heard too that the Indians were making the most of the absence of the army in the West by raiding trains, ambushing wagons of supplies and killing settlers. It was generally thought that they should be forcefully suppressed, then herded into reservations.

Matilda wondered how people who were themselves born in other countries had the cheek to wish to sweep their adopted country clear of its native people. They seemed to have entirely forgotten that but for Indians helping the first settlers to cross America, it would still be a wilderness.

But when a discussion came up about the draft amongst a group of wealthy people she found herself travelling with, she was incensed to hear them boast openly that they'd paid for their sons to be excused enlistment. She thought this was the most dishonourable thing she'd ever heard of and said so, loudly. She wondered how the country could get back on its feet when the war was over, when the brave and loyal had died for a cause few truly believed in, and the fate of its future was left to carpet-baggers, cowards and bigots.

Private Newton died a few minutes after she'd held the letter to his mother for him to sign it. She closed his eyes, folded his arms across his chest, and pinned the tips of his socks together, in the manner she'd been taught to lay out the dead. But she kissed his cheek too, not caring that Miss Dix would regard such an act as unprofessional. As she walked away to order a stretcher, her mind slipped back to the day she arrived in Washington.

It was a grey, damp November day, but she was so eager, so excited to be in Washington at last, that she leaned out of the window as the train chugged into the station. The billowing smoke and steam obscured the view for a minute or two, but even over the noise of grating wheels on rails, she could hear hundreds of voices.

As the smoke cleared, she saw a sea of blue-uniformed men on stretchers, on crutches, many of them with missing limbs, patches over a missing eye, slings and bandages, every pale face turned towards the train. Her legs turned to jelly and a cold, tingling sensation crept up and down her spine, for if these men were well enough to be transported somewhere, what would the ones back at the hospital be like? She pulled her cape tighter round her, jammed her plain bonnet more firmly on her head, and taking a deep breath, picked up the one small bag she'd brought with her and stepped down from the train.

The scene was far worse on a level with the men. She could see blood staining bandages, livid, unhealed scars on faces, and empty sockets where an eye should be. One young boy on a stretcher held out his hand to her, perhaps in his pain he thought she was his mother.

It was so frightening and overwhelming. Reading about casualties in the newspapers hadn't prepared her for seeing so many of them in the flesh. But then Tabitha called out her name and came dodging through the men to greet her, and it was too late to back away.

'Oh Matty,' Tabitha exclaimed, before enveloping her in the tightest, warmest hug. 'I can't tell you how proud I was of you when I got the telegraph saying you were on your way. I'd been on tenterhooks for so long, sure you'd refuse.'

The terror inside Matilda abated as Tabitha held her. She told herself that if she could drive a wagon over 2,000 miles, nurse her own child dying of cholera, and run a saloon, she could dress wounds and soothe the dying.

'When could I ever refuse you anything?' she managed to say. All at once she knew she must try to match Tabitha's courage and enter into nursing wholeheartedly.

Somehow the stark horror of the injured all around them highlighted what she felt for Tabitha. She had loved her from a tiny child; some of the happiest hours in her entire life, and some of the most traumatic ones, had been spent with her. And by being with her now she felt she could draw on the strengths of both Lily and Giles, which Tabitha had in abundance.

Tabitha didn't seem the least fazed by the men all around her, she could have just been standing in a busy market. 'I've got us lodgings,' she said, picking up Matilda's bag with one hand and tucking the other through her arm. 'They aren't very nice I'm afraid, but folk around here aren't very kind to those who work at the hospital. I suppose they think we'll bring infections back with us.'

She said so much in those first few minutes that much of it was a jumble to Matilda. All she really took in was that they were to be on A1, the ward where the most seriously wounded men were taken, Tabitha because of her medical knowledge and Matilda because of her maturity.

It was only once they were away from the crowds that Matilda stopped Tabitha. 'I want to get a good look at you before we go any further.'

Tabitha giggled. 'I don't look any different to when you last saw me in Ohio.'

'That's for me to decide,' Matilda said. 'I've missed so many years of you growing into a young woman, I'm entitled to study you carefully now.'

She was taller than Matilda by a couple of inches, and thinner than she had been back in Ohio. Her plain brown unhooped dress, the regulations Miss Dix insisted on for her nurses, made her skin look sallow, and her severe hair-style, parted in the middle and plaited into two coils over her ears did nothing to flatter her. Yet those mournful dark eyes which even as a small child had always dominated her face were so expressive and beautiful.

'What you see outwardly isn't important,' Tabitha replied with a touch of indignation. 'I hope you hadn't expected me to turn into a beauty, I'll never be that.'

'Tabby, my love,' Matilda laughed, 'you will always be beautiful to me. Just that you are here and wanted to nurse wounded men so badly is enough for me to know I was a good nursemaid. But I'm not so sure I'll be a good nurse.'

As Matilda walked out of the ward she saw Tabitha at the last bed, bent over, washing the stump of an amputated leg. Such sights no longer distressed either of them, they were ordinary duties they performed day after day. But seven months ago, on that first terrifying day on the wards of The Lodge hospital, such a sight made them avert their eyes and clamp their hands over their mouths in nausea.

Matilda still had the sights, smells and sounds of that day firmly locked in her mind, the disgusting stench of putrefying flesh, blood in pools on the floor, the screams of men in agony. That day alone there had been over twenty deaths. Suddenly she was seeing the real face of war, brave young men crying for their mothers as the surgeon hacked off their leg or arm with a saw. Men with their guts spilling out beneath dirty bandages, pools of blood and vomit, pus, and wounds so putrid they almost defied cleaning.

She remembered how on their first night together in their lodgings Tabitha had raged about a doctor who had dropped a surgical instrument on the filthy floor, wiped it on his already blood-soaked gown, then delved into the patient again. She couldn't believe from what she'd learnt so far in her medical studies, that all the wounded got here before major surgery was a few drops of ether to calm them. She kept saying it was as barbaric as the Middle Ages, and they had to do something to make people realize how bad it was here.

But in the weeks that followed they came to see that the nurses and doctors did the best they could for their patients, despite grave shortages of medicine, bandages and linen. They learned too that it was the brutal field hospitals to which the men were taken first which were responsible for the worst of the horror. There men bled to death for lack of a tourniquet, they were left for so long on the ground that flies laid eggs in undressed wounds, and limbs were often cut off rather than precious time being spent on removing bullets. They heard how some soldiers kept a gun beneath their pillow, to warn off butcher doctors intent on amputation.

There were sixteen hospitals in Washington, but only a few had been purpose-built, the rest, like The Lodge, were just ageing, empty buildings pressed into service. The tin roof at The Lodge leaked, many of the broken windows were boarded over, the old floors were bare planks and impossible to keep clean, in the cold weather it couldn't be heated adequately. Even sixteen hospitals weren't enough, some casualties were cared for in the Senate House and chambers, even in Georgetown jail.

They got used to the long hours, the hard work, the smells, the screams of pain, and the ravings of the delirious. They learned to eat the disgusting hospital food and put up with their cramped, cheerless room, but it was the feeling of helplessness that affected them and all the other nurses the most. Even the most tender care couldn't save many of their patients, all they could do was make their last hours as comfortable as possible. But as fast as one man died, and his corpse was removed, so another man was moved into the bed. Sometimes they lived for such a short time the nurses never even got a chance to speak to them, let alone soothe them in their last moments.

Sometimes when Matilda and Tabitha left the hospital in the early evening, they had to stop and sit down somewhere, just to breathe in some fresh air and take a rest before they had the strength to walk home after a twelve-hour shift. It was only when they were in bed together, in the tiny airless room of the house they boarded at, that they talked. They would reminisce about Tabitha's childhood, Primrose Hill, the voyage to America, the times in New York and Missouri. It was the happy times they reflected on most, funnier aspects of the trail to Oregon and the good times with Cissie and John at the cabin.

In time Matilda came to tell Tabitha the things she'd hid from her as a young girl. Why she led her to believe she was running a restaurant, who Zandra really was, why she felt compelled to help prostitutes and how she came to have a love affair with James and that she didn't care if they could never be married, just as long as she could spend the rest of her life with him.

Just a couple of years ago Matilda couldn't ever have imagined herself talking about such things to Tabitha, for there had always been a clear demarcation line between woman and child. But Tabitha was a woman herself now. She might have been protected from the hardships Matilda had endured, never had a passionate love affair, but she had great sensitivity and intelligence, and her father's gift of being able to put herself in others' shoes.

'When you were my age you'd already done so much,' Tabitha said one night as they lay in bed. 'I don't seem to have done anything.'

'You call going to medical college nothing!' Matilda exclaimed. 'I think that amounts to far more than anything I've done.'

'But even when I've got the degree, I won't be able to practise medicine,' Tabitha said in a forlorn voice. 'Well, I suppose I'll get to deliver babies, and maybe treat the poor in a big city. But women doctors just aren't acceptable to most folk.'

'That will change,' Matilda said stoutly. 'You wait and see! Maybe it won't be for years yet, but I'm sure it will come. Most women would rather have a lady doctor, if they had a choice.'

'I expected you to say "you'll be married with children to look after in the few years," that's what most people think,' Tabitha replied.

'People used to say that to me too.' Matilda laughed softly. 'I know I'm getting old now because no one says it any more.'

'Would you have liked that?'

'Yes, I would more than anything,' Matilda admitted. 'But what about you?'

'If a very special man came along,' Tabitha said, the slight catch in her voice proving this was something she hoped for. 'And if I could feel about him the way you did about Papa and do now about James. But I don't attract men, Matty, special or otherwise. I guess I'm too smart and too plain.'

'It's not that,' Matilda said quickly. She had noted the respectful way men reacted to Tabitha, and she knew its meaning. 'It's because they can tell the minute they meet you that you have something important to do.'

Tabitha was silent for a moment as if mulling that over in her mind. 'You know what I like best about you, Matty?'

'No, do tell me,' Matilda whispered back.

'How you always tell the truth. Mama said that about you one day, when we were in Missouri. She said, "If Matty tells you something, you should always believe it." That day when we buried Cissie and the girls, do you remember the things you said to me afterwards?'

'That I wanted you to stay in Oregon, is that what you mean?'

'Not so much that, it was more what you said about always thinking of me as your daughter. I remembered what Mama had said then, and I knew I could believe you. I was sad I had to stay in Oregon. But I knew you weren't casting me off. That gave me such comfort.'

'That was a terrible time,' Matilda sighed. 'If I hadn't had you and Peter to think about, I don't know what I would have done.'

Tabitha put her arms right around her and cuddled her tightly. 'I wish I could take away that hurt,' she whispered. 'I was too young then to really understand what it must have been like for you. But I do now.'

'I wonder if we'll get any letters today,' Tabitha said thoughtfully on the morning of 1 July. It was half past five, and she was plaiting her hair in preparation for a day on the wards. 'It seems so long since we heard anything from the boys.'

Letters tended to arrive in batches. Sometimes they were miraculously written only a couple of weeks earlier, but mostly they were months old. When they'd last heard from Sidney back in April, he was at Fort Henry in Tennessee. An injury to his foot had resulted in him getting a job in the stores, and, still firmly unpatriotic, he hoped he'd get to stay there. He voiced no concern about the war, win or lose, only for those he loved and getting through the weeks so they could all be together again.

James and Peter always seemed to be on the move, back towards Virginia, and said little about any fighting they had encountered on the long march, or even what lay ahead of them. Peter's letters never had a serious note in them, and centred mainly on the men he'd met, mud, digging ditches, and army rations. He described the hardtack as so tough you could use it as armour. He said the only way to eat it was to soak it in coffee, then skim off the weevils which came out of it.

James's letters immediately after Shiloh were cheerful, amusing ones too, but after the Union's defeat at the Battle of Fredericksburg in Virginia, his own home town, a bitterness had crept in. Fortunately he and Peter had been spared being involved in that battle, the humiliating defeat and the loss of some 12,600 Union men, for they were still on the march to Virginia. But James was not only furious that 'Poppycock Generals' had ordered their men into a situation where they could only be massacred, he was also appalled that the town had been looted by Union men after the Confederates had urged the townspeople to leave their homes for safety. Six thousand civilians left the town, trudging through snow with nowhere to go. The victorious rebels finished what the Union had started after the battle, burning and ransacking till there was nothing left for the owners to return to. He said he could never understand such wickedness if he lived to be a hundred.

The letter he penned on New Year's Day, after President Lincoln had announced the Emancipation Proclamation, was even more troubled. While delighted in principle that it was to end slavery, he pointed out the loopholes, that Lincoln hadn't set all slaves free, only those in Confederate States. The ones in the loyal states such as Maryland, Delaware, Missouri and Kentucky were left out of it because Lincoln was too anxious to retain the goodwill of the slave owners there. He added that no decision had been reached about what to do with the thousands of Negroes who were flocking to the Union army for refuge either. He said Lincoln was weak, and unless he addressed the problems immediately there would be worse trouble in the future.

But while Matilda sympathized that James often found himself with an unsteady foot in both Yankee and Confederate camps, her primary concern was that he and Peter should stay unharmed. Infuriatingly, he didn't say exactly where they were or which battles they were involved in, and each time a new batch of injured were brought to the hospital, both she and Tabitha were always quizzing the men to see what they knew, and worse still scanning the men's faces in terror as they arrived, in dread that one day Peter or James might be among them.

Just as Matilda and Tabitha were leaving the ward to go home that day, word arrived that a battle had begun in Gettysburg. Matilda didn't even know where this was, but while lingering outside the hospital to listen to the gossip, they heard it was just a little cross-roads town further upstate.

They heard that the battle had begun over boots. There was rumoured to be a large supply of them in this town, and both armies had made their way to it, and when they met, fighting had broken out.

To Matilda it sounded like just a mild skirmish, and she and Tabitha walked home laughing about men fighting over boots.

They heard nothing more about Gettysburg the next day, but the following morning as they arrived for duty, there was talk of nothing else. Apparently vast numbers of troops on both sides had all converged on the area, and at four on the previous afternoon battle had commenced. Some of the nurses volunteered to go and help in the field hospitals, but this idea was turned down as no one had any idea of casualties, and anyway, everyone was needed here at The Lodge.

As it was the Fourth of July the following day, some of the men in the convalescence ward had made bunting to hang up, and they came into A1 to hang some in there, and talk to the badly injured men. Matilda thought as they made their way home that evening that it was one of the best days she'd known. Not one death, and no new arrivals. Yet she had a queasy feeling in her stomach that it was just the lull before the storm.

There was no celebration for the Fourth of July, for by mid-morning the storm Matilda had anticipated began with the first batch of wounded soldiers from Gettsyburg brought in. As the nurses worked at the jobs they'd become so familiar with, cutting uniforms from injured flesh and bathing wounds so the doctors could see the full damage, they heard from the men that this was the worst battle yet. These men were mostly from 20th Maine, and they seemed to want to speak of how they had advanced on the enemy with fixed bayonets and taken the Confederates by surprise. 'Some of them dropped their weapons,' one young private whispered to Matilda. 'I thought we were home and dry, but then I got a bullet through my knee.'

He was one of the luckier ones, it turned out, as he had been put in a wagon and hauled away to the safety of the tents of the field hospital, then quickly despatched here to Washington before even a scalpel was put near his knee, let alone the surgeon's saw.

Neither Matilda nor Tabitha left the ward till midnight. The story was circulating that there would be thousands of casualties in the next day or so. That was, if there were enough wagons to get the men to a hospital.

Hell was the only word Matilda felt was appropriate for what she saw in the next few days. A constant stream of wagons was coming into Washington, all heavily laden with wounded. Many of them had lain for two days in open fields in hot sunshine alongside the corpses of both their comrades and their foes, watching the bodies bloat and putrefy in the heat.

They didn't only use the beds now, but the floor and corridors too. The less badly wounded were left outside on the ground until they could be seen. All the nurses worked sixteen-hour shifts, every pair of hands was needed. There was no time for writing to someone's mother, no time to coax a man to drink if he didn't do so willingly. Often they couldn't even change the bloody sheets on the beds between patients.

They heard that 51,000 men had been killed, 23,000 of them Union men. The Confederates were limping back to Virginia, taking their wounded with them in the wagon train seventeen miles long.

Then Peter was brought in.

It was his voice that Matilda recognized, not his face, for like most of the men he was so blackened with gunpowder that his features were blurred.

'Aunt Matty!' she heard as the stretcher was carried by her. 'Is that really you, or am I dreaming?'

She was so startled she almost spilled the pitcher of water in her hands. The right leg of his pants was split right up his thigh and the dressing around the wound was soaked in blood.

'Peter!' she exclaimed, rushing up to his stretcher, hands instinctively reached to wipe his brow. 'Oh my poor love, I never wanted to see you here.'

She immediately organized for him to be given the bed in the corner, it was the one they called lucky, as more men seemed to make it who'd been put there. Tabitha came rushing over, greeted Peter, and quickly stripped off the blood-soaked dressing which the field hospital had applied over the bullet wound in his thigh.

'The bullet is still in there,' she said as she probed into the wound. 'But it looks reasonably clean compared with the other men's. Matty will wash you, and I'll get the doctor to come as quickly as possible. Were you lying outside for long?'

'No, the Brigadier saved me,' he said, wincing with the pain.

Both women wanted to know more, and to ask where James was, but Peter was in terrible pain, he'd lost a great deal of blood, the wound needed cleaning, and there were many other men needing even more urgent help.

Peter passed out with pain as Matilda washed the wound. Once she had it and the surrounding area of his thigh clean, she put a fresh dressing on it, then began undressing and washing him. She had done the same thing to hundreds of men before, but this time she was choked by emotion, remembering him as a baby and how he'd howled in that cellar while Cissie fed little Pearl. She remembered too her delight in seeing him every time she went to the Waifs' and Strays' Home in New Jersey. He'd been such a delightful, fat, bonny baby. But that was twenty years ago, he was a man now. No dimpled fat thighs that invited her to kiss them, just hard, taut muscle.

Yet as she washed his face, the boy she'd brought back to San

Francisco after the death of his mother came back, still only downy hair on his chin, the little scar he'd got on his right cheek when he'd fallen from a tree out at the cabin still there amongst the freckles. He came to again, light brown eyes looking at her in wonder.

'It really is me, Peter,' she whispered. 'And I'm going to make you better. Just go back to sleep, you are safe now.'

She wasn't going to let him die, she had promised Cissie she would care for him. If she had to bribe the doctor to get that bullet out, then she'd do it.

The bullet was removed at eight that evening. Matilda held his hands while the doctor dug it out, and she stitched the wound herself. He didn't cry out, and his endurance reminded her so much of the way he had been when Cissie and the girls were dying.

'You are a brave man,' she said, as she and Tabitha lifted him from the stretcher, back into his bed. 'I've never been prouder of you.'

Matilda sent Tabitha home to bed, but she remained on the ward. There were many men much more gravely wounded than Peter, few would last the night and they needed someone to comfort them, but it was Peter she stayed for.

He slept intermittently, yet each time he opened his eyes and saw her still there, he half smiled and closed his eyes again. At dawn his colour had improved slightly, and when she changed the dressing on his leg, she rejoiced to find no sign of infection.

'Can you tell me about what happened now?' she asked around six, knowing that soon a senior nurse would come to ask how he was, and perhaps move him to one of the other wards where the patients needed less attention than the men in here.

'The rebels came up Cemetery Hill to us,' he said in a whisper. 'They were waving their flags, the sun was gleaming on their bayonets, it looked like a sloping forest of flashing steel. They came like they were one, silent and bold, it was the most beautiful, awesome sight. They looked invincible even though their uniforms were in rags and some had no boots. Then General Gibbon came down the line, cool and calm, and ordered us to hold our fire until they were real close.

'He gave us a signal to fire when they were so close you could almost smell their breath. As we fired, so all the cannons went off at once. You wouldn't believe it, Matty! Arms, heads, caps and knapsacks were thrown up into the clear air above the smoke.' He paused, wincing at the memory. 'But still the rebels came on. It was hand to hand, face to face after that. Men cutting with sabres, thrusting with bayonets, guns fired right into faces. So terrible!'

He stopped, then gave a long-drawn-out sigh. 'I got hit, but I kept on shooting and reloading because I knew if I fell I'd be bayoneted. Then out of nowhere James came roaring through on his horse. He was like an avenging angel, Matty, slashing out with his sabre. I didn't think he'd even see me, but he'd come to get me, Matty, he grabbed hold of my arms and hauled me up on to his horse.'

Matilda covered her mouth with her hands, eyes wide with shock.

'I guess I must have passed out, 'cos next thing he was dropping me down on the grass, away from it all. He said I'd got to go to the field hospital,' he said in an emotional croak. 'He saved my life.'

Matilda was reeling from the vivid and dramatic picture he'd painted for her.

'Did he go back to the fighting?' she asked weakly.

''Course he did, Matty,' Peter retorted. 'I saw him riding off swirling his sabre in one hand, shooting with his pistol from the other, clinging on to his horse with his knees, the way he said an Indian taught him.'

He stopped suddenly, his face clouding over. 'But he got hurt real bad later, Matty.'

Matty felt as if her heart had just stopped. For a moment she could only stare at Peter in horror. 'Are you sure?' she whispered.

''Fraid so,' he said, with pain in his eyes. 'Captain Franklin, came to tell me. That's why I got here so quick. Seems James gave instructions that I was to be brought right here, to this hospital, and you.'

Matilda had already discovered the previous night that most of the wounded were still up there at Gettysburg, taken into people's houses, and she thought it was just luck that brought Peter here. But there was no luck in it, just James looking after her boy for her, as he'd always promised he'd do.

'So where is James?' she asked, panic overwhelming her.

'I guess he's been taken wherever the officers go,' Peter replied. 'That's if – ' He stopped short, but he didn't have to finish the sentence, he'd said enough.

'Would you mind if I go and find him?' she said hurriedly. 'Tabby will be on duty very soon, she'll look out for you.'

'You go and find him,' Peter said. 'Tell him.' Again he stopped short and tears filled his eyes.

'Tell him you love him?' she whispered.

He nodded, and swiped angrily at his tears. 'And tell him he's the bravest man I ever knew.'

It took Matilda only minutes to discover that officers were taken to the Federal Hospital, and she took off, running like a hare. It was going to be another very hot day, the sun was climbing rapidly into the sky, and the sound of wagon wheels bringing more wounded was all around her.

Only as she reached the doors of the Federal Hospital did she remember that her apron was stained with blood, and felt her hair coming loose under her cap, but it was too late to do anything about that now.

She was told by a starchy lady on a desk that Brigadier James Russell had indeed been brought in late last night, but that she couldn't possibly see him now.

'I insist,' she said, looking at the woman as if she might knock her down if she refused again. 'I am his wife.'

He was in a room at the end of a long corridor, with five other men, and as Matilda rushed in, a stout nurse tried to restrain her.

'Let go of me,' she said, pushing the woman to one side.

James was in the bed nearest the window, and recognizing her voice he turned his head towards her. 'Matty!' he whispered.

For a moment she thought whatever injuries he had were only minor ones, for his fair hair was gleaming in the early morning sun, his face was tanned, moustache trimmed, and his naked upper chest and arms rippled with muscle. He looked exactly the way he had three years ago, on the last night they spent together. But as she ran to him she saw it wasn't a sheet pulled up over him, but a bandage around his middle, and his eyes had that dull, faraway look of approaching death she'd seen so often before.

She felt as if she'd been hit by a mortar shell, her mouth went dry, her heart was thumping too loudly. Stomach wounds were always the worst. She'd never known one man survive them. It wasn't fair, everything she'd planned and dreamed of was for him and with him, her life would be worth nothing without him.

Yet somehow she managed to smile and kiss him, to say she'd run all the way here as soon as she heard he had been wounded. She wondered why she wasn't crying, or even berating him for not keeping back from the action the way senior officers were supposed to, but all she did was continue to smile, stroke his hair back from his face and whisper that she loved him.

'Is Peter going to make it?' he asked, gripping her hands. His voice was so husky and weak it made her feel weak too.

'Yes, thanks to you, my darling, he told me what you did,'

'He turned out to be a fine soldier,' James said softly. 'He does you credit, Matty.'

'He told me to tell you he loves you,' she said, close to him and stroking his face. 'He said you were the bravest man he ever knew. But even if he recovers enough to be sent back into the war, I'll fight tooth and nail to prevent it.'

James nodded in agreement. 'Tell Tabitha she's to go back to her studies after this, and nothing must stop her becoming a doctor, and tell Sidney I'm sorry I can't be Elizabeth's godfather, and to look after you for me.'

She wanted to say he would get better, and he'd see Elizabeth soon for himself, and James too, the new baby who had been named after him, but she'd had too much experience of death now to stop a man saying the things he needed to say before he went.

He picked up her hands and looked at them.

'Don't,' she said, trying to pull them back. 'They look so ugly.'

'I love these hands,' he whispered, drawing them up to his lips. 'For I know how they got that way. Every mark tells a story of a brave woman with a big heart. I can't tell you how often I've dreamed of them in the last three years, they say more about you than your beautiful face.'

'I look a fright,' she said, looking down at her stained apron and drab brown dress.

'You look like an angel to me,' he whispered, clinging on to her hand. 'I'm so sorry I couldn't keep my promises.'

'You gave me more happiness than a woman has a right to,' she said. 'What's a few broken promises?'

She noted how different this ward was from the one she worked in. It was the same size, but here there were six beds, in hers sixteen. There were screens for privacy, the floor was waxed and polished, but for once she didn't mind that a privileged few got special treatment. Not when James was one of them.

'I've asked to be buried at Gettysburg, with my men,' he said suddenly. 'I couldn't bear to be taken back to Fredericksburg.'

For just a second she wanted to protest, but she saw the look in his eyes and understood. It wasn't just that his home town was sacked, or he had no allegiance to it or his people there any more. His men were what counted to him, and if they had to be buried in crude mass graves, then he wished to be there with them.

'May I be there?' she said, tears welling up in her eyes.

'I was counting on you to be there,' he whispered, clinging on to her hand. 'And Tabby too. Your family always meant so much more to me than my own.'

'If only,' she started, then checked herself.

'If only what?'

'We'd had a child of our own, I guess,' she said, and tried to smile.

He gave her a sad look. 'I thought you believed in never looking back?'

'It's an easy thing to say, but not so easy to do,' she whispered. 'Not after all we've been to one another.'

He winced with sudden pain. The nurse came to say the doctor was on his way to examine the Brigadier, and as she wheeled the screen around the bed, her look was kindly, she even apologized for having to ask Matilda to wait outside.

The doctor was small and old and walked with a cane but he stayed a lot longer with James than the doctors at The Lodge spent with their patients. When he came out, he looked at Matilda with real sympathy. 'I'm so sorry, Mrs Russell,' he said. 'We've done all we can, but as a nurse you'll know that serious stomach wounds like his are beyond help.'

She nodded, glad at least that he'd treated her as an equal. 'How long does he have?' she asked.

'Only minutes, I fear,' he said gently. 'Go back to him, Mrs Russell, and God be with you both.'

James hung on for ten minutes, his eyes wide open, his hand squeezing hers, and at last she found the words she'd never been able to say before. 'You gave me purpose, James, you've made me strong enough to withstand anything. Loving you has been everything I ever wanted. If I could go right back to the beginning, the only thing I'd change is that I'd have followed you everywhere, to the most distant, dirty fort, to the mountains and desert. I'll carry you with me for always, in my heart, mind and body.'

Tears rained down her cheeks unchecked, she ran one finger round his lips, his nose, his chin and ears, impressing every small detail into her mind for all time.

His chest was making a rattling noise, and his hand squeezed hers. 'Kiss me,' he whispered.

His lips were dry and cracked, but she kept hers on them until she felt his last breath go and his hand in hers went limp. 'Farewell, my love,' she whispered.

She closed his eyes herself, sealing them with a kiss, then called the nurse.

'Would you like to take his belongings with you now?' the woman said gently. 'I know that might sound a little hasty, but sometimes it helps to have something to hold on to.'

Even in her grief, Matilda sensed this stout, plain woman had suffered great loss recently too, and she embraced her silently for a moment.

'There's his sabre and pistol, and the things which were in the pockets of his uniform,' the nurse said, her lips trembling.

Matilda nodded. Peter should have his sabre, and she'd keep the pistol.

She sat beside James's bed while the nurse went away. He looked just the way he had that day on the beach at Santa Cruz, when he fell asleep on the sand beside her, and it was hard to imagine those eyes would never open again, or those lips smile at her. She'd met him fifteen years ago, been his mistress for ten, yet if she put all the time they'd actually spent together it would only amount to perhaps six months in all.

Death had become so commonplace to her that she had begun to imagine she'd lost some of her sensitivity. But that wasn't so, she felt mortally wounded, that her heart would give out at any moment. Amelia's death had crushed her, yet it had been bearable in as much as she knew it was inevitable once the disease caught hold of her. She had the other children to think of then too. But ever since Amelia died, James had been her guiding star, he had promised they'd grow old together, and she had believed it.

He was her love, her life, nothing was worth anything without him.

The nurse returned just a few minutes later, with the sabre and pistol bundled together in a piece of cloth tied up with string and 'Brigadier Russell' written on a label.

'There was this too,' the nurse said, handing her a brown leather wallet. 'He was holding it in his hands when they brought him in.'

A lock of Matilda's hair fell out as she opened it. Inside was the picture of her that they'd had taken back in San Francisco seven years earlier. It was faded now, worn from constant handling. As she opened a small pocket, she saw the red garter he'd snatched from her that night in Santa Cruz. That too was faded, now just pale pink. She had the other one back home in a drawer, still bright red. She'd planned to wear it on their first night together when he came home.

Tears ran down her cheeks as she picked up the lock of hair, and tucked it back into the wallet with the picture and the garter, then handed it back to the nurse. 'I think he'd like to take that with him,' she said simply. 'Will you make sure it stays with him?'

The nurse nodded, and put one hand on Matilda's shoulder. 'I'm so sorry,' she said in a soft voice. 'He was a fine man and a brave soldier.'

'The very finest,' Matilda said, sniffing back her tears. Picking up the heavy parcel and cradling it in her arms, she looked once more into the nurse's eyes. 'I'm in Ward A1 at The Lodge hospital. I am known as Nurse Jennings there. Will you ask that I'm told when his funeral will be?'

The streets were jammed with wagons, soldiers everywhere, and it was desperately hot and noisy. There was nowhere to go to be alone but back to the boarding-house. She put the parcel away unopened in the closet, then sank down on the bed, so numb and desolate that she was beyond tears.

The clamour from the street outside, the rumbling wagon wheels and shouts of street vendors and newspaper boys was deafening, yet even above it she could hear a fly buzzing at the window, trying to get out.

So many memories flitted through her mind. The tough, often insolent wagon master. The friend who had cradled her new baby in his arms. She remembered the first time she danced with him at London Lil's, the way her body had stirred as he held her close. His troubled face when he told her he was married to another woman. The frantic love-making in the rain up by the Presidio. So many unforgettable kisses, endless nights of passion, laughter, happiness and tears.

She had believed she knew everything about him, his past, dreams and aspirations. She knew every mark on his body, every line on his face, the shape of his toes, the little whistling noise he made as he fell asleep. Yet now he was gone she could see that the biggest part of him, his soldiering, was something she knew nothing of. She had never discovered if he was scared before a battle, if he prayed, drank or played cards. Did he wash and shave for it? When he leaped up on to his horse did he ever wonder if it would be for the last time? How did he feel after the battles, win or lose? Did he sometimes cry?

All she had of that part of him was a bundle of letters, and although they revealed his thoughts of her, his views about so many things, and his plans for the horse ranch, he'd never touched on how it felt to be ordered out to kill.

She would never get the answers to these questions now, but she did know that even in the thick of battle he'd kept his promise to her and looked out for Peter. She would keep the vivid picture in her mind of him sweeping her wounded boy up on to his horse. That was a far better image to hold on to than dwelling on how he got his own fatal wounds.

And he wanted to be buried with his men. That was perhaps the finest epitaph of all.

The tears came flooding out then, so hot they stung her face and soaked the pillow beneath her. They said she was the woman who never cried – well, she was crying now because her heart was in pieces and she had nothing further to live for. What reason could she find to get up each day? Where could she call home with the knowledge he would never share it with her?

Let the two armies kill and go on killing till there's no one left. They'd taken her man, her love, her future. There was no point to anything any more.

Chapter Twenty-six

The stage-coach lurched from side to side on the mountain road over the Sierra Nevada mountains. If the eight occupants hadn't been so tightly packed together they would have been tossed around inside like apples in a basket.

Matilda, in a black gown, cape and bonnet, had the seat nearest to the window, facing the front of the coach. A cushion tucked down beside her hip shielded her from the worst of the jars, and the breeze from the open window kept her reasonably cool, but it was her numb state of mind which was her greatest protection from the discomfort of the long journey.

It was June 1865. General Lee had surrendered back in April and the war was over. Two whole years, all but one month, since Gettysburg, and James's death, but for Matilda it could have been a week, several months or even many years ago.

Time and place had no real meaning for her any more. Since that summer's day when James died all her responses had become automatic. She had gone back to the hospital to nurse the wounded beside Tabitha. Worked round the clock where she was needed, giving the sick and dying as much tender care as she had always done, just because she knew James would have wanted her too, but inside she felt cold and empty.

Tabitha had asked her on many an occasion to explain how she felt. She was extremely anxious because Matilda ate and slept very little and she couldn't bear to see her so thin and gaunt. Matilda tried to describe how it was, but words failed her; to say she just felt empty didn't quite cover it.

Nothing was the same any more now James was gone. The taste of food, the smell of flowers, the sound of birdsong, all less somehow. Extremes of temperature, seasons, comfort, discomfort, didn't affect her. It was almost as if she were inside a bubble, seeing and hearing everything, but nothing quite touched her.

She observed the wild excitement in Washington when the

war ended as if from very far off, unable to understand why the joy and happiness all around her didn't move her. She was very glad the soldiers could now go home to their wives and families, and so very relieved that there would be no further casualties, but how could she delight in a victory won at the expense of six million dead?

There was only one clear picture in her mind as the people of Washington cheered, hugged and kissed one another and celebrated. That of James's funeral, and the long, long trenches, some already filled with bodies, others lying empty, waiting to be filled.

Because of James's rank, someone had covered the mounds of waiting bodies with sacking. But that didn't prevent Matilda and Tabitha smelling them, or seeing the black cloud of buzzing flies around them. She didn't think she would ever get that smell out of her nostrils, or wipe the image from her mind.

Tabitha had gone back to Ohio now, to pick up her medical studies again, and as they had parted at Washington station some six weeks ago, Matilda pretended for Tabitha's sake that she was excited to be going home to San Francisco. The truth of the matter was that she didn't really care where she went; if she'd been ordered to go to nurse in another town, she would have gone willingly. It was easier to be with strangers than to face people who loved her.

As a series of trains carried her across America, and California became closer, she told herself she must snap out of this apathy and look forward. She was lucky that she had a home to go to, the whole South lay in ruins, people were starving, their homes sacked, crops destroyed, and so many women had lost not only their man, but their sons too.

Sidney had managed to get himself sent home because of his infected foot, and in the last letter she received from him he'd been joyfully anticipating Peter's arrival. She knew she should be mentally making plans for the future, she had London Lil's to open again, the Jennings Bureau, and the girls' home in Folsom Street, but instead of planning she just stared out of the window, watching the miles go by without even noticing the scenery.

It was only when she boarded this stage-coach in Denver, and passed by the hotel where she once stayed with James, that she felt something. They had been so happy there, and she knew he wouldn't want her to go on mourning him this way. She could almost hear him whispering, 'There will always be people who need your strength, Matty, you can't let them down.'

Suddenly the stage-coach lurched sideways, making everyone inside it gasp. Matilda glanced round at them, all at once aware that she had been completely oblivious to her fellow passengers, despite travelling with them for several days.

There was nothing particularly unusual about any of them, they were just a bunch of quite ordinary people, such as you'd see on any street, in any town anywhere in America.

A fat man in a checked suit, his companion a somewhat worn-looking woman with a pinched, narrow face. Two young soldiers returning home, their uniforms shabby, yet their boots highly polished. A young woman in a smart red dress and matching bonnet, travelling with an older lady who might be her mother, and finally a small, rather wizened clergyman, who was holding his broad-brimmed hat in his hand and twisting it nervously.

Matilda had been aware of them talking to one another most of the way. At first, some of them had tried to engage her in conversation too, but due to her lack of response they had soon given up. Even when they pulled in at coach stops, Matilda had kept herself aloof.

The sideways lurch had been caused by the coach reaching the summit of the hill and they were now going down the other side, right beside them a steep rocky chasm. For the first time in the entire trip she felt a stirring of excitement for it was very reminiscent of travelling in the wagon all those years ago.

The young soldier sitting opposite her must have observed her sudden interest because he leaned forward in his seat. 'Scared?' he asked.

He was just a boy, perhaps twenty, pale and thin, with a lock of fair hair falling over his eyes. Something about him touched her and she smiled. 'No, not scared,' she said. 'I trust the coachman. I expect he's been this way hundreds of times.'

It was a funny thing, but just making that remark cheered her. If she still had faith in a coachman, then she could get back her faith in herself.

'Are you going home?' she asked the boy.

He nodded. 'My folks live in Sacramento. I hope to hell they ain't moved on, I ain't had no letters for two years.'

'They'll be there,' she said reassuringly. 'Do they know you're safe?'

He shrugged, and somehow that little gesture summed up the whole folly and heartbreak of war. Letters were sent and never arrived, countless families all over the country had no idea if their men would come back to them.

'Well, there's going to be one happy mother in Sacramento tomorrow,' she said, her smile now coming from deep inside her. 'You hurry on back to her now, don't dawdle on the way.'

He laughed, a little embarrassed. 'Have you got sons coming back to you?' he asked.

'I'm going back to them,' she said, and found herself telling him about Sidney and Peter. 'I guess they were both luckier than most,' she finished up. 'So many men were forced back into the action even with bad injuries.'

She lapsed back into silence then, looking out at the view and straining her eyes for the first glimpse of the ocean through gaps in the mountains. That brief conversation, the first she'd had with anyone since leaving Washington, had made her see she was glad to be going home after all. Maybe her apartment and London Lil's were going to bring back more painful memories of James, but with her family around her again, perhaps she could rise above them.

'Matty!'

Matilda was just stepping down from the coach in San Francisco when she heard Sidney's joyous bellow. Her head swivelled round and she saw him racing towards her through the crowds of people, his mop of red hair a welcoming beacon.

He flung his arms around her and lifted her right off her feet, almost crushing her, and all at once she was crying.

'Oh Matty,' he sighed, planting a kiss on both her cheeks. 'It sure is good to have you home again. Now, what are you cryin' for? This ain't no time for tears, Mary said I'd got to get you and rush you home right away. Why, she's been cleaning and polishing for days in your honour.'

Matilda reached up and just held his face in her two hands for a moment. He seemed so much bigger than she remembered, his face rounded out, and the freckles less pronounced. It was over three years ago that he enlisted, and he was a thirty-year-old man now, the boy gone forever. But his exuberance was unchanged, and she could almost feel a thaw beginning around her heart.

'I love you, Sidney,' she said simply, resting her head on his broad chest for a moment. 'It's so good to be back.'

She had expected everything to have changed, but it hadn't. Still the same jostling crowds, the sunshine, noise, smells, music and gaiety. Her little gig was waiting, bright with a coat of fresh paint, and even Star snorted a welcome when she saw her mistress.

As they drove up California Street Hill and Matilda saw London Lil's up ahead, a lump came to her throat. The paint was dull and peeling, the shutters still closed on the saloon windows, but despite its neglected appearance it still dominated the hill, reminding her of what an important role it had played in this town.

There was a big brown hound lying on the veranda. As Sidney pulled up the gig, it stood up, stretched and yawned before bounding over to greet Sidney. Treacle had died at a very old age soon after Matilda left to go nursing, and she guessed Mary had got this dog as a replacement.

'This is Lincoln,' Sidney said, patting him. 'Say hullo to the boss,' he said. 'Come on, the way I taught you.'

The dog held up one paw, looking at her with questioning eyes. Matilda took his paw and shook it. 'I'm so pleased to meet you, Lincoln,' she said with a chuckle. 'I do hope no one shoots you!'

The saloon door opened and there was Mary, her arms open in welcome, her smile as wide as a slice of water-melon. 'Matty!' she shrieked, and ran down the steps to hug her.

An hour or two later, Matty felt almost bruised by the sheer number of hugs and kisses she had received. The upstairs parlour had been decorated with a 'Welcome Home' banner, Chinese lanterns, paper streamers, and so many flowers. The table was laid with party food, and people kept arriving to see her.

Peter was still limping badly and he needed a stick to walk with, but he looked strong and healthy again. Mary was expecting a third child, and it seemed impossible to Matilda that Elizabeth was now four and James, the baby she'd helped deliver just before leaving San Francisco, was now three, walking and talking. Both children had Sidney's red hair, with Mary's curls, and they shared their parents' happy dispositions.

Dolores' hair was peppered with grey, and she looked every bit as severe as she always had, but she had burst into emotional tears as she embraced Matilda and in a hoarse voice said she had missed her so much that sometimes she felt she was going crazy.

But of all the surprises, Fern was the greatest, for she'd changed from a skinny girl into a beautiful woman while Matilda had been away. Her coppery skin had a delicate sheen, her body had filled out with voluptuous curves, and her soulful eyes were framed by the thickest, darkest lashes. Gone were the timid, frightened glances, she was self-assured and poised, even in male company, and just looking at her made Matilda's heart swell with pride.

All day people came and went. Henry Slocum, on two walking sticks, old and tired now, was so thrilled to have Matilda home. Shop-keepers, ex-gold miners, and some of the business men she'd sold timber to right back in 1850 came to see her. She had thought it would be unbearably painful if anyone spoke of James and offered her their condolences on his death, but they did speak of him, and their heartfelt sorrow for her filled that empty space inside her.

That night she shared her old bed with Elizabeth, and as she lay with her arms around the sleeping child, caressing her silky hair, the few tears she shed were ones of happiness. No one could ever take the place of Amelia or James, she would never stop mourning them, but she could see now she still had a great deal to live for.

At seven the next morning she was dressed and sitting at her desk in the parlour. The apartment was silent, everyone still asleep, but then Peter came in, still in his night-clothes and a dressing-gown.

'I thought you'd be resting up today after the hectic time yesterday,' he said. 'Couldn't you sleep?'

'I slept like a baby,' she smiled. 'But I had to get up, there is so much I want to get started on.'

'Already,' he groaned, running his fingers through his tousled hair. 'I would have expected you to want to catch your breath first.'

Matilda was very glad of this opportunity to speak to Peter alone. He was the only one who hadn't mentioned James yesterday, or spoken of his plans for the future. She guessed his state of mind was much like hers had been.

'It's almost two years since you were wounded and James died,' she said gently. 'It's time we both got going again, Peter. You have to plan a career for yourself, I have to pick up the reins here.'

He sat down on the armchair next to her desk, his light brown eyes looked troubled. 'What can I do walking with a stick?' he said.

'I know you are still in pain, and that perhaps you feel you are a cripple, but you survived that wound, you are only twenty-two, and there are a great many things you can do.'

'Like what, Aunt Matty?' he said dejectedly. 'I can't run, lift anything heavy, I'm so slow.'

'There's nothing wrong with your brain,' she said. 'You were always so good at figures, how about accountancy?'

He gave a cynical smile. 'So I can do your books?'

'Yes,' she grinned back. 'But other people's too, it's a good way to earn a living, now the war's over, all businesses will be picking up.'

'It wasn't what I planned,' he sighed, and she knew that even after all the horror of war he still saw himself as a soldier.

She reached out and put her hand on his shoulder. 'I know. But there's nothing cissy about being an accountant, Peter. Armed with knowledge you can fight people's battles for them, raise and manage money for causes you care about. I think if James were still with us, he'd say the same.'

He was silent for a moment or two and she guessed he wanted to say something about James. She waited.

'I loved and admired him more than any other man in the whole world,' he said at last, his lips trembling. 'I wanted to be just like him.'

'But you are,' she said, her eyes filling with tears. 'It wasn't being a soldier that made him a great man, it was his goodness, intelligence, courage, and his love of humanity. You have all those qualities too, Peter.'

He looked right into her eyes, saw her tears, and reached out tenderly to wipe them away. 'We're both scarred, aren't we? We lost Cissie, Amelia and Susanna, and now I've got to live with a limp, and you've got to get by with a broken heart. But we did come through it. I guess you're right, the only way to make sense of it all is for us to pull together and make a whole new life for ourselves.'

'That's the spirit,' she said, taking his hand and kissing the tips of his fingers. 'Now, it just so happens I've made a list of things that need to be done. Shall we look at that now?'

Peter laughed then.

'What's so funny?' she said indignantly.

'You, Aunt Matty! Right from when I was a little boy you always had something up your sleeve, whatever happened. Ma said once that you were always two jumps ahead of everyone else.'

On 1 September, London Lil's opened again with a huge party. The outside had been repainted, new gas lighting installed, and the interior revamped entirely. The old worn mural of London scenes had been painted over, and another had taken its place. The bar and floor had a new coat of varnish, the cracked mirrors, old tables and chairs replaced with new ones, the stage rebuilt and the floor sprung.

Matilda wanted Sidney, Mary and the children to stay with her permanently, so she had two new rooms added to the apartment upstairs, with a private staircase leading down to the back yard. She called in a gardener to turn part of the yard into a garden, and on the rough ground at the front of the saloon, he'd planted a few trees and shrubs. Maybe it would be noisy in the evenings for small children, but as Mary pointed out, it was better to have their pa, Aunt Matty and Uncle Peter close to hand, a garden of their own to play in, than a silent, and dull home.

Matilda remembered with nostalgia how hard it had been to find dancers and entertainers for the first opening, the hours of fruitless auditions and the agony of thinking they would never get anyone good. It was all so different this time – as soon as word got around she was re-opening, there were theatrical agents beating a path to her door, offering everything from snake-charmers to opera singers.

This time, too, the opening was by invitation only. Matilda heard with some amusement that many of the leading socialites in the town, who wouldn't have dreamt of coming in during the early days, were now offering bribes to anyone they thought could get them invited.

The band struck up at seven in the evening and the doors were flung open. Sidney, in a green jacket and embroidered waistcoat, was ready behind the bar with his new staff, the waiters in red jackets, the waitresses in red flouncy dresses, each with a simple feathered headdress.

Almost all the girls had previously been residents in Folsom Street, and moved on to become maids or waitresses. But as soon as they had heard Matilda was back in town, they had gone to see Dolores with the hope she might persuade her mistress to take them on. It gave her so much pleasure seeing their glowing faces, but at the same time it was a reminder that soon she'd have to pick up her crusade against the evils of 'the Coast' again, for Dolores had told her that since the emancipation of slaves, hundreds of very young Negro girls were coming into the clutches of the brothel owners.

In a new black velvet gown, and a feathered and sequinned headdress similar to the waitresses', Matilda greeted all the guests personally. She had vowed that she would stay in mourning for James for the rest of her life, but as Dolores had dryly commented as she dressed her hair, 'It sure is lucky you look good in black, ma'am. Some ladies, they look like an old crow. You's jist look like a fallen angel.'

But beneath her gown and petticoats, Matilda was wearing the one remaining red garter. It had made her cry when she took it from the box, remembering where its partner was, buried with James up in Gettysburg. Yet by putting it on, she felt she was drawing on his spirit to get her through the night.

Everyone she had really wanted here came. Old miners, now turned shop-keepers, hotel owners, carpenters and bricklayers, stevedores and businessmen, almost all with their ladies. There were no flannel shirts and muddy boots as there had been on her first night, everyone looked scrubbed and polished. Even

Alicia accompanied Henry, and it gave Matilda just a little pleasure to see she wasn't ageing well. Her teeth were gone, her cheeks caving in, and her gown of lavender silk was very matronly and old-fashioned.

The show opened with the dancing girls doing the cancan, and though everyone had seen the dance countless times before, they were still as spellbound as when Zandra launched it here originally. A troupe of tumbling clowns came next, making everyone shriek with laughter as they seemingly fell off the stage, only to land on their hands and quickly jump up again. Their finale was making a human pyramid, and they played for laughs right to the end, wobbling and threatening to hurl themselves into the audience.

The waiters and waitresses were run ragged filling up glasses, for all the drinks were on the house tonight. But clearly everyone had enough to drink, for when the Negro minstrel band called for a sing-song, everyone uproariously joined in with 'Oh Susanna' and many other old songs from the gold rush days.

Dolores slipped down from the apartment to watch the dancing girls come on for their final routine. She was minding Elizabeth Rose and James, so Mary could be with Sidney. As the girls whooped around the stage one last time before running off to the changing-room, she squeezed Matilda's arm. 'Reckon Mizz Zandra's come back to be with us tonight, along with the Captain. I sure can hear them laughing.'

Matilda couldn't speak. She could hear Zandra's last words on that first night.

'Know what that smell is? It's the smell of success.'

Late that evening, after everyone had gone, Matilda, Sidney, Peter and Mary had one last glass of champagne together before retiring. The floor was dirty, awash with spilt drinks and cigar butts. There were hundreds of empty bottles everywhere, and even more glasses.

'To absent friends,' Peter said, raising his glass.

Sidney looked at him sharply, perhaps thinking this was no time to be casting gloom on a wonderful evening, for the only living person missing was Tabitha.

'Yes, to absent friends,' Matilda agreed. 'And may we hold

them in our hearts, remember them with love, but look to the future always, and treasure what we have now.'

'So what's the next project?' Sidney asked Matilda after the solemn toast had been made.

'Plural,' she said, and grinned. 'I've got several up my sleeve.'

Peter groaned. 'What now?'

'A hostel for single working girls,' she said. 'A fund for widows of ex-servicemen. A united effort to get "the Coast" cleared up. Is that enough to be getting on with?'

Sidney chuckled. 'I guess I'll have to make sure this place makes a heap of money then,' he said.

'And I've got to learn to manage it,' Peter laughed.

Matilda grinned. 'That's my boys!' she said. Then, putting her hand gently on Mary's swelling belly and leaning down, she whispered. 'And make sure you are strong and smart, we'll need reinforcements before too long.'

Chapter Twenty-seven

New York 1873

Tabitha was stiff with tension, sitting on the edge of the couch, waiting for the guests to arrive to celebrate her engagement to Dr Sebastian Everett. It was February, and silent out on Fifth Avenue because thick snow was muting the sounds of horses' hooves and carriage wheels. She wished Matilda had accepted the Everetts' invitation to stay here in their house, instead of insisting on staying at a hotel, perhaps then she wouldn't be so nervous.

Matilda was probably right in saying that she needed time alone with her future in-laws to get to know them, and that she would only be a distraction. Yet even after four days, Tabitha still didn't feel comfortable with them. Mrs Everett had been welcoming in the sense that she lavished attention on her, but at the same time it felt very much like critical scrutiny. Tonight it would be Matilda's turn, for Tabitha was only too aware that Mrs Everett was intensely curious about her step-mother. She had asked a great many questions about her, and though she hadn't actually voiced any disapproval that her business was a saloon, or that her charitable work was with fallen women, Tabitha sensed it.

Tabitha was anxious too about her appearance. Sebastian said she looked beautiful, but then he said that even when she was wearing the most drab outfit, and he was certainly no judge of whether her dark red velvet evening gown was just a little *too* bold for a woman of thirty-three, or if her ringlets would droop before the evening was over.

She glanced anxiously across the drawing-room towards Anne Everett who was giving some last-minute instructions to her butler. She was in her mid-sixties, with white hair, but a slender body, pert turned-up nose, fashionable clothes and good skin made her look much younger. Tonight she was wearing a royal blue velvet evening gown and a stunning diamond necklace, a tiny lace cap held in place with still more diamond-headed pins. But just as her age was disguised, so were her true feelings. She chattered brightly about inconsequential matters, asked many pointed questions, yet revealed little about herself.

Tabitha thought Anne was like most of her class and imagined that any woman who was still unmarried by twenty had to have some hidden defect. No doubt the fact that Tabitha was thirty-three, plain, didn't come from an illustrious family and had the gall to enter the male-dominated world of medicine all heightened her suspicions. Only yesterday Tabitha had voiced these thoughts to Sebastian, but he just laughed and said his family wasn't illustrious either, just rich, and if anything his mother was in awe of Tabitha's intelligence.

Albert Everett was equally difficult to reach. He was sitting by the fire, staring into the flames, nursing a large whiskey. He must have been very like Sebastian at the same age, he too was tall and slender, with the same big nose and ears, and dark blue eyes, but he had stooped shoulders, and very little hair left.

He had said very little to Tabitha since she'd arrived, but then she didn't think he'd really taken in that she was to marry his son in the near future. Anne had said that he'd withdrawn from his business interests, become muddled and lost his appetite when their youngest son, Aaron, a West Point graduate, died of an infected wound in the last year of the war. Tabitha could sympathize wholeheartedly with that, for the war was responsible for so much misery.

She remembered the joy she felt when General Lee surrendered in April of '65. But just a few days later that joy was shattered by the shocking news that Abraham Lincoln had been assassinated while at The Ford theatre, just a stone's throw from the hospital.

That seemed the point when the true evil and futility of war finally struck home for everyone in America, whichever side they were on. Six million men dead, and countless more so badly injured that they would never be able to work again. The whole of the South lay in ruins, farms and plantations plundered, houses sacked and burned by the victorious army.

The slaves were free at last, but for many of them it was the beginning of an almost worse era, for those who remained in the South were then a target for more persecution at the hands of the Ku Klux Klan. Those who had gone north or west fared no better. They were still discriminated against, for now white men feared they would take their jobs. If they made it to the cities the only shelter they could get was in the grimmest slums, and any work offered was of the most menial kind and poorly paid. Those who stayed in rural areas found themselves on infertile land and their homes were little more than makeshift tents or shacks.

Tabitha knew a great deal about discrimination herself. She had returned to medical school in Ohio after the war, burning with the desire to qualify as a doctor and to use her skill to help the suffering she saw all around her. She passed her final exams with flying colours, but she soon found that qualifying as a doctor didn't necessarily mean she could practise medicine. She applied to just about every hospital in North America, but was turned down purely because she was a woman.

It was Matilda who finally persuaded her to join her in San Francisco. With her support and influence, Tabitha was finally able to start a small practice there.

However disappointing it was to find that most of her patients came to her only in emergencies when no male doctor was available, being close to Matilda, Peter, Sidney and his family more than made up for it. Yet with patience and perseverance her practice had grown enough to enable her to support herself. She liked California's mild climate, and came to love the lively, fast-growing city which for all its faults at least suffered less from hypocrisy than any other place she'd been in America. She might have stayed there for ever, but for meeting Sebastian.

They met three years ago while she was at a conference in Denver where Sebastian was giving a lecture on infectious diseases. She was enraptured initially by his controversial view that women should be welcomed wholeheartedly into the medical profession, and by his beautiful, deep, melodious voice. He wasn't a handsome man, tall, thin and rather ungainly, with a mop of untidy grey-streaked black hair and an equally untidy beard. But after his lecture he stopped her, and asked her to tell him her experiences as a lady doctor, and within minutes they were talking as if they'd known each other all their lives.

That talk led to dinner at her hotel. As they laughed, argued and chatted, she found she no longer noticed his sticking-out ears, or his over-large nose, but saw instead his lovely dark blue eyes, long slender fingers, and a smile that made her feel like a young girl again.

The next morning some flowers were delivered to her hotel from him. The card with them was simply inscribed *'I've spent my whole life waiting for you to come along. Sebastian.'*

He had a practice in New York, she was 3,000 miles away in San Francisco, and common sense told her that an eminent physician of over forty could well be married, and a plain, dedicated spinster would not make a suitable mistress.

But he wrote to her as he travelled back to New York, and said he'd hardly had a wink of sleep through thinking about her. He said he was coming to San Francisco as soon as he could, to woo her. Matilda said that married men did not use words like 'woo', and that life was too short to be coy and girlish, so if Tabitha felt the same way as he clearly did, she must write back and tell him so.

Now, three years later, she was here in his parents' New York mansion, awaiting guests for their engagement dinner party. The ring on her finger was a single small diamond, but now, in the splendour of this drawing-room, she could understand why Sebastian had been amused by her restrained choice. Above her a crystal chandelier twinkled, paintings by renowned artists hung on the walls, there were dainty little side tables holding exquisite silver and porcelain ornaments, priceless oriental rugs covered the floor. Just the velvet drapes at the vast windows would buy a small row house, and everyone of the fourteen rooms she'd seen in this mansion were just as beautiful.

Sebastian had never told her his father was a multi-millionaire. She knew of course that to live on Fifth Avenue, New York's smartest address, he had to be rich, but Sebastian hadn't given her the impression he had been born with the proverbial silver spoon in his mouth. His clothes were plain, he was seriously committed to his work, and he was very at ease with ordinary people. So she had been taken aback by the size and splendour of his parents' home when she arrived here, and wished he'd given her some prior warning as to how this wealth had been acquired.

She knew now that Mr Everett's business was railroads,

although Brett, his elder son, had taken over running the company since the war, and completed the much-needed and long-awaited track right through to the west coast. The initial capital which started this company had come from Mrs Everett's grandfather who had once owned huge cotton plantations in the South. Tabitha knew that most of the richest and most powerful families in America had made their fortunes by exploitation of the poor in one way or another. But as railroads were essential for the greater good of the country, she was inclined to overlook the morality of the vast personal profits made by the Everetts. However, she wasn't sure Matilda would take such a liberal view.

Since the war, Matilda had become something of a firebrand on social injustice. If tonight's conversations should drift into dangerous waters, she was likely to air her hard-held views on railroad coolie labour, the plight of the Negroes and Indians, and once she got going, she wasn't a lady to mince her words.

'Stop worrying,' Sebastian whispered in her ear as the butler announced that the first guests, Mr and Mrs MacVeeney, had arrived. 'I know what you are thinking, but you know as well as I do that Matty can be the soul of diplomacy when she chooses to be!'

Tabitha smiled, she was always surprised by Sebastian's ability to tune into her thoughts. He looked almost handsome tonight, for his hair and beard had at last been given a dramatic pruning, and he wore his dinner jacket with style. But then she wasn't marrying him for his looks, position or his ancestors, what she loved about him above all else was his belief that he was set on this world to help the sick, and whether they were rich or poor, he gave them the same attention.

He had as little time for mealy-mouthed philanthropists as he did for self-seeking capitalists. He saw his wealthy patients in their homes or at his smart surgery in Washington Square, and if they believed he rarely set foot out of the two-mile radius surrounding it, he didn't choose to enlighten them otherwise. In fact he also gave his medical services free at a clinic in the Lower East Side, and acted as a surgeon at two charity hospitals.

On each of his three visits to San Francisco, he had grown to love and admire Matty as Tabitha did. He knew too that her early influence on Tabitha would mean she would want to treat the very poor when she moved to New York, and although perhaps he hoped this would be in the same inconspicuous way he did it, he had never said as much. This diplomatic stance was both sensible and endearing to Tabitha – like Matilda she had never had time for folk who wore their good works like a badge.

Tabitha jumped to her feet to meet the MacVeeneys. Mrs Emily MacVeeney was Anne's younger sister and Tabitha thought they were remarkably alike. But Emily's smile appeared very much more sincere, and she kissed Tabitha's cheek with warmth when they were introduced.

'I am so very pleased to meet you at last,' she said, her brown eyes sweeping over Tabitha as if she liked what she saw. 'My nephew has told me so much about you, my dear, and we're so very happy that you are soon to become one of our family.'

Mr George MacVeeney was small and stout with a ruddy complexion and a bulbous nose. He pumped Tabitha's hand vigorously and beamed at her as he made similar welcoming remarks.

Emily admired Tabitha's gown, and said that red had been her favourite colour as a young woman. 'It's a great disappointment to me that as one gets older one can no longer wear such vivid colours.' She looked down at her own rose-pink gown which was sprinkled with tiny seed pearls and grimaced. 'Pink is a poor substitute for red.'

'You look lovely,' Tabitha said truthfully. 'Both you and your sister are so elegant, I hope I can count on some advice from you both when choosing clothes for my trousseau. I am overwhelmed by the amount of shops here in New York, I really don't know where to start.'

Matilda arrived on the dot of seven, simultaneously with Brett, Sebastian's older brother, his wife Amy, Rupert, a cousin, and his wife Sophia. As Tabitha had met Brett, Rupert and their wives just the day before, she greeted them quickly and turned her entire attention on Matilda.

She was stunned by how magnificent she looked, and touched that she had clearly spent the last four days preparing for tonight to create the best possible impression. Her black velvet evening gown was trimmed with fluffy feathers around the low neck, enhancing her delicate pinky-toned skin, and a beautiful sapphire necklace and ear bobs, left to her by Zandra, matched her eyes. As always she wore lace gloves; tonight's ones reached to her elbows, with tiny jet buttons at the wrists. Her blonde hair had been carefully arranged up in loose curls by an artful hairdresser, and it shone like gold under the chandelier. She was forty-seven now, but her figure had remained taut and slender, and the few lines on her face had only added softness, not age.

Every man in the room turned to look at her in admiration, and Tabitha felt her heart swell with tenderness and pride, for ten years ago when James was killed, she had been fearful that Matilda would never recover her spirits or her looks. She had worn black from that day since, and in that last year of the war, Tabitha had seen her grow thinner and thinner, until she was just skin and bone. She hardly slept, did as much work as three other nurses, and so often Tabitha woke in the night to see her sitting by the window crying silently.

Yet grief-stricken as she was, when she returned to San Francisco, she put on a brave face. She opened London Lil's again with a lavish celebration party and within weeks it was as famous and popular as it had been during the Gold Rush years, the shows she put on even more spectacular. Yet however much she might have appeared to be only interested in making her own personal fortune, those who knew her well saw that her real motivation was to use this wealth to improve the lot of the underclasses.

When she saw how many girls had fallen into prostitution during the war, she bought the empty neighbouring house in Folsom Street, in order to offer sanctuary to more of them. She opened a working girls' boarding-house for the same reason, and expanded the Jennings Bureau to find work for the many soldiers who came back to the city with disabilities.

Tabitha was away in Ohio at that time, but Peter, who was then training as an accountant, wrote to her, often in anger because Matilda was still slighted by 'polite society' in the city and he claimed that the malicious rumours about her came from this quarter. One was that Matilda was supposed to be a procuress herself, that she lured fallen girls to her doors to polish them up, then sent them off to brothels in other cities. They said she had a string of lovers, and that she made huge profits from her so-called charitable works, and that much of the donations from the public went into her pocket along with the fortune she made from London Lil's.

As Peter did all Matilda's book-keeping, he knew that the small profit Matilda made from the bureau and boarding-house, along with all donations, went straight to the girls it was intended for. A third of all profits from London Lil's went to several charities, the one closest to Matilda's heart was to aid war widows and their children.

But then a great many of these socialites who reviled her had increased their wealth by speculation and carpet-bagging during the war. Their sons had wriggled out of the draft, some of them were the unscrupulous owners of properties on the Barbary Coast and shareholders in the Union Pacific Railroad.

When they saw Matilda vigorously speaking out at rallies on behalf of the Chinese who were used in their thousands almost as slave labour on the building of the railroad, or read her impassioned articles in newspapers about the need for free medical help for the poor, for Negroes to have the same rights as white men, for the Indians to be treated with respect, and for the Barbary Coast to be policed and cleaned up, they quaked.

Yet Tabitha, Peter and Sidney had in time learned to ignore the salacious gossip about the lady they loved, just as Matilda herself did, for the work she did brought its own rewards, and she was content. For every lie spread about her there were ten people with a debt of gratitude to her who told their true stories. It became widely known that on nights she was missing from the saloon, she was either down at Folsom Street teaching girls to read and write, harassing police into raiding brothels to check on their girls' ages, or looking out for girls who were in need of help.

Peter often said that if she had been a plain woman, with a less flamboyant nature, she might have gained sainthood by now, for the poor knew her true worth and loved her. But a woman who could laugh, dance and take a drink with customers in her saloon, who drove a smart gig and knew personally most of the shady characters in town, including the politicians, and who aroused female jealousy, was bound to be vilified. Matilda liked it that way, she didn't want the status of saint, she identified too often with the sinners.

'You look wonderful,' Tabitha said, embracing Matilda, and suddenly not caring a jot if she upset a few people later tonight. 'Let me introduce you to everyone.'

'First let me look at you!' Matilda said, her smile as vivid as her eyes. 'That dress, Tabby, is inspirational!'

They both laughed, for Matilda had had it made for her by her own dressmaker back in San Francisco. While they were choosing the material, Matilda had related the tale of how Lily had worn red for passion when Giles proposed to her. She said Tabitha must keep up the family tradition.

'You don't think it's just a wee bit too bold for me?' Tabitha whispered.

Matilda shook her head. 'It's perfect, the colour warms your skin and empathizes with your lovely eyes.'

Perhaps it was true that love made all women beautiful, she thought. She didn't know who had arranged Tabitha's hair in ringlets, so that they jiggled on her bare shoulders seductively, but she deserved praise, for it set the gown off to perfection.

She wondered for just one moment what Miss Dix would have made of this dramatic change in her nurse's appearance. She certainly wouldn't have let Tabitha into her hospital if she knew she was capable of looking like this!

'Now,' she said, her eyes dancing, 'I'm ready to be introduced, and more than ready to tell them all how much you will enhance their family.'

'You see, I was right, she's charming everyone,' Sebastian whispered in Tabitha's ear a little later. Matilda was at the centre of the family group, sparkling and vivacious as she found out who everyone was, asked about their children, and told funny little anecdotes about the long and cold journey she'd shared with Tabitha from California.

As they all went into dinner, Tabitha felt more relaxed. She and Sebastian were seated next to each other at one side of the beautifully laid table, Matilda and Anne opposite them, with Albert and George at the head and foot, the other guests in between. The first course was a consommé, followed by a fish dish, and Matilda was being so very gracious, taking care to compliment Anne on the superb food, her lovely home, and also chatting to Brett, who sat on her immediate right. Tabitha had noticed Anne kept looking at Matilda's gloves, as if wondering why she hadn't removed them, and she wished she had confided in Anne why she wore them.

Sebastian led most of the conversation, he spoke of the brownstone house he had just purchased close to Central Park, and got Tabitha to describe some of the furniture they had bought the previous day. Their wedding was to be in early April at Trinity Church, followed by a reception here at the house. His three young nieces were to be bridesmaids, and Amy, his sister-in-law, spoke up to say her girls were terribly excited, and she just hoped Tabitha could get them all to agree on what colour dresses they were to wear.

'I really don't mind,' Tabitha laughed. 'What colour have they got in mind?'

Amy groaned and said one wanted red, one blue and the other pink. She'd already told the youngest one that red wasn't a suitable colour for a wedding.

Matilda looked at Tabitha, her lips quivering with silent laughter, clearly remembering how Tabitha herself had asked if she could wear red when her father was making the plans for their wedding.

'I agree, we have to rule out red,' Tabitha said, giving Matilda a sly wink. 'But as all the girls are so blonde and angelic, why don't we settle for pink?'

Amy, who was blonde too, of German descent, beamed.

'I believe your father was once minister at Trinity Church?' she said. 'That should make the day extra special for you, Tabitha.'

'Yes, indeed,' Tabitha smiled. 'That's why we chose it. When Sebastian and I went there to make the arrangements, I was quite overcome by all the memories it brought back. I thought I'd forgotten everything about it. But I hadn't. We walked round to State Street where we used to live, but the house has been pulled down now, and there's an insurance company there instead.'

Everyone spoke of the dramatic changes in what was now just a financial district, and George MacVeeney spoke of when most of the area was gutted by the fire of 1845. He said he had owned a warehouse at that time and he lost everything.

'It was a terrible sight,' Matilda said, commiserating with him. 'We were choking on the smoke in the house in State Street. Lily,

Tabby's mother, was terrified the fire would reach it too, but fortunately for us the wind blew it towards the river.'

'You were there then?' Anne said in surprise, turning in her seat to look at Matilda, brown eyes like gimlets.

'Of course,' Matilda said. 'I was Tabby's nursemaid. I came to America with the Milsons.'

'I haven't gone back that far with my family history,' Tabitha said, looking across the table to Anne. 'Matty became my nursemaid back in London when I was only two. She held our family together through thick and thin. Both Mama and Papa always said they didn't know what they'd do without her.'

Anne gave Matilda a sideways stare. 'And you stepped into the breach and married Reverend Milson when his wife died too.'

That remark had more than a tinge of sarcasm and Tabitha heard alarm bells ringing in her head. Matilda was too honest to be an entirely successful liar, and she was already blushing.

'I loved both Lily and Giles,' she said, but as all other conversations around the table had stopped suddenly her voice sounded unnaturally loud. 'I couldn't stay and care for Tabitha alone in the house with Giles, there would have been talk. So we decided to marry.'

'So it was a marriage of convenience?' Anne probed.

Tabitha gulped. She knew Matilda would never agree to that, not even to smooth things over.

'No, for love,' she said. 'It grew out of our shared grief. Sadly Giles was killed just a few weeks later, and because Tabby and I could no longer stay in the minister's house in Independence, the following spring we joined a wagon train to take us to my friends in Oregon.'

Tabitha breathed a sigh of relief. She thought Matilda had handled that superbly, as she hadn't spoken of an actual wedding, she hadn't even told a lie.

'We had a pretty terrible time on the way,' Tabitha said, and giggled from nervousness. 'Amelia, my half-sister, was born in the wagon just before we got to The Dalles.'

There was a chorus of sympathetic noises from all the women, and surprisingly from Brett too, who had seemed rather pompous and chilly when she first met him yesterday. Sophia, Cousin Rupert's wife, a vivacious, dark-haired woman, remarked on how hard it must have been for Matilda to make such an arduous journey at such a time, and asked whether Amelia was going to be a bridesmaid too.

'Sadly no, Amelia died from cholera when she was six,' Tabitha said. 'Aunt Cissie, and her daughter Susanna too. You may have heard me speak of Peter, he was another of Cissie's children. Matilda took him back to San Francisco, and brought him up as her own. I think of him as a brother.'

There was a moment's embarrassed silence, broken only by Sophia apologizing profusely for being so tactless.

'You weren't to know,' Matilda said, giving Sophia a gentle smile. 'There is so much sadness in everyone's family, but I hope with more good doctors like Sebastian and Tabby, perhaps one day a cure will be found for such terrible diseases.'

Tabitha thought Anne had run out of loaded questions, and as the main course – roast pheasant – was brought in and served, she moved back to speaking about the house Sebastian had bought, and her view that they would need to hire a housekeeper and a cook if Tabitha was *really* going to practise medicine in New York after the wedding.

'Of course she is, Mother,' Sebastian laughed. 'We are intending that she should have her surgery in our house, and I shall be relying on you to send along all the women you know who have been harshly treated by male doctors.'

Anne made no reply to this, and Tabitha thought the odd expression on her future mother-in-law's face was irritation that her son had chosen to make such an announcement in public, rather than tell her himself first in private. But to her surprise she turned to Matilda again. 'Why don't you call yourself Mrs Milson?' she asked.

This was something neither Tabitha nor Sebastian had thought of, and Tabitha wished they had.

But Matilda just shrugged. 'Jennings is my family name. When I started up my business in San Francisco, I decided to revert back to it.'

'Because you were afraid that people would find it shocking that a minister's widow would run a saloon?'

Neither Tabitha nor Sebastian had sought to cover up what Matilda's business was, even though they knew genteel folk were invariably affronted by it. Sebastian had said his family were open-minded and once they met Matilda they would see what a fine woman she was for themselves.

But Anne's remark was clearly designed to belittle Matilda. Was it jealousy because she sensed everyone was captivated by this attractive, interesting woman?

'I've never been afraid of anything, or anyone,' Matilda retorted, fixing Anne with a chilling look. 'I had two children to support, so I just did what I could for them.'

'And a fine job she made of it too,' Sebastian said stoutly. 'Look at my lovely Tabitha, one of the first few women doctors in America. I'm so very proud of her, but it is to Matilda much of the praise should go, for without her determination to give Tabby a fine education, she never would have got there. Did you know Matilda joined Tabby in nursing during the war too?'

Tabitha was touched by Sebastian's effort to move the conversation on to safer ground, and as none of the guests knew about this, she told them a little of the hospital in Washington and about their cramped lodgings there. As medical matters weren't considered a suitable topic for the dinner table she kept off the horrors, but she did add that after the Battle of Gettysburg the number of casualties were so vast they worked almost round the clock.

Albert Everett had said almost nothing during the entire meal, in fact he hadn't appeared to be even listening to the conversations either, but just as Tabitha thought all difficulties had been surmounted, he suddenly spoke up.

'Were you two the nurses at Brigadier Russell's funeral?' he said, leaning forward. His dark blue eyes, so very like his son's, were suddenly animated. He looked towards George, his brother-in-law, at the far end of the table. 'You must remember that funeral, George? Brigadier Russell was the man who insisted on being buried with his men at Gettysburg. None of his family attended, just two nurses. We read about it in the papers, it was just a couple of months before we heard Aaron had died.'

George looked a little bewildered and flustered. 'I recall reading about the funeral, Albert. We thought it was very noble of the man to wish to be buried there, and a comfort to the families of his men. But I don't remember about two nurses.'

'You do,' Albert insisted. 'We were sitting in the library that afternoon and we talked of nothing else. There was a great deal of controversy because Russell's wife was the daughter of Colonel Harding and they weren't informed of his request.'

Tabitha felt a chill run down her spine. She wasn't surprised Albert remembered about it, war correspondents had made much of James's funeral, and as Aaron had also been at West Point, like James, it would have had special significance. But then the story had touched people all over America. Many considered it to be one of the most moving incidents of the war. Many notable generals, including Grant, paid homage to James's gallant leadership and unswerving courage in battle. Even President Lincoln was quoted as having said that 'Brigadier Russell was an inspiration to his men, and his request that he should be buried with those who fell alongside him must surely acknowledge his deep respect for them.' Yet some of the correspondents who sided with the rebels had brought up the Union defeat at Fredericksburg, James's home town, and implied this was the true reason he didn't wish his body to be returned there for burial.

Tabitha caught hold of Sebastian's hand under the table and squeezed it, hoping he'd think of something to say to prevent this going any further.

But before he even had a chance to say anything, Matilda spoke. 'You have a very good memory, Mr Everett, Tabby and I were indeed the two nurses at the funeral. Brigadier Russell was an old and very dear friend. We had met him when he was a captain, he led our wagon train to Oregon. When I heard he had been brought to Washington wounded, I went to see him, indeed stayed with him until he died. He asked me if we would attend his funeral and we were proud to be there.'

'Well!' Anne Everett gasped, her slender body as stiff as a fire iron. 'It's all coming back to me. He came from Virginia, one of the oldest families. There were many who felt he should have fought for the Confederacy.'

'He couldn't have fought for them,' Tabitha said. 'He was against secession and slavery.'

'I think we should change the subject,' Sebastian said. He knew the whole story of Russell and Matilda, and what they had been to one another. While he thought the story very moving, and one he intended to tell with pride to his own children, he was afraid that it would only bring back sad memories for Matilda, and also of Aaron for both his parents.

'But why, Sebastian darling?' his mother said, fixing him with an overbright smile. 'Because it was rumoured that one of the nurses was Russell's mistress?'

There was a gasp from some of the women round the table. But before Tabitha could catch her breath, Matilda turned in her chair to face Anne.

Tabitha knew Matilda loved James far too much ever to deny her relationship with him. Their love affair was her most treasured memory. Tabitha could see her bracing herself to speak of it, and she had never looked more lovely: such pride in her clear blue eyes, defiance in her chin, only the faint quiver of her lips proving that her love for James ran as deep today as it had ten years ago.

'Mrs Everett,' she said in a clear, unwavering voice, and Tabitha felt as if her heart was breaking for her, 'rumours about me abound, most of them founded on ignorance or jealousy, and usually I ignore them. But I will put you straight on this one, because it is not something I am ashamed of, and if Tabby is to marry your son it is best that there are no secrets between us.

'It is true that I was James Russell's mistress, and I loved him more than life itself.'

'I can really make no comment about your behaviour, but didn't you stop to think what such a scandal could do to your daughter?' Anne retorted, two bright red spots appearing on her cheeks. 'Taking her with you to your lover's funeral!'

Matilda's eyes narrowed and darkened, she had the expression on her face which Tabitha had seen so often as a child. It was a mixture of anger and scorn, and it always precipitated a verbal tongue-lashing.

'My dear Mrs Everett, Tabitha went to the funeral to pay her last respects to an old friend. She was twenty-two then, hardly a child,' she said, her voice like ice.

There was a little sniff from Anne. Matilda looked across the table at Tabitha and Sebastian first, then her eyes swept right round the table at all the shocked faces.

'I am sorry if my bluntness offends you,' she said, 'but I have always believed one should tell the truth. However, whatever you choose to think of me, you must not allow that to reflect on your opinion of my step-daughter. She has a spotless character, she is an excellent doctor, and comes from better stock than anyone else at this table.'

Mrs Everett gave a sniff of disbelief.

Tabitha's blood ran cold, for she knew Matilda always fought to win, and her tongue could be as sharp as any sword when her blood was up.

'You don't agree?' Matilda said with a faint smirk. 'Well, let me put this to you. Does a family fortune made by the work of slaves, and the building of railroads which took the lives of hundreds of Chinese and Irish labourers, mean one is superior to a poor but enlightened church minister, who spent his whole life working for the good of others? I surely doubt it.'

There was utter silence for a moment, not a clink of a glass or the rustle of a napkin. Every face turned towards Anne Everett and Matilda.

Tabitha hadn't discovered how the Everetts' fortune had been made until she'd arrived here in New York. She wondered when and how Matilda had discovered this.

The silence was broken by Sebastian clapping his hands. 'Well said, Matilda,' he exclaimed. 'You are not only right of course, but very brave to speak out. But this evening was intended to celebrate the engagement of Tabitha and myself, not to look back on the rights and wrongs of either of our families. I wish to propose a toast to that effect.' He picked up his glass of wine and looked around the table. 'I propose that we should all look forward to a bright new future in which sadness and old prejudices will be laid aside.'

Brett was the next to raise his glass, and gave his mother a scathing glance. 'To the future!' he said.

George and Albert at opposite ends of the table looked a little puzzled, perhaps they hadn't fully heard everything that had been said. But they raised their glasses, and everyone else followed suit.

Tabitha wondered how the dinner party could possibly continue harmoniously, but to her surprise Matilda turned to Anne and smiled. 'We really should have got together earlier to sound one another out, shouldn't we? But it's done now, and let's put it aside. Now, do please tell me where you got that beautiful gown made, it's so stylish, it could have come from Paris.'

Perhaps Anne Everett realized she had made a grave mistake in trying to humiliate Matilda, for she made no further sarcastic remarks, and surprisingly, seemed to warm to her outspoken guest. By the time the dessert was served, the matter had been put aside, for Matilda had drawn everyone out by suggesting everyone told their favourite comic story about someone they knew.

George's was about a good friend of his involved in landscaping Central Park who was tricked into parting with an enormous sum for trees, expecting them to be well-established ones of at least four or five feet in height. When they arrived they were seedlings, no more than three inches high. Rupert, who was in banking, told a tale about a man who posed as an English lord, got himself invited to all the society events, where he charmed everyone, and managed to swindle thousands of dollars from the bank. By the time it was discovered the man was in fact Irish, a penniless immigrant when he first arrived in New York, he had skipped off to South America.

Brett prompted his father Albert to tell them all about the disastrous ceremonious opening of the railroad into Chicago. The dignitaries, including two Senators, were to arrive by train. A band was playing on the station, Albert and Brett waiting to receive them with a champagne reception. When the dignitaries and their train never arrived, Brett and Albert had to go out on a handcar, pumping themselves down the line to inspect, only to find that several miles out of town, some wild railroad men had decided to remove a length of the track as a prank. The train with its load of dignitaries was stranded there, not hopping mad and indignant as Brett and Albert expected, but drunk, as there had been large supplies of whiskey on board.

It was almost midnight when the party finally broke up. Matilda was last to leave, and as Tabitha and Sebastian escorted her to the front door where her carriage was waiting, Matilda suddenly enveloped Tabitha in a tight hug.

'I'm sorry if I embarrassed you,' she said. 'But I had to set the record straight.'

'I'm very glad you did,' Tabitha said, hugging her back. 'It's all out in the open now, and I'm so very proud of you.'

Sebastian grinned. 'It turned out to be the best and liveliest dinner party Mother's ever thrown,' he said. 'I bet we'll all be talking of it for months.'

Matilda disengaged herself from Tabitha and took Sebastian's two hands in hers, looking up at him. 'You are a good man, Sebastian,' she said. 'I couldn't imagine any man being more worthy of my precious Tabby. I really don't mind your mother thinking I'm a common upstart, I guess I am. But I had to point out to all your family, for Giles and Lily's sake, that Tabitha is their equal. That was the really important issue.'

Sebastian was touched by the sincerity in her words. He could feel the roughness of her hands in his, even through her lace gloves. They said so much about her character and he hoped his mother would one day see them too, for then perhaps she'd really understand what made him love and respect this woman so much.

'You are more of a real lady than all of Lady Astor's cronies put together,' he said. 'Now, go on back to your hotel before you catch cold and sleep tight. Tabby and I will meet you for lunch tomorrow.'

As Matilda's carriage bowled away through the snow to the Fifth Avenue Hotel, she smiled to herself. All things considered, she decided, Tabitha was marrying into a good family. The men were principled and fair-minded, and Tabitha's modern views would almost certainly bring a welcome breath of fresh air to the younger women. She thought it would be advisable, though, to keep her distance from Anne Everett. Tonight's sharp exchanges might have been necessary to clear a few cobwebs, but she guessed that in the next few weeks before the wedding, Anne would be eagerly waiting for her to make a social blunder, and if it came she would be all too gleeful.

Not that Matilda had any intention of getting involved with any more society folk while she was here, that was the main reason she'd opted for staying in a hotel. That way she was free to come and go as she pleased, wander around the city, and see Tabitha and Sebastian on her own.

She was astounded at how much New York had grown and changed since she first came here as a young girl. The vast and beautiful Central Park had replaced that awful shantytown Flynn had once shown her, blocks and blocks of smart new houses on both sides of it. There was a train which ran overhead, lighting on all the streets, and many wonderful shops. So far the snow had prevented any real exploring on foot, but maybe she'd buy some stout boots if it didn't clear soon.

Peter and his wife Lisette, Sidney, Mary and their children would be joining her for the wedding, and after the bride and groom had gone off on their honeymoon, they were intending to make the return journey a holiday, stopping off in different towns they'd always wanted to visit.

Sidney had three more children now, John, Cissie and Ruby. All five children had freckles and red curly hair, and Matilda adored them. Peter had married Lisette only last year after a long courtship; she had the looks and style of her French mother, and the brains of her lawyer father, Henry Pollock.

The war and a close brush with death had changed Peter, just as it had so many of the brave young men who entered into it thinking it was the ultimate adventure. While still as outwardly jovial and devil-may-care as he'd always been, those who knew him well saw greater sensitivity, caution and ambition. He had taken Matilda's advice and studied accountancy, and he now had a flourishing practice with dozens of extremely prosperous clients. His good education and the circles he mixed in now had given him a sophistication which Sidney lacked, yet he had retained his integrity and a social conscience. He had used the money he'd inherited from Cissie to buy a very comfortable house, but along with handling all Matilda's financial affairs, he was her confidant, aide and supporter in all her charity work too.

It had been Peter more than anyone who had helped her to come to terms with losing James, for he truly shared her loss. He was the one who always knew when she was thinking about him, and his little stories about James during the war gave her back the small part of the man she hadn't seen.

As the organ at Trinity Church began to wheeze into life and the wedding march began, Matilda turned to look at Tabitha being led up the aisle by Sidney, and tears pricked her eyelids.

It seemed impossible that this tall, slender woman in white satin was that plump little tot she'd rescued from the path of the horse and carriage over thirty years ago. Matilda had never managed to hold any real faith in God, but today she was prepared to acknowledge that perhaps he had orchestrated that near tragedy for a purpose.

Had she not met the Milsons, she would never have come here to America. Without her assistance Giles might never have gone into Five Points and found Sidney, or Cissie. But for Cissie she would never have set out to Oregon and met James. All their lives seemed to have been inextricably linked, and today it did seem to have been pre-ordained.

She glanced back along her pew, putting her finger to her lips to warn the children to stay quiet. Mary looked lovely in emerald green, her red curls peeping becomingly from her bonnet. She smiled serenely as she held Ruby, the youngest, in her arms, perhaps thinking back to her own wedding. Sidney often said he felt blessed by having her and his five beautiful children; he said that being able to give his own children the love and security he'd never had as a child had wiped out any remaining bitterness about his early life.

She glanced over her shoulder to Peter and pretty, dark-haired Lisette in the pew behind. Lisette was tucking her arm through her husband's and looking up at him in some surprise as his eyes were glinting with emotional tears at seeing Tabitha in all her wedding finery. Was it possible that this elegant young man in his tail-coat and striped trousers had begun his life in a filthy cellar just a couple of miles from here?

Matilda gulped to rid herself of the lump in her throat. They were her children, even if not one of them had been born to her, bound together as brothers and sister by the hand of fate. Her father's advice never to look back might have stood her in good stead for most of her life, but it was right to look back now, for here in the church she knew so well as a young nursemaid, she could see the sense in the long and sometimes impossibly hard road which had led her back here again.

While she felt sadness that she'd never been a bride herself, she had been blessed in so many other areas of her life. She had known the kind of passion which most women only dream of, and love in so many different forms. She'd had adventure, good friends, excellent health, and become wealthy too. She wasn't ashamed of anything and she had no real regrets. If she was to die tomorrow she could go happily knowing she *had* made a difference in other people's lives.

Tabitha and each of the three bridesmaids were holding posies that Matilda had made herself this morning. She'd gone down to the flower market and bought the flowers herself, far grander posies than she ever sold on the streets, with pink rosebuds, white carnations, and delicate freesia. But the old skill hadn't left her, she'd picked the glossy leaves which enclosed the flowers from a bush in Central Park, wrapped the twine tightly around the stems and added a circle of lace and ribbon to finish them off. The scent of them brought back a whiff of England and in some odd way seemed to evoke Lily and Giles's presence.

There was pain inside her that James hadn't lived to see this day. It would have been just perfect if he was by her side now, his hand in hers. But he was tucked into her heart, and if heaven was the way Giles used to describe, he was here somewhere watching, along with all those other dear ones who loved her and Tabitha.

As Tabitha came alongside Matilda, she turned to smile. Her face was partially concealed by her veil, but her happiness shone through it. As she continued forward, Sebastian turned round at his position at the altar rail, and the look of naked love on his face was unmistakable.

'Don't you dare start crying yet!' Mary whispered to her, above her small children's heads. 'You'll start me off!'

Brett was Sebastian's best man, and they both cut fine figures in their tail-coats. Matilda glanced across the nave to the Everett family. They had at least ten times more people on their side, from young children right up to very old folk. Anne was dabbing at her eyes too, and she looked a picture in pink silk, the crinoline skirt so wide it filled the pew, and her bonnet trimmed with small white flowers.

Matilda's gown and small veiled hat were pale blue. She had abandoned her customary black just for the wedding as she didn't think James would approve of her in mourning on such a happy occasion.

After the minister had pronounced Tabitha and Sebastian man and wife, he mounted the pulpit for his sermon, and Matilda hoped he'd make it a brief one for the children were beginning to fidget. She had never really been bored when Giles preached, but he was the only minister she remembered, apart from the Reverend Darius Kirkbright', who could manage to hold her interest for more than a few minutes. She closed her eyes for a second and remembered Kirkbright's speech of farewell to the Milsons, and how the congregation had applauded. She wondered if he was still alive. He'd be at least eighty now, so she doubted it.

The Waifs' and Strays' Home was still there in New Jersey, she'd taken the ferry to see it soon after she got to New York. Perhaps it was a mistake to go back, as it wasn't as welcoming as she remembered, icy cold, the children too quiet and cowed, and she suspected they were hungry too. But then few things were the same. New York was all grown up, most of the old wooden houses she remembered gone, replaced by brick and cast iron, an elevated train service whizzing along overhead, belching out thick smoke into the tenements of the Lower East Side it passed by.

Sebastian had told her that these tenements, most of them built just a few years earlier, were a public disgrace, designed purely to make as large a profit as possible for the landlords out of the smallest amount of space. Even if only one family occupied each tiny three-room dwelling, with only one window on the outer wall, they would be cramped and unsanitary, but the rent was too high for the poor immigrants, and they all sub-let, with sometimes as many as three or four families squeezed into one apartment. With great sadness Sebastian had pointed out that while the elegant brownstones in the blocks around Washington Square and Central Park and of course the mansions on Fifth Avenue had water piped right into their homes, the poor of the tenements still had to make do with one privy and tap between hundreds of them.

Matilda had steeled herself against going to look at these tenements, for she knew once she'd seen them, she wouldn't be able to contain her desire to do something to help. So instead she had made several trips to Macy's, the fine dry goods store which had opened on Sixth Avenue, to buy lengths of cotton and flannel to take home for her girls to make up into baby clothes and dresses for themselves. She reminded herself that she was here in New York just for Tabitha, that San Francisco had enough problems for her to deal with, and she was better placed to give her help there.

The sun was shining when they eventually emerged from

the church, and as all the wedding guests waited while the photographer set up his camera to take pictures of the happy couple, Matilda was reminded of Dolores, and of her words that day she had found Matilda crying over her picture of James. It was still a mystery to both of them that a likeness of a person or an object could be transferred to a sheet of paper, just as it was equally puzzling how a message could be sent by telegraph from one side of the country to the other. But she supposed the young understood such things.

Dolores was sixty now, but still running the home on Folsom Street with as much energy as she'd shown when they first began it, and Fern was thirty-two, and still her housekeeper at the working girls' hostel. What wonders they both were!

As Matilda stood in the sunshine of the old churchyard, the other wedding guests all around her, memories of Flynn flitted through her mind. They had never dared walk through here for fear of running into Giles, but almost every street surrounding the church held poignant memories of him. Most of the tea and coffee shops they'd spent so much time in were gone now, but many of the alleyways he'd kissed her in were still there. She'd walked down to Castle Green one day and looked out across the bay, remembering all the dreams they wove together there.

She wondered what happened to him. Did he make his fortune? Or did he join the rebel army as so many Irishmen did, only to be killed too?

'Why such a sad face?' Sidney asked her, taking her by surprise.

It seemed improbable that Sidney was thirty-eight, married with five children. His face had grown fatter and ruddy in the last few years, there was a paunch under his tail-coat, and deep lines around his eyes. Only his red hair was the same, it still shone out like a torch.

'Just memories,' and she laughed lightly. 'Has it brought back any for you?'

'Too many! I slept here in the churchyard in the summer on many a night,' he said with a wide grin. 'And down on Castle Green! But I shan't be telling any of these smart people that! I had it in mind to take Mary and the children out to New Jersey before we leave and see the Home again though.'

'Don't,' she said, taking hold of his arm and squeezing it. 'It's not how you remember it, there's nothing good to see and it will upset the children.'

He looked surprised, amber eyes widening. 'Okay, I won't do that, not if you think it might upset them. But you won't talk me out of taking Peter to Five Points.'

'You can't, Sidney,' she said in horror. 'That won't be good for either of you.'

Sidney's mouth was set in a determined straight line. 'Peter needs to see where he was born. It's as much part of his life as the trip to Oregon, Cissie and the girls dying, or the Battle of Gettysburg. We're both grown men now, Matty. Don't try to stop us.'

Matilda woke early the next morning to the sound of whispering outside her hotel room door. Recognizing the voices as belonging to Peter and Sidney, she guessed they had both crept out of their own rooms and were planning to go to the Lower East Side, now, before their wives woke.

She was out of bed in a flash and opened her door. They were bending over to put their boots on. 'Come in here, both of you,' she said sternly.

Although the previous day's wedding ceremony had been a joyful occasion, the reception in the afternoon at the Everetts' mansion had proved an unhappy experience for Sidney and Mary. Neither of them was accustomed to sophisticated events, and the splendour of the mansion and the elegant guests made them awkward and gauche. Perhaps their children had sensed their discomfort too, for they played them up, touching everything and climbing on furniture, which had in turn made the couple even more uneasy.

Matilda had whisked the children away later, taking them for a carriage ride in Central Park, but on her return she was grieved to find that though removing the children to allow them to let off a little steam had calmed them down, Sidney and Mary still hadn't been able to relax enough to enjoy themselves. She understood why. Back home in San Francisco they were well known and respected, their origins or class immaterial, but their strained faces showed that in just a few hours, the day had been spoiled for them by feelings of inferiority.

Matilda sympathized, she could remember only too well her

own dilemma at finding she was neither fish nor fowl. In truth she knew she was still in the same position, she might have learnt how to look and behave like a lady well enough to pass muster, but closer inspection always gave her origins away.

She thought that maybe this was why Sidney was so determined to take Peter to Five Points. Was there just a tiny bit of rivalry because Peter could fit in so easily with the upper classes, when he couldn't?

'You are intending to go slumming, I take it?' she said, closing the door once they were inside.

They nodded like two schoolboys caught stealing apples.

As boys they had shared many similar characteristics, and even now as grown men they could pass for real brothers. They both had freckles and impudent grins, they were the same height and stocky build, though Sidney had grown fatter of late. Peter's hair was sandy rather than red, and his eyes were a pale brown while Sidney's were tawny, but they were very similar.

What set them apart was their different motivation. Sidney lived for the moment; running a busy saloon, with all that entailed, was as far as his ambition stretched. His security was all centred on his wife and family. He had a generous and sometimes flashy nature which showed in his superbly cut green coat and colourful necktie.

Peter, on the other hand, wore quiet clothes, his voice was softer, he was a thinker and he acted with caution. Yet he was the ambitious one, meticulously planning ahead rather than rushing. Just the way he had courted Lisette for so many years before finally marrying her was evidence of this. No doubt when children arrived he would be working out a plan for their education before they were even out of napkins.

Matilda loved them both, and knew all their strengths and weaknesses. Sidney was the fun one, a mad-cap who radiated sunshine. Peter was solid, utterly dependable, and she leaned on his intelligence. Together they created a very strong force.

Her first thought was to forbid them to go to Five Points. They might be grown men but they still always obeyed her when she put her foot down. Yet she wasn't sure she had the right to force them to her will. Maybe they did need to face where they came from! Would she allow anyone to stop her from seeing Finders Court if she went back to England?

'We're going, whatever you say,' Peter said, sticking out his chin in just the same determined way he had as a small boy.

'We're not going to come to any harm,' Sidney chimed in. 'It might be dangerous at night, but not this early in the morning!'

Matilda looked from one face to the other and realized nothing she could say, short of throwing a tantrum and waking up their wives, would stop them.

'Then I'm coming with you,' she said.

They argued with her, but Matilda held her hand up to stop them. 'If you go alone you might get into trouble. Besides, without me you won't see the things which might make it a valuable lesson to you.'

Ordering them to stay where they were, she went into her adjoining dressing-room to put her clothes on. She chose her plainest black dress and cape, a pair of stout boots, and a black untrimmed bonnet, for these were clothes she'd bought to go exploring herself.

Taking her small repeater pistol from a drawer, she quickly loaded it and slipped it into a hidden pocket at her waist. It had been some time since she last had occasion to threaten anyone with it, but she always carried it with her back home, and it had become a habit she couldn't break.

She slipped on her gloves as she came back into the bedroom and looked appraisingly at Sidney's green coat and grey derby hat. They were too conspicuous, but she knew he hadn't anything more sober here in New York. Peter's tweed coat was an expensive one, but quietly so. Yet as Sidney had pointed out, it was very early, and thugs and thieves were hardly likely to be out and about. But as a precaution she ordered both of them to leave their pocket watches and wallets behind.

The previous day's warm spring weather had vanished overnight. Outside on Fifth Avenue a chilly wind was blowing hard, and although it was only eight in the morning the street was busy with omnibuses, carts and gigs. Matilda hadn't been out this early before, and it was quite a revelation to see the street sweepers, servants scurrying to the stores and markets for their masters and mistresses, maids polishing door-knockers and washing down steps. A great many of them were Negroes, yet by mid-morning they would have vanished out of sight, to leave New York's most fashionable street mainly white.

The cab they called took them down Broadway, but as it turned on to the Bowery, Sidney became silent, staring intently out of the window, clearly remembering.

All at once Matilda realized that it was he who needed to see this area again, far more than Peter. It was almost thirty years ago that she had led him and his little band away from here, but for the first eight years of his life these streets had been home, and no doubt he had a million memories he'd never spoken of. Sidney claimed at the time he was rescued that his mother had died, and she had accepted it as true. Only now she wondered about this, for he'd never told her one thing about her. He could have just run away from her, many children did when a new man came into their mother's life. Maybe having children of his own had made him feel guilty about it?

If that was the case, maybe it was a good idea to come here again after all. It might prompt him to talk about that very early part of his life.

The cab slowed right down in the heavy traffic and up ahead Matilda could see a band of ragged, bare-footed small boys eyeing up a display of fresh fruit outside a store. Just the way they were discussing something and looking all around them made her certain they were about to pounce.

'Watch them,' she said to Peter, pointing them out. As they watched, all but one boy moved away slightly, leaving the one on his own to sidle up to the display and begin to pocket fruit. The shopkeeper spotted him, yelled and ran out, and the boy ran off with the man in hot pursuit. Meanwhile the rest of the gang rushed to the shop, grabbed what they could, then ran off in the opposite direction.

Peter laughed heartily. 'That was almost a military operation,' he said.

Matilda nodded sagely. To Peter it might look like boyish mischief, but she knew better. 'That might be the only food they get for a couple of days,' she said.

'Is that what you used to do, Sid?' Peter asked.

'Worse than that sometimes,' he replied with a smirk. 'My favourite target was the sausages hanging up on hooks. I used to get another smaller kid on my shoulders, rush by and get him to grab them. But once we did that, and I didn't notice there was a barber's pole sticking out right next door. The poor kid was knocked right off my shoulders, and we ran off. Later on I heard he'd died, must have cracked his head right open on the sidewalk.'

'But that's terrible,' Peter gasped.

'It was all terrible round here,' Sidney said with a shrug. 'Only the quick and the tough survived.'

'Sure this is where you want to go?' the cab driver asked as he dropped them off at the start of Mulberry Street. ''T'ain't a good place to be.'

'We have business here,' Sidney said, handing him the fare. The driver cracked his whip at his horse and drove off, looking stunned that anyone staying on Fifth Avenue should have any business here.

Mulberry Street had once been a winding cow path for cattle coming home from pasture. The old wooden houses which lined it in later years had been the homes of the wealthy, but like all the streets in the neighbourhood it had been taken over by the poorest immigrants. When Sidney was a boy, it had been almost as rough an area as neighbouring Five Points, but its quaint and almost picturesque appearance had given it a certain charm.

Matilda remembered almost fondly the hot sunny day she came here to collect the two little orphaned boys to take them out to New Jersey. But there was nothing quaint or picturesque about it now.

'The Bend', as the crooked elbow at the middle of the street was called, was lined with pedlars' carts and shops, where people were selling things as diverse as cigars, bread, second-hand clothes and fish. But these were not real shops, mostly just open doorways of the dilapidated buildings and boarding houses above, the seller plying his wares from an upturned ash can or a wooden box. A great many people were already milling around, and the contrast between them and the sort of folk they'd mixed with on the previous day was so marked it was like being in another country. Dirty old hags in rags crouched in doorways smoking clay pipes, whiskered, grim-faced men in shirtsleeves, often with a piece of sacking to serve as a jacket, hobbled along in worn-out boots. Younger women were haggling noisily over baskets of fish, their faces as grey as the slimy creatures they were bartering for.

The smell was so appalling, Peter covered his nose. 'What is it?' he asked.

'Human and animal excrement, unwashed bodies, putrid meat and stale beer,' Matilda said simply. 'San Francisco smelled just the same back in 1850, but at least there wasn't the poverty too. Just look at that bread!'

They were coming up to two old Italian women squatting by a basket. Their faces resembled dried prunes, and they pulled bread shaped like plaited wreaths out of filthy sacks with hands so dirty it made Matilda's stomach heave. The bread must have come from some fancy baker's uptown, several days before, and had almost certainly been retrieved from a garbage can.

They saw another two ancient crones hacking offal into lumps and shoving it into newspaper for their customers. It already smelled high, and their clothes and hands were encrusted in blood from several previous days' sales.

Sidney recognized an old wooden house as one which had marked one of the Five Points. A group of desperate-looking men were sitting on the ground outside, one trying to fix some cardboard into an almost sole-less boot. They scowled as Peter's eyes lingered on them just a little too long, and Matilda hurried him along.

But Five Points as Matilda and Sidney had known it was gone. The Old Brewery, Rat's Castle and all those other decayed wooden houses had been torn down and replaced by row after row of five-storey tenement blocks with rickety wooden stairs that snaked up the outside. Matilda and Sidney stood stock-still in surprise. She felt they ought to be glad that the terrible place they remembered was gone, yet she could feel no joy, because the new buildings were almost as bad, built so close together that precious little fresh air and sunshine could get in.

Sidney, however, seemed disappointed that he couldn't show Peter his birthplace. He used the word 'improvement' with a tone of regret.

Peter looked up at the grim buildings, ragged washing festooned along each wooden landing in horror. 'This is an improvement to where I was born?' he said.

'No improvement, Peter,' Matilda said, seeing rats playing on a pile of refuse out of the corner of her eye. 'Except perhaps for the landlords who get even more rent for each square yard. I can't believe that such a wealthy city would use its poor so badly. Just look at those children!'

Although it was early, they were everywhere, thin, barefoot, dirty, with matted hair, ghostly faces and wearing rags. Their hungry, bleak eyes, runny noses and apathetic stares were so very disturbing, and it was doubtful they'd been sent out to go to school, more likely just to give the adults indoors more room.

Sidney failed to pin-point exactly where Rat's Castle had been, or the cellar in Cat Alley where Peter was born, and they wandered back towards 'The Bend'. Peter had already seen enough and said he wanted to go back to the hotel, but Sidney insisted on going further.

'You gotta see it all, Peter,' he said, taking his arm and leading him into one of the many alleys which led off Mulberry Street. 'I reckon it's important to know where you came from, if only to see how lucky we were in getting out.'

The stench was even worse here, for this was the domain of rag-pickers. Matilda had to explain to Peter how they went about the city collecting up rags, then sorted them in the cellars of these places, and sold them on when they had a full load. She tried to make light of it, telling him about the day she'd run into such a yard and met Sidney for the first time, but it seemed even more ghastly than her old memories. Another alley was full of bottles of every shape and size, and small, thin children with hollow eyes patiently sorting them.

There were wounded ex-soldiers, some blind, others with missing limbs, arranging matches or cigars on a tray ready to go and sell them on the street. In a dank corner they saw a group of small boys all curled up together, still sleeping. Matilda guessed their lives were just the same as Sidney's had been, and unless someone stepped in and offered them a home, they'd be hardened villains by the time they were twelve.

They saw children no bigger than four or five carrying a 'growler' home, a pint or two of beer in a tin can. One burly man was skinning a small goat outside his doorway, while three or four others stood by, clearly waiting for their share of the animal they'd no doubt stolen.

But over and above the smell and the squalor was the infernal noise: babies crying, women yelling to one another from upstairs windows, men bellowing, and constant banging and scraping from work going on unseen in the buildings. So many, many people too, despite the early hour, women slumped on doorsteps, a baby at their breast, their dark-rimmed eyes and hollow cheeks suggesting they were as much in need of nourishment as the baby. Men huddled in groups, smoking pipes, looked suspiciously at Matilda and her two men as they passed, and all the time children were dodging around them, begging for money.

'Have you seen enough?' Matilda said a little later, for the narrow alleys were making her feel nauseous. Some they went through were full of Negroes, others Irish, Italians or Jews, but whatever the dominant nationality, they all shared appallingly similar conditions. She felt ashamed at coming here like a sight-seer, knowing that in an hour she could be back in her fancy hotel tucking into a big breakfast. It was adding insult to the burden of misfortune these people already had to bear.

She had pointed out to Peter that if everyone was to come out of the buildings at one time, she doubted there would be room for them to pass. In truth she thought it was worse than the old Five Points, there at least the residents in the main were rogues, thieves and the flotsam and jetsam that society had rejected. But she could see for herself by the endless washing being hung up, the women with brooms, and the noise of work being done inside the dingy, rotting buildings, that for the most part these were decent enough people who had come to America with empty pockets and a head full of dreams. All they had achieved was to swap a slum in Cork or Dublin, Naples, or Rome, for something even worse.

'I've seen more than enough,' Peter said in a weak voice. His face had turned pale and he looked very shaken. 'I had no idea.'

Sidney was still intent on exploring further, but Matilda refused, and taking Peter's arm began leading him away in the direction of Broadway, assuming that Sidney would follow them.

'It was very like this in the part of London where I grew up,' she said as they picked their way carefully through the alleys. 'But it's worse for these people, Peter, so many of them don't even speak English, they don't understand how this country works, and often they've brought ideas from their own countries with them which are at odds with ours here.

'Sebastian told me a story a while ago about a distraught Italian woman who came rushing into his clinic with her sick baby begging him to make the child better because she couldn't afford a funeral. He said it took him a minute or two to understand what she really meant. But it was just that! You see, it's a matter of pride to the very poor to have a proper funeral, they will sell or pawn everything they own, even borrow money they can't hope to pay back just to give their dead a good send-off. That woman wasn't so upset at the thought of her baby dying, child death is a common enough event, only that the expense of a funeral would put her entire family at risk of starvation. Isn't that terrible?'

Peter agreed it was, and told her that Tabitha had examined many immigrant women's small children and found them to be suffering from rickets and other complaints that sprang from poor nutrition. He said Tabitha had asked them what they fed their children and they had admitted to feeding them with what they ate themselves. That, Tabitha had discovered, was often just pretzels, doughnuts, beer and coffee. These poor, ignorant women who so wanted to become true Americans, had abandoned the sort of simple, cheap wholesome food they'd eaten back in the old country, instead they had embraced what they saw as an American diet.

A pail of water thrown from an upstairs window, narrowly missing them, made them turn to see Sidney wasn't right behind them.

Matilda sighed. Sidney was an inquisitive man, and very friendly, so she expected he'd struck up a conversation with someone. They had reached a wider lane which didn't smell quite so bad, and as Peter's colour was coming back, she was loath to go back again to the narrow alleyways. 'We'd better wait for him here,' she said wearily. She desperately wanted a cup of coffee, her stomach was rumbling from missing her breakfast, and she really didn't think they had achieved anything by coming here, except perhaps to give Peter a guilty conscience that he had so much when others had nothing.

After a wait of five or ten minutes, and still no sight of Sidney, they reluctantly turned back the way they had come. But as they turned into a particularly fetid alley, all at once they heard the sound of fighting, men shouting and women screaming.

Matilda's sixth sense told her Sidney was in the thick of it, and she began to run towards the noise, pushing through women turning out of doors, all intent on seeing what was going on.

As she came into a small yard between two very old houses, she could see Sidney's unmistakable red hair over the heads of the crowd gathered there. Frantically elbowing her way through, she got to the front and to her horror saw two men were holding on to each of Sidney's arms, while a third was hitting him around the head and middle with what looked like a long axe handle. Blood was pouring down the side of Sidney's head, and he didn't appear to have any strength left to fight the men off. A small child of perhaps five or six, standing near, was wearing his grey hat.

'Stop!' she yelled at the top of her voice. 'He's done nothing to you.'

Peter ran past her, straight up to the man hitting Sidney, and tried to grab the axe handle from him.

Matilda glanced around her. From every direction more and more people were coming, filling the small yard. She knew that it would be only seconds before someone set about Peter, and perhaps her too if she didn't do something.

She pulled out her gun from her pocket and fired a warning shot into the air.

'I said stop it,' she yelled at the top of her voice. 'The next person to touch either of my sons gets the next bullet.'

There was a sudden hush, people close to her edged away, but the two men holding Sidney merely glowered at her, and continued to hold him. It was clear they'd been hitting him for some time, for his eyes were almost closed and even his legs were swaying as if he'd been partially knocked out.

Peter managed to wrest the axe handle from the third man, giving him a warning whack with it, but as he moved in to try to frighten off the two men holding Sidney, Matilda saw two more very big men with dark beards and filthy oilskin waistcoats dash forward out of the crowd to grab Peter.

'Get the police, someone!' she shouted. But there was no time to wait for help, one of the men had already caught hold of Peter's coat lapel, his fist raised to strike him. Matilda aimed her gun at the man's leg and fired again. He hopped like he had been stung, screamed out some abuse, but moved away.

'That's better,' she shouted, moving closer. 'You two holding my son, let him go, or one of you gets it. I aimed for your friend's leg, but I shall aim right for your heart.'

One man let go, and backed away, but Sidney suddenly sagged, and the remaining man lifted his foot to kick him in the belly.

Matilda didn't stop to think, just fired at him without aiming. The man lurched, reeled a few feet, then fell on to the ground. Peter leaped over to Sidney who had now collapsed on the ground, but although Matilda wanted to run to him too, she didn't dare. She had witnessed scenes very like this one in the 'Barbary Coast.' Fights were sport, and no one would side with or come to the aid of a stranger. They were likely just to watch and cheer while all three of them were slaughtered.

Turning to the crowd behind her, she tried to appeal to their better nature. 'Please help us,' she implored them.

'Don't look like you need much help, missis,' a man called out. 'Not the way you fired that gun. Whatcha come down this way for anyway?'

All at once Matilda became aware of the malevolence in the air. The houses on all sides leaned in on the yard, the flapping washing on lines above their heads shutting out much of the natural light. There were faces at every window, she even caught sight of a woman wielding a slop pail, ready to throw its contents at her if she came within range. She could feel the animosity towards her and her boys, her gun alone was what was holding them back.

Matilda slowly edged across the few yards towards the boys, keeping the gun cocked and ready in case any one rushed them, her eyes swivelling around watching for sudden movement. Just a glance at Sidney's crumpled figure and Peter's stricken face was enough to know he was seriously injured.

She was only a few feet from them now, but the mob was edging ominously closer too, packing in on all sides. She didn't need to hear what their indistinct rumbling voices were saying, the hatred in their gaunt faces was enough to know they were spoiling for real action, to beat her and the boys and strip the clothes from their backs.

She walked in safety around the alleys of the Barbary Coast for people knew who she was. Here she and her boys were just well-dressed and well-fed strangers, and as such they were a target for hatred.

The man she had hit in the leg was now propped against a wall, holding his bleeding wound and still hurling abuse at her. The second man was prone on the ground. Her heart was pounding with terror, she had to hold the gun with both hands to stop herself shaking. She had never felt more helpless.

Suddenly she heard a shrill whistle. The crowd heard it too, for all heads jerked round.

'Police!' someone hissed, and as the sound of metal-tipped boots came running in their direction, suddenly there was pandemonium. Women shrieked and ran for doorways, men fled into alleys, others unable to get away because of the sheer numbers shrank back against the walls.

As a dozen policemen brandishing cudgels burst into the yard, Matilda stood alone in the centre, gun in hand.

'Thank God you've come,' she gasped.

Many a time in the past Matilda had complained bitterly about the police's different treatment for rich and poor, but for once she was glad of it. She had no doubt that if she had been in rags with a smoking gun in her hand, she would have been dragged away to the cells without even having time to explain what had happened. But as it was, the police listened to her, even before checking on those that were hurt.

Their care and sympathy was all for Matilda and her boys. Sidney was hastily placed on a stretcher and she was told she was free to accompany him to the hospital. As Matilda ran along beside the men carrying the stretcher, she saw some of the police disperse to look for the other men involved, while others dealt with the two remaining injured men.

The small hospital close by was as grim as the old Marine Hospital in San Francisco, dark, dirty and crowded with desperately poor people waiting patiently for treatment. Normally Matilda's sympathies would have been aroused by the sight of a mother holding a limp, clearly very sick child in her arms, but all she could think of right then was Sidney. She ordered the nurse in charge that her son needed immediate attention, then turned to Peter and insisted he should rush to get Sebastian and Matilda, regardless of the fact that this would mean they would have to delay their honeymoon.

It seemed like hours while she waited for them to come. On seeing how dirty the nurses were, she declined their help, and bathed his wounds herself. His skull was broken on the right side of his head, small pieces of splintered bone embedded in the bloody mass beneath. His chest and belly were covered in weals too, and she thought his ribs were broken. He regained consciousness fleetingly, but he didn't seem to know her.

Then suddenly Sebastian and Tabitha were there. In a trice they had Sidney whisked into a smaller private examination room, and at their insistence Peter led Matilda away out to a cab so they could go back to the hotel and tell Mary what had happened.

It was eight when they left that morning, by the time they got back to the hotel it was three in the afternoon. Both Mary and Lisette were angry rather than anxious. When they woke to find their husbands and Matilda gone, with no note of explanation, they had assumed the trio had gone out on some private business with no thought for them and the children. It was Lisette who launched into a tirade of complaint at Peter.

'How could you leave us without any warning? You know we don't know our way about,' she said, dark eyes flashing with rage. 'Mary and I had to take the children out to the park all alone, then we had such a miserable time at luncheon because the little ones played us up in the restaurant.'

'And where's Sidney?' Mary snapped, her eyes flashing dangerously. 'If he's in a saloon somewhere I'll do for him when he gets back.'

There was nothing for it but to tell them straight out where he was and that he was badly hurt. The explanations as to why and how would have to come later.

Mary's face lost all its high colour, anger vanishing as fear took its place. She pulled on her coat and hat and insisted they were to take her to the hospital immediately.

'Mary, you can't go yet,' Matilda said, trying to restrain her, glancing round at the children who were all looking at their distraught mother in shock. Elizabeth was twelve, James eleven, and John eight, all old enough to understand, but the other two were just babies. 'For one thing Sebastian and Tabitha are operating on him right now, for another Peter and I have to explain how it all came about before you see him.'

Nothing had ever been so difficult for Matilda to explain. In the light of what had happened to Sidney, any reasons she could give for their actions sounded feeble and entirely foolhardy.

'It's all your fault,' Mary screamed at Matilda. 'You and your do-gooding!'

Lisette's dark eyes swept from Mary to Matilda. As the only real outsider in the group, in as much as her whole life had been a pampered one, she had often been a little embarrassed by the nature of Matilda's charity work and wished her husband would distance himself from it.

'Mary, it wasn't Matty's idea to go,' Peter said, kneeling down in front of her and trying to take her hands. 'Sidney and I planned it right back in San Francisco. Don't blame Matty, please, but for her we could all have been hurt.'

'But she could have stopped you going,' Mary spat at him, snatching her hands away from his. 'Ain't there enough slums back home without her leading you to the ones here too?'

'She couldn't have stopped us.' Peter shook his head. 'We needed to see it. We'd have gone whatever she said and she knew that, that's why she came, hoping we'd be safer.'

'Well, I hope you're satisfied now,' Mary sobbed. 'If Sidney dies you can tell his children *you* were responsible. But then I expect we'll end up somewhere like that ourselves without him to provide for us.'

Matilda couldn't even bring herself to assure Mary that she'd take care of her and the five children if that happened. To voice the possibility would make it seem inevitable, and she couldn't accept that.

'Sidney's not going to die. He's a strong man,' she said instead. 'With Sebastian and Tabby looking after him he'll pull through.'

Peter and Lisette took charge of the children later so that Matilda could take Mary to the hospital. She had stopped her hysterical outbursts, even saying she was sorry she'd blamed her, but a plaintive statement about how she wished they'd stayed home and never come to the wedding cut Matilda to the quick.

Sebastian was still operating on Sidney when they got to the hospital, but on his instructions they were shown to a private room to wait. While they were there a burly Irish policeman called in to tell Matilda Sidney's assailant had died from his gun-shot wound, and that in all likelihood the first man she'd shot would probably lose his leg. The policeman told her this most cheerfully as if she'd rid the city of some of its vermin. He praised her courage, and said that no charges would be brought against her as it was a clear case of self-defence. But Matilda felt nothing, not relief she wouldn't be charged nor even guilt that both those men might have had wives and children. All her thoughts were centred on willing Sidney to survive.

As they waited in silence, fingers linked together for mutual comfort, Matilda found herself thinking back over the twenty-odd years she'd known Mary. Maybe in the early days of London Lil's Mary's loyalty was out of gratitude for Matilda giving her a new start, but they had become friends later. When Cissie and the girls had died, Mary had such sympathy for her, Sidney and Peter, and later when Matilda opened up the house in Folsom Street, she was always so ready to help in any way she could.

Matilda could remember well the delight she felt when Mary and Sidney wanted to get married. The first two years of the war would have been so bleak but for her moving into the apartment with baby Elizabeth. Shared fear for their men drew them even closer; when Matilda helped deliver James, they became like mother and daughter.

She didn't know how she would have fared without Mary in the years after the war. Her gentle, loving ways, her deep understanding of her loss, were so comforting. Then there had been the births of her other children, each one bringing happiness back to the family and pushing out the sadness.

Matilda guessed what Mary was thinking now. Sidney had managed to sail through the war without harm, even his infected foot had occurred through a simple accident, not from an injury by a weapon. Was it really possible that a boy who had survived such a terrible childhood and grown to be one of the most popular characters of San Francisco could be snatched from her now, in his prime, just for going back to where he was born?

When Sebastian and Tabitha came in together, both with drawn faces, Matilda feared the worst.

'He's pulling through,' Sebastian said, but though that was meant to cheer them, Matilda saw a defeated look in his blue eyes. 'I can't say right now that he will make a full recovery, the beating he took was a very brutal one. But he's strong and healthy, so I'm hopeful.'

Mary gave a little hiccuping sob, and Tabitha enfolded her in her arms to comfort her.

Matilda could say nothing. She could see that head wound in her mind's eye. Sebastian may have managed to get out all the splintered bone, and keep out any infection until it healed, but what she'd seen protruding was brain. Like Sebastian and Tabitha, she wanted to believe in miracles, but was something as delicate as a brain able to heal itself?

Why hadn't she stopped the boys going there? Wasn't it just because she was as curious as them? She would have to pay dearly for that curiosity if Sidney didn't recover, for she knew it would be on her conscience for ever.

Chapter Twenty-eight

New York 1900

As the clock on the mantelpiece struck seven, Tabitha put down her book on her lap and sighed deeply.

It was dark and very cold outside, and still Matty hadn't come home. 'It's too bad of you worrying me like this,' she said aloud.

She smiled faintly at her own words, for irritating as Matty's behaviour had been lately, she saw the humour in their now reversed roles. Tabitha had become the mother figure, Matty the child.

For so many years Matilda had seemed so very much older than herself, an adult when she was a child, a mature woman while she was still a girl. But in fact there was only fourteen years between them, nothing once you were sixty yourself, with three grown-up children and five grandchildren.

Tabitha stood up and studied herself in the over-mantel mirror. She looked like a grandmother too, her once dark hair was snow-white, and she was plump, with a double chin and wrinkles. In many ways she liked the way she looked now, for while patients viewed a young female doctor with suspicion, they felt they could trust someone of her age, gender didn't really enter into it.

She smiled at herself, imagining how amused Sebastian would have been at such a statement. It was the year he was sixty, eleven years ago, that they sold the brownstone they bought when they married, and moved into this elegant, spacious apartment overlooking Central Park. He had found the stairs in the house difficult, but he would never admit that was the reason they moved. He told everyone it was because he wanted to live somewhere with a view.

Two years ago he had passed away in the armchair looking at the view of the park. She had been sitting right here by the fire, and thought he was asleep, it was only when she got up to pull the drapes that she found he had died.

She missed him so much, his gentle ways, beautiful deep voice, his common sense and his diplomacy. In twenty-five years of marriage they'd hardly had a cross word – heated arguments sometimes, but they were always just a difference of opinion, medical matters, politics or religion, nothing personal.

Yet she wasn't lonely, for their children all lived quite close by. Giles, now twenty-six, had gone into the Everett family business started by his grandfather, and had married a society girl, Lucy Harkness, who despite being five years older than Giles, and considered a little 'fast', surprised everyone by quickly producing twin boys, then a little girl the year after, and becoming a superb mother.

Twenty-four-year-old Alfred was training to be a doctor, and hoped to be a surgeon. He was as committed to medicine as both Sebastian and herself, but he favoured his grandfather, Giles Milson, with the same doleful dark eyes, dark curly hair and strong social conscience.

Lily, their only daughter, was twenty-two, and very like Grandmother Everett. She had met John Dearing, the heir of a prominent banker, at a ball when she was only seventeen. Within a year they were married, within three they had two sons, and their life was a constant social whirl.

A ring on the front-door bell made Tabitha start, and she ran out into the hall to find Alice the maid had reached the front door before her, and there stood Matilda in her fur coat and hat.

'Oh, Matty! Where have you been? I've been so worried about you,' Tabitha said, rushing up to her and touching Matilda's cheeks. 'You're frozen! Now, come right in by the fire and I'll pour you a brandy.'

'I'm fine, really I am,' Matilda insisted. 'Don't fuss.'

Tabitha took Matilda's arm and led her into the drawing-room. She took her coat and hat and nudged her into the armchair closest to the fire, then knelt down in front of her to unbutton her boots. 'These are damp,' she said, looking up at the older woman reproachfully. 'And there's salt stains on them. Have you been down by the docks again?'

'Yes. I had a trip around the bay in a tug,' Matilda said airily.

Tabitha made no comment. Try as she might to keep Matilda

away from the docks, because she considered it dangerous, the older Matilda got, the more obsessed she seemed to be with that area.

She rubbed Matilda's feet with her hands, then slipped out to the bedroom to get her slippers. She brought them back, warmed them by the fire for a minute or two, then put them on her feet. It was only after she'd put a warm shawl around her shoulders and given her a brandy that she spoke again.

'It won't do, Matty,' she said firmly. 'I can't have you wandering around the city all the time. You could be attacked by someone, you could fall and hurt yourself, and it worries me because I don't know where you are.'

'I can still look after myself, I haven't gone crazy yet,' Matilda said, looking up at Tabitha with hurt-filled eyes. 'I like to talk to people. You know I can't stand your grand friends for very long.'

Tabitha wasn't the least hurt by that remark, she had heard Matty say such things almost all her life. The older she got, the more she sought out the company of ordinary people. She liked nothing better than a chat with Alice, or Jackson the coachman.

'Maybe you should have stayed in San Francisco,' Tabitha said, perching on the arm of the chair. 'You had so many people there that you liked.'

'It wasn't the same after Sidney died,' Matilda said, and her eyes filled with tears. 'I was glad when Mary married again, but she didn't need me sticking around reminding her of the past. Dolores and Henry Slocum had gone too. Besides, Peter and Lisette came here, and Mary's children are all off in different places.'

Tabitha and Sebastian's worst fears about Sidney's recovering from that beating were realized. It left him brain-damaged. He recovered enough to walk, talk, feed and dress himself, even his red hair grew back over the scar, but he was just like a big, amiable six-year-old.

Once Matilda and Mary knew how it was going to be, Matilda had the apartment above London Lil's extended further, so there was more room for all of them, and took Sidney home. He could still lift beer barrels, sweep the floor and do simple jobs, but there was no question of him running the saloon any more, or being a real husband and father. Mostly he sat out out on the veranda and stared at the view of the bay. Matilda hired a permanent manager, and she and Mary looked after the children together.

Sidney died fifteen years ago when he was fifty, his five children were then ranging between sixteen and twenty-four, and Mary still a very attractive woman of forty-seven. The man she married a year later had been her lover for almost ten years, but the only person who had known that was Matilda, and it was only a short while ago that Mary had told Tabitha herself.

Ten years ago, when Matilda was sixty-four, she finally sold London Lil's. Since the miraculous cable car was run up California Street Hill, right past her place, land up there had suddenly become the most sought after in the entire city. Millionaires began to build mansions, and it soon became known to everyone as Nob Hill. To Peter and Tabitha it seemed very ironic that London Lil's, which had supported so many people, and been such a major part of Matty's life and character, should finally make her a millionairess when it was torn down.

But once it was gone, with all its memories, there seemed to be little to keep Matilda in San Francisco. She stayed for a while, set up trust funds to enable her working girls' hostel and the two houses in Folsom Street to keep running, and when Peter came to New York, she decided that was where she belonged too.

Tabitha knew that Matilda had always blamed herself for Sidney's brain damage, though she never said as much. She had loved and protected Mary and her children, and nursed Sidney right to the end. It was another, rather sweet irony that the shooting, rather than causing outrage, had finally brought her not only acceptance in San Francisco's society, but the admiration she so richly deserved. In her own time she had become a legend of the Old West, and where once people whispered salacious stories about her, now they loudly proclaimed her courage, good deeds, her sparkling personality and her beauty.

Tabitha smiled fondly at Matilda and wiped her eyes dry. Old as she was, she had retained the essence of her youthful beauty. Her blue eyes were still lovely, she still had her teeth, and her smile as warm as it had been when she was a girl. 'Now, you old fraud,' she said. 'I know the real reason you came here, and it wasn't because you had no friends left there. It was because you were too vain to let anyone in that town see you grow old!'

Matilda smiled. She knew there was some truth in that. 'I should have gone back to England,' she said. 'I think I will go too.'

Tabitha shook her head, her eyes smiling. 'You don't really want to go back, you belong here, where you are wanted and needed. Now, I guess Alice has the supper ready. I'll tell her we'll have it in front of the fire tonight. Then you can have a nice hot bath and I'll read you some *David Copperfield* in bed.'

'It's funny how we get used to things,' Matilda said thoughtfully. 'Like turning on a tap and getting hot water, then pulling out a plug and seeing it run away. Back in Primrose Hill I had to lug so many buckets of water up the stairs for your bath. I thought it would always be that way. I was looking at the Brooklyn Bridge today and I had a job to remember what the river looked like before it was built. I've forgotten what it's like to clean the oil lamps, and to go to a privy outside.'

'I don't think I want to remember that sort of thing.' Tabitha laughed. 'Every time I switch on the electric light here in this apartment I think it's a miracle. I'm not a bit nostalgic for the old days.'

'I am, but I suppose that's because I'm getting so old. Sebastian always said folk revert to children again once they are past seventy.'

'You'll never be really old.' Tabitha patted her cheek affectionately. 'Now, I'm going to see about the supper.'

Tabitha had her ears pricked as she heard the bath water running away later. Matilda loved baths, she would wallow in one for hours. She still liked beautiful clothes too, and dainty underwear, try as she might, Tabitha could never get her to wear a woollen vest, or a flannel petticoat. Matilda loved the feel of silk, and as much lace and embroidery as possible.

Tabitha didn't hear the bathroom door open, but she knew when it had by the waft of expensive French perfume, and again she smiled. Perfume was another of Matty's luxuries, she put it on even to go to bed. She would give her half an hour to brush her hair, and rub cream into her hands, then she'd go in to her and read.

Sadly Matilda's eyesight was fading fast, she could no longer see to read, and this was one of the reasons why Tabitha worried about her ordering the carriage and going wandering around by the docks. Jackson always insisted he never let her out of his sight, but Tabitha knew he was lying. Matilda charmed him, just as she had been doing with people all her life.

She sat back in her chair and closed her eyes for a moment. There was hardly a day in her life that Tabitha didn't thank God for Matilda. Thanks to her she'd escaped an orphanage, become a doctor, encouraged Sebastian enough for him to ask her to marry him, reared three children and had over twenty-five years of loving and being loved.

Marriage had been the best part of her life, she loved her children and her home, yet Sebastian had given her the freedom to have a career of her own too. She'd got her wealthy women clients with their female problems, but she'd also had the satisfaction of becoming respected in her own right as a good doctor, regardless of the fact that she was a woman. Since Peter had come to New York, the pair of them had made many inroads into improving the health of the immigrants in New York. While he had raised money for free clinics, she had manned them and persuaded others to join her.

Tabitha and Sebastian had expected that Peter would turn his back on the poor after what happened to Sidney, and few would have blamed him. But it had the reverse effect, making him care still more. As the years had gone by, his was the voice of thunder which roared among the wealthy socialites, and made them open their eyes to the true evils of poverty. He campaigned for better housing, hospitals, schools, holidays in the country for slum children. He made the rich open their wallets and gave them a conscience, so they volunteered to help, yet he did it with such charm and grace that he retained their friendship.

There was still a great deal more to do, but Tabitha knew her son Alfred would join them in the fight before long, for he had heard Matilda's tales since he was a little boy and she was his idol. Tabitha often thought the boys' names should have been switched around. Alfred was so like her father, while Giles was like Sebastian. Lily was just like the flower, tall, elegant and poised. Perhaps time would tell if she had inherited the gentle qualities of her grandmother along with the name.

Tabitha came to with a start, and realized she had fallen asleep.

It was now after ten and she hadn't gone in to read to Matty as she'd promised.

She jumped up and went out into the long passage which led down to Matty's room. A beam of light shone out from under her door, and Tabitha guessed she'd fallen asleep waiting. She tiptoed down the hall, for Matty was a light sleeper and she didn't want to wake her.

Matty was asleep, her hands in their white cotton gloves which she put on nightly after anointing them with cream, spread out on the sheets. Her hair was brushed, still blonde, though faded now and a little thin, like pale gold satin embroidery thread. She was wearing her newest night-gown, a turquoise-blue silk, the ruffled neckline hiding the neck she complained was growing crêpey.

Tabitha stole in to turn out the bedside light, but paused a moment because she saw a note-pad by Matty's hands. It looked like a list, and she picked it up out of curiosity.

'What I need for England' was what she'd written at the top in her thin, spidery writing. 'Four ballgowns, matching slippers, riding habit (velvet). Fur coat and hat. Walking shoes. Two suits for country, four town, with suitable hats. 6 afternoon dresses.'

The list stopped abruptly, the pencil still beside the pad. As Tabitha looked at its position she realized Matilda had fallen asleep while writing it, her right hand slightly away from the left.

All at once she was doctor rather than daughter, and a sixth sense told her Matilda had slipped away. She took her hand to feel her pulse, but even before her fingers touched the bare skin, she knew Matilda was dead.

It was sheer professionalism which stopped her calling out for Alice. But she sank to her knees beside the bed and bent her head on to it and sobbed.

For fifty-eight years, almost to the day, from tiny tot through to becoming a grandmother, she'd loved Matty. She had been by her side at all the major points of her life – the first day at school, the death of her parents, her first steps in nursing, when she got her degree in medicine, her wedding, the birth of her first child – and on Sebastian's death she'd been there to comfort her. Yet it wasn't all those major events that were so important now, it was the little kindnesses, the caring, sharing and laughter. She was indeed mother, sister and friend, the dearest, most precious person in her life.

'What are we going to do without her?' Peter said, tears running down his cheeks as he embraced Tabitha. Alice had run round to his house to get him, and he'd run here so fast he was still panting.

'She wouldn't want us to say that,' Tabitha whispered, and slid her arms around him. They held each other tightly, crying on each other's shoulders, both aware in their grief of all the others who had loved this woman, but had gone before her. 'She'll be reunited with them all now,' Tabitha murmured. 'Her father, Lily, Giles, John, Cissie, Amelia, Susanna, Zandra, Dolores and Sidney, but most of all James.'

After Peter had gone in to see Matty, they went into the drawing-room and sat down by the fire, cried together and talked, Tabitha of her memories from when she was a little girl, of Missouri when her parents died, and the wagon train.

'I wish I'd been old enough to understand that James was in love with her even then,' she said sadly. 'I adored him, I would have given anything to have him as a father. How different things might have been if he'd only told Matty how he felt.'

'But then we wouldn't have all become a family, would we?' Peter said. 'Imagine if Cissie hadn't had Matty around when John died.' He went on then to talk about how terrible it was when he lost his mother and sisters, his first memories of San Francisco, and seeing Matty in love with James.

'She would light up when he was there,' Peter said. 'And he was the same. You could feel something in the air between them, it made you tingle just to be in the same room.'

'She was so brave at his funeral,' Tabitha said, tears running down her cheeks. 'It was so awful, all those long mounds of earth, and still more trenches to be dug so the rest could be buried. We could smell the bodies, even though they covered them so we couldn't see them. She kept her head up, and her back straight, she was as much a soldier as the men who came to pay their last respects.' She paused to dab at her eyes.

'I never saw such courage, Peter. When they sounded the last post, she was trembling, but she walked forward to lay her posy of flowers on his grave. She'd made it that morning, wrapped a wet bandage round the stems so the flowers wouldn't die too fast. She kissed it and put it down, her tears were glinting on the petals like dew.'

Peter drew her into his arms. Neither Tabitha nor Matilda had ever spoken before about the funeral. He guessed it had been too painful to relive it.

'It wasn't fair that she should lose so many times,' he said, his voice croaking with emotion. 'She deserved better.'

They were overcome with grief, both constantly saying they couldn't believe she'd gone. But by talking about all she'd been to them, of how she'd been as a young woman, and how frustrating she'd found it to be growing old, losing her once keen sight, slowly it came to them that a quick and painless death, as hers had been, was what she would have wanted.

'She once told me all she cared about was that she'd made a difference in people's lives,' Tabitha said at length. 'Well, she did, didn't she, Peter? Not just to you and me, but all who were touched by her. If we were to make a list now of all the people she made life better for, it would take all night.'

'There was even your mother-in-law.' Peter half smiled as he remembered. 'Do you remember how outraged she was by Matty shooting those men? Sebastian thought she'd have a heart attack. But how she changed her tune once Matilda was said to be a heroine! She loved that, she dined out on her connection to Matilda for years!'

Tabitha smiled too. She had never really grown to like Anne Everett, however hard she tried to, and some of the hateful things she'd said about Matty at the time still made her angry.

'Do you know, she used to tell people that the man Matty killed had robbed and murdered countless rent collectors. She just made that up. I don't think the police ever discovered anything much about the man. Anne used to say, "Of course she could have been sent to prison, but with our family connections they wouldn't dare do that." As far as I know there was never any question of Matty being charged with murder!'

Peter smirked. 'Even if they had sent her to prison, I dare say she would have even used her time in there constructively. She was never one to waste an opportunity.'

'Do you think she was serious about going back to England?' Tabitha asked, suddenly remembering not only the list of clothes but the remark she'd made earlier in the evening about returning home.

'Who can say?' Peter shrugged. 'She did tell me once she intended to go back when Queen Victoria died, just to watch the funeral. I said that was morbid, but she just laughed and said she was still common enough to enjoy a good lavish funeral.'

'Well, that old lady's still alive.' Tabitha smiled. 'Sometimes I think she'll outlive me! I wish I knew the secrets of her diet, I might be able to keep some of my patients going a little longer.'

Peter lapsed into thoughtful silence for a moment. He was remembering his time in hospital and how Matty had returned to the ward later that day after James died, and carried on nursing the wounded almost as if nothing had happened. Even when she told him James had died, she offered him comfort, regardless of the fact that she needed it far more. She was tough outwardly, but both Peter and Tabitha knew how soft she was inside. All those years she cared for Sidney, never complaining, never even considering putting him into an asylum when he became incontinent, just shouldering it all with a smile. He reminded himself to find that six cents Sidney had given her all those years ago. She'd want them in her coffin with her, just as she'd want Amelia's rag-doll, the quilt she made with Lily, and the picture of James.

'You know how she always used to say "*Never look back*",' he said eventually. 'Well, it seems to me she stuck with that right to the end. I guess that list was her intention to have one last adventure. It's rather comforting to think she slipped away planning it.'

Tabitha sighed deeply. 'For all those years here in America, she was still so very English, wasn't she? The emotions kept in check, that indomitable pride and courage.'

'We must go there later this year, for her,' Peter said. 'See all the places she used to tell us about, the palace, the Thames, and the Tower of London.'

Tabitha began to smile, a sparkle coming back into her eyes. 'I saw some of them when I went to England before, but it will be so much better with you, Peter. We'll go to the top of Primrose Hill and take a boat down the river to where her father and Dolly lived. Maybe we could even go to one of the newspapers and tell them her story. Wouldn't she just love that?'

Peter caught hold of Tabitha's hand and squeezed it. 'Do you know, I can almost hear her laughing.'